PRAISE FOR

IMAGINARY FRIEND

Goodreads Choice Awards Finalist, Best Horror

"Twenty years after his smash hit novel, *The Perks of Being a Wallflower*, Stephen Chbosky returns... An ambitious tale narrated through multiple perspectives, mashing together horror, fairy tales, and the (rewritten) Bible... But Chbosky's true skill is in turning a book of absolute horrors—both fantastical and real—into an uplifting yarn. [This is] a book about so much—fate, destiny, redemption, power... Chbosky has his eye firmly on humanity."

—*New York Times Book Review*

"*Imaginary Friend* is an all-out, not-for-the-fainthearted horror novel, one of the most effective and ambitious of recent years... To be sure, the underlying sensibility that characterized *Wallflower* is present in the new book, particularly in its empathetic portraits of people struggling to recover from personal tragedy... Perhaps its most impressive aspect is the confidence with which Chbosky deploys the more fantastical elements of his complex narrative... A very human story with universal implications."

—*Washington Post*

"Chbosky's horror writing stands on its own... a gleeful meditation... The nine years Chbosky reportedly spent writing the book shows in his well-crafted scares, snappy pacing, and finely tuned plot. *Imaginary Friend* is well worth the time for those who dare."

—*TIME*

"A haunting and thrilling novel pulsing with the radical empathy that makes Chbosky's work so special."

—John Green, #1 *New York Times* bestselling author of *The Fault in Our Stars*

"An epic work of horror...Ambitious and compulsively readable...A Grand Guignol exploration of what it means to have faith, even in the face of absolute hopelessness...His willingness to pursue and present answers to such meaningful queries is what elevates *Imaginary Friend* from a more than competent attempt at the horror genre to a formidable work on par with other genre operas that also tackle spiritual matters, like Stephen King's 1978 behemoth *The Stand* or Justin Cronin's The Passage trilogy. *Imaginary Friend* is a book that far outstrips the expectations of his chosen genre...a book full of its own light."

—Pittsburgh Post-Gazette

"With *Imaginary Friend*, Stephen Chbosky has written another classic, setting a new high watermark for fantasy horror. It is the greatest story ever told of love and salvation, in which a little child shall save them. It is as spine-tingling sinister as a Stephen King tome, as ghastly as any ghost story by Peter Straub, as gothic as any Neil Gaiman title. It should become a horror perennial, taken out at Halloween and Christmas or any other time a reader wants a proper fight."

—Washington Independent

"Like *The Perks of Being a Wallflower*, *Imaginary Friend* says that no matter how dark the places you have been or the things you have seen, no one and nothing and nowhere is beyond redemption. What is astonishing and laugh-out-loud genius is that Chbosky has disguised all this wisdom in an entertaining thriller. In true Stephen Chbosky style, he gives you the bran and the doughnut. Spiritual enlightenment and horror. I don't know how he did it. But he did it. It's a masterpiece."

—Emma Watson, actor and activist

"If you aren't blown away by the first fifty pages of *Imaginary Friend*, you need to get your sense of wonder checked."

—Joe Hill, #1 *New York Times* bestselling author of *The Fireman* and *NOS4A2*

"If you grew up reading *The Perks of Being a Wallflower*, you won't want to miss this spooky, surreal thriller...You'll feel locked in the battle between good and evil as Kate and Christopher fight for their lives."   —Good Housekeeping

"*Imaginary Friend* is simply an extraordinary reading experience—it reminded me of discovering a classic Stephen King novel from two decades ago, but all funneled through Chbosky's utterly unique style. A tremendous read, every bit worth the wait."

—Blake Crouch, *New York Times* bestselling author of *A Dark Matter* and *Recursion*

"Chbosky brings deep humanity to his characters and creates genuinely unsettling tableaux." —*Publishers Weekly*

"The author of *Perks of Being a Wallflower* goes full Stephen King in his new supernatural thriller of epic proportions . . . This is my kind of Christmas novel!"

—*LitHub*

"It's not just horror that Stephen Chbosky is tackling: it's religion, too, [which] makes the world-building all the more richer . . . Thrilling." —*Variety*

IMAGINARY FRIEND

ALSO BY STEPHEN CHBOSKY

The Perks of Being a Wallflower

IMAGINARY FRIEND

STEPHEN CHBOSKY

GRAND CENTRAL
PUBLISHING

NEW YORK   BOSTON

Copyright © 2019 by Stephen Chbosky

Reading group guide © 2020 by Stephen Chbosky and Hachette Book Group, Inc.

Cover design by Gray318. Cover copyright © 2020 by Hachette Book Group, Inc.

Grand Central Publishing
Hachette Book Group
1290 Avenue of the Americas, New York, NY 10104
grandcentralpublishing.com
twitter.com/grandcentralpub

Originally published in hardcover and ebook by Grand Central Publishing in October 2019

First trade paperback edition: October 2020

Grand Central Publishing is a division of Hachette Book Group, Inc. The Grand Central Publishing name and logo is a trademark of Hachette Book Group, Inc.

The publisher is not responsible for websites (or their content) that are not owned by the publisher.

The Hachette Speakers Bureau provides a wide range of authors for speaking events. To find out more, go to www.hachettespeakersbureau.com or call (866) 376-6591.

Library of Congress Cataloging-in-Publication Data

Names: Chbosky, Stephen, author.
Title: Imaginary friend / Stephen Chbosky.
Description: First Edition. | New York: Grand Central Publishing, 2019.
Identifiers: LCCN 2019004169| ISBN 9781538731338 (hardcover) | ISBN 9781538733851 (large print) | ISBN 9781549143182 (audio book) | ISBN 9781549143199 (audio download) | ISBN 9781538731345 (ebook)
Classification: LCC PS3553.H3469 I43 2019 | DDC 813/.54—dc23
LC record available at https://lccn.loc.gov/2019004169

ISBNs: 978-1-5387-3135-2 (trade paperback), 978-1-5387-3134-5 (ebook)

Printed in the United States of America

LSC-C

10 9 8 7 6 5 4 3 2 1

For Liz
and mothers everywhere

ACKNOWLEDGMENTS

I just wanted to say about all those listed that there would be no book without them, and I thank them with all of my heart.

Liz, Maccie, and Theo Chbosky
Wes Miller
Karen Kosztolnyik
Ben Sevier
Emad Akhtar
Luria Rittenberg
Laura Jorstad
Laura Cherkas
Eric Simonoff
Jeff Gorin
Laura Bonner
Kelsey Nicolle Scott
Ava Dellaira
Randy Ludensky
Jill Blotevogel
Robbie Thompson
Stacy, John, and Drew Dowdle
Fred and Lea Chbosky

And finally...
Emma Watson, who inspired the ending on the Perks of Being a Wallflower set and Stephen King, who inspired everything else.

IMAGINARY FRIEND

50 years before...

Don't leave the street. tHey can't get you if you don't leave the street.

Little David Olson knew he was in trouble. The minute his mother got back with Dad, he was going to get it. His only hope was the pillow stuffed under his blanket, which made it look like he was still in bed. They did that on TV shows. But none of that mattered now. He had snuck out of his bedroom and climbed down the ivy and slipped and hurt his foot. But it wasn't too bad. Not like his older brother playing football. This wasn't too bad.

Little David Olson hobbled down Hays Road. The mist in his face. The fog settling in down the hill. He looked up at the moon. It was full. The second night it had been full in a row. A blue moon. That's what his big brother told him. Like the song that Mom and Dad danced to sometimes. Back when they were happy. Back before David made them afraid.

Blue Moon.

I saw you standing alone.

Little David Olson heard something in the bushes. For a second, he thought it might be another one of those dreams. But it wasn't. He knew it wasn't. He forced himself to stay awake. Even with his headaches. He had to get there tonight.

A car drove past, bathing the fog in headlight. Little David Olson hid behind a mailbox as rock 'n' roll poured from the old Ford Mustang. A couple of the teenagers laughed. A lot of kids were being drafted into the army, and drunk driving was on the rise. That's what his dad said anyway.

"David?" a voice whispered. Hisspered. Hisss.

Did someone say it? Or did he just hear it?

"Who's there?" David said.

Silence.

It must have been in his head. That was okay. At least it wasn't the hissing lady. At least he wasn't dreaming.

Or was he?

David looked down the hill at the street corner with the big streetlight on Monterey Drive. The teenagers passed it, taking all the sound with them. That's when David saw the shadow of a person. A figure stood in the middle of the pool of streetlight. Waiting and whistling. Whistling and waiting. A song that sounded a little like

Blue Moon.

The hairs on the back of David's neck stood up.

Don't go near that corner.

Stay away from that person.

Little David Olson cut through the yards instead.

He tiptoed over an old fence. *Don't let them hear you. Or see you. You're off the street. It's dangerous.* He looked up in a window where a babysitter was making out with her boyfriend while the baby cried. But it sounded like a cat. He was still sure he wasn't dreaming, but it was getting harder and harder to tell anymore. He climbed under the fence and got wet grass stains on his pajama bottoms. He knew he couldn't hide them from his mom. He would have to wash them himself. Like how he was starting to wet the bed again. He washed the sheets every morning. He couldn't let his mother know. She would ask questions. Questions he could not answer.

Not out loud.

He moved through the little woods behind the Maruca house. Past the swing set that Mr. Maruca had put up with his boys. After a hard day's work, there were always two Oreos and a glass of milk waiting. Little David Olson helped them once or twice. He loved those Oreos. Especially when they got a little soft and old.

"David?"

The whisper was louder now. He looked back. There was no one around. He peeked back past the houses to the streetlight. The shadow person was gone. The figure could be anywhere. It could be right behind him. *Oh, please don't let it be the hissing lady. Please don't let me be asleep.*

Crack.

The twig snapped behind him. Little David Olson forgot about his hurt foot and ran. He cut through the Pruzans' lawn down onto Carmell Drive and turned left. He could hear dogs panting. Getting closer. But there were no dogs. It was just sounds. Like the dreams. Like the cat baby crying. They were running after him. So, he ran faster. His little booties hitting the wet pavement. Smack smack smack like a grandma's kiss.

When he finally got to the corner of Monterey Drive, he turned right. He ran in the middle of the street. Like a raft on a river. *Don't leave the street. They can't get you if you're on the street.* He could hear the noises on either side. Little hisses. And dogs panting. And licking. And baby cats. And those whispers.

"David? Get out of the street. You'll get hurt. Come to the lawn where it's safe."

The voice was the hissing lady. He knew it. She always had a nice voice at first. Like a substitute teacher trying too hard. But when you looked at her, she wasn't nice anymore. She turned to teeth and a hissing mouth. Worse than the Wicked Witch. Worse than anything. Four legs like a dog. Or a long neck like a giraffe. Hssss.

"David? Your mother hurt her feet. They're all cut up. Come and help me."

The hissing lady was using his mom's voice now. No fair. But she did that. She could even look like her. The first time, it had worked. He went over to her on the lawn. And she grabbed him. He didn't sleep for two days after that. When she took him to the house with the basement. And that oven.

"Help your mother, you little shit."

His grandma's voice now. But not his grandma. David could feel the hissing lady's white teeth. *Don't look at them. Just keep looking ahead. Keep running. Get to the cul-de-sac. You can make her go away forever. Get to the last streetlight.*

"Hsssssss."

David Olson looked ahead to the last streetlight in the cul-de-sac. And then, he stopped.

The shadow person was back.

The figure stood in the middle of the pool of streetlight. Waiting and whistling. Whistling and waiting. Dream or no dream, this was bad. But David could not stop now. It was all up to him. He was going to have to walk past the streetlight person to get to the meeting place.

"Hiiiiiissssssssss."

The hissing lady was closer. Behind him. David Olson suddenly felt cold. His pajamas damp. Even with the overcoat. Just keep walking. That's all he could do. Be brave like his big brother. Be brave like the teenagers being drafted. Be brave and keep walking. One little step. Two little steps.

"Hello?" said Little David Olson.

The figure said nothing. The figure did not move. Just breathed in and out, its breath making

Clouds.

"Hello? Who are you?" David asked.

Silence. The world holding its breath. Little David Olson put a little toe into the pool of light. The figure stirred.

"I'm sorry, but I need to pass. Is that okay?"

Again there was silence. David inched his toe into the light. The figure began to turn. David thought about going back home, but he had to finish. It was the only way to stop her. He put his whole foot into the light. The figure turned again. A statue waking up. His whole leg. Another turn. Finally, David couldn't take it, and he entered the light. The figure ran at him. Moaning. Its arm reaching out. David ran through the circle. The figure behind him. Licking. Screaming. David felt its long nails reaching, and just as it was going to grab his hair, David slid on the hard pavement like in baseball. He tore up his knee, but it didn't matter. He was out of the light. The figure stopped moving. David was at the end of the street. The cul-de-sac with the log cabin and the newlywed couple.

Little David Olson looked off the road. The night was silent. Some crickets. A little bit of fog that lit the path to the trees. David was terrified, but he couldn't stop. It was all up to him. He had to finish or the hissing lady would get out. And his big brother would be the first to die.

Little David Olson left the street and walked.

Past the fence.

Through the field.

And into the Mission Street Woods.

Part I

Today

CHAPTER 1

*A*m *I dreaming?*

That's what the little boy thought when the old Ford station wagon hit a speed bump and knocked him awake. He had that feeling of being cozy in bed, but suddenly needing to go to the bathroom. His eyes squinted in the sun, and he looked out over the Ohio Turnpike. The steam from the August heat came off it like waves at the pool that Mom took him to after saving up by skipping lunches for a while. "I lost three pounds," she said and winked. That was one of the good days.

He rubbed his tired eyes and sat up in the passenger seat. He loved riding in the front seat when his mom drove. He felt like he belonged to a club. A special club with him and this cool skinny lady. He looked over at her, framed by the morning sun. Her skin was sticking to the hot vinyl seat. Her shoulders red around her halter top. Her skin pale just under the cutoffs. She had her cigarette in one hand, and she looked glamorous. Like the old movie stars in their Friday Night Movies together. He loved how the ends of her cigarettes had red lipstick. The teachers back in Denver said cigarettes were bad for you. When he told his mom that, she joked that teachers were bad for you and kept on smoking.

"Actually, teachers are important, so forget I ever said that," she said.

"Okay," he said.

He watched her stub out her cigarette and light another instantly. She only did that when she was worried. She was always worried when they moved. Maybe it would be different this time. That's what she always said since Dad died. This time it will be different. Even though it never was.

And this time, they were running.

She took a drag, and the smoke curled up past the beads of August sweat on her upper lip. She peered out over the steering wheel, deep in thought. It took her a full minute to realize he was awake. And then, she smiled.

"Isn't this a great morning?" she whispered.

The boy didn't care about mornings at all. But his mom did. So he did.

"Yeah, Mom. It sure is."

He always called her Mom now. She told him to stop calling her Mommy three years earlier. She said it made him small, and she never wanted her son to be small. Sometimes, she told him to show her his muscles. And he would take his skinny little arms and strain to make his biceps be anything other than flat. Strong like his dad in that Christmas picture. The one picture he had.

"You hungry, buddy?" she asked.

The boy nodded.

"There's a rest stop right up the turnpike over the state line. I'm sure there's a diner there."

"Will they have chocolate chip pancakes?"

The boy remembered the chocolate chip pancakes back in Portland. That was two years ago. There was a diner under their apartment in the city. And the cook always gave them chocolate chip pancakes. There had been Denver and Michigan since. But he never forgot those pancakes or the nice man who made them. He didn't know men other than his dad could be nice until him.

"If they don't, we'll get some M&M's and throw them in the middle of the stack. Okay?"

The little boy was worried now. He had never heard her say that. Not even when they moved. She always felt guilty when they moved. But even on her guiltiest day, she told him that chocolate was not a breakfast food. Even when she had her chocolate SlimFast shakes for breakfast, she told him that. And no, those shakes do not count as chocolate. He had asked her that already.

"Okay," he said and smiled, hoping this wasn't a one-time thing.

He looked back at the turnpike. The traffic slowed as they saw an ambulance and a station wagon. The emergency men wrapped a man's bloody head with gauze. He looked like he cut his forehead and might be missing some teeth. When they drove a little farther, they could see the deer on the station wagon's hood. The antler was still stuck in the windshield. The eyes of the deer were open. And it struggled and twitched like it didn't know it was dying.

"Don't look at it," his mom said.

"Sorry," he replied and looked away.

She didn't like him to see bad things. He had seen them too much in his life. Especially since his dad died. So, he looked away and studied her hair under her scarf. The one she called a bandanna, but the little boy liked to think of it as a scarf like the ones in the old movies they watched on Movie Fridays. He looked at her hair and his own brown hair like his dad's in the one picture he had from Christmas. He didn't remember much about his father. Not even his voice. Just the smell of tobacco on his shirt and the smell of Noxzema shaving cream. That was it. He didn't know anything about his father other than he must have been a great man because that's what all fathers were. Great men.

"Mom?" the little boy asked. "Are you okay?"

She put on her best smile. But her face was afraid. Like it had been eight hours ago when she woke him up in the middle of the night and told him to pack his things.

"Hurry," she whispered.

The little boy did as he was told. He threw everything he had into his sleeping bag. When he tiptoed into the living room, he saw Jerry passed out on the sofa. Jerry was rubbing his eyes with his fingers. The ones with the tattoos. For a moment, Jerry almost woke up. But he didn't. And while Jerry was passed out, they got in the car. With the money in the glove compartment that Jerry didn't know about. Jerry had taken everything else. In the quiet of night, they drove away. For the first hour, she looked at the rearview mirror more than she did the road.

"Mom? Will he find us?" the little boy asked.

"No," she said and lit another cigarette.

The little boy looked up at his mom. And in the morning light, he finally saw that her red cheek was not from makeup. And this feeling came over him. He said it to himself.

You cannot fail.

It was his promise. He looked at his mother and thought, *I will protect you*. Not like when he was really little and couldn't do anything. He was bigger now. And his arms wouldn't always be flat and skinny. He would do push-ups. He would be bigger for her. He would protect her. For his dad.

You cannot fail.

You must protect your mother.
You are the man of the house.

He looked out the window and saw an old billboard shaped like a keystone. The weathered sign said YOU'VE GOT A FRIEND IN PENNSYLVANIA. And maybe his mother was right. Maybe it would be different this time. It was their third state in two years. Maybe this time, it would work out. Either way, he knew he could never let her down.

Christopher was seven and a half years old.

CHAPTER 2

They had been in Pennsylvania for a week when it happened.

Christopher's mother said she chose the little town of Mill Grove because it was small and safe and had a great elementary school. But deep down, Christopher thought maybe she picked it because it seemed tucked away from the rest of the world. One highway in. One highway out. Surrounded by trees. They didn't know anyone there. And if no one knew them, Jerry couldn't find them.

Mill Grove was a great hiding place.

All she needed was a job. Every morning, Christopher watched his mom put on lipstick and comb her hair all nice. He watched her put on her smart-looking glasses and fret about the hole under the right armpit in her only interview blazer. The rip was in the fabric, not the seam. So, there was nothing to do except throw on a safety pin and pray.

After he ate his Froot Loops, she would take him over to the public library to pick out his book for the day while she looked over the want ads in the paper. The book of the day was his "fee" for eating Froot Loops. If he read a book to practice his words, he got them. If he didn't, he got Cream of Wheat (or worse). So, he made sure to read that book, boy.

Once Mom had written down a few promising leads, they would climb back in the car and drive around to different interviews. She told Christopher that she wanted him to come along so they could have an adventure. Just the two of them. She said the old Ford was a land shark, and they were looking for prey. The truth was that there was no money for a babysitter, but he didn't care because he was with his mom.

So, they went "land sharking," and as she drove, she would grill him on the state capitals. And math problems. And vocabulary.

"Mill Grove Elementary School is really nice. They have a computer lab and everything. You're going to love second grade."

No matter where they lived, Christopher's mother hunted for great public schools the way other moms hunted for bargains on soda (they called it "pop" here in Mill Grove for some reason). And this time, she said, he would have the best. The motel was near a great school district. She promised to drive him every day so he wouldn't be called a "motel kid" until she saved enough to get them an apartment. She said she wanted him to have the education she never got. And it was okay that he struggled. This was going to be the grade when he'd be better at math. This was the year that all of his hard work would pay off, and he would stop switching letters when he read. And he smiled and believed her because she believed in him.

Then, when she got to each interview, she would take her own private moment and say some words she read in her self-improvement books because she was trying to believe in herself, too.

"They <u>want</u> to love you."

"<u>You</u> decide this is your job. Not <u>them</u>."

When she was finally confident, they'd go into the building. Christopher would sit in the waiting rooms and read his book like she wanted, but the letters kept switching, and his mind would wander, and he would think about his old friends. He missed Michigan. If it weren't for Jerry, he would have loved to stay in Michigan forever. The kids were nice there. And everyone was poor, so nobody knew it. And his best friend, Lenny "the Loon" Cordisco, was funny and pulled down his pants all the time in front of the nuns in CCD. Christopher wondered what Lenny Cordisco was doing now. Probably getting yelled at by Sister Jacqueline again.

After each interview was over, Christopher's mother would come out with a shaken look on her face that acknowledged that it really was <u>their</u> decision to hire her. Not <u>hers</u>. But there was nothing to do but climb back in the car and try again. She said that the world can try to take anything from you.

But you have to give it your pride.

On the sixth day, his mother pulled into the middle of town in front of a parking meter and took out her trusty paper bag. The one that said OUT OF ORDER on it. She threw it on the meter and told Christopher that stealing was bad, but parking tickets were worse. She'd make it up to the world when she got back on her feet.

Normally, Christopher had to go into the waiting room to read his book. But on the sixth day, there was a sheriff and his deputy eating across the street in a diner. She called out to them and asked if they were going to be there for a while. They gave her a salute and said they'd keep an eye on her boy. So, as a reward for his reading, she let Christopher in the little park while she went into the old folks home to interview for a job. To Christopher's eyes, the name of the home read like . . .

Sahdy Pnies

"Shady Pines," she corrected. "If you need anything, call out to the sheriff."

Christopher went to the swings. There was a little caterpillar on the seat. He knew Lenny Cordisco would have smushed it. But Christopher felt bad when people killed small things. So, he got a leaf and put the caterpillar under a tree where it would be cool and safe. Then, he got back on the swings and started to pull. He may not have been able to make a muscle. But boy could he jump.

As he began to swing, he looked up at the clouds. There were dozens of them. They all had different shapes. There was one that looked like a bear. And one that looked like a dog. He saw shapes of birds. And trees. But there was one cloud that was more beautiful than all the rest.

The one that looked like a face.

Not a man. Not a woman. Just a handsome pretty face made of clouds.

And it was smiling at him.

He let go of the swing and jumped.

Christopher pretended that he landed on the warning track. Top of the ninth. Two outs. A circus catch. Tigers win! But Christopher was near Pittsburgh, Pennsylvania, now. And it was time to switch teams so the kids would like him. Go Pirates!

After ten minutes of swinging, his mother came out. But this time, there was no shaken look. There was only a big smile.

"Did you get the job?" Christopher asked.

"We're having Chinese tonight."

After she thanked the sheriff for his help, and was warned about her OUT OF ORDER bag, she got her son back in the land shark and took him out for Movie Night. Friday was their night. She wouldn't miss it. Not for anything. And this was going to be the best one in a long time. No Jerry. Just their special club with only two members. Junk food. And old movies from the library.

So, they drove to the 7-Eleven to play her numbers like they did every Friday. After picking up some beer, they went back to the library to get Christopher his two practice books for the weekend and a couple of videos for their night. Why do people pay for things that are free? They went to China Gate like the sheriff said since cops know food better than anyone, and she gasped when she saw the prices, but tried her best to hide her expression from him. Then, she smiled. She said she had a little left on the Visa that Jerry didn't know about, and in a week, she'd have a paycheck. And as they drove back to the motel, with the smell of Egg Rolls and Orange Chicken and Christopher's favorite Lo Mein (Chinese Spaghetti you like! said the menu), they planned what they would do with the lottery money like they did every Friday before they lost.

Christopher said he would buy her a house. He even made blueprint plans with graph paper. Christopher had video games and a candy room. A basketball court and a petting zoo off the kitchen. All painstakingly planned. But the best room was his mom's. It was the biggest one in the house. It had a balcony with a diving board that went to her own private pool. And it had the biggest closet with the nicest clothes that weren't ripped under the arm.

"What would you do with the money, Mom?" he asked.

"I'd get you a tutor and all the books in the world."

"Mine is better," he said.

When they got home, the mini fridge in the motel room wasn't working too well, so her beer was not getting cold in time for their feast. So, as she watched the lottery on the little television, Christopher went to the ice maker down the hall. And Christopher did the thing he learned from the old movies they watched. He got some ice and poured her beer over it to make it cold for her.

"Here, Mom. On the rocks."

He didn't know why she laughed so hard, but he was glad to see her so happy.

*

Christopher's mother sipped her beer on the rocks, and made yum yum sounds until her son beamed with pride for his clever—if somewhat misguided—solution to her warm beer problem. After her lottery numbers came up short...AGAIN...she tore up the lottery ticket and put a DVD in the old player she got at a garage sale back in Michigan. The first movie started. It was an old musical she loved as a kid. One of her few good memories. Now one of his. When their feast was done, and the Von Trapps were safely in Switzerland, they opened their fortune cookies.

"What's yours say, Mom?" he asked.

"You will be fortunate in everything you put your hands on."

. . . in bed, she thought and did not say.

"What about yours, buddy?" she asked.

"Mine is blank."

She looked. His fortune was indeed blank except for a series of numbers. He looked so disappointed. The cookies were bad enough. But no fortune?

"This is actually good luck," she said.

"Really?"

"No fortune is the best fortune. Now you get to make up your own. Wanna trade?"

He thought about it long and hard and said, "No."

With negotiations over, it was time for the second movie. Before the film had finished, and the good guys had won the war, Christopher had fallen asleep on her lap. She sat there for a long time, looking down at him sleeping. She thought back to the Friday Night Movies when they watched Dracula, and he pretended he wasn't scared even though he would only wear turtleneck sweaters for a month.

There is a moment childhood ends, she thought. And she wanted his moment to happen a long time from now. She wanted her son to be smart enough to get out of this nightmare, but not smart enough to know that he was actually inside one.

She picked up her sleeping boy and took him to his sleeping bag. She kissed his forehead and instinctively checked to make sure he didn't have a fever. Then, she went back to the kitchenette. And when she finished her beer on the rocks, she made another just like it. Because she realized she was going to remember this night.

The night she stopped running.

It had been four years.

Four years since she found her husband dead in a bathtub with a lot of blood and no note. Four years of grief and rage and behavior that felt out of body. But enough was enough. Stop running. Stop smoking. Stop killing yourself. Your kid deserves better. So do you. No more debt. No more bad men. Just the peace of a life well fought and won. A parent with a job is a hero to someone. Even if that job was cleaning up after old people in a retirement home.

She took her beer on the rocks out on the fire escape. She felt the cool breeze. And she wished it weren't so late or she'd play her favorite Springsteen and pretend she was a hero.

As she finished her drink and the last cigarette she'd ever light, she was content, watching the smoke curl and disappear into the August night and the beautiful stars behind that big cloud.

That cloud that looked like a smiling face.

CHAPTER 3

The week after his mom got the job was the best Christopher had in a long time. Every morning, he looked out the window and saw the Laundromat across the street. And the telephone pole. And the streetlight with the little tree.

And the clouds.

They were always there. There was something comforting about them. Like the way that leather baseball gloves smell. Or the time Christopher's mom made Lipton soup instead of Campbell's because Christopher liked the little noodles better. The clouds made him feel safe. Whether he and his mom were buying school supplies or clothes, erasers or stationery. The clouds were there. And his mom was happy. And there was no school.

Until Monday.

The minute he woke up Monday, Christopher saw the cloud face was gone. He didn't know where it went, but he was sad. Because today was the day. The one day he really needed the clouds to comfort him.

The first day of school.

Christopher could never tell his mom the truth. She worked so hard to get him into these great schools that he felt guilty for even thinking it. But the truth was he hated school. He didn't mind not knowing anyone. He was used to that. But there was this other part that made him nervous about going to a new school. Simply put,

He was dumb.

He might have been a great kid, but he was a terrible student. He would have preferred it if she had yelled at him for being dumb, like Lenny Cordisco's mom. But she didn't. Even when he brought home his failed math tests, she always said the same thing.

"Don't worry. Keep trying. You'll get it."

But he did worry. Because he didn't get it. And he knew he never would. Especially at a hard school like Mill Grove Elementary.

"Hey. We're going to be late for your first day. Finish your breakfast."

As Christopher finished his Froot Loops, he tried to practice reading the back of the box. Bad Cat was the cartoon on it. Bad Cat was the most funniest cartoon on Saturday mornings. Even in this cereal box version, he was hilarious. Bad Cat went up to a construction site and stole some hard hat man's sandwich. He ate it all up. And when they caught him, he said his famous line.

"Sorry. Were you going to finish that?"

But this morning, Christopher was too nervous to laugh at the cartoon. So, he immediately looked for other things to distract himself. His eyes found the carton of milk. There was a picture of a missing girl. She was smiling without her two front teeth. Her name was Emily Bertovich. That's what Christopher's mom told him. To him, the name looked like . . .

Eimyl Bretvocih.

"We're late. Let's go, buddy," Mom said.

Christopher drank the little bit of sugar milk left in the bowl for courage, then zipped up his red hoodie. As they drove to school, Christopher listened to his mother explain how "technically" they didn't exactly "live" in the school district, so she kind of "lied" that her work address was their residence.

"So, don't tell anyone we live in the motel, okay?"

"Okay," he said.

As the car rolled over the hills, Christopher looked at the different sections of town. The cars in the front lawns on blocks. Houses with chipped paint and missing shingles. The pickup truck with the sleepaway camper in the driveway for hunting trips. Kind of like Michigan. Then, they moved to the nicer section. Big stone houses. Manicured lawns. Shiny cars in the driveways. He would have to add that to the graph paper sketch of his mom's house.

As they drove, Christopher searched the sky for clouds. They were gone, but he did see something he liked. No matter the neighborhood, it was always close by. Big and beautiful with tons of trees. All green and pretty. For a moment, he thought he saw something run into it. Fast as lightning. He wasn't sure what. Maybe a deer.

"Mom, what is that?" he asked.

"The Mission Street Woods," she said.

When they arrived at school, Christopher's mother wanted to give him a sloppy kiss in front of all the new kids. But he needed his dignity, so she gave him a brown bag and fifty cents for his milk instead.

"Wait for me after school. No strangers. If you need me, call Shady Pines. The number is sewed into your clothes. I love you, honey."

"Mom?" He was scared.

"You can do this. You've done it before. Right?"

"Mommy—"

"You call me Mom. You're not small."

"But they're going to be smarter than me—"

"Grades and smarts are not the same thing. Keep trying. You'll get it."

He nodded and kissed her.

Christopher got out of the car and approached the school. Dozens of kids were already milling about, saying hello after their summer vacations. These twin brothers were pushing and shoving and laughing. The smaller one had a lazy-eye patch. A couple of girls itched at their new school clothes. One of them had pigtails. When the kids saw him, they stopped and looked at him like they always did in new places. He was the shiny new thing in the store window.

"Hey," he said. And they nodded the way the kids always did. Quiet and mistrustful at first. Like any animal pack.

Christopher quickly walked into his homeroom and took a seat near the back. He knew not to sit up front because it's a sign of weakness. His mother said, "Never mistake being nice for being weak." Christopher thought maybe that worked in the grown-up world.

It didn't in the kid world.

"That's my seat, Squid."

Christopher looked up and saw a second grader with a rich boy's sweater and haircut. He would soon know Brady Collins by name. But right now, he was just this kid who was mad that Christopher didn't know the rules.

"What?"

"You're in my seat, Squid."

"Oh. Okay. Sorry."

Christopher knew the drill. So, he just got up.

"Didn't even fight back. What a Squid," Brady Collins said.

"And look at his pants. They're so short you can see his socks," a girl said.

When the teacher took roll call later, Christopher would hear her name, Jenny Hertzog. But right now, she was just a skinny girl with an overbite and a Band-Aid on one knee, saying,

"Floods! Floods!"

Christopher's ears turned red. He quickly moved to the only open seat left. Right in front of the teacher's desk. He looked down at his pants, and he realized that he must have grown because he looked like Alfalfa in the Little Rascals. He tried to pull them down a little, but the denim wouldn't budge.

"Sorry I'm late, boys and girls," their homeroom teacher said as she quickly entered the room.

Ms. Lasko was older like a mom, but she dressed like she was still a teenager. She had a short skirt, Sound of Music blond hair, and the thickest eye makeup Christopher had ever seen outside of a circus. She quickly put her thermos down on the desk with a thump and wrote her name on the blackboard with perfect penmanship.

Ms. Lasko

"Hey," a voice whispered.

Christopher turned around and saw a fat kid. For some reason Christopher couldn't figure out, the kid was eating bacon.

"Yeah?" Christopher whispered back.

"Don't listen to Brady and Jenny. They're jerks. Okay?"

"Thanks," Christopher said.

"Want some bacon?"

"Maybe not during class."

"Suit yourself," the kid said and kept chomping.

As it was in the kid world, that is how Christopher replaced Lenny Cordisco with a new best friend. Edward Charles Anderson ended up being in Christopher's remedial reading class, lunch period, and gym. He ultimately proved to be as bad at reading as he was at kickball. Christopher called him Eddie. But everyone else in the school already knew him by his nickname.

"Special" Ed.

CHAPTER 4

For the next two weeks, Christopher and Special Ed were inseparable. They had lunch every day in the cafeteria (trade you my baloney). They learned remedial reading from the sweet old librarian, Mrs. Henderson, and her hand puppet, Dewey the Dolphin. They failed math tests together. They even went to the same CCD two nights a week.

Special Ed said that Catholic kids have to go to CCD for one reason . . . to get them ready for what Hell is really going to be like. Marc Pierce was Jewish and asked him what CCD stood for.

"Central City Dump" was Special Ed's hilarious reply.

Christopher didn't actually know what CCD stood for, but he had learned a long time ago never to complain about it. There was one time back in Michigan that Christopher hid in the bushes so he didn't have to go. His mother called his name over and over, but he didn't say anything. Then, finally, she got really mad and said,

"Christopher Michael Reese, you get out here . . . NOW."

She used his three names. And when she did that, there was no choice. You went. That's it. Game over. With a stone face, she told Christopher that his father was Catholic. And she had promised herself that his son would be raised Catholic, too, so he would have some connection to his father besides one picture at Christmas.

Christopher wanted to die.

When they were driving home that night, Christopher thought of his dad reading the Bible. Christopher's dad probably didn't scramble his letters like Christopher did. He was probably much smarter because that's what dads were. Much smarter. So, Christopher promised that he would learn to read and know what the Bible words meant, so he could have another way to be close to his dad besides the memory of the tobacco smell on his shirt.

*

As for picking the church, Christopher's mother always followed the Cold War strategy of her grandmother's favorite president, Ronald Reagan. Trust but verify. That was how she found St. Joseph's in Mill Grove. The priest, Father Tom, was fresh from seminary. No scandals. No former parishes. Father Tom checked out. He was a good man. And Christopher needed good men in his life.

But for her own faith, it didn't matter who the priest was. Or how beautiful the mass. Or the music. Her faith died in the bathtub next to her husband. Of course, when she looked at her son, she understood why people believed in God. But when she sat in church, she didn't hear His word. All she heard were whispers and gossip from all the good Catholic women who regarded her as that working-class mother (aka "trash").

Especially Mrs. Collins.

Everything about Kathleen Collins was perfect. From her tight brown hair to her elegant suit to her polite contempt for "those people" Jesus would have actually loved. The Collins family always sat up front. The Collins family was always first in line for Holy Communion. And if her husband's hair slipped out of place, her finger would be there instantly to put it right back, like a raven's claw with a tasteful manicure.

As for their son, Brady, the apple didn't fall too far from the tree.

If Christopher's mother only had to deal with Mrs. Collins on Sundays, it would have been tolerable. But Mr. Collins was a real estate developer who owned half of Mill Grove, including Shady Pines, the retirement home where she worked. He put his wife in charge of the place. Mrs. Collins claimed that she took the position to "give back to the community." What it really meant was that it allowed Mrs. Collins to yell at the staff and the volunteers to make damn sure that her own elderly mother, who was suffering from Alzheimer's, got the finest care possible. The best room. The best food. The best of everything. Christopher's mother had traveled enough to know that Mill Grove was a very small pond. But to the Collins family, it may as well have been the Pacific Ocean.

"Mom, what are you thinking about?" Christopher whispered.

"Nothing, honey. Pay attention," she said.

Right before Father Tom turned the wine into blood with a few well-chosen words, he told the flock that Jesus loved everyone, beginning with Adam and Eve. This prompted Special Ed to begin singing the jingle for Chili's restaurant.

"I want my baby back baby back baby back! Adam's baby back ribs!"

This was met with thunderous laughter, especially by Special Ed's parents.

"Good one, Eddie. My baby is so clever!" his mother said, her fleshy arms jiggling.

Father Tom and the CCD teacher, Mrs. Radcliffe, sighed, as if realizing that Special Ed's discipline was now entirely their job.

"First Holy Communion is going to be awesome," Special Ed said in the parking lot after church. "We get money. And we even get to drink wine."

"Really?" Christopher asked. "Is that true, Mom?"

"It's part of Communion. But it'll be grape juice," she said.

"That's okay. I can get wine at home. Bye, Mrs. Reese," Special Ed said before leaving to hit up the bake sale table with his parents.

*

On the drive home, Christopher thought about mass. How Jesus loved everyone. Even mean people. Like Jenny Hertzog and Brady Collins. And Jerry. Christopher thought that was amazing because he could never love someone like Jerry. But he would try because that's what you were supposed to do.

When they got back to the motel, Christopher held the door open for his mother, and she smiled and called him a gentleman. And when he looked up before going inside, he saw it. Drifting. A shooting star looked like a twinkle in its eye.

The cloud face.

Normally, Christopher wouldn't have thought much about it. Clouds were normal. But every day when his mother drove him to school. Every time they drove past the Mission Street Woods. Every sunset when they drove to CCD. The cloud face was there.

And it was always the same face.

Sometimes big. Sometimes small. Once it was even hidden behind the other shapes in the clouds. A hammer or a dog or an inkblot like the ones the man showed him after his father accidentally drowned in the bathtub. It was always there. Not a man. Not a woman. Just a handsome pretty face made of clouds.

And Christopher could have sworn it was watching him.

He would have told his mother that, but she had enough worries about him already. He could stand her thinking he was dumb. But he didn't dare risk her thinking that he was crazy.

Not like his dad.

CHAPTER 5

The rains began on Friday.

The thunderclap woke Christopher up from a nightmare. The dream was so scary that he instantly forgot it. But he didn't forget the feeling. Like someone was right behind his ear. Tickling it. He looked around the motel room. The neon from the Laundromat outside turned the front curtains on and off like a blink.

But there was no one there.

He looked at the clock next to his mother sleeping in the other twin bed. It flashed 2:17 a.m. He tried to go back to sleep. But he couldn't for some reason. So, he just lay there with his eyes closed and his mind going.

And listened to the pouring rain.

There was so much rain, he couldn't figure out where it was coming from. He thought it would dry the oceans.

"Floods! Look at his pants! Floods! Floods!"

The words came to him, and Christopher's stomach tied itself into knots. He would be going to school in a few hours. School meant homeroom. And homeroom meant . . .

Jenny Hertzog and Brady Collins.

Every morning, they waited for him. Jenny to call him names. Brady to fight him. Christopher knew his mother didn't want him to fight anyone. She always said he wasn't going to become some violent roughneck like the men in her family. She wouldn't even let him have toy guns.

"Why not?" asked Special Ed during lunch.

"Because my mom is a packfist," Christopher said.

"Do you mean a pacifist?" Special Ed replied.

"Yeah. That's it. Pacifist. How did you know that word?"

"My dad hates them."

So, Christopher turned the other cheek, and Jenny Hertzog was right there waiting to make fun of him and the other kids in the dumb class. Don't say dumb, his mom would say. Don't you ever say dumb. But in the end, it didn't matter. He was in the dumb class, and Jenny was especially mean to the dumb students. She called Eddie "Special Ed." Matt got the name "Pirate Parrot" on account of his lazy-eye patch. His twin brother, Mike, was the best athlete in the school, but Jenny liked to call him "Two Moms Mike" or "Mike the Dyke" depending upon her mood, since he and Matt had two mothers and no dad. But Christopher was the new kid, so he got it the worst. Every homeroom started with Jenny Hertzog pointing at his short pants and chanting,

"Floods! Floods!"

It got so bad that Christopher asked his mom for new pants, but when he saw in her face that she couldn't afford them, he pretended that he was kidding. Then, during lunch, he told the cafeteria lady that he didn't want milk, so he could save his fifty cents every day and buy pants on his own. Christopher had already saved up $3.50.

He just wasn't sure how much pants cost.

He went to ask Ms. Lasko, but her eyes were a little bloodshot and her breath smelled like Jerry's after a night at the bar. So, he waited until the end of the day, and went up to sweet old Mrs. Henderson.

Mrs. Henderson was mouse-quiet. Even for a librarian. She was married to the science teacher, Mr. Henderson. His first name was Henry. Christopher thought it was so weird for teachers to have first names, but he went with it. Henry Henderson.

So many e's.

When Christopher asked Mrs. Henderson how much pants cost, she said they could use the computer to look it up. Christopher's mom didn't have her own computer, so this was a real treat. They went online and searched the word "pants." They looked at all these stores. And he saw that things were a lot of money. $18.15 for pants at JCPenney.

"So, how many fifty cents is that?" he asked Mrs. Henderson.

"I don't know. How many?" she asked.

Christopher was almost as bad at math as he was at reading. But like a good teacher, instead of giving him the answer, Mrs. Henderson gave him a pencil and a piece of paper and told him to figure it out. She'd be back in a bit to check on him. So, he sat there, adding up 50 cents at a time. Two days is 100 cents. That's a dollar. Three days is 150 cents. That's a dollar and fifty cents. With the seven dollars in his piggy bank, that meant he could . . .

hi

Christopher looked at the computer. It made a little sound. And there was a little box in the left-hand corner. It said INTSATN MSESGAGE. But Christopher knew that meant instant message. Someone was writing to him.

hi

Christopher turned to look for Mrs. Henderson, but she was gone. He was all alone. He looked back at the screen. The cursor blinked and blinked. He knew he wasn't supposed to talk to strangers. But this wasn't talking, exactly. So, he pecked with the pointer on his right hand. Peck peck.

"Hi," Christopher typed back.

who is this?

"Christopher."

hi, christopher. it's so nice to meet you. where are you right now?

"I ma in teh library."

you have trouble with letters, huh? which library?

"At scohol."

which school do you go to? don't tell me. mill grove elementary, right?

"How did yuo konw?"

lucky guess. are you liking school?

"It's oaky."

when are you leaving for the day?

Christopher stopped. Something felt wrong to him. He typed.

"Who is this?"

There was silence. The cursor blinked.

"Who are you?" Christopher typed again.

Silence again. Christopher watched the cursor blink and blink. The air was still and quiet. But he could feel something. A tightness in the air. Like staying under the covers too long.

"Hello?" Christopher asked the empty library.

Christopher looked around the stacks. He thought someone might be hiding. He started to get a panicked feeling. Like back in Michigan when Jerry would come home from the bar in a bad mood.

"Hello?" he called out again. "Who's there?"

He felt this prickle on the back of his neck. Like when his mom used to kiss him good night. A whisper without words. He heard the computer beep. He looked over. He saw the person's reply.

a friend

When Mrs. Henderson came back, the screen went blank. She looked at his math work and told him that he should ask Ms. Lasko for help. In the meantime, she gave him three books for the weekend to help with his reading. There was an old book with a lot of words. Then, there were two fun books. Bad Cat Eats the Letter Z and a Snoopy. Snoopy wasn't as good as Bad Cat. But Snoopy was still great. Especially with his cousin Spike from Needles. That word. Needles.

So many e's.

When the bell rang, Mrs. Henderson walked Christopher to the parking lot. Christopher waved goodbye as she and her husband got in their old minivan. Ms. Lasko got in her cherry-red sports car that must have cost a million fifty-cent milks. One by one, the teachers left. And the students. The twin brothers—"Pirate Parrot" and "Two Moms Mike"—threw their little plastic football as they got on the school bus. Special Ed blew a raspberry from the bus, which made Christopher smile. Then, the last buses left. And when everyone was gone, Christopher looked around for the security guard.

But he wasn't there.

And Christopher was alone.

He sat down on a little bench and waited in the parking lot for his mother to come pick him up for Movie Friday. He tried to think about that instead of the bad feeling he was having. The feeling that something could get him. He was nervous waiting outside. And he just wanted his mom to get there early today.

Where was she?

The thunder clapped. Christopher looked at his math test. 4 out of 10. He had to work harder. He picked up the first book. A Child's Garden of Verses. It was old. Kind of dusty. Christopher could feel the spine creak a little. The leather cover smelled a little like baseball gloves. There was a name in the front cover. Written in pencil.

D. Olson

Christopher turned the pages until he found a picture he liked. Then, he settled in and started reading. The words were scrambled.

Up itno the cehrry tere
Woh shuold cilmb but ltitle me?

Suddenly a shadow cut across the page. Christopher looked up. And saw it drifting overhead, blocking out the light.

It was the cloud face.

As big as the sky.

Christopher closed the book. The birds went silent. And the air got chilly. Even for September. He looked around to see if anyone was watching. But the security guard was still nowhere to be seen. So, Christopher turned back to the cloud face.

"Hello? Can you hear me?" he asked.

There was a low rumble in the distance. A thunderclap.

Christopher knew it could be a coincidence. He may have been a poor student, but he was a smart kid.

"If you can hear me, blink your left eye."

Slowly, the cloud blinked its left eye.

Christopher went quiet. Scared for a moment. He knew it wasn't right. It wasn't normal. But it was amazing. A plane flew overhead, shifting the cloud face and making it smile like the Cheshire Cat.

"Can you make it rain when I ask you to?"

Before he got out the last word, sheets of rain began to pour over the parking lot.

"And make it stop?"

The rain stopped. Christopher smiled. He thought it was funny. The cloud face must have understood he was laughing, because it started to rain. And then stop. And rain. And then stop. Christopher laughed a Bad Cat laugh.

"Stop. You'll ruin my school clothes!"

The rain stopped. But when Christopher looked up, the cloud started to drift away. Leaving him all alone again.

"Wait!" Christopher called out. "Come back!"

The cloud drifted over the hills. Christopher knew he shouldn't, but he couldn't help himself. He started walking after it.

"Wait! Where are you going?"

There was no sound. Just sheets of rain. But somehow, it didn't touch Christopher. He was protected by the eye of the storm. Even if his sneakers got soaked from the wet street. His red hoodie remained dry.

"Please, don't leave!" he yelled out.

But the cloud face kept drifting. Down the road. To the baseball field. The rain trickling on the clay-caked dirt. Dust like tears. Down the highway where cars honked and skidded in the rain. Into another neighborhood with streets and houses he didn't recognize. Hays Road. Casa. Monterey.

The cloud face drifted over a fence and above a grass field. Christopher finally stopped at a large metal sign on the fence near a streetlight. It took him a long time to sound out the words, but he finally figured out they said...

COLLINS CONSTRUCTION COMPANY

MISSION STREET WOODS PROJECT

NO TRESPASSING

"I can't follow you anymore. I'll get in trouble!" Christopher called out.

The cloud face hovered for a moment, then drifted away. Off the road. Behind the fence.

Christopher didn't know what to do. He looked around. He saw that no one was watching. He knew it was wrong. He knew he wasn't supposed to. But Christopher climbed under the construction site's fence. Snagging his little red hoodie. Once he untangled himself, he stood on the field, covered in wet grass and mud and rain. He looked up in awe.

The cloud was HUGE.

The smile was TEETH.

A happy SMILE.

Christopher smiled as the thunder clapped.

And he followed the cloud face

Off the cul-de-sac.

Down the path.

And into the Mission Street Woods.

CHAPTER 6

Christopher looked up. He couldn't see the cloud face anymore. That's how thick the trees were. He could still hear the rain, but not a drop fell to earth. The ground was still dry. Cracked like old skin. It felt like the trees were a big umbrella. An umbrella keeping something safe.

Christopher

Christopher turned around. The hairs on his neck stood up.

"Who's there?" he said.

There was silence. A quiet, shallow breathing. It might have been the wind. But something was here. Christopher could feel it. Like the way you know when someone is staring at you. The way he knew Jerry was a bad man long before his mother did.

He heard a footstep.

Christopher turned and saw that it was just a pinecone falling from a tree. Thump thump thump. It rolled down the ground and landed on

The trail.

The trail was covered by tree needles. And a few twisted branches. But it was unmistakable. A trail worn into the earth by years of bikes and ramps and races. By kids taking shortcuts to the other side of town. But now it looked abandoned. Like the construction fence outside had kept the kids away for months. Maybe even years. There wasn't a pair of fresh footsteps on it.

Except one.

He could see the imprint of a shoe in the dirt. Christopher walked over and put his little sneakers next to it. They were about the same size.

It was a little kid's footprint.

That's when he heard a little kid crying.

Christopher looked down the trail, and he saw that the little-kid tracks went on for a long, long time. The sound was coming from that direction. Far away. In the distance.

"Hello. Are you okay?" Christopher yelled out.

The crying got louder.

Christopher's chest tightened, and a voice inside told him to turn around, walk back to school, and wait for his mother. But the little kid was in trouble. So, he ignored his fear and followed the footprints. Slowly at first. Cautiously. He walked toward an old creek with a billy goat bridge. The footprints went through the water and came out on the other side. They were muddy now. The little kid must be close.

Help me.

Was that a voice? Was it the wind? Christopher picked up his pace. The little-kid tracks led him past an old hollow log that was carved out like a big canoe. Christopher looked ahead of him. He saw no one. The voice must be the wind. It didn't make sense to him. But there was no other explanation because he saw nothing.

Except the light.

The light was far down the trail. Bright and blue. The place where the crying was. Christopher began walking toward it. To help the little kid. With every step, the light got bigger. And the space under the trees got wider. And pretty soon, there were no trees above his head.

Christopher had reached the clearing.

It stood in the center of the woods. A perfect circle of grassy fields. The trees were gone. And he could see the sky. But something was wrong. He had gone into the woods a few minutes ago when it was day. But it was nighttime now. The sky was black. And the stars were shooting a lot more than usual. Almost like fireworks. The moon was so big that it lit the clearing. A blue moon.

"Hello?" Christopher called out.

There was silence. No crying. No wind. No voice. Christopher looked around the clearing and saw nothing but the trail of footprints leading to

The tree.

It stood in the middle of the clearing. Crooked like an old man's arthritic hand. Reaching out of the earth like it was trying to pluck a bird from the sky. Christopher couldn't help himself. He followed the foot-steps. He walked up to the tree and touched it. But it didn't feel like bark. Or wood.

It felt like flesh.

Christopher jumped back. It hit him suddenly. This horrible feeling that this was wrong. Everything was wrong. He shouldn't be here. He looked down to find the trail again. He had to get out of there. His mom would be so worried. He found the trail. He saw the little-kid tracks. But there was something differ-ent about them now.

There were handprints next to them.

Like the little kid was walking on all fours.

Crack!

Christopher turned around. Something had stepped on a branch. He could hear creatures waking up all around him. Surrounding the clearing. Christopher didn't hesitate. He started to run, following the trail out. He reached the edge of the clearing. Back into the woods. But the minute he stepped under the trees, he stopped.

The trail was gone.

He looked around for it, but the sky was getting darker. The clouds were covering the stars now. And the moon was shining through the cloud face like a pirate's good eye.

"Help me!" Christopher called out to the cloud face.

But the wind moved, and the cloud covered the moon like a blanket. Chris-topher couldn't see. *Oh, God. Please, God.* Christopher fell to his knees and started digging through the pine needles. Frantic. Looking for the trail under-neath. The needles sticking to his palms.

He could hear the little kid now.

But it wasn't crying.

It was giggling.

Christopher found the trail with his hands and began to crawl on all fours. *Get out of here! Faster!* That's all he thought. *Faster!*

The giggling was closer now.

Christopher started running. He moved so fast that he lost the trail. He ran in the darkness. Past the trees. His legs buckled when he stumbled into the creek. Past the billy goat bridge. He fell and ripped up his knee. But he didn't care. He kept running. A full sprint. He saw the light up ahead. This was it. He knew it. The streetlight. He had somehow found the street again.

The giggling was right behind him.

Christopher ran faster toward the street. Toward the light. He ran under the cover of the last tree. And he stopped when he realized he wasn't in the street.

He was back in the clearing.

The light was not the streetlight.

It was the moon.

Christopher looked around and could feel things staring at him. Creatures and animals. Their eyes glowing. Surrounding the clearing. The giggling was closer. Louder. Christopher was surrounded. He had to get out of here. Find a way out. Find any way out.

He ran to the tree.

He began to climb. The tree felt like flesh under his hands. Like climbing arms instead of branches. But he ignored the feeling. He needed to get higher to see a way out. When he reached halfway up the tree, the clouds parted. The moon made the clearing glow.

And Christopher saw it.

On the other side of the clearing. Hidden behind the leaves and bushes. It looked like a cave mouth. But it wasn't a cave. It was a tunnel. Man-made. Wood-framed. With old train tracks in the ground running through it. Christopher realized what that meant. Train tracks led to stations, which led to towns.

He could get out!

He climbed down the arms of the tree. He reached the ground. He felt a presence in the woods. Eyes on him. Waiting for him to move.

Christopher ran.

All of his might. All of his speed. He felt creatures behind him. But he couldn't see them. He reached the mouth and looked into the tunnel. The train tracks went through it like a rusty spine. He saw moonlight on the other side. An escape!

Christopher ran into the tunnel. The wooden frames held up the walls and ceiling like a whale's rib cage. But the wood was old. Dilapidated and rotting. And the tunnel wasn't wide enough for a train to pass through it. What was this place? A covered bridge? Sewer? Cave?

A mine.

The word hit him like water. A Pennsylvania coal mine. He saw a movie about them in class. Miners using handcarts and rail track to bring out earth to burn. He ran deeper. Racing to the moonlight on the other side. He looked down at the tracks to get better footing. That's when he saw the little-kid footprints were back. And the giggling was back. Right behind him.

The moonlight faded ahead as the clouds played hide-and-seek. The whole world went black. He groped into the darkness. Trying to find the walls to guide his way out. His feet scraped the tracks as he reached out like a blind man. And he finally found something. He finally touched something in the dark.

It was a little kid's hand.

Christopher

was

not

seen

heard

from

for

six

days.

Part II

Dreams Come True

CHAPTER 7

Mary Katherine was guilty. That was nothing new. She had been guilty ever since her first CCD class with Mrs. Radcliffe over ten years ago. But this was really bad. She couldn't believe she let it get so out of control. The law clearly stated that kids were not allowed to drive alone after midnight. It was 11:53 p.m., and she was at least ten minutes from home. How did she let this happen?

"You just got your license! You're so stupid!" she berated herself.

How long did it take her to get her license? Remember?! She had to beg her mother to even bring it up to her father. Then, when her mom finally mustered enough courage to throw back a couple of (boxes of) white wine and have the talk, it took both of them working on Dad for weeks to even allow a learner's permit. When the other kids only took one Driver's Ed class, Mary Katherine had to take two. When the other parents let their kids drive on McLaughlin Run Road or even Route 19 for gosh sake, Mary Katherine was still stuck in the church parking lot. Not even the big parking lot at Holy Ascension. She was stuck at St. Joseph's! Hello!

By the time slutty Debbie "Done Him" Dunham and that notorious drunk Michele Gorman were driving all the way to downtown Pittsburgh, Mary Katherine was pulling in and out of her own driveway.

"Hey, Virgin Mary," Debbie would say in the locker room. "Could you give me a lift up my driveway?"

Mary Katherine was used to kids calling her names. "The more devout the child, the more devout the insult," her mother liked to say when Mary Katherine couldn't keep the tears down with the usual "sticks and stones" advice. But Debbie Dunham was the worst. When it came to Christians, she cheered for the lions. So, when Mary Katherine graduated from her Catholic middle school to the public high school, she had found the transition more than difficult. In the end, being a true believer was not an easy path in a multiple-choice world.

But the good thing about Catholic guilt was that it worked both ways. Mary Katherine's perfect attendance, straight A's, extra credit when she already had a 99, and 2020 SAT score eventually wore down her father. Eventually, even he had to admit that he had the most responsible daughter a man could ever hope to have. He allowed her to take her driver's test. She aced it! Thank you, Jesus. And when her permanent license came in the mail, her picture was drop-dead gorgeous. She was guilty because vanity is a sin. But this quickly passed. Because she was seventeen. She had her license. It was senior year. She was applying to Notre Dame. Life was endless with the possibilities of freedom.

She had to make it home by midnight.

Or else she was going to ruin it all.

The clock read 11:54 p.m.

"God dammit!" she said, then immediately crossed herself.

"Gosh darnit," she corrected, hoping it would be enough.

Mary Katherine retraced her mistake. She had met Doug at the movie at 9:30. The theater manager said the running time was two hours. That would have brought her to 11:30. It would be 11:27 if she left before the credits ended, which made her feel guilty because those people work so hard. But either way, she had plenty of time, right? But the theater kept playing commercials. And more trailers for Bad Cat 3D (as if we needed another one!). By the time the movie started, she actually forgot what movie they were supposed to see. She wanted to see the new romantic comedy from Disney. But oh, no. Doug needed his disaster movie.

Stupid Doug.

Why do the smartest boys like the dumbest movies? Doug had gotten straight A's since kindergarten. He would be valedictorian and get into every college he applied to—even the secular ones. But he just had to see the world almost destroyed again.

"And no, Doug," she said aloud to herself in the car, practicing for a fight she would never actually start, "I don't like it when you put the Junior Mints in the popcorn. I don't think it tastes better at all!"

The clock read 11:55 p.m.

God dammit!

Mary Katherine considered her options. She could exceed the speed limit, but if she got a ticket, she would be grounded for even longer. She could blow off a stop sign or two, but that was even worse. The only plan that made sense was going on Route 19, but her father forbade her from driving on highways. "Honor thy father and thy mother" worked on most days, but this was an emergency. It was either jump on Route 19 for two minutes or be late.

She turned onto the highway.

The traffic was so fast. Her heart beat with all of the cars rushing by in the left lane with her doing the legal 45 miles per hour in the right. She couldn't risk a ticket. No way. Especially on Route 19. Her father would take her license away for that. And she would never drive her mother's Volvo again.

"God," she said, "if You get me home by midnight, I promise to give extra money to the collection plate this Sunday."

After she said that, something gripped her. It was an old guilt. An old fear. The first time she'd thought it was after Doug and she went parking near Mill Grove Elementary School last Christmas. They were tongue kissing, and out of nowhere, Doug touched her left breast over the fuzzy sweater her grandmother had given her. It only lasted a second, and he claimed he slipped. But she knew better. She was very upset with him. But the truth was, she was more upset with herself.

Because she liked it.

She would never tell Doug that. But when she went home that night, she couldn't stop herself from replaying the moment over and over. Thinking about his hands under her shirt and over her bra. And under her bra. And naked. She was so guilty that she actually thought she could get pregnant from Doug's hand on top of her fuzzy sweater. She knew that was crazy. She knew you could only get pregnant from sexual intercourse. She went to health class. Her parents weren't <u>that</u> crazy Catholic. But still, she couldn't shake the fear. So, she promised God that if He spared her the humiliation of being pregnant, she would confess her sins and give all her babysitting money to the collection plate. The next day, she got her period. And she was so relieved, she cried. That week, she confessed her sins to Father Tom and gave all her babysitting money to God.

But the experience left her shaken. After all, to think sin is to commit sin. That's what Mrs. Radcliffe taught in CCD. So, what would have happened if she had died before she could have gone to confession and cleansed herself? She knew the answer, and it terrified her.

So, she had to figure out an early warning system. Something that would make her know that what she had done was so sinful that God would send her to Hell. For weeks, she couldn't think of it. And then, when she started driving by herself, she passed a deer on the road, and it came to her.

Hit a deer.

"God," she said, "if I am going to Hell, make me hit a deer with my car."

She knew it sounded crazy, but the agreement instantly took away her fear. She promised to never speak of it to anyone. Not her mother. Not Mrs. Radcliffe. Not Father Tom. Not even Doug. This was a private understanding between her and her Maker.

"God, if I hit a deer, I will know that I have sinned against You so terribly that You have given up on me. This will give me time to make it up to You. I am sorry that I enjoyed him touching my sweater (he never touched my breast!). I am so sorry."

11:57 p.m.

Over and over she said it. So much so that it became background noise. Like the baseball games her dad played on the radio in his study while he built his model ships or her mother's vacuum keeping their rugs spotless. Whenever she saw a deer on the side of the road, she would slow down and pray it would stay where it was.

11:58 p.m.

She turned off the highway and headed onto McLaughlin Run Road. The moon was dull and dark. She kept her eyes wide open. There were a lot of deer nearby. Especially after Mr. Collins started to cut down part of the Mission Street Woods for his new housing development. So, she had to be extra careful.

11:59 p.m.

Her heart raced, and her belly tightened. She was two minutes from home. If she didn't speed, she would be late. But if she did speed, a deer might dart in front of her car. The only other choice was to run that last stop sign at the crest of the hill. She could see deer fifty yards away there. The woods were far off the street. So, she could blow off the stop sign and still be okay.

12 midnight

This was it. She had to choose. Blow off the stop sign and be on time or follow the rules and be late and be punished.

"God, please tell me what to do," she said in her most humble and earnest voice.

The feeling hit her at once.

She tapped the brakes.

And made a full and complete stop.

If she hadn't done that, she wouldn't have looked over the hill. And she wouldn't have seen the little boy coming out of the woods. Covered in dirt and malnourished. The little face that was on the Missing posters all over town. If she had blown off the stop sign, she would not have seen him at all.

And she would have absolutely killed him with her car.

CHAPTER 8

C hristopher?" a voice spoke. "Christopher?"

The boy was cold. There was a blanket on top of him. Hospital-thin and scratchy.

"Christopher? Can you hear us?" the voice continued.

The little boy opened his eyes. But his eyes hurt like leaving a movie in the afternoon. He squinted around the room and saw shapes of grown people. There was a doctor. Christopher couldn't see his face, but his stethoscope felt like ice on his chest.

"His color is returning," the doctor said. "Can you hear me, Christopher?"

The little boy squinted and found his mother. All hazy with light. He felt her smooth, warm hand on his forehead. Like the times he got sick.

"I'm here, honey," his mother said, her voice breaking a little.

Christopher tried to speak, but the words got caught in his dry throat. Every swallow was sandpaper.

"Honey, if you can hear us, wiggle your toe," his mother said.

Christopher didn't know if he wiggled it or not. He couldn't feel his toes much. He was still very cold. But he guessed it worked.

"Excellent," the doctor said. "Can you move your hands?"

He did. They felt a little numb. Like a funny bone all over.

"Christopher," another man's voice said, "can you speak?"

Christopher squinted up and saw the sheriff. He remembered him from the day in the park when his mother got the job at Shady Pines. The sheriff was a strong man. As tall as the tetherball pole at school.

"Can you speak?" the sheriff repeated.

Christopher's throat was so dry. He remembered when he had strep throat and the medicine tasted like a weird cherry. He took a swallow and tried to force out a word. But it hurt his throat too much.

Christopher shook his head no.

"That's fine, son," the sheriff said. "But I need to ask you a few questions. So, just nod your head yes or no, all right?"

Christopher nodded yes.

"Very good. You were found on the north end of the Mission Street Woods. Did someone take you there?"

All of the grown-ups were on pins and needles. Waiting for his answer. Christopher searched his mind for a memory, but there was nothing but empty space. He couldn't remember anything. Still, he didn't think anyone took him to the woods. He would have remembered something like that. After a moment, he shook his head. No. And he could feel breath return to the room.

"Did you get lost, then?" the sheriff asked.

Christopher thought really hard, like when he was practicing reading. If no one took him, then he must have gotten lost. That made sense.

He nodded. Yes, he got lost.

The doctor traded his cold stethoscope for rough, fleshy hands. He checked Christopher's limbs and joints, then put blood pressure Velcro over his skinny arm. Christopher got scared that he would have to pee in a cup later. He always felt so ashamed when he had to do that.

"In the woods . . . did anyone hurt you?" the sheriff continued.

Christopher shook his head. No. The doctor hit the button and the blood pressure machine made a grinding noise, strangling his arm. When it was done, the doctor took the Velcro off with a r-r-r-ip and jotted down some notes. Christopher heard the pen.

Swish swish swish.

"Did you hear the cars? Is that how you found your way out of the woods?"

Christopher looked at the doctor's notepad. He began to get an uneasy feeling. A pressure in his head. A dull little headache that usually went away when his mom gave him the aspirin that tasted like orange chalk. But this one was different somehow. Like he had enough headache for the both of them.

"In the woods . . . did you hear the cars? Is that how you found your way out of the woods?"

Christopher snapped out of it. He shook his head. No.

"So, you found the way out on your own?"

Christopher shook his head. No. The room got silent.

"You didn't find the way out? Did someone help you out of the woods?"

Christopher nodded. Yes.

"Who helped you, Christopher?" the sheriff asked.

He gave Christopher a pad of paper and a pencil to write down the name. Christopher took a hard swallow. He whispered. Barely audible.

"The nice man."

CHAPTER 9

Dr. Karen Shelton: Where did you see the nice man, Christopher?

Christopher: Down the trail from the clearing. He was far away.

Dr. Karen Shelton: When you saw him . . . what happened then?

Christopher: I screamed for help.

Dr. Karen Shelton: Did he hear you?

Christopher: Nuh-uh. He just kept walking.

Dr. Karen Shelton: And you followed him?

Christopher: Yes.

Dr. Karen Shelton: You said before you thought it was daylight?

Christopher: Yes. He was walking out of the woods. And the light was bright. So, I thought it was the day.

Dr. Karen Shelton: But it turned out to be the headlights of Mary Katherine's car.

Christopher: Yes.

Dr. Karen Shelton: And what happened to the nice man once you left the woods?

Christopher: I don't know. He must have run away.

The sheriff pressed stop on the tape and stared at the Mission Street Woods. He had been parked outside of them most of the afternoon. Watching through the windshield. Listening to the recording. Over and over. He actually didn't know what he was listening for anymore. Something else. Something he couldn't quite put his finger on.

He had worked a double already. He didn't know if the budget could stand any more overtime from him or his men (and two women). Especially considering there wasn't money in the budget to replace the old tape system. But it didn't matter. They had to find this "nice man."

That is, of course, if he existed.

The sheriff had his suspicions. It didn't take a lot to imagine being a seven-year-old boy, dehydrated, hungry, scared. Needing someone to hold you and convincing yourself that tree branches looked like arms.

But he had to be sure that there wasn't a nice man.

Not to thank this Good Samaritan.

But to see if he took Christopher in the first place.

Dr. Karen Shelton: What did the nice man look like, Christopher?
Christopher: I don't know. I never saw his face.
Dr. Karen Shelton: Do you remember anything about him?
Christopher: He had white hair. Like a cloud.

The sheriff had seen it enough in his old job. In the worst neighborhoods in the Hill District. He had seen bad things done to children. He saw them lie to protect the guilty out of fear. Or even worse . . . loyalty. But the doctor said that Christopher looked to be in good health. Nothing happened to the boy that left any physical marks.

But the sheriff had seen from experience that not all wounds leave marks.

Dr. Karen Shelton: Can you think of anything else?
Christopher: He walked with a limp. Like his leg was broken.

The sheriff stopped the tape and looked at the sketch artist's rendition. Dr. Shelton tried every trick in the book, but Christopher could never remember seeing the nice man's face. The rest of his description was consistent. Tall. Walked with a limp. And white hair.

Like a cloud.

The sheriff took a swallow from his old Dunkin' Donuts cup and let the cold, bitter coffee slosh in his teeth. He studied the sketch for another minute. Something was wrong. He knew it in his guts.

The sheriff opened the door.

He got out.

And walked into the Mission Street Woods.

He didn't know the woods very well. He wasn't from around here. After that last case in the Hill District, he put in for a transfer. He chose Mill Grove for the quiet. And other than a small-time meth lab run by a couple of science fair judges, he got what he wanted. No crimes but underaged drinking and the occasional naked teenager in the back of Daddy's leased sports car. No guns. No killing. No gangs.

It was heaven.

A heaven that barely lasted a year. That's when he got the call that a boy named Christopher Reese had gone missing, and the mother wanted to speak to the sheriff right away. So, he got himself out of bed and threw stale coffee into the microwave. He added three pinches of salt to cut the bitterness and drank it all the way to the station. When he arrived, he was fully prepared to take the mother's statement, mobilize his department, and offer her a trained, uniformed shoulder to cry on.

But there were no tears with Christopher's mother.

She was fully prepared with a recent photo. A list of friends. Activities. And his normal daily routine. When the sheriff asked if there was anyone who would wish the mother or child harm, she mentioned one name. An ex-boyfriend named Jerry Davis back in Michigan.

The sheriff only needed one click of the mouse to see that Jerry was a potential suspect. It was a petty sheet. But there was enough violence. Bar fights. An ex-wife with some bruises. He hit Christopher's mother after he got drunk. He passed out. She left him that night. The sheriff respected her for not waiting to verify his promise to "never do it again." Most women he knew didn't make that call until it was too late.

"Do you think Jerry could have taken Christopher, Mrs. Reese?"

"No. I covered our tracks. He'll never find us."

But the sheriff wanted to make sure. He used the landline with the blocked caller ID. He spoke to Jerry's foreman, who told him Jerry had been at the plant all week. And if he didn't believe him, there was security video to back it up. The foreman asked what this was all about, but the sheriff figured he better not give Jerry a trail to find Christopher or his mother. So, he lied and said he was calling from California. Then, he thanked the man and hung up.

After Jerry Davis was cleared, the sheriff did his due diligence. He questioned teachers and classmates while his deputies combed all of the security footage and traffic cameras in a ten-mile radius. But there was no trace of the boy. No signs of abduction. Not even a footprint left by the rain.

The only fact he was able to establish was that Christopher had been outside waiting to be picked up from school. Christopher's mother said the rain was terrible. There was no visibility. Fender benders everywhere. She said it almost felt like the weather was trying to keep her from getting to her son.

Dr. Karen Shelton: Why did you leave school, Christopher?
Christopher: I don't know.
Dr. Karen Shelton: But you knew your mother was coming to pick you up.
So, why did you leave school?
Christopher: I can't remember.
Dr. Karen Shelton: Try.
Christopher: My head hurts.

By the end of the sixth day, the sheriff had this ache in his gut that someone in a car had simply grabbed the boy. He would keep searching, of course, but with no new leads, clues, or potential suspects, the case was threatening to go cold. And the last thing he wanted to do was give bad news to a good woman.

So, when word came in that Mary Katherine MacNeil found Christopher on the north side of the Mission Street Woods, no one in the sheriff's department could believe it. How the hell did a seven-year-old wander all the way from Mill Grove Elementary School to the other side of those massive woods without being seen? The sheriff was too much of a city mouse to understand just how big 1,225 acres really was, but suffice it to say the woods made South Hills Village Mall seem like a hot dog cart by comparison. The locals joked that the woods were like New York's Central Park (if Central Park were big). It seemed impossible. But somehow, that's what happened.

It was a miracle.

When the sheriff rushed to the hospital to question the boy, he saw Mary Katherine MacNeil with her parents in the reception area. She was crying.

"Dad, I swear to God I was going to be home early when I saw the little boy. I would never drive after midnight! Don't take my license! Please!"

The sheriff's aunt, who'd raised him after his mother passed, had been something of a Bible-thumper herself. So, he took a little pity on the girl and approached with a big smile and a bigger handshake.

"Mr. and Mrs. MacNeil, I'm Sheriff Thompson. I can't imagine how proud of your daughter you must be."

Then, he looked at his clipboard to make the next part feel very official.

"My men told me Mary Katherine called the sheriff's department at five minutes to midnight. Lucky it happened then. It was right before shift change. So, next parking ticket, you just bring it to my office, and I'll tear it up personally. Your girl is a hero. The town is in your debt."

The sheriff didn't know if it was the clipboard. The handshake. Or the free parking ticket, which always felt like more than the $35 it actually was. But it did the trick. The mother beamed with pride, and the father patted his daughter's shoulder as if she were the son he would have preferred. Mary Katherine looked down instead of relieved, which instantly told the sheriff that the girl was lying about being early. But after saving a little boy, she deserved to keep her license.

"Thank you, Mary Katherine," he said, then added a little something to ease the girl's guilt. "You did a real good thing. God knows that."

Once he left the MacNeil family, the sheriff walked down the hall to check in on Christopher and his mother. When he looked at her holding her sleeping boy, he had the strangest thought. In the split second before his job kicked in, he realized that he had never seen anyone love more than that woman loved that little boy. He wondered what it would be like to be held like that instead of chastised by an aunt about what a burden he was. He wondered what it would feel like to be loved. Even a little bit. By her.

Dr. Karen Shelton: What made you walk into the woods, Christopher?
Christopher: I don't know.
Dr. Karen Shelton: Do you remember anything about those six days?
Christopher: No.

The sheriff walked under a canopy of branches on his way to the clearing. The thick trees blocked out the light. Even in the daytime, he needed his flashlight. His feet snapped the twigs like wishbones at his mother's Thanksgiving table. God rest her soul.

snap.

The sheriff turned around and saw a deer watching him from a distance. For a moment, the sheriff didn't move. He just watched this peaceful creature study him. The sheriff took a step, and the deer ran in the other direction. The sheriff smiled and kept walking.

Finally, he reached the clearing.

The sheriff looked up and saw the beautiful autumn sun. He slowly walked the scene, looking for any evidence of Christopher's story. But there were no twigs snapped or broken. There were no footprints except for Christopher's.

The sheriff kicked at the dirt.

Looking for trapdoors.

Looking for hidden passages inside the coal mine.

But there was nothing.

Just a single tree and a whole lot of questions.

Dr. Karen Shelton: I'm sorry your head hurts, Christopher. I only have one more question, then you can stop. Okay?

Christopher: Okay.

Dr. Karen Shelton: If you never saw his face . . . what makes you think he was a nice man?

Christopher: Because he saved my life.

The sheriff pressed STOP on the tape. He left the woods and drove back to the hospital. He parked in the space reserved for law enforcement, right next to the ambulance. Then, he walked the familiar hallway to Christopher Reese's room. He saw Christopher's mother at her son's side. But she did not look like the sleep-deprived woman he had known for close to a week. Her hair was no longer in a ponytail. Her sweatpants and hoodie were replaced by jeans and a blazer. If he weren't so focused on his work, she might have taken his breath away.

"Excuse me, Mrs. Reese?" the sheriff asked after a soft knock on the door. "I just got back from the woods. Do you have a minute?"

She sat up quietly and led him to the waiting room to let Christopher sleep.

"What did you find, Sheriff?"

"Nothing. Look, I promise I'll have my deputies comb the woods again, but I'm almost positive they'll confirm what my gut is telling me."

"What is it?" she asked.

"Maybe it was a combination of malnourishment and dehydration. Whatever it was, ma'am, in my professional opinion, there was no nice man. Just a scared little boy who got lost and in his desperation, saw something that he turned into an imaginary friend of sorts. How else can you explain no footprints other than Christopher's? On the bright side, Dr. Shelton said that imagination like his is a sign of extreme intelligence," he said, trying to be nice.

"Tell that to his teachers," she joked.

"Will do," he joked back.

"But you'll keep your eyes open," she said more than asked.

"Of course. I'll have those woods patrolled every day. If we find anything, you'll be my first call."

"Thank you, Sheriff. For everything."

"Yes, ma'am."

With that, Kate Reese smiled and went back to being Christopher's mother. As the sheriff watched her return to her son's room, he remembered her back in August. He was having lunch with his deputy when she brought Christopher to the little swing set in the park and asked them to watch her son. The thing that struck him was that she only asked after she quickly looked at their sandwiches with one bite each and concluded that she had at least thirty minutes of premium babysitting time by two policemen. Nothing safer than that. So, whether she was educated or not, the sheriff knew that she was smart. And he didn't need her change of clothes to know she was beautiful. The sheriff promised himself he would give the case time to be closed properly, then he would ask Kate Reese to dinner. And he hoped she would wear that beautiful blazer. The one with the tear under the arm that she tried so desperately to hide.

CHAPTER 10

Christopher was staring out of the window when Kate entered the room. She had seen his father do the same thing many moons ago. And for a moment, she forgot about the hospital and thought about his future. He would look more like his father every day. And one day, his voice would change. And one day, he would be taller than her. It was unreal to think that Christopher would start shaving his face in six years. But he would. As all boys do. And it was her job to make sure he would be as good a man as he was a boy.

That and to protect him.

He turned and smiled at her. Her hand found his, and she whispered while she talked. Like a secret.

"Hey, honey. I have a surprise for you."

As she reached into her purse, she saw his eyes light up. She knew her son well enough to sense his little prayer to Jesus and Mary that she was pulling out a box of Froot Loops. It had been days of hospital food. Days of his second-worst nemesis. Oatmeal.

"It's from the school," she continued and watched his heart sink.

Instead of Froot Loops, Christopher's mother pulled out a big white envelope and handed it to him. They opened it together and saw Bad Cat eating the words "Get well soon" off the front of a huge greeting card.

"Your whole class signed it. Isn't that nice?"

Christopher said nothing, but somewhere in his eyes, she could see that he understood that all the kids were forced to sign the greeting card, like how they were forced to give Valentines to everyone so no one would feel left out. But still, he smiled.

"Father Tom had the church say a prayer for you on Sunday. Isn't that nice of him?"

Her boy nodded.

"Oh, and I almost forgot," she said. "I got you a little something, too."

Then, she reached into her purse and pulled out a little box of Froot Loops.

"Thanks, Mom!" he said.

It was one of those wax-lined boxes that didn't need a bowl. He greedily broke it open while she took out a plastic spoon and milk from the cafeteria. When he started eating it, she would have thought he was feasting on Maine lobster.

"The doctors said you can go home tomorrow," she said. "What is tomorrow? I can't remember. Is it Wednesday or Thursday?"

"It's Movie Friday," he said.

The look on his face nearly broke her. He was so happy. He would never know about the $45,000 hospital bill. The health insurance that denied coverage because she hadn't worked at Shady Pines long enough. The lost wages from the week of work she missed to look for him. And the fact that they were now financially ruined.

"So, what do you want to do tomorrow?" she asked.

"Get movies from the library," he said.

"That sounds boring," she said. "Don't you want to do something different?"

"Like what?"

"I heard that Bad Cat 3D is opening tomorrow," she said.

Silence. He stopped eating and looked at her. They never went to first-run movies. Not ever.

"I spoke to Eddie's mom. We're going tomorrow night."

He hugged her so tightly she felt it in her spine. The doctors told her that there was no sign of trauma. No sign of sexual or any other abuse. Physically, he was fine. So what if her son needed some father figure or imaginary friend to make him feel safe? Considering that people sometimes saw Jesus' face in a grilled cheese sandwich, her seven-year-old boy could believe anything he needed to believe. Her son was alive. That's all that mattered.

"Christopher," she said. "The rain was terrible. There were accidents. And this deer jumped in front of the truck ahead of me. I would never leave you in front of that school. I would never do that. You know that."

"I know," he said.

"Christopher, this is you and me now. No doctors. Did anything happen to you? Anyone hurt you?" she said.

"No, Mom. No one. I swear," he said.

"I should have been there. I'm sorry," she said.

And then, she held him so tightly, he couldn't breathe.

*

Later that night, Christopher and his mother lay side by side like they used to before she told him he was big enough to beat up the monsters by himself. As she fell asleep, he listened to the breath that she had given him. And he noticed that even here in the hospital room, she smelled like home.

Christopher turned back to the window, waiting for his own eyelids to get sleepy. He looked at the cloudless sky and wondered what had happened to him for six days. Christopher knew that the grown-ups didn't believe the nice man was real. Maybe they were right. Maybe he was a "fig newton of his imagination" like Special Ed said.

Or maybe not.

All he knew was that he woke up in the middle of the woods. In a giant clearing. With one tree. He had no idea how he got there or how to get out. That's when he saw what he thought was the nice man in the distance and followed him out of the woods.

The sun became the nice girl's headlights.

And she screamed, "Thank you, God!"

And she rushed him to the hospital.

Right before Christopher's eyelids drooped closed, he looked out of the window and saw the clouds drift by, blocking out the moon. There was something familiar about the clouds, but he couldn't quite remember what. In the quiet, he noticed that he had a little headache. And drifted into a peaceful sleep.

CHAPTER 11

N o!" he shouted and bolted up from a dream.

It took his eyes a tick to adjust to the darkness. He saw the little carton of milk with the picture of Emily Bertovich. He saw the old fuzzy TV bolted high above the room. And his mom asleep in the big chair right next to him. And he remembered.

He was in the hospital.

It was quiet. The only light came from the clock. It glowed green and hummed 11:25 p.m. Christopher almost never woke up in the middle of the night.

But the dream was terrifying.

His heart pounded against his breastbone. He could hear it like a drummer hitting sticks inside his body. He tried to remember the nightmare, but for the life of him he couldn't recall a single detail. The only proof was a slight headache that felt like bony fingers pushing on his temples. He crawled under the covers to feel safe, but the minute his body relaxed under the thin, scratchy blanket, he could feel a familiar pressure under the drafty hospital robe.

Christopher had to pee.

The balls of his feet hit the cold tiles beside his bed, and he tiptoed to the bathroom. He was about to open the door when he got this strange feeling. For a second, he thought that if he opened his bathroom door, there would be someone there. He put his head against the wood of the door and listened.

Drip drip drip went the faucet.

He would have called out, but he didn't want to wake his mother. So, he gave the door a slight tap. He waited, but there was no sound. Christopher gripped the handle and started to open the door. Then, he stopped. Something was wrong. It felt like there was a monster in there. Or something else. Something that hissed. The hiss reminded him of a baby rattle. But not from a baby. From a rattlesnake.

He went into the hallway instead.

Christopher walked through the darkness and the quiet hum of machines. He peeked up at the night desk where two nurses were sitting. One of them was on the phone. It was Nurse Tammy, who was always so nice and brought him extra desserts.

"Yes, Dad. I'll get the wine at the state store for Mum's birthday. MerLOT it is. Good night," Nurse Tammy said and hung up.

"Does your father know it's pronounced mer-LOW?" the other nurse asked.

"No, but he put me through nursing school," she said with a smile. "So, I'll never correct him."

Christopher swung the door open for the men's room.

The room was dark and empty. Christopher went to the urinal. The short one. It took him a while to navigate the hospital gown. As he peed, he remembered how Special Ed always went to the bathroom right after remedial reading class. He would stand about four feet from the urinal and try to sink his "long shots." Christopher missed Special Ed. He couldn't wait to see him for Bad Cat 3D tomorrow!

Christopher was so excited daydreaming about the movie, he didn't hear the door open behind him.

He went to the sink to wash his hands. He couldn't exactly reach, so he strained to stand up tall enough to get the soap. The automatic soap made a groaning sound and threw a small dollop on his wrist. He got his hands coated in the soapy goo and reached up to trigger the automatic sink. But he wasn't tall enough. He reached and he strained but nothing worked.

And then, the withered hand came from behind him to turn on the water.

"She's coming," the voice said.

Christopher screamed and spun around.

He saw an old woman. Her face was wrinkled, her back crooked as a question mark.

"I can see her. She's coming for us," she said.

She lit a cigarette, and in the flicker of light, he saw her stained dentures. Perfectly straight and yellow. A cane in one hand. The cigarette shaking with age and arthritis in the other. Her hand moving her cane. Tap tap tap.

"Little boys need to wash their hands for her," she said.

Christopher backed away from her as she puffed like a dragon.

"Where is the little boy going?" she said and walked toward him. "Little boys need to wash their hands clean!"

His back hit the handicapped stall. The door opened like a rusty gate.

"You can't hide from her! Little boys need to get clean for her! Death is coming! Death is here! We'll die on Christmas Day!" she said.

Christopher backed into the wall. He had nowhere to go. He could feel her smoky breath on his face. Christopher started to cry. The words wanted to come out. Help! Stop! Anyone! But they were frozen in his throat. Like those nightmares he had after his dad died when he couldn't get up.

"DEATH IS COMING! DEATH IS HERE! WE'LL DIE ON CHRISTMAS DAY!"

Finally, his voice unclenched, and he screamed, "HELP ME!"

Within seconds, the overhead light flickered on. Christopher saw an old man with coke-bottle glasses open the bathroom stall and walk into the light.

"Mrs. Keizer, what the fuck are you doing? Stop sneaking cigarettes and scaring this poor boy and get your old ass to bed," he said.

The old woman glared back at the old man.

"This is none of your business. Go away!" she said.

"It is my business when you are scaring the shit out of little kids right across the hall when I'm trying to watch The Tonight Show," he barked.

He grabbed the cigarette out of her arthritic hand and tossed it into the toilet. It hit the water with an angry hiss.

"Now stop being crazy and go back to your room." He pointed to the door.

The old woman looked at the water turning cloudy with cigarette ash. She turned back to Christopher. Her eyes were coal black and angry.

"There is no such thing as a crazy person, little boy. It's just a person who is watching you."

For a moment, her eyes seemed to flicker. Like a candle when someone opens the door.

"Oh, go fuck yourself, you scary old bat," the old man said as he ushered the old woman out of the bathroom.

Christopher stood still for a moment, feeling his heart find its way back into his chest. Once he was convinced no one was coming back, he walked over to the sink and somehow got the water going. He quickly rinsed off his hands and left the bathroom.

He looked down the long, dark hallway. The only light came from a single room across the hall. The only sound was the television playing The Tonight Show. The host made a joke about the president's slow response to the crisis in the Middle East. And the grown-ups in the audience laughed and cheered.

"Damn right," the old man laughed from his hospital bed. "Throw the bum out."

"Turn that down, Ambrose," a man's voice said behind the curtain next to him. "Some of us are trying to sleep."

"No. Some of you are trying to die. So, why don't you go f—"

Suddenly, the old man's eyes snapped to Christopher standing in the doorway.

"—screw yourself."

The old man did not wait for his neighbor's response.

"How you doin', son?" he asked. "Old Lady Keizer scare the piss outta you?"

Christopher nodded.

"She's got Alzheimer's. That's all. She lives down the hall from me at the old folks home. Good times. But she's harmless. It's best not to be too scared. Okay?"

"Okay, sir."

"Stop calling me sir and start calling me Ambrose. Deal?"

"Deal."

"Good. Then, have a seat or go to your room. Either way, shut up. I'm missing the monologue," the old man said.

Christopher never got to stay up late to watch The Tonight Show. He smiled and climbed up onto the visitor's chair. He looked at the old man's tray. He still had his dessert on it. A big fat chocolate chip cookie.

"You like chocolate chip cookies?" the old man asked.

"Yes, sir," Christopher said.

"Well, so do I. And that one is mine. So keep your paws off," he barked.

Christopher nodded and watched the old man take the cookie. Without a word, Ambrose broke it in half and gave Christopher the bigger half. Christopher smiled and ate the cookie and watched television with the old man. Most of the time, Christopher didn't know what was so funny, but he wanted to fit in, so he laughed anyway. At one point, he looked over at the old man and saw his leathery skin and a faded tattoo of an eagle.

"Where did you get that tattoo, sir?" Christopher asked.

"Army. Now shut up. I gave you that cookie so you would <u>stop</u> talking."

"Were you ever in a war?" Christopher asked, undaunted.

"A couple," the old man grunted.

"Which ones?"

"The good ones."

The Tonight Show host said something about the crumbling economy and Mr. Ambrose laughed so much he started coughing. Christopher looked at his face.

"Sir, what's wrong with your eyes?" he asked.

"Cataracts," the old man said. "I have cataracts."

"Do those come from a cat?" he asked.

The old man grumbled. "A cat? For Christ's sake. <u>Cataracts.</u> I don't see too well. It's like my eyes are full of clouds."

Christopher froze.

"What do you mean, clouds?" he asked.

"I see shapes. But they're covered over with clouds. That's why I'm here. I hit a deer with my car. I didn't even see the God damn thing. Banged my head on the dash. They're going to take my license this time. I know it. I won't even be able to get away from that home for five minutes now. Fuckers."

Christopher smiled at all the swearing. He loved it. It felt like breaking the law. So, he kept quiet and listened to the running commentary as he watched the lights from the television dance on the old man's face. After a while, Mr. Ambrose "rested" his eyes in a grumpy old man way, and eventually he started to snore. Christopher turned off the TV with the chipped plastic remote in Mr. Ambrose's hands.

"Thanks, junior," he said. Then, he turned over and fell back to snoring.

No man had ever called Christopher "junior" before. And it made him smile. He went back into the hallway. But for some reason, it wasn't scary anymore. He walked past the nurses' station. Nurse Tammy was on the phone again. She didn't see him.

"Dad, please stop calling. I have to do rounds. I promise to bring the merLOT," she said, exasperated.

Just before he went into his room to go back to sleep, he looked down the hall and saw Father Tom. He had never seen a priest outside of church, so he was curious. He tiptoed down the hallway and looked in as Father Tom made the cross over an old man. The old man's family was there. His wife. Two middle-aged daughters. Their husbands. And some grandchildren, who looked like they were in middle school. They were all crying as Father Tom performed last rites.

"Christopher," Nurse Tammy whispered. "Back to bed, hun. This is nothing for a little boy to see."

She ushered him down the hall back to his room. But before he settled in, they passed Mrs. Keizer's room. The old lady was sitting up in bed, watching static on the television. Her yellow teeth drowning in a jar on her nightstand. She turned to Christopher and smiled a sick, toothless grin.

"She took another one. She'll kill us all before the end," she said.

"Don't pay attention to her, Christopher. She doesn't know what she's saying."

CHAPTER 12

W hen Christopher woke up the next morning, he didn't remember when he had fallen asleep. But he saw the light coming through the blinds. And that meant Friday. And that meant no more hospital. And that meant Bad Cat 3D!

He turned to the bathroom. The door was open.

His mother was washing her hands.

And the hissing feeling was gone.

"Wake up, lazy bones." She smiled. "You ready to go home?"

When the nurse pushed him in the wheelchair out of the hospital, he pretended he was Bad Cat's rival, Ace, the flying squirrel who always got motion sickness. The vinyl seats of their old car never felt better. His mother brought him to the diner next to the motel, and he ordered chocolate chip pancakes. Normally, that would be the highlight of his day.

But this was not normal.

This was Bad Cat 3D day. All morning and afternoon, Christopher thought about Bad Cat and his best friend, Ice Cream Cow, who made delicious soft serve. He looked at the clock on the wall and used Ms. Lasko's lessons about telling time. As the seconds ticked away to their tickets at 4:30, it was worse than the waiting on Christmas Eve.

"Why can't Christmas be a day earlier?" he would ask his mother.

"Then, you'd be groaning on December twenty-third," she would reply.

At three o'clock, they headed over to the movie theater near South Hills Village to get in line. By four o'clock, the line was around the block. Special Ed arrived with his mother, both of them dressed as Bad Cat characters. Christopher's mom thought Special Ed probably browbeat his mom into making a fool of herself. At least, she hoped that was the case. The kid had enough struggles ahead of him without having a mom who voluntarily dressed like a donkey named Kicker.

When the usher finally opened the doors, Christopher was so excited. He got his chunky 3D glasses. "Just like a rich kid!" he said. They found their perfect seats right in the middle. Christopher's mom left to get snacks and returned with every bit of junk food that Christopher loved.

He had finished half the snacks by the time the trailers ended. But with each trailer and each chomp of popcorn, his excitement only grew. And when the movie finally started, the children erupted into applause.

*

This would forever be their childhood, Christopher's mother thought.

She remembered the movies she loved when she was a girl. Back when she believed that maybe she was a long-lost princess who belonged to a much nicer family than her own. It wasn't true, but somehow, she still gave birth to a prince.

"I love you, Christopher," she said.

"You, too, Mom," Christopher whispered, distracted by the movie.

She looked up at the screen and smiled when Bad Cat walked up to his crab neighbor, Leonardo di Pinchy, who was halfway through painting his girlfriend, Groan-a Lisa.

Bad Cat said, "Nice painting, Leonardo. Were you going to finish that?"

And all the kids cheered.

When the movie was over, Special Ed's mother "absolutely insisted to Christ" that she take all four of them to TGI Fridays for dinner. Her treat.

"So, the kids can have wings, and we can have our 'mommy juice,'" she said with a wink.

All through dinner, Christopher's mother listened to Special Ed's mother "for Christ's sake, call me Betty" as she margarita'd (it's a verb now) her way through stories of almost finishing college and marrying Special Ed's father, who just opened his sixth "count 'em. Sixth!" hardware store in the tristate area.

She leaned over and whispered through her boozy breath, "You know that C-U-Next-Tuesday, Mrs. Collins? Well, her husband—the notorious P.I.G.— keeps developing housing plans and people keep borrowing money to fix 'em up nice, so God bless is all I have to say. Suck it, Home Depot! My husband is rich! Waitress, the bottom of my glass is dry, and I can still remember my troubles!"

Christopher's mother thought that maybe she made something of a friend in Betty Anderson. Some people are born to talk. Others are born to listen. And it's wonderful when the two meet.

"I like you, Kate," Betty said as they walked to the parking lot. "You're a great listener."

On the drive home, Christopher fell asleep, his belly full of food. His mother carried him up the stairs to their motel room and put him in bed.

"Mom?" he said from his sleep.

"Yeah, honey?"

"Can we see Bad Cat again?"

"Sure, honey. Anytime you want."

She kissed his forehead and left him to dream. She made a beer on the rocks and savored the night. Because she knew that tomorrow, the bill was due, and she couldn't possibly pay it.

CHAPTER 14

When Christopher woke up Monday morning, his "vacation" was over. He was going back to school. Back to Brady Collins and Jenny Hertzog saying "Floods." But most importantly, he was going back after missing two whole weeks.

Even Special Ed is going to be smarter than me now, he thought. He looked down. One little Froot Loop floated like a life raft in the milk.

"I will be here to pick you up at three," his mother said as she dropped him off. "Do NOT leave this school."

"Yes, Mom," he said.

Christopher's mother gave him an extra-long hug, then he walked to the entrance. Normally, he was ignored until he reached homeroom, but this morning, he was the "missing" kid. When the pigtail girls saw him, they stopped jumping rope and stared. A couple of the kids said "Hey." Then, the twin brothers ran up to the school. The minute they saw him, something amazing happened.

"Hey, Christopher. Heads up," Mike said and tossed him their little plastic football.

Christopher couldn't believe it. Matt and Mike wanted to play with him. He looked up, and saw the ball sailing down at him. He was so bad at sports, but he prayed with all his heart that he wouldn't miss the ball. It came down, and right before it almost hit him in the nose . . .

He caught it!

"Hey, Chris. Hit me deep," Matt with the lazy-eye patch said. Then, he started to run.

Christopher knew he couldn't throw, so he thought really quick about how to keep himself in the game.

"Flea flicker," he said and tossed the ball underhand to Mike.

It worked! Mike grabbed the ball and sailed it twenty yards down the sidewalk to his brother. A perfect spiral.

They spent the next three minutes throwing the ball together. But to Christopher, it was as fun as a whole Saturday. He ended up being pretty good at catching the ball.

Mike and Matt, who liked to be called the M&M's, actually said he was pretty fast, too. Mike was older than Matt by three minutes and taller by two inches. And he never let him live that down. But if anyone else made fun of Matt, look out. Especially Matt's lazy-eye patch. Jenny Hertzog somehow got away with "Pirate Parrot." But if anyone else said it, Mike would simply beat them up.

Even fifth graders.

When Christopher got to homeroom, the chatter stopped, and all eyes were on him. Christopher sat down next to Special Ed, trying to blend into his desk. But the M&M's hovered, asking what happened to Christopher when he went missing.

Christopher was normally very shy when kids talked to him, but the brothers were being so nice. So, as the class waited for Ms. Lasko to be her usual five minutes late, he told them the story. As he spoke, he noticed that no one else in the room was talking. All ears were on him.

Suddenly, Christopher felt a little more confident. So, he started to add details about the hospital and getting to stay up late and watch The Tonight Show, which was very impressive to everyone.

"You stayed up past midnight?! Holy shit," Mike said.

"Holy shit," Matt said, trying to be as tough as his brother.

Christopher was in the middle of the story of the old woman in the men's room when he suddenly heard a voice.

"Shut up, faker."

Christopher looked up and saw Brady Collins. He'd gotten a haircut in the two weeks Christopher was gone. He looked even meaner without bangs.

"You pretended to get lost. I know you met your boyfriend in the woods, you big faker. Now shut up," Brady said.

Christopher's face turned red. He immediately got quiet.

"He's telling us a story, Brady," Mike said.

"Yeah, he's telling us a story," Matt echoed.

"So, shut up," Special Ed said with newfound bravado, knowing that Mike was there to back him up.

The room got pin-drop tense.

Christopher immediately tried to keep the peace. "It's okay, guys. I'll stop."

"No, Chris. Screw him," Mike said.

"Yeah. Screw him," Special Ed said, beating Matt to the punch.

Mike finally smirked and whispered, "Sit your ass down, Brady, before I give it a new crack."

Brady's eyes narrowed to slits. He looked violent. Until the girl with the freckles laughed. And then, the geek with glasses laughed. And pretty soon, everyone was laughing. Except Brady. He looked angry and embarrassed and suddenly small. But he was still as dangerous as seventy-five pounds could be. Christopher had seen that kind of violence in someone's eyes before. Jerry was just a lot bigger.

"So, what happened after the old woman?" Mike asked.

Christopher started to tell the story again, and he was so grateful for new friends that he did something daring. He did his impersonation of Leonardo di Pinchy from Bad Cat 3D.

"Were you going to finish that story?" he finished, switching to Bad Cat.

All the kids laughed. Story time was over when Ms. Lasko finally came into class with her thermos and bloodshot eyes. She fished out a couple of aspirin from a tin in her desk, then said the worst two words in the English language.

"Pop quiz."

The kids groaned. Christopher's heart fell. First period was math. Dreaded math.

"Come on now. We've spent the last two weeks working on addition. You can do this, boys and girls," she said as she gave a small stack of quizzes to each kid in the front row. The tests moved back like a wave at a football game. Christopher sank in his chair. He felt Ms. Lasko's manicure on his shoulder.

"Christopher, I don't expect you to know how to do this. Just give it your best shot. You can always retake it. Okay?" she said.

Christopher nodded, but it wasn't okay. He was always terrible at math, and now he was almost two weeks behind. He was going to fail, and his mom was going to have to say, "Don't worry. Keep trying. You'll get it."

He wrote his name in the upper-right-hand corner with a big green pencil. Then, he looked up at the clock. The red seconds hand swooshed past the twelve, and it was exactly eight o'clock in the morning.

Christopher looked at the first problem.

$2 + 7 = $ _____

Ms. Lasko always liked to start with a really easy one to give the kids confidence.

$2 + 7 = 9$

He was sure that was right. Christopher looked down at the test. Only six more problems. He was determined to get at least one more right. At least one more.

$24 + 9 = $ _____

Christopher stopped. Normally nines were really tricky because it never got all the way to ten. If it were twenty-four plus ten, that would be pretty easy. Thirty-four. No problem. But then Christopher figured out something. Just add ten and take off one. That made sense. That was easy. His big green pencil put down the answer.

$24 + 9 = 33$

He couldn't believe it. He got the first two right. If he could just get one more, that would be three of seven. Three plus seven is ten. Ten minus seven is three. He looked at the next problem. It was a money problem.

If you had two nickels, one dime, and one quarter, how much money would you have? _____ cents.

Ms. Lasko always liked to challenge them on the third one. And normally, this was the time Christopher would feel stupid. But not this time. Christopher realized the money was just numbers. And if he could add two numbers, he could add four numbers.

45 cents!

Christopher was so excited, he almost jumped out of his chair. He never got the first three on a pop quiz. Never.

36 - 17 =

Ms. Lasko was being smart again, but he knew what to do now. Thirty-six minus sixteen minus one.

36 - 17 = 19

Slowly, he got this feeling. A small, quiet hope that maybe, just maybe he could get a perfect for his mom. He never got a perfect on a test. Not in any subject. Not in his whole life. His mom would buy him Froot Loops for a year.

If you were at the baseball game for 1 hour and 6 minutes, how many minutes is that?

This was Ms. Lasko being nice again. Any kid could look up at the clock and count around the clock face if they wanted to. But Christopher didn't need to. Sixty tick tick ticks. With six more.

66 minutes

Two more to go. He wanted that perfect so badly. He wanted his mom to be proud of him. He didn't even care about the Froot Loops. He looked at the next problem, tap tap tapping the green pencil.

There are 91 people on a boat, but only 85 life jackets. How many more life jackets are needed?

Christopher took the numbers out of the words and saw ninety-one minus eighty-five. And this time, he didn't even need to do ninety-one minus ten and add four. He didn't need to do anything. He just understood.

6 life jackets

The last question. Christopher could barely bring himself to look. He only needed one more answer to get a perfect. Brady Collins got them all the time. So did Dominic Chiccinelli. Kevin Dorwart. Even Jenny Hertzog. But this was his.

Bonus Problem:
12 x 4 =

Christopher's heart sank. He had only started to learn multiplication before he went to the woods. There was no way he could figure this out. So, he just thought about the number twelve. And how there were twelve people in the jury box in his mom's old movies on Friday nights. And how if there were four movies, that would be four sets of twelve jurors. And how that would be forty-eight jurors.

Christopher stopped breathing.

The answer was forty-eight.

He knew it. Like the moment he learned how to tie his own shoe or know his left from his right (your left hand makes an L!). His mind went CLICK. Everything in his brain that had been cloudy was lifted.

Bonus Problem:
12 x 4 = 48

Christopher had to make extra sure he would get that first perfect, so before he put down his pencil, he went back over the whole test. He did each problem again. And when he got to number three, he stopped.

If you had two nickels, one dime, and one quarter, how much money would you have?

It didn't even occur to Christopher the first time through. This was a math test after all. Not a reading test. But there were so many letters. And he realized he didn't switch his letters back. Not once. He had read the sentence without even sounding it out. He thought there must be something wrong, so he read it again.

If you had two nickels, one dime, and one quarter, how much money would you have?

45. Or forty-five. There were so many e's. Seven, to be exact. But that didn't stop him. And nickels didn't look like . . .

ncikels

They were nickels. And one quarter was one quarter, not . . .

Qautrer

His chest was pounding now. He looked up at the posters around the room. The ones that had given him trouble all month.

RAEIDNG IS FNUDAEMANTL

He didn't even have to sound it out. He did it all in his brain.

READING IS FUNDAMENTAL

All the sound faded away.

DRAE TO KEEP KIDS FOF DRUGS

There was only the room and the sound of Christopher's mind.

DARE TO KEEP KIDS OFF DRUGS

Christopher could read!

He put his head on his desk and tried to hide his excitement. He wasn't stupid anymore. And his mom didn't have to pretend anymore. She would never need to say, "Don't worry. Keep trying. You'll get it." He finally got it. He would make his mother proud with his test.

Not Mom proud. Real proud.

Christopher was about to put his big green pencil on his desk and raise his hand for Ms. Lasko when he stopped. Christopher looked around and realized all the other kids were still taking their tests. Heads were down. And big green pencils were going swish swish swish like the doctor's pen in the hospital. Most of the kids were still on problem number two, including Brady Collins.

That's when Christopher finally looked up at the clock. The test had started at eight o'clock that morning. Christopher didn't even need to do the math in his head. He just knew.

He had taken the test in forty-two seconds.

He was so proud that he didn't even notice the beginning of a headache.

CHAPTER 15

By the end of the day, Christopher's headache was pretty bad. But he was too excited to show his mother his new reading skills to care. He went to the library to pick out his practice books. Mrs. Henderson was there to help him as always. He chose Bad Cat Steals the Letter E, which she set aside for him special. She was about to give him another Snoopy when he stopped her.

"Mrs. Henderson, is there a harder book I can try?"

"Let me see what I can find," she said with a smile.

Mrs. Henderson came back with Treasure Island by Robert Louis Stevenson. Christopher couldn't believe how thick it was. For a moment, he thought he should pick something a little less advanced. But when he opened the old book, all of the letters stood still long enough for him to read.

Fifteen men on the dead man's chest—
Yo-ho-ho, and a bottle of rum!

Not bad. Plus, the cover looked promising. Pirates and treasure? Win win.

"Do you want something easier?" Mrs. Henderson asked.

"No. This looks fun," he said.

He thanked her and threw the books in his backpack. The clock finally hit three. And the bell rang. And the students filled the hallways like ants in an ant farm. Christopher grabbed his windbreaker from his locker. He said goodbye to Special Ed and the M&M's.

And when he got outside, the sky was filled with clouds.

When his mother pulled up, he climbed in the car, excited to show her his first grown-up book. Until he saw that she had a sad face.

"What's wrong, Mom?"

"Nothing, honey," she said.

But Christopher knew better. She looked tired and worried. Just like the week before they ran away from Jerry. Something was wrong. But he knew his mother well enough to know that she would never tell him what it was. She didn't want to worry him.

And that's what always worried him.

He wanted to tell her about his reading all day, but it never seemed to be the right time. She barely talked on the drive home. She talked even less during dinner. And she was in a bad mood about the motel getting so messy and how she "couldn't be the only one who cleaned up around here." By the time the nightly news finished the lead story about the Middle East, she had apologized for being cranky and was already asleep in her twin bed.

So, Christopher let his mom sleep, and he picked up around the motel room. He was hoping if she woke up to a clean room, she wouldn't be so worried that week. Then, they could have a great Friday night together. He had it all planned. Christopher would wait until Movie Friday to give her the special surprise. Not only would he show her his reading. But he would have his pop quiz back by then, too, and he could show her his perfect math score. She would be so proud that she would insist they go to Bad Cat 3D again. He might even get McDonald's. Probably not. But maybe!

Christopher turned off all the lights and then slowly turned down the volume on the TV, so as not to wake her from "resting her eyes." He went to the desk to read Treasure Island by the window light. He wanted to make it through a chapter by Friday for her. Maybe even two. The desk was messy with stacks of paper. At first, he just picked up the coffee cup, which left a ring on the top. But then, he looked a little closer and realized what they were.

They were bills.

Christopher had seen his mom do bills before. She hated them more than anything except maybe parking tickets. But whenever Christopher would ask what was wrong, she would always smile and say the same thing.

"Nothing, honey."

Christopher picked up the first bill. It was from the phone company. In the past, he wouldn't even have tried to read grown-up words like this. But now, he saw them.

Third Notice
Past Due

He turned the bills over. One at a time. Until the coffee mark went from a wet spot to a small circular dent. On every bill, he saw the late payments and the penalties and the past dues.

If you had two nickels, one dime, and one quarter, how much money would you have?

Not enough.

Christopher couldn't add all the numbers together. They were way too big. But he knew she couldn't afford to take him to Bad Cat 3D again no matter how well he did on a test. And she probably couldn't have afforded it last week, either.

He suddenly felt very ashamed for all the things he wasted, like Froot Loops. And his hospital and doctors. He cost her too much. Just like his dad did. She put his father's funeral on a credit card, so he could be buried with some dignity. And she never recovered. He overheard her talk about it to a nice neighbor back in Michigan over one too many beers. And later, when he asked her what was wrong, she smiled and said, "Nothing, honey."

Just like she did today.

So, he promised himself that when she saw his perfect math test and wanted to take him to McDonald's, he would say no. And if they went to a restaurant with Special Ed's mom again, he would only buy things that were "market price" on the menu because if they only charged the same price they did at the supermarket, then that would be a good deal for his mom. But most of all, he would never go to a rich 3D movie again. He would get an old movie from the library. And he would read a book out loud to her, so she would know that all of her hard work paid off.

With this thought, Christopher tiptoed to his sleeping bag. He got out one of his old tube socks. He reached in and pulled it out.

His pants money.

Then, he tiptoed around his mom and put it at the bottom of her purse. Jenny Hertzog could say "Floods!" to him for the rest of his life for all he cared.

CHAPTER 16

F loods! Floods!" Jenny Hertzog called out in the hallway.

But this time, it didn't bother Christopher. He just felt sad for Jenny like he would for his mom. That didn't make sense. But that was how he felt. He just thought Jenny was someone who had a lot worse things than "Floods" said to her. Or maybe her dad had a lot of bills at home and was cranky all the time. Whatever it was, he was glad he gave his mom the money. And he couldn't wait for Ms. Lasko to give them their tests back today, so he could show his mom his first perfect.

When math period began, Ms. Lasko passed back all of the tests. Christopher looked around the room. He saw Kevin Dorwart got a 7 out of 7. Brady Collins got a 6 out of 7. Special Ed got a 2 out of 7. Matt and Mike got 5 each. But Christopher's test didn't come back. He didn't know why. When the bell rang, and all the kids left for recess, Ms. Lasko kept Christopher after class.

"Christopher," she said gravely. "I know you were gone for two weeks, and that you didn't want to get behind. So, did you . . . did you look at anyone's answers when you took the math quiz?"

Christopher swallowed. He shook his head no.

"I won't be mad. But I don't want you to cheat yourself out of learning how to do this for yourself. So, one more time, did you look at anyone's answers for the pop quiz? Maybe Kevin Dorwart's paper?" she asked.

"No, Ms. Lasko."

Ms. Lasko studied his eyes closely. Christopher felt like a frog on a dissection table.

"You know, I've seen students who feel so much pressure to do well on tests that they always did badly. And when they were told it didn't matter, they ended up doing really well," she said.

Then, she smiled and gave him his pop quiz back.

"I'm proud of you. Keep it up."

It had a big 7/7 on it with big red marker. And a gold star. And a big sticker of Bad Cat saying, "You are purrrrrrfect!"

"Thank you, Ms. Lasko!"

Christopher smiled so big, he couldn't contain himself. He couldn't even wait for Movie Friday. When his mother pulled up into the parking lot, she waved. And Christopher waved back with the paper in his hand.

"What's with you?" she asked. "You look like the cat that ate the canary."

And that's when Christopher handed her the test.

"What is this?" she asked.

He didn't say anything. She opened it up. And read it. And stopped. Quiet. His first perfect. 7 out of 7. She studied the test again for a private moment, then she turned to Christopher. Her eyes had a look of pride instead of worry.

"See! I told you you would get it!" she said.

That's when he showed her his Treasure Island book.

"I'm on chapter three," he said.

She was so proud, she let out a shout and hugged him.

"This is what happens to people who don't give up," she said.

As he predicted, she offered to take him to Bad Cat 3D again.

"No, thanks. Let's get movies from the library," he said.

She looked puzzled at first, then relieved. Especially when he said he wasn't in the mood for McDonald's or any restaurant food for that matter. He wanted her grilled cheese sandwiches. So, they went to the library and scored with a fresh copy of Bad Cat 2 ("This time it's purrrrsonal") and The African Queen for her.

Then, they got groceries at Giant Eagle for their grilled cheese feast. Christopher saw his mom reach into her purse. This was it! He watched as she pulled out the hidden money. Her face crinkled with confusion. She didn't know where it came from. But she was happy it was there. She was about to put it back in her purse for a rainy day when Christopher stopped her.

"Mom, you should get something for you," he said.

"No, I'm okay," she said.

"No, you really should," he insisted.

He squeezed her hand softly. Like his mom buying tomatoes. She seemed surprised. Christopher was not one for insisting on much. She paused for a moment, then shrugged.

"What the hell," she told the clerk. "Get me a Sarris pretzel and a lottery ticket."

The teenage clerk gave her the world's best chocolate pretzel and a lottery ticket. To honor her son, Christopher's mom decided to play the answers from his first perfect test. She handed the girl five dollars. She got seventeen cents back. He saw nothing else in her wallet. She looked at a little tin for charity. A child was staring back at her from a refugee camp in the Middle East. She gave the tin seventeen cents, and they left the store with her purse empty.

On the drive home, Christopher saw his mother eye the gas tank. 1/4 full. He was grateful it was Special Ed's mom's turn to carpool to CCD, or they might not have made it to payday.

When they got home, the night was quiet and cool. They stood side by side in the kitchenette. Christopher watched his mom drop the grilled cheese onto the hot plate and smiled when the butter sizzled. He listened to the ice cubes clink in the glass as he poured his mom her beer on the rocks. And as always, they planned what to do with their untold riches. Christopher added a sports car in the driveway of their dream house for his mom like Ms. Lasko's car. For her part, Christopher's mother was so impressed with his selection of Treasure Island that she pledged she would get him a bookshelf to go with his very own library.

Christopher turned on the television, which filled the motel room with sounds of the evening news. Christopher's mother was flipping the grilled cheese sandwiches when the sports coverage ended, and it was time for the lottery. She was so focused on cooking, she almost didn't hear the first number called out.

It was a nine.

Christopher unfolded the TV trays they bought at a garage sale and dragged them in front of the beds. He looked at his math test stuck to the motel mini fridge with a couple of alphabet magnets.

"Mom, would you like—"

She held up her hand to shush him. He got quiet and looked at her. She grabbed his math test from the mini fridge and walked to the television. The

lottery balls danced in the glass vacuum. Christopher hadn't been paying attention.

The second number was 33.

"Mom?" he said.

"Shh," she said.

She dropped to her knees. Looking at the newsman. Christopher had seen
her get two numbers before. That had happened. But now her hands were
wringing. The third ball got sucked into the vacuum.

45

"Oh, God," she said in a whisper.

Christopher had never seen his mother pray in church. But now, she laced
her fingers together so tightly, her knuckles turned white. The fourth number
got sucked out. And the newsman announced,

19

"Oh, Jesus, please," she said.

Christopher looked at his perfect test, shaking in her hands. The next answer
was 66. His mother had stopped breathing, waiting for the next number to be
drawn.

"Sixty-six!" the newsman announced.

Christopher's mother didn't know it, but she was rocking back and forth.
She held him so hard, he could barely breathe. But he didn't say anything. He
didn't dare. She was tense as a board. He looked at the next answer from his
test. It was 6. The next number was drawn.

It was 9.

"No!" she gasped.

It felt like an eternity before the newsman turned the ball upside down to
put the line on the right side.

"Six!" the newsman said.

"Oh, my God," she said.

There was one number to go. One single number. The balls danced in the
glass box. Christopher looked at the last answer on his perfect test. It was 48.
Christopher's mother closed her eyes. As if she couldn't bear to look. Couldn't
bear one more loss after so many.

"Tell me," she said.

"Mom, you won."

He didn't see it. But he felt her tears on his neck. Her arms held him so tightly that he thought his spine would snap. They would have stayed there all night if the smoke alarm didn't start chirping. They ran back to the hot plate and saw the grilled cheese sandwiches were now as black as raisins. His mom turned off the burner and opened the window, letting the smoke out.

"It's okay. We can still eat it. The grilled cheese isn't that burnt," Christopher said.

"Fuck that," his mother replied. "Grab your coat. We're going out for steak."

They went to Ruth's Chris downtown. And even though his mom said to order anything he wanted, he still chose the lobster because it was listed as "market price."

CHAPTER 17

T his is the nicest house we've seen," Mrs. Soroka said as they pulled into the driveway.

She was a classy lady. Elegant on the outside. But it was learned. Kate knew that. The way some people could throw on a bigger vocabulary than their father and pretend they came from somewhere else. Some people's fake is more honest than other people's real. She might have talked fast, but Mrs. Soroka meant every word.

"The driveway is a little ragged, but you're a few years from repaving. And I know people who can cut you a deal. We girls have to stick together."

She said that with a wink and opened the car door. It was their third house that day. The first house was too big. The second was too small. And like Goldilocks, they were hoping the third would be just right.

"The door sticks a little," Mrs. Soroka said, jangling the keys and popping them into the lock. "But we can add that to the inspection list, and they'll pay for it."

Mrs. Soroka clicked the lock and opened the door with a shoulder bump. Kate stayed behind with Christopher for a moment, looking around the crisp fall neighborhood. All the houses on the cul-de-sac looked clean and rich. As pretty as the changing leaves. There was even a log cabin on top of the little hill across the street. It reminded her of Christopher's old Lincoln Logs. There was an old lady sitting in the attic, staring out the window. Even at a distance, Kate could hear the creak of her rocking chair.

"Christopher? Earth to Christopher?" Kate said. "Let's go."

Christopher turned away from the log cabin and followed her inside.

The house was beautiful. What Mrs. Soroka called a _real_ Craftsman. The living room had built-in bookshelves and a fireplace with enough space for a really nice TV. The whole place smelled like chocolate chip cookies from a dozen open houses. Mrs. Soroka told them that cookies were a trick that real estate agents used to sucker people into feeling at home.

"Well, it's working," Kate joked.

"Tell me about it. I was skinny before I got into this business."

Mrs. Soroka moved through the house, turning on lights. Kate's excitement grew with each room. The dining room was perfect for four, but could easily fit eight. She could even have company over for Christmas dinner.

And the kitchen.

Oh, God, that kitchen.

This wasn't a microwave and a hot plate in a motel room. This was heaven. Brand-new stainless-steel appliances. A dishwasher that didn't leak. A fridge with an ice maker rather than a bucket and a trip down the hall of a motel. The place even had a kitchen island. A God damn kitchen island!

"What do you think, Mom?" Christopher asked.

"Not bad," she said, trying to sound casual.

Mrs. Soroka kept talking about washer/dryer hookups and maintenance, but Kate had stopped listening. What had started as a crush in the living room had grown into a full-blown love affair by the time they mounted the stairs to the bedrooms. She had never had stairs. Only walk-ups. And fire escapes.

She could finally tell her son not to run on the stairs.

"Let's see the master first," she said.

"You're the boss," Mrs. Soroka said with a smile.

Kate loved the beautiful staged bed and large windows. But the walk-in closet finally did it. Her face broke into a Cheshire grin, and her palms started to sweat with the anxiety of having to fill so much closet space. Her guilt couldn't take this many trips to the mall. Outlet or otherwise. But maybe she could go to Goodwill and get some things.

Stop it, Kate. You deserve this. Breathe.

"Now, the second bedroom is a little cozy. That's code for small," Mrs. Soroka joked. "So, maybe that could be a guest bedroom for relatives."

There were no good relatives. There would never be guests. But Mrs. Soroka didn't need to know that. The guest room would make a perfect office when Kate finally went back to school. It was right above the two-car garage. No more parking tickets during street cleaning days. No more brown paper bags on parking meters. Their brand-new (certified pre-owned) land shark would have its own dock.

"And this would be Christopher's room," Mrs. Soroka said as she opened the door.

It was perfect.

A little bed with a desk. A big bay window with room for a child to sit and stare and wonder. A large closet for clothes. A separate storage closet for toys. Nice clean carpet. The whole room smelled like spring. Like lemons without the sour.

"You like it, honey?" she asked.

"I love it, Mom."

"I love it, too."

"So, are we happy?" Mrs. Soroka asked.

"We're very happy," Kate said.

"Are you ready to make an offer?"

Kate got quiet. Her heart beat with thoughts of being given the pen to sign her name. But she had already collected her winnings, and when it was all added up and taxes were taken out, she was completely out of debt. She paid for Christopher's stay at the hospital. She paid for her late husband's funeral. Then, she paid off all of her credit cards like Suze Orman said to on TV. She started a college fund (for both of them). And when it was all said and done, she still had enough money left for a down payment on the one thing Christopher always promised to buy her.

Their very own house.

No more running. No more moving. Her boy was going to have a home.

Slow down, Kate. Ask the questions.

"Is it a good deal? Be straight with me. We girls have to stick together, right?"

"Right. And it's a great deal. The only reason they're selling is they bought a condo in Palm Springs to get away from the winter and the son-in-law. This location is about to explode. Even if you went above the asking price, it's a steal."

Kate knew she was telling the truth. She had done her homework.

"What do you think?" she asked Christopher.

"It's the nicest place I've ever seen," he said.

"Then, let's make an offer," she said.

Mrs. Soroka clapped her hands.

"You're doing the right thing! And do you want to know something? I haven't even shown you the best part!"

Mrs. Soroka walked across Christopher's bedroom to the large bay window. She threw open the curtains and let in the view. Right under Christopher's bedroom was a big backyard with a tree and a tire swing and a jungle gym and a sandbox. It was every boy's dream. Flat and well manicured. Perfect for football. Perfect for anything.

"Just think," Mrs. Soroka said. "You get that backyard, and then take a look right behind it."

It was the Mission Street Woods.

Christopher may have forgotten the six days he was lost in them, but Kate never would.

"I don't want to live near those woods," she said.

Mrs. Soroka nodded, as if remembering Christopher's picture in the newspaper when he went missing.

"Look, me, you, and the wall . . . Mr. Collins is planning a new housing development a stone's throw from here."

"I know," Kate said.

Mrs. Soroka nodded, then dropped her voice to a conspiratorial whisper.

"Yes, but did you know that he hired my boss to sell those houses? And he's going to build a road to connect both sides of town? In six months, you will have a house in the hottest neighborhood in Mill Grove that will be worth a hundred thousand dollars more than you paid for it. I like you, Kate. And I'm a mother, too. So, I don't want you to miss this opportunity. Two words . . . Ker ching."

"Are you sure?"

"Trust me. Those woods will be gone by Christmas."

CHAPTER 18

They moved the day after Halloween.

Christopher and his mom were on their knees as they packed their lives in boxes. They were used to moving by now. Michigan was only a couple of months ago. But this was not running away in the middle of the night to get away from Jerry. It wasn't escaping a town where every signpost reminded her of her late husband.

This was her own home.

This was her new life.

Kate packed up the old hot plate and dishes. She was so excited with thoughts of her new kitchen that she almost accidentally wrapped the cereal bowls with Christopher's picture from the newspaper.

The Pittsburgh Post-Gazette had run the story about him. Kate didn't want her picture in the paper, but she wanted her son to have the glory. So, he went to the jungle gym at recess for the photo with his teacher Ms. Lasko. The photographer, an aspiring filmmaker, took the snap. And on Sunday, Kate proudly got every single copy at the Giant Eagle where she bought the lottery ticket.

Boy's Test Wins Lottery

She looked at her seven-year-old son dragging his Bad Cat sleeping bag into the small pile of boxes near the door. There wasn't a lot from the old life. Just a few things she was able to sneak into the trunk of the old land shark to get ready to run from Jerry. And a few new things to mark the beginning of this era.

The posse arrived shortly after. Kate was actually rather proud that they were able to make so many friends in so little time. Special Ed and his mother Betty brought her husband to help them move. Big Eddie had a heart almost as big as his man boobs. He spent the afternoon entertaining everyone with stories about how he put himself through college working for a moving company.

"Back then, I was ripped," he kept saying.

"You're ripped now, baby," Betty said, blinded by love.

The M&M's pitched in, too, with the help of their two moms. A quiet lady named Sage. And a not-so-quiet lady named Virginia. One a vegan from Connecticut. The other a carnivore from Texas. They were made for each other.

Little by little, the gang sweated and muscled their belongings into a small truck, generously supplied by Big Eddie's Hardware Stores.

When it was all packed, Christopher and his mom went back to look for anything they might have left behind. When they realized the only things left in the motel room were memories, they said their goodbyes to their old life.

"I will never pay rent again," Kate said and closed the door.

When the new land shark pulled up to 295 Monterey Drive at the end of the cul-de-sac, Kate and her son were given a special treat. Special Ed's mom and dad ("I said call us Betty and Eddie, for Christ's sake!") had bribed Mrs. Soroka with a bottle of Chardonnay for the keys to the garage. Two of Big Eddie's finest employees had set up the automatic garage door. And when Christopher's mom was about to get out of the car to open it manually, Betty hit the button. Eddie pretended it was a ghost, much to everyone's delight, and then everyone went inside to begin unpacking.

It didn't take long, considering how little they had. The trips to the truck became even shorter once the sheriff came to help after his shift had ended. He and Kate had kept in touch since Christopher had left the hospital. When his deputies found nothing in the woods, the sheriff made sure to call her. And before she put the offer in on the house, she made sure to call him. Christopher's safety came first. The sheriff did his due diligence, and after combing the last decade of police reports, he assured her that the house was safe. The neighborhood was safer. But if she'd like, he'd walk the area with her to make triple sure.

"Not necessary," she said, much to his disappointment. "But if you want to come on moving day, I'm buying the pizza."

Deal.

All day, Kate watched Christopher and his friends try to act like real men. When the sheriff helped her carry in the new furniture (from the outlet mall), the four boys were there to volunteer. When Big Eddie stopped to have his beer, they stopped to have their lemonade. And when the house was done, and Big Eddie fired up the grill to cook his famous "pancake dogs" to "wash down" the pizza, the boys studied his technique with a trained eye and listened to him talk to the sheriff and nodded along as they pretended to be grown men.

After all, Eddie was the only father any of them had known in a couple of years.

And the sheriff was the sheriff.

When their feast was over, the family of friends said their good-nights. Sage and Virginia promised to swing by that week to help Kate clean. Betty promised to swing by to help her drink and watch them clean. Big Eddie said that if she ever needed any hardware to fix the usual first-month-in-a-new-house pain-in-the-ass problems, he'd help out. And Christopher told his friends he'd see them all Monday.

The sheriff was the last to go.

"It was nice of you to come and help, Sheriff," she said, shaking his hand.

The sheriff nodded, then turned his eyes to the floor. He shuffled his feet like a middle school kid, and his words suddenly sounded as if his chest was beating like a ball in a racquetball court.

"Yeah, well. I know what it's like to move to a new place and have no one pitch in. I only came from the Hill District a year ago."

She nodded. And he swallowed. And he tried.

"Mrs. Reese . . . have you been to Primanti Brothers yet? It's a real Pittsburgh institution."

"No."

"Can I take you?"

Maybe not as elegant as he'd planned. But there it was.

She looked at him. This big bear of a man who suddenly looked small. She had known enough bad men in her life to recognize a good one when she saw one. But she wasn't ready. Not even close. Not after Jerry.

"Give me some time, Sheriff," she said.

That seemed to be enough for him.

"I have plenty of that, Mrs. Reese," he said, smiling. "Good night."

With that, he walked to his car. Kate stood on the porch and watched him drive away through the first few drops of rain. Then, she went inside her very first house and locked the door.

As she listened to the rain pitter-pat the roof, she walked up her very own stairs to her son's bedroom. Christopher was already in his pajamas, curled up in bed, reading Robinson Crusoe. Mrs. Henderson recommended the book after Christopher loved Treasure Island so much.

Kate couldn't believe how far he had come with his reading in the past month. His math, too. He had started preschool shortly after his father died. After struggling for so long, he was finally thriving. So, maybe his early learning problems had as much to do with stress as anything. Whatever it was, she promised herself to get Mrs. Henderson and Ms. Lasko extra-special gifts at Christmas.

Those women were miracle workers.

She sat next to him and read a few lines over his shoulder, tucking his hair behind his ear. She looked around his bedroom at the two things she'd promised to get him with the lottery money.

The first was a bookshelf.

This didn't come from an outlet mall or IKEA, either. Oh, no. For her son's first real bookshelf, she had combed all over town until she found a lovely antiques shop. She said he could have any he wanted. There were beautiful ones. Oak. Pine. Cedar. But instead, Christopher picked out an old one covered with this ridiculous duck wallpaper. It was the bookshelf equivalent of Charlie Brown's Christmas tree.

"You can have any bookshelf you want. Why do you want that one, honey?" she asked.

"Because it smells like baseball gloves."

The second was a silver frame for the picture of his father. He proudly put it on top of the bookshelf as the centerpiece of his room. She stared at the photograph. A moment frozen in black and white. Christopher's father smiling next to the Christmas tree. That was one of the good days.

Kate lay there for twenty minutes, listening to her son read his book, his voice as soft as the rain outside. When they were done, she kissed his cheek and tucked him into bed for sleep.

"Christopher . . . you bought your mother a house. Do you know who does that?"

"No."

"Winners do that."

And with that, she turned off his light with a "One two three...ah-choo!" Then, she went down to the kitchen. After a couple of swigs of beer on the rocks, she started to tackle her bedroom. Her very own bedroom. Other than a few years with her husband, she'd never known a safe home in her entire life.

And now she was giving one to her son.

When she finally unpacked the last of her clothes, she realized that they only filled up one-third of her walk-in closet. Normally, Kate Reese would wait for the other shoe to drop. But this was heaven. Sheer heaven. She retraced every decision, every moment that led to her standing in her very own house listening to the clouds drop rain on her roof.

She felt like it couldn't have worked out any better if someone had planned it.

CHAPTER 19

Christopher was curled up in his Bad Cat sleeping bag. He listened to the pitter-pat rain, and he felt warm and toasty. The moonlight winked through the streaks of rain on the bay window, casting little shadows on his new bookshelf and picture of his dad. His mom said he could paint his walls any color he wanted because they never had to worry about getting a security deposit back ever again. He told her he wanted blue with clouds. Like the sky. Or Mr. Ambrose's eyes.

Without a sound, Christopher got out of his sleeping bag.

He walked to the bay window and climbed up. He sat there, cross-legged, looking out over his backyard. With the tire swing. And the big field perfect for baseball with the guys.

And the Mission Street Woods.

A streak of lightning broke across the sky. The rain leaving impressions of itself on the glass like tears down a windshield. In CCD, someone said that rain is God's tears. He wondered if Noah's Ark was from anger.

Or God's sobbing.

Christopher opened the bay window. He looked up and saw the clouds. Little drops of rain fell on the ledge. They were cold on his cheeks, rosy and red. He sat there for half an hour just looking and listening, feeling special and happy. There was something familiar about the clouds. He just couldn't remember what. But they felt like they were smiling. And Christopher smiled back.

It wasn't a voice. It was the wind. It was a whisper. Not like a voice. Like an impression of a voice. Christopher didn't hear it so much as remember someone saying it to him. But it was there. It was coming from the woods.

Asking him to come.

Christopher grabbed his boots and red hoodie off the floor. He quickly glanced at his father framed in silver. Then, he opened his bedroom door. He looked down the hallway. His mother's room was dark. He tiptoed down the staircase and walked through the kitchen. There was no cookie smell anymore.

Christopher opened the sliding glass door to the backyard. The fog was thicker now, but he could still make out the trees swaying in the breeze. It was soothing to him. Like a lullaby or the nice side of the pillow.

His feet hit the wet, cold grass. He walked through the fog, past the tire swing, to the very edge of his backyard. He looked back at his house. He saw the log cabin across the street. Every window was dark. Then, he turned back to the trees. And there it was. One foot away.

The Mission Street Woods.

Christopher watched them. The trees swaying all pretty and bare and still. Like arms waving in church. Back and forth. Back and forth. He couldn't see anyone, but he could feel them there. And he could smell the baseball-glove smell even though his baseball glove was packed in the living room in a box.

"Are you there?" Christopher finally whispered.

The trees rustled. He heard the sounds of twigs crackling. Christopher's ears turned red. He knew he should have been afraid, but he wasn't. He took in a breath, feeling relieved. Because he knew something was in there. Watching him.

"Thank you for getting my mother a house," Christopher whispered.

There was silence. But it wasn't silence. It was listening to him. Christopher thought that maybe it was right behind him. The tickle on the back of his neck.

"Are you trying to talk to me?" Christopher asked.

The breeze wrestled with the leaves. Christopher felt a voice on the wind. It didn't speak. But he still felt words on his neck. As if the wind pushed through the trees just barely enough to understand.

Christopher entered the woods.

The rain hit the tops of the leaves and ran down the trunks in small rivers. Christopher didn't know where he was going, but somehow, his feet did. It felt like riding a bike. His brain might have forgotten, but his body never would.

His feet were taking him to the voice.

Christopher's heart skipped a beat. He couldn't see anyone, but he could feel something. Like static that goes crack when hands finally touch. He followed it through the woods, and the light on the trail became brighter. A smell came to him. A delicious autumn smell. Like bobbing for apples. He saw names carved into the trees. Initials of teenage lovers from a hundred years ago. People who were old now.

Or people who were dead.

Christopher reached the clearing. He stood silent, staring at the giant tree shaped like an arthritic hand. He saw a plastic bag on the ground, covered in dirt. He picked it up and lovingly washed it in the rain, fresh and cold. He rubbed it with his red hoodie until the dirt gave way to white. Then, he walked over to the tree and put the white plastic bag on a low-hanging branch. Christopher stared at it, dancing like a kite on a string. He couldn't remember, but there was something about it. Something safe and comforting. Like an old friend.

"Hi," Christopher said to the white plastic bag.

you can hear me?

The white plastic bag sounded so relieved.

"Yes, I can hear you," Christopher said.

i can't believe it. finally someone can hear me.

Christopher's face went flush. He took a long, hard swallow.

"Are you really real?" Christopher asked the white plastic bag.

yes.

"You're not a fig newton of my imagination?"

no.

"So, I'm not crazy?" Christopher asked.

no. i've been trying to talk to everyone. but you're the only one who listened.

Christopher was so relieved.

"Why can I hear you now?"

because we're alone in the woods. that's why i got you that house. do you like it?

"It's the greatest house I've ever seen."

i'm so glad.

"When can I see you?"

soon. but first, i need you to do something for me. okay?

"Okay," Christopher said.

Then, the little boy knelt down at the foot of the tree and stared at the white plastic bag, dancing like hair in the breeze. Christopher sat there for hours. Oblivious to the cold. Talking about everything. With his new best friend.

The nice man.

Part III

Best Friends Forever

CHAPTER 20

"Do you guys want to build a tree house?"

"A tree house?" Special Ed said, washing down his bacon with a chocolate Yoo-hoo. "My dad made me one from a kit once. He got really drunk, and it broke."

They were in the cafeteria. Salisbury steak day. Christopher didn't know what Salisbury meant exactly, but his mom had given him lunch money to buy a real hot lunch instead of his usual brown-bag peanut butter and celery. Especially because it was getting a little colder in November. The Halloween decorations had been taken down and Thanksgiving decorations had been put up.

"Not that kind of tree house, Ed," Christopher explained.

Christopher opened his notebook and carefully slid the plans over to his friends. The M&M's looked at the blueprints, all perfectly drawn on graph paper in painstaking detail. The roof. The black shingles. The hinges. Red door. And the little 2x4s snaking up the tree like a ladder of baby teeth.

"Wow. That's like a real house," Matt exclaimed behind his eye patch.

"You drew all this?" Mike asked, impressed.

Christopher nodded. He woke up with the plans on Sunday morning. An image in his brain he could almost scratch. He spent the whole day drawing them with colored pencils and graph paper the way he used to plan his mother's dream house. But this time, there were no video games or candy room or petting zoo off the kitchen.

This time, it was real.

"You would have a front door that locks and everything?" Mike asked.

"Yeah. And shutters. And real glass windows. And a secret trapdoor with a rope ladder on the bottom," Christopher said excitedly.

"But why would you need a secret door?" Matt asked.

"Because it's cool. Duh," Mike said.

"Let me see those," Special Ed said, grabbing the papers out of Matt's hands.

He studied them skeptically, like a surveyor, in between sips of Yoo-hoo. Christopher saw that Special Ed was getting bacon grease on the corners of the blueprints. It made him a little mad, but he didn't say anything. He needed his friend's help. After a moment, Special Ed slid the papers back to Christopher.

"Impossible. We could never build anything like that by ourselves," he said.

"Yes, we could," Matt said. "Our uncle George is a—"

"—handyman," Mike said, stealing his little brother's thunder. "We helped him last summer. We could figure it out."

"But it's already November. It's cold as hell," Special Ed cautioned.

"Are you a girl?" Mike asked.

"I don't know. Are you?" Special Ed replied skillfully.

"Come on, Eddie. It'll be our own private clubhouse," Christopher said.

"What's so fun about going out into your backyard and building some stupid tree house thirty feet from your warm living room with a real TV?"

"Because we're not building it in my backyard," Christopher whispered. "We're building it in the Mission Street Woods."

You could have heard a pin drop. Suddenly, the gravity of the plan was revealed. This was not some backyard excursion. This was high adventure. This was breaking rules. This was . . .

"Awesome," Special Ed whispered.

"But that's trespassing," Matt said.

"No shit, Sherlock. That's what's so awesome," Special Ed replied.

"I don't know," Mike said. "The Collins Construction Company has fences everywhere."

"Are you a girl?" Special Ed asked. The "touché" was silent.

"Not everywhere," Christopher said. "There is a path to the woods in my backyard. We don't need to jump the fence there or anything. But we'll need tools."

"Easy," Special Ed said, now the plan's biggest champion. "My dad has a garage full. He never uses them."

"What about wood?" Christopher asked, although he knew the answer.

"Collins Construction has scrap piles all over the place," Mike said.

"And our uncle has plenty of loose nails," Matt added, as if trying to matter.

The planning went on like that for the rest of lunch. The boys figured out that they could beg, borrow, or steal almost everything they needed except for shingles and a doorknob and windows. But Special Ed's dad had a collection of old Playboy magazines and a color Xerox and a neighborhood full of older kids.

So, money could be raised.

Of course, the Collins Construction Company had a strict no-trespass policy. And Special Ed knew from his dad that Mr. Collins had been cutting down parts of the woods to build subdivisions. So, this was illegal. But somehow, that was part of the appeal.

"Breaking the law! Breaking the law!" Special Ed said, singing a line from one of his mother's favorite songs from her college days.

"But what about our parents?" Matt asked.

Oh, right. Their parents. Hmmm.

They didn't see how their parents would ever agree to let them run around in those woods alone. Especially after Christopher went missing. Maybe Special Ed's father could be conned, but their mothers? Never.

His friends were stumped, but the problem actually felt good in Christopher's brain. Kind of like a combination of a long stretch in the morning and a back scratch. As he thought of solutions, he realized that for the last two minutes, his head wasn't hurting. He actually had an idea.

A sleepover.

Of course.

They could bring sleeping bags and have a sleepover at the tree house. If they each told their parents they were staying with the other, they could work Saturday night all the way through Sunday. It was a risk. The moms would call to check on them. But with cell phones, maybe they could get away with it. Either way, they could work for almost two whole days without interruption.

Mike loved the idea. Matt seemed scared to be in the woods, but he didn't dare say anything in front of his brother. So, he agreed.

"Can I be in charge of the food?" Special Ed asked.

"Sure, Eddie."

With the plan settled, Christopher sat back and looked at his friends, giddy and loud with excitement. But to Christopher, the room was almost silent as the pain quietly crawled back into his mind. He didn't mind the headache. He was getting used to them by now. He was just relieved that his friends were helping him build the tree house because without them, he knew he couldn't have finished it in time.

"Come on, Chris," Special Ed exclaimed.

Christopher snapped out of it and realized they were waiting for him, their drinks hoisted and ready for the toast. Christopher raised his drink, and Special Ed's Yoo-hoo came together with three little milk cartons to toast the glory of the tree house. As he drank the cold milk, Christopher looked at the picture of the missing girl on the carton.

Emily Bertovich.

Her name was so easy to read now.

Christopher was so excited about the tree house, he barely paid attention when he got on the school bus to take him home. He didn't know any of the kids on his new bus route or neighborhood. Except one.

Jenny Hertzog.

"Floods! Floods!" she teased, even though Christopher's mom got him new longer pants from the outlet mall.

Their bus stop sat at the end of a long street, next to an old house on the corner. Jenny ran into her house next door with the aluminum siding. Christopher walked down to his cul-de-sac. He looked at the log cabin across the street and the Mission Street Woods that surrounded all of them.

The woods where they would build the tree house.

Christopher felt bad that he didn't tell his friends everything. But he didn't want them to think he was crazy. Like his dad. He also didn't want to frighten them. But there were other things the nice man had told Christopher as they stayed up all night, talking. Most of them were confusing. Some of them were scary.

But Christopher trusted the nice man. There was something about his voice. A kindness. A warmth. And even when Christopher was skeptical, everything the nice man told him was true. As it turned out, Special Ed's father did have a garage full of tools. Mike and Matt did help their uncle George build things. Christopher was taken out of Mrs. Henderson's remedial reading class that day. Jenny Hertzog was at his bus stop.

And he had to finish the tree house before Christmas.

"But what's the hurry? What does the tree house do?" he asked.

you'd never believe me. you'll have to see it for yourself.

CHAPTER 21

They began on a Saturday.

It was freezing, late November, and the trees blocked out whatever sun the clouds had spared. But the boys were too excited to care. The week could not have gone any better. The M&M's found the place where the Collins Construction Company stored building supplies. And the team figured out a way to move everything to the clearing.

"You ever heard of a wheel barrel?" Special Ed said in CCD.

"You mean a wheelbarrow?" Christopher said.

"I know what I meant," Special Ed said with a huff.

What he lacked in vocabulary, Special Ed made up for in business savvy. He had raided his father's tool chests and found two dirty magazines to boot (great for resale value!).

On Saturday morning, Christopher woke up early and got out his favorite backpack. The special one with Bad Cat asking, "Do you have any food in here?" He went downstairs and sat next to his mom on the couch. She was as warm as her coffee and smelled even better.

"Where are you off to so early?" she asked.

Ever since Christopher had gone missing for a week, his mother was extra protective of him leaving.

"I'm hanging out with Eddie and the M&M's," he said. "We're meeting at Eddie's house. We were going to play all day. Maybe have a sleepover."

"Does his mother know that?" she asked with a raised eyebrow.

And sure enough, a text chirped through almost on cue.

Kate. Eddie is bugging me for a sleepover. Virginia and Sage already said yes. OK with you?

Christopher's mom had no idea that Special Ed was the one typing and then immediately erasing the texts at precisely 8:30 a.m. Nor did she suspect that the M&M's had already done the same thing on their end to free Special Ed for the night. The boys didn't know how kids got away with anything when people actually talked to each other. But their texting plan worked like a charm. Christopher's mom typed back.

Sure, Betty. I'll grab an extra shift at work now. Thanks.

Phew.

"Keep your phone on," she said as she dropped him off at Special Ed's house. "I'll pick you up tomorrow morning at ten sharp."

"Mom, please—"

"Fine then. Nine thirty."

"Okay. Ten. No problem!" he said before things went south.

"You be careful," she said. "No leaving Eddie's house. No wandering off. No kidding."

"Yes, Mom," he said.

She put him out of the car with a hug.

Christopher found the boys in the garage, where Special Ed's father stored all of the camping gear that his family had used exactly zero times. Eddie was proudly showing the M&M's his Playboy-funded windows stacked on the wheelbarrow.

"I told you my dad had a wheel barrel," he said.

With that, they set to work.

The boys grabbed flashlights, lanterns, and old sleeping bags that Special Ed's mother was too lazy to remember to make their housekeeper throw out. They stuffed one of the bags with bread and peanut butter and chipped ham. They threw paper plates and plastic spoons on top with milk and Froot Loops. And of course, two bags of Oreos. The sleeping bag looked like a lumpy cigar.

There was barely enough room in their backpacks for the tools.

So, as Special Ed's mother slept off her "bridge night," the boys walked to the Collins Construction entrance to the Mission Street Woods. As luck would have it, the guard was making his rounds and the workers were too busy excavating a nearby site, so the boys had their pick of the woodpile. They filled their arms with 2x4s and headed to the fence. They pushed their cart under the wire and hopped over, making a small path through the field. Past the COLLINS CON-STRUCTION COMPANY sign.

Right to the edge of the Mission Street Woods.

They stopped. Cautious and silent. Like Hansel and Gretel in their old bed-time stories. When they believed in such things as witches and wolves.

"Guys, maybe we should have told our parents where we're going," Matt said.

"Are you kidding? Mom would never let us," Mike said.

"But if we get lost, no one knows where to find us."

"Christopher got lost in here for six days. He knows his way around," Special Ed said.

Matt looked to Christopher for some backup, but Christopher was staring at the big colorful leaves. The wind slow-danced around them. It felt like the woods were breathing.

"Yeah. So, stop being a wimp," Mike said to his little brother by three minutes.

"I'm not a wimp."

"Then, prove it. Go first."

"Fine. I will," Matt said without moving.

"Come on. What are you waiting for? Trees don't bite."

"I said I'm going!"

But Matt wouldn't take a step. He was too afraid.

"Come on, guys. Follow me," Christopher finally said.

Christopher went in first, ending the game and saving Matt his dignity. The boys followed him under the canopy of trees and were swallowed by the Mission Street Woods.

Christopher walked down a footpath, trying to find the trail from the Collins Construction site to the clearing. But all he saw was that their feet weren't leav-ing footprints. Maybe the ground was that dry. And if they got lost, no one could find them. With the clearing hidden behind acres of trees, no one would ever know that they were even there.

For a moment, he had a sense of déjà vu. Footprints of a little kid. Lying on the ground like a trail of bread crumbs. In his mind, he saw himself walk-ing down a trail. Following the tracks. He didn't know if that was a dream or not. All he knew was that he probably shouldn't tell his friends about it because they would say he was crazy. Something cracked up ahead. Branches like bones.

"Look, Chris," Matt whispered.

Matt pointed up ahead on the trail.

A deer was looking at them.

It stood in the path, still as a lawn ornament. It locked eyes with Christopher, then slowly began to walk into the deep woods. A direction that Christopher had never been.

"Where is it going?" Matt whispered.

Christopher didn't answer. He just followed. Step after step. The headache creeping up his neck. Finding his temples. Pushing him farther. Down a narrow path. Christopher looked to his left and saw . . .

. . . an abandoned refrigerator.

It lay on the ground like a rusted skeleton. It was filled with twigs and leaves. A nest for something. Or someone.

"Chris?" Special Ed said, pointing ahead. He sounded scared. "What is that?"

Christopher looked up ahead and saw the deer walk into a large tunnel. It looked like a cave mouth. Wood-framed and rotting. Christopher approached the old coal mine. There was something so familiar about it.

"We shouldn't go in there," Matt said.

But Christopher didn't listen. He felt compelled to keep moving. He entered the dark tunnel. The boys followed. The world went black. The old mine cart tracks were bumpy under their feet. The whole place smelled like pee from a "long shot" bathroom.

Special Ed turned on his flashlight. Christopher grabbed the flashlight and clicked it off.

"Don't. You'll scare it away," Christopher whispered.

"*I'll* scare <u>it</u>?" Special Ed asked.

The boys followed the deer out of the mine tunnel. Christopher looked down and saw the footprints of what looked like hundreds of deer. And other creatures who lived and died for generations in these woods, never knowing that there was such a thing as man. Then, he looked up.

The four boys had reached the clearing.

They hadn't realized how dark the footpath was because their eyes needed time to adjust to the light. They blinked and covered their eyes for just a moment.

That's when they saw the tree.

It was the only tree for a hundred yards. It sat dead center in the middle of the clearing. A crooked hand ripping out of the earth's cheek like a pimple.

The boys were silent. They had forgotten all about the deer, who stood still, staring at them. They began to walk. Little by little. Moving silently toward the tree. Mike's arms, which had been so heavy under the weight of the wheelbarrow, suddenly felt light. Matt's throat, which had been scratchy with thirst and the last gasp of strep throat that antibiotics had wiped out, swallowed and felt no pain. Special Ed, who had been scheming for the last five minutes as to how to avoid sharing the two bags of Oreos, suddenly didn't care if he ever ate again. And Christopher's dull headache, the kind that couldn't be drowned with Children's Tylenol or Advil mixed with applesauce, finally left the space behind his eyes, and he felt relief. There was no pain. No fear. Not anymore.

Christopher arrived at the tree first. He reached out his hand, half expecting the bark to feel like flesh. But it felt right. Strong, weathered bark with ridges like wrinkles. It reminded him of Ambrose, that nice old man from the hospital.

"We'll build it here," Christopher said.

"It's so creepy," Special Ed said, following it with a quick "Awesome."

Christopher unrolled his blueprints, and the boys began. While they unloaded the supplies, Christopher peeled the Bad Cat backpack off his shoulders and let the tools fall with a clank. He pulled out a hammer and a nail.

"Matt. You get dibs on the first nail," Christopher said.

"No," Matt said. "It's yours, Chris. You do it."

Christopher looked at his friends. They all nodded in agreement. Mike and Matt held the first 2x4 up to the tree. Right next to a century of initials that teenagers had carved on their way to adulthood. WT + JT. AH + JV. Names in rows like identical houses. Johnny and Barbara. Michael and Laurie. Right before he struck the first nail into the tree, Christopher saw the freshest initial carved into it. A single letter.

D.

After the first nail had punctured the tree, the boys started hammering the 2x4s. One on top of the other. A little ladder reaching up the tree like a row of baby teeth. They would have run out of wood quickly, but Christopher had foreseen this problem. The boys never asked him where the big pile of wood came from. Maybe they didn't notice. Or maybe they just assumed.

But he had already started building.

He had actually worked on it for three weeks. Talking to the nice man. Making trips back and forth to the Collins woodpile. Preparing and planning. Stocking up for this moment with his friends. The nice man said it was best to keep quiet about these things until you had to make noise.

Luckily, the security guard was always in the foreman's trailer, watching sports on a little portable TV. He was so busy screaming "Yes," "No," and "You call that interference, you blind asshole?!" that he never saw the little boy raiding his boss's woodpile.

Christopher wanted to talk to the nice man now, but he didn't want to frighten his friends. They had no idea he was there, watching them. At one point, Mike reached out to grab the white plastic bag and fill it with nails.

"Don't touch that," Christopher said.

Mike immediately put the bag back on the low-hanging branch and returned to work. It was never said that Christopher was in charge. But nobody questioned him. Not even Mike, and he was the strongest.

Somehow, children always know who the leader is.

As they worked, the sky got so windy that the trees swayed back and forth like teenagers' arms at a concert. But despite the wind, every time Christopher looked up into the sky, the cloud face never moved.

It just seemed to watch them, building.

CHAPTER 22

After she dropped her son off at Special Ed's house, Christopher's mother had a little time, so she took the scenic route to work. She looked into the sky. The clouds were glorious, like big fluffy marshmallows left in the microwave right before they burn. But they weren't nearly as beautiful as the Mission Street Woods. The leaves had already started to change, and the trees looked like an artist's palette, messy and clean at the same time. She rolled down the car window and took a deep breath. The crisp autumn air was that refreshing. The sky was that blue. The trees were that gorgeous. The moment was that perfect.

So why was she so anxious?

Over the years, she had considered her mother's intuition a blessing. No matter the circumstances, she always believed that the quiet voice in her head kept her son safe, kept her sane, kept them surviving.

And right now, it was humming like a tuning fork.

Of course she was overprotective. What mother wasn't? After that hellish week Christopher went missing, she could have kept him under lock and key for the rest of his young life, and nobody would have blamed her. But the little voice that kept things pointing north told her that she had to let him live his life, not her fear. "Mother" is just one letter away from "smother." Right now, her son was safely at Eddie's house eating bad food and playing video games. He would be there for the rest of the night. So, why did she feel so bad?

Maybe because you don't have your own life, Kate.

Yeah. Maybe it was that.

She arrived at Shady Pines, punched the clock, and got busy. Whenever Christopher's mom got worried, Super Kate got manic. She turned over beds.

Cleaned the bathrooms. Helped the nurses with Mr. Ruskovich, who used his degenerative muscular disorder as an excuse to "accidentally" grope the women all day.

"A thousand pardons," he would say in his broken English, tipping an invisible hat.

After breakfast, the manic had burned through all of her chores, and there was precious little to do but worry about her son. Luckily, today was "New Candy Day." That's what the nurses called it. One Saturday a month, Shady Pines welcomed new volunteers to train as candy stripers or kitchen help or whatever horrible chore Mrs. Collins could imagine for the low low price of college credit (or community service hours).

The volunteers were usually the same crop. Local high school kids who realized that their college applications were looking a little too thin because outside activities such as "texting," "pot," and "compulsive masturbation" didn't exactly wow Harvard. The kids would work a few afternoons a month. Then they would get a certificate for college. And then they were never heard from again. That is, except for a few guilty Catholics who might stay two months. The record was four.

It was a great quid pro quo.

The owner of Shady Pines, Mr. Collins, would get free labor. His wife, Mrs. Collins, would get fresh children to torment for not taking proper care of Mrs. Keizer, also known as her demented seventy-eight-year-old mother, all the while telling her frenemies at the country club that she just wanted to "give back to the community that had given her family so much." And the kids would get to pad their college applications for a bright future of thinking they would be young forever.

Win. Win. Win.

Father. Son. Holy Ghost.

Since college applications were due in the new year, the holiday season was the holy grail of volunteerism. Before one could say "Ivy League," Shady Pines was swamped with eager young faces looking to trick colleges into thinking they cared. Kate counted about twenty faces. Ten times more than usual.

Normally, Christopher's mom would have skipped orientation, but she had a vested interest in this "New Candy Day." Because right in the front of the pack, wearing a long skirt, a fuzzy sweater, and a nervous smile, was the beautiful teenage girl who had found Christopher on the road after he had been missing for six days.

Mary Katherine MacNeil.

She was standing next to her boyfriend, a poor whipped kid named Doug. They were both so nice. So wholesome. So legitimately God-fearing Catholic that they had no idea what Mrs. Collins had in store for them. Christopher's mother wanted to make sure they got the least painful assignments, so she quietly approached them.

"Hi, Mrs. Reese," Mary Katherine said. "How is your son doing?"

"Great," Christopher's mom whispered. "Now, move to the back. Don't interrupt her orientation speech. Volunteer for the kitchen."

With that, Christopher's mom winked and slinked into the adjacent room, pretending to turn over a bed as she watched Mrs. Collins pretend to smile.

"Welcome to orientation," Mrs. Collins said.

And thus began the speech Christopher's mom had heard twice already. How Shady Pines is an institution of caring. How a society will be judged by how it takes care of its elders. How her family bought this elder care facility because seniors deserve dignity (even if the workers who provide it do not). Bullshit bullshit. Yadda yadda. Country club country club. Christopher's mom waited for the first kid to make the dreadful mistake of interrupting the speech. And like clockwork, it happened . . .

"Excuse me, Mrs. Collins? When do we get our certificate?" a boy asked.

Christopher's mother saw that the voice belonged to none other than . . .

Doug.

Stupid Doug.

Mrs. Collins smiled. "You'll get it at the end of the month."

Doug smiled back. "Good. I'm applying to schools in December."

"That's wonderful. You are so eager to help. What a nice young man. Is that your girlfriend?" she asked, pointing to Mary Katherine.

"Yes, Mrs. Collins. Hello," Mary Katherine said.

They were doomed.

"Would you two like a special assignment?" she asked.

Doomed.

Mary Katherine looked like a deer in headlights. She turned to Christopher's mom, who quietly shook her head no. She turned back to Mrs. Collins.

"Well, uh . . . I am good in the kitchen. I'd love to volunteer there," she said sweetly.

"Are you sure? This would be very special. You'd be taking care of my very own mother."

Fucking Doomed.

"Well, uh . . . that's quite an honor," Mary Katherine said. She turned to Doug to think of something. Bail them out. Anything. But he was silent.

And then, a miracle.

"Yes, it's quite an honor, kids," a voice said sarcastically. "Her mother is a mean old bitch just like her."

There was a collective gasp, a nervous laugh, and a turn to the voice. Everyone looked at the owner of the coke-bottle glasses.

It was Ambrose.

The old man from the hospital.

The old man with the cataracts.

The clouds in his eyes.

Mrs. Collins turned to him. "How dare you," she said.

"How dare me? Mrs. Collins, these kids have to listen to your bullshit for their college applications. I don't. So, go fuck yourself, you dime-store bully," he said.

The kids laughed.

"Sir, you will watch your language in front of the children, or you will leave Shady Pines."

"Promise?" he said sarcastically.

Then, he turned to the group.

"Hey, kids. You're here for your future, right? Well, look at all the old people here. That is your future. So, don't fuck around and waste time. Go to college. Get laid. Make some money. Travel. Then, get married and raise your kids to be nothing like Mrs. Collins or her husband. Capiche?"

Without waiting for a response, the old man hobbled on his bad knees back to the parlor, leaving behind a room full of adoring fans. Of course, it did nothing to stop Mary Katherine and Doug from getting the worst assignment in the place. It didn't stop Mrs. Collins from being even more abusive to the kids and the staff because she couldn't get her mani-pedi'd claws on Ambrose. But it did give them all a little ray of sunshine to pass the time.

Like a song to a chain gang.

Right after lunch, Christopher's mom went into Ambrose's room to clean. He was watching Jeopardy! on his television. He knew every answer and called them out. When the commercial break came on, he turned to her.

"I saw you try to help that poor girl," he said.

"Yeah. I heard you help her, too," Kate said back.

Christopher's mom knew a lot about Ambrose from the nurses. Between his cataracts, glaucoma, and age, she heard that his eyes were not healing. His eye doctor told him that he would be blind soon. Probably by Christmas. He took the news with a bark of "Fuck it. No one to see anyway." He had no relatives. No visitors. No one to take care of him. Nowhere to go for Christmas.

And yet, somehow, he was the brightest light in the place.

"Mrs. Reese...this is your future, too, you know? You're a nice lady, and your kid is great. So, don't fuck around."

She smiled at him and nodded. Then, Christopher's mom left the room, taking Ambrose's smile with her.

*

Ambrose turned off the television and took a sip of water. He put the plastic cup by his bedside. Next to the photograph of the pretty old woman with the wrinkles. She was still beautiful after forty years of marriage.

It had been two years.

She was gone. Like his brother when he was a kid. Like his parents when he was a middle-aged man. Like the men he served with in the army. The only person he ever dared to love as a grown man was gone. And now, his only companionship came within the walls of Shady Pines. All of these old people like kids left in day care with Mom and Dad never coming to pick them up again. All of these nurses and doctors who tried their best to give them some quality of life. And that nice Mrs. Reese with the great smile.

His wife was gone.

By this point, everyone had told him in one manner or another that he needed to move on. "Move on to what?" was his response. He knew they were right. But his heart refused. He woke up every morning remembering the sound of her breathing. The way she wouldn't throw away anything (except his things, of course). And right now, he would give anything for one more morning of a good fight with her over bacon and eggs. For the chance to see her flesh wither. As his did. And telling each other the lies about how beautiful their bodies still looked. But the truth of how beautiful their bodies actually were to each other.

That's the kind of thing that Anne would say. A mixture of self-help and "walk it off" working-class Irish. Every morning now, he would wake up and turn over on the bed. And instead of her face, he would see a plastic cup of water. The old people weren't allowed to have glass here. Not after Mrs. Collins' mother cut herself up in a bout of dementia. The old man kept his wits about him. Thinking about escaping this place like Clint Eastwood and Alcatraz. He could escape Shady Pines, but there was no escaping old age. Not with two bad hips, two worse eyes, and enough arthritis to make a thirty-year-old cry. Not to mention war wounds, inside and out. Growing old was not for sissies indeed. And the physical pain was the least of it. He could take watching boyhood heroes become footnotes. He could even handle seeing his color memories become black-and-white footage. But the old man knew he would never get over the death of his wife as long as he lived.

Ambrose was raised Catholic, but ever since his brother died when they were kids, he thought that no God could let what happened happen. Seeing an empty room where his brother used to be. Seeing his mother cry like that. Even his father. Since that moment, there were no thoughts of God. There was only a staunch belief that we are carbon and electricity and that was that. When you're dead, you're dead. And his Anne was in a beautiful plot that he visited when the shuttle could take him. And when he was lying in the ground next to her, her photographs would be thrown in the trash because her face wouldn't mean anything to anyone else. He was the last person alive who knew her and loved her. Like his little brother. Like his mom and dad. Like his wife, who said, "Don't worry. Dead is just an asleep you don't wake up from." His wife, who made him promise to throw her a traditional Irish Wake with the joke, "You can't have a good Sleep without a proper Wake."

Right before he closed his eyes for the afternoon nap, he lay in bed like Clint Eastwood on Alcatraz. Trying to figure out a way to escape old age. He squinted through the clouds in his eyes and prayed in his heart just like he did every nap and every sleep that he wouldn't wake up. He whispered, "God, if You're up there, please let me see my family again. I beg You." He wouldn't know when his eyes closed. He would simply open them and realize that God was keeping him alive for a reason only God could say. For purpose or punishment. Or both. Then, he would turn...

And see a plastic cup where his wife used to be.

*

Kate was thinking what a nice man Ambrose was as she walked through Shady Pines. She looked at the old folks in the parlor. Some playing checkers. Some chess. A little Saturday afternoon television. Some talking. Some knitting. Mostly sitting. A few eager beavers lining up for lunch early to have first dibs on the Jell-O.

Mrs. Reese...this is your future, too, you know? You're a nice lady, and your kid is great. So, don't fuck around.

The thought was not depressing. It was realistic and sobering. She felt the tick tock in her chest. And she remembered a line from one of her self-help books. One of the early ones that got her out of her horrible small town with a horrible small family.

We have this time. We have no other.

She knew that Friday nights would always be for her son Christopher.

But maybe Saturday nights could be for her.

She got up and went to the phone. After a moment, she dialed.

"Hello. Sheriff's office," the voice said.

"May I speak to the sheriff, please? It's Kate Reese," she said.

"One second, ma'am."

She stood there, listening to the Muzak. The song was Blue Moon. After a moment, the phone clicked.

"Hello?" the sheriff said. "Everything okay, Mrs. Reese?"

"Yeah. Everything is fine," she said.

She could hear him realize that she wasn't calling for police work. His voice changed.

"Oh. Good. That's good," he said.

He waited.

"Yeah. So, look, uh . . . I don't have work tonight," she said.

"Me neither," he said.

She waited. Be a man. Step up.

He did.

CHAPTER 23

Y ou smell like going out."

That's what Christopher used to say when he was little. She would put on her red lipstick and little black dress. She would spray a cloud of perfume on her wrists and rub them together, making the cloud disappear. And her son would follow her around the apartment on his little feet and say, "You smell like going out."

But he wasn't there right now.

She opened her closet door and looked at her new dress for her new life. That afternoon, she decided that none of her old outfits fit anymore. Not her body. Not her life. The cutoffs. The tight dress. The trashy denim skirt. All of those belonged to the old Kate Reese. New Kate Reese might deserve a little better.

She still had savings with the lottery money. She couldn't quit her job anytime soon, but this month's mortgage was paid. The retirement accounts maxed, along with the college fund. Of course, she still felt guilty and wasteful like she always did when it came to spending money on herself. But this time, she decided to take a chance and see what it was like to splurge. Just a little.

So, right after work, she drove to the Grove City Outlet Mall.

After ten stores, one hot pretzel, and an iced tea, she finally found it. A designer dress. On the clearance rack. $600 retail that she could have for only $72.50. She couldn't believe it. She went into the dressing room. It had a skinny mirror, thank God. She slipped off her work whites and slipped the dress over her frame. Then, she stopped when she saw herself in the mirror.

Oh, my God. That's me.

She looked beautiful. She looked like she had never been mistreated in her life. She looked like men always called her back. And they were always kind. And her husband hadn't quit on her. And she had never met Jerry.

She bought the dress and found the greatest pair of shoes on the clearance rack for $12.50.

That's right. $12-fucking-50.

She celebrated in the food court with her favorite frozen yogurt. TCBY Strawberry. Then, she went home and spent the rest of the day feeling possible. At 7:30, she put the dress and shoes on. She studied herself in the full-length mirror. And even though it wasn't as skinny as the store mirror, she didn't mind admitting to herself.

She looked good.

When she drove to the restaurant to meet the sheriff (her idea—always good to have a getaway car), she decided she wasn't going to talk at all about Jerry. How many first dates had she gone on since her husband died where the topic of conversation was the last bastard she dated? She thought she was getting a sympathetic ear. What she was actually doing was giving the next bastard a trail of bread crumbs as to how much shit she was willing to put up with for what grief convinced her was love.

But not with the sheriff. She would leave no more bread crumbs. No more tips as to how to mistreat her. Yes, he knew some facts about Jerry from the time Christopher went missing. But that's all he knew. As far as he was concerned, she was a widow. Her late husband was kind and honest and treated her like women are treated in the movies. He didn't need to hear the word suicide. And more importantly, she didn't need to say it.

She pulled into the parking lot. She got a great spot right next to the handicapped stall. The "filet mignon" of parking spaces. Good sign. She went into the restaurant ten minutes early to be sure she was the first to arrive. But the sheriff was already sitting at the good table by the window. She guessed he got there twenty minutes early and tipped Mr. Wong a few extra dollars to get the best seat in the house.

The sheriff didn't see her. Not at first. So, she took a moment to study him. Kate Reese knew that people were themselves when they didn't know someone was watching. Like her husband when she came home and found him talking to the wall. Or Jerry when she came home and saw him with an empty six-pack.

She had been hurt too many times to not take this thirty seconds to cram for the date as if it were a final exam.

The sheriff didn't look at his phone. He didn't read the menu. Instead, he scanned the room. Over and over. As if by habit. Seeing if there was any threat. Seeing if there was anyone suspicious. Maybe it was just his police training, but she thought it was more than that. Some kind of primal response to a world he knew to be dangerous. A world she knew as well. He was a real man. Solid. Blue-collar handsome. Sexy in the way that workingmen can be.

And those hands.

Kate Reese was not a sentimental woman about anything except her son. But she was partial to hands. Call it what you will. That's what she liked. She liked real men with strong hands that could make her feel held.

The sheriff had beautiful hands.

And he was blowing on them.

His hands are sweating. He's nervous.

"Hi, Sheriff." She waved.

"Oh, hi," he said a little too eagerly and stood up.

Instinctively, he wiped his hands off on his dress pants and shook hers. His hand was smooth and dry and strong.

"I got us a table by the window. I hope that's okay," he said.

"It's great."

He got up and pulled her chair out for her. She couldn't believe it. Her husband used to do that for her. It hadn't happened since.

"Thank you," she said.

She took off her jacket, revealing the designer dress, and took her seat.

"You're welcome. You look beautiful. That's some dress," he said.

"Seventy-two fifty at the outlet mall," she said.

Shit. Why am I telling him this?

"Clearance rack. The shoes, too," she added.

Stop talking, Kate.

It hung in the air for a moment. And then, the sheriff smiled.

"Which outlet mall? Grove City?" he asked.

She nodded.

"That's the best one. I get all my clothes there," he said matter-of-factly.

And with that, Kate Reese settled into the greatest first date she'd had since

Christopher's father. She never brought up Jerry. She didn't even think of him. The old Kate Reese who put up with Jerry was wearing that interview blazer with the hole under the arm. The new Kate Reese was in a beautiful designer dress with a man with great hands that he kept blowing on all through dinner because for once in her life, a man was nervous to impress her. Instead of the other way around.

CHAPTER 24

When Christopher called his mom, he was confused. She hadn't picked up their home phone. She picked up her new cell phone. And the music in the background didn't sound like television at home. It sounded like restaurant music.

"Hello, Mom?" he said.

"Hi, honey."

"Where are you?" Christopher asked.

"China Gate."

"Are you alone?" he asked, already suspecting the answer.

"No. I'm here with a friend."

Christopher knew what that meant. She always called a new guy she was dating a "friend." She made sure not to give him a name until it became more serious. He remembered when they were in Michigan. After a month of not talking about it, she finally said her friend's name was Jerry.

"Oh. That's nice," Christopher said.

"What about you? You having fun? Enjoying your sleepover?"

"Yeah. But I miss you," Christopher said.

"I miss you, too, honey."

"Maybe after church tomorrow, we can do something fun," he said.

"Sure, honey. Whatever you want. Dave & Buster's even."

"Okay, Mom. I love you," he said.

"I love you, too, honey. See you tomorrow."

With that, they hung up. And there was silence.

Christopher handed the phone to Special Ed and returned to work. Out of the corner of his eye, he could see Mike and Matt text their moms from Special

Ed's mom's phone (which Eddie smartly "lost" for the weekend). Out of the corner of his ear, he could hear Special Ed call his dad from Mike and Matt's phone and say they were having the best time at Mike and Matt's house. And oh, no . . . he hadn't seen Mom's phone. Maybe she left it at the salon during her mani-pedi.

But Christopher barely paid attention. He just wanted this new "friend" to be nice to his mom. Unlike the others. He thought about all the screams he heard through the walls. All the times she had been called names that he was too young to understand. A few months later, he heard some older kid say "bitch" on the playground. Maybe two months after that, the word "crap" became "shit." And "jerk" became "asshole." And the words made them all older and uglier. If he could just make the walls of the tree house thick enough, no one could hear those bad words through them. If he could make them strong enough, no one could ever hear "Fuck you, bitch" ever again. So, he stared at the white plastic bag as he hammered and hammered nail after nail after nail after . . .

"Come on, guys. Break is over," he said.

Nobody questioned him. The boys just fell into line and returned to the tree. They had worked like that all day, pausing only to take a drink of cherry Kool-Aid or a bite of chipped ham. The floor beams had been secured by late morning. The secret door with the rope ladder by lunch. By midday, the beams for the four walls were up. Even as the temperature dropped twenty degrees, they kept building with an almost religious focus. The autumn chill had worked its way into their bones as they let their minds go to the big thoughts of little boys.

Special Ed talked about cheeseburgers. He wondered why the ones at McDonald's were so much better than the ones in the cafeteria. He had a bone to pick with McDonald's about their apple pies, though. "Ever heard of caramel? Hello!" His rant quickly turned to daydreams of Thanksgiving dinner with his one grandma's famous apple pie. Only five days away. Mmmmmm.

Matt wondered when his eye would stop being lazy, so he could take off his eye patch. He hoped it was soon so Jenny Hertzog would stop yelling, "Pirate Parrot! Pirate Parrot!"

Mike did not talk about being called "Mike the Dyke." His focus was building the tree house. He said these nails were perfect. They went in every time, no problem. Normally, nails were difficult. They would bend, and you'd have to pull them out and straighten them. But not these nails. They always found footing in this tree. Mike looked at his little brother, who smiled at him. For some reason all their own, he smiled back.

"Remember that time you stepped on a rusty nail and needed a tetanus shot?" Mike said to his little brother.

"You mean a tennis shot," Special Ed corrected.

"Yeah. That hurt," Matt said.

"You didn't cry, though," Mike said.

"No. I didn't."

The discussion quickly found its way to a heated debate about which Avenger was best. Special Ed was a Hulk man himself. Matt liked Iron Man until his older brother liked Thor, and then Matt agreed Thor was best. Nobody could figure out what it would look like if the Hulk ever took a crap. But everyone agreed that it was the funniest thing they ever heard.

They decided they should each get their own character. Special Ed got his beloved Hulk after convincing the group Mike was the perfect Thor since he was the best with a hammer. Matt had to be Captain America because he started as a pipsqueak but became big and powerful. The whole group said there was only one Iron Man. Christopher. He was the leader. The smartest. The mastermind.

"The vote is anonymous then," Special Ed said.

And that was that. The boys didn't say another word for the rest of the afternoon. The tree was like a mom with babies in her arms. Safe and warm. It was only when they left the tree that the cold caught up to them, and they would realize how freezing it really was. They didn't know where the hours went. The clearing was its own little world. A big circle protected by trees and clouds. An island in the middle of the ocean.

The only person who didn't feel safe was Christopher. As day became dusk, he found himself watching the clearing like a deer with eyes on each side of its head to see predators approaching. The predator wasn't visible, but he could still sense it. With every tap of the hammer, he could feel a whisper working deep into his mind. The same words echoing over and over like the congregation repeating the Lord's Prayer with Father Tom and Mrs. Radcliffe on Sundays.

We're not going fast enough.

Christopher asked the guys to go that much faster. And they did. Their hands raw. Their faces sunburnt despite the November cold. They all looked more exhausted than they would ever admit. Especially Matt, who never wanted to seem weak in front of his big brother. But even Mike looked tired. Still, they had kept working. Silently humming a song in their hearts. Blue Moon. Until finally, around eleven o'clock that night, their bodies began to give out, and the unlikely voice of reason spoke.

"This is nuts. I'm hungry," Special Ed exclaimed.

"We're not stopping," Christopher said.

"Come on, Chris. Put down the whip. It's the first night," Mike said.

"Yeah," Matt added.

"Guys, we need to finish before Christmas," Christopher said.

"Why?" Special Ed asked in a huff. "What's the big deal?"

Christopher looked at the white plastic bag. Then, he shrugged.

"It's nothing. You're right. Let's eat," he said.

The four boys sat on the longest branch, side by side, like the men who built Rockefeller Center. Christopher had seen that picture in the library once with his mom. All those men hovering above the city on a beam. One false move and they would all die.

At dinner, they passed around the canteen filled with Kool-Aid, eating peanut butter sandwiches with grape jelly on Town Talk bread. For dessert, they snacked on Oreos with ice-cold milk kept in the stream near the billy goat bridge. After a full day's work, they were the most delicious Oreo cookies any of them had ever had. They spent the next hour making each other howl with laughter with the latest and greatest burp or fart.

All the while telling ghost stories.

Matt told the one about the guy with the hook that everyone had heard a million times. And without Matt pretending to be the guy (since no one had a hook), it didn't get much of a scare. But Christopher did his best to act afraid so that Matt wouldn't feel too bad for his failure.

Christopher then recounted the plot of the movie The Shining, which was on TV one night when Jerry had fallen asleep on the couch. His mom was working the late shift at the diner, and Jerry was supposed to be babysitting. Christopher liked the black cook the best and didn't understand why if he could see the future he would walk directly into the ax. But otherwise, it was really good.

Mike's story was really good, too. He started with the flashlight under his chin.

"Do you know why they bury bodies six feet deep?" he asked like those spooky guys who host the horror nights on TV.

"Because they start to smell," Special Ed said. "I saw it on TV."

"No," Mike said. "They bury them six feet deep so they can't get out. They're all awake under there. And they are crawling like worms to get out. And eat your brains!"

Mike proceeded to tell the story of how one zombie woke up underground and crawled out to get back at the guy who shot him and his girlfriend. It ended with the zombie eating the guy's brains with a knife and fork. All the guys loved it!

Except one.

"I have a better story," Special Ed said with confidence.

"The hell you do," Mike said.

"Yeah," Matt added, trying to sound tough.

"I do. I heard it from my dad," Special Ed assured him.

Mike nodded, prodding Special Ed to "Do your worst." Special Ed took the flashlight and put it under his chin.

"A long time ago. In this town. There was a house. The Olson house," Special Ed said.

Mike and Matt got instantly quiet. They had heard this one.

"Mr. and Mrs. Olson were away at dinner. And they left their oldest son in charge of his crazy younger brother, David. All night, he kept coming down the stairs while the older brother was trying to make out with his girlfriend, and David would say these crazy things.

" 'There is a witch outside my window.'

" 'She has a cat who sounds like a baby.'

" 'There is someone in my closet.'

"Every time he came down, his big brother would make him go back upstairs, so he could keep making out with his girlfriend. Even when David came down with pee stains in his pajamas from being so scared, the older brother thought he was just faking it for attention because David had been so crazy lately. So, he took him upstairs and changed his pajamas. Then, he walked him all over the upstairs and showed David that there was nothing scary up there. But David wouldn't listen. He kept screaming. It finally got so bad that the older brother locked David in his bedroom. It didn't matter how much David screamed or kicked at the door, the older brother would not let him out. Eventually, the kicking and screaming stopped. And the older brother went downstairs to be with his girlfriend again.

"That's when they heard the baby crying.

"It sounded like it was on the porch. But they didn't know who would bring a baby here this late at night. Or why. So, they walked to the front door.

" 'Hello?' asked the older brother.

"The older brother looked through the peephole in the door. But he could see nothing. All he could hear was the sound of that baby crying. He was just about to open the door when his girlfriend grabbed his arm.

" 'Stop!' she said.

" 'What's wrong with you?' he asked. 'There's a baby out there.'

" 'Don't open the door,' she said.

" 'What are you talking about? What if it's alone? It could wander out into the street,' he said.

" 'It's not a baby,' she said. Her face was pale. She was terrified.

" 'You're crazy,' the older brother said.

"She started walking up the stairs toward David's room.

" 'Where are you going?!' he screamed.

" 'Your brother is telling the truth!' she said.

"The older brother opened the front door. There was a little baby basket on the porch. The older brother crept up to it and took off the little blanket. And saw it . . .

" . . . A little tape recorder playing a baby's crying. The older brother ran upstairs and found his girlfriend in David's room, screaming. The window was shattered. There were muddy handprints all over the glass and walls. His little brother was gone. They never found him."

The boys were silent. Christopher took a deep swallow.

"Did that really happen?" he asked.

The three boys nodded.

"It's a local legend," Special Ed said. "The parents all tell us that story to make us go to bed at night."

"Yeah, but in our uncle's version of it, there was a killer on the porch with the baby recording," Mike said.

"Yeah," Matt agreed. "And there was no girlfriend."

Either way, it didn't matter. Special Ed was crowned the king of the ghost story. By that point, it was well past midnight. The day's labor and their full bellies made everyone sleepy. Since they were all spooked by the stories, they decided that one of them should stand guard while the others slept. Like a good leader, Christopher took the first shift to let his crew get a good night's rest.

And give him a chance to be alone with the nice man.

Christopher watched his three friends unroll their sleeping bags on the cold ground. They climbed in and huddled together for warmth. Within minutes, the chatter died down. The flashlights clicked off. And there was darkness. And there was silence.

Christopher sat in the tree house. He looked around the clearing for any signs of babies or cats or witches. But all he saw was that deer. It stared at him for a moment, then went right back to sniffing the ground for things to eat.

Christopher wrapped the sleeping bag around him a little tighter and crunched a cold Oreo, his tongue finding the gooey white middle. He looked at the woods in the moonlight. The changing leaves red and orange like a campfire. And the minute he saw them, he could smell the leather baseball-glove smell and his father's tobacco shirt and mown grass and damp leaves and chocolate chip pancakes and everything else that ever smelled great to him. He looked up and saw that the clouds had parted, letting in the moonlight. Behind the moon were thousands of stars.

He had never seen so many. So bright and beautiful. He saw a shooting star. Then another. And another. One time in CCD, Mrs. Radcliffe said that a shooting star was someone's soul going up to Heaven. He also saw a science show on TV that said a shooting star was a meteor burning in the Earth's atmosphere. But his favorite theory came from the playground back in Michigan. Christopher had heard once that a shooting star was nothing but a dying star's last breath and how it takes six million years for the light to travel to Earth so that we know the star is dead. So, he wondered, which was which. A soul or a star? And what if all of the stars had burned out already and it was just taking Earth six million years to know it? What if that six million years happened tomorrow? What if they were all alone? And there were no stars except the sun? And what would happen if the sun burned out? And our shooting star could be seen millions of years from now? By a little boy with his friends building a tree house.

And eating cold Oreo cookies or whatever it was that people out in the universe ate. Do all stars and all souls go to the same place in the end?

Is that what the end of the world would look like?

That thought made his head hurt a little, which was strange because he never got headaches when he was at the tree. But this thought was different. And it led to nicer ones. Like toasty fires. And his warm bed at home. And how nice his mother's hand felt when she stroked his hair while he fell asleep. He had barely slept for over twenty days now, as he stayed up late every night bringing wood out to the tree to prepare for the build. But now he couldn't remember ever feeling sleepier.

As his eyes closed against his will, Christopher had déjà vu about the tree. Like he'd slept here before. He thought he could feel his mother's hand touching his hair like she did sometimes when he had a fever. But his mother wasn't here. There were only the tree branches. And tree branches didn't move enough to rub people's hair.

And they certainly didn't feel like flesh.

CHAPTER 25

christopher. wake up.

Christopher opened his eyes. He looked down at the white plastic bag, crinkling in the breeze.

hi.

He was so happy that the nice man was back, but he didn't dare say anything. He didn't want his friends to think he was crazy.

don't worry. your friends are asleep. they can't hear us.

Christopher looked down at the clearing. He saw his friends curled up on the ground.

"Where have you been?" Christopher whispered.

i've been right here watching you. you are doing such a great job.

"Thank you," Christopher said.

are you tired or can you keep building?

Christopher looked down at his phone. He had been asleep for only ten minutes, but somehow he felt like he'd just slept in on a Sunday. His muscles were sore and strong. But for some strange reason, he wasn't tired.

"I can keep building," Christopher said cheerfully.

great. let's go to the woodpile. stock up for tomorrow.

Christopher climbed down the 2x4s like baby teeth. Then, he grabbed a skinny stick and scooped up the white plastic bag.

Christopher and the nice man left the clearing together.

Christopher had made this trip to the woodpile dozens of times by now. But something was different. Something was wrong. He felt eyes on him. The whites of deer's eyes. And little creatures. The twigs cracked under his feet like brittle bones. And he thought he could hear breathing behind him. Like the times he played hide-and-seek and tried to make himself not breathe too loud. He thought someone was near him. Shallow breath. A little kid's breath.

He remembered a little kid's hand.

A little kid giggling.

Was that a dream? Or was it real?

i found a shortcut. turn here.

Christopher followed the white plastic bag. He stepped over logs and tripped on a branch. He turned the flashlight deep into the woods and thought the branches were two arms coming to strangle him. He wanted to scream, but he didn't dare. The nice man had warned him about this feeling. When the wind didn't feel like the wind, you had to be extra careful.

especially when it feels like someone's breath.

"Chrisssssstopher?" the wind kissed behind him.

He felt it on his neck. He wanted to turn around. But he knew he couldn't. If he did, he was afraid he could turn into a pillar of salt. Or stone. Or all the bad things Father Tom and Mrs. Radcliffe talked about in church and CCD. A snake. A little kid.

"Hisssss," the wind kissed behind him.

Christopher broke into a sprint to the Collins Construction site. He saw the streetlight up ahead. Tall and blue. He ran with all his might and just as the kissing hissing found the back of his neck, he burst out of the woods . . .

. . . and onto the street.

He looked back. He saw nothing but trees. No eyes. No bodies. His mind must have been playing tricks. Or not.

"What was that?" he asked the nice man.

we need to hurry.

Christopher went to the woodpile. Luckily, the security guard was asleep in the foreman's trailer. Christopher took the longest 2x4 he could find and dragged it off the top. The wood fell with a splat on the ground. Christopher saw the security guard shift in his chair, but he didn't wake up. He was just talking in his sleep like Jerry used to after he drank too much.

"Christopher?" the man said in his sleep.

The hair stood up on the back of Christopher's neck. He saw the man's eyes twitch under his lids like he was dreaming.

"What are you doing with the wood?" the guard whispered.

Christopher started to back away.

"What are you doing out there?" the guard whispered in his sleep.

Christopher tiptoed back into the woods. He grabbed the long piece of wood and dragged it back under the cover of darkness.

"You really shouldn't be out here," the guard whispered. "Or else you're going to end up just like him."

Christopher felt his heart in his throat.

oh, god.

The nice man sounded terrified.

stand still. don't move.

The guard rose and began to sleepwalk.

"Just like him, Chrissstopher," the guard hissed.

don't speak. it'll be over soon.

The guard walked right toward Christopher. Sniffing the air. He stopped right in front of Christopher and dropped to his knees. He opened his eyelids, but his eyes had rolled back into his head. There were no pupils. Just white like a cue ball.

Or a cloud.

"JUST LIKE THE BABY!" the guard screamed. "WAAAAAAAAAA!"

With that, the guard closed his eyes and walked back to the trailer.

pick up the wood. hurry.

Christopher bolted like a colt. He dragged the long piece of wood back under the trees all the way down the path. When they were finally safe in the clearing, he turned to the white plastic bag.

"What was that?"

The nice man was silent.

"What did he mean when he said 'You're going to end up just like him'?"

i don't know.

"Yes you do. I'm going to end up just like the baby. What does that mean?"

please, christopher. don't ask me that.

"Tell me," Christopher hissed. "Or I'll stop working."

The white plastic bag floated in the wind on the stick in his hand. There was a long silence. And then, a sad, resigned voice.

i can't tell you. but i can show you. just remember . . .

we can swallow our fear or let our fear swallow us

CHAPTER 26

What was that sound?

Matt sat up. He turned. He was in the sleeping bag. Rolled up like a man in a hollow log. His hand instinctively found his forehead, which was covered in sweat.

From the nightmare.

He was stuck to the ground like flypaper. The street turned to quicksand. He couldn't stand or run. He just kept drowning in the street. The sand coating his lungs.

Screaming as his brother died.

Matt stuck his head out of the sleeping bag and looked up at the stars. The blue moon lit the clearing like a lantern. As bright as a sun dying in the sky. There was a deer looking at him. Matt bolted up. The deer startled and ran toward the old mine tunnel, which looked like a giant's mouth, swallowing the animal whole.

Matt stepped out of the sleeping bag, and the freezing November air hit his pants. That's when he felt it. The wet spot. He had wet the bed again. And this time, he didn't do it at home. He did it on a sleepover in front of his friends. Like a baby, he thought. Like a stupid baby.

Mike was going to tease him forever for this.

Panicked, he looked over at the wheelbarrow near the tree. He thought maybe if he could get to his backpack, he could put on the extra thermals before Mike woke up. He moved to the tree, avoiding every twig that might crack. He tiptoed past his brother sleeping soundly and grabbed his backpack. He moved away from Mike. Back toward the tunnel. With each step, he got closer until his eyes caught something in the moonlight. A figure huddled in the shadows. Digging in the dirt.

It was Christopher.

And he was talking to himself.

"Yes, I can hear the baby," he whispered.

Matt forgot all about the fresh clothes. He tiptoed toward Christopher, who was digging in the dirt like a dog burying a bone. When he got closer, he noticed a thin branch with the white plastic bag on it.

"I don't want to see. It's too scary," Christopher whispered.

"Christopher? Are you okay?" Matt said.

Christopher turned around quickly. He looked startled.

"How long were you standing there?" he asked.

"Just now. What's wrong with your eyes?" Matt asked.

"What do you mean?" Christopher said.

"They're so bloodshot."

"It's nothing. Don't worry, okay?"

Matt nodded, but he did worry about it. Christopher rubbed his exhausted eyes. Then, he looked down at Matt's pants and saw the streak of urine staining the denim a dark blue. Matt's face went hot with shame.

"Don't tell. Please," Matt said.

"I won't," Christopher whispered.

"No, I really mean it. My brother would never stop teas—"

Without a word, Christopher pointed down to reveal the pee stain on his own pants.

"You had a nightmare, too?" Matt asked.

"Yeah. So don't worry."

Christopher smiled at him. And somehow, Matt felt better.

"What were you doing?" Matt asked.

Christopher paused for a moment.

"Digging for treasure," he finally said.

"Can I help?" Matt asked.

"Sure. Grab a shovel."

"Can we change our pants first? I don't want Mike to see that I wet the bed, okay?"

Christopher smiled, and the boys quickly rummaged through their backpacks and pulled out fresh underwear and pants. They peeled their underwear off like bananas. The cold air hit their willies (Matt's word), which retreated back into their bodies like scared turtles. Then, they quickly put on the fresh clothes, which felt warm and soft and dry. Christopher opened up the tools and handed Matt a small shovel. They began to dig for treasure. Side by side.

"Who were you talking to?" Matt asked.

"Myself," Christopher said. "Now hurry. You don't want anyone else to get the treasure, do you?"

They spent the next half hour digging. They didn't talk much. Matt noticed that Christopher kept looking at the white plastic bag, but he didn't think too much of it. Matt knew that Special Ed was Christopher's best friend, but Matt secretly thought Christopher was his. And he didn't mind coming in second to Special Ed. He was used to it by now. He had come in second to Mike his whole life. The only thing that bothered him was a nagging question in his mind. The thing that woke him up in the first place.

What was that sound?

It was on the tip of his tongue.

"What are you guys doing?" Special Ed asked before Matt could place it.

Matt and Christopher turned to see Special Ed and Mike approach, rubbing the sleep out of their eyes. Their breath making clouds.

"Digging for treasure," Matt said.

"Can we help?" Mike asked Christopher.

"Sure, Mike."

"I'll make breakfast," Special Ed said, finding his niche.

Mike picked up the shovel and used his strong arms to cut through the frozen earth. Matt looked at Christopher to see if he would tell Mike about wetting the bed. Christopher smiled as if to say, "Your secret is safe with me."

*

Later, the boys had their breakfast of Froot Loops with cold milk from the stream. Christopher said nothing of the terror. Nothing of the guard whispering his name. Or the sound of the baby crying, which had woken up Matt. He knew that the truth would scare Matt. And he didn't want anyone but him to be scared. So, Christopher said nothing of the nice man explaining what would happen to him if he didn't finish the tree house in time. The less they knew, the better. And the safer for everyone. And he knew that if he did tell them, they might get scared and run away. And he needed their help.

When they finished the Froot Loops, he made sure Mike got the sugar dust, and Matt got the prize. Then, Christopher thanked Special Ed for a great breakfast.

It was important to keep his troops happy.

When morning came, the sun warmed their cold bones. They worked in shifts. Two boys building the tree house. The other two boys digging. After a snack of frozen Oreos and the last of the milk, Special Ed joined Christopher, hacking at the frozen earth looking for treasure.

No treasure came.

But at about 7:06 a.m., they did find a child's skeleton.

CHAPTER 27

The call came in at 7:30 a.m.

And the news began to spread.

The sheriff's night deputy went to church that Sunday morning to pray. He told Father Tom, who changed his homily to speak about how the remains of a child were found in the Mission Street Woods. He said that the child was in Heaven now, and as sad as the town was, they should rejoice in the power of Christ's forgiveness.

The homily was so powerful that Mrs. Radcliffe couldn't contain herself. She kept dabbing at the corners of her eyes all the way through Holy Communion. How many times had she and Mr. Radcliffe prayed for a child of their own? How many times did she miscarry? And how many times did Mr. Radcliffe hold her and say that her body was not broken? It was beautiful.

Mary Katherine prayed for the child and within minutes, her seventeen-year-old brain played hopscotch. That poor child. It should have had a chance to grow up like her and go to college. Like Notre Dame. She chastised herself for thinking of her own life at all. But she was afraid she wouldn't get into Notre Dame. And her father would be so disappointed in her. She promised God to pray for the child and focus on service at the old folks home. But Mrs. Collins was so mean, and her mother was so crazy. The old woman screamed at her all weekend about how "they" were watching. How was she going to listen to that for a month? Especially after Doug quit, saying that nothing was worth this torment. Not even Cornell. Mary Katherine quickly reprimanded herself to stop being so narcissistic and think about the child.

You don't want to hit a deer with your car, do you?

When mass let out, people called relatives and checked on their kids away at college. Moms held their children a little tighter and made mental notes to include extra-special treats on Thanksgiving. Dads decided to limit their football games to one (instead of three) to spend more time with their families instead of their fantasy football leagues. And kids found themselves getting whatever candy they wanted all day. Some felt guilty that it was for all the wrong reasons, but hey . . . candy was candy.

The only person who didn't seem rattled was Mrs. Collins.

Kathleen Collins had been sitting in the front pew with her son Brady during mass. Of course, she'd already heard the news. As landowner, her husband was the first person notified after the sheriff. He immediately left the house and went to the scene. He had too much money tied up in the Mission Street Woods project to leave its future in the hands of bureaucrats. Mrs. Collins found herself a lot more concerned about her family's potential bankruptcy than she was about the family of the child in the woods. After all, these things happen for one reason.

Bad parenting.

Simple. If you are a good parent, you watch your children. You make sure they are safe. If you fail at your job, you do not blame some outside force. You look right in the mirror and take responsibility. That was the problem with the world. No one took responsibility. Someday, the police would catch the psychopath who committed this horrible crime. And when they did, she knew that the monster would cry his crocodile tears and say he was abused by his parents. Well, that is—excuse her French—bullshit. There is such a thing as insane. There is such a thing as evil.

Not one for chicken-and-egg arguments, Mrs. Collins wondered if somewhere in the world, there was a parent who abused his children who was not abused himself. She would bet a million dollars that there was. And if someone could find just one of these mothers or fathers to prove it once and for all, she would die a happy woman.

As for her husband, Mr. Collins spent Sunday arguing with the sheriff. The Mission Street Woods project was turning from his greatest dream into his worst nightmare. First that little Christopher Reese kid went missing in them. And now a skeleton? Fuck. Everywhere he put his foot in the Mission Street Woods, he either stepped in dog shit or a bear trap. Environmental groups bitched about the deer losing their natural habitat. Historical societies bitched about the town losing its "centerpiece." Even preservation societies bitched to have him turn that shitty old tunnel into a coal mine museum. Yeah, that made sense. Everyone loves those. Fuck them all. He knew he had to start building by Christmas because the loans would come due. But did the sheriff (aka "government employee") understand anything about that? Hell no. The sheriff was telling him that he had to close the woods down because it was a crime scene.

"When are you going to let me dig? When I'm buried under two feet of snow?! Well, fuck you very much, Sheriff. It's like you and the rest of the universe don't want me to finish the God damn thing!"

As for Mrs. Collins' mother, she sat in the parlor of the old folks home. She couldn't remember how she got there. Or who she was. Or who her daughter was. Or her rich son-in-law. She thought for a moment that the woman on the news was telling her that a child had died, but no other details were being released at this time. Then, a loud man named Ambrose came into the room and told her that it wasn't her child. He said that her daughter was alive and well and waiting to torment teenage volunteers later that afternoon. Now shut up. He was trying to listen to the news.

Mrs. Collins' mother didn't like Ambrose. She didn't care if he was losing his eyesight. Vulgar was vulgar. She turned back to the television and tried to remember something else. Something important. But she couldn't. And then, right when the news ended, and the football game started, she remembered what it was.

They were all going to die soon.

Yeah. That was it.

They were all going to die.

Death was coming.

Death was here.

We'll die on Christmas Day.

CHAPTER 28

The entire parking lot was filled with camera trucks and news vans when the boys arrived at the sheriff's office. It had only been forty-five minutes since they ran to the Collins Construction security guard to call the police, but the skeleton was already big local news. Special Ed smiled when he saw the news vans.

"Wow. We're going to be famous!"

Then he turned to the deputy driving.

"Can I see your shotgun?" he asked.

"No," the deputy said.

"Did you know that the term 'riding shotgun' came from covered-wagon times when the man sitting next to the driver literally held a shotgun to protect the wagon?"

"No, I didn't." The deputy sighed as if wishing any of the other three boys had called shotgun.

"Can I use your radio then? My dad has a scanner in his Hummer. He uses it to know where the speed traps are. I know all of your codes. Ten-six means you're going to the bathroom, right?"

The boys were ushered into the sheriff's office without comment to the media. Well, except for Special Ed, who happily yelled out to the reporters, "We found a body!" A few of the local papers—most notably the Post-Gazette— were able to get a couple of snaps for the front page. The news vans took their B roll for the five o'clock news. Four boys find a skeleton in the woods. It was a great local story.

"If it bleeds, it leads," Special Ed said thoughtfully. "That's what my mom says."

The boys entered the sheriff's office and saw their parents waiting for them.

From the looks on their faces, the boys knew that their sleepover cover story had been blown to smithereens. It probably took the grown-ups all of three seconds to realize that they'd been had by a series of texts, and their boys had run around unsupervised for an entire night.

"We're so dead," Mike said.

But Special Ed proved to have more than media acumen. He immediately burst into tears and rushed over to his mother.

"Mommy, we found a skeleton! It was so scary!"

He cried and held her. Whatever anger she felt at him for lying melted as quickly as the chocolate in her purse.

"Where the hell were you, Eddie? We were worried sick," she said.

"Yeah!" Big Eddie said, checking the scores on his phone.

"We heard there was treasure in the woods. We wanted to find gold rings to give to our moms for Christmas," he said.

"Oh, baby," she said and held him tightly. "You're so thoughtful."

Mike and Matt followed his lead and rushed to their two moms. The boys apologized for lying and said they really wanted to find the treasure as a surprise. The M&M's moms weren't as forgiving as Betty, but they still hugged their boys within an inch of their lives and said it was going to be okay.

Then there was Christopher's mom.

Christopher waited for her to yell at him. Or hold him. Or be angry. Or sad. But she did the worst thing she could have possibly done.

Nothing.

"I'm sorry, Mom," he said quietly.

She nodded and looked at him as something she didn't quite recognize. Christopher wanted to hug her and make this horrible feeling of being in trouble go away. But it wouldn't. Because she was more than mad. She was hurt. Her little boy was lying to her. When did that start? What did she do so wrong that he didn't think he could tell her the truth anymore? When he saw that she was more disappointed in herself than him, the guilt he felt for deceiving her was almost unbearable.

"Boys, I need to ask you a few questions," the sheriff said, mercifully ending the standoff.

They spent the next fifteen minutes "being given the third degree" as Special Ed told everyone in school that Monday. In reality, the sheriff just asked them a couple of questions each. He wasn't interested in punishing seven-year-olds for trespassing or stealing a few scraps from the woodpile. He left the discipline to their parents.

He only wanted to know about the skeleton.

About that, the boys had precious little information. The sheriff went back and forth between the boys to make sure they were all telling the same story. When he was satisfied they were, he concluded they were just a bunch of kids who went out to the woods to build a tree house and, instead, found a body. There was only one thing that puzzled him.

"Christopher," he finally asked. "What made you dig in that spot?"

Christopher could feel all eyes in the room on him. Especially his mother's.

"I don't know. We were just digging for treasure. Mom, can we go now? I have a really bad headache."

"Okay, son," the sheriff said, patting his shoulder.

That's when Christopher sensed it. The sheriff smelled just like Christopher's mother when she was "going out." There was the faintest hint of his mother's perfume on the sheriff's jacket. Maybe from a hug or a kiss. Either way, Christopher knew the sheriff was mom's new "friend." His mother would mention the sheriff by name soon. And then he would be over at the house. Probably not for Thanksgiving. But maybe for Christmas. He hoped the sheriff was a good guy, who would be nice to his mom. But this time, Christopher promised himself that if the sheriff got mean like Jerry, he would do something about it.

*

That night, Christopher's friends were snuggled up with their families. Warm in their kitchens like cookies on a plate. Of course, they were still grounded. Appearances must be maintained. But there was too much relief that their boys were not the ones buried out in the woods for their mothers to be too mean to their sons.

Especially since their sons were being so nice.

The M&M's two moms made their favorite lasagna and were shocked when their sons cleaned up their own dishes. Special Ed's parents couldn't remember the last time their son only had one helping of dessert—and this was Mom's special chocolate delight.

All through dinners and bedtimes, the families chitchatted the way families chitchat. About a lot of nothing that somehow adds up to everything. The parents were all surprised when their sons wanted to read a book instead of watch TV. But the evenings ended up being lovely. And when the books were read, and their sons went off to bed, each of the parents had the same thought that they would never speak out loud . . .

My boy is growing up. It's almost like he got smarter overnight.

That is, except for Christopher's mother.

*

Of course, Kate felt proud the way other parents did. Ever since his perfect math test, she saw how happy he was. Christopher was never that good at sports. He was never that good at school. And he beat himself up for it. But she knew her son was a world-class person. If they gave gold medals for being a good human being (and they should), then Christopher would be singing the national anthem on the podium every four years. And now, he was the same little boy she had always known and always loved.

But he was different.

No, he wasn't possessed or a pod person or a doppelgänger. She knew her son. And this was her son. But how many times did she see Christopher struggle with remedial reading books? How long did she coach him through math drills? How many years had she seen her son cry because he didn't know why the letters switched on him? He felt like a failure. He felt like an idiot. Then, suddenly, almost overnight, he turned it all around. But it didn't happen overnight.

It took six days.

She forgave herself for not noticing at first, because she was swept up in it. She was so happy to have him back. So happy to see him safe. So proud of his sudden academic improvement. The reading. The perfect math test. The lottery. The new house. The new clothes. The bookshelf with the duck wallpaper filled with books that Christopher suddenly couldn't read fast enough. But deep in her heart, something always bothered her about it.

When something seems too good to be true, it always is.

And that was it. It was more than the reading. More than the grades. It was the way he looked around. The way he saw people interact. It reminded her of the moment when adults start spelling to trick their toddlers. "Hey, honey, should we take her to the t-o-y-s-t-o-r-e?" "Hey, should we give him some i-c-e-c-r-e-a-m?" As soon as their children were old enough to spell, adults had to find other ways to hide the world under their noses. Sins and sweets and sex and violence tucked away with looks and gestures and sleights of hand like a magician's misdirection.

Christopher never used to notice these things.

And now, he noticed them all.

Her son was suddenly bringing home straight A's when there used to be C's. Her son was speed-reading Treasure Island instead of stumbling through Dr. Seuss. Christopher studied the world with a knowing eye that simply hadn't been there in Michigan. There was a manic quality to his intelligence now.

Just like with his father.

And now he was lying to her.

When they left the sheriff's office, they fought their way through the reporters and cameras. Christopher's mother finally got him in the car. She was quiet for a moment as she turned on the motor and let the defroster work its invisible magic erasing clouds from the windshield.

They drove home in half silence.

Christopher apologized all the way home. But she said nothing in return. Not to punish him. But to get back the higher ground. Her son was growing up too fast, and she needed to know why. She'd already lost a husband to an overactive mind. She was not about to lose a son. When they reached their garage and were finally alone, she stopped the car.

"Christopher," she said softly. "I have to ask you something."

"Sure," he said, sounding relieved to have her talk again.

"Why did you lie to me?"

"I don't know."

"Yes, you do. It's okay. Tell me."

She saw his eyes twitch. She saw the response being measured.

"I, um . . . I knew you wouldn't let me go out to the woods."

"Why?"

"Because I could have gotten lost out there again. I could have frozen to death."

"But you did it anyway. Why?"

"My head hurts."

"Tell me why, Christopher."

"To build a tree house."

"Why? What's so important about a tree house?"

"Nothing, I guess," he said.

"So, you risked your life to build a tree house that meant nothing?"

He suddenly went silent. Then, he did the best impression of a smile she had ever seen.

"I guess it seems kind of silly now that you say it," he said.

"I'm glad you feel that way. Because you're never allowed in those woods again."

"But, Mom—"

"You're grounded until Christmas."

"But Mom!"

"Christopher. Your friends can lie to their parents. Every kid on earth can lie to theirs, too. But you don't lie to me. There is no debate. There is no time out. There is no big hug, and 'I understand.' I'm the fucking boss. And my only job is to keep you safe. SO, YOU ARE GROUNDED. YOU ARE NEVER TO STEP FOOT IN THOSE WOODS AGAIN. You got it?!"

"I'm sorry," he said desperately.

"Sorry isn't good enough. Not for me."

His eyes filled with tears. "I'm sorry."

"GO TO YOUR ROOM!"

Christopher went up to his bedroom, not knowing that once the door closed, his mother felt much worse than he did. She hated being that hard on him, but since she was unwilling to raise him with the leather belt she got growing up, it was the best discipline she had in her arsenal. She couldn't let him lie. Her rules were still black and white. She couldn't let him go grey. And she couldn't let him out in the woods where they found the skeleton of a child.

She kept him in punishment all day. Other than a brief respite of a grilled cheese dinner and Children's Tylenol for his headache, he stayed in his room. No TV. No books. He just lay in bed, looking at the picture of his father in the silver frame. She wondered if he wished his father were here. Maybe his father could explain what was happening to him. Maybe he would tell his father the truth. Right before bed, she came into the room.

"Listen," she said. "I'm still mad, but I'm sorry I yelled at you."

"That's okay," he said.

"No, it's not. We don't keep secrets from each other. And the only way that works is if we don't yell at each other. Right?"

Christopher nodded.

"You can tell me anything, Christopher. Always know that. Okay?"

"I know," he said.

She waited to see if he would. But Rome wasn't built in a day.

"I love you," he finally said.

"I love you, too."

With that, she kissed his forehead, closed the door, and went down the hall. She turned on The Tonight Show to distract herself. The host told funny jokes, but Kate Reese didn't laugh at any of them. She just looked at the screen, having a pretend fight with her son.

"You lied to me. You're still not telling me everything. I know it. You know I know it. So, what the hell is going on inside that head of yours, Christopher?"

And as she closed her eyes for sleep, she could almost hear his answer.

That's for me to know and you to find out.

CHAPTER 29

The sheriff entered the woods alone. It was Thursday night. The air didn't feel like Thanksgiving. It was too warm, too dry, too perfectly wonderful. The only signs of autumn at all were the leaves. Yellow and red like blood. The trails were soft under his leather shoes. Quiet as a mouse.

Something was wrong.

It had been five days since the skeleton was discovered, and he couldn't quite put his finger on it. He thought about his old captain's dog back in the Hill District. How every now and then, Shane would sit up and start barking for no reason. The captain would always say, "Quiet, boy. There's nothing there." But maybe there was something there. Dog whistles have a pitch that only dogs can hear.

Maybe there's something that only dogs can see as well.

The sheriff didn't understand why he was having those thoughts. He was a practical man. To him, this was an investigation like any other. Yes, it was a dead child, and that was a horrible tragedy. But it was nothing new to him. In the city, people die every week. Including children. In his old job, he'd seen children living in filth and closets and basements. He'd seen things so bad that it took the department shrink a couple of mandatory sessions to whitewash it out of his brain.

Except that little girl with the painted nails.

He'd never forget her.

But why was he thinking about her so much this week?

That he couldn't explain.

Nor could he explain the voice inside him. Something that just said this case was important. That's what people didn't understand about police work. They see a crime committed on television and truly believe there are enough man-hours to throw ten full-time detectives at a single homicide. In the real world, choices were made. Resources allocated. The sheriff was good at that. Sometimes too good. But this time, something in him said to bet the farm. So, once the skeleton was discovered, the sheriff called in a favor.

His old friend Carl was as good at forensics as he was bad at physical exercise. And since they were investigating a child, the sheriff had asked Carl to come to the crime scene immediately, even though it was on a Sunday. Double time be damned. He wanted to know everything he could about this skeleton. If anyone could tell him, Carl could. The Feds at Langley had tried to poach him several times over the years, but Carl's wife was a lot scarier than the FBI.

"The government can go screw itself, Carl. I'm not leaving my mum in Homestead!"

Case closed.

When Carl arrived at the scene, the two walked around and compared notes. Both of them thought it was a child of about seven or eight judging from the missing front teeth. And both of them thought the body had been buried a long time.

How else could you explain the tree roots wrapped around the body like a snake?

At the end of the evening, Carl and his team took the body away to do as much of an autopsy as they could. Carl said he had a full plate around the holidays, especially with his mother-in-law needing to be driven to mass three times a week, but he would try to squeeze in the work and get back to the sheriff by Friday.

The sheriff spent the rest of the week dealing with fallout. In the city, people don't stop when they hear news of a dead body. But this was a small town. And in a small town, people get scared.

Scared like the girl with the painted nails.

The sheriff shook off the thought and looked up ahead on the trail. There was a deer eating some grass near a little bridge that looked like something out of the Billy Goats Gruff. God, he hadn't thought of that in years. He was so scared of that troll when he was little. Scared like Hansel and Gretel.

Scared like the girl with the painted—

"Stop it. Focus," he said to himself out loud.

The sheriff didn't know what he was looking for exactly. After all, he and his men had walked almost every inch of these woods that week, despite Mr. Collins' rage. They didn't find much. No carvings. No strange symbols. Nothing to indicate that these woods were home to some cult or a ritual killer.

Just a bunch of trees.

And some deer.

And a bunch of beer cans.

Of course, he had expected that. Once the news began to spread about the skeleton, the morbidly curious (aka teenagers) started using the woods to drink beer and fool around. Rubberneckers, he thought. They left cans everywhere. He told his men to start collecting them to make up for the double time in the budget. They laughed when he said that. And when he didn't laugh back, they started collecting the cans.

The sheriff reached the clearing.

He looked up at the clouds drifting in the sky. Such a pleasant evening for November. It was amazing to think that Christmas was less than a month away. He stared at the tree in the middle of the clearing. It looked like a hand stretching to the sky. Some of its branches were strong. Others twisted like fingers crippled by arthritis.

The sheriff walked up to Christopher's tree house. He still couldn't believe how sophisticated it was for a seven-year-old. The ladder. The foundation. The framing. Kate Reese's son was a genius. It was like a real house.

But this time, the tree house looked different.

As if someone had been working on it all week.

But when he looked down, he saw no footprints.

No evidence.

Just a white plastic bag drifting from a low-hanging branch.

The sheriff touched the tree. The bark was cool and rough to the touch. Like the trees he climbed when he went to elementary school. He had his first kiss under a tree like this. Justine Cobb had braces and a summer dress and beautiful blond hair.

Just like the girl with the painted nails.

Daddy.

The sheriff took his hand off the tree. He shook off the cobwebs and tried to get back to center. He picked up the white plastic bag, fully intending to put it in his pocket and throw it away like litter. But for some reason, he found himself moving the bag in his hand like a kid trying to break in a new leather baseball glove. Over and over and over and

Crack.

The sheriff turned. He saw a deer staring at him. The sheriff looked down at the white plastic bag. He suddenly wanted to get the hell out of these woods. Some voice told him that he had to get out. Right now. The voice wasn't threatening him.

It was warning him.

He put the bag back on the branch and hurried away. He quickly passed through the mine tunnel hiding the clearing from the other side of the woods. He turned on his flashlight and saw initials etched into the metal tracks. Old names spray-painted on the wood frames like hieroglyphics. As he left the mine, he saw something disturbing.

An abandoned refrigerator.

He didn't know how his men could have missed this, and they were going to get a piece of his mind when he got back. A kid could play in this, get trapped, and suffocate.

The sheriff walked toward the refrigerator. It was big and white and old with rust on the edges like greying temples. Temples like churches. Like Carl's wife's mother's mass. The refrigerator was filled with a nest. He couldn't tell if it was for a bird or a raccoon. But there was no sign of either. The sheriff grabbed the refrigerator door to close it.

That's when the snake jumped out.

It was a rattler. Coiled. Hissing. Hissss. Hissss.

The sheriff backed away. The snake slithered toward him. Hissing like a baby's rattle. The sheriff stumbled on a log and fell. The rattler came at him. Its fangs out. Ready to strike. The sheriff pulled out his revolver just as the snake jumped for his face.

Bang.

The snake's head exploded with the bullet.

The sheriff stood and looked at the snake twitching on the ground. Coiled like the tree branches wrapped around the child's skeleton. After a quick just-in-case shot to the body, the sheriff went to close the refrigerator door. That's when he looked down into the nest and saw baby rattlers wiggling in their eggshells. He closed the door, locking them in, then checked his neck for anything squirming.

He quickly moved away, making a mental note to put in a call to pest control to send their team out. He had no idea why there were baby snakes in November. It was a long time since spring. Nothing was born in winter.

Something was wrong here.

He couldn't see it, but he could feel it, like his captain's old dog hearing a whistle. It sounded like the wind. But it wasn't exactly wind. The sound was more like a snake coiled in the tree branches. Like . . . like . . .

Invisible hissing.

The sheriff quickly moved down the hill to the construction site. There were stumps everywhere. Carcasses of trees. Giant roots torn out of the frozen earth. Several bulldozers were parked down the road. Each had a COLLINS CONSTRUCTION COMPANY sign on its door. The bulldozers sat there, lifeless, after the sheriff had shut down the woods for the investigation. Mr. Collins had already gotten his lawyers on the case, and if the sheriff knew anything about power and politics (and he did), construction would resume shortly. Soon enough, Mr. Collins would turn the trees into lumber to build the houses. The sawdust would go to another company to be mixed with flammable glue to make fake fire logs for Christmas. It was as if Mr. Collins were making the Mission Street Woods dig its own grave. As massive as the woods were, they couldn't exactly fight back.

The sheriff walked past the police tape. Past the field of tree stumps, already cut short by Mr. Collins back in September. They looked like little tombstones that eventually, no one would visit.

Like the girl with the painted nails.

As he drove back to the station, the sheriff looked at the little drops of rain falling from the clouds onto his windshield. He thought about the lovely time he had with Kate Reese just five days ago. God, it felt like a year. He wanted to see her again, but it was Thanksgiving with her kid. And tomorrow would be their Movie Friday together. So, it would have to wait for Saturday when maybe she'd get a babysitter, and she could erase the nightmare of his week with two hours of her company. She looked so nice last Saturday. With that new dress from the Grove City outlets. And her lipstick.

Like the girl with the painted nails.

Daddy.

When the phone rang, the sheriff almost jumped out of his skin.

It was Carl.

"Hey, Carl. You're a day early. I'm surprised to hear from you on Thanksgiving."

"You wouldn't be if you met my mother-in-law," he said.

The sheriff didn't laugh. That joke was as old as their friendship.

"What do you got for me?" the sheriff asked.

Carl went on to spew his trademark technical jargon. The sheriff always wondered why geniuses couldn't talk like normal people. But maybe that's what made them geniuses. After wading through biological data and DNA and carbon dating factoids for ten minutes, the sheriff was able to put together the facts about the skeleton.

The child was about eight years old.

The child was a boy.

The child had been in the ground for around fifty years.

And most impressively, Carl was able to figure out the cause of death.

The sheriff was stunned when he heard that. Technology had come a long way in the two decades he had been an officer. But still, he had never heard about a cause of death from a fifty-year-old skeleton when there was nothing to test but bones.

But that's just it. There was.

Carl figured there must have been something in the soil. With enough pressure, coal becomes a diamond. So, maybe it had to do with the coal mine. Or the tree roots. Or some temperature regulation he could not understand yet. A medical mystery that someday would be as routine as fingerprints or DNA. Whatever it was, it kept enough of the brain preserved. The autopsy was conclusive.

The sheriff was ready for anything. A stab wound. A gunshot. He had seen worse. Much worse. But when Carl told him the actual cause of death, the answer was so shocking that the sheriff stopped for a moment. He looked at the phone in his hand.

"Carl, I think I have a bad connection," the sheriff said. "Say that again."

"The victim was buried alive."

CHAPTER 30

On the other side of the woods, Christopher sat at the dining room table with his mother for their first Thanksgiving in their new house. It was not the festive evening either of them hoped it would be.

And it was all his fault.

Christopher barely ate his dinner. He told his mother that he had no appetite because his head hurt, but the truth was, he didn't want to get sleepy. So, after he consumed enough apple pie to avoid suspicion, they watched A Charlie Brown Thanksgiving in silence, and both went up to bed.

After she tucked him in with a kiss and tried to jump-start a conversation that would not come, she finally went to her room. Christopher listened to his mother's television turn on. He waited for hours until his mother's television turned off. And she fell asleep. And it was safe. Then, Christopher got out of bed.

As he had all week.

He went to his dresser to get warm clothes. He put them on over his PJs, dressing in layers to make sure that he could work in comfort. He put his pillow under his blanket to make it look like he was still there.

Then, he tiptoed downstairs.

Once he was clear of the creaky stairs, he slipped on his boots and went outside through the sliding glass door. He looked up at the black sky. A shooting star shot across the clouds. Christopher walked to the far side of the lawn, right up to the edge of the Mission Street Woods. The woods that the sheriff closed down to investigate, which made it impossible for Mr. Collins to keep ripping them up. It would give Christopher the time to finish the tree house before Christmas.

that's why i showed you the skeleton
i wouldn't have done that otherwise
i don't want to scare you, christopher

Christopher could have helped with the sheriff's investigation. He knew how he found the skeleton. He knew that the bones had been there for a long time. He even thought he knew the name of the kid who died. But he couldn't tell the grown-ups that. Because eventually, they would ask him how he knew everything. And he only had one truthful answer.

"Because my imaginary friend told me."

There were moments that Christopher's faith wavered between fact and fantasy. He was becoming too smart not to understand that either the nice man existed, or he was a crazy kid wandering around the woods alone.

But Christopher still kept building the tree house.

He felt like his head would rip apart if he didn't.

Sometimes, the headaches were dull. Sometimes sharp. And other times, he could eat Children's Tylenol all day, and it would do nothing. Christopher's headaches were now just a part of his life. Like school or Froot Loops or Bad Cat cartoons on Saturday morning. The only thing that made it livable was working on the tree house.

So he did. Thanksgiving night. And the night after that. And the night after that.

He never got headaches at the tree house.

He never got headaches near the nice man.

For the next week, every night, Christopher waited to hear his mother's television go silent. Then, he put the pillow under his covers, grabbed his coat and gloves, and ran out to the tree house to get one more nail into the frame or paint one more wall. All the while talking to the white plastic bag. He stayed out until his hands got too numb to paint. Too sore to hammer. Then, at dawn, he'd race back to his house to make sure he was in his bed when his mother got up. The fatigue was so brutal that eventually, he had to take his mother's makeup and blend it under his eyes, so that she would think he was still sleeping at night.

But he kept building.

He didn't dare stop.

The fatigue finally caught up to him after Movie Friday. His mother served him a huge spaghetti dinner with meatballs and butter rolls and an ice cream sundae for dessert. By the time he reached the tree house, his eyes were already closing on their own.

Christopher tried to fight the sleep. He needed to stay awake. He needed to drag the windows up to the tree house. He needed to finish the roof. He needed to . . . sleep. I can't. But you're so tired. No, I'm not. Then, maybe you should just rest your eyes. Yes. That's all. Just lie here at the tree. Make the headache go away by resting your

eyezzzzzzzzz.

When he finally woke up on Saturday morning, he was back in his bed. He didn't know how he got there. Christopher was upset that he let a whole night get away. But there was nothing to be done about it. His mother would be with him all Saturday. So, he couldn't sneak off to the woods. He couldn't talk to the nice man. He would just have to endure the headache until night came.

Christopher walked downstairs. He went to the kitchen cabinet and pulled out his mother's bottle of Excedrin. He ate four of the aspirin, crunching them in his teeth like Smarties. The chalky taste was horrible. So, he grabbed the box of Froot Loops. It was a new box. No sugar dust. But when Christopher poured the cereal, a special surprise fell out. It was a little plastic Bad Cat figurine. Christopher laid it on the counter and smiled. A rare moment of joy before the headache started knocking on the door again. He got the milk carton, drowned his cereal, and stared at the picture of Emily Bertovich. He made a mental note to ask the nice man why her picture seemed to change a little every time they bought a new carton.

Christopher put the milk back into the refrigerator and sat down for his Saturday morning cartoons. He remembered when he was younger, he used to turn off the TV and think that when he turned it back on, it would be in the same spot he left it. It took him a while to figure out that Bad Cat and the rest of TV kept going without him. It made him feel sad, but his mom cheered him up and said that he did things, too, and the rest of the world would have to catch up to him.

Christopher turned on the television. It warmed up and started showing his favorite Saturday morning cartoon.

Bad Cat.

Christopher was so happy. The Avengers might be his new favorite movies, but Bad Cat would always be his favorite TV show. He was just in time to see the opening credits. A big parade of all the characters marching down Broadway, singing.

Who's the one and only-est?
Who's the never lonely-est?
Who's the meat and bone-iest?
Bad Cat!
Who's the whack and snack-iest?
Who's the catty cattiest?
The "going to finish that?" iest?
Bad Cat!
Bad Cat!
Bad Cat!

Then, Bad Cat ran in front of the parade and screamed, "Are you going to finish that song already? I'm trying to eat!"

Christopher laughed every time because it was simply that funny. He even laughed a little harder this time because he needed to let out some steam from the stress of the week like the whistle on his mom's teakettle.

The episode began. Christopher was a little disappointed because it was a repeat where Bad Cat steals fish from the butler of a rich lady cat he's in love with. Christopher had already seen it a dozen times, but it did have one funny part where the butler chases Bad Cat screaming, "Come back here, Gato!" And Bad Cat says, "That's Mr. Gato to you, Raoul." So, he sat down to watch the episode anyway.

But this time it was different.

Bad Cat didn't say those lines. Instead, as Christopher watched, Bad Cat kept looking at the camera. Finally, Bad Cat stopped and looked at the screen.

"Oh . . . hi, Christopher. Enjoying the show?"

Christopher looked around the empty house. His mother was still asleep upstairs. He was all alone.

"Don't worry about your mom. It's just us. Don't be afraid. How ya doing, buddy?" Bad Cat asked him, all friendly.

"How do you know my name?" Christopher finally whispered.

"Are you kidding? You're my number one fan. How could I not know your name? I heard that my TV show is your favorite ever. Gosh, that's so nice. Thank you!" Bad Cat bellowed.

"Shhh. You'll wake my mom up."

"Now, that's just a pile of whiskers. Your mom talked to the sheriff on the phone for a couple of hours last night after you fell asleep. Gosh, he's super nice. Much better than Jerry, don't you think?"

The hair stood up on Christopher's neck.

"How do you know about Jerry?"

"I know everything about you, buddy. I know Jerry is looking for your mother. Gosh, he would hurt her if he ever found her. So, we can't let that happen, can we?"

"No," Christopher said.

"Gosh, you're brave. Your mother raised you well. She must be so proud of you. So, don't be afraid. I promise we'll keep your mother safe. No fuss. No muss."

"How?" Christopher said.

Bad Cat looked left and right. Trying to see out of the TV like looking around a blind corner.

"Oh, gosh. Christopher, I'm afraid we're almost out of time. I'll tell you how to keep your mother safe, but I need to ask you one question first, okay?"

Christopher nodded. Bad Cat narrowed his eyes.

"How did you find the skeleton, buddy?"

Christopher's heart began to pound.

"What?" he said.

"Somebody showed you where the skeleton was, right? Who's helping you? Oh, gosh, we need to know."

"Nobody," Christopher lied.

"I don't think that's altogether true. I think somebody told you about that old skeleton. I need to know who told you, buddy. Oh, gosh, I do. Because it's getting bad in here. She's so mad right now. My gosh . . . is she ever mad."

"Who?"

"Sorry. We're not allowed to tell you that, buddy, or we'll get in trouble. She keeps giving people boo-boos to find out who's helping you. All that screaming really hurts my ears. So, it would sure make things a lot nicer in here if you'd just tell us how you found the skeleton. You can tell old Bad Cat. It'll be our little secret."

"Nobody told me. I was digging for treasure."

"Gee whiz, that is fucking disappointing, buddy. That's the same lie you told to the sheriff and your mom. You don't want to be like Pinocchio, do you? Lies made his nose grow. Do you want to know what your lies will do?"

"What?"

"If you don't tell me who is helping you, something bad will happen to your mother."

Christopher's throat closed, like the time he tried to swallow a marble and almost choked. His face turned red.

"What will happen to her?" he asked.

"I can't tell you, but if you turn up the TV, I can show you. Would you mind turning up the volume on the TV?"

Christopher held the remote and turned the volume up.

"Gosh, no, Christopher. Not on the remote. On the actual TV. Or else it doesn't work."

Christopher hesitated, but he had to know what would happen to his mother. He slowly walked to the television.

"That's it, buddy. It's okay. I won't bite."

Christopher reached out his hand to the volume button. Bad Cat's eyes glowed. He licked his lips.

"Gosh, we can't wait to meet you, buddy. She's going to show you everything."

Bad Cat started to reach his paw across the screen. Closer to the volume button. Closer to Christopher.

"All you have to do is touch the screen, and we'll save your mother together. Cross my heart. Hope to dieeeeee."

Christopher reached out his hand as Bad Cat reached out his paw. They were centimeters away. Their fingers almost touching. The headache began to go away. And Christopher could feel the Zzzz.

"Christopher!" his mother yelled. "What did I tell you about sitting so close to the TV?"

Christopher opened his eyes and turned around. It was his mother. Dressed in her bathrobe. She looked confused. His nose was literally an inch from the television.

"I'm sorry, Mom," he said.

"All right. Well, finish breakfast at the table like a normal person. I didn't raise an ape."

Christopher nodded and turned back to the TV. Bad Cat was no longer staring at him. He was being chased by the butler.

"Come back here, Gato!"

"That's Mr. Gato to you, Raoul," Bad Cat said. Then, he ran into the sewer, bringing the delicious fish with him.

Christopher sat at the kitchen table and ate his cereal while his mom made herself scrambled eggs. He looked at her, terrified as to what would happen to her. He would have said something, but now he knew something was watching him.

Either that, or he was completely insane.

Christopher wanted to believe that all of this was just a figment—not a Fig Newton—of his imagination. Especially Bad Cat. He hoped that he was just a crazy person like his father. And the blinding headache was just the lightning that used to make "Daddy dance funny." That's what Mom used to call it when Dad had seizures. Dad took pills for them, and sometimes the pills would make it so he wouldn't get out of bed for weeks. Mom took care of him, but she had to work late at the restaurant.

That's when he died in the bathtub.

Late that night, after his mother turned off Saturday Night Live, Christopher snuck out of the house and went to the Mission Street Woods. He ignored the breath that played hide-and-seek with the wind and sprinted to the tree.

"Are you there?" he asked the white plastic bag.

There was no response.

"Please answer me. I'm afraid," he said. "What was that? Who is she? What is Bad Cat going to do to my mom?"

In that moment, Christopher stepped outside himself and looked back like a spectator. What he saw was a little boy on his knees begging a white plastic bag for answers to things that no one could possibly explain. If given the choice of having this be real or crazy, Christopher would pick crazy. Because even though his mom would be sad that she had a crazy son like her crazy late husband, at least nothing bad would happen to her.

"Am I insane?" he asked the white plastic bag.

Nothing.

"Please, tell me I'm insane."

Silence.

Christopher sat there all night, begging the white plastic bag for an answer that would not come. The nice man seemed to have disappeared. Christopher didn't know where he went. Maybe he was in hiding. Maybe he was running from Bad Cat. Or maybe he was just a white plastic bag.

Whatever it was, Christopher was alone.

As dawn streaked the sky, he ran back to his bed, lay under the covers, and stared at the picture of his father framed in silver. The more he looked at his father smiling near the Christmas tree, the more the question echoed in his mind like an old record stuck in a groove. Am I insane? Am I insane? Am I insane? Twenty minutes before his mother's alarm clock woke them up for church, Christopher finally closed his eyes. And just before he fell asleep, he thought he could hear the vaguest whisper. It could have been a thought. It could have been a voice. It could have been neither. All it said was . . .

Finish the tree house and you'll know.

CHAPTER 31

Are you nuts? My dad almost took the HBO out of my room," Special Ed whispered.

Christopher followed Special Ed through the church parking lot as their parents shouted their greetings.

"You don't understand. We have to finish it," Christopher said.

"Do you have HBO money?" Special Ed asked.

"No."

"Then finish it yourself."

They went into church, and after being grounded all Thanksgiving weekend (and the week after that for good measure), the boys sat through an especially long mass. Father Tom talked about how Jesus loves the refugees in the Middle East. But all Christopher could notice were the people staring at him. And their whispers.

"That's the little boy who found the skeleton."

"Those were the boys on the news."

"They were in the paper."

"He won the lottery a couple of months ago."

Christopher's head ached with their voices. Every minute he spent away from the tree house only made his head worse. At one point, Father Tom switched from English to Latin. The language swirled around in Christopher's head. And "diem" was "day." And the words made sense. But they brought with them a terrible wave of pain.

O Deus Ego Amo Te

O God I Love You, Christopher knew.

When church ended, Special Ed's mother went out to the parking lot and lit a cigarette. She took a deep breath in and exhaled a cloud.

"Jesus Christ, that was a long mass," she said. "Doesn't Father Tom know we all have Christmas shopping to do?"

She said it without a hint of irony, which Christopher's mother admitted made her love Betty all the more. Then, after Betty cleaned the bake sale out of snickerdoodles, she offered to take everyone out for pizza to celebrate the good news.

"What good news?" Christopher's mother asked.

"Eddie was promoted out of the dumb class!" she said.

"Hey!" Special Ed sulked.

"Sorry, honey. But it's true. You were in the dumb class," she said, patting his hair. "But that Mrs. Henderson is a genius because you're reading at a fourth-grade level now. We're so proud. Right, Big Eddie?"

"So proud. So proud," Special Ed's father said, watching the Steelers highlights on his phone.

Christopher saw his mother lock the information about Special Ed away in her mind. Then, the two families joined Matt and Mike and their two moms, who had just finished doing what Betty referred to as "whatever it is that Lutherans do" at their church off Route 19.

They may have had their religious differences, but hey . . . same God. Same pizza.

As the adults plowed through a pitcher of Iron City beer, the boys played video games.

"I just need help with the windows and roof," Christopher offered. "I'll do the rest myself."

"Sorry, Chris. Our moms grounded us," Matt said.

"Yeah," Mike said, wanting their dessert privileges restored.

But Christopher wouldn't let it go. The headache wouldn't let him. After his mother went to sleep that night, he tried to carry the windows up the ladder by himself. But they were too heavy. So, Christopher stashed them away and tried to fit the roof, but it was impossible with only one person. He had reached the limit of what one kid could do. The minute he stopped building, his headache returned with a vengeance.

And the nice man was nowhere to be seen.

The next day in school, Christopher found his friends in homeroom.

"The roof is a four-man job. I can't finish alone," he begged.

"Dude, we told you. We're grounded," Mike said, exasperated.

"Yeah, Chris. Leave us alone. You're being crazy," Special Ed said. "And you look terrible. Get some sleep."

Christopher looked over at Matt, the one person he knew he could count on. Matt quietly looked down at his desk.

"Matt?" he said.

"Leave my brother alone," Mike said.

"Let him answer for himself," Christopher said to Mike.

Mike had twenty pounds on him, but Christopher didn't care. The two boys squared off. Matt didn't want a fight to break out.

"Sit down, guys. We're already in trouble," Matt said.

Christopher turned to Matt. He looked him dead in the eye.

"Are you going to help me or not?"

Matt was silent. He looked up at his brother.

"No, Chris. I'm sorry."

The headache forced the words out of Christopher's mouth before he even thought them.

"Fuck you then," he said.

The minute he said it, he felt ashamed. He didn't know what he was doing anymore. By the end of the day, Christopher's head was screaming. It didn't matter that he snuck his mother's Excedrin into school and ate them all day like candy. It didn't even matter that the final period of the day was canceled so all the kids could go outside to the playground for the special event. Christopher's head would not stop hurting.

Not even for Balloon Derby.

He looked around the playground at all the kids in their winter coats and hats. Each of them held a different-colored balloon with a little card attached to the end of a string. Mrs. Henderson told them all to write their names on the card with the school's contact information. Whoever's balloon traveled the farthest got the prize. The kids would find out the last day of school before Christmas break. He suddenly remembered Mrs. Keizer sneaking up on him in the hospital, screaming, "Death is coming! Death is here! We'll die on Christmas Day!"

Don't cry.

The pain in his head was so terrible. He was never going to finish the tree house. So, either Bad Cat was going to hurt his mother, or he was completely insane.

Don't cry.

Christopher tried to shake off the pain and just write his name. But the first tear hit the card and smudged the pencil.

Stop crying, you baby.

But he couldn't. He just hid himself behind the slide, put his throbbing head in his hands, and began to sob. After a moment, he felt a shadow cut across his eyelids. He looked up and saw Matt put a hand on his shoulder.

"What's wrong, Chris?"

Christopher couldn't speak. He just kept crying. Mike and Special Ed ran up next.

"What happened?" Mike asked. "Was it Brady? I'll kill him."

Christopher shook his head. No, it wasn't Brady. Special Ed looked around. A little paranoid.

"Well, stand up. You don't want Brady to see you crying, right?"

The boys helped him to his feet. Then, he wiped his eyes on the sleeve of his jacket.

"I'm sorry," Christopher said. "I didn't mean to swear at you. I didn't mean to get you guys in trouble."

"Hey, don't worry about it," Matt said.

"Yeah. Our moms aren't so mad anymore," Mike added.

"Yeah, my mom thinks I'm a genius now," Special Ed exclaimed. "Plus, we got to spend a whole night camping out by ourselves. Win win."

"So, will you guys help me finish it?"

"Why is it so important to you?" Matt asked.

"Because it's our place. Because we're the Avengers," Christopher said, knowing they would never believe the truth.

The blacktop got quiet. The boys thought a minute.

"Okay, Chris," Special Ed said. "We'll help you."

"Of course," Matt agreed. "But we have to figure out how. We're still grounded."

"What if we skipped school?" Mike proposed.

"I can't skip," Special Ed said, quickly embracing his new academic success. "If I get an A on a test this year, my dad said he'd get me Showtime in my room. Showtime has a lot of naked ladies."

"What if we all pretend to be sick?" Matt offered.

"Too suspicious," Special Ed said.

The more the boys thought, the more they realized that there was no plan that worked. Christopher was the only one who lived close enough to the woods to sneak away at night. Their moms were with them every day after school and on weekends, and they would never allow another sleepover.

"Boys and girls, get ready with your balloons!" Mrs. Henderson called out.

"Come on, guys," Special Ed said. "We've got a Balloon Derby to win."

The boys held their balloons for Christopher. He tied his balloon to theirs. The four looked over at Brady Collins and Jenny Hertzog, whose popular friends had so many balloons tied together, it looked like the movie Up! But Christopher and the Avengers didn't care. They were best friends again.

"One. Two. Three! Go!" Mrs. Henderson cheered.

All of the children let their balloons go. The white sky was filled with little dots of color like a painting. The sky was beautiful and vast and quiet as a prayer. Christopher looked up at the floating cloud. White like the plastic bag. The words came to him in an instant.

A snow day.

The headache stopped with the answer. Christopher hadn't realized how much pain he was in until it was gone.

"What if we had a snow day, guys?" Christopher asked.

"That would work!" Special Ed said. "Too bad you don't control the weather, Chris."

That night, after his mother fell asleep, Christopher marched out to the woods. He walked right up to the white plastic bag.

"I don't know if you're real or not. But if you exist, you have to help me finish the tree house. And if you don't exist, then I will stop building it. I don't care if my head explodes. Because I am not doing this alone anymore. I need proof. So, talk to me. Please, talk to me."

In the silence that followed, he stared at the white plastic bag, floating silently on the low-hanging branch. Christopher's voice rose.

"This is your last chance. I need a snow day to finish the tree house. So, you better make it snow, or I swear I will never believe in you again."

CHAPTER 32

A blizzard.

God dammit, the sheriff thought. *The last thing I need now is a blizzard.*

The weatherman predicted two inches of snow. He was off by a foot. The schools had already been closed for the day. Mill Grove Elementary. Both middle schools. The high school. The snow was so bad that even the Mt. Lebanon School District closed down as opposed to saddling its youth with one of their legendary "three-hour delays (no morning kindergarten)."

The kids were outside with their sleds and their snowmen. The sheriff would have much rather been a kid running around with a sled than a grown-up trying to figure out if the town would have enough money in the budget for additional road salt. When he was a kid, he hated the salt that took away the snow. Now he hated the salt even more.

Because it took him away from the case.

Maybe it was the fact that it involved Kate Reese's kid. Maybe it was the fact that the sheriff was used to a city pace, and as much as he initially wanted the quiet life of a small town, he wanted to do real police work again.

Whatever it was, it seemed like the more time he spent in those woods, working the crime scene and looking for clues, the more engaged, focused, and passionate he felt. If he didn't know any better, he would say that he was almost becoming smarter. Because even with all the distractions, he was able to turn four basic pieces of information . . .

A boy.

Eight years old.

Fifty years ago.

Buried alive.

. . . into a near-positive ID of the child. He would need a DNA test to confirm it. But he was almost sure of the victim's name.

David Olson

The sheriff sat at his desk. He opened the cold-case file and unfolded the brown, faded Missing poster. David Olson was such a cute little boy. Big cheeks. Big smile. Even with the missing front teeth.

The same missing teeth they found on the skeleton.

The sheriff moved the poster aside and looked at copies of all the newspaper clippings from the Pittsburgh Post-Gazette and the old Pittsburgh Press before it shut down. There was even a mention of it in the local Pennysaver.

According to the papers, David Olson was at home with his older brother and the brother's girlfriend. His parents were downtown, enjoying a show at Heinz Hall after a dinner at the Duquesne Club. According to the initial police report, the older brother said that someone had placed a baby carriage on their porch with a tape recorder playing a baby's cries. The perp (or perps) must have used this diversion to take David Olson from his bedroom.

The police pulled out all the stops (and spent most of the town's budget, the sheriff knew) to close down roads and highways. Deputies and volunteers walked through the entire town, including the Mission Street Woods. But in the end, they couldn't find so much as a footprint.

It was as if David had been taken by a ghost.

When they were unable to find a suspect, the suspicion turned to the family. To sell a few papers, some muckraking reporters accused David Olson's father of killing his own son. The "Mad Dad" story stuck for a little while, especially when it was discovered that the family had taken out a whole life policy on David. But without any proof, the story quickly died (along with the newspaper sales), and the reporters focused on the older brother.

The worst of them accused the older brother of murder. The best of them simply asked the question, "How does it feel to know you were there when David was taken?" The older brother, to his credit or detriment, was very open with the reporters to keep the story alive. But eventually, other news became more interesting, and the family was left with the burden of being the only people who knew how the story ended. How the crime was never solved. How the perp (or perps) were never caught. How the family was left to find meaning in the place of answers. How the town stopped looking because they were out of leads and needed the money for road salt to keep the rest of their population safe.

The sheriff put the case file away with the Missing poster on top. Then, he looked up at all the current Missing posters on his bulletin board. Faces of men, women, and children. Sheriff's departments would send these pictures to one another like boys trading baseball cards. All in the hope (vain or real) that by some miracle, a child taken in Hershey would wind up in Philadelphia. Or the old man with dementia who wandered off in Harrisburg would somehow find his way to Pittsburgh. Sometimes, the faces changed when a child was rescued, Grandpa was found, or a teenage runaway decided that the hell at home was nothing compared with the hell on the street. But as much as the faces changed, the bulletin board never did. It was always full like the opening of The Brady Bunch.

The board was such a constant that the sheriff rarely noticed a particular face above the others. But there was one Missing poster that stood out to him now. Maybe it was her age. Or her blond hair. Or the fact that she looked a little like the girl with the painted nails. Whatever it was, the sheriff was always aware of one missing girl.

Emily Bertovich.

She had gone missing four months ago, but her parents must have had some pull in their hometown of Erie, Pennsylvania (or a whole lot of money). Because her case was still treated like it was twenty-four hours fresh. New pictures. New posters. Even the old milk carton campaign came back for this girl. Her poster looked as new and freshly printed as David Olson's was brittle and faded. Someday, Emily's poster would be old, too. And hopefully, she would be safe in her mother's arms. The sheriff could feel his mind wandering again from Emily Bertovich back to the girl with the painted nails, but he quickly stopped himself.

He had work to do.

The sheriff went outside to dig his car out of the snow. Then, he drove his cruiser over the salted roads, looking at the children playing on the 3 Hole Golf course with that amazing sledding hill. He saw the little kids in their colorful jackets running up the white, snowy ridge.

Just like balloons in the sky.

He cracked the window a little to take the fog off his windshield. Fresh, cold air filled the car. He heard the children and their screams of delight as they raced down the hill and ran back up only to race down it again. The sound made him smile. A bright moment in a grey day.

The sheriff finally arrived at the old folks home. Mrs. Collins was on the porch, standing next to her mother in the wheelchair. Her mother was saying something nonsensical about the end of the world as Mrs. Collins berated three teenage volunteers to "put their backs into it" and shovel all the snow from the front porch. The sheriff felt especially bad for one of them.

"We don't want my mother falling and breaking her hip, do we, Mary Katherine?"

"No, ma'am," Mary Katherine said, her face red and snotty from the cold.

The sheriff was not looking forward to this little chat with Mrs. Collins. He remembered when he first took the job, the Collins family invited him over for dinner in their ten-thousand-square-foot McMansion with the long driveway and swimming pool and tennis court and wine cellar that was slightly bigger than his apartment. Just a nice, cozy dinner to politely remind him that the second word of "civil servant" was "servant." And if he was the town's servant, then they were the masters. Nothing was ever said. But it was understood. The sheriff endured their tense "We are normal. We are fine" display. Especially when Brady spilled his soup on the fine linen and tensed up like a guy caught skimming from his drug-dealing boss. The sheriff knew the minute the door closed, Brady was going to catch hell. But at least he had a ten-thousand-square-foot mansion to be miserable in. The girl with the painted nails didn't get a hundred.

And Brady's mom could cook. He had to give her that.

Everything had been just fine between master and servant until a skeleton was found, and the sheriff ordered the woods shut down pending further investigation.

"Sheriff, I don't have another week to lose," Mr. Collins had told him. "But I do have a team of lawyers."

"Great. Then, maybe you can get them out here to help us dig for more skeletons on your land. You're building family-friendly suburbs. You don't want those news vans to think you don't care about a dead child, right?" the sheriff said.

It wasn't exactly the shot heard 'round the world, but it was enough to prompt Mr. Collins to go "new sheriff shopping" the next election. But the sheriff didn't care. As long as he solved the case, the community would stand by him, and he would keep his job. And if not, then not. He had seen worse things than second place.

"Hello, Mrs. Collins. How is your husband?" the sheriff said politely.

"Wonderful. He's so pleased that you've stopped his construction . . . for another week."

"Just trying to keep the town safe, ma'am," the sheriff said, tipping his cap with the tone of giving her the finger.

"Well, you're doing a <u>wonderful</u> job," she said with a smile.

When the sheriff entered the home, he saw Kate Reese at the end of the hallway. She was taking out Christmas decorations from a box. And she looked just as beautiful as she did the night of their date that had started at 8:00 p.m. and ended when Mr. Wong said in his broken English that "we close now." The sheriff didn't know how three hours had passed, but they had, and then it had been time to break open their fortunes.

"What does yours say?" he had asked.

"A Friend in Need Is a Friend Indeed. How about yours?"

"You Will Find Happiness with a New Love."

Ten minutes later, they were making out in his car in the parking lot like sixteen-year-olds. They had only kissed, but that only made it better.

"What are you doing out in this storm?" Kate Reese asked.

"I'm the sheriff. What are you doing?"

"I've got a mortgage. And Christopher is out with his friends, sledding."

The sheriff could feel the shift in her. Once she learned that the skeleton had been in the ground for fifty years, she had relaxed with her son. A little.

"No more house arrest?" the sheriff asked.

"Parole," she said. "If he goes in those woods again . . . solitary."

The sheriff could feel eyes prying into their conversation from every corner of the place. From the old ladies playing cards through their arthritis to the staff sneaking cigarettes outside. So, he leaned over privately and whispered the reason he was here. She nodded and walked him down the hallway into one of the rooms. Then, she left him to his police business. The sheriff saw the old man sitting in his chair, bandages wrapped around his head from his exploratory eye surgery.

"Excuse me, sir? This is Sheriff Thompson," he said.

"Well, hello, Sheriff. Nice to know you actually work, since I voted for you," Ambrose said. "How can I help you?"

The sheriff took his hat off out of respect, even though the old man couldn't see him do it. He took a seat across from him.

"Sir . . . my men combed the woods and found the body of a little boy."

"Yes?"

"I believe it's your little brother David."

David Olson's older brother, Ambrose, sat still as a statue. The sheriff couldn't see his eyes. But slowly, he noticed that tears started running from the bottoms of his bandages.

CHAPTER 33

Christopher looked at the sky filled with clouds. He couldn't remember ever seeing so many. Big beautiful clouds spilling snow on them like confetti at a parade.

His friends couldn't believe their luck.

A snow day!

A big, delicious snow day.

"Jeez, Chris. Maybe you really do control the weather," Special Ed joked.

Christopher forced a smile. Of course, he knew the snow could have been a coincidence.

Or not.

His mother had dropped him off at the 3 Hole Golf course that morning to meet his friends for "sledding" with a hug, a kiss, and a stern reminder.

"No woods. I'm not playing around."

"Thanks, Mom," he said.

"There's no thanks here. The only reason I am letting you do this at all is that half the town is on this hill. Do not leave this spot until I come back."

"Yes, ma'am," he said.

The mothers told their boys they would pick them up after work (or a day of beauty, in the case of Special Ed's mom). Either way, that gave them more than eight hours to get back to the tree house and finish.

This was their chance.

They waited for their mothers to drive away, then walked back through the parking lot with their red plastic sleds. They passed parents grumbling about longer commutes and road conditions while their children made plans with their friends to squeeze the most out of God's unplanned vacation day.

Fueled by Special Ed's thermos of hot chocolate and backpack of junk food, the boys trudged through the snow all the way back to the Mission Street Woods. They stopped just outside. The trees were limp under the weight of the snow. Silent witnesses to history. Christopher thought these trees had been here for hundreds of years. Maybe thousands. These trees were older than their country. These trees would be here long after they were all dead.

Unless Mr. Collins got to them first.

Christopher led the boys to the spot where he hid all the windows. As they dug them out, the snow got caught on their wrists, giving their arms an ice cream headache. But Christopher felt nothing.

They reached the clearing within five minutes, dragging the windows behind them on their red plastic sleds. The boys fought their way through the snowdrifts. Cutting through the beautiful white powder that seemed to hide the clearing away from the world. Like a mountain before anyone ever thought to ski.

They reached the tree.

They did not speak. They just worked in silence, occasionally grunting a word to coordinate tying the rope off to hoist the windows up. Or get the right screwdriver. Or seal the windows with weather stripping.

The boys used their muscle to move the planks of the roof into place. Their hammers pushed the nails through the wood like a knife through warm butter. The wind whipped around, turning their cheeks red and wet with cold. Special Ed and Mike finished the roof within two hours while Matt and Christopher put black shutters on the windows. When the roof was laid down, all four boys climbed on top of the tree house and began nailing down the shingles. One by one. As fast as they could. Tap tap tap like four manual typewriters.

Until they were done.

When he reached the last shingle of the roof, Christopher stopped. There was one more nail to drive home. He asked the guys who would like to finish it.

"You do the honors," Mike said.

"Chris! Chris! Chris!" his friends cheered.

Christopher grabbed the hammer and struck the last nail. They all carefully climbed down off the roof to the ground. The four boys stood, looking up at their creation with silent reverence. A perfect little tree house with shutters and windows and a real door with a lock. The floor with the secret door and a rope ladder for emergencies. It was beautiful. Exactly as Christopher pictured it in his mind. It was better than his graph paper drawings. Better than any house he ever planned except for the ones for his mom.

The tree house was done.

"Who wants to climb first?" Matt asked.

There was no debate.

Christopher climbed.

His friends followed.

The boys moved up the 2x4 stairs like baby teeth. They reached the little porch. Christopher opened the door like a doorman and let his friends walk in first. One by one. Special Ed, then Mike, then Matt. The three boys huddled in the tree house and started talking about how they were going to bring out furniture and iPads to watch movies. Maybe even a little propane stove to make Jiffy Pop.

As his friends made their excited plans, Christopher looked back at the clearing. He saw deer poking their heads through the bushes. Grazing on the last patches of green before the winter threatened to starve them. He listened. There was no sound. No wind. Just a steady pouring of snow from the clouds in the sky. Christopher saw that the cloud face was back. Smiling and drifting as it dropped snow on him like cotton candy. The snow was so thick, it covered all their footprints.

As if they were never there.

"Come on, Chris. Close the door. It's freezing," Special Ed said.

Christopher turned back to his friends. But not before staring at the white plastic bag, which had been silent all day. He looked at it, hanging on the low branch. Waiting patiently. Then, he stepped his foot over the doorframe and entered the tree house. Christopher knew the minute he closed that door, he would have his proof. Either he was crazy, or there was something on the other side. Either there was no nice man, or he was about to meet him in person.

"But what does the tree house do?" he had asked the nice man once.

you'd never believe me. you'll have to see it for yourself.

Christopher closed the door.

*

After a moment, a small bird landed on the doorknob. It looked around at the deer slowly crawling in a circle toward the tree house. Each step in unison. The bird did not like things it was not used to seeing, so it flew away. It flew up through the snowflakes and freezing air. It flew up past the tops of the trees and kept going higher and higher until it had reached the bottom of the clouds that looked like faces.

Then, it turned.

The bird looked back down at the earth. It saw the woods, the snowy white clearing with the deer, and the little tree with the tree house. And if it had words to describe what it saw, it would have sworn that it looked like a stark white iris with brown flecks and the black pupil of . . .

A giant eye.

Part IV

Seeing Is Believing

CHAPTER 34

hi. how are you? are you okay? don't worry. just breathe. you'll adjust. just remember a couple of things. are you listening? calm down. i know you can't see. you're not blind. you're passing to the imaginary side.

your friends are not with you. they still think you're with them on the real side. but you are not alone. i am waiting for you. i will never let you come in here alone. i am your friend forever.

oh, god. you've passed through. get ready. you can do this, christopher. I know you can do this. there. that's the doorknob. you're about to see. please remember something. i will do everything i can to protect you. but if you die in here, you die on the real side. so, whatever happens, don't ever come in here if i am not there to meet you. never come in at night. and if we ever get separated, don't leave the street.

she can't get you if you don't leave the street.

CHAPTER 35

Christopher opened his eyes.

At first glance, everything looked the same. He was standing in the tree house. He was still in the clearing. The snow was on the ground. For a moment, he thought he was just a crazy kid in a tree house listening to a figment of his imagination.

Except for that smell.

When he went into the tree house, the air was winter cold. The kind of freezing that made his nostrils stick together. But when he opened his eyes, the air smelled sweet. Like cotton candy.

"Hey, guys, do you smell that?" he asked.

No response.

"Guys?" he repeated.

He turned and almost screamed. Because sitting there, right next to Special Ed, Mike, and Matt, was his own body. Christopher watched the four boys sitting cross-legged, rubbing their hands together for warmth. He called out to them, but they could not hear him. He waved his hand in front of their eyes, but they didn't even blink. They were busy making plans about what furniture they could bring to the tree house. Their voices sounded far away. Like how his mother's voice echoed when he put his ears under bathwater. Christopher strained to hear them. Until . . .

knocK. knocK. knocK.

Christopher turned toward the door. The sound vibrated through his teeth like chalk on a blackboard. Christopher looked back to his friends. They couldn't hear the knocking. They just kept talking about how they were going to get power in the tree house for their toys and gadgets. Maybe batteries? Can refrigerators run on batteries?

knocK. knocK. knocK.

He inched toward the door. He put his ear up against it. At first, there was silence. Then, he heard a voice as clear as his friends were muddy.

christopher. psst. out here.

Christopher's heart pounded. He went to the window. He strained his neck to see, but he could see nothing.

knocK. knocK. knocK.

Christopher stood on his tiptoes, trying to see the person, but he just heard the voice through the door.

christopher. it's okay. it's me. open the door.

Christopher took a hard swallow and inched toward the door. He didn't want to open it, but he had to know if there really was a person standing there. Or if it was just another figment of his imagination. Was he outside of his own body? Or was he out of his mind?

Christopher opened the door.

The light outside was blinding. But Christopher could still see the face. The scars running up and down from a thousand cuts. A young man with an old soul. Or an older man with a young heart. The eyes were so blue. The face was so handsome.

It was the nice man.

"You're real," Christopher said in amazement.

"Hi, Christopher," he said. "It's so nice to finally meet you."

The nice man offered his hand. Christopher took it and shook it. The nice man's skin was soft and smooth. Like the cool side of the pillow.

"We only have an hour of daylight," the nice man said. "Let's go to work."

Christopher looked back to see if his friends noticed the change. Could they see the nice man? Could they feel the open door? Did they know that there was a whole other side to the woods and the world? But their conversation never changed. They saw nothing. Just a tree house built by eight little hands. Christopher followed the nice man out of the tree house and closed the door. He walked down the little 2x4s like baby teeth. And followed the nice man through the clearing and out into the imaginary world.

CHAPTER 36

W hat happened to your fingers?" Christopher's mother asked when she picked him up.

They were in the parking lot of the 3 Hole Golf course, standing with his friends and their mothers. The sun had finally set. The air was cold and crisp. Like a sensitive tooth.

"Nothing. Just some splinters," Christopher replied.

"From a plastic sled?"

"A kid from school let us use his wooden one."

Christopher's mother looked at him for a quiet moment. Suspicion was too strong a word for the look in her eyes. But it was a close enough cousin.

"Which kid?" she asked.

"Kevin Dorwart. He's in my homeroom," he said without a blink.

That ended the questions for now. Just as he knew it would. Because there was something else he brought with him out of the imaginary world along with the splinters and the memory of the conversation that his body had with his three friends in the tree house. His mind was only in the imaginary world for an hour, but ever since he left it, there was this . . .

Itch.

An itch on his nose that he just couldn't scratch because it wasn't on his nose. It was in his brain. But even itch wasn't the right word. Because an itch doesn't also tickle and whisper and scratch. An itch doesn't leave thoughts behind. The thoughts were like his old flash cards.

2 + 2 = 4

The capital of Pennsylvania is . . . Harrisburg.

But these flash cards were different. As he looked at his friends and their mothers, the itch flipped the flash cards quickly, like the man he once saw playing three-card monte on the street.

Special Ed's mother is...
Special Ed's mother is...a drunk.

Mike and Matt's moms are...
Mike and Matt's moms are...seeing a couples therapist.

"Christopher, are you all right?"

Christopher turned around. All of the mothers were staring at him. Worried. Christopher smiled a reassuring smile.

"I'm fine. Just a little headache," he said. "I want to keep sledding."

"Yeah. Can we?" the boys asked.

"Sorry, it's getting late," his mom said.

"Yeah. Say good night, boys. I have a bottle of white Zin at home with my name written all over it," Betty said.

They all said their goodbyes, and Christopher got into the car with his mom. He turned the car vents onto his face and let the hot air melt his cold apple cheeks. He looked over and saw his mother furrow her brow.

"Hey, Mom. What are you thinking about?" he asked.

"Nothing," she said.

My mother is thinking about...
My mother is thinking about...the splinters in my fingers.

When his mother pulled onto their street, a shudder went through his body. He remembered the things he saw on the imaginary side. How it was like a one-way mirror that lets you spy on people on the real side.

And know things.

He tried to distract himself from the things he'd seen by looking at the houses, but the itch only got louder. They passed the old house on the corner. Christopher's mother told him that a young couple had just bought it. The wife was painting over the red door.

The house on the corner is...
The house on the corner is...

Nothing. His mind was blank. There was no answer. Only the itch and the scratch. Christopher's mother pulled into their driveway. She hit the automatic garage door opener with the remote and forced a smile.

My mother is…
My mother is…worried about me.

Christopher watched his mother put soup on the stove. Chicken with the little noodles he loved. And grilled cheese sandwiches. Like she used to make for her late husband.

My father had…
My father had…voices in his head. Like me.

The whisper scratch lingered, then died. Christopher had a little headache and a slight fever. But it wasn't too bad. He felt cozy in the kitchen, slowly filling up with the smell of soup and grilled cheese. When his mom asked if he wanted to watch The Avengers or Bad Cat, he said no. He didn't want to watch a movie at all. No television, either.

"Then, what do you want to do?" his mother asked.

"Can we look at my baby book together?"

Christopher's mother smiled, surprised. They hadn't looked at it in years. And maybe this was the perfect night for it. With snow on the roof and soup on the stove.

"Of course. What made you think of your baby book, honey?"

"I don't know."

And for once, he didn't. He had no idea why the baby book was suddenly so interesting. He just wanted to look. So, when the soup was done and the grilled cheese was perfectly golden brown and toasty, his mother got down the baby book.

My mother knows…
My mother knows…I am different than I was.

And they sat on their new sofa.

My mother knows…
My mother knows…I am smarter than I should be.

With a fire in the fireplace.

My mother knows…
My mother knows…I am keeping secrets from her.

"This is really good grilled cheese, Mom," he said to make her smile.
"Thanks, honey," she said, pretending to.

Christopher just wished that he could give his mother the power he brought back from the imaginary side. He wished that she could see the thoughts that played hide-and-seek between people's words, and she would know what was really going on inside his mind.

I can't tell…
I can't tell…you what is happening, Mom.

It would…
It would…terrify you.

The nice man said that he had to be careful. The more time he spent on the imaginary side, the more he would know on the real side. But the power would come at a price. At first headaches. And then fevers. And then worse. He made Christopher promise to stay out of the tree house for a few days to recover.

He didn't want to train him too quickly.

So, Christopher put his head on his mother's shoulder and tried to forget the things he saw on the imaginary side. The man in the Girl Scout uniform near the bushes in the cul-de-sac. The other man rolled in the hollow log near the billy goat bridge. Luckily, it was daytime, and the imaginary people were sleeping. The nice man said that at night, the imaginary world wakes up.

And then it gets really scary.

"So, never come in here without me. Never be in here at night. Promise me."
"I promise, sir."

Christopher gave his eyes to the baby book, but his thoughts went back to the sunset. It was only two hours ago, but it felt as far away as Michigan. When sunset had come, the nice man brought Christopher back to the tree house. He apologized for not answering him for so long, but said he couldn't risk it because the imaginary people were getting suspicious of him. He said to be very careful if Christopher had a bad dream because bad dreams were the imaginary side poking around to see if you knew about them. So, if things got really scary in a dream, Christopher was supposed to just run to the street.

She can't get you if you're on the street.

"Who?"

"The less you know about her, the better. I don't want her to find you."

Christopher then asked the nice man to come to the real side with him, but the nice man said he couldn't. He had a job to do. Then, the nice man mussed his hair and closed the door.

In an instant the cotton candy smell turned back to cold air. Christopher returned to his body on the real side. He saw Special Ed with the tree house door open in his hand.

"Come on, Chris," Special Ed said. "It's almost six. We're going to be late."

"Yeah," Mike said. "We gotta get back to the golf course."

"We don't want to get grounded again," Matt agreed.

Christopher followed his friends out of the tree house. He was the last one out. He closed the door behind him, shutting the imaginary world inside like a coffin. Then, he climbed down the little 2x4s like baby teeth. When they reached the ground, Christopher looked at the white plastic bag back on the low-hanging branch.

And he smiled.

Because he wasn't alone.

"Chris, are you okay?" Matt asked.

"What do you mean?"

"Your nose is bleeding."

Christopher reached up and dabbed at his nose. He brought his fingers back into his field of vision like rabbit ears and saw them spotted with blood.

The power will...

The power will...come at a price.

"It's nothing. I'm fine. Let's go."

Then, he knelt down to wash the blood off in the pure, white snow.

"Christopher, are you asleep?" his mother asked.

Christopher followed her voice back to the present. He didn't know how much time had passed, but his mother had already reached the end of the baby book.

"No, I'm wide awake," he said.

Then, he asked her to go back to the beginning of the baby book and look at the old pictures again. It was the only thing that made his brain stop itching.

He had no idea why.

CHAPTER 37

Ambrose opened the baby book.

It was one o'clock at night. His room was still. He opened the window and listened to the snow falling outside. It was barely audible. Someone without gauze covering their eyes probably couldn't have heard any of it. But he could. Wet, heavy drops falling on the ground like feathers. David used to love to play in the snow. God, his little brother loved to play in the snow.

Ambrose held the baby book.

He remembered the time David begged him to take him sledding on the 3 Hole Golf course. "You're not old enough, kid." But David could be persuasive. And that time, he won out. They went sledding. David wore his favorite hat. It was a ski hat with the Pittsburgh Steelers logo on it and a yellow tassel on top. Back before the Immaculate Reception, when the Steelers were a terrible football team. But Ambrose won the hat at Kennywood and gave it to his little brother. That hat was still David's favorite. That and the baseball glove Ambrose bought him. He still remembered that baseball-glove smell.

Ambrose stood up.

He remembered going down the steep hill of the 3 Hole Golf course. The wind turning their cheeks red like the apple that scared David when he saw Snow White. They went sledding all day, the snow sneaking its way under David's mittens, making his wrists ache with cold. When they finally left for home, his nose was caked in frozen snot. Mom and Dad were out, so Ambrose made them two TV dinners with the tinfoil peas and lumpy mashed potatoes. They sat down and ate together and watched the Steelers lose to the Bears.

"God damn Steelers," Ambrose said.

"God damn Steelers," David said.

"Watch your mouth. And take off that hat while we eat."

David took off the old Steelers hat and smiled when his big brother mussed up his hair.

Ambrose was getting older, and over the years, it was getting harder to remember details about his little brother. But some things he would never forget.

David's hair.

Ambrose could still remember the color. Not quite black. Not quite brown. Textured so perfectly that a bad haircut was an impossibility. Ambrose remembered his mother taking a lock of the hair to put on the front page of David's baby book. It sat proudly right next to the little hospital bracelet with D. OLSON printed on it. Right next to the little handprints and footprints. The hair and bracelet pasted with clear plastic tape that yellowed over time.

Ambrose couldn't believe that the lock of hair from his little brother's baby book was now in a plastic evidence bag on its way to a forensics lab in Pittsburgh to confirm that the skeleton they found in the Mission Street Woods was, in fact, David. If it was, Ambrose would finally be able to bury his kid brother after fifty years. His mother and father had never allowed a funeral.

They always said David was coming home.

For years, Ambrose had tried to make that dream come true. He looked for David everywhere. For years, he thought he saw him in other children. Sometimes he had to look away so that no one would think he was a creep. Eventually, though, deep in his own quiet, Ambrose understood that David was never coming home. He knew that David was taken like children are. Not for ransom. But for something far more evil. He watched his mother and father lie to themselves that David was taken in by some childless family. Not a monster with a van. Or some freak making movies. Or some coward who needed to destroy something small to feel big. Eventually, Ambrose was forced to trade his parents' war at home for another war abroad. In the army, Ambrose had seen worse things than a child gone missing. He had seen villages of them torn apart by bombs. He had seen girls sold to pay for rice and men disgusting enough to buy them. And when he returned from the war, and his wife wanted children, he said he couldn't go through that much pain again. He failed his little brother. And he could never forgive himself. And he didn't deserve his own son.

Ambrose took the bandages off his eyes.

He squinted through the haze. He looked at his reflection in the window and the snow falling behind it. Ambrose studied his bald head. And the single strip of grey hair that wrapped around his scalp above his ears like Mrs. Collins' mink stole. David never saw his hair go grey. He never saw it fall off his head and leave traces of itself like pine needles on a pillow every morning. He never heard his wife lie to him about how great he still looked.

Ambrose stared at the baby book.

He turned the pages and saw his little brother grow up all over again. He saw a picture of a baby with no teeth become a little boy crawling and walking and eventually running into the coffee table so many times that he called the hospital the "stitches store." He saw his little brother crying in Santa's lap. A little boy smiling under the family's Christmas tree when he got the baseball glove from his big brother Ambrose. The one that smelled like new leather.

"Ambrose, can we go play catch?"

"It's snowing outside."

"I don't mind."

Ambrose turned the pages. Over and over. Trying to see as much as he could. His eyes were not healing. He would be blind soon. His eye doctor warned him that it could happen as soon as Christmas. But as long as he could squint, he would look at this baby book. And remember everything he could about his little brother. Not the crazy stuff at the end. Not the headaches. The fevers. The talking to himself. The bed-wetting. The nightmares that got so bad that by the end, he didn't know if he was asleep or awake.

No.

He would remember the David from these photographs. The kid who loved that old Steelers hat and had to play catch in the snow because he loved the baseball glove that his big brother gave him. The kid who begged to go everywhere with Ambrose and loved every minute he got to spend with his big brother. The kid who sat down next to Ambrose at the barbershop and smiled when the barber pretended to shave him and said,

"David . . . you have a great head of hair."

Ambrose got to the end of the baby book. The last picture was David at the age of eight. Then, there were dozens of pages that were going to be blank forever. Fifty years ago, they were clear white from Sears. Now, they were yellow and cracked like the skin on his hands. Ambrose went to his bed and lay down on the pillow. He took out his teeth and put them in the glass by his bed. He dropped in the tablet of Efferdent to wash away his sins. The hissing of the water was soothing to him like the rain on the roof during a thunderstorm. The thunder would clap and David would open his bedroom door.

"Ambrose, can I sleep in your bed?"

"It's just thunder."

"I had a nightmare."

"Another one? Okay. Climb in."

"Thanks!"

Ambrose remembered the smile on David's face. Those missing front teeth. He looked so relieved to be climbing into bed with his big brother. He used that old baseball glove as a pillow.

"Ambrose . . . let's go to the woods tomorrow."

"Go to bed, David."

"I want to show you something."

"I'm seventeen. I'm not going to the woods like a little kid."

"Please. It's something special."

"Fine. What is it?"

"I can't tell you, or they'll hear me. You have to see it for yourself. Please!"

"Fine. I'll go with you. Now go to sleep."

But he never did. No matter how much David begged him. Because he didn't want to encourage more of his crazy shit. He had no idea what David did out there. He had no idea what happened in those woods. But someone did. Someone put a tape recording of a baby crying on his porch and took his little brother away.

And someone buried his little brother alive.

A primal rage took the old man. A young, inexhaustible anger came back to him like an old song on the radio. He saw the faces of the newspapermen who accused him of murdering his own brother. The classmates who avoided him. The enemy's armies that shot at him. His mother on her deathbed saying David was coming home. His father on his deathbed saying nothing because the cancer ravaged his brain worse than his own denial. He saw the doctor who said his wife was dead. The judge who told him he could no longer take care of himself. The gum-snapping bureaucrat who finally took his license. The government that couldn't solve the refugee problem in the Middle East. And the God who let all of this happen for a reason all His own.

They all took on one face.

The person who buried his brother alive.

Ambrose took a deep breath of it. Then, he exhaled and stared at the ceiling through the clouds in his eyes. He was done crying. He was done feeling sorry for himself. He was done being a feeble old man who was just waiting to be blind before waiting to die. He was being kept alive for a reason. And he wasn't going to waste it. He was going to figure out what happened to his brother if it was the last thing he ever did.

Which he was almost certain it would be.

CHAPTER 38

*W*ho murdered David Olson?

That's what the sheriff thought as he drove through the Fort Pitt Tunnel until the blizzard almost took his tires off the bridge. He had never seen snow like this in his life. Two days with no signs of stopping. It was like the earth was angry at them or God Himself really needed some Head & Shoulders for all that dandruff. There were droughts in Africa, a crisis in the Middle East, and Western Pennsylvania was throwing its hat in the ring to become the next North Pole.

What the hell was going on?

The sheriff pulled in front of the precinct and parked. He looked up at the old, grey building where he spent his eager twenties and less than eager thirties. The grey building where he put a lot of bad people behind bars and where a lot of innocent people lay lifeless on a cold metal table in the coroner's office.

Innocent people like David Olson.

The sheriff got the call an hour before. His buddy Carl had run the DNA off the books as a favor. The hair from the baby book matched the DNA of the body found in the woods. The skeleton belonged to David Olson. The sheriff hoped that the final proof might give some comfort to Ambrose. He had seen grown men cry before, but there was something about Ambrose that got him behind the throat. Something about seeing this old war veteran cry through the gauze over his eyes that would never heal.

"Did he suffer? Were any of his bones broken?" Ambrose asked.

"No, sir."

"Was he hurt . . . in other ways?"

"Other than the manner of death, there was no sign of foul play, Mr. Olson."

"How was my little brother murdered?"

The sheriff was silent at first.

"I'm a soldier, Sheriff. The only thing I can't handle is bullshit. Tell me the truth."

"He was buried alive, sir."

Even without seeing his eyes, the sheriff would never forget the look on Ambrose's face. It began as confusion spreading across his forehead, then blossomed into a white-hot rage. The sheriff had been the bearer of bad news to many families over the years. These were always the hardest words to speak. He would come back to this old grey building after seeing a single mother in the Hill District. Or a nice wealthy couple in Squirrel Hill. And the reaction was always the same. That mixture of disbelief, grief, guilt, and despair.

Except for the girl with the painted nails. Her mother was dead.

The sheriff met Carl in the coffee shop in the lobby of the grey building to collect the lock of David's hair, get the official paperwork, and arrange for the body to be sent to the funeral parlor. They got their favorite booth. The one underneath the picture of the owner shaking hands with Steelers legend Terry Bradshaw. The first time they sat under that picture, Carl spent lunch telling him about this hot Catholic girl he met at Metropol down on the Strip. And they laughed about girls the way that young men always do (and older men never do). The autograph was faded now, along with the color, and the hot girl Carl met at Metropol was now the overweight Catholic woman who had given him three kids and made his life a happy, living hell. The sheriff smiled as he listened to Carl complain about spending another Christmas with his mother-in-law in Homestead.

"The woman can make a mean mushroom soup, though. You wanna join us?" Carl asked.

"No, thanks. Too much to do."

"Come on. You worked all the way through Thanksgiving. Don't be alone on Christmas again."

The sheriff lied and said he had been invited to one of his deputies' houses. He thanked his old friend, then got back to his car, already covered with another inch of snow.

Where was it all coming from?

As he started the car and let the defrosters clear the windshield, his mind settled back. He looked at the evidence bag, the lock of hair, and the official report before putting it to rest in the passenger seat.

Then, he started driving.

He knew where he was going. He did this every time he came downtown. He was going to drive past the hospital where he took the girl with the painted nails. Even with the blizzard and the bad roads. He would drive past it because he promised God that he would. His logical brain knew that it didn't make any difference whether he parked in front of Mercy Hospital or looked at that Charlie Brown tree in the front or not. But in a rare moment of grief, he had made a deal with God that if he did that, the girl with the painted nails would be in Heaven. So, he was going to do this forever. If he couldn't save her life, at least he could save her soul. He owed her that much.

He parked in front of Mercy Hospital. He stared at that tree for the better part of an hour. The tailpipe making clouds in the cold air. The windshield wiper and defroster turning fat snowflakes into streaks of water. He reached over and grabbed David Olson's report from the seat next to the lock of the boy's hair.

Who left the baby carriage on the porch?

The question stuck in the sheriff's mind like a fly in a jar. Somebody planned all this. Someone went through a lot of trouble to wipe down a baby carriage and leave it out there with no prints. This wasn't the work of some kids playing a prank. This was the work of a person (or persons) who took David to do horrible things to him.

Ambrose said there was no one he suspected. No neighbors. No teachers. No parents of friends, because David didn't have any friends. He was just a weird, lonely kid who spent his time reading in the library. Back then, the polite people in the neighborhood called him "off" or "special," or "touched" if their roots were Southern. Today, David might have been diagnosed anywhere from "on the spectrum" to "schizophrenic," depending upon the doctor. Whatever his diagnosis would have been, it didn't provide the one thing the sheriff needed to solve the case.

A motive.

David Olson wasn't found in a ditch. He wasn't at the bottom of a creek. They found David Olson's body twisted under a tree root. Buried alive. So, if David Olson was murdered, then who fucking buried him?

Because it wasn't the trees.

CHAPTER 39

Christopher stared at the trees.

He lay in bed, watching the moon wink through the bare branches. He was too afraid to sleep. Too afraid to dream. He didn't want the imaginary people poking around in his nightmares to see if he knew about them.

So he stayed awake by reading.

He went to the duck paper bookshelf three times that night. The words worked through him, quieting his mind, and distracting him from the itch. And the fear.

And that fever.

It started slowly. Just a little sweat on the back of his neck. Then it got so hot that he had to take off his pajama bottoms and lie above the blanket, reading with his bare skinny legs.

By the time morning came, he had almost finished The Lord of the Rings.

Christopher's fever climbed the minute he entered school. He looked at the kids, who all felt gypped that they only got three snow days. He remembered his mother telling Jerry that "gyp" was a bad word. "Gyp" comes from "gypsy." It's not nice to say "gyp."

Jerry is...
Jerry is... looking for my mother.

Christopher felt the hallways go quiet. The itch pounded his ears. Flipping the flash cards faster and faster, like a ten-speed bike changing gears.

The janitor is...
The janitor is... talking to his wife.

I don't speak Spanish, but I know what he says.
"It's a sin to get divorced. I will not give up custody of my son."

"Hi, Christopher," the voice said.
He turned around and saw Ms. Lasko smiling pleasantly.

Ms. Lasko was…
Ms. Lasko was…standing in line at the clinic.

"Are you okay, Christopher? You don't look well," said Ms. Lasko.
"I'm fine, ma'am. Thank you."

Ms. Lasko got…
Ms. Lasko got…rid of her baby.

"Then come on. We're all going to the auditorium for the state exam."

Ms. Lasko went…
Ms. Lasko went…straight from the clinic to the bar.

Christopher followed her into the auditorium. He sat down in his alphabetical seat as all the teachers passed out the state exam. They were supposed to do this last week, Mrs. Henderson explained, but the snow days threw off their entire schedule. She told them they would have to complete all of their work in this last week of school before break. She told them not to feel any pressure. This exam did influence state funding, but Mrs. Henderson and the other teachers were really proud of their progress this year.

Mrs. Henderson is…
Mrs. Henderson is…lying.

The school needs…
The school needs…the money.

When all the tests were passed around, Christopher took out his number 2 pencil and started working. The itch went away, and there was nothing but answers. Beautiful, calm answers. He filled in the little circles row after row until they looked like stars in the sky. Shooting stars that were either a soul or a sun (or a son). In that moment, Christopher couldn't hear thoughts. All the kids were too busy thinking about the test. There were no flash cards. No itch. Just the test answers, which felt like a warm bath. His mind the cool side of the pillow. Christopher finished the test and looked around the room. All of the other kids were still on page five. Christopher was the only one who had finished his test.

Until Special Ed finished and put his pencil down.

And Mike put his pencil down.

And Matt put his pencil down.

The four boys looked at each other and smiled. Proud that four of the dumbest kids in school had somehow become four of the smartest.

"If you're done with your test, please put your head down," said Mrs. Henderson.

Christopher put his head on his desk as he was told. His thoughts drifted to the tree house. To the nice man. And the training they would do. His mind floated away like the clouds up in the sky. Like the sheep he used to count when he couldn't sleep after his dad died.

Just rest your eyes.

Like your daddy did in the bathtub.

Like the voices told him.

Just rest your eyes and you will sleep forever.

"Christopher!" a voice shouted. "What did I tell you?"

Christopher took his head off his desk and looked up at the front of the class. Ms. Lasko was staring at him with a stern expression, which was strange because Ms. Lasko never got mad at the kids. Not even when they spilled paint in class.

"Christopher! I said come up to the blackboard."

Christopher looked around the auditorium. All of the kids were staring at him. They looked like they wanted to say things . . .

You heard her, Christopher.

Come on.

We don't have all day.

. . . but they couldn't because their mouths were sewn shut.

Christopher searched for his friends, but Special Ed was asleep at his desk. The M&M's had their heads down, too. Christopher looked back as Ms. Lasko bent her finger, beckoning him to the front of the class. There was dirt under her fingernails. A silver key hung from a little noose around her neck. Christopher's heart started to pound. He knew what had happened.

I fell asleep. Oh, God. I'm dreaming.

"Christopher, if you don't come to the board right now, everyone in this auditorium will have no choice but to eat you alive," Ms. Lasko said in a calm voice.

Get to the street.

Christopher turned. All of the exits were guarded by teachers. Standing with their eyes and mouths sewn shut. There was no way out.

"Christopher, you come right now!" Ms. Lasko hissed.

Christopher didn't want to walk to her. He wanted to get out of here. So, he moved away from the blackboard. But every time he moved away, he somehow moved closer. Everything was opposite day. He stopped. He breathed calmly.

He took a step away from the blackboard.

And his feet took one step closer.

"No!" he cried.

He took another two steps away.

And he moved two steps closer.

He stopped. And thought. "Okay. It's opposite day. If I move closer to the blackboard, then I'll move away."

So, he took two steps toward the blackboard.

And he moved four steps toward it.

It didn't matter what he did.

He kept walking to the front of the auditorium.

"Help me! Please!" Christopher shouted.

Christopher looked at all of the kids for help. Their mouths were sewn shut, but their eyes smiled at him. Christopher moved down the aisle. Every row he passed looked up at him and hissed.

Don't mess up the test.

Don't blow the curve.

Christopher walked up to the blackboard where Ms. Lasko stood, her thick eye makeup the right color. But somehow wrong. Everything was wrong. She didn't smell like her usual cigarettes. She smelled like burning skin. Ms. Lasko smiled and held up a perfect piece of white chalk. It was in the shape of a finger.

"Take it, Christopher," she said, rubbing her dirty fingernails over his brown hair.

She handed him the chalk.

"Now, write on the board, Christopher."

"What do you want me to write?" he asked.

"You know what to write," she said.

The chalk screeched on the blackboard as Christopher began.

I WILL NOT FALL ASLEEP IN CLASS.

He turned to Ms. Lasko. She pulled out a pair of scissors.

"That's not what you're supposed to write, Christopher."

"What do you want me to write?" he asked.

"You know what to write," she said calmly.

Christopher turned to see Ms. Lasko walk to the front row of students. She knelt down in front of Jenny Hertzog, picked up the scissors, and quietly snipped away the thread covering her mouth. Jenny loosened her jaw. She began to salivate. Like little babies do when they are starting to grow teeth. Little baby teeth.

I AM SORRY I FELL ASLEEP IN CLASS.

"That's not what you're supposed to write, Christopher," Ms. Lasko said.

"Ms. Lasko, please. I don't know what you want me to write," he begged.

"Yes, you do. The bell is going to ring for lunch period. Would someone like to help Christopher at the board?"

All the kids raised their hands and opened their mouths to say "Me! Me! Me!" But no words came. Just the sound of babies crying to be fed their mother's milk.

Mother's milk is blood without the red corpuscles.

Milk is blood. The babies want your blood.

"Thank you, children. You. You in the red hoodie. Why don't you help him?" Ms. Lasko said.

A raised hand came out of a little red sleeve. Christopher couldn't see the kid's face. All he saw was Ms. Lasko moving down the front row, cutting all of the children's mouths free. Snip. Snip. Snip. The babies were howling for blood.

Christopher turned back to the board. Desperate. The chalk shook in his hand. He knew he could never write anything about the tree house or the nice man or the training or the imaginary world. So, he started to write furiously. Anything he could think of.

I'M SORRY YOU DRINK YOURSELF TO SLEEP, MS. LASKO.

"THAT'S NOT WHAT YOU WRITE, CHRISTOPHER!" she hissed.

Ms. Lasko moved to Brady Collins. Snip. Snip. Snip.

I'M SORRY FOR MS. LASKO'S BABY. IN HEAVEN.

"That's not where my baby is," Ms. Lasko said in a baby voice. "HELP CHRISTOPHER WRITE WHAT HE NEEDS TO WRITE!"

Christopher saw the kid in the red hoodie move next to him at the blackboard. He saw a little hand grab some chalk and begin writing. He followed the hand to the arm to the face of a little boy. The little boy turned to Christopher and smiled. With his missing front teeth. His eyes glowed as he wrote in big, bold letters,

WHO IS HELPING YOU?

"That's all we need to know, Christopher. Just write it down like a good little boy, and you'll get out of here alive," Ms. Lasko said with a cheerful smile.

Ms. Lasko quietly moved to the second row. Cutting all the threads with scissors. Snip. Snip. Snip.

"I don't know what you're talking about," Christopher said.

"Yes, you do," Ms. Lasko said. "Lunch period is almost here. Tick tock."

The little boy in the red hoodie dragged his chalk against the blackboard, screeching each letter.

WHO IS HELPING YOU?

"No one! I swear!" Christopher said.

Ms. Lasko went to the back row, cutting the last of the thread free. Snip. Snip. Snip.

"Now, who wants to eat him first?!" she shrieked.

"Oh! Me! Me! Me!" the piglets squealed.

Christopher turned to the little boy in the red hoodie. Desperate.

"How do I wake up?" he whispered.

The little boy said nothing. He just turned to Christopher with his glowing eyes and smiled. With his missing front teeth. The same missing teeth Christopher saw on the skeleton. Christopher felt the hair on the back of his neck stand up.

This <u>thing</u> was David Olson.

"David, please help me wake up," Christopher begged.

David Olson stopped, shocked to hear his name spoken aloud.

"Please. I know your big brother Ambrose."

The boy looked bewildered. For a moment, his eyes blinked and stopped glowing. He wasn't a thing. He was a little boy. He opened his mouth, trying to speak, but his serpent tongue flicked through the gap like a snake. And nothing came out but hissing.

"I don't know what you're trying to say," Christopher whispered.

David Olson moved to the board. He wrote in big capital letters.

RING.

The bell rang. Christopher turned. He saw the mob of kids running at him at full speed. Their teeth exposed. He ran to the exit door where Mrs. Henderson stood guard in the hallway, holding a stack of library books.

"Mr. Henderson doesn't love me anymore, Christopher. He always goes out at night."

She dropped the library books and grabbed his arm. Her eyes were lost and desperate.

"Why does he think I'm so ugly? Christopher, help me!"

Brady Collins and Jenny Hertzog rushed at them. Howling like baby dogs needing to nurse. Christopher wrenched his arm free and ran out of the auditorium. But Mrs. Henderson did not move. She just stood there, looking at herself in the glass of the display case stuffed with decades of trophies and class photos.

"When did my hair turn grey? When did I become so old and ugly?" she said just as the pack of children jumped on her. Their teeth gnashing. Thirsty. Starving.

Christopher ran down the hallway, looking for an exit. Some way to get to the street. Just get to the street. He turned the corner and saw the exit far in the distance. On each side of the hallway were rows and rows of lockers. Eyes peeking out through the vents. Whispers behind the metal frames. Christopher ran toward the exit. The locker handles began to jiggle.

The lockers started to open.

Like the lids of coffins.

Christopher ran past them as fast as he could. He raced through the hallway. Just get to the exit. Just get to the street. He was just about to open the exit door when . . .

A locker opened, and a hand pulled him back into the darkness.

Christopher started to scream. The hand covered his mouth.

don't. it's a trap.

It was the nice man.

Suddenly the front door burst open. Ms. Lasko ran back into the school. Somehow, she had doubled back. She stalked around the hallways. Her face smeared with blood.

"Chrisssssstopher," she whissspered. "Is your friend here now? I think he might beeee."

don't scream. that's how she finds you.

Christopher peered out through the vent. He saw Ms. Lasko walk to different lockers and rap her bloody knuckles.

Bang. Bang. Bang.

"Eeny. Meeny. Miny. Moe."

Bang. Bang. Bang.

"Catch the new friend by his toe."

Bang. Bang. Bang.

"He will holler, can't let him go."

Bang. Bang. Bang.

"Eeny meeny miny . . ."

Silence.

Christopher stood breathlessly, waiting for her to open the locker. But she didn't. She went to the gymnasium across the hallway and disappeared behind a door. The nice man waited for a moment. Then, he lowered Christopher down and whispered.

we need to get to the street.

Christopher opened the locker.

The entire hallway was filled with children. Too short to be seen from the vents. They all pointed and screamed at once.

"MOE!"

The gymnasium door slammed open. Christopher saw Ms. Lasko enter the hallway. But she was all wrong. Her eyes glowed green like the fakest of green contact lenses. Like no color an eye should be. A sick puke green. A broken-arm green. She stared at him and smiled, revealing dog's teeth.

"YOU'RE OFF THE STREET!" she cackled.

She ran at him.

Christopher fell down in the hallway. He couldn't get up.

With every step, he heard a sick click as her neck began to break. It was like a giraffe's neck growing out of her shoulders one vertebra at a time. The children parted like the Red Sea as she moved at him with a click. Sick. Click. He could smell her breath. Hot and rancid. There was no more Ms. Lasko. There was only this woman in her true form. Covered in burns. Her hair matted and insane. A silver key hanging from a little string noose around her neck.

She launched herself at Christopher, digging her nails into his neck. Suddenly the nice man sprang out of the locker. The two collided and fell to the ground.

"I knew it was you!" she hissed.

That's when Christopher realized that it was a trap. But the trap wasn't for him. The lady reached her dirty fingernails and grabbed the nice man. The children jumped up and down. Howling. All except David Olson, who stood as far away as he could down the hallway, then slipped into a locker out of sight. Hiding. The nice man tackled the woman. She opened her mouth, baring her razor-sharp dog teeth. She was stronger. Faster. Her eyes glowed. Screaming and licking and hissing. Hiss. Hisssss!

The nice man looked at Christopher.

He was about to speak.

"STOP HELPING HIM!" the hissing lady screamed as her dog teeth buried themselves into the nice man's neck.

CHAPTER 40

Christopher was screaming before he even opened his eyes.

He looked up and saw the face of Ms. Lasko, rushing at him. There was no time to lose. He got up and pushed her.

"Get away from me!" he screamed.

"Christopher, calm down!" Ms. Lasko said.

"You're going to kill me!" he shrieked as he grabbed her arm. His forehead became hot with fever, which he immediately pushed down his arm through his fingers. His fingers heated up like little ovens through the fabric of Ms. Lasko's cotton blouse.

"Christopher, stop! You're hurting me," she shrieked.

"Please! Don't let them eat me!" he said.

The laughter was what finally snapped him out of it.

Christopher looked around the auditorium. The kids were all sitting at their desks, taking the state exam. Their mouths were no longer sewn shut. They were wide open and laughing at him.

"Please! Don't let them eat me!" Brady Collins mocked.

"Shut up, Brady!" Special Ed said.

"If they want to eat someone, Special Ed is the juiciest," Jenny Hertzog said.

The kids laughed harder. Christopher looked back at Ms. Lasko. Her fingernails were clean. There was no more dirt. No more puke-green eyes. No more hissing lady. This was the real Ms. Lasko. And she was . . .

Terrified of him.

"Christopher, you had a nightmare. Please, let go of my arm."

Christopher let go. Ms. Lasko quickly pulled her blouse off her arm and looked just as little blisters began to form. She turned back to Christopher, who seemed even more terrified than she was.

"I'm sorry, Ms. Lasko," he said.

"Don't worry," she said. "It's just a brush burn. Let's take you to the nurse."

"I don't need the nurse," he said. "I'm fine now."

"For your neck," she said.

Christopher didn't understand what she meant until he noticed the little smears of blood on her white blouse in the shape of his fingers. Christopher looked down at his fingernails, raw like hamburger. Then, he reached up and felt his neck. The place where the hissing lady scratched him was the same place that it seemed he'd ripped his own neck with his fingernails.

"Come now," she said kindly.

The minute Christopher stood up, the laughter began anew. It started as little snickers from the kids around him. Within moments, it had spread through the entire auditorium as kids laughed and pointed and whispered. Christopher looked down at his pants and saw it.

The urine stain.

It had spread over his corduroy pants, turning the tan color into a dark chestnut brown. He had wet the bed in front of his entire school. He looked up at Ms. Lasko, who quickly snapped her attention away from the mild pain on her arm and into the eyes of a mortified little boy. She took his hand and led him to the nurse's office.

Ms. Lasko is . . .

Ms. Lasko is . . . putting vodka in her thermos.

Ms. Lasko is . . . chewing gum to cover the smell.

Christopher lay on the hard plastic cot in the nurse's office. His head ached and his forehead was hot with fever. He tried to see the thermometer over the bridge of his nose, but his eyes crossed. He could barely see the numbers climbing.

99. 100. 101.

He looked over at the nurse treating the burn on Ms. Lasko's arm. She slowly rubbed a cream on the blisters and wrapped it loosely with gauze.

"Just keep it wrapped," the nurse said. "The blisters will be gone in a day or two."

The thermometer beeped. The nurse came back and grabbed it out of Christopher's mouth.

"One hundred and two degrees," she said. "Stay here. We'll call your mother."

The nurse thinks…
The nurse thinks…I hurt my neck on purpose.

Ms. Lasko and the nurse walked into the office next door to call Christopher's mother. Christopher suddenly panicked. If his mother knew he was sick, she would never let him out of the house. No school. No tree house. No way to help the nice man. But it wasn't just the fever. His mother would see the urine stains on his corduroy pants and the cuts on his neck. She would ask him questions. Questions he could never answer. Because the hissing lady was watching him now.

"Excuse me, Ms. Lasko? May I clean up in the bathroom?" Christopher asked.

"Of course, Christopher." She smiled.

Ms. Lasko is…
Ms. Lasko is…thinking about the drink in her thermos.
Ms. Lasko is…drunk drunk drunk all day in school.

Christopher slipped into the hallway and rushed to the first-floor boys' bathroom. There were no kids in there. No boys doing "long shots" into the urinals. Christopher was finally alone. He looked up at the clock. The test wouldn't be over for another five minutes. There was time. He quickly stripped off his pants and ran the cold water. He put his corduroy pants into the water and started to rub them back and forth. Throwing in a little soap. Trying to rub out the urine stains. But they wouldn't come out. He scrubbed over and over. Manically cleaning and rinsing and cleaning and rinsing. But nothing worked. His pants got wetter and wetter. His cheeks redder and redder. His face flushed with shame.

It's not working. She's going to see my pants.
She's going to see my neck.
She won't let me go to the tree house.

Christopher knew he had to get back to the tree house. Promise or no promise, he needed to find the nice man before the hissing lady killed him. What if he was too late? What if the nice man was like the autumn leaves of the woods? When the branches went bare, the nice man would be gone. And Christopher would be alone.

He looked up at the clock. He had two minutes left. He stopped the water and wrung out his pants. He held them up to the hot-air dryer. He hit the button and let the hot air fill his corduroys like balloons in the Balloon Derby. He looked at himself in the mirror, and rolled his turtleneck sweater up to cover his neck like he did when he was afraid of vampires. He hit the dryer again and saw the brown chestnut color get a little more faint. But it wasn't drying fast enough.

It needs more heat.

Where am I going to get more heat?

Christopher closed his eyes and felt the heat rising on his forehead. He pictured the Mission Street Woods. The branches bare except for the evergreens like Christmas trees. Christmas trees all in a row.

And they were burning.

Christopher looked up at the clock. Two minutes had gone by in a daydream, and he was standing in his tighty whities, holding his pants up to the blow dryer. The pants were so dry, they were hot in his hands. Brady Collins and his group of friends stepped into the bathroom as Christopher tried to put his pants back on.

"No, we'll take those!" Brady said, snatching them out of his hands.

"Give them back, Brady," Christopher said.

"Give them back, Brady," Brady Collins mocked. His friends joined in a chorus of mocking. "Please, don't eat me!" "Please, don't kill me!" They walked forward, pushing Christopher out into the hallway. Christopher landed on the ground in front of Jenny Hertzog and a group of girls, who began to laugh.

"I've heard of floods, but this is ridiculous," she mocked.

Jenny Hertzog is afraid . . .

Jenny Hertzog is afraid . . . of her stepbrother's room.

"Brady, give them to me!" Jenny Hertzog squealed. "Floods! Floods!"

Brady threw the pants over to Jenny, who slipped them over her legs and under her skirt. Christopher's face flushed hot with fever. He barely had time to think before the itch pushed the words out of his mouth.

"Why don't you sleep in your own room, Jenny?"

He said it innocently. Like a child asking his mother why the sky is blue. But Jenny Hertzog stopped laughing. Her eyes narrowed to slits. She felt all the kids turn from Christopher to her, waiting for a response. Jenny Hertzog stared through Christopher, her eyes burning with hatred.

"Fuck you," she said.

Brady started to walk toward him, pinning him against a locker. The itch came back, pushing words into Christopher's mind.

Brady Collins is afraid . . .
Brady Collins is afraid . . . of the doghouse.

"What's in the doghouse, Brady?" he asked.

Brady Collins stopped. All of the kids looked at him as his face went flush with embarrassment. Christopher looked at them. He saw they were scared. And somehow, he couldn't get mad at them. Somehow, he knew that they were more afraid than he was.

Brady Collins did not speak. He just glared at Christopher with murderous eyes.

"It's okay, Brady. It'll be okay," Christopher said.

Brady Collins hit Christopher in the mouth. It wasn't a soft hit. It wasn't a warning. It was real. But the strangest thing was . . . when Brady hit him, it didn't really hurt. It felt like a tickle. But Brady wouldn't stop. He was so angry, he wanted to kill Christopher. Brady rushed at him, both fists out, ready to do real damage. Christopher did not lift his arms. He merely stood there, waiting to receive the blows.

A statue waiting for the impact of a feather.

Brady wound up and was about to hit Christopher again as hard as he could when a fist came out of nowhere and punched him in the jaw. Brady turned around and saw Special Ed.

"Get away from him!" Special Ed said.

Brady's eyes turned to rage. Mike stepped out from behind the crowd with his little brother Matt, backing up Special Ed.

"Back off, Collins!" Mike said.

And within seconds, a brawl started.

Brady and Jenny's gang had Christopher's friends beat three to one, but it didn't matter. Special Ed and the M&M's stood back-to-back just like the

Avengers. Brady ran at Special Ed first, fists flying. Mike took his book bag and swung it, hitting Brady in the gut. Brady fell to the ground in front of Jenny Hertzog. Jenny jumped on Mike and bit his hand. Matt grabbed a handful of her hair and yanked her down on the ground. Everyone was biting and kicking and screaming.

Just like a war.

Christopher watched all of this in silence, his head throbbing with a fever that felt like their rage. After a moment, he forced himself to his feet. Then, he calmly approached the fighting. He reached out and grabbed Brady's arm in his feverish hand.

"It's going to be okay," he said softly.

The heat shot through Christopher's arm. It tickled like little needles reaching through his fingertips to Brady's funny bone.

Until they turned to heat.

"Stop! It hurts!" Brady said.

Christopher looked Brady in the eye. The boy was terrified. Christopher let go and Brady saw little blisters form on his arm. Christopher moved to Jenny Hertzog, who was scratching Matt's face. She got her fingers under his lazy-eye patch when Christopher grabbed her arm.

"It's all going to get better, Jenny. You'll see," he assured her.

The heat shot its way through his fingertips and burrowed under her long-sleeved shirt. She grabbed her arm in pain. She rubbed the small blisters on her right arm, screaming.

Christopher reached down and helped his friends back to their feet.

"Come on, guys," he said.

The heat from his hands moved down their arms, but it did not blister. It was soothing, like Vicks VapoRub on a sick chest. The warmth spread to their faces, making their cheeks rosy. Special Ed's brain started to feel light and fizzy as soda pop. Mike's arm suddenly felt stronger. Matt's lazy eye began to tingle. Christopher's forehead began to cook. The pain was blinding.

"What is going on?!" a voice yelled from the door.

Christopher looked up and saw Mrs. Henderson, the librarian, rushing down the hallway. The itch pushed the flash cards through Christopher's throbbing forehead at a dizzying speed.

Mrs. Henderson is . . . sad.

Mr. Henderson . . . doesn't love her anymore.

Mr. Henderson . . . always goes out at night.

Mr. Henderson . . . doesn't come back until breakfast.

Christopher turned to Mrs. Henderson and smiled.

"It'll be okay, Mrs. Henderson. I promise," he said.

The last thing he remembered was grabbing her arm with one hand. He tried his best to hold the heat in, but it escaped like a water balloon full of pinholes. Within seconds, he felt the wet liquid kissing his fingertips. He took his fingers back in plain sight and saw it.

His nose was gushing blood.

CHAPTER 41

When Christopher's mother arrived at the school, Special Ed's mother Betty was standing outside, hoovering a last-minute cigarette to endure the unscheduled parent-teacher conference. Mrs. Henderson stood impatiently next to her.

"The other parents are already in the principal's office," she said.

The not-so-subtle hint was completely lost on Betty, who took in one last massive puff, and then crushed the Capri out with the heel of her Ugg boot.

"Can you believe this shit?" she said to Christopher's mother, her breath still sweet from her lunchtime Chardonnay. "I was in the middle of a massage."

"Where's my son?" Christopher's mother asked Mrs. Henderson.

"He's in the nurse's office with the other children, Mrs. Reese. You can see him shortly," Mrs. Henderson said, sounding grateful to have someone who could wrangle Betty.

The two women followed Mrs. Henderson to the principal's office and took their seats next to the other parents. Mike and Matt's two mothers looked weary, as if Mrs. Collins had been yelling at them for the last fifteen minutes. They looked up and smiled when their reinforcements arrived.

"... then how do you explain the burn on his God damn arm?!" Mrs. Collins said.

"Mrs. Collins, I understand you're upset," Principal Small said.

"You don't understand a God damn thing," Mrs. Collins said. "When my husband's lawyers get done with this school, you'll understand how upset I am."

"You're going to sue the school because your son started a fight?" Betty groaned.

"My son didn't start anything. It was <u>her</u> son," she said, pointing at Christopher's mother.

"Mrs. Collins," the principal said firmly, "I already explained to you. Christopher had wet his pants, and Brady was teasing him, playing keep-away."

"And that gives her kid the right to burn my son's arm?" Mrs. Collins hissed.

"I was there, Mrs. Collins," Mrs. Henderson said gently. "When Christopher held their arms, he was trying to make everyone stop fighting."

"My son doesn't fight, Mrs. Collins," Christopher's mother finally said.

The room fell silent. They could see Mrs. Collins spinning through all the options in her mind. Finally, one voice cut through the tension.

"Let me translate this for you, Mrs. Collins," Betty said. "Your son is a little sociopath who started a fight and ruined my deep tissue massage."

Thank God Christopher's mother was able to stifle her laugh, or she would have been out of a job instantly. But the M&M's mothers had no such trouble. Both let out a laugh so loud that it doubled back to Special Ed's mom, and soon, the three women filled the office with their cackles. Mrs. Collins' face became flush, but her eyes told the real story. The Collins family was used to getting its way. There was not a problem they couldn't get rid of with a stack of money or the right friend. But having a "problem child" was another matter entirely. And the silence that followed their laughter was deafening.

"Then I owe Mrs. Reese an apology," Mrs. Collins said. "We'll talk more about it tonight at work."

"That's very kind of you, Mrs. Collins, but it's not necessary."

"No, it is. We'll talk after your shift is over," Mrs. Collins said pleasantly.

"I'll get my shift covered. I want to stay home with my son tonight."

"I'm afraid my mother has been having a difficult time. She really needs the best attendant on the floor tonight. And you are the best."

"But my son has a fever."

"And my mother has Alzheimer's."

The silence returned to the room as the others realized that they had laughed Christopher's mother right into the worst holiday-season detail at Shady Pines.

"Come on, Kathleen. Don't be a bitch. I made the joke. Punish me," Betty said.

"This isn't a punishment. We just can't all have time off when our children get the sniffles," she said.

Mrs. Collins waited to see if Kate Reese would say something and give her grounds to fire her. But Christopher's mother said nothing. Because the lottery paid off the past, not the future. She still had a mortgage. She still needed the job. She still had to provide for her son.

"Kathleen," Betty said. "How the hell do you sit in the front row of church and not hear a God damn thing?"

"I hear more than you think," Mrs. Collins said.

After another tense minute of "she said, she said," all the mothers were led to the nurse's office to collect their young and take them home. When Kate saw Mrs. Collins drag her son Brady out to the parking lot, her insides tightened. She was used to hating little snot-nose kids who picked on Christopher, but this was a different feeling. What she saw was a violent, angry kid being shoved into his mother's Mercedes by an exasperated, angry woman.

"You get in there, God dammit," Mrs. Collins said.

"Mom . . . they started it. I swear to God," Brady said.

And by God, if Kate didn't know better, she would have believed him. Of course, she knew that Brady was too small and Sunday-school charming to do any real damage now. But God help the deli line of cute girls who would climb into the backseat of Brady Collins' car in high school. Girls like Jenny Hertzog in her stepbrother's pickup truck. Girls who see something worth saving and never stop to notice that the boy doesn't want to be saved. Girls who never admit that some boys are perfectly happy treating them like shit because they seem to be perfectly happy taking it. She once saw Jerry's picture when he was little. Jerry had a cute innocent-boy look. And that cute little boy grew up and just had this thing for punching things that were smaller than him. Kate Reese shivered when she realized the sad truth: Even monsters are adorable when they're little.

Kate turned back to Christopher, who covered his corduroy pants with her jacket and his bandaged neck with his turtleneck like he did when he was little and afraid of vampires. They told her he had fallen asleep after the state exam and had such a terrible nightmare, he had wet his pants and tore up his own neck with his fingernails.

Just like he did after his father died.

Back then, it wasn't just his neck. It was a bruise on the arm. Or sleepwalking into a wall and sending himself to the ER. Kate managed to scrape together enough money to take him to a few different psychologists. The doctors had different approaches, but the bottom line was that Christopher needed time to work through the trauma of his father's death.

After all, Christopher found the body.

It took a while, but eventually, the nightmares had stopped. And with them, the self-harm. She had no idea why it was all coming back now. And every attempt she made to get a straight answer from him was met by a monosyllabic answer. Occasionally, she would get three syllables:

"I don't know."

Kate Reese had a million questions, but she had to work. And her son didn't look like he could handle the third degree right now. So, she made the strategic decision to give him space and ask him the only question she knew he wanted to answer.

"Hey . . . before I go back to work . . . you want to get some ice cream?"

His smile almost broke her heart.

Christopher didn't know it, but his mother had already done many things to try to figure out what was happening to him. Including some things she'd promised herself she would never do. She'd snooped around his room for clues. A drawing. A letter. A diary. Anything. But all she found was the picture of his father on the bookshelf with duck wallpaper and the books that looked like her son had already read several times over.

When everything in his room proved fruitless, Kate Reese threw on a jacket and went outside. She walked through the backyard and stood on the edge of the Mission Street Woods. She stared at the trees. Watching the breeze kiss the branches.

Kate Reese walked into the woods. She did not stumble. She knew exactly where she was going. She wasn't sure why it had taken her this long to do it. Maybe fear. Maybe focus. After all, the sheriff assured her the woods were safe. He said what happened to Ambrose's brother was an unspeakable tragedy, but it happened a long time ago.

But that didn't mean it couldn't happen again.

It didn't take long for her feet to find the path. She passed the billy goat bridge and the hollow log until she found herself in the heart of the woods.

The clearing.

The tree.

The tree house.

She was astonished. When her son had told her that he built a tree house, she pictured a ramshackle hut with more gaps in it than her great-uncle's teeth. But this thing was extraordinary. Every detail perfect. The paint. The craftsmanship. This was the work of an obsessive mind.

Just like her husband's.

Everything had to be right, or he would be very wrong. She was grateful that her husband was innately kind because his manic energy never turned on her.

But it had turned.

Kate stared at the tree house. The tree. The clearing.

"Is there someone there?" she said out loud.

There was silence. Still and breathing. She waited to see if something would blink.

"I don't know if you're there or not," she said. "But if you are, leave him the fuck alone."

She stood her ground for a moment more to let whatever might be on the other side of the wind know that her rage was far bigger than her fear. Then, she walked home, never once looking back over her shoulder.

When she got home, she went immediately to the internet. Two months ago, she might have dismissed it as a ridiculous phrase to search, but after putting Christopher's tree house together with his sudden math and reading talent, she found herself typing in the letters anyway.

Spontaneous genius.

Whatever hesitation she felt evaporated quickly when she saw the results.

The search warranted almost a million hits. She studied some cases, and she almost WebMD'd herself into madness when she found a few potential reasons for this "miracle." Tumors. Cysts. Or the one that sent her into a two-hour anxiety attack . . .

Psychosis.

She had already called every pediatrician in town after she went online, but they were booked. It was flu season, they all said. So, she would have to wait a couple of weeks. But as she watched her son devour his vanilla cone at 31 Flavors, she was back on that phone, demanding an earlier time. She was put on hold, and her mother's intuition screamed in her ear.

Help him, Kate. He's in trouble.

As she listened to the horrible Muzak version of Blue Moon, she remembered something her husband told her right after he came out of one of his worst spells.

What are the two types of people who can see things that aren't there, Kate?

And his quiet whisper of a punch line.

Visionaries and psychopaths.

CHAPTER 42

W hen the call came in that afternoon, Mary Katherine was sitting in her bedroom, dreading her life. Christmas break was right around the corner, and she was woefully behind on her Notre Dame application essay. Not only that, but she had the late shift at the old folks home. She had already volunteered long enough to get her certificate for college. But she felt guilty that she was only volunteering for her college application, and if that was true, it wasn't real charity work. And if it wasn't, then God would punish her by making her not get into Notre Dame like her father and mother and grandfather and grandmother and so on and so forth did. So, she was determined to keep volunteering to help the old people to prove that she wasn't just volunteering to get into college so that God would help her get into college. It was a perfectly reasonable plan, but there was only one problem.

She really hated the old people.

"Don't get me wrong," she whispered to Jesus in prayer. "There are some nice ones. Mr. Olson is sweet and funny. And Mrs. Epstein taught me how to bake snickerdoodles and make something called matzah balls. But it's hard to focus on them when Mrs. Collins' mother screams 'We're all going to die' at the top of her lungs for four hours straight. I could manage when Doug was there, but then he quit volunteering. He's already finished his applications to MIT and Cornell. I asked if he would ever go to Notre Dame with me, and he said he would apply to it as a 'safety school.' I could have killed him. I know it's wrong to ask You for this, but I just have to get into Notre Dame. Am I going to get into Notre Dame?"

She waited, but no sign came. Just the wind blowing through the trees outside her bedroom window. Mary Katherine thought more about her night shift at the old folks home. Her stomach churned with the guilt that she really didn't want to go. They were just so old. And they smelled. And the demented ones frightened her. Sometimes, she would stop and look at the hall and think . . . "Jesus loves every one of these people. Every single soul."

"How do You love everyone, Jesus?" she asked. "Give me a sign."

When her cell phone rang, she let out a little scream.

"Hello?" she said, half expecting Jesus to be on the other end of the phone (hopefully with good news).

"Mary Katherine," Mrs. Reese said. "Is there any chance you are available to babysit Christopher tonight?"

Mary Katherine weighed her options. Take care of nice Mrs. Reese's son or listen to Mrs. Collins' mother scream about how the "witch lady" is going to kill us all on Christmas Day.

"I'm sorry, Mrs. Reese, but I'm signed up to volunteer at Shady Pines," Mary Katherine said sadly.

"I can cover your shift. I need someone to come to my house right away. Please. You'd be a lifesaver."

"Then, of course! I'd love to babysit your son!" Mary Katherine beamed.

She wrote down the address and hung up. She knew that Jesus would notice that she chose the old folks home first. The fact that Mrs. Reese needed her to watch her son was outside of her control. And Mrs. Reese knew what the old folks home needed more than she did. So, this was a win win. Mary Katherine was respecting her elders by babysitting instead of volunteering. And she would have hours of babysitting time to work on her Notre Dame application.

She took all this as a very good sign.

As she drove over to Mrs. Reese's house, she quickly scanned the side of the road for deer. She felt like she had made a good decision to babysit. After all, Christopher was the missing little boy that she had saved, and Father Tom said that in some cultures, once you save a life, you are responsible for it. But still, she couldn't be too careful.

"Jesus, if I made a mistake, make me hit a deer."

When no deer came, Mary Katherine turned on the radio to enjoy the rest of the drive. She was planning on listening to Christian rock, but Doug had left the dial on 102.5 WDVE. The station was playing a song by The Doors that she was uncomfortable admitting she liked as much as she did.

This is the end, my only friend, the end
Of our elaborate plans, the end

She arrived at the house before the song ended without seeing a single deer.

"He has a fever," Mrs. Reese explained. "So, he's not allowed out of bed. Understood?"

"Don't worry, Mrs. Reese. I took first-aid courses at youth group, and I'm a trained lifeguard. He won't leave the bed."

"But Mom, it's still daylight," Christopher pleaded. "Can't I go outside?"

With a cold "No" and a warm "I love you," Christopher's mother kissed her son and left his bedroom. Mary Katherine followed her down to the garage. Mrs. Reese went through her checklist of emergency contact numbers and instructions and rules.

"I just gave him some Tylenol. You can give him some Advil in two hours with his dinner. Hopefully, he'll fall asleep, but if he doesn't, his bedtime is eight thirty. Don't let him work you a minute past nine," she said.

"Don't worry, Mrs. Reese. I'm tough on bedtimes. I won't let you down."

After Christopher's mother drove away, Mary Katherine went back inside the warm house. She walked through the kitchen and living room, trying to figure out the best place to work on her Notre Dame application. Once she settled on the kitchen table, she put down her books and went to the refrigerator.

As she grabbed the carton of milk, she thought about her Notre Dame essay. They wanted her to write about a hero, but she couldn't figure out which one. Her mom and dad were too obvious. Political ones were too risky. It would be great to write about Jesus, but since Notre Dame was a Catholic school, she was worried that too many kids would pick Him. But if she didn't pick Jesus, then who would she pick? Pope Francis? John Paul II?

The Virgin Mary.

The thought came to her from out of nowhere. Jesus' mother. Of course. What an inspired choice. That would be perfect!

She finished pouring the milk and closed the carton. She looked at the picture of the missing girl, Emily Bertovich. Poor thing. She wondered if Emily Bertovich would ever be found. Would she ever apply to college? Who were Emily Bertovich's babysitters?

That thought chilled her blood.

Mary Katherine stopped and looked around the house. Suddenly something felt wrong. It was too quiet. Too warm. Like something was in the house. The cuckoo clock clicked away the seconds on its march to 4:00 p.m. Tick tick tick.

"Hello?" she said. "Who's there?"

Mary Katherine waited for a response. None came. She looked back at the carton of milk. The picture of Emily Bertovich stared back at her. Smiling with those missing front teeth. Mary Katherine's heart began to pound. She didn't know what was wrong, but she could sense something. Like her father's knee that knew there would be a storm an hour before the weatherman did.

"Christopher? If that's you, you better go back to bed," she said.

The silence was deafening. Mary Katherine quickly returned Emily Bertovich to the cold refrigerator. Then, she hurriedly walked through the kitchen, the dining room, the living room. But there was nothing there. Just that feeling. She was about to go upstairs to check the bedrooms when she looked through the sliding glass doors to the backyard. And there it was, standing in the snow, staring at her.

A deer.

The clock struck 4:00 p.m. Cuckoo. Cuckoo. Cuckoo. Cuckoo. Mary Katherine knew something was terribly wrong. She raced upstairs to Christopher's room.

"Christopher!" she said. "Christopher! Answer me!"

She opened his bedroom door and saw that Christopher was not in the bed. His window was open, the curtain fluttering in the breeze. Mary Katherine rushed to the window and stuck her head out.

"Christopher! Where are you?!" she screamed.

She looked down and saw the trail of his little footprints through the snow.

Right past the deer.

And into the Mission Street Woods.

CHAPTER 43

Something was watching.

The moment Christopher closed the door to the tree house, he felt it. A big eye. Smothering like a blanket. Just watching and drifting. Looking for something.

Hunting.

Christopher knew it was a terrible risk coming into the imaginary world alone. He'd promised the nice man he would never do this, but he had no choice. The nice man was imprisoned somewhere. Or he was already dead. Christopher had to find some information. Proof. A clue. Anything. But he had no idea what was waiting for him on the other side of that door.

Never come in here without me. Never be in here at night.

Christopher turned to the window and saw the sun low in the sky. He didn't have much time before night fell. It was now or never. He put his ear up against the door. At first, everything seemed all right. Then, he heard a faint noise.

sCratch. sCratch. sCratch.

Something was under the tree.

sCratch. sCratch. sCratch.

Christopher turned back to the window. He saw deer crawling through the clearing, leaving trails in the winter snow. The deer walked up to the tree and scratched with their hooves.

sCratch. sCratch. sCratch.

"Remember, Christopher," the nice man had told him. "The deer work for her."

The deer sniffed around the base of the tree for something. Maybe food. Maybe him. Christopher only had an hour of daylight. He needed to find a way around them. He saw a six-point buck chew a small leaf off the low-hanging branch. Right next to something that caught Christopher's eye.

The white plastic bag.

Christopher was so used to seeing the bag on the real side that he didn't pay it any attention. But something about it looked different on the imaginary side. The bag was hanging lower on the branch than usual. Like a fish bending a pole. The bag must be weighed down. Because . . . because . . .

Something is inside it.

Christopher's heart skipped. The nice man must have left him something. He was sure of it. What was it? A map? A clue? He had to know. Christopher waited until the deer had satisfied their hunger (or curiosity) and moved away from the clearing.

Then, he slowly opened the door.

Christopher quickly walked down the 2x4 ladder. Little baby teeth nailed into the tree. His boots landed on the crunchy ground, and he tiptoed over to the white plastic bag. He reached inside and pulled out what the nice man had left behind.

A Christmas card.

On the front was a picture of Santa Claus yelling at Rudolph the Red-Nosed Reindeer as he pulled his sleigh through the snow.

WHAT DO YOU MEAN YOU FORGOT YOUR GLASSES?!

Snap.

Christopher turned around. The deer were back. The six-point buck stared right at him, but its ears perked up as if listening for a predator. The wind whipped through Christopher's hair, then died like a bird in flight. Christopher held his breath, waiting for the deer to react. But they never did.

Because they can't see me.

Christopher looked back at the Christmas card. Santa screaming at Rudolph.

WHAT DO YOU MEAN YOU FORGOT YOUR GLASSES?!

This was the clue. Christopher looked back up to the tree house and saw that his body was still there. To the deer, it looked like he was still in the tree house on the real side. Just a little boy playing alone.

But in here, he was invisible.

"The more time you spend in the imaginary world, the more powerful you will become," the nice man had told him. "But the power will come at a price."

Christopher waited for the deer to move on, then he quietly opened the card. He hoped to find a note from the nice man, but all he saw was the caption that came with the card...

WHEN YOU CAN'T SEE THE LIGHT...
JUST FOLLOW YOUR NOSE!

Christopher began to walk.

He moved out of the clearing and into the woods. He found the footpath, clean and smooth. He followed it until he reached the hollow log near the billy goat bridge. There, he saw the man wrapped inside like a pig in a blanket. The man was asleep. His eyes twitching. Whimpering like a child:

"Please make it stop. I'm not helping him."

Christopher looked around to see if the hissing lady was near. But he couldn't see anyone. So, he quietly backed away from the man in the hollow log and took off running. He rushed out of the Mission Street Woods, his boots slapping the muddy trail, until he reached the cul-de-sac in front of his house.

Christopher scanned his street, looking for a clue. In the fading daylight, his street looked like the old negatives from the picture of his dad. It was his neighborhood. But the left was right. And the right was left. And the sun was a lightbulb after a long stare, leaving traces of itself behind.

He was looking at the world from the other side of a one-way mirror.

He saw Mary Katherine running through his backyard. She was panicked.

"CHRISTOPHER!" she screamed. "WHERE ARE YOU?!"

Mary Katherine is...watching the deer.
Mary Katherine doesn't know...the deer are watching her.

Mary Katherine raced into the Mission Street Woods past the deer. Christopher turned back to the street and saw the man in the Girl Scout uniform. The man was sleepwalking, turning around and around like water leaving a drain. His body twitching, whimpering:

"Please make it stop. I'm not helping him."

Christopher didn't know where to go or what to do. The daylight was fading.

Mary Katherine would find him. He was running out of time. He opened the Christmas card again.

WHEN YOU CAN'T SEE THE LIGHT...
JUST FOLLOW YOUR NOSE!

He looked up and saw the clouds drifting. For a moment, he remembered a handsome pretty face made of clouds. Christopher felt the wind in his hair. And under the wind, barely detectable, was the smell of grilled cheese sandwiches.

WHEN YOU CAN'T SEE THE LIGHT...
JUST FOLLOW YOUR NOSE!

It was coming from the log cabin across the street.

Christopher turned to the cabin and saw the old lady in the attic. He walked up the driveway. Cautious as a mouse. He didn't know if he would find a clue or a trap or the hissing lady, but an instinct kept his feet moving. He opened the front door. The family was having an early dinner on the real side. He could smell tomato soup and grilled cheese sandwiches browning in the pan.

"Do you think Mom wants some?" the wife asked.

The words flooded into Christopher's mind. He staggered. The itch was far more powerful on the imaginary side. Like a dentist's drill wrapped in sandpaper.

He instantly understood that the husband hated his wife's mother. The man wanted her to die just so they could have a life again. He was not a bad man. But he wondered what would happen if he only pretended to feed "the thing in the attic." He would never do it, of course. But sometimes while he watched a Steelers game, he wondered how long it would take his mother-in-law to starve and give them some peace.

"Do you think Mom wants some?" the wife repeated, frustrated.

"I'm sure she's hungry," the husband said. "You want me to take her up a plate?"

"No. I'll do it, just like I do everything else around here," the wife huffed.

I offered. What the fuck do you want from me? the husband thought in silence.

God, why doesn't he just ask me to do it with him? the wife thought in silence.

The wife went to the kitchen. Christopher quietly moved upstairs to the attic. The old lady was turned to the window in a wicker chair. Rocking back and forth and back and forth. Like a metronome on a piano. She looked out the window at the clouds. Grunting in frustration as she struggled with a stack of papers in her hands.

They were Christmas cards.

Christopher was startled, but he did not back away. It was another message from the nice man. He was sure of it. He moved to the old woman. The Christmas card on the top of the stack was old and yellow. The dyes and ink faded.

TOO OFTEN WE UNDERESTIMATE THE POWER OF A TOUCH...

Christopher touched the woman's shoulder. In an instant he closed his eyes and felt the stroke that took half of her mind and most of her speech. He saw that the old woman was young once. She was beautiful. Christopher looked down at her hands and saw that the old woman's fingers were now crippled with arthritis. Jagged like the branches of the tree in the clearing. He took her hands into his and held them. The warmth from his body seemed to move through him to her.

Christopher let go. The old woman moved her fingers like butterfly wings waking up from a cocoon. She suddenly remembered when she could play the piano and how the beautiful boy in her mother's parlor complimented her song choice. Blue Moon. Later, on their honeymoon, they found a piano in that big hotel in Niagara Falls, and she played him the same song. The old woman smiled. Her fingers were now relaxed enough to turn the page of the Christmas card.

A HUG, A SMILE, A KIND WORD, ALL WITH THE POTENTIAL TO TURN A LIFE AROUND COMPLETELY.

Christopher saw a personal message written in black ink right underneath it.

*So, go see your mother right now.
She needs you.*

Suddenly the old woman's daughter walked into the attic with grilled cheese and soup on a TV tray.

"Remember when your father gave you this card?" the old woman said and smiled.

"Yes, Mom. We talked all about it yesterday. Don't you remember?" the daughter said.

"I played the piano for him. Your father was such a beautiful boy. We swam in the Ohio River together," the old woman said.

The wife gently took the Christmas card out of her mother's hands.

"Hey, Mom," the wife said, pleasantly surprised. "Your hands seem a lot better. And your words are much clearer. How are you feeling?"

"There's someone in the room right now," the old woman said.

"Okay, Mom. Let's not get upset."

"Go see your mother right now! She needs you!" the old woman yelled.

"Mom, please calm down," the wife begged.

"See your mother! She needs you! Right now! Right now!" the old woman screamed.

"Gary! Help!" the wife yelled downstairs.

If the first card told Christopher to follow his nose, the second was unmistakable. He had to see his mother at Shady Pines. As the husband ran into the attic, Christopher backed out of the room and quickly exited the house.

He looked back across his neighborhood and almost screamed when he saw them. The streets were suddenly lined with people. They all stood still as mailboxes. Lining the yards. A woman in a blue dress. A man in a yellow hat. A wrong yellow. A sick yellow.

Their eyes were sewn shut.

Some with zippers.

Others with thread.

Just like the kids in his nightmare.

The mailbox people were all holding a string. Each one. A string leading to the next person and the next. All the way. Down the street. For as far as Christopher could see. Where did they all come from? Where were they all going?

Never come in here without me. Never be in here at night.

Christopher looked up at the sky. The sun had moved down the horizon. Hanging low like the white plastic bag on the branch. He had maybe forty-five minutes until the sun set. He had to get to his mother, but he couldn't possibly run to Shady Pines fast enough. He didn't know how to drive a car. He needed some kind of transportation. He scanned the neighborhood, and his eyes finally landed on...

A bicycle.

It was a three-speed. The kind that used to come with a basket on the front. But this bike was older. Rusted. Sitting alone on a kickstand in the middle of a driveway.

At the house on the corner.

Christopher ran down the street toward the bike. He passed a couple standing in the middle of the road. They were asleep like two mannequins, kissing one another, blood running from their mouths. Whispering:

"Please make it stop. We're not helping him."

Christopher grabbed the bike and stopped when he saw the little nameplate on the handlebars.

D. OLSON

The house on the corner is...
The house on the corner is...
David Olson's house.

Christopher swallowed hard. He knew it could be a trap. It could be a message. The hissing lady could be waiting to ambush him. But the instinct screamed for him to get to his mother at Shady Pines before the sun set.

He began to pedal. He moved up the road quickly, locking into first gear. Once he started pedaling downhill, he snapped the bike into second, then third. He moved faster. Gaining speed. Heading toward the highway. His legs growing stronger and stronger with each rotation as he saw more and more mailbox people lining the street. Twin little girls, an older Asian man, and a Middle Eastern woman who looked skinny from hunger.

Their eyes and mouths were sewn shut.

They were sleepwalking.

For now.

At night, the imaginary world wakes up. And then it gets really scary.

Christopher moved the bike. Faster and faster. At first, he didn't notice his speed. All he thought about was the fading daylight and his mother at Shady Pines who needed him. But once he looked at the road moving past him in a blur, he couldn't understand it. The hill wasn't that steep. The bike wasn't that light. But he had never gone so fast in his life. He turned onto Route 19. The cars whizzed down the highway on the real side.

And he was riding right next to them.

The pavement whipped by at blinding speed. The freezing air climbed into his eyes, making them water. The power coursed through his legs. Christopher saw an old Mustang up ahead filled with teenagers. He pumped his bike right behind it. Then he pedaled alongside it. Then, he passed the teenagers, pumping his legs as if all their blood were in his veins. Christopher moved the bike off the highway and down the road to Shady Pines. He saw the sun chase the horizon and more mailbox people lining the street.

Like a guardrail.

I don't have much time.

Christopher hid the bike down the road, then ran the rest of the way to Shady Pines. He looked through the window to make sure he wasn't walking into a trap. Then, he crept into the old folks home, opening the door with a . . .

Crrrreak.

He tiptoed down the long hallway. Into the parlor. A nurse played the piano in the corner. The song was Blue Moon. Several of the older people played chess and checkers.

"I found them, Mr. Olson," a woman's voice said.

Christopher knew that voice. It was his mother. Christopher turned around. He saw his mother walking up from the basement with a small box.

"They were in storage right where you said they'd be," his mother said.

Christopher watched his mother walk to Ambrose Olson, sitting in a rocking chair in the parlor. She handed a shoe box to him. The old man took off the lid and pulled up a stack of something wrapped in old white string.

Christmas cards.

A cold breeze moved through the old folks home. Christopher heard some of the older ladies complain to the nurses about the temperature and wrap themselves in their shawls. Christopher saw Ambrose Olson take the first Christmas card out of its envelope. The front of the card was a picture of Santa yelling at Rudolph the Red-Nosed Reindeer:

WHAT DO YOU MEAN YOU FORGOT YOUR GLASSES?!

The room stopped. Christopher watched Ambrose crack open the faded, yellow card. The same card that was left in the white plastic bag.

WHEN YOU CAN'T SEE THE LIGHT...
JUST FOLLOW YOUR NOSE!

And a personal note written in a scrawl...

I'm sorry if I scare you sometimes.
I never mean to.
Merry Christmas
Love, David
P.S. Thank you for the baseball glove. But especially
the books.

The nice man wasn't the one giving him clues.

WHEN YOU CAN'T SEE THE LIGHT...
JUST FOLLOW YOUR NOSE!

David Olson was.

"What is that?" a voice asked. "Did you hear something?"

Christopher looked down the hallway as the hissing lady entered the parlor. David Olson was wrapped around her shoulders like a mink stole. He was her pet. A little demon with two missing front teeth. He was terrifying.

I'm sorry if I scare you sometimes.
I never mean to.

"What lovely handwriting," Christopher's mother said.

Merry Christmas
Love, David
P.S. Thank you for the baseball glove. But especially
the books.

"Thank you," Ambrose said, closing the card. "David loved to read."

Christopher's heart pounded. He shifted his weight. The floor creaked just a little. The hissing lady turned.

"What is that? Who's there?" the hissing lady whispered.

She looked right at Christopher, who froze like a deer in headlights.

WHAT DO YOU MEAN YOU FORGOT YOUR GLASSES?!

But she could not see him.

The hissing lady looked around the room. Sniffing the air. Sensing something.

"Are you in here?" the hissing lady whispered. "Are you in here, Christopher?"

Christopher started to inch back out of the parlor. Little steps. *Don't breathe. Don't let her hear me.*

"Just say something. I won't hurt you," she whispered.

Christopher looked outside. The sun was setting. He was running out of daylight. The mailbox people lined both sides of the road now. The hissing lady moved to Christopher's mother.

"Are you watching, Christopher?" she asked calmly.

The blood pounded his temples. He knew it was a trap. His mother was the bait. He stood in the hallway, crouched down. Ready to rush at her if she did anything to his mother. The hissing lady whispered in Christopher's mother's ear. Christopher saw his mother scratch her ear absentmindedly.

"If you don't come out, your mother is going to die," she hissed.

The hissing lady pursed her lips and blew on his mother's neck. She instantly shivered and found herself reaching for the thermostat. Christopher's heart pounded.

"Ready? Now, watch this, Christopher," the hissing lady said.

Mrs. Collins burst into the room, angry as a snake.

"Your son burns my son's arm, but that's not good enough for you," Mrs. Collins barked at Christopher's mother.

"I'm sorry, Mrs. Collins. I don't know what you're talking about."

"You left my mother alone in her room. She wandered off again!"

"I'm sorry, Mrs. Collins. I had to help Mr. Olson. The volunteers are gone. We're understaffed tonight," she replied wearily.

"If you had a dollar for every one of your excuses, I'd be working for you!"

"Why weren't <u>you</u> watching her, Mrs. Collins?" Ambrose barked. "She's <u>your</u> God damn mother."

Christopher could feel the anger in the room rising higher and higher.

"This is just the beginning, Christopher . . ." The hissing lady smiled. "It will keep going . . . and going . . . and going . . . Now, watch this!"

Suddenly Mrs. Collins' mother came into the room in her wheelchair.

"Mom, thank God," Mrs. Collins said.

The old woman stood up on her crooked legs. She looked right at Christopher.

"Oh, hi. You're here. You can see me," the old woman shouted.

"Who can see you?!" the hissing lady asked.

"The little boy. He's standing right there." She pointed. "They all think I'm talking nonsense. But he knows. He knows."

The hissing lady leaned and whispered into the old woman's ear.

"You're all going to die."

"We're all going to die," the old woman repeated.

"It's okay, ma'am," Christopher's mother said. "Calm down."

"Death is coming. Death is here. We'll die on Christmas Day!" the hissing lady whispered.

"Death is coming. Death is here. We'll die on Christmas Day!" the old woman screamed.

"Mom, get back to your room!" Mrs. Collins barked. "Mrs. Reese, help me!"

But the old woman would not stop. She chanted over and over. Screaming at the top of her lungs.

"Death is coming. Death is here. We'll die on Christmas Day!"

The hissing lady left her and turned in Christopher's direction. She smiled.

"I'm surprised you haven't made a sound," she said. "But that's not why I showed you all this. I just had to keep you entertained until nightfall."

The sun dipped below the horizon. David Olson uncurled from her neck.

Christopher could feel the room turning cold around him. The cotton candy smell turning to blood. He looked back at the hissing lady, who smiled.

"Because we can see you at night, buddy. There you are. What a handsome boy."

The hissing lady started running right at Christopher.

"You're off the streeeeeeeet!" she screamed.

Christopher ran to the front door. The hissing lady jumped at him just as Christopher opened the door, and his eyes were hit with the flashlight.

"CHRISTOPHER! THANK GOD!" Mary Katherine exclaimed as she opened the door to his tree house.

The flashlight from her cell phone blinded him. For a moment, Christopher didn't know where he was. He grabbed her arm, thinking she was the hissing lady. The heat from his fever shot from his forehead through his fingertips.

"Ow!" Mary Katherine screamed. "Stop it! You're burning me!"

Christopher looked around and realized that he wasn't in the old folks home anymore. He was back in his tree house. The hissing lady wasn't grabbing him. It was Mary Katherine. Christopher let go of her arm. She ripped off her jacket and rolled up her sweater. Her skin was red. Tiny blisters popped up over her arm.

"I'm sorry," Christopher said.

"Where the heck have you been?" Mary Katherine asked, angry and frightened, rubbing the burn.

"I couldn't sleep, so I thought I'd come out here and play," he said.

"Well, you could have gotten us both in a ton of trouble, you know that?"

"I'm sorry. Can you forgive me?"

"Only God can forgive you. But He would. So yes, I forgive you. Come on. Let's get you back home. We have to deal with your nose."

Christopher brought his hands up to wipe his nose, and he saw the blood, wet and red on his fingertips. His face flushed with fever. His joints ached. And the itch split into a blinding headache. He had never felt so sick in his life. Not even when he had the flu.

Christopher thought about the speed he had on the highway. The invisibility. The clarity of thought that came with the itch. If those powers led him to feeling this ill on the real side, he didn't think he could stand much more.

Before it killed him.

Mary Katherine kindly helped Christopher out of the tree house. His joints creaked with every step. Christopher looked up at the sky. There was no more daylight. He saw a star shooting across the sky. One more sun. One more soul.

When he reached the ground, he looked at the white plastic bag hanging on the branch next to the tree. He instinctively opened it, but there was nothing inside. No Christmas cards. No hidden messages. Just the itch. Christopher thought about the trail of bread crumbs that led him to Shady Pines and the last lines of David's card.

P.S. Thank you for the baseball glove.

Christopher remembered the times a baseball-glove smell had come to him. Sometimes he was in his room. Sometimes on the bus. The more he thought about it, the more he realized how present the smell had been. Baseball season was long over. He couldn't remember kids carrying their gloves. Just footballs—Nerf or plastic. But the baseball-glove smell was always around.

I'm sorry if I scare you sometimes.
I never mean to.

Christopher closed his eyes. He let the itch work its way through his mind. He saw the trail of bread crumbs laid out in front of him. He saw the space between the words. The thoughts playing hide-and-seek. Leading him down the trail. The first card telling him to FOLLOW YOUR NOSE to the lady in the attic whose card told him to *go see your mother right now. She needs you.* And the bicycle that was left in David Olson's driveway to give Christopher the time to get to his mother at the precise moment when she handed Ambrose David's Christmas card that ended **P.S. Thank you for the baseball glove** and the final clue of the puzzle . . .

But especially the books.

The itch stopped. Christopher opened his eyes. He could feel the blood running from his nose so deeply, he could taste it on his lips. But he didn't care. Because he finally caught the thought playing hide-and-seek. David was not a demon. He was a little boy passing notes. And there was one place in town where a kid could leave a note for another kid. Even if there were five decades between them. The one place where every kid in Mill Grove got their books.

Mrs. Henderson's library.

Mary Katherine turned the flashlight back to the trail. She saw a couple of deer frozen in the light.

"Oh, God. Jesus. I hate deer," Mary Katherine said, crossing herself. "Now, how do we get out of here?"

Christopher led Mary Katherine away from the clearing. Far away in the distance, he could hear bulldozers ripping up the trees. Mr. Collins had won his court battle. Construction had resumed. Just as Christopher thought it would.

It wouldn't be long before Mr. Collins ripped down most of the woods on his march to Christopher's tree house.

"But what does the tree house do exactly?" he had asked the nice man.

you built a portal to the imaginary world.

Christopher didn't know if the nice man was captured or being tortured.

He didn't know if the nice man was dead or alive.

All he knew was that as long as the nice man was missing, there was nobody to protect the world from the hissing lady.

Except him.

CHAPTER 44

Special Ed woke up. He scratched his arm and stared at the tree outside his bedroom window. The tree was covered in snow. The weight of the snow pulled the branches down, so that they all looked like a sick smile.

Sick smile, Eddie. That's what a frown is. It's just a smile that got sick.

His grandmother used to say that to him before she got all skinny and died. He didn't know why he was thinking of her now. It was like she was there in the room with him. She smelled like an old dress. And she was whispering.

Listen to Grandma.

Special Ed got out of bed.

His feet didn't feel the cold wooden floor. He went to the window. He opened it and looked at the wet snow gathered on the windowsill. He gathered it in his hand and made a snowball. Perfectly round. Perfectly smooth. Like the Earth. It didn't make his hands cold for some reason. It felt nice, actually. Like cotton candy from Kennywood put in the freezer.

Don't eat too much, Eddie. Your stomach will get sick. Listen to Grandma.

Special Ed closed the window. He hadn't felt how cold his face was getting in the frosty air. But now his cheeks were red, and he wanted a glass of water. Not bathroom water. Kitchen water. Special Ed walked down the hallway. He passed his father sleeping in the guest bedroom. The snowball was melting in his hand, dripping little water spots on the hardwood floor like a trail of bread crumbs. Special Ed passed his mother sleeping in the master bedroom.

"Why do you sleep in different beds?" he asked his mother once.

"Because your father snores, honey," she said, and he believed her.

Special Ed walked down the stairs. He went to the kitchen and poured himself a glass of kitchen water. He used his favorite glass. *Hulk...drink!* He drank it up in ten seconds. He still felt thirsty. He drank another. And another. He felt like he was getting a fever. But he didn't feel bad. He just felt hot. It was just so stuffy in this kitchen.

I can't breathe, Eddie. Go outside. Listen to Grandma.

Special Ed opened the sliding glass door.

He stood there, filling his lungs with cold Popsicle air. For a moment, it took away the stuffiness. And he didn't feel like his grandmother with the tubes in her nose making him promise never to smoke like her. He wondered if his grandmother had been buried alive and couldn't breathe in her coffin. Was she knocking on her coffin lid right now? He walked into the backyard and sat on the swing hanging from the old oak tree like a Christmas ornament. What did his grandmother call ornaments again? Something from an old song she liked.

Strange fruit, Eddie.

Special Ed just sat there, thinking about his grandmother as he packed the snowball tighter and tighter. He put the snowball at the bottom of the old oak tree. And he made another snowball. And another. And another. He thought he might need them to defend Christopher and the tree house. Because people take things that don't belong to them. Bad people like Brady Collins.

A man must protect his friends, Eddie. Listen to Grandma.

When Special Ed finished the last snowball, he looked down and realized he had made a little clearing around the old oak tree. The grass was green and crunchy with frost. And there was a little stack of snowballs like the cannonballs that he had seen on the field trip about the Revolutionary War.

Good guys win wars, Eddie.

He couldn't remember where he heard it, but he was pretty sure that the word "infantry" came from the word "infant." Just like how the word "kindergarten" came from the German word "kinder," meaning "child," and "garden." So, everyone in the infantry was just some mother's infant.

That made sense.

Special Ed went back inside. He closed the sliding glass door, locking the chill outside. He looked into the kitchen and saw the cupboard door was slightly open. Was it always like that? Or did someone just open it? Just a little? Like a coffin lid with an eye peeking out to look at the living. A dead person trying to remember what food tastes like because skeletons don't have tongues. He remembered when they had to take out his grandma's tongue from her being sick with cancer. His grandmother couldn't speak. So, she wrote things down on pieces of paper.

I miss the taste of Dutch apple pie, Eddie.

Eat some apple pie for me, Eddie. Listen to Grandma.

Special Ed went to the refrigerator. He cut a big slice of Dutch apple pie. He looked at the milk carton with the picture of that missing girl on it. Emily Bertovich. He closed the refrigerator and stared at his reading test stuck on the door with four magnets like Jesus on the cross. It was the first time his test was good enough to move from the junk drawer to the fridge. His first A. Special Ed smiled and closed the refrigerator door.

Before he went back upstairs to bed, Special Ed walked to his father's den. He opened the door and smelled the years of pipe tobacco and scotch ground into the walls. He went to his father's wood desk. The second drawer was locked, so he took off the top drawer and slid it out. Then, he reached in and pulled out a little leather case that smelled like a fresh baseball glove. He carefully laid the case on the desk and opened it. Then, he looked inside, and he smiled when he finally saw it.

The gun.

Special Ed picked it up. The .44 went heavy in his hand. Without a word, he opened it and saw that there was one bullet left in the chamber. Special Ed held the gun like his heroes in the movies. The moon reflected off its metal like a twinkle in the eye.

Take it upstairs, Eddie.

He walked upstairs and stood outside the master bedroom, watching his mother sleep. Then, he walked past his father sleeping in the guest bedroom. Special Ed noticed his father wasn't snoring at all. He didn't know why they had lied to him.

Special Ed went to his room. He looked at the old oak tree outside. The tree with the smile that got sick. Special Ed sat on his bed, eating his Dutch apple pie. When he was finished, he wiped the crumbs from his blanket to the floor. Then, he put the gun under his pillow and put his head down. He looked at the clock: 2:17 a.m. He closed his eyes and thought about the first Avengers movie. How all of the Avengers stood in a circle and won the war. Because they were the good guys. And good guys are the only ones who win wars.

The war is coming, Eddie. A man must protect his friends. Listen to Grandma.

CHAPTER 45

The clock read 2:17 a.m.

Brady Collins sat huddled up with his back against the cold wooden wall. Something was bothering him. Like the itch on his arm. He kept scratching at the blisters Christopher left behind, but nothing would get rid of that itch. He just kept scratching and thinking about the day. His mother picked him up from the principal's office and drove him home from school. She screamed at him about getting into a fight with new-money trash like Christopher and Special Ed. She screamed that he would never embarrass the family like that ever again. He was a Collins, God dammit. When they got home, she made him take off his coat and go into the doghouse in the backyard. It wasn't so bad in the summer, but this was winter. He begged her not to make him go into the doghouse, but she told him that when he wanted to behave like a human being, he could sleep like one. He had been in the doghouse ever since. All because of Christopher and Special Ed. Those two losers made his mother hate him again. And he couldn't have her hate him anymore. He couldn't sleep in the doghouse anymore. He had to do something to make her love him. Shivering, he took his arms out of his sleeves and tucked them into the middle of his shirt. The heat of his chest started to warm up his arms, but it couldn't get rid of that itch. He just kept scratching and scratching, and thinking and thinking. One thought. Over and over. That those two fucking kids would pay for making his mother hate him so much.

The clock read 2:17 a.m.

Jenny Hertzog woke up in her bed. She thought maybe someone was in her room. She could hear breathing. Or was it the wind? She thought that her stepbrother Scott had snuck in, but a quick scan of the room showed that she was alone. She looked at the bedroom door, waiting for him to walk through it. Scott had picked her up from school that day since his mom was at work. Jenny begged him not to tell her dad that she got in another fight. Her dad might not let her go to camp that summer if he did. And camp was the only thing that got her away from Scott. So, when he told her that she would have to dance for him, or else he would tell, she had no choice. He made her take off her clothes. She was naked except for the bandage covering the burn on her left arm. It was so itchy. She kept scratching it and scratching it, but it wouldn't stop. Like bugs on her skin. She got out of bed and walked to her door. She moved the chair from under the doorknob. Then, she walked down the stairs to the kitchen. She got a knife out of the drawer. She scratched the itch a little with it and walked past Scott's room. For a moment, she thought about plunging the knife into Scott's neck. That thought made the itching stop for a little while. She went back to her bedroom and put the knife under her pillow. In case Scott came into her room as he had the night before. He talked about her pajama bottoms being too short as he threw them in the corner. They were "floods, floods."

The clock read 2:17 a.m.

Matt sat up in bed and scratched his arm. He should have been happy about the news, but he wasn't. After school, he had gone to the eye doctor with his mothers. They were angry that he and Mike got in a fight, but when Mike explained that they were only protecting Christopher, their moms laid off a little bit. He went to see the eye doctor about his lazy eye, and the doctor told him the good news. It should have taken his eye patch until the summer to make his eye stop being so lazy, but somehow, it was already fixed. "It's a miracle," the doctor said. Matt should have done cartwheels knowing that Jenny Hertzog couldn't call him "Pirate Parrot" anymore. But something was wrong. Matt thought about Christopher grabbing his arm. How the heat soaked through his arm and tickled its way up to his eye. He would never tell the guys this out loud. They would think he was crazy. But as he scratched his arm, he couldn't help but think that Christopher fixed his eye somehow. This thought scared him. Because he knew that if anyone found out, then someone might try to kill Christopher. So, he promised himself that he would keep wearing the eye patch at school, so no one would suspect. He would listen to Jenny Hertzog call him "Pirate

Parrot" forever to keep his friend safe. He just had to keep Christopher alive. He felt like the whole world depended on it.

The clock read 2:17 a.m.

Mike sat in his bed. The itching was driving him crazy. He got up and went into the bathroom looking for that pink lotion his mothers used on him when he and Matt both had chicken pox. But he couldn't find any. All he saw were his one mother's vitamins. The ones that made her happy. He left the bathroom and went to the basement, where no one could hear him. He turned on the television and put on his favorite movie, The Avengers. Anything to take his mind off the itching. He was really enjoying the movie, and the itching almost went away, but then something happened. In the middle of the movie, Thor stopped and talked to Mike. They stayed up all night. Thor was so nice. Thor said Brady Collins was dangerous and that Jenny Hertzog was about to do something very scary. Thor told him to protect Special Ed and Matt. But especially Christopher. Because Mike was the strong one. And the war was coming. And the good guys had to win the war this time. Or the bad people would take over the world. Mike woke up on the couch. He didn't know if it had been a dream.

The clock read 2:17 a.m.

Ms. Lasko sat at the bar in Mt. Lebanon. The bar closed at 2:00 a.m., but Ms. Lasko knew the owner very well, and she begged him to let her stay. She just couldn't go home. She scratched her arm, and for a moment, she reminded herself of her own mother back when they lived in the city. Her mother would scratch herself all the time until she got her medicine. Ms. Lasko thought of it as "Mommy's itch medicine." Because the minute she put it into her arm, she stopped itching. She hadn't thought of that for years. Ms. Lasko looked at all the empty bottles and glasses in front of her. She counted seventeen, which would normally send her home in a taxi with a blackout. But all night, it didn't matter how much she drank. Bottle after bottle. Shot after shot. She could not get drunk. She just kept itching and itching. And thinking and thinking. What if she could never get drunk again? Oh, God. Why couldn't she get drunk today? She recounted the day, and she thought about Christopher. She knew it was crazy. There was no way a little boy could touch her arm and make her unable to feel drunk. But the thought was there like the itch on her arm. And she needed to find her own version of "itch medicine." She had to get her drunk back before sobriety drove her insane.

The clock read 2:17 a.m.

Mrs. Henderson sat in the kitchen. Her perfect kitchen. Her dream kitchen. She had spent years creating it. Finding every knickknack. Every antique. She was not a rich woman, but she had taste. And over the decades, every Sunday, she would go out into the world of yard sales and flea markets and find pieces for ten dollars that would have gone for thousands at Christie's. Little by little, bit by bit, she created the perfect home for herself and her husband. It was her life's work. She taught children to read and love books during the day. And she created the perfect home for her husband at night. But now her husband was never in it. It was 2:17 a.m., and her husband was still out somewhere. So, Mrs. Henderson sat in her kitchen, just staring at the front door. She stared at the little WELCOME HOME antique plaque and the perfect little curtains on the brass railing. She stared and scratched and thought about the day she got engaged on top of the Ferris wheel at Kennywood. Mr. Henderson couldn't keep his hands off her back then. She would tell him "no" in the backseat of his car even though her body screamed "yes." Because she was not that kind of girl. Men don't marry those kinds of girls, her mother told her. But her skin itched whenever he kissed her. Her skin burned for him. Like it burned now. Like it burned in her first year teaching at Mill Grove Elementary School. She would never forget that little boy. That little frightened boy. How smart he was. How sad she felt when he went missing. Why was she thinking of him now? She had no idea. But it made her arm stop itching to think of him. It made her stop asking when her husband stopped touching her. It made her remember that this was going to be her last year of teaching. She was going to retire and have a great life with him. Yes. Her husband would walk through that door eventually. Eventually, he would get hungry and need her warm kitchen again.

CHAPTER 46

The clock read 2:37 a.m.

Mary Katherine lay alone in her bedroom. She had been awake for twenty minutes now. She woke up because her arm was itchy. She tried to put on some lotion, but that didn't work. She drank a glass of water because sometimes itchy skin means dehydration. But that didn't work, either. The itch just stayed on her skin.

The strange thing was that she enjoyed it.

Her skin was warm. Soft and quiet like silk sheets. And the itch felt good against it. Nice and scratchy like the one time when Doug forgot to shave and kissed her cheek. The scratching kind of hurt, but she liked it, and kind of wished that Doug could grow out his beard. He tried once for their production of Fiddler on the Roof. All the boys in the cast did. The results were varying degrees of tragic. Why were boys boys? she wondered.

Why couldn't they just hurry up and become men?

Mary Katherine lay on her bed in her cotton nightgown and looked around the room. The wind was blowing outside. A little more than usual. Mary Katherine pictured the wind sneaking into her bedroom and blowing the itch on her arm all over her body. She pictured it moving down her forearm to her wrist to her fingers.

Five little fingers on her right hand.

Mary Katherine took her fingers and started to move the itch around. Inch by inch. She started on her arm, then slowly moved her itchy fingers up her shoulder to her neck to her mouth. She stopped there. Just grazing her fingers back and forth across her lips. They were dry and cracked from her walk through the cold Mission Street Woods. Every time she grazed them, the itch became warmer and softer and scratchier all at the same time. Kind of like how she pictured a real beard feeling on her skin. A real beard belonging to a real man. A man like the sheriff who lied for her on the night she found Christopher. Mary Katherine stuck out her tongue and licked the tips of her fingers. Slowly, she moved one of her fingers into her mouth. Then, she moved the finger in deeper and added another and another. She pictured the sheriff kissing her. She pictured taking the sheriff into her—

STOP.

Mary Katherine sat up in bed. The itch on her skin turned to a burn. What the hell was she doing? This wasn't right. It would have been a sin to think of Doug that way because they weren't married. But the sheriff? That was disgusting. Mary Katherine had never had sex. She had never masturbated because she knew that would lead to shameful thinking. She knew the rules . . . To think it is to do it. That's what she was taught by Mrs. Radcliffe in CCD for over ten years.

TO THINK IT IS TO DO IT.

Mary Katherine got on her knees at the foot of her bed and prayed to take these sinful thoughts out of her mind. She was kneeling in front of God. Using her mouth to speak His words. But the itching only got worse. She could feel it under the cotton of her nightgown. The skin of her breast could feel the itch on her fingers. Nothing but a little slice of cotton in between them. It wasn't a sin to rub her nightgown. Right? It's just cotton. It's not like it's her body. So, that would be okay. That wouldn't be a sin. So, she got off her knees and rubbed the cotton of her nightgown. Her breast was only scratched by accident. By the coarse cotton. Like a beard. Like the sheriff's stubble as he picked her up and put her on the bed and—

STOP.

THIS IS A TEST.

Mary Katherine stood up. Her chest was aching now. Her face flushed red. She told herself that it was okay. She was only touching her nightgown. Not her breasts. She didn't do anything wrong. She had come close, but she hadn't gone all the way. Not yet. But Mary Katherine was still terrified. She had to get out of her bedroom before she thought something that would send her straight to Hell. She had to go outside. That's it. Yes. She would go outside in the cold air, and it would stop all of this heat.

Mary Katherine went to her closet and took off her nightgown. She stood in front of her closet in nothing but panties. The draft in her bedroom moved across her skin like little kisses. The wind blowing on her neck. Gooseflesh popped up wherever it touched her. She didn't know why the wind was allowed to touch her, and she wasn't. But she wasn't. But she still wanted to touch herself. Over and over again. She wanted to put her itching fingers into her panties and—

"Stop it, Mary Katherine!" she hissed at herself. "To think it is to do it! Just stop thinking!"

She had to get out of there. Cover her body. Forget she had one. She threw on the thickest white sweater and pair of blue jean overalls she owned along with her thickest socks and boots. Mary Katherine left her room and tiptoed past her parents' bedroom, then down the stairs. She walked outside, but it was too freezing to stay there. Luckily, her mother parked in the driveway. Mary Katherine wasn't allowed to drive past midnight. But it wasn't a sin to sit in a car, right? Right.

Mary Katherine got in the car.

The cold of the car seat ate its way through her thick clothes. The cold made her gooseflesh return and turned her nipples into pebbles under her overalls. She thought about warm hands on her breasts. Crawling into the backseat. Steaming up the windows.

THIS IS A TEST. STOP IT.

But she couldn't. Mary Katherine was on fire. She couldn't stand it anymore. She took out her cell phone and dialed.

"Hello?" Doug said, half-asleep.

"Doug! Are you at home?" she asked desperately.

"Of course. It's almost three," he said.

"Is the key under the mat?"

"Yes."

"Then I'm coming over."

"But I have a final tomor—"

Mary Katherine hung up. She started the car. She knew she would get in the worst trouble if her parents found out, but she didn't know what else to do. She had to get rid of these thoughts. She had to get the itch off her skin.

Mary Katherine drove to Doug's house, checking for deer the whole way. She parked in front. Before she could get out of the car, he appeared on the porch. He walked over to the car in a robe and snow boots, the frost on the lawn crunching with each step.

"What the hell are you doing, Mary Katherine?"

"Let's go inside."

"Are you crazy? My parents would hear us. What's going on?"

"I need your help, Doug. Pray with me."

"About what?"

"Just pray with me. Please."

"Okay," he said.

Mary Katherine opened the door. Doug got in and shivered. The two clasped hands and closed their eyes in prayer. Mary Katherine wanted to speak. She wanted to tell him about the itch on her skin and all of her impure thoughts, but she couldn't. She knew to speak it is to think it and to think it is to do it, and to do it is to hit a deer and spend eternity in Hell.

But Doug's hands felt so warm.

And he smelled so good.

"What are you doing, Mary Katherine?" Doug asked.

Mary Katherine opened her eyes and realized she had reached under Doug's seat and slid it all the way back to make room for herself in front of him. She got on her knees and parted his robe. Mary Katherine reached for his boxers and slid them down his body. She looked down and saw it. She had never seen one before. Not in person. Only drawings in health class.

But there it was.

"What are you doing?" he asked quietly.

She didn't say a word because she had no words. Just the heat on her body and the itch and the shame that felt so terribly bad in the best kind of way. Mary Katherine slowly moved her hand to Doug. *Stop. It's a test.* She touched it. *To think it is to do it.* She started moving her five itching fingers up and down. *So you may as well do it.* Up and down. Up and down. She couldn't believe this was happening. She didn't know what was possessing her. But she wanted it. She wanted him to grab her. And be a man already. Just be a God damn man already, Doug. He looked over at his house. The lights turned on.

"Oh, God. My mother is awake," he said.

But Mary Katherine didn't stop. She put Doug into her mouth. He was hard as a diamond. The itching stopped. The voices stopped. The words stopped.

She didn't know what to do with it other than hold it in her mouth. But it didn't seem to matter. Within three seconds, he pulled out, and he finished all over her sweater.

They were both silent.

She looked up at Doug, who was filled with desire and disgust, shame and confusion. The look on his face horrified her. She realized that in that moment, Doug had no idea who she was. Neither did she. He pulled up his underwear and closed his robe.

"I have to go," he said.

He got out of the car and ran back to his house. Mary Katherine didn't know what to do. She couldn't believe what just happened. Her grandmother had given her that white sweater. For her sixteenth birthday. Her grandmother was dead now. Her grandmother could see what she had just done. So could Jesus. The sweater was dirty now. She was dirty. Like Debbie Dunham or any other girl at school. Her face was flush with shame. She looked back at the house as Doug walked through the front door without turning around to wave goodbye.

Mary Katherine drove away.

She turned on the radio to distract herself. The radio was set to her mother's favorite religious station. The priest told Mary Katherine that Jesus loved her and would wash away her sins. The sins of sex. The sins of adultery. She changed the channel. Every station spoke of God. God was watching her. God could see everything.

A deer ran in front of her car.

Mary Katherine hit the brakes and skidded. The deer looked right into the headlights and froze. Mary Katherine screamed. The deer came closer and closer into the headlights.

"PLEASE, GOD! NO!" she screamed.

The car stopped an inch from the deer.

Mary Katherine looked through the windshield. The deer stared at her. The deer was soon joined by a doe. And a fawn. It was a little family like Mary and Joseph after the manger. Mary Katherine's heart raced. If she hit a deer with her car, she was going to Hell. This was God's warning. He gave her a body as a vessel for His spirit. Not the other way around. She had better stop her sinful thinking. And get home, Mary Katherine. Now.

But the deer were blocking the road.

Mary Katherine had no choice but to turn around. She quietly put the car in reverse. She backed into a driveway and drove back the way she came. It would take a little longer to get home, but if she took a left at the next fork, she would be home before her parents knew she was gone.

But when she got to the fork, she saw more deer blocking the road.

Mary Katherine idled the car at the stop sign. She looked back into the rearview mirror and saw that the family of deer had followed her. On every street she scanned, there were deer. Blocking her path home. Leaving her only one street to drive on.

The street toward the Mission Street Woods.

Mary Katherine moved down the street. She reached the Collins Construction site. She turned the car around and saw them. Dozens of deer walking slowly toward her. Threatening to scrape the car with their antlers. Mary Katherine leaned on the horn.

"Get away from me!" she screamed.

The deer did not scatter. They did not run. They just inched closer and closer. Mary Katherine had no choice. She opened the car door and stepped out into the freezing night. The deer began to run at her. She climbed over the security fence and landed on the muddy ground. The deer stopped at the security fence, their antlers poking through the metal grate.

She took off into the Mission Street Woods.

Mary Katherine didn't know if this was a dream or real. She prayed it was a dream. She prayed that she would wake up in her bed and never have had these thoughts. Never have taken the car out past midnight. Never have taken Doug into her mouth. She prayed that all of this was some horrible nightmare and that she was still a girl worth loving.

She could hear more deer in the woods running behind her. Scattering like cockroaches on a fresh kitchen floor. She ran aimlessly, looking for a path she might recognize. She ran past an abandoned refrigerator, right into a tunnel.

She dropped her cell phone. The tunnel went dark, the water from the melted snow squishing under her feet. Mary Katherine reached down and fished out her cell phone. She shook it. Nothing happened. She prayed for light. She dried the cell phone off on her overalls. Suddenly, the cell phone came back to life.

That's when she saw the deer.

Dozens of them.

In the coal mine.

"Ahhhhh!" she screamed.

Mary Katherine ran. Lighting the way with her cell phone until she finally found the moonlight again in the clearing.

Mary Katherine saw the tree house. She remembered finding Christopher in there earlier that night. He grabbed her arm, and the heat shot through his fingers and made those tiny blisters. The blisters were warm. Like the tree house would be. Yes. That's where she needed to go. The tree house would keep her warm and safe from the deer. Mary Katherine ran to the tree house just as the deer reached the clearing. She moved up the 2x4 steps. She opened the door and looked inside. The tree house was empty. Mary Katherine turned back around and saw the deer circling her like sharks in a tank.

Then she began to pray.

As she spoke the Lord's Prayer, she looked up at the beautiful field of stars past the clouds. A shooting star flew across the sky. She remembered when Mrs. Radcliffe said that every shooting star was a soul going to Heaven. The memory soothed Mary Katherine. She thought about being a child in CCD with all those lessons about Jesus. God, she loved Jesus with all her heart. She was a child, and she did not know there was such a thing as a body that could do dirty things. Wouldn't it be great to be that child again? To be pure of thought and deed. She whispered the Lord's Prayer and crossed herself after the final line.

"And deliver us from evil. Amen."

Mary Katherine closed the door to the tree house.

The instant the door snapped shut, she felt better. Calm and quiet. She realized it was not too late. God could have made her hit a deer, but He didn't. He just warned her and led her to a child's tree house. To remind her to love as a child loves. Because children don't go to Hell.

sCratch sCratch sCratch

She heard the deer outside, but they couldn't get her up here. And she still had a few hours until her mother would be awake. So, she could set the alarm on her phone and just wait for the deer to go away. Then, she could go home safely. Yes. That's what she'd do. She would sleep inside the tree house. And in the morning, she would be safe as a child in her mother's arms.

sCratch sCratch sCratch

Mary Katherine ignored the deer and set her alarm for two hours. She laid her head on the floor of the tree house, and she suddenly felt as snug as a child in bootie pajamas. Warm and safe as if Jesus were holding her. Spooning her the way they do in movies. Telling her that she was forgiven. And that she was loved. She curled up, and as she fell asleep, she dreamed that she could almost hear Jesus whisper in her ear. His voice was soft.

Almost like a woman's.

CHAPTER 47

Christopher sat up in bed. He looked outside his window and saw the Mission Street Woods in the wind. The bare branches swaying back and forth like arms in a church, worshipping. He could feel the itch stirring in the breeze.

Waiting for the town to wake.

Christopher took a deep breath and tried to quiet his mind. The last trip to the imaginary side had made the itch much more powerful. But with it came the pain. Christopher had gotten used to the headaches and nosebleeds.

But this fever was a little scary.

The heat rose from his skin like steam off highway asphalt. His temperature climbed until the town started going to bed. Christopher thought he could feel lights being switched off. Televisions going dark. And with the silence, his temperature dropped a little. The itch died down. And the flash cards slowed because most of the town was sleeping. But he knew that when the town woke up, the flash cards would come through his mind like a jackhammer. And he couldn't let that happen. He had to focus on one thing and one thing only today.

He had to find the message David Olson left for him at school.

But making it to school was another matter entirely.

Christopher didn't know how much of a fever he had, but he knew it was bad enough to make his mother keep him home. So, he dragged himself out of bed and walked down the hall. He tiptoed past his sleeping mother to her bathroom. He climbed onto the sink, opened the medicine cabinet, and took out the bottle of aspirin she kept on the top shelf. He had gone through the kitchen supply a long time ago. He took other bottles, too. Aleve, Advil, Tylenol, and any cold medicine with the term "non-drowsy" on it. After wrestling the child-proof caps off, he took a few pills from each bottle to avoid the suspicion of an empty. Then, he returned them all to the cabinet and tiptoed back through her room.

"Honey? What are you doing?" the voice asked.

Christopher turned and saw his mother sleeping.

"I had a bad dream," he lied.

"About what?"

"I dreamed you had gone away. I just wanted to make sure you were still here."

"I'll always be here," she whispered. "Do you want to sleep here tonight?"

Yes.

"No, thanks. I feel better now."

"Okay, I love you," she said and rolled back over to dream.

Christopher went back to his bedroom and waited for morning to come. He would have read his books to pass the time, but the truth was that he had memorized all of them already. He saw them all like flash cards in his mind. Pages turning like generations from birth to death. Beginning to end. Trees to paper.

As dawn broke, the itch broke with it. And with it, the pain. Christopher felt his neighborhood wake. Each stretch and yawn. Cups of coffee being poured and cereal crunching. He wondered how there could possibly be enough coffee for everyone to drink all the time. He remembered his father loved coffee and doughnuts with sugar on them. Christopher thought about his father's funeral. How there were white headstones as far as the eye could see. He wondered about all those graves. If every soul who ever lived took up a grave, then eventually...

Wouldn't the entire earth be covered in graves?

Half an hour before his mother's alarm went off, Christopher crushed all thirty pills into a fine powder and ate it like a rancid Pixy Stix.

Christopher went to the kitchen.

He threw a stopper into the sink and ran the water quietly. He took the two ice trays out of the freezer, cracked them like knuckles, and dumped the ice into the water. He filled the trays and returned them to the freezer to cover his tracks.

Then, he took his pajama top off and dunked his entire head, neck, and shoulders into the freezing-cold water. He wanted to scream, but he kept himself in that freezing soup for twenty-five Mississippis. Then, he pulled out his head, took a deep breath, and did it all again. And again. And again.

The cold bit through his skin like little needles until his body went numb, but he didn't dare get out. It was either this or the doctor. There was no plan B. Christopher knew plenty of kids who pretended to be sick to get out of school. He remembered when Special Ed showed him how to fake out a thermometer with a lightbulb and a heating pad. He just never thought he would be the first kid in history who faked being well to get back in. When his mother's alarm clock went off (thank God she always hit SNOOZE), he quickly dried himself with a dish towel, pulled out the plug, and raced back upstairs to climb back into bed and pretend to be awakened by her.

"Hey, how are you feeling?" his mother asked.

"Much better," he said, pretending to open his eyes. It wasn't a lie. The thirty pills were starting to work. He did technically feel better.

"Good. How did you sleep?" she asked.

"Great. I can't wait for school. It's Taco Tuesday," he said brightly.

Then, he braced himself for the moment of truth. Christopher's mother instinctively put her hand to his forehead. She felt his hair, still slightly damp from the water. Christopher thought he had blown it.

Until she smiled.

"I think your fever broke," she said. "Let's double-check."

She put the thermometer under his tongue. He looked down when the digital readout beeped.

It was 98.6.

"Sorry, kid," she said. "I'm afraid you have to go to school."

It was a miracle.

My mother wants...
My mother wants... to invite the sheriff for Christmas dinner.
My mother won't... because of me.

"Mom?" Christopher asked. "Where do people without families go for Christmas?"

"Depends. Some visit friends. Others go to church. Why?"

"Because I want people like Mr. Ambrose and the sheriff to have somewhere to go this year," he said.

"That's nice," she said. "You want to invite them over?"

"Yes."

"Okay," she said. "Now hurry up. You're going to be late."

My mother is . . .
My mother is . . . so happy right now.

The school bus opened its doors.

The minute Christopher stepped onto the bus, the voices began to pick up speed. He saw the students stare at him like a thing at the zoo. To them, he was just the boy who pissed his pants in front of the whole school.

To him, they were something entirely different.

The boy with the red hair . . . dresses in his mother's clothes.
The girl with braces . . . doesn't eat as much as she should.
The little girl with brown eyes . . . worries about her family in the Middle East.
They are suffering. The whole world will be suffering soon, Christopher.

You have to find the message from David Olson.

Christopher passed the bus driver, Mr. Miller. He saw the tattoo on Mr. Miller's arm. The tattoo from the marines. He could feel Mr. Miller bracing himself for the holidays. Every holiday he would think about the men he killed in a desert somewhere.

Mr. Miller thinks . . .
Mr. Miller thinks . . . he doesn't deserve to live.

"Mr. Miller?" Christopher said.

"Sit down!" Mr. Miller barked.

"I'm sorry. I just wanted to thank you for keeping us safe on the way to school."

For a moment, Mr. Miller was silent. Christopher knew it was the nicest thing anyone had said to him in five years. Certainly the nicest thing any of these brats had ever said to him. Period. He would have thanked Christopher then and there, but he was afraid that if he spoke, he would burst into tears, and have no authority with these kids ever again. So, he said the only thing that he could think of.

"It's my job. So, stop distracting me and sit down," he barked.

Christopher simply nodded and sat down. The gesture helped Christopher.

It calmed his mind long enough that he made it to school without thinking about every family in every house. When the bus stopped in front of school, Christopher smiled.

"Have a good day, Mr. Miller," he said.

"You, too, kid," the gruff man said.

Mr. Miller won't...
Mr. Miller won't... kill himself this Christmas.

Christopher looked ahead at all of the children walking into the school with their thick coats and hats. There were hundreds of them. Hundreds of babies who were born to hundreds of parents. Every one of them the hero of their own life. All of those voices and secrets and thoughts. Christopher took a deep breath and put his head down. He tried to concentrate on David Olson, but the voices itched their way through his mind. He felt like he was standing in a batting cage while a machine gun shot baseballs at him. Most of the chatter was innocent. Rod Freeman was worried about his test. Beth Thomas wondered what was for lunch. But occasionally, there would be a violent thought. A memory. A daydream. Some kids wondered where Brady Collins was. Why Jenny Hertzog was absent. Where Special Ed and the M&M's were. Christopher saw Ms. Lasko walking up the hall. She was scratching her arm. She looked very sick.

Ms. Lasko didn't... sleep last night.
Ms. Lasko got... naked with the bartender because she can't get drunk.

"Ms. Lasko, are you okay?"

"Sure, Christopher. Just feel a little under the weather is all," she said, but her voice sounded like it was drowning in syrup. Too low and too slow.

"Maybe you should go home," Christopher said.

"No. It's worse there," she said.

Ms. Lasko patted the top of his head and moved on as the hallways became flooded (Floods! Floods!) with students. Father Tom said that God was angry, and He flooded the world. Christopher saw the kids all swimming upstream, their voices blending together into a white noise like ocean waves. He wondered if that's how God created the sound of the oceans. He just took billions of voices and carried them out to sea. The energy moving through still water. The energy moving through otherwise dead flesh. All of these people connected.

Like the mailbox people.

Christopher fought the voices as best he could, but his brain couldn't stop them anymore. So, he did the only thing left to him. He submitted. He let his mind go, and the voices took him like a surfer on a wave. Hundreds of voices carrying him out to sea. Moving him through the school hallways like the blood in their veins. In science class, Mr. Henderson said that our bodies are 70 percent salt water. Like the oceans. We are all connected.

Like the mailbox people.

Christopher followed the voices, racing down the hallway to the library, moving past the lockers standing side by side like little coffins. The library was empty of students in the morning. There was only Mrs. Henderson. The moment Christopher saw her, he became concerned. Mrs. Henderson was standing on top of her desk, adjusting a white panel in the ceiling. Her skin was pale and shiny with a thin layer of sweat. Christopher knew she was terribly sick. Just like Ms. Lasko.

Mrs. Henderson . . . waited in the kitchen all night.
Mr. Henderson . . . didn't come home until breakfast.

"Are you okay, Mrs. Henderson?" he asked.

For a moment, she did not speak. She just looked down at Christopher and scratched her arm. The skin was red and raw. Like it was missing a dozen layers. She got down off her desk. Woozy.

"Yes, Christopher. I'm fine. Thank you for asking," she said.

Her voice sounded wrong. It was slow and distant. She was in a daze.

"Mrs. Henderson, are you sure you're okay? You look sick," he said.

Christopher reached out and touched her hand.

In an instant she stopped scratching her arm. Mrs. Henderson looked down at his little face. For a moment, she forgot her husband didn't love her anymore. She still had red hair. They got married at the fire hall. They helped each other through college. Back then, she couldn't imagine all of the kids she would teach. Over the last fifty years, class after class moving through time like energy through ocean waves. She had helped thousands of kids become better people. Each of those kids took a little red out of her hair until it turned grey. They held those strands of hair like the strings of the Balloon Derby balloons every year. Mrs. Henderson just couldn't stop thinking about how it all started with that first year. That first class. And that first student. She smiled when she thought of that little boy. Asking for another book. And another. And another. There was always hope with a sweet little boy like that.

"You know, you remind me of someone, Christopher," she said. "What was his name again? I was trying to think of it all night."

The room went cold, and the itch started crawling up his neck.

"David Olson," she said slowly. "That's it. God, I've been trying to remember that name all night. It was driving me crazy."

Mrs. Henderson sighed. She was still talking slowly, as if her whole body were underwater. But she felt such a relief that she remembered his name.

"He loved to read books. Just like you," she said.

"What books?" Christopher asked.

"Oh, gosh. Everything. He couldn't check them out fast enough," she continued, suddenly lost in memory. "'Mrs. Henderson, do you have Treasure Island? Do you have The Hobbit?' He would read them in a day. I'll bet if he hadn't gone missing, he would have read every book in the library."

Her face suddenly changed with the memory of David's disappearance. Christopher saw the wrinkles come back around her eyes and mouth. Deep lines that she earned with a lifetime of pretending to smile.

"Do you know that when he went missing, there was one book he threw into the return bin. I just didn't have the heart to check that book back in. I knew if I ever did, he would be gone forever. God, that sounds so strange now, doesn't it? I kept it checked out for the rest of the school year hoping that he would come back. But he didn't. And when we did our year-end inventory, I was finally forced to check the book back in."

"What book was it?" Christopher asked, his voice stuck in his throat.

Mrs. Henderson put her other hand on Christopher's. It felt so warm and dry to her. She felt so good all of a sudden. So peaceful.

"Frankenstein," she said, smiling. "God, David checked that book out a dozen times. It was his favorite. I never had the heart to replace it."

Mrs. Henderson stopped for a moment. Tears began to well up in her eyes.

"I went home that night for the start of summer vacation. Mr. Henderson surprised me with our first color television set. He had saved his money all year to buy it. We watched television together on the couch all summer. Old movies. Baseball games. We even saw Frankenstein. It was part of a double feature. And

I thought about David and lay on my husband's chest. And I knew how lucky I was just to be alive."

"You're still lucky, Mrs. Henderson," he said quietly.

"Thank you, Christopher," she said. "Tell Mr. Henderson that."

With that, she let go of his hands. She blinked twice and looked around the library, as if suddenly realizing she was crying in front of a student. Embarrassed, she excused herself and rushed away to the bathroom to fix her makeup.

Christopher was alone.

He knew the solitude was temporary. He felt the voices trapped in homerooms swirling around him in a circle. Hundreds of classmates busy daydreaming or paying attention to their lessons. Teachers with sins and secrets busy instructing children how to know what they knew. He was an island in the eye of a hurricane.

Just like the tree house in the middle of the clearing.

Christopher steadied himself and moved as quickly as he could on wobbly legs to the computer. He clicked on the search engine to look for David Olson's book. He began to type rapidly . . .

F-R-A-N-K-E-N-S-T-E-I-N

Christopher saw the section where the book was. He moved over to the shelves and found an old hardcover copy, beaten and worn with the same years that took the red out of Mrs. Henderson's hair. He cracked it open and looked at the title page. There was nothing. No notes. No writing. He turned the page. And the next. And the next. There was nothing. Just a few underlines. Christopher didn't understand. He was sure that David Olson left him a message in the book. Why else would he come to the library? Why else did he listen to Mrs. Henderson's story? There had to be a message in here somewhere, but there was nothing but these stupid underlines.

Christopher flipped back to the title page of the book. He looked again and thought maybe David wrote in invisible ink. Maybe David was afraid that the hissing lady would find his messages, so he hid them somehow. Christopher stopped and looked closely at the underlined passages of the book. The underlines were strange. They weren't full sentences. They were words. Sometimes, letters within a word. Christopher looked at the title page again.

Frankenstein by Mary <u>She</u>lley.

The phrase that was underlined was . . . *She*

Christopher turned the pages until he found the next underline. He saw the word was . . . *thinks*

The temperature rose. Christopher could feel a presence in the room. He looked back to see if anyone was watching him. But no one was there. Christopher quietly turned back to the book and flipped pages until he found the next underlines.

The first two underlines were . . . *She thinks*

The next two underlines were . . . *you are*

And the next . . . *reading*

And the next two . . . *right now.*

And the next . . . *Do not*

And the next . . . *write this down*

And the next . . . *or she*

And the next . . . *will know,*

And a series of letters . . . *C-h-r-i-s-t-o-p-h-e-r.*

Christopher got silent. And still. He knew the hissing lady was watching him right now from the imaginary side. So, Christopher did his best imitation of reading a book as he flipped through the pages and read nothing but David Olson's underlines. This is what it said.

> *She thinks you are reading right now. Do not write this down or she will know, Christopher. She is watching you right now. She is always listening. You can never speak your plans out loud, or she will kill your mother. Do not contact my big brother Ambrose. She will kill him instantly if she finds out I'm helping you.*

Christopher kept turning the pages at lightning speed.

> *I know you have questions, but we cannot speak directly, or she will know that I have turned on her. I'm sorry that I scare you in nightmares, but I have to prove my loyalty. I will leave you clues when I can, but if we are going to defeat her, you must rescue HIM. He is the only person who can help us. I called him the soldier. You call him the nice man. He was put here to fight the hissing lady. Without him, your world is doomed.*

Christopher thought about the nice man. The soldier.

When you see him, tell him that the hissing lady has found the way. It's already started. You have seen some of it. You haven't seen other things. But it's spreading beyond the woods. Beyond the town. She is only getting stronger without him to check her power. And when the time is right, she will shatter the mirror between the imaginary world and yours. And there will be only one world left standing. She doesn't know that I know, but I can tell you the exact moment WHEN everything will be revealed.

Death is coming.
Death is here.
You'll die on C-h-r-i-s-t-m-a-s Day.

The words flew through Christopher's mind. He looked up at the calendar. Tuesday, December 17. He went back to the book.

The soldier is our last chance. If we can get him out of the imaginary world and back to the real one, then he can stop her. But if we can't, all is lost. I will do what I can to help you, but you must rescue him alone. She keeps him chained in my house. Go in during the day. Be absolutely silent. She will test to see if you are there. DO NOT FAIL THAT TEST. If she catches you, she will never let you out of the imaginary world again.

Christopher, I have been here for 50 years. I don't want you to be trapped like I was. So, please be careful. And if you do find a way to get HIM out of here, PLEASE TAKE ME WITH YOU.

Your friend,
David Olson

Christopher turned the pages and reached the end of the book. There were no more underlines. No more words. Christopher returned the book to its shelf and casually left the library. Then, he went to his locker, grabbed his coat, and slipped into the "long shot" bathroom on the first floor. There was an open window the fifth graders used to skip school. He didn't know if he had heard that or simply read it in someone's mind. All he knew for sure was no one would see him leave, and he could make it back before the final bell. After all, it was only a two-hour walk to the tree.

Then, another ten minutes to David Olson's house.

CHAPTER 48

The house was smaller than he remembered it.

Ambrose had not been back since he moved to Shady Pines, but when he woke up that morning, something compelled him to go. It was more than a hunch. It was more than grief. He simply knew he had to see the old house before his eyesight was completely gone.

And he had to go today.

He would have left that morning if it hadn't been for the funeral. That's what was so troubling to him. Ambrose had spent days planning it. Without any heirs, he did not worry about money. His brother didn't get the best in life, so Ambrose made damn sure he would get the best in death. The casket and headstone were as lavish as he could buy while still remaining tasteful, a quality that his mother regarded above all others.

"You can't buy class," she loved to say.

"You can't buy life, either," he thought out loud.

Kate Reese and the sheriff both attended the funeral. The sheriff had been kind enough to drive to Ambrose in person to tell him that the DNA was indeed a match. When the sheriff brought out the evidence bag with the lock of David's hair, Ambrose squinted up at him and shook his head. The two looked at each other. Soldier and cop.

"Keep it in the evidence bag, Sheriff. We're going to solve this crime."

That was it. The sheriff nodded and put the evidence bag back into his pocket.

"Sheriff," Ambrose finally said, "would you come to my brother's funeral?"

"I would be honored to, sir."

Ambrose did his Catholic best at the funeral. He listened to Father Tom's mass about peace and forgiveness. He ate the Communion wafer, which tasted like a stale Styrofoam cup. He willed himself to help carry the casket—let his back and two arthritic knees be damned. He would have broken his back before he let David be put in the ground without him. Father Tom delivered a final word at the grave. Ambrose put a rose on the headstone.

But there was no peace. There were no tears.

There was only this uneasy feeling.

That this was not over.

His little brother was not at peace.

And Ambrose had to go to his old house. Right now.

He still had a car, but with his bad eyes, the state had already taken his license. Luckily, Kate Reese offered to drive him since she lived in the old neighborhood. Ambrose was grateful for the company because another feeling had started to bubble up inside him as he got closer and closer to the old house.

It was something close to terror.

Don't open the door. It's not a baby! Your brother was telling the truth!

Ambrose put his foot on the old porch. He rang the doorbell. As he waited, he looked down at the exact spot where he had found the baby carriage. He could still hear the sound of the baby's cries. He could still hear the police speaking to his father.

We found no fingerprints on the tape recorder, sir. No prints on the carriage.

Then, who put it there?!

And his mother speaking to him.

Why didn't you watch your little brother?!

Ambrose turned his sights back to the neighborhood to get the bad out of his body. For a moment, he could remember that final summer before David started getting sick. All the fathers worked on their cars in the driveways with their sons. Barry Hopkins was trying to turn that old piece-of-shit '42 Dodge into something. The street was safe. People looked out for each other. All the men listened to the Pirates game on the radio while all the women busied themselves in the living rooms with games of bridge, white wine, and gin. The following summer after David had disappeared, people did not spend as much time in their driveways. Kids were almost never outside. And as far as the bridge games went, if they were happening, no families invited the Olsons. It hurt his mother's feelings deeply, but Ambrose always understood that people are afraid that tragedy is contagious. Still, it would have been nice if his mother hadn't lost her friends along with her son.

"Hello? May I help you?"

Ambrose turned around to see a young woman. She was maybe thirty years old. Pleasant and pretty. He instinctively took off his hat and felt the winter air settle on his bald scalp.

"Yes, ma'am. I'm sorry to bother you. I used to live in this house with my family. And uh . . ."

Ambrose trailed off. He wanted to ask her if he could look around, but now being here, he didn't know if he wanted to go inside. His chest tightened. Something was wrong here. Kate Reese jumped right in.

"Mr. Olson wanted to know if he could look around. I'm Kate Reese. I live right down the street," she said, pointing down the hill.

"Of course. Please, come in, Mr. Olson. My house is your house. Or should I say your house is my house," the woman joked.

Ambrose forced a smile and followed her inside. When the door closed behind him, he instinctively turned to the corner to hang up his coat and hat. But of course, his mother's coat-tree was gone. So was her wallpaper. So was she.

"Would you like some coffee, sir?" the woman asked.

Ambrose didn't want coffee, but he wanted to be left alone to gather his thoughts. So, he agreed to a cup of Vanilla Hazelnut (whatever the hell that was) and thanked the woman for her kindness. Mrs. Reese followed the woman, who introduced herself as Jill, into the kitchen, chatting up a storm about neighborhood property values.

Ambrose walked through the living room. The fireplace was still there, but the carpeting on the floor was torn up, revealing the hardwood underneath. He remembered when wall-to-wall carpeting was a sign of status. How proud his mother was when his father's raise made the carpeting affordable. He was sure that Jill was just as proud of her hardwood floors because he had learned that what is old is new again. He wondered if someday when Jill became an old lady and sold her house the status would already have changed back to carpeting, and the new couple would laugh at the old people's funny hardwood floors.

He heard the floor creak behind him.

Ambrose turned quickly, expecting to see Jill with the coffee. But no one was there. Just the empty house and the sound of his own breathing. Ambrose saw that Jill had chosen the west corner for the sofa. His mother preferred the east for the evening light. Back when the focus of a living room was living. Not television. He remembered when his father brought home their first black-and-white television. His mother thought it meant the end of the world.

Ambrose, can we watch a movie tonight?

Sure, David. Find a good one.

His little brother would get the TV Guide and pore through it. This was years before people could get anything they wanted anytime they wanted it. Kids had to work for a movie, and the movies were more sacred somehow because of it. David would read every line of that TV Guide, trying to find a good movie to please his big brother. That's how Ambrose Olson got to see Dracula, The Wolf Man, The Mummy, and of course David's all-time favorite, Frankenstein. David would see Frankenstein any chance he got. He must have gotten the book out of the library a hundred times. Ambrose finally broke down and planned to buy David his own copy for Christmas, but David only wanted to read the library's copy for some reason.

So, Ambrose got David a baseball glove instead.

When the movie was over, David was usually asleep. Ambrose would scoop him up and carry him upstairs to bed. That is, until David started having nightmares about things a whole lot scarier than Frankenstein's monster.

Ambrose heard the floor creak upstairs. He didn't want to go up there. But he had to see the room again. His feet started to move before he was consciously aware that he was going. He grabbed the banister and forced his knees to forget his age.

Then, he started to climb the stairs.

The Sears portrait of the family that Mom bought on layaway was gone. Pictures of Jill and her husband on a family trip stood in its place.

Ambrose, I'm scared.

Calm down. There's nothing in your room.

Ambrose reached the top of the stairs and walked down the hallway. Every step of the hardwood floor creaked. Ambrose stood outside David's bedroom. The door was closed. The memories flooded back to him. David yelling, kicking, and screaming behind that door.

Don't make me go to bed! Please don't make me, Ambrose!

David, there is no witch in your room. Now stop, before you scare Mom.

Ambrose opened the door to his brother's old bedroom. The room was empty. Quiet. It was already set up as a nursery. Ambrose could smell the new yellow paint. The lumber and drywall from the renovations. Ambrose looked at the crib sitting against the wall. The wall that David used to draw on. There was no more wallpaper. No more terrifying drawings of his nightmares. No more ranting and raving from a mentally ill child. Just a lovely nursery for Jill and her husband's happily ever after instead of a bedroom covered with crayons and madness.

Mom, he needs a psychiatrist!

No. He just needs a good night's sleep.

Dad, he hid under his bed for two days! He is talking to himself all the time!

I'll teach him to act like a man!

Ambrose looked in the corner where David's bookshelf used to be. The bookshelf that housed Frankenstein and Treasure Island from the library. He remembered how much his brother struggled to read when he was younger. Back before there was such a word as "dyslexia." They just called the kids like David "slow." But David kept working at it, and he became a great reader.

When Ambrose moved out of this house, he couldn't bear to bring that old bookshelf, so he sold it to an antiques dealer. He would give all of his money to have it back now. He would put it up in his room at Shady Pines and put David's baby book on the top shelf.

Creakkkkkk.

Ambrose stopped. He heard the floorboard behind him. Ambrose turned quickly. The door was closed behind him. But he hadn't closed the door.

"Jill? Mrs. Reese?"

There was no one there. But Ambrose could suddenly feel something in the room. A wind on his skin. Little whispers on the hairs on the back of his neck.

"David?" he whispered. "Are you in here?"

The temperature in the room suddenly dropped. He could smell the old baseball glove. He squinted through the clouds in his eyes. The cataracts that turned the whites into cracks in a windshield. It was only a matter of time now. His eyes would go, and he wouldn't be able to see the wallpaper replaced with paint. The area rug replaced with hardwood floors. The old bookshelf replaced with a crib. His old family replaced with Jill's new one. His little brother David replaced with their baby. The baby was crying on the porch.

Let me out, Ambrose! Let me out!

Ambrose could feel his brother in the room.

"I'm sorry," he whispered.

Ambrose, please!

"David, I'm sorry," he whispered.

Ambrose could feel the draft shooting through the floorboards. The wind howled outside the window where David left, never to return again. Ambrose traced the draft along the gaps in the floorboards. He reached the corner of the room. The corner where David's bed used to be. The corner where David read Frankenstein and drew terrifying pictures on the wall that his mother papered over with her promises of "He's fine. He's fine." Ambrose bent his arthritic knees and knelt down in the corner. And that's when he felt it.

The floorboard was loose.

Ambrose took out his army knife and jammed it into the gap. He sawed back and forth, creating more space. He finally loosened it enough to pivot the knife and create a little crowbar. He lifted the board out and stopped when he saw it. Sitting there. Hidden in the crawl space.

David's old baseball glove.

Ambrose lifted the glove out of its hiding place. He held it to his chest like a lost child. He took a big deep breath. The leather smell poured through Ambrose, bringing with it memories. And that's when he noticed the glove was too thick.

Something was hidden inside the glove.

Ambrose took a quick breath and opened it like a clamshell. There he saw a little book wrapped carefully in plastic. A little book covered in leather. It was bound with a strap and held together with a little lock and key. Ambrose had never seen it before, but he was almost positive he knew what it was because his brother talked about it. It was David's best-kept secret.

Ambrose was looking at his little brother's diary.

CHAPTER 49

Christopher stood on the street, looking up at the old Olson house. The nice man was in there somewhere. He had to rescue the nice man. Christopher had gone straight from school to the woods. When he went into the tree house, it felt like Superman's phone booth from the old movies. A place to change. Once he closed the door and crossed to the imaginary side, he immediately felt better. His fever and headaches were replaced with clarity and power.

But the hissing lady could be anywhere.

Christopher crouched low and watched Ambrose standing in David's old bedroom. The old man was holding a baseball glove. David Olson was standing right next to him, trying to put his hand on Ambrose's shoulder. But Ambrose did not know that his little brother was there.

David is...
David is...helping us.

Be absolutely silent. She will test to see if you are there.
DO NOT FAIL THAT TEST.

Christopher stepped onto the porch. Silently. He looked into the little windows on either side of the front door. The entry hall was empty. But the hissing lady could be waiting for him. She could be crouched on the other side of the door. He tried to calm his fear by reminding himself that he was invisible in the daylight when he walked through the tree house. But she saw him in his nightmare at school, and that was in the daylight. He didn't understand the difference. He needed the nice man to explain the rules. He needed to rescue the nice man. Now.

If she catches you, she will never let you out of the imaginary world again.

Christopher listened for another minute. Then, he quickly opened the front door, making as little sound as possible. He shut it behind him and stood still for a moment just in case the hissing lady heard him. The living room was silent. The grandfather clock stood in the corner of the room. Precious seconds passing in a tick tick tick.

Christopher tiptoed through the empty living room. The hardwood floor squeaked under his feet. He quickly knelt down and took off his sneakers. He tied the laces together and threw them over his neck like a scarf. He stood on the hardwood floor in his stocking feet. A draft rose through his toes. He could hear the wind picking up outside. A few mailbox people stood at the end of the driveway.

They were little kids playing jump rope with the strings.

With their eyes sewn shut.

Christopher moved to the bottom of the staircase. He stared up at the second floor, waiting to see if she would appear. He was just about to walk up the stairs when a noise stopped him.

"The school is excellent," the voice said.

Christopher stopped. He knew that voice.

"You picked a great place to raise a family."

It was his mother.

Christopher quickly moved to the kitchen and saw his mother sitting at a small table with a woman.

Her name is . . . Jill.
She bought the house with her husband . . . Clark.
They are trying to have a baby.

"Well, Clark and I have been working on having a family," Jill said.

"Nice work if you can get it," Christopher's mother joked.

Jill laughed and poured Christopher's mother a steaming cup of coffee.

"Would you like some milk?" she asked.

"Love some."

Jill and Clark...almost had a baby last year.
She lost the baby. But they kept the crib.
And changed the color of the walls to make it good for a girl or a boy.

Jill brought the carton of milk over to the table. Christopher saw the picture of the missing girl, Emily Bertovich. The little girl sat frozen in a photograph. Smiling with the gap in her teeth. Suddenly her eyes darted over his shoulder. Her smile turned to terror. Then, quick as a blink, she quietly turned and ran away, disappearing out of frame.

Christopher froze.

He looked up at the windows in the kitchen. And the reflection inside them. The hissing lady was right behind him.

She had walked up from the basement, carrying a dog bowl that smelled like rotten food. The hissing lady stood, the key on the noose around her neck, her ear to the air. Waiting. Listening. Christopher held his breath.

The hissing lady can't...
The hissing lady can't...see me.

She waited. Searching with her ears. After a minute, she was satisfied. He watched the hissing lady move to the sink and throw the dog bowl into fetid water. The bowl made a horrible clanking noise.

"What was that sound?" Christopher's mother asked.

"The house is still settling," Jill said.

Jill and Christopher's mother kept talking, completely unaware of what was happening around them. The hissing lady sat right next to Jill as she put a spoonful of sugar into her coffee. The hissing lady touched Jill's arm. Jill immediately got an itch and started to scratch her arm.

"God, this cold weather. Murder on my skin," she said.

"Tell me about it. I can't moisturize enough."

The hissing lady looked straight at Christopher's mother. She slowly moved toward her. Christopher wanted to scream, "MOM! GET OUT! PLEASE!" but he knew it could be a test. So, he silently took hold of his mother's left hand from the imaginary side. He closed his eyes and thought as loudly as he could.

Mom. Leave this place. Now.

The heat began to rise on his forehead. The wind picked up outside. The hissing lady instantly looked up. She knew something had changed, but she didn't know what it was.

MOM. LEAVE THIS PLACE. NOW.

Christopher's head began to cook. His fingers and arms felt like they were birthday candles melting onto a cake.

The hissing lady swung at his mother's right hand, holding the coffee cup. Christopher's mother suddenly tipped the cup over, scalding herself with coffee.

"OW!" she shrieked.

"Are you okay?" Jill said, grabbing a dishrag.

Christopher's mother moved to the sink and put her hand under the cold tap. The water poured over the burn.

"Let me see that. Oh, you need first aid," Jill said.

The hissing lady stood in the kitchen, waiting to see if there would be a re-action. Christopher said nothing. He just followed Jill over to the sink to cover the sound of his footsteps. Then, he took hold of his mother's hand in the water, closed his eyes, and thought as loudly as he could.

MOM! LEAVE THIS PLACE! NOW!

Christopher's mother suddenly checked her watch.

"God, is that the time?" she said, alarmed.

"Please, let me get you a bandage," Jill said.

"No, I'm fine. Thank you. I need to get Mr. Olson back if I'm going to be home in time for my son's school bus."

Christopher's mother stood up, leaving Christopher breathless, his forehead dripping sweat. Jill followed Christopher's mother out into the entry hall.

"Well, why don't you bring your son up for dinner sometime?"

"I would love that," Christopher's mother said, then she called up the stairs. "Mr. Olson! I'm sorry to rush you, but I have to get you back. My son will be coming home."

Christopher watched as Ambrose came downstairs, carrying the baseball glove. His little brother David followed him, playing hopscotch on his shadow.

"DAVID! WHAT HAVE YOU BEEN DOING?!" the hissing lady shrieked.

David said nothing and ran back upstairs, afraid. Christopher watched silently as Ambrose and his mother thanked Jill, then left the house. They walked to the car. Away from the hissing lady. Away from danger.

Jill walked back to the kitchen with her mug of coffee. The hissing lady followed. Christopher didn't have a moment to lose. Quiet as a mouse, he tiptoed on his stocking feet to the basement door. He opened it quickly and slipped through. He could hear Jill on the other side of the door.

"Clark, could you bring home some Lanacane? I've got an allergy or something. I can't stop itching. And did you call the exterminator? It still smells like shit in the basement."

The basement was dark. Christopher stood at the top of the long staircase. He squinted to try to see what was down there, but he could see nothing. He could hear nothing. But he knew that whatever was down there was horrible.

From the smell.

The smell of rotten food was everywhere, mixed with a leather baseball glove and what felt like hundreds of years of "long shots" that missed the urinal. The hissing lady had come up with a dog bowl full of rotten food. Was it for a prisoner?

Or an animal.

Christopher heard a chain clank in the basement. He looked down the wooden staircase. With open stairs. Open for hands to grab him.

"Sir, are you down there?" Christopher whispered.

There was silence. And Christopher didn't trust it. Something was terribly wrong. He knew it in his bones. He took a little step to get a closer look, but he almost slipped. He looked down at his feet and saw something wet and sticky on the bottom of his socks.

It was blood.

A trail of it ran down the staircase like a river. Christopher wanted to retch, but he held it in. He wanted to run, but he could feel the hissing lady in the kitchen blocking his escape.

There was nowhere to go but down.

Christopher slowly moved down the stairs. Into the darkness. The wood planks creaking beneath his feet. He almost slipped in the blood, but he steadied himself on the railing. He took another step. He heard shallow breathing. He squinted, trying to see if anyone was standing in the room. He couldn't make out any shapes. Just darkness. And that stench. Rot and copper. More pungent with every step.

He reached the bottom of the stairs.

Christopher put his stocking feet on the cold cement floor. He reached out to flick on the light. But the light was broken. He thought he heard someone breathing in the corner. Christopher groped in the darkness, his eyes trying to adjust. He took another blind step into the basement.

That's when he tripped over the body.

It was the nice man. His wrists and ankles shackled. Soaked in the rust-smelling blood.

"Sir?" Christopher whispered.

The nice man did not move. Christopher reached around in the darkness. His hands found two buckets placed against the wall. The first was a bathroom. The second had clean water and an old ladle. Christopher picked it up. He took the nice man's head in his hands. He dipped the ladle to the very bottom of the bucket and brought the cool water to the nice man's cracked lips. He tried to give sips of water, but the nice man was motionless.

The nice man is…
The nice man is…dying.

Christopher didn't know what he was doing, but instinctively, he reached out and put his hands over the nice man's wounds. He closed his eyes. Immediately his head began to ache and a fever ran through his forehead and down his arm to his fingertips. Christopher felt the blood run from his nose and trickle onto his lips. The blood tasted rusty like a copper pipe. It was the nice man's blood. The fever became too hot and Christopher was forced to let go. He reached out to use the water to clean the wounds. But the wounds were gone. There was nothing but healthy, healed skin.

That's when the nice man grabbed him.

"Leave me alone! Stop torturing me! I'll never tell!"

The sound would have brought the hissing lady running downstairs, but the nice man was so weak, his voice was barely audible.

"Sir, it's okay. It's me. Christopher," he whispered.

"Christopher?" the nice man whispered. "What are you doing here? I told you never to come in without me."

"We have to get you out of here," Christopher said. "There has to be something we can use to pick the lock."

"Christopher, it'll be dark soon. She'll be able to see you. You have to get out. Now."

"I'm not leaving without you," Christopher said.

The stubborn silence hung in the air. The nice man finally sighed.

"The table," he said.

"Where? I can't see," Christopher said.

"The light is above it," the nice man said. "Reach for the string."

The nice man took Christopher's hand and gently pointed him toward the darkness. Christopher crawled on his hands and knees until he came to a cold metal table. He groped in the darkness. His fingers reading the contents of the table like a blind man's book. It took a moment for his brain to process what all the edges, corners, and points were.

Knives and screwdrivers.

All wet with blood.

The hissing lady...
The hissing lady...tortured the nice man.

Christopher pulled himself onto the table. He stood in the wet blood. Reaching up for the light. After a moment, his fingers found the lightbulb with a long string hanging from it. Like the noose holding the key around the hissing lady's neck. Christopher pulled down the string, bathing the room in sick, yellow light.

What he saw almost made him scream.

The room was not a finished basement. There was no beanbag chair or wood paneling. There was only a cement floor. A metal table. And four walls covered in saws, knives, and screwdrivers. Every surface was dripping blood.

This was a torture room.

The nice man was chained in the corner like an animal. Covered in dirt and blood and bruises. His skin had been ripped apart and put back together a dozen times. He squinted at the light as if waking from a nightmare. Christopher had seen that look before when he went to the dog pound back in Michigan with Jerry. Some dogs get beaten for so long, they don't remember how to do anything but flinch.

Christopher quickly climbed down. He grabbed a knife and screwdriver. He rushed back and handed them to the nice man, who began to pick at the lock on his wrist. His fingers trembled with pain.

"How did you find me?" he whispered.

"David Olson."

"David? But he's with . . . her."

The way the nice man said "her" sent a shudder down his back.

"No. He's helping us. He wants me to take you both to the real side."

The news spread across the nice man's face. Confusion at first. Then, hope. The nice man was pale and drawn, deathly ill from all of the blood loss. But for the first time, Christopher saw him smile.

The hissing lady had ripped out some of his teeth.

The nice man freed one of the shackles. The screwdriver slipped out of his slick, bloody hand and clanked on the cement floor. A board creaked above them in the kitchen. The hissing lady stopped moving. Listening to the basement.

"Yes, Dr. Haskell," Jill said. "Can I get a referral to a dermatologist? I can't stop itching."

Christopher picked the screwdriver off the floor and handed it back to the nice man.

"Can you do it?" he whispered.

"Yes," the nice man said weakly.

While the nice man picked the locks, Christopher turned back into the basement, searching for a way out. His eyes finally settled on a small, filthy window covered with a curtain on the other side of the room. The window was at least ten feet off the floor. Too high for even the nice man to reach. They needed something to stand on. A chair. A bookshelf.

A metal table.

Christopher rushed over to the bloody table and started moving the instruments quietly to the floor. When he had cleared the table of anything that could fall, he put his shoes back on for traction. He grabbed a few blood-soaked towels and threw them under the legs to cut the noise.

Then, he waited for Jill's voice to cover his tracks.

"No, Dr. Haskell. It started suddenly. I don't know what it is."

Christopher dragged the table painfully across the floor. Moving with each word. Stopping with each silence.

"I don't think it's allergies. Not in December."

Every inch like pulling a tooth.

"Is there something going around?"

The rags left deep, red streaks on the concrete. Christopher pushed the table flush against the wall. His hands making little prints in the blood.

"Flu season? Does that usually come with a rash?"

He rushed over to the nice man, who had managed to get three of the shackles loose.

"Well, thank you, Dr. Haskell. I'll see you tomorrow then," Jill said, hanging up the phone.

Christopher could hear Jill walk back to the living room. But the kitchen floor still creaked. The hissing lady was waiting in the kitchen. The nice man desperately hacked at the lock on his ankle with the screwdriver.

"I can't do it," he whispered, delirious with pain. "Just leave me here."

"No!" Christopher whispered.

"You're invisible in the daytime. You can escape."

"I'm not leaving you."

Christopher took the wrist shackle in his bare hands. The heat broke out on his forehead. The power moved through his fingers. Christopher began to split the shackles like breaking a deck of cards for a shuffle. He tore the metal shackle off the nice man's ankle and dropped it gently to the ground. The nice man was speechless.

"How did you do that? Only she can do that," the nice man whispered.

"I don't know," Christopher said. "Come on."

He propped the nice man up against the wall. The nice man looked woozy. On the verge of passing out. Christopher splashed some water on the nice man's face. The water trickled down his filthy neck like a mudslide.

"I can't stand," the nice man said.

"Yes, you can. Get up."

Christopher took the nice man's hand and pulled him to his feet. The nice man's knees buckled, but he put his hand on Christopher's shoulder to steady himself.

With Christopher as a crutch, he limped to the window.

The nice man reached the table. Christopher sprang to his feet and turned. He took the nice man's hand to help him climb and stand, almost slipping on the slick blood. The nice man opened the window curtain. He saw dozens of mailbox people standing guard around the house. Their strings stretched like demented laundry lines hanging the world out to dry.

"Her guards," the nice man whispered.

Christopher put his hands together for the nice man's foot.

"I'm too big," the nice man said.

"Not for me," Christopher said.

The nice man put his foot into Christopher's hands. He looked skeptical. Like he couldn't believe the little boy could carry his weight. Until Christopher pushed. The nice man inched up the wall and grabbed the windowsill with his fingertips. He used whatever strength he had left to pull himself up. The nice man opened the filthy window and let the fresh air into the basement. He put his chest halfway through the opening and collapsed. Panting like a dog left in a car.

"Get up!" Christopher begged.

Christopher grabbed the nice man's bloody feet and pushed the rest of his body out of the window with all his might.

Then, Christopher slipped on the bloody table. He reached out, trying to find his footing. But the force was too great. Christopher fell to the ground.

Bringing the metal table down with him.

Crash!

The kitchen floor creaked upstairs. Christopher scrambled to his feet. The table lay upside down like a dead cockroach. There was no way to climb the legs.

"Stay here, David," the hissing lady said upstairs.

"She's coming," the nice man whispered. "You can make it!"

Christopher looked up at the window. Ten feet off the ground. The nice man stretched his body down from the window. Christopher ran. Jumped. Their bloody hands met for a moment, then slipped. Christopher fell to the ground.

"Turn off the light!" the nice man whispered.

The hissing lady turned the doorknob.

Christopher leapt up and grabbed the string hanging from the lightbulb. The nice man closed the curtains. In an instant, the world went black.

The door opened at the top of the stairs.

The kitchen light poured into the basement. Christopher crawled like a mouse and hid under the staircase.

The hissing lady walked down the stairs.

Creak. Creak. Creak.

Christopher's heart pounded. There was nowhere to run.

He watched her bloody shoes through the slits in the wooden stairs.

Creak. Creak. Creak.

Christopher held his breath. The blood pounded his temples. The hissing lady's feet came right to eye level. He reached through the slits and braced himself. One second. Two seconds. Three seconds. Four.

Swallow your fear or let your fear swallow you.

Christopher yanked back on the hissing lady's feet. She fell down the stairs, slamming her head on the bloody floor.

"AHHHH!" she hissed.

He only had seconds. Christopher ran from under the stairs and jumped over her outstretched arms. She reached up, tripping him. Christopher screamed and landed on the stairs above her. She reached for him. Her hands smearing blood up his pants as she climbed his body as if scaling a wall.

"There you are!" she hissed.

Christopher kicked back. The adrenaline coursing through his veins like the world's blood. He connected with her chest. Sending her backward. She hit the wall and screeched. He ran to the top of the stairs and turned. The hissing lady was already on her feet. Racing up the stairs after him. Faster than anything he'd ever seen. Christopher slammed the door shut.

BOOM.

The hissing lady charged into the door. Like a caged animal.

Christopher braced his body between the door and the kitchen wall.

"Mill Grove Plumbing?" Jill said on the telephone. "Can you come out immediately? I think something is wrong with my pipes."

BOOM. BOOM.

Christopher dug his heels into the ground. The hissing lady reached for the doorknob. It turned. Christopher reached for the dead bolt. Stretching his fingers above his head.

"YOU ARE GOING TO DIE!" she hissed.

Christopher reached as far as he could. He could feel the tendons in his shoulder ripping like taffy. But the dead bolt was too far. He could not reach it. His legs strained to keep her inside. But she was too powerful. His legs began to buckle.

BOOM. BOOM. BOOM.

Suddenly Christopher saw a bloody hand reach up his arm. He screamed. Until the hand passed him and snapped the dead bolt shut.

It was the nice man.

His face was pale and drawn. His eyes blinking, exhausted with pain.

"Come on," he said.

BOOM. BOOM. BOOM.

"DAVID, WHERE ARE YOU?!"

Her voice echoed through the house. The nice man crouched down and led Christopher through the kitchen. Jill was at the stove, making hot dogs in a large soup pot. But they weren't hot dogs.

They were fingers.

"DAVID!"

Christopher turned to see David Olson walk from the living room. The hissing lady pounded on the door. David flinched. Terrified. David reached for the dead bolt. Christopher was about to run back to stop him. The nice man grabbed Christopher's shoulder.

"She can't know David helped us. She'll kill him," he whispered.

Christopher nodded and followed the nice man outside.

"She'll search the streets first," he said. "Follow me."

The nice man limped, leading Christopher through the backyards. A huge deer ran out of a doghouse, howling bloody murder at them. The deer leapt for the nice man's throat. Until the chain yanked it back, and the deer landed on the slush-covered ground, whimpering.

"Guard dog," the nice man said. "Come on."

Christopher walked behind the nice man. They crept into a backyard. Next to a tire swing. Christopher heard the pitter-pat of feet.

He turned and saw Jenny Hertzog.

Dressed in her nightgown.

Hiding in the backyard.

Freezing to death.

He wondered if Jenny would ever believe what was happening in the backyard she used as a hiding place. Soon, the cold became too much. He saw Jenny Hertzog open the back door of her house and creep into the kitchen. The nice man gestured, and Christopher followed behind her. The house was smoky and dark. Jenny tiptoed into her entry hall, trying to go undetected. Her stepmother was in the living room. Asleep. Her Marlboro Red smoking in the ashtray. A daytime talk show was on. They were doing paternity tests.

"You ARE the father," the host said.

Jenny crept up the stairs without waking her stepmother. She passed her stepbrother's room. Quiet. She was just about to turn the corner when his door opened. He was older. With angry acne. And braces that he kept licking with his tongue.

"Jenny, you weren't in bed. Where have you been?" he asked.

She shrugged.

"I thought you were too sick to go to school. I stayed home to take care of you," he said.

She froze.

"So, let me take care of you," he said. "That nightgown is too small. Floods. Floods."

"Shut up, Scott," she finally said, defiantly.

"Don't tell me to fucking shut up, you slut. Come here."

Defeated, she went into his room and closed the door behind her. Christopher put his ear to the door and heard nothing other than music. Scott was playing an old song. Blue Moon. Christopher grabbed the doorknob to help Jenny.

"Don't. It's a trap," the nice man said.

But it was too late. Christopher opened the door. Standing inside were a dozen deer. Their fangs exposed. They rushed at the door. The nice man slammed it shut.

BANG. BANG. BANG. BANG. BANG.

The nice man raced Christopher through the house and opened the side door. There they saw . . .

. . . a baby basket.

A mailbox person held it. Thick zippers kept his eyes closed, but the black stitches on his mouth were just loose enough to sound the alarm. The mailbox person opened his mouth through the stitches and made the sound of a baby crying.

"Waaaaaaaaa!"

The nice man grabbed Christopher's hand. He dragged him past the mailbox person, toward the street. They ran together down the lawn. The hissing lady ran up the driveway, chasing after them. David Olson crawling like a dog behind her.

"STOP HIM!"

Her voice boomed through the street. The mailbox people fanned out through the neighborhood. Groping blindly with their arms outstretched. Hunting for the escaped prisoner. They made a solid wall along the street. Blocking both sides.

"We can't make it!" Christopher said.

"Hold on to me," the nice man said.

The nice man summoned all his strength. Just as he and Christopher were about to smash into the wall of mailbox people, the nice man jumped. They hurdled the mailbox people and landed safely on the street.

"STOP HELPING HIM!" she cursed the nice man.

The hissing lady jumped after them, trying to grab the nice man, but she missed. She landed on the street. Her feet started to smoke and burn. Leaving liquid skin on the pavement like a chemical spill. She peeled herself off the asphalt and dragged herself back to the lawn. Screaming in pain like a deer that had been hit by a car.

"She will heal in a minute," the nice man said. "Hurry."

The nice man ran with Christopher down the street. They raced past the mailbox people, each holding the string of the next, going on for miles with no end in sight. Christopher could feel the nice man's energy through his skin. The healing spreading across his body like static electricity on a wool sweater. The nice man closed his eyes, his eyeballs shifting back and forth under his eyelids like he was dreaming. In seconds, he jumped over the mailbox people again.

"How did you do that?" Christopher asked.

"I'll teach you."

They moved off the street and disappeared into the Mission Street Woods. The nice man led him down a path. The deer crashed the trail behind them. Nipping at their feet. A team of cats with two little mice. The nice man made a sharp left past the billy goat bridge. The sleeping man popped his head out of the hollow log.

"They're here!" the man screamed in his sleep.

The nice man jumped over the log and led Christopher down a narrow path of dead, jagged branches. The deer behind them got wedged in the bottleneck. The hollow log man screamed as the deer dragged their tongues across his face like a salt lick. Drowning him in spit. Right before they began to eat his face.

"Don't look at them," the nice man said.

They left the narrow path and ran across the clearing. To the tree. The nice man collapsed on the ground, straining to breathe. Exhausted.

"We only have a few seconds," the nice man said. "She knows you helped me now. She will do anything to get you back here."

"Then come with me," Christopher said.

"I can't. The hissing lady has the only key. I can't leave here without it. Neither can David."

A great shriek went up to the heavens as the hissing lady searched the woods.

"So, let's get the key. I'm invisible now. I can handle her," Christopher said.

"Listen to me," he barked. "However strong you become, she is stronger. And the next time she catches you, you will never get away. So, focus your mind. Do not daydream or fall asleep. I will work with David to get the key. I'll let you know when it's safe to come back."

"But I came here to save you."

"You did. Now go."

The nice man grabbed Christopher and pushed him up the tree. Plank by plank. Baby tooth by baby tooth. He reached the tree house door just as the hissing lady jumped into the clearing with David and the deer.

"STOP HELPING HIM!"

The nice man jumped down and rushed away into the shadows. The hissing lady ran at the tree. Christopher dragged his body into the tree house and quickly closed the door behind him.

Within seconds, the cotton candy air turned back to frozen December. Christopher opened the door and looked back down at the clearing. The hissing lady was gone, along with the rest of the imaginary people. He was back to the real side.

And Christopher had rescued the nice man.

CHAPTER 50

The moment Christopher came back from the imaginary side, he felt the price of his new powers. The tearing of the chain was now a throbbing in his hands. The lifting of the nice man to the window was now a pain in his shoulders that felt like torn ligaments.

But the worst was the headache.

It felt like a knife pushing his eyes through his eyelids. Compelling him to walk. Take a step. Take the next step.

He had to keep going.

He had to get back to school.

He climbed down the ladder and grabbed the white plastic bag from the low-hanging branch. He put it in his pocket for safety. Then, he limped his way back through the snow to school, making only one stop.

Jenny Hertzog's house.

He walked up to the door, rang the bell, then ran away. He knew that would be enough to wake up Scott's mother and buy Jenny Hertzog one more afternoon of peace.

He finally arrived at school five minutes before the final bell. Christopher snuck back in through the open window in the boys' bathroom. Then, he waited outside his homeroom until the bell rang and the hallway was flooded with students.

"Where have you been all day?" Ms. Lasko asked him suspiciously.

"I've been in class all day, Ms. Lasko. Don't you remember?"

Christopher smiled and sweetly touched her hand. Letting a little heat move from his fingers to hers.

"Yes," she said. "You've been in class all day. Good work, Christopher."

She patted the top of his head, and his brain soaked up the entire day's lesson plan like a sponge.

Ms. Lasko is...
Ms. Lasko is... going straight to the bar after work.

Christopher went home on the bus and sat behind Mr. Miller, the bus driver.

Mr. Miller called... his ex-wife.
Mr. Miller is... going to spend Christmas with his children this year.

"Hello, Mr. Miller." Christopher smiled.

"Sit down. Don't distract me!" the man barked.

Christopher went home, where his mother was waiting for him with hot bread and chicken soup. He made sure not to eat the bread. Because he knew he would have to stay awake until the nice man told him it was safe.

My mom's arm...
My mom's arm... still hurts from the hissing lady's coffee.

"How was school today, honey?" she asked.

"It was okay," he said.

I can't tell...
I can't tell... my mom or the hissing lady will hear.

"What did you learn?" she asked.

"Not much," he said, then recounted a few details from Ms. Lasko's lesson plan.

My mom doesn't know...
My mom doesn't know... I will do anything to keep her safe.

That night, when his mother went to sleep, Christopher slipped down into the kitchen. He grabbed the milk carton and poured a big glass of milk. He looked at Emily Bertovich's picture, searching for any clue as to whether or not the hissing lady was watching him.

But all he saw was Emily smiling.

He put Emily back, then quietly searched the cupboard and found some Oreo cookies. He put them on a paper plate. Then he grabbed the loaf of Town

Talk white bread and chipped ham and made a sandwich with lettuce and mayonnaise. He put the evidence away and tiptoed down to the basement.

The basement was dry and clean. The furnace in the corner kept the room nice and toasty. Christopher didn't think the nice man would ever come here. It would be the first place the hissing lady would look. But he wanted it to be ready for him just in case. And the truth was, Christopher was scared without him. He didn't want to stay up all night by himself.

Christopher walked with the big glass of milk and the cookies and sandwich over to the sofa. He remembered when he used to leave out cookies for Santa Claus. Christopher's mother made delicious peanut butter blossoms with a Hershey's Kiss right in the middle of each one. The heat from the cookie melted the Kiss just a little bit. She would kiss his cheeks and ask, "Where are my kisses?" And he would laugh, and then Christopher gathered the cookies on a plate with a nice glass of milk and left them under the tree for Santa.

He suddenly remembered waking up really early one Christmas. It was still dark out. And even though his mother warned him not to leave bed or else Santa would know he was being naughty, Christopher couldn't help himself. He had asked Santa for a Bad Cat stuffed animal, and he just had to know if Santa brought it. Christopher tiptoed down the hallway of their railroad apartment and peeked his head into their living room.

That's when he saw his father.

Eating the cookies and drinking the milk.

Christopher's father put down Santa's snack, then went to the closet. He grabbed a big, white pillowcase hidden behind ordinary bedsheets. Then, he pulled a bunch of wrapped presents out of the case and put them under the tree. The last was a nice big present, wrapped in Bad Cat paper. Christopher's father then went to the kitchen, where he finished the cookies. One by one in silence. Then, Christopher went back down the hallway and went to sleep.

The next morning, Christopher chose that big present with the Bad Cat wrapping paper as his very first gift.

"What do you think it is, Christopher?" his mother asked.

"I don't know," he said quietly.

Christopher opened the gift wrap and saw his beloved Bad Cat stuffed animal.

"Isn't that a nice present from Santa?" his father asked.

Christopher nodded dutifully even though he knew his father was the only person who put presents under the tree. Christopher went to church later that day and heard the other kids excited for the presents that Santa brought them that morning. Christopher didn't have the heart to blow it for the other kids. He never told anyone that Santa was an imaginary friend. He just pretended for the rest of the day and smiled when his mother took a picture of his father in front of that old Christmas tree. The picture that rested in the silver frame on his bookshelf upstairs. That was the last year his father was there at Christmas. His father died in the bathtub a week later. And when the next Christmas came around, his mother made the cookies with the Hershey's Kiss in the middle. She said, "Where are my kisses?" as she put them under the tree. And the next morning, the cookies and milk were gone, replaced by presents. Christopher didn't have a father anymore. But he still had Santa Claus.

Christopher set down the milk and cookies on the side table and went to the old suitcase. He opened it up and looked at the old clothes, which still smelled a little like tobacco smoke. His father had a favorite sweater that was warm but not scratchy. He also had a pair of smooth cotton slacks that he'd owned for so long, they were as soft as pajamas. Christopher took the outfit, an old sleeping bag, and a pillow, and laid them on the sofa. Then, without making a sound, he tried to think as loud as he could for the nice man to hear him.

I don't know if it's safe for you to hide here. And I know I can't talk to you out loud because she might be listening. But I hope you can hear me thinking. I got you some food because you must be hungry from eating that dog food all the time. I will pretend I forgot it here in case she's watching. And I'll leave you a sleeping bag so you can rest on the couch.

Christopher laid out his father's old clothes.

These are my dad's clothes. I don't know if they'll fit you, but I know that your clothes are covered in blood and dirt. So, I hope you can fit in them and be more comfortable. Oh, and one last thing...

Christopher reached into his pocket and pulled out all the aspirin he had.

I always have a headache now, so I take these all the time. They also make my fever stop a little. But I saw how much she hurt you, so I want you to have them to take away your pain. I'll get more tomorrow. I know you need to heal so you and David can get the key and escape.

Christopher took the old plastic bag out of his pocket. He put it right above the sweater where the head should have been, then covered it with a pillow. Just in case. Christopher walked to the basement stairs, but before he climbed, he turned back to the little recovery bed he made for the nice man. He looked at the cookies and milk left for his real-life Santa Claus. His real imaginary friend.

CHAPTER 51

Something had changed. The sheriff could feel it. He had been in the Mission Street Woods since early that afternoon. He had walked the crime scene for the hundredth time when out of nowhere, it felt like the woods woke up around him. Rodents who had been hiding in holes suddenly made digging sounds. The birds flew off the branches as if someone had shot a gun that only they could hear. The temperature instantly dropped to below freezing. It felt like someone had left a window open and a draft was running through the world.

If David Olson was buried alive, then who buried him?

Because it wasn't the trees.

The sheriff shook off the uneasy feeling and went back to his work. He walked up and down the footpath, looking for clues. Of course, the case was fifty years old, so he knew he wouldn't find a fresh scene. No sign of abduction. No hole in the ground. No trapdoor. But maybe he would find something else. An idea. An insight. Some reasonable explanation that would allow the sheriff to put David Olson to rest in his own mind the way that Ambrose had put him to rest that morning.

But nothing came.

Except that uneasy feeling.

The sheriff passed the spot where David's body was found. He looked at the torn earth and remembered standing next to Ambrose and Kate Reese at David's funeral. It was only that morning, and yet it felt like it happened two years ago. Father Tom gave a beautiful eulogy. Ambrose insisted on carrying his little brother's casket. The sheriff had to give the old man credit. He couldn't think of a lot of men who could have been a pallbearer on two arthritic knees.

When they reached the cemetery, they walked the casket over to the grave.

As Father Tom spoke, the sheriff looked out over the cemetery. He could barely hear the words "love" and "forgiveness" and "peace." He could only think about the thousands of headstones with generations of families lying side by side. Husbands. Wives. Mothers. Fathers. Daughters. Sons. The sheriff thought about all those families. All those Christmas dinners and presents and memories. And then, he had the strangest thought.

God is a murderer.

The sheriff had no idea where it came from. There was no menace to it. No malice. Nothing sacrilegious. It was just a thought that drifted there quietly like the clouds that had gathered above the cemetery. One cloud was shaped like a hand. Another like a hammer. And one looked like a man with a long beard.

God is a murderer.

The sheriff had arrested murderers before. Some begged that they were innocent or cursed him or screamed that it was all a misunderstanding. Some just sat there, still as statues, calm and sometimes covered in their victim's blood. They were the truly frightening ones. Except of course the worst of them. The one woman who killed her own daughter. The girl with the painted nails. Not with a knife or a gun. But with neglect.

If God were arrested for murder, what would the people do with Him?

The sheriff looked out over the graves and thought about the girl with the painted nails. Hers was the last funeral he had attended before David Olson's. The sheriff was the only person at the girl's funeral other than the priest. The sheriff couldn't bear to have the girl laid to rest in the plain pine casket that the city provided. So, he cashed out some of his savings and bought her the best he could afford on an honest cop's salary. When the funeral was over, he drove home and sat in his apartment. He wanted to pick up the phone and call his mother, but she had passed years ago. He wanted to take his father out for a drink, but his father was gone, too, along with his aunt, who died right after his high school graduation. The sheriff was an only child. He was the only one in his family left alive.

God had taken the rest.

If God were arrested for murder, would people ask for the death penalty?

The sheriff left Ambrose and Kate after the funeral and drove straight to the Mission Street Woods. The answer to David was in here. He was sure of it. He parked his cruiser and walked past the bulldozers of the Collins Construction

Company. The judge (aka Mr. Collins' golfing buddy of the last thirty years) had given the Collins Construction Company "temporary" permission to begin working again so long as they didn't disturb the crime scene. The "temporary" permission lasted just long enough to put the Collins team back on schedule. Lucky them. The security guard told the sheriff that since the blizzard ended, they had cleared off a huge section of trees. Most of the trees would be gone by Christmas.

If David Olson was buried alive, then who buried him?

Because it wasn't the trees.

The security guard explained that all of the bulldozing had torn up a lot of fresh earth. And the crew kept finding strange things buried out there. They found an old hacksaw, the kind the Amish still used. They found old hammers and rusty nails. A bunch of broken shovels, one of them with the shaft burnt. Tools going back to the 17th century, when England gave the entire state of Pennsylvania to William Penn to settle a debt.

At least a hundred years before men ever thought to mine coal.

The sheriff looked at the collection of old tools. Saws, hammers, and shovels. And that's when he started to have an idea. He could feel it. An itch forming in his mind. As good as a back scratch.

What were these tools for?

The sheriff moved the questions around his brain. There was an answer here.

Were the tools for building?

The sheriff walked down the narrow path.

Or were the tools for burying?

The sheriff reached the clearing.

Or were the tools for murdering?

The clearing was still. Almost as if the wind was holding its breath. The sheriff looked up. And there it was. The tree house. Resting on the old tree.

If David Olson was buried alive, then who buried him?

Because it wasn't the trees.

The sheriff approached the tree. He looked up. The sunlight poured through the clouds above, making the frost on the branches glow with golden light. Instantly the thought came to him. As clear as the sun.

If God were arrested for murder, the people would ask for the death penalty.

The sheriff stared up at the tree house. The wind returned, moving through his hair like a whisper.

But the people could never kill God, so they killed His Son Jesus instead.

Some deer started to walk toward the sheriff.

Did Jesus die for our sins?

Or did He die for His Father's?

He held this thought like a smoker cradling his last match.

The people didn't put Jesus to death as a martyr.

They put Him to death as an accomplice.

He could feel the answer on the tip of his tongue.

Jesus forgave us for killing Him.

His Father never did.

The sheriff stopped. He knew that in one second, he would see how it was all connected. David Olson. The old tools. The Mission Street Woods. The clearing. The clouds. All wrapped together like the tree roots around David Olson's skeleton. One more second and he would know how David Olson really died.

And that's when he heard the sound of a baby crying.

Coming from inside the tree house.

CHAPTER 52

Hello?" the sheriff shouted. "This is the Mill Grove Sheriff's Department."

The sheriff waited to hear if anyone in the tree house would acknowledge him. There was no answer. Only the sound of the baby crying.

The sheriff drew his gun and walked toward the tree house. He called into his radio for backup, but he got nothing but static. Maybe he was too far in the middle of the woods. Maybe it was the thick clouds.

Or maybe it was something else.

The sheriff reached the tree. He looked down and saw footprints that belonged to a child. They were fresh prints. It looked like someone was just here. The sheriff touched the tree. It didn't feel like bark. It felt like . . . like a baby's soft skin.

The baby was inside the tree house. Crying.

"Who's up there?!" he demanded.

There was no response. Just wind. Like hissing. The crying reached a fever pitch. Did someone abandon their baby out here? He'd seen worse. The sheriff looked up at the ladder of the tree house. Little 2x4s nailed into the tree. The sheriff holstered his gun and put his hands and feet on the ladder. He climbed a few steps. The baby was screaming.

Ambrose was at home with his girlfriend.

They heard a baby crying.

Someone left a baby carriage on the porch.

There was no baby.

The sheriff stopped. All of his training screamed at him to keep climbing that ladder to help that baby. But his instincts told him to stop. He felt like a dog reacting to an invisible whistle. That's what the baby cries were. They were a dog whistle. A dinner bell. An ambush.

He knew this was wrong.

There was something evil here.

If his deputies had done what the sheriff started to do next, he would have suspended them. But the sheriff was no fool. He started to climb back down the ladder. Away from this tree. Away from these woods. Away from whatever that dog whistle was. And that's when he heard the voice.

"Daddy."

The instant he heard the sound, his blood froze.

It was the girl with the painted nails.

"Daddy."

She sounded exactly like she did that day in the hospital. The day before she died. She touched his hand with her little fingers and smiled with those broken teeth and called him that word.

"Daddy."

The sheriff climbed. He reached the top of the ladder. He looked through the little window. The tree house was empty. Just little footprints on the wood floor.

"Daddy, help."

The sheriff heard her voice right behind the tree house door. He pulled out his gun with one hand and reached for the doorknob with the other.

"Daddy, please help me."

The sheriff threw open the door.

He saw her hiding in the corner.

The girl with the painted nails.

Her teeth weren't broken. Her little body wasn't broken. She was an angel. With a key around her neck.

"Hi, Daddy. You never finished the story. Do you want to read to me?" she asked, smiling.

The sheriff smiled, his eyes welling with tears.

"Of course I do, honey," he said.

"Then, come inside," she said.

She started to walk toward him. She took her little hand and gently helped him into the tree house.

The door closed behind him.

The sheriff looked around the tree house. It was no longer empty. It looked like her old hospital room. The little girl with the painted nails climbed into the bed. She got under the covers and brought the blanket under her little chin.

"The book is on the nightstand," she said.

When the sheriff saw the book, he got an uneasy feeling. He remembered that her mother never read to her. She was never allowed to go to school. So, the book of fairy tales that he read to her in the hospital was the only book she ever heard. It was the book he read to her the night she died. She fell asleep before he could finish the last story. She never got to hear the ending.

"I want to know how it ends," she said. "Start reading from here."

She pointed to a page. The sheriff cleared his throat and read.

"Grandma, what big eyes you have!"

"All the better to see you with, my dear."

The girl with the painted nails closed her eyes. When the sheriff finished the story, he realized that she was asleep. She still didn't get to hear the end of the story. The sheriff touched the hair on her head and smiled. He turned out the light. Then, he watched her rest until he fell asleep in the chair right next to her.

When the sheriff woke up, he had no memory of the tree house looking like her hospital room. No memory of reading that story. He didn't know why he had fallen asleep in the tree house. The only vague recollection he had was the memory of the girl with the painted nails calling him "Daddy."

When the sheriff left the tree house, he looked up. The clouds were gone. The day was night. And the moon was a sideways smile. The sheriff felt like he had fallen asleep in the tree house for an hour at most.

But when he looked at his watch, it read 2:17 a.m.

The sheriff walked down the 2x4 ladder, and his boots hit the snowy ground with a crunch like broken bones. He looked around the clearing and saw that the deer were long gone. It was just him and the moonlight. Alone with his thoughts.

Why didn't I save her?

The sheriff walked back through the Mission Street Woods. He looked at the footpath and saw the years of neglect. Old rusted beer cans. Condoms. Bongs made out of plastic honey bears. Stuffed with the resin of the marijuana kids were growing in their parents' basements. Along with things that were much worse. Things that make people crazy. People like her. The girl with the painted nails' mother. Things that made her do terrible things to her daughter.

I should have saved her.

The sheriff shoved his freezing hands in his pockets and moved through the woods. The cold bit at his ears. Worming into his brain. If the neighbor had smelled the apartment one day earlier, he could have saved her. Why didn't God let him know one day earlier? He could think of a hundred people who deserved to die more than the girl with the painted nails. A thousand. A million. Seven billion. Why did God kill her instead of other people? And then, the answer came to him. Cold and quiet. God didn't kill her instead of other people. In the end, He kills everyone.

Because God is a murderer, Daddy.

CHAPTER 53

Brady Collins woke up in his bed. His mother had finally let him out of the doghouse when he woke up with a bad fever and couldn't go to school. She asked him if he was ready to act like a human being, and he said yes. They all ate breakfast at the table. His father complained about "that fucking sheriff" delaying the Mission Street Woods project and how the loans were coming due. If the project died, the family was bankrupt. "So, why do you spend so much God damn money, Kathleen?!" As his father railed against the small pond he mistook for the world, Brady finished his breakfast, then spent the rest of the day in bed. He slept the whole time, stopping only to take one long pee that smelled sweet like baby aspirin. Then, he went back to bed and slept all the way through lunch and dinner. When he woke up, he was covered in sweat. His fever had broken, but the itch on his arm was worse than ever. Brady looked at the alarm clock to see what time it was. The date looked right. December 18. But the time was all wrong.

An hour can't have more than sixty minutes.

Maybe he was still asleep. Maybe he was still having that nightmare. The one with his mother luring him off the street and killing him while Special Ed laughed. Brady walked down the hall into his parents' bedroom. His parents were asleep. They were so much nicer when they were asleep. His father's nightstand was covered with business papers. His mother's nightstand was covered with invitations and thank-you cards. And her letter opener. It was sterling silver. It cost a lot of money. She fired their old housekeeper for stealing it. But it turned out his mother just lost it. And when she found it a week later, she didn't give their old housekeeper her job back because the new one was from the Middle East and worked harder for less money. Desperate people do that, she told a friend on the phone. Brady picked up the letter opener. He looked at the reflection of the moon in the silver. It looked like a row of smiling teeth. Brady tucked it into the string of his bathrobe. Then, he knelt down and held his mother's hand. The itch on his arm began to heat up. It became warm and soft like his mother's smile the times she loved him. He put her hand on his head and pretended that she was patting it and telling him he was good. Good boy, Brady. It felt so much better than the nightmares where she killed him, saying the same thing over and over, while Special Ed laughed.

"You're such a bad little dog, Brady. Somebody should put you down."

2:17

Special Ed pulled the gun out from under his pillow. That's how scary that nightmare was. He and his friends were out on the street playing baseball with fresh baseball gloves. But the cars kept coming faster and faster as the deer kept chasing them. His mother reached her arm out to get them off the street, but just as Special Ed took his mother's hand, Brady Collins and Jenny Hertzog jumped out of nowhere and stabbed her. Her blood ran into the street, and Brady took his little serpent's tongue and lapped it up like a dog in a toilet. That's when Special Ed woke up. He was covered in sweat. His fever had broken. All day, it didn't matter how many times he turned the pillow over and back. He could still feel the fever on his forehead. But now, all he felt was the itch on his arm. He looked at the five empty chambers and scratched his arm with the barrel. It didn't matter how much he scratched it, his arm kept itching. And he kept thinking. About one thing.

You need more than one bullet, Eddie. Listen to Grandma.

Special Ed got out of bed and walked pitter-pat downstairs. He went to the study, got a nice leather chair, and leaned his ear against the cold metal of his father's gun safe. He started to turn the dial in three-number combinations. 1-1-1. 1-1-2. 1-1-3. All night. Because the war was coming, and the good guys needed to win the war. When dawn broke, Special Ed stopped his quest at 2-1-6 and went to his mother, asleep in the master bedroom. Alone. He was so happy that she was alive. He held her hand. The itch moved down his fingers to hers. Special Ed's mother opened her eyes slowly. She looked at him sleepily and smiled. "What's wrong with my Eddie?" she asked.

"Nothing, Mom. I feel much better," he said.

"Good. I love you. I left you a slice of cake in the fridge," she said. She patted his head, closed her eyes, and went back to sleep. Special Ed waited until she had drifted far away. Then, he kissed her forehead and whispered in her ear.

"Mom, what's the combination to Dad's gun safe?"

2:17

Jenny Hertzog stood over her sleeping stepbrother. The fever that had kept her home from school was gone. And there was nothing in its place except the itch, which twitched its way to the knife in her hand. She stared at her stepbrother. As angry as he had been after somebody ding-dong-ditched their house, woke up his mother, and stopped his afternoon fun. The moonlight made his face pasty and pale. His acne stood out like stars in the sky. She thought his blood would do his face some good. She could take his blood and color his cheeks rouge red like the whores in the movies he loved to watch on his computer. Or a clown. She took the knife and gently pressed it in the middle of his palm. He turned a little in bed, but he did not wake. Jenny closed her eyes and pushed the itch down her arm through the knife and into his skin. As the itch ate its way into her stepbrother's filthy hands, she thought about her beautiful dream. Her mother was still alive. And Jenny's father had never married that horrible woman with her even more horrible son. In her dream, Jenny saw her mother running through the backyard, hunting for Christopher. Jenny's mother came rushing up with a little pet boy, but Christopher was too fast, and he disappeared down the street. Jenny's mother chased after him, but she couldn't catch up. So, she came back to Jenny's back-yard. She scaled the ivy walls into Jenny's bedroom. She smelled so nice. Like Chanel No. 5. She held Jenny in her arms and listened to Jenny tell stories about school and dance practice. Jenny's mother then explained that Jenny shouldn't stab her stepbrother Scott. Because there was a war coming. And their side needed all the soldiers they could get. Jenny asked if she could kill Scott after the war was over. Her mother explained that she wouldn't have to. All she would have to do was look up at the moon staring back at the Earth and say a little prayer.

"Wash him away, God. Wash him away in Floods. Floods."

2:17

Mrs. Henderson stared at the clock as she stood in the warm kitchen. Mr. Henderson had finally come home. Without an explanation. Or an apology. But still, he was home. So, she made him his favorite meal, as she had more than a thousand times over the last fifty years. He didn't notice. He didn't care. Mrs. Henderson asked her husband if he remembered what today was. She waited for him to remember lifting the veil off her beautiful young face. Her red hair tumbling down over her shoulder on their wedding night. She waited for him to remember it was their anniversary. But he never did.

Because he doesn't love you anymore.

Mrs. Henderson tried to kiss Mr. Henderson like it was their wedding night, but he pushed her away. Mrs. Henderson started crying when he said he didn't want to kiss her anymore. She had kissed her husband for the last time, and she didn't even know it, so she could cherish it. She gave him fifty years. Mrs. Henderson went to the counter. She looked at herself in the glass of the window. She was worse than ugly now. She was invisible. Her husband had taken her youth, and he hated the snakeskin that was left behind. This was her last year of teaching. At the end of the school year, there would be nothing left. No school. No job. No husband. No children. She would have nothing but these walls. She started to scratch her head. God, it wouldn't stop itching. Why wouldn't it stop itching?

Mrs. Henderson stood behind her husband. She waited to see if he would turn around. If he would say anything. But he kept eating as if nothing had happened. He made his little yum yum moan sounds when he chewed. God, that chewing. That awful chewing. Those moans he made when he ate his favorite meal. Didn't he remember that she had to ask his mother how to cook that meal? Didn't he remember that a beautiful young woman with gorgeous red hair worked like a God damn slave to perfect that meal that he keeps chewing and chewing like a God damn dog? Did he think that the men he ran around with were going to learn to cook him that meal?

You better turn around. You better ask me how I'm feeling.

Mr. Henderson didn't turn around. Mrs. Henderson thought so loudly she didn't understand how he couldn't hear her.

If you pick up that newspaper, I'm going to make you remember lifting the veil off my face.

Mr. Henderson picked up the newspaper.

Okay, you just picked up the newspaper. Let's see how the Steelers are doing while your wife cries behind you. Well, guess what? Your wife just stopped crying. Did you notice that I stopped crying? Do you have any idea what is happening behind you? Do you think your little mousy wife is standing there just begging for whatever crumbs you call love? Well, just turn around, and you will see who your mousy wife really is. Turn around, and you will know I am not invisible. I am a BEAUTIFUL FUCKING WOMAN AND I DESERVE YOUR FUCKING RESPECT.

"Honey?" Mrs. Henderson whispered sweetly.

"What now?" her husband groaned.

Then, he turned around, and she plunged the kitchen knife straight through his neck.

CHAPTER 54

Mary Katherine woke up in a cold sweat. Her fever had broken, but her body didn't feel good. In fact, it felt worse. She was bloated. Her joints ached. Her breasts were tender. The itch on her arm was driving her crazy. And she felt a little queasy. It was probably the fact that she had stayed in bed all day and slept without eating.

Or maybe it was that dream.

In her dream, it was still three days ago. And none of the horrible things that had happened to her had happened yet. She was babysitting Christopher. She found him in the tree house. She went home. But this time, when the sinful thoughts came to her, she didn't fantasize about the sheriff. She didn't put Doug's awful thing in her mouth. She didn't wake up in the tree house with no memory of how she got there. She didn't come home at eight o'clock in the morning to find her parents seething in the living room. And she didn't have to spend two days taking finals with a 102-degree fever from staying out in a freezing tree house all night. In her dream, none of that happened.

Because the Virgin Mary stopped her.

In her dream, Mary Katherine was back in her room. When the sinful thoughts started, she heard a knocking on the window. She turned to the window and saw a woman floating outside.

"Please let me in, Mary Katherine," the woman whispered.

"How do you know my name?"

"Because your parents named you after me," the woman said.

"I thought I was named for the Virgin Mary."

The woman said nothing. She simply smiled and waited for two plus two to find its way to four. Mary Katherine studied her face. The woman didn't look like an angel. She didn't look like all of those paintings and statues that Mary Katherine had seen in churches her whole life. She had no makeup. Her hair wasn't perfect. She was a simple woman. Poor and dignified. With dirt on her clothes from giving birth in a manger. She was real.

"Please, open the window, Mary Katherine," the woman whispered.

Mary Katherine walked over to the window and slowly unhooked the lock. When the window opened, the freezing air of December hit her white cotton nightgown. The cold made her flesh stand up all over her body.

"Thank you. It's so cold out there. And no one would help me," the woman whispered.

The woman sat in Mary Katherine's white wicker chair and shivered. Mary Katherine took the extra blanket from the foot of her bed and gave it to her. The woman took Mary Katherine's hands. She was ice-cold, but a warm itch ran through her fingers.

"What are you doing here?" Mary Katherine asked.

"I'm here to save you, Mary Katherine," the woman said.

"From what?"

"From Hell, of course."

"Yes, please. How do I keep from going to Hell?" Mary Katherine asked.

The woman smiled and opened her mouth. But when she spoke, there were no words. All Mary Katherine could hear was the sound of a baby crying.

That's when she woke up.

Mary Katherine sat up in bed. For a moment, the dream occupied her mind. But soon, the memories of everything she had done flooded back. Her horrible sexual thoughts. Doug's thing in her mouth. Waking up in the tree house and rushing home to her parents, who had never been more disappointed in all their lives. Mary Katherine's face was hot with shame. The pit in her stomach felt permanent.

She felt like she was going to throw up.

Mary Katherine rushed to the bathroom. She opened the toilet and knelt in front of it like an altar. She started to throw up, but it was a dry heave. There was no food in her stomach. There was only that pit. After a moment, the nausea passed.

But the taste was still there.

Mary Katherine took the mouthwash out of her medicine cabinet. She filled the cap to the rim with blue liquid and filled her mouth with it like her Irish grandfather did with whiskey sours at Christmas. The Listerine sat in her mouth like a cold blue ocean.

Then, it started to heat up.

The heat covered her tongue like the itch on her arm. Tears began to fill her eyes as seconds turned to minutes, but she wouldn't stop. She couldn't stop. The mouthwash burned like Hell, but she didn't dare spit it out. She just held it there, begging God to take it all away. Burn the taste off her tongue like a memory killed by time.

Make me forget.

Make me a child.

Make me forget Doug's thing.

Make me forget I liked it.

Eventually, her flesh won, and she spit the liquid out in a gasp of pain. She left the bathroom and moved down the hall to the master bedroom. She looked at her parents sleeping in the king-size bed. All she wanted to do was crawl in between them the way she did when she was little. She knelt in front of her father and took his hand. She closed her eyes and asked for his forgiveness. The itch moved through her fingers to her father's hand. He stirred for a moment, then turned over and started snoring.

She spent the rest of the night writing her essay for Notre Dame about Jesus' mother, the Virgin Mary. She thought if she could get into Notre Dame, her parents would forgive her.

In the morning, her mother came downstairs and made breakfast. Mary Katherine tried to engage her in conversation, but her mother was too disappointed to speak. The only thing her mother told her was that she was allowed to go to school and volunteer at Shady Pines. Then, it was right back home.

"No friends. No Doug. No nothing."

"Yes, ma'am. I'm sorry," Mary Katherine said. "Where's Dad?"

"He's in bed. He doesn't feel well this morning," her mother said.

Mary Katherine rode the bus to school. She looked up at the sky and saw the beautiful clouds floating above her. For a moment, she remembered a rhyme Mrs. Radcliffe taught them in CCD.

Clouds gave us rain.
God gave us floods.
Mary gave her son.
Jesus gave His blood.

When she arrived at school, Doug was outside, waiting for her. He was the last person she wanted to talk to right now. Just seeing him made her want to throw up. So, she snuck around the side entrance to avoid him and waited under the stairs for ten whole minutes while the world passed above her.

When the bell rang, Mary Katherine ran down the hall. She was late for first period. She had been so wrapped up in her life for the last three days, she had completely forgotten that today was the history final. It was her last final before Christmas break. She needed this grade to keep her straight-A average. She needed this grade to get into Notre Dame. She needed Notre Dame for her parents to forgive her.

Mary Katherine tried to focus on the test, but all she noticed were the aches in her body. The itch on her arm was screaming. And she just didn't understand why her boobs hurt so much. Was that what happened to girls after they became orally sexual? She didn't know. But she didn't dare look it up on the internet because her parents monitored her search history. And she couldn't use the library's computer because the administration monitored everything since some boys were caught downloading porn last year. She wished she knew a counselor she could ask, but counselors were for girls with problems or reputations. Like Debbie Dunham. Mary Katherine never had any problems. Not until now.

She felt like she was going to throw up again.

She somehow managed to finish her test and get through the school day by skipping lunch and swatting away Doug's texts like flies. After school, she came home to an icy silence. The only thing her parents said to her was that they were going to church.

"Do you want to join us or do you want to rot in Hell?" her father asked.

Mary Katherine rode in silence all the way to church. She sat dutifully on the hard bench despite her physical discomfort. She didn't know why Father Tom was holding mass on a Thursday night, but she didn't dare question it. Mary Katherine had come to this building fifty-two Sundays (plus Christmas Eves and Christmas Days and Good Fridays and Ash Wednesdays and CCD) every year since she was born. And yet, she realized she had never really seen the people who came here at night when everyone else was home and safe. She didn't even know these people existed. But there they were, some dressed as homeless people. Some were bickering with each other. Some of them seemed a little crazy. Or a little sick. So, Mary Katherine paid particular attention to Father Tom's homily. When he asked the congregation to pray for the refugees in the Middle East before another war broke out, Mary Katherine turned off all noise about Notre Dame, Doug, and her parents, and prayed to deliver those poor people.

When they started the profession of the faith, she saw Mrs. Radcliffe with the collection basket. Mary Katherine remembered all of those years in CCD. Mrs. Radcliffe told her parents she was such a good student. Such a good little girl. She wanted to be that girl again. The girl in the white gown receiving her first Holy Communion. The girl who learned from Mrs. Radcliffe that the Communion wafer was the body of Christ and the wine was His blood. The little girl who told the boys to stop making fun of Mrs. Radcliffe after her big boobs brushed against the chalkboard in CCD and for the rest of the class, she had two perfect white chalky headlights on her blouse.

When Mrs. Radcliffe brought the collection basket to her row, Mary Katherine gave her all of the money she had.

"Thank you for teaching me about God, Mrs. Radcliffe," she said.

Mary Katherine smiled.

Mrs. Radcliffe did not smile back.

She just scratched her arm.

The rite of Communion began. Father Tom led the congregation in the Lord's Prayer. Mary Katherine stood up with her parents to receive Communion. She suddenly had a terrible feeling in the pit of her stomach. Mary Katherine reached the front of the line. She stood in front of Father Tom with her hands open.

"Body of Christ," he said.

Mary Katherine brought the wafer to her mouth. She made the sign of the cross and chewed it as she had at least fifty-two times a year since she was seven years old. But this time, the wafer didn't taste like bland Styrofoam.

It tasted like flesh.

Mary Katherine stopped chewing. She looked up and saw her parents staring at her. She wanted to spit the wafer out, but she didn't dare. She went to Mrs.

Radcliffe, who was holding the goblet of wine. Mary Katherine normally didn't take the wine, but she had to wash this taste out of her mouth. Mrs. Radcliffe handed her the goblet. Mary Katherine made the sign of the cross and drank the wine. But it didn't taste like wine.

It tasted like blood.

Mary Katherine forced a smile and a sign of the cross and ran to the bathroom. She went to the sink and spit out the flesh and blood. But when she looked into the sink, all she saw was a wafer and wine.

Mary Katherine suddenly felt her stomach come up. She rushed to the handicapped stall. It was always the cleanest. She got on her knees and threw up the eggs she had for dinner. She sat there for a moment, catching her breath. Then, she flushed the toilet and went to the sink.

She wiped away the thin layer of sweat that had broken out on her forehead with a coarse paper towel. Then, she fished in her purse for peppermint Tic Tacs to wash the wretched taste out of her mouth. She couldn't find any mints, but she did find a stray tampon hidden on the bottom of her purse.

That's when she realized her period was late.

Mary Katherine stopped. She thought about her aching body. Her tender breasts. The horrible nausea she felt all morning. The pit in her stomach. If she didn't know any better, she would have thought she was pregnant. At first, the thought terrified her, but quickly, her mind calmed down. She couldn't be pregnant. It was impossible.

After all, she was a virgin.

And virgins can't get pregnant.

Everybody knows that.

CHAPTER 55

The wind howled outside. The lights began to turn off. And it was almost time for the old people to sleep. Ambrose had been reading his brother's diary every minute since he'd found it. He wanted to stop several times, but he wouldn't allow himself. His eyes could handle this much information, but he didn't know about his heart. The feeling was more than guilt or regret. He had experienced plenty of each over the last fifty years. It was the diary itself. Everything about it reminded him of David. It smelled like him. It felt like him. And of course, it had that handwriting.

It looked like the walls of an insane asylum.

Most little kids have a chicken scratch scrawl, but when David's mind turned, he took the prize. He wrote in the weirdest combination of capital letters, lowercase, cursive, and printing Ambrose had ever seen. Everything was a little off. Just like David was a little off. Ambrose had expected to finish the diary in a couple of hours. But somehow, one day stretched to two, and Ambrose wasn't even halfway done. Every page was filled with so many sketches, drawings, and hieroglyphics that sentences couldn't be read.

They had to be excavated.

But if there was a clue in here, he was going to find it. Ambrose rubbed his tired eyes and opened the diary again. The leather cracked. He continued to read.

April 1st

Ambrose said he was too busy to come to the woods today, but that's okay. He is on the varsity baseball team and has important things to do. I just wish I could show him the inside of my tree house. It took me so long to build it by myself. But maybe that's what makes it special. When you go in, you can walk around town. But it's not really town. It's a copy of town. People think they are alone, but they're not. Imaginary people are with them all the time. Some people are very nice. Some are very bad. But none of them can see me, though, so it's okay. In the daylight, I'm invisible like Wonder Woman's jet. So, I am safe until night falls. That's when the woman with burnt feet can find me. She always makes that terrible hissing noise. I just wish Ambrose would come and see it for himself.

April 13th

I am becoming a superhero. When I am on the imaginary side, I can jump really high if I think about it hard enough. But then, when I leave, I feel sick. I woke up today with a very bad headache. I thought the headaches were over. But they aren't and now I have a fever. My mother is starting to get worried, but I can't tell her what's going on because I think the woman with the burnt feet is watching me. So, I pretended I was okay. But I don't know if I'm okay. I'm starting to get scared.

April 23rd

I am having trouble sleeping because I'm so sick. And I'm afraid of the nightmares. I thought they were mine for a long time, but now I think I am having the whole town's nightmares at the same time. The things people dream are terrifying. Everyone is so unhappy. The woman with the burnt feet keeps finding me. I am afraid to go to sleep tonight.

May 3rd

The deer are looking at me again. They are working for the woman with the burnt feet. I know it. I want to tell Ambrose the truth, so he can help me. But I know I sound crazy. And I know she is listening. I want to run away, but I can't leave Ambrose.

<u>May 9th</u>

I don't want to sleep anymore. The nightmares have been so bad that I see them when I'm awake. I don't remember how many I've had by this point. Several a night because they keep waking me up. They are always different, but the ending is always the same. Somebody tries to kill me. Usually it's the woman with the burnt feet. But sometimes, she has other people do it. Last night was the worst. I was on the street because she can't walk on it without burning her feet. So, she pretended to be my mom to bring me over to the lawn. And when I wouldn't come to the lawn for her, she sent Ambrose out to the street with a knife. I couldn't get up. The hissing woman made Ambrose stab me. It was so real that when I woke up, I had to get the baseball glove Ambrose bought me for Christmas to remember that he still liked me. I slept with the glove all night, and this morning, I asked Ambrose if he wanted to play catch. He said yes! We played catch for 5 whole minutes! He said he was too busy with finals to play longer, but we'll catch more in the summer. That would be so great. It's important to have things to look forward to.

Ambrose closed the diary. He wanted to keep reading, but his cataracts couldn't take another word. He closed his eyes to get the sting out and the moisture back. In the darkness, he could hear the world around him. The wind rustled the tree branches. The lady across the hallway coughed. The radiator hummed. Otherwise, Shady Pines was covered in an eerie silence. It reminded Ambrose of sitting in a foxhole. The quiet was never really quiet. It was just the coming attraction for the storm.

Ambrose opened his eyes and looked at David's old baseball glove resting on the nightstand. He suddenly felt very frightened and didn't want to be alone. He stood up on his arthritic knees and left his bedroom with his brother's diary in hand.

When he reached the parlor, Ambrose took his normal spot near the fireplace. He sat in the big easy chair and looked around the room at all the old faces. Mr. Wilcox and Mr. Russell played chess. Mrs. Haggerty knitted a new stocking for her granddaughter's first Christmas. A few spinsters watched a trashy reality show.

Ambrose took out a magnifying glass and opened the diary. His eyes were burning, but he had to force another page into them. He squinted through his cataracts and focused to decipher his brother's haunted handwriting.

May 20th

I don't know if I am asleep or awake right now. My head hurts so much. My family thinks I am eating cereal in the morning, but it's really a bowl of aspirin that I've put in milk so they can't tell the difference when I chew them. But it does no good. I am in constant pain. I am so ashamed. Yesterday, I got so sad that I wanted to die. So, I went into the tree house, walked out to the middle of the clearing, and waited for night to come. I knew the woman with the burnt feet would be able to see me at night, and she could kill me once and for all. But right before sunset, a man came out of hiding and saved me. He threw me back into my tree house right before the woman with the burnt feet attacked me. She ripped him apart instead.

May 21st

I went back into the tree house and looked for the man who saved me. I found him near the creek washing the cuts from his hands. He looked like he had been whipped a thousand times. I was so relieved to see someone who would talk to me. He said that he understood why I got sad yesterday, but that I had to be strong. He said he was a soldier, who promised his father to keep us all safe from her, and he would never give up. So, I couldn't give up, either. I asked him what he knew about the woman with the burnt feet. He said she rules the imaginary world.

May 22nd

Her plan has started. No one on the real side can see it, but it's there. I tried to help them see things the way they really were, but the kids think I'm crazy. I was walking home from school because I didn't want them to make fun of me on the bus anymore. I went to the imaginary side through my tree house. I saw a woman yelling at her son on the porch. She hit her son really hard. She didn't know that the hissing woman with the burnt feet was moving her arm and whispering in her ear.

June 1st

It's spreading everywhere. The soldier and I have tried to keep people safe from inside the imaginary world, but it's not working. The hissing woman is so much stronger than us. She gets stronger every day. It's like the thing I heard in science class. The teacher told us that if you put a frog in boiling water, it knows to jump out. But if you put a frog in cold water and slowly turn up the heat, it can't tell until it's too late. So, it boils to death. Right now, the town thinks it's a flu, but it's something much worse. I would ask Ambrose to help me, but I know that deep down, even Ambrose thinks I'm crazy. And I really hope he's right. I really hope I am just a psycho kid who goes into the woods and talks to himself. Because if this is real, the world is in a pan of cold water right now, and the heat is getting turned up. And I'm the only one on earth who can stop it.

"Nurse!" a voice called out.

Ambrose closed the book and looked up in the parlor. He saw Mrs. Haggerty stop knitting her granddaughter's Christmas stocking to put her hand to her forehead to check her temperature. The nurse came rushing up.

"What is it, Mrs. Haggerty?"

"I have the flu."

"Okay. Let's get you to bed, love."

Ambrose studied the parlor. Mr. Wilcox and Mr. Russell loosened their sweaters and asked someone to turn down the heat. Mrs. Webb scratched her neck, which was coated in a thin sweat like cooking spray on a skillet. Ambrose heard one of the spinsters cough as they watched the trashy reality show. The complaints and requests for water and Advil and cold washcloths spread throughout the room.

People were getting sick.

Except Mrs. Collins' mother.

She stared right at Ambrose from her wheelchair. Ambrose felt the room go cold around him. A breeze tickled the hair of his neck. Like a whisper.

"That woman is standing right next to you, whispering in your ear," she said. "Can you hear her?"

"What is she saying, Mrs. Keizer?"

Mrs. Keizer smiled like the Cheshire Cat and wheeled herself down the hallway with a squeak. Squeak. Squeak.

"Death is coming. Death is here. We'll die on Christmas Day."

CHAPTER 56

The Christmas Pageant was supposed to be great.

That's what everyone told Christopher's mother. The Christmas Pageant was a proud tradition between Shady Pines and Mill Grove Elementary School going back all the way before they had to start calling it the "Winter Pageant" for legal reasons. On the last Friday before Christmas, Mill Grove Elementary would send kids to sing "winter" (aka holiday) songs and make cookies for the old folks. Then, the old folks would give the kids different prizes for Balloon Derby. The rule was whoever's balloon flew the farthest by the pageant would get the best prize, but all the kids would get a little something. Everyone knew the prizes were actually Christmas and Hanukkah presents, but the Balloon Derby excuse was a great way around the separation of church and state.

"That's like keeping God out of God dammit!" the nurses liked to joke.

No matter on which side of the aisle one stood, the old people loved the pageant because it was a distraction from checkers and daytime TV. The kids loved it because they got out of school. But nobody loved it more than the staff because it meant that for a few blissful hours, the old people would stop complaining.

There aren't a lot of win-win-win situations in life.

This was one of Mill Grove's finest.

"Did you hear news, Mrs. Reese?" one of the nurses asked in her broken English.

"What?"

"Mrs. Collins...she call in sick with flu. She won't be in all day. Christmas miracle!"

For the rest of the morning, the folks of Shady Pines were excited about the pageant the way children are the night before Christmas. Christopher's mother tried her best to join in their festive mood. Since it was her son's last day of school before "winter" break, she was planning to whisk him away after the pageant and take him to whatever movie he wanted—her good taste be damned. Then, they would spend the whole weekend decorating their very own home for Christmas.

But she couldn't shake it.

That uneasy feeling.

"Hi, Mrs. Reese."

Christopher's mother turned and saw Mary Katherine walking through the door. The girl looked scared. This was nothing new, of course. Poor Mary Katherine was so skittish, so guilty, so unbelievably Catholic that sometimes, she said the Lord's Prayer before her dessert, thinking somehow her "these, Thy gifts" prayer before dinner didn't last long enough. But this look was different. The girl was downright ashen.

"You okay, honey?" Christopher's mother asked.

"Oh, yes. I'm fine," the girl said.

But she wasn't fine. The poor thing looked like she might burst into tears.

"You sure? You can talk to me."

"I'm sure. Just a little sick to my stomach. That's all."

"Then go home. You already got your certificate. You don't need to keep volunteering. No one will judge you, you know?"

"Yes, they will," she said.

With that, Mary Katherine nodded a quick goodbye and slipped into Mrs. Keizer's room to begin her volunteer shift. Christopher's mother would have followed, but she was distracted by the noise from the parlor.

"They're here! The children are here!" the voices yelled.

The excitement worked its way through the room as the school buses pulled into the parking lot. Within seconds, the doors opened, and the teachers did their best to shepherd the kids into single-file lines. Christopher's mother instinctively looked for the kids she knew, but she couldn't find them in the sea of wool knit caps and Steelers beanies.

The first person through the door was Ms. Lasko. Christopher's mother had just seen her in the principal's office when Christopher got into the fight with Brady Collins. It was only a few days ago, but she remembered that Ms. Lasko had looked healthy and vibrant and pink-faced.

The difference was shocking.

Ms. Lasko was pale and drawn. The bags under her eyes were so black that she looked like she'd been punched. She was so exhausted that Christopher's mother didn't think she had slept since the principal's office. She looked as tired as . . .

As Christopher.

"Are you okay, Ms. Lasko?" Christopher's mother asked.

"Oh. I'm fine. Thank you, Mrs. Reese. Just a little headache."

That's when Christopher's mother noticed it. Ms. Lasko smelled like a fifth of vodka covered up with a gallon of peppermint mouthwash. Christopher's mother knew that smell. She had grown up with it. That smell used to read her bedtime stories. And beat the shit out of her when she spilled things.

Christopher's mother was ready to tell the other teachers that her son's homeroom teacher was drunk as a skunk.

Except that Ms. Lasko wasn't drunk.

She wasn't even buzzed.

She looked like someone who was going through withdrawal.

Ms. Lasko turned back to the kids marching into the old folks home. She clapped her hands together to get their attention.

"Okay, kids," she said. "Let's go into the parlor."

Christopher's mother watched the kids trudge up the porch. She finally found Christopher and his friends in the sea of snow hats. The boys were acting like soldiers. Special Ed flanked Christopher, looking around to make sure the coast was clear. Mike stayed a few feet behind them to make sure no one snuck up. Matt walked out front like a scout.

The boys were playing army.

And Christopher was their king.

Christopher's mother saw Matt enter the parlor first to make sure that everything was safe. Then, he nodded to Special Ed, who escorted Christopher into the old folks home. Mike turned around and scoped the entire scene. She had seen the sheriff do the same thing on their first date. She had witnessed that instinctive need to make sure the coast was clear.

But never in a seven-year-old.

Mike's gaze finally found their enemy. Brady Collins and Jenny Hertzog looked at Christopher, then whispered to their friends. Christopher's mother would have smiled at the antics except both sides were taking their roles so seriously, it unnerved her. This didn't feel like a game.

It felt like a war.

Back in the parlor, Ms. Lasko sat down at the old upright piano and started warming up her hands by playing scales. Every now and then, she would stop and scratch her arm. At first, Christopher's mother thought it was just another itch of withdrawal.

Until she saw Special Ed scratching his arm.

And Matt. And Mike.

Everyone but Christopher.

Christopher's mother noticed that Brady and Jenny were scratching their arms, too. As were some of their friends. And a couple of teachers. She had seen illness and rashes travel around a school before. But this was ridiculous.

"Hey, boys . . . how are you feeling?" she asked.

"Good, Mrs. Reese. Fine." Mike spoke first.

"Are you sure? You keep scratching your arm," she said.

"Yeah. I guess Matt and I got poison ivy or something." He shrugged.

In December? she thought but did not say. She touched his forehead instead.

"But you're burning up. Do you want me to call your moms?"

"No. They're really sick. It's better if we're here."

"My mom, too," Special Ed said.

Normally, Christopher's mother would think there must be a flu going around. The same flu that made her son burn up with fever only a few days before. But nothing about this felt normal. She could tell that all of the boys seemed a little under the weather. Christopher especially.

"Christopher, are you okay?" she asked, concerned.

"Yeah, I'm fine, Mom," he said.

She instinctively put her hand to his forehead. What she felt shocked her. When she had checked his forehead that morning, he seemed fine. His forehead was even a little cool. And now he was burning up. She didn't want to make a scene in front of his whole school, so she kept quiet. But in that moment, she decided there would be no movie. There would be bed and rest and visits to every doctor in the tristate area until someone could tell her what the hell was making her son so sick.

"Okay, honey. Go join your friends," she said.

Christopher and his gang moved over to the piano as Ms. Lasko started playing the first song. It was a long musical introduction with her opening remarks about the proud tradition of the "Winter" (wink wink Christmas and Hanukkah) Pageant.

"Ladies and gentlemen, boys and girls, we are so pleased to be here at Shady Pines. I am your musical director, Ms. Lasko. We will be handing out the prizes for the Balloon Derby winners soon, but first . . . let's go . . . Up on the Housetop!"

> Upon the house, no delay, no pause
> Clatter the steeds of Santa Claus;
> Down thro' the chimney with loads of toys
> Ho for the little ones, Christmas joys.

The start of the children singing brought the rest of the old folks into the parlor. All except Ambrose Olson. He had barely left his room since they returned from visiting his family's old house right after David's funeral. The night nurse said Ambrose stayed up all night, reading, then fell into a deep sleep. He had specifically requested that he be woken up for the Christmas Pageant. He said he didn't want to miss the children under any circumstances. But for some reason, when they went into the room, none of the nurses could wake him. They figured he was just exhausted from being up all night.

Or maybe he had the flu.

> Leave her a dolly that laughs and cries,
> One that can open and shut its eyes.

As laughter and song spread through the room, Christopher's mother saw Mary Katherine push Mrs. Keizer in her wheelchair. The old woman seemed a lot more agitated than usual.

"There's something wrong with you," she said to Mary Katherine.

"Please, Mrs. Keizer," Mary Katherine begged.

"You smell wrong. You're different," she said.

"Your grandson Brady is standing right over there. Let's find you a nice seat, so you can watch him sing," Mary Katherine offered.

"She's dirty. This girl is dirty!" the old woman screamed.

Christopher's mother quickly got the wheelchair out of Mary Katherine's hands and parked it down the hallway.

"Mrs. Keizer, I don't care if your daughter owns this place. You do not speak to anyone that way. Least of all our teenage volunteers. Do you understand me?"

The old woman was quiet for a moment, then she smiled at Christopher's mother.

"Everything is wrong. You feel it, too," she said calmly.

Christopher's mother looked at the old woman sick with Alzheimer's. Gooseflesh rose on her arms.

O! O! O! Who wouldn't go.
O! O! O! Who wouldn't go,
Upon the housetop, click! click! click!
Down thro' the chimney with good St. Nick.

Christopher's mother shook off the creeps. She locked off the old woman's wheelchair, then she went over to Mary Katherine, standing at the table with the punch and cookies.

"She's a sick woman, Mary Katherine. She doesn't know what she's saying," she whispered.

"Yes, she does," Mary Katherine said.

"What's wrong, honey? You can talk to me."

Mary Katherine was silent. Christopher's mother knew that the girl was suffering with some terrible secret. She had grown up with enough of her own. So, she was about to ask Mary Katherine to step into the kitchen to have a real heart-to-heart.

Then it happened.

Christopher's mother had no idea how it started, but Special Ed and Brady Collins were standing nose-to-nose in the middle of the parlor.

"Get away from him, Brady!"

"Fuck you, fat boy!"

Out of nowhere, Brady Collins wound up and hit Special Ed in the face. Special Ed fell hard to the ground. Mike and Matt rushed to his side as Jenny Hertzog jumped on top of him. Special Ed threw her back and charged at Brady.

"If you touch Christopher again, I'll fucking kill you!"

Christopher's mother rushed to the boys.

"BOYS! STOP IT RIGHT NOW!" Christopher's mother screamed.

But they wouldn't stop. They kept hitting and biting and tackling each other to the ground. All except Christopher, who sat down, paralyzed with a headache.

"MS. LASKO . . . HELP ME!" Christopher's mother screamed.

Christopher's mother tried to pull her son's friends off Brady and Jenny, but they kept fighting and biting like dogs. She looked over at Ms. Lasko, who just sat there, holding her head like she had a hangover after a dry drunk.

"Stop making so much noise! My head is killing me!" she screamed.

The scene was so chaotic that nobody noticed the old woman.

Except Christopher.

*

Christopher was frozen on the ground. The itch was beyond anything he had ever felt before. The thoughts were flying through his mind at such a dizzying speed that he didn't have a hope of keeping up with them. He heard no voices. Except one.

Hello, little boy.

Christopher looked down the hallway. He saw Mrs. Keizer staring at him from her wheelchair. She pulled out her false teeth and stood up on her spindly legs. She took a step and urinated on the floor. He wanted to scream, but the voice kept coming.

There is no such thing as a crazy person.

The old woman limped toward Christopher. She smiled, but it looked wrong. No teeth. Like a little baby. Christopher wanted to stand, but he was pinned to the ground by the voice.

It's just a person who is watching you.

For her.

The old woman hobbled toward him. "Chrissstopher . . ." she hissed. She put her teeth back in the wrong place. Her tops on the bottom. Her bottoms on the top.

She is very angry.

Christopher wanted to scream, but he couldn't find his own voice. There was just the whisper and the scratch and the old lady coming at him. Her legs got weak, so she knelt down and started crawling on all fours. Like a dog.

You took the nice man from her.

The woman scratched the floor, crawling at him. Christopher looked over as Jenny Hertzog dug her nails into Matt's face, trying to get to his eyes. Brady Collins and his friends were kicking Special Ed in the stomach. Mike threw Brady down.

She wants him back.

The old woman's eyes were insane with dementia.

Tell us where he is.

Christopher couldn't move. He was stuck to the floor. The itch took him until he wasn't there anymore. He was all of the old people in the room. Their aches. Their pains. Their cancer. Disease. Alzheimer's. Madness. The old woman crawled at him, slobbering like a dog with no teeth.

"Tell us where he is!" she screamed out loud.

The old woman grabbed his hands in her brittle fingers. Christopher stared into her eyes. He saw an old woman screaming gibberish. But it wasn't gibberish. Like a newborn. It knows what it means even if no one else understands.

"Death is coming! Death is here! We'll die on Christmas Day!"

Christopher pushed the itch through his hands into her skin. He saw her sitting in her room, looking out of the window, seeing the clouds. For years. He took her back in time. Before her mind was covered in a fog. They went back to the very last day when she had all of her faculties. She looked so relieved. Like an ice pack on a swollen joint. But this was her mind. The fog lifted. She looked at Christopher.

"Where am I?"

"You're in an old folks home."

"Is my name Mrs. Keizer?"

"Yes, ma'am."

"Is that my grandson Brady over there?"

"Yes, ma'am."

"How long have I been sick?"

"Eight years."

"I'm sorry I'm so frightening," she said.

"You're not frightening to me," he replied.

With that, Christopher pushed the itch deep into the woman's mind. His nose began to gush blood. The children stopped fighting when they saw the old woman lying on Christopher. The silence spread through the room. Christopher's mother rushed toward them.

"Mrs. Keizer! Let go of my son!"

"Of course," she said. "I beg your pardon, Mrs. Reese."

With that, the old woman let go of Christopher. The entire staff stared at her. The woman had been ravaged for eight years by Alzheimer's. And now, she was lucid, bright, and happy.

It was a miracle.

Christopher looked up at his mother. His face was covered in blood. From his nose to his neck. He locked eyes with her.

"Mommy," he said. "I think I'm dying."

CHAPTER 57

Christopher's mother was so panicked when she entered the emergency room that at first, she didn't notice. All she saw was the step right in front of her.

She had blown through every red light and stop sign on the way to the ER. She saw the deer on either side of the road, but she didn't slow. Her son was gushing blood from his nose. His skin was so feverish that it gave her hands little blisters.

And he was talking to himself.

They weren't sentences. Just little phrases. Words strung together like ants at a picnic. Christopher's mother prayed it was a fever dream and nothing worse. She had one when she was younger. She was on a hike with her one good uncle and she reached under a rock. She was bitten by a snake and spent two days not knowing what was real and what was make-believe.

"Hang in there, honey," she said.

But her son kept muttering. Delirious. The only phrase that made any sense was . . .

"No dreams."

Christopher's mother pulled into the loading zone of the hospital and ran into the ER, holding her son like a laundry bundle. She went straight to the admissions desk. Nurse Tammy listened dutifully, asked for her insurance card, and told her to take a seat in the waiting room.

"Fine. Fine. How long until he can see a doctor?"

"About ten hours."

"What the hell do you mean, ten hours?"

Nurse Tammy pointed into the waiting room. Christopher's mother quickly turned. And that's when she finally saw it.

There was not a single chair left in the ER.

She was used to waiting rooms being desperate places. The times when she didn't have health insurance, the ER was where she was forced to go. She had seen strung-out couples moaning. Poor people crying and screaming to be seen immediately. But now she had health insurance. She wasn't in a city. She was in a small town.

And she had never seen anything like this.

The entire room was packed. Fathers stood against the walls so their wives and children could sit. Old people sat on the floor.

"I'm sorry, Mrs. Reese," Nurse Tammy said. "So many of our doctors and nurses called in sick today. I'm even working the desk. We'll see him as soon as we can."

"Where's the next nearest hospital?" she asked.

"It's the same everywhere, ma'am. Christmas is flu season. Please have a seat."

Christopher's mother wanted to scream at her, but all she saw was a tired woman who looked sick herself. She wasn't about to yell at one of the few nurses who actually came in that day. So, she swallowed her rage and nodded.

"Thank you, Nurse," she said.

"You're welcome, ma'am," Nurse Tammy replied, then went back to the phone. "Sorry, Dad. I can't leave. We're short-staffed. I'll buy the merLOT for the party tomorrow."

Christopher's mother walked up and down the rows. She expected at least one person to give up their seat for a sick child. The fact that no one did was very unsettling to her. The people were too busy loosening their clothes to cool down their own fevers. Too busy scratching their arms. Christopher's mother saw one man holding a bandage to his face.

"God damn deer ran right in front of my truck," he said to the guy next to him.

She passed a stabbing victim. A housewife who inexplicably fell asleep in her backyard and woke up with frostbite. A couple of guys who got into a bar fight over "some Indian woman," who said she could drink anyone under the table. She got them both drunk. As a joke, she thought it would be funny if they fought to the death for the right to sleep with her. And for some reason neither of them could explain, they broke beer bottles and tried it.

When the glass hit their skin, they woke up from their madness.

"You will see my mother NOW!"

Mrs. Collins stood next to Brady and her mother at the admission desk. Mrs. Keizer was passed out in a wheelchair. Mrs. Collins looked deathly ill herself. Her forehead glistened with sweat, but she refused to take off her fur coat or jewelry. She scratched her neck under her necklace as she continued to berate Nurse Tammy.

"Look up there," Mrs. Collins hissed. "You see what that sign above the door says? It says COLLINS EMERGENCY CARE WING. I'm Collins. So, if you don't get my mother a bed right now, guess what that sign will read tomorrow? LEASE AVAILABLE."

Christopher's mother didn't think Mrs. Collins understood what was happening around her. Her mind wandered to Marie Antoinette right after her "cake diet" failed to poll well. A couple of bigger guys stood up. They walked toward Mrs. Collins. Some of the older people quickly took their chairs.

"Why don't you wait your turn, lady?" one of the men said to Mrs. Collins.

Mrs. Collins turned her head and glared at the men fearlessly.

"Why don't you build your own fucking hospital?" she said.

A murmur shot through the room. No one knew what would happen next.

Christopher's mother saw their anger spread like an echo. For a moment, she wondered if echoes ever really died out, or if they just became impossible to hear. Like a dog whistle. Always there. Always around us. Forever.

"Bitches like you make me sick—" the man said.

Mrs. Collins' son Brady walked right up to the men. He was a third of their size, but he was fearless in his rage.

"Leave my mother alone!" he said.

Brady's presence quieted the room down enough for the security guards to get the Collins family away from the angry mob and into a nice, clean hospital room. With no Collins family to focus on, the group turned their anger back on each other. The angry men returned to their seats and ordered the old people out of them. Including the women. The old women found space on the floor and stared at the young women with their sick children. Openly judging them. Saying how they should have taken better care of their kids. The young women shot back.

"Don't tell me how to raise my kids."

"Don't talk to my wife that way."

"You better sit down, or I'll make you sit down."

"Turn that TV up."

"No, turn it down. I'm tired of that shit about the Middle East."

"Watch your mouth in front of the children."

"Make me, old man."

The whole room was becoming as angry as Jerry.

The ambulance pulled up and the EMTs raced in with a man whose wife had stabbed him through the throat with a kitchen knife. She had dressed his wounds with the curtains from their kitchen and waited to call the authorities. His legs kicked wildly. Christopher's mother backed away as she shielded her son from the horrific image. He was still feverish, muttering to himself.

"She's here. What? Okay."

"Hold on, Christopher," she whispered. "I'll get you to a doctor. I promise."

She stood in the corner, so she could see if anyone came at them. She held her son in her arms, waiting for a chair. She refused to feel sorry for herself.

Sorry doesn't survive. People do.

So, instead, she counted her blessings because right now, blessings were all she had. She looked up at the TV and was grateful that she was not in a refugee camp in the Middle East. Those people would have given everything they had just to be stuck in this emergency room for ten hours with vending machines full of food.

To them, it must have seemed like the world was coming to an end.

CHAPTER 58

*D*addy.

When the phone rang, the sheriff didn't know when he had fallen asleep again. That had been happening ever since he left the Mission Street Woods. He had passed the Collins Construction site, then driven back to the station. He traded in his black-and-white cruiser for his Ford pickup the way Mr. Rogers would trade loafers for tennis shoes when he got home.

But the sheriff didn't go home.

He could barely keep his eyes open, but the sheriff forced himself to bring the old tools they found in the Mission Street Woods to his friend Carl downtown. The sheriff knew that he could have left the job to a deputy, but something told him that he needed to deliver those tools immediately.

Call it a voice.

After the sheriff dropped off the tools, he found himself parked outside Mercy Hospital. He stared at the place where he said goodbye to the girl with the painted nails. She touched his hand and called him "Daddy." He stared at the Charlie Brown tree for what felt like hours.

He fell asleep in the car.

God is a murderer, Daddy.

When he woke up, the sheriff was deathly ill. At first, he thought it must be the flu, but there were no aches. No pains. No swollen glands. If it was the flu, it was the weirdest God damn thing he'd ever had. Because a flu doesn't usually cook your skin with a fever and spare the rest of your body everything except a little itchy part of your hand.

Either way, all the sheriff wanted to do was drag his bones home and rest. His grandfather had given him a great recipe for any illness. "Down a few shots of scotch, wrap yourself up in five blankets, and sweat it out. It's hell for ten hours, but then it's gone."

The sheriff was about to buy the scotch when his cell phone rang. He looked down at the caller ID, hoping it would be Kate Reese. But it was dispatch. He shook himself alert and took the call. He'd told his deputy that he was down with the flu and to only call him in an emergency.

But the emergency had already started.

His deputy informed him that half of the department called in sick with the flu. To make matters worse, some librarian from the elementary school stabbed her husband. There were a couple of bar fights. Some car accidents. It was like the whole town woke up on the wrong side of the bed.

"We need you to come in as soon as possible, Sheriff."

It was the last thing the sheriff wanted to do.

"On my way," he said.

As the sheriff drove back to Mill Grove from downtown, he noticed how terrible the traffic was. It reminded him of Monday mornings as a boy. Whenever the Steelers won on Sunday, people would happily share the road. "No, please. After you, sir . . ." But if the Steelers lost, the only sharing involved middle fingers and honking horns. That's how much the city loved its team. Monday morning traffic lived and died with the Pittsburgh Steelers.

But this was Friday.

And the Steelers were on a winning streak.

When the sheriff arrived at the station, his fever was unbearable. The sweat ran in trickles down his back. But any hopes of him downing a little Nyquil and grabbing a catnap were crushed the minute he walked through the door. He couldn't believe how busy it was. Mill Grove was a nice little town. But one look into that room, and he would have thought it was the Hill District on New Year's Eve.

For the next few hours, the sheriff dealt with everything from the librarian stabbing her husband to several car accidents involving deer. The minute he put out one fire, another would pop up. Robberies. Bar fights. Vandalism. The owner of the gun shop called to say he'd had a break-in overnight. The burglars didn't even try to open the register. He wasn't missing any money. He was only missing guns.

It's like the town was going crazy.

The sheriff had seen enough to know that when things go south, death is usually around the corner. But luckily, none of the car accidents were fatal. The flu hadn't killed any children or old folks. And while the deer might have totaled a few cars, no people had died. Not even the librarian's stabbing victim. The knife sliced through his throat and vocal cords. Mr. Henderson would never speak again, but he was still breathing.

It was a miracle.

By the end of first shift, the sheriff was dead on his feet. It didn't matter how much aspirin he chewed, he couldn't get his fever under control. He had already given up hope that any lotion could make the itch on his right hand stop driving him crazy. He knew that if he didn't get a little rest, he would be useless for the upcoming week. And he couldn't afford to be sick the week of Christmas. So, he waited for a small dip in activity, then went to his office. He downed a shot of Nyquil and let the thick cherry syrup slide down his throat. He turned off the light, lay down on the couch, and closed his eyes.

He lay there for a good ten minutes, but he just couldn't get comfortable. The sticky sweat from the fever had already made a swamp of his clothes. He turned the pillow over and over again, but if there was a cool side, he couldn't find the God damn thing. In desperation, he threw the pillow to the floor and put his head directly on the leather couch.

The sheriff forced himself to lie back and make his eyes heavy. But it was no use. He looked around his office, and he found himself staring at his bulletin board with the Missing poster of Emily Bertovich. He wondered if the police over in Erie had any new leads. Or maybe they were so distracted by flu and hospitals and bar fights and car accidents they couldn't find her. Just like he was too distracted to figure out who buried . . . who buried . . . what was his name? That kid. The little brother of the older guy. It would come to him. He just needed to get some sleep. What was his name? He was a nice kid. Missing those two front teeth. Just like the girl with the painte . . .

Daddy.

When the phone rang, the sheriff didn't know when he had fallen asleep. His fever was worse, and his head throbbed behind the eyes. He looked down at the caller ID, and his mood instantly picked up. It was Kate Reese.

"Hello," he said.

"Hey," she said. She sounded worried.

"What's wrong?"

"I'm at the hospital. Christopher has the flu."

"Yes. It's going around. I woke up with it," he said.

"You, too?" She sounded alarmed.

"Don't worry. I called around to all of the hospitals. It's not fatal. It just feels like hell. That's all."

He expected that news to put her mind at ease, but he could tell there was something else going on. Her silence just lay there like the itch on his hand.

"Could you send a deputy to the ER?" she asked.

"Why?" he asked.

"The people here are too..." She paused, searching for the right word. "...angry."

"Everyone hates hospitals," the sheriff said.

"Are you going to patronize me, or are you going to listen?" she shot back.

"Listening," he said, chastened.

"I've been to ERs. In much poorer places, too. This is different. We've almost had a few fights. People seem really off. Sometimes just seeing a police car on the side of the road is enough to make drivers slow down—you know what I mean?"

He nodded. Smart.

"Okay. I'll send someone right away," he said. "And I'll come by the hospital as soon as I can leave work."

"Thank you," she said, finally sounding relieved. "I have to get back to my son. Good night, Bobby."

His first name never sounded so good.

"Good night, Kate," he said and hung up.

The sheriff really couldn't spare a deputy, but he told dispatch to send one to the ER anyway. The sheriff felt such a primal desire to protect her that he couldn't explain it. He just had to keep Kate Reese and her son safe.

He felt as if the world depended on it.

When the sheriff left his office, he noticed that the station was even busier than it had been that morning. There had been more fights and accidents and disputes between neighbors. The flu had spread even farther. The people in the holding cells were all feverish. They would have moved them, but hospitals were filled to capacity.

The sheriff walked past the holding cells to survey the day's damage. He saw a few guys nursing wounds they got in a bar fight. A couple of others were arrested for refusing to get out of their cars or hand over a driver's license when they got pulled over for speeding. Or reckless driving. Or a hit and run. All of them shouted things at the sheriff. Their anger was unsettling. But it was nothing compared to what he saw in the last holding cell.

The one with Mrs. Henderson.

The old woman had such a sweet face. It was impossible to believe that she'd stabbed her husband through the neck. Right now, the only thing standing between her and first-degree murder was her husband hanging on for dear life in the ICU.

Mrs. Henderson looked up at the sheriff and smiled pleasantly.

"Is my husband still alive?" she asked.

"Yes, ma'am. He's hanging in there," he replied.

"Good," she said. "I hope he lives."

The sheriff nodded. The old woman smiled.

"Because I really want to stab him again."

With that, Mrs. Henderson went back to reading the Bible.

The sheriff knew from experience that the holidays bring out the extreme sides of people. Some feel a deep connection to love and charity while others feel murderous or suicidal. To the sheriff, darkness was as common to Christmas as Santa Claus.

But this was different.

This was scary.

The sheriff headed downstairs. He knew he couldn't count on the flu to keep the blood off its hands forever. And he didn't like the idea of Kate Reese and Christopher being surrounded by it in the hospital. So, he wanted to review the emergency plans he made when he started the job. He had to make sure they were ready. For what? He didn't exactly know.

But something told him he had to prepare for the worst.

The sheriff kept moving. Downstairs. Into the records room. He told Mrs. Russo to get him anything she had on previous flu outbreaks while he looked at the emergency plans. He knew that he had to keep Route 19 open under any circumstances. If the highway was open, the state police could get in and people could get out. If that road shut down, Mill Grove may as well be an island. The town was like a person's body. The roads were the arteries and veins pushing blood back and forth from the heart.

But in this case, the heart of Mill Grove was the Mission Street Woods.

The sheriff suddenly remembered that he was investigating something from the Mission Street Woods when the flu outbreak hit the town. What was he going to do again? It took him a moment to remember. The tools. That's right. Those old tools. He had brought them to his friend Carl. He thought they might have something to do with . . . with . . . what was that kid's name again? The old man's little brother. The one who went missing. Every time he tried to think of the kid's name, his hand would start itching again and the sweat would break out on his brow. God, he really was sick. It would come to him.

The sheriff went back to the emergency plan. He had to focus. He had a flu epidemic on his hands. He couldn't spend all of his time worrying about fifty-year-old cold cases about Ambrose Olson's little brother. What was his name again? Oh, that's right. It was . . .

Daddy.

The sheriff didn't know when he fell asleep again, but Mrs. Russo woke him up. The sheriff looked down at the emergency plan. It was covered in the sweat from his forehead. He was too sick to even try to save face. He had fallen asleep on the job. He would have suspended any of his deputies without pay for as much.

"Sheriff, maybe you should go home," Mrs. Russo said kindly.

The sheriff wanted to go home, but he couldn't. He was the dog who knew that a storm was coming long before the master does.

"Thank you, Mrs. Russo. I'm fine. Let's work," he said.

The two sat down and went over the records of old flu outbreaks. The worst was the Spanish flu in 1918, but there had been others. An Amish settlement was hit so hard in the 1800s that the surviving members left town and moved to parts of Ohio. There was another smaller epidemic just after the Revolutionary War.

But the most recent outbreak caught the sheriff's eye. It happened in the summer, not the winter. People got very sick, but no one died. The sheriff stopped. The itch and fever spread, but he wouldn't be distracted this time. He read the entire manila envelope cover-to-cover. He didn't find any helpful information as to how the sheriff's department handled the emergency back then. But he did find one interesting piece of information.

The flu outbreak happened the year a little boy went missing.

The name of the boy was David Olson.

The sheriff couldn't remember exactly how, but that name meant something to him.

CHAPTER 59

Christopher couldn't remember if he was asleep or awake. He looked down at his legs. He didn't understand why they were so short. Or why he was in a hospital gown. Or why he was in a hospital room. He looked down at his hands expecting to see an old woman's wrinkled hands. The hands that belonged to Mrs. Keizer. But he didn't.

"Why do I have little boy's hands?" he wondered to himself.

After all, ever since the Christmas Pageant, he could have sworn he was Mrs. Keizer. He didn't know why. All he did was touch her arm. Maybe it was the meds they gave him. But her life passed before him like a home movie, playing on the inside of his eyelids.

I'm a little girl. I am an honors student. I am going to college. Look at that boy over there in the gymnasium. What's your name? Joe Keizer? My name is Lynn Wilkinson. It's nice to meet you. Yes, I'm free this Saturday night. And the Saturday after that. I am looking down at my hands. Oh, my God. The engagement ring is going on my finger. We are holding hands in the church. I am not Lynn Wilkinson anymore. I am Mrs. Joseph Keizer now.

Christopher sat up in bed. He looked into the window and saw a little boy's reflection. But when he closed his eyes, the reflection was Mrs. Keizer's home movie.

Joe! Joe! I'm pregnant. It's a girl! Let's name her Stephanie after my mother. Okay. Fine. Kathleen after yours. Kathy Keizer, you come here right this minute! Wait until your father sees what you did. Joe, stop it. She's freezing. Let her come into the kitchen. Fine, then I will! Joe, stop! You're hurting me. Joe, please. Our baby is a teenager. Our baby is graduating. Our baby is getting married. She won't be Kathy Keizer anymore. She'll be Mrs. Bradford Collins. Joe, she's pregnant! Joe, we have a grandson! Bradford Wesley Collins III! What a regal name. Joe, what's wrong?! Joe! Joe! Wake up! Joe!

Christopher opened his eyes and saw that nice woman coming out of the bathroom. What was her name again? Mrs. Reese. Yes. That was it. Kate Reese.

"Can you hear me, Christopher?" she asked.

Mrs. Reese turned the pillow to the cool side to make him more comfortable. Christopher closed his eyes, and her concerned face was replaced by Mrs. Keizer's memories. Flickering like an old movie with each blink of the eye.

No, Brady. Grandpa died. I know. I miss him, too. We had been married for forty...forty...God, how long had it been? Forty something? It's on the tip of my tongue. God, why can't I remember? I'm not feeling right. I can't remember where I put my...my name. What do you mean my name is Lynn Keizer? Since when? I don't remember getting married. No, you're wrong. I'm not Mrs. Keizer. My name is...my name is...Lynn...I don't remember. Who are you? Kathleen who? Who is that little boy with you? He's not my grandson. I don't know that kid. Nurse! Someone stole my memories! Someone stole my name! Don't tell me to calm down! Don't you know what's happening? Don't you understand? Death is coming. Death is here. We'll die on Christmas Day!

Mrs. Reese brought a straw to his mouth to drink. He tasted ice-cold apple juice. It was the most delicious he'd ever had. He loved it more than even Froot Loops. But old women don't like Froot Loops. So, he wasn't an old woman, was he? He was a little boy with little-boy hands.

"That's it, honey. How are you, Christopher?"

His name was Christopher. That's right. Mrs. Reese wasn't a nurse. She was his mother. They were in the hospital together. The doctor was holding a chart. The doctor thought it was a fever, but Christopher knew it wasn't. He had just had Alzheimer's for a couple days. That's all.

"How are you feeling, son?" the doctor asked.

"I'm fine," he said.

"Are you sure, Christopher?" his mother asked.

He wanted to tell his mother the truth. He wanted to tell her that he could still feel Mrs. Keizer's suffering. Her illness ravaged his joints. He didn't know if he could walk. Let alone stand. But he couldn't tell her with the doctor here.

Not the doctor who was scratching his arm.

"Yes, Mom. I'm fine," Christopher said.

The doctor brought the stethoscope to Christopher's chest. The cold metal touched his skin, and the itch shot through him. The doctor's entire medical school education flowed into Christopher's mind in an instant. The doctor thought it was the temperature of the stethoscope. He shook it and tried again.

I don't understand this. The boy's lungs are fine. His heart rate is normal. I've run every test, and everything checks out. He has no fever according to the thermometer, but it looks like this kid is . . . dying.

Christopher forced a smile. They couldn't know how sick he was. Sick meant drugs, and drugs meant sleep, and sleep meant the hissing lady. But the itch was so powerful that it was going to sweep him out to sea. Christopher had nowhere to put it, so he took a massive breath and brought it deep into his lungs.

"That's a good deep breath, son," the doctor said kindly.

The itch spread through Christopher's body, bringing with it all the people the doctor saw that day. Their aches and pains. Their fevers and headaches. Christopher could feel the blade going into Mr. Henderson's neck. Fifty years of marriage all thrown into one plunge of a kitchen knife.

I made you ten thousand dinners with this knife!

The flu was everywhere. But it wasn't the flu. It was the hissing lady on the other side of the glass. He was sure of it. Christopher's mother gave him another sip of cold apple juice. It tasted like Mr. Henderson's blood running down the kitchen table. Christopher wanted to throw up, but he couldn't. They would never let him out. He had to get out of here.

"That's delicious, Mom. Thank you."

Christopher could feel the hissing lady in the room. Watching them all. Playing them all like puppets with strings. Strings like the mailbox people. Strings like the Balloon Derby. She is beginning to get inside people's minds now to use their eyes. The giant eye is getting bigger. The evil is inside the doctor now. He is scratching his palm. The one where he kept the cheat sheets in medical school.

"Mrs. Reese, there is nothing physically wrong with your son."

"Doctor, feel his forehead . . ."

"The thermometer says ninety-eight point six degrees."

"Then, it's broken . . ."

"We've tried three of them. They're not all broken. He doesn't have a fever."

"You could cook an egg on his forehead."

"Mrs. Reese, your son doesn't have a fever."

Christopher could feel his mother's outrage growing. She kept a steady voice.

"What about the nosebleeds?"

"He's not a hemophiliac, Mrs. Reese."

"But his nose won't stop bleeding . . ."

"We ran tests. He's not a hemophiliac."

"Then, what does he have?"

"We don't know."

Her anger was growing. All of their anger was growing.

"You don't know? You've pricked and prodded him for two days . . . and you don't fucking know?!"

"Mrs. Reese, please calm down."

"I will not fucking calm down. Run some more tests."

"We have. Blood work. PET scans. Brain scans."

The hissing lady is . . .
The hissing lady is . . . getting stronger.

"Run some more fucking tests!"

"There are no more tests! We've run them! He has nothing, Mrs. Reese!"

"BUT LOOK AT HIM!"

She pointed to her little boy, and Christopher saw himself through her eyes. He was pale as a ghost. His nose crusted with blood. He wanted to tell her that the hissing lady was in the room right now making everyone hate each other. But he didn't dare because then . . .

"Mrs. Reese, is there a history of mental illness in the family?"

. . . he might sound insane.

"Is there a history of mental illness in the family?" the doctor repeated.

The room was quiet. Christopher watched his mother sit very still. She gave no response. The doctor seemed grateful to have a calm moment. He began to speak, his voice as tentative as if he were tiptoeing his way through every syllable.

"Mrs. Reese, the reason I ask is that I've seen psychosomatic illnesses in children many times. Whenever I can't find a physical reason, it's usually because there is a psychiatric one."

Christopher looked at his mother. Her face was expressionless, but as he held her hand, he could see a glimpse of the home movie she kept so guarded. On her knees. Cleaning the bathtub. Her hands raw from Clorox. Her husband's blood never came out. So, she moved away. And she never stopped moving.

"My son is not crazy," she said.

"Mrs. Reese, you said he ripped apart his own neck in school. Self-harm is one of the signs—"

"It was a nightmare. Kids have nightmares."

The doctor held his tongue. For a moment.

The doctor thinks...the doctor thinks...I have something serious. He has seen schizophrenia in children. It can show up in kids younger than me. The doctor is...the doctor is...working for the hissing lady. But he doesn't know it.

"Mrs. Reese, I'm trying to help your son. Not hurt him. I could call the child psychiatrist right now. He could do a quick evaluation. If he rules out mental illness, I'll run all the physical tests again. Deal?"

The silence hung in the room. Ten seconds that felt like an hour. But eventually, Christopher's mother gave a nod. The doctor returned the favor and made a quick call to the child psychiatrist. After he hung up the phone, he tried to put a positive spin on the situation.

"I know this seems like a dark cloud, Mrs. Reese, but there is a silver lining," he said. "There isn't anything wrong with your son physically."

He scratched his palm and smiled.

"We can thank God for that."

CHAPTER 60

Mary Katherine looked at the portrait of Jesus on her wall and said a prayer.

She knew that she would be grounded for life if her parents caught her leaving, but she had no other choice. She wasn't allowed to use the car anymore. She couldn't think of a good excuse to go to the pharmacy. But she couldn't scrub Mrs. Keizer's words out of her mind.

"You smell wrong. You're dirty. This girl is dirty!"

Mary Katherine pulled up her jeans under her nightgown. When she buttoned them, she noticed the button was a little tight. She hoped she was just putting on weight. *Please, God, I'm just putting on weight, right?* She took off the nightgown and threw on her letter jacket. The one she got for playing the flute in the marching band.

She went to her bed and stuffed the pillow under the sheets to make it look like she was still there. Then, she went to her piggy bank. The one that Grandma Margaret gave her before she died. Mary Katherine wanted to stop using it. She wasn't a child, after all. But it was the last thing her grandmother ever gave her, so she felt too guilty to let it go.

She took out all of the cash, including the change.

She combined it with her babysitting money.

She had around forty-three dollars.

It would be enough.

Mary Katherine left her bedroom. She walked down the hallway and stopped outside her parents' door. She listened to the silence on the other side until she heard her father snoring. Then, she went downstairs, grabbed the car keys from the ring underneath the portrait of Jesus, and went outside to the driveway. She turned on the station wagon. Quietly. She didn't wait for it to warm up. She got in and her hands nearly froze to the steering wheel until her fever warmed up the leather.

She didn't know where to go. She couldn't drive to the Rite Aid near South Hills Village because people might know her there. Debbie Dunham worked at the Giant Eagle where the other late-night pharmacy was. Mary Katherine couldn't afford to let anyone she knew see her.

She decided to get onto Route 19.

Far away from Mill Grove.

Mary Katherine drove through the Liberty Tunnels and saw the lights of downtown to her left and the prison on the right. She had driven on this bridge on her way to Mercy Hospital when her grandmother died. Her grandmother left her a lot of money that she never got to see or touch. That money was for Notre Dame, her dad said. All she had left was that piggy bank. She didn't even know what her grandmother's maiden name was. Why was she thinking about her so much? She hardly ever thought about her anymore. She felt so guilty about that.

Mary Katherine drove on Highway 376 and took the Forbes Avenue exit to Oakland, where the colleges were. Pitt University and CMU. No one would know her there. She drove until she saw a 24-hour pharmacy. She parked the car and sat in the parking lot, looking at the building for a good five minutes to see if anyone she knew was inside. She saw nothing but the security cameras. So, she put on a thick wool hat and some sunglasses, which still smelled like the family's trip to Virginia Beach. It was such a simple time then. So warm and sunny. And her parents weren't mad at her. And she had never done anything wrong.

The automatic doors saw her coming and opened like a whale's mouth.

Mary Katherine walked into the pharmacy. Her heart pounded. She didn't know what section it would be in. She had never been in this situation.

"Can I help you find something, hun?" the saleswoman asked her.

"No, thank you. I'm fine," Mary Katherine said.

Her heart pounded. *She knows. She knows.*

Mary Katherine did her best to walk casually down the aisles. She stopped and looked at a bag of Christmas candy. Then, she browsed some Christmas cards. Then, she stopped at the bookshelf and browsed the titles. When she passed the cold medicine, she noticed that it had been picked clean. She figured this flu must be everywhere, but she didn't give the matter much thought. She finally found what she was looking for right next to the tampons.

The pregnancy test.

She had no idea what the good brands were, and she didn't dare ask. So, she grabbed the three most expensive ones. She wanted to shoplift them, so that the lady behind the counter wouldn't know. But she couldn't add another sin to what she had already done. She felt guilty for even thinking about theft.

To think it is to do it.

She walked up to the counter. The lady looked down at the pregnancy tests, then back up at Mary Katherine. Her tense little grin said it all.

"Good thing you didn't need no cold medicine, hun. We're clean out. Christmas flu season 'n' that," she said.

Mary Katherine nodded and tried to say something in return, but she knew if she spoke, she'd burst into tears.

"How 'bout them Steelers today? I think they're going to win it all this year."

Mary Katherine nodded and looked at the woman. She was so kind. Nearly as kind as her grandmother.

"Thanks, hun. Merry Christmas to ya," the woman said.

"Merry Christmas, ma'am," she replied.

The woman rang up the tests and put them in a bag. Mary Katherine gave her the money in quarters, dimes, and crumpled dollar bills. She didn't wait for her change.

As Mary Katherine left the pharmacy, some college boys pulled up in a loud Ford Mustang. Mary Katherine could hear their stories of their latest conquests. That "dumb slut" from the Kappa house. And that "hot bitch" was so wasted, she would have given it to anybody. Mary Katherine quickly got back into her mother's station wagon and locked all the doors. She took off the hat and glasses and opened the first box. The directions were too small to read in the dark car, but she didn't dare turn on the light because someone might see her. She had to find someplace secluded. So, she started up the car and retraced her steps to Mill Grove.

As she drove back, she thought about all the times coming back home from Christmas Eve at Grandma's house. Laughing to the song "Grandma Got Run Over by a Reindeer." The radio man would finish the song and then say that there was a sighting of a sleigh just outside the North Pole. Mary Katherine would tell her dad to hurry up and get home before Santa came. If she weren't in bed, Santa would get angry and skip the house.

Please, Daddy. Hurry.

Mary Katherine drove back past the prison, through the Liberty Tubes, Dormont, and Mt. Lebanon until she arrived back in Mill Grove. She turned off Route 19 and drove around the suburban streets until she finally found a perfectly secluded spot.

Right outside the Mission Street Woods.

Mary Katherine looked through the foggy windshield to make sure no one was around. All she saw was the fence guarding the bulldozers and equipment for the Collins Construction Company. But there were no security guards. No cameras. She was safe.

Mary Katherine grabbed the directions. She unfolded them neatly and read everything until she had reached the Spanish translation. When she realized what she had to do in order to take the test, she couldn't believe it.

Pee on a stick?

She almost wanted to cry. It was so disgusting. Why was everything involving a girl's body so degrading? Boys got to stay clean and dry. And girls had to put up with being so dirty and pretending they weren't.

You smell wrong. You're dirty.

Mary Katherine was at her grandmother's house when she got her first period. She thought she had cut herself down there. She didn't know what to do. So, she used toilet paper. And when that wasn't enough, she went to her mother's bathroom and stole a tampon. She was so ashamed. When she put it in, she started to cry. A part of her thought it was a sin. And when she pulled it out, she couldn't believe her eyes. It wasn't this blue liquid on blotter paper like in the commercials. It was clumpy. And bloody. It disgusted her. She was so dirty.

You're dirty. This girl is dirty!

She opened the car door. The air was freezing cold. Mary Katherine pulled down her jeans and felt the little dent that the button made in her belly. She crouched down next to the car, bent her knees, and squatted. She let her bladder go. She peed on the stick. Her mind racing.

It's okay. You only had oral sex one time. You can't get pregnant from that. You can't, right? No one ever got pregnant through their mouth. It doesn't work that way,

Mary Katherine. You know that from health class. You didn't get pregnant the time Doug touched your breast, either. It's the same thing. Right? Right.

If I'm wrong, God, make me hit a deer on the way home.

Mary Katherine turned on her phone to get a little light. She looked at the stick. Blue meant you were pregnant. White meant you weren't. The instructions said it would take a few minutes. Every second felt like an eternity.

Don't panic. Yes, he did get sperm on your sweater, but you can't get his sperm on your sweater and get pregnant. It doesn't work that way. It doesn't, right? Even if I touched it and then went to the bathroom hours later. Can you get pregnant that way? No, of course not. I took health class. It doesn't work that way. You know it doesn't.

God, if I'm wrong, make me hit a deer on the way home.

She looked around the construction site. The trees swayed in the breeze. And her arm was so itchy. Her skin was just so itchy. She pulled her jeans up over her freezing skin and got back into the car. She didn't even bother to turn off the light. She just sat there, looking at the stick. Scratching her arm. Waiting. Praying,

Please, God. Make it white. Make me not pregnant. I swear I didn't do anything. I didn't touch myself. I thought about it. And I know that to think it is to do it, but I didn't do it! I stopped myself! Please, God, help me! Make this white. I swear I will go to church more. I swear I will volunteer at Shady Pines for the rest of the year. I'll confess to Father Tom. I'll tell my parents I snuck out tonight. Please, God. I'll do anything. Just please make it white.

Mary Katherine looked down.

It was blue.

She began to sob.

Mary Katherine was pregnant.

CHAPTER 61

Aripiprazole.

Christopher's mother held the prescription bottle in her hand. She didn't even know how to pronounce the name of the drug. But after the child psychiatrist spent an hour with Christopher, he assured her that it was the right one to try first. It had been used on children and adolescents. It had an excellent track record.

"What is it?" she asked.

"It's an antipsychotic," he explained.

"Christopher is not psychotic."

"Mrs. Reese, I understand how you feel, but your son spent an hour refusing to talk to me because..." He fished for his notes and emphasized his quoting. "'...the hissing lady is listening.' I have treated mental illness in children for three decades, and help is available for your son. I just need your support."

Christopher's mother did her best to stay present as the doctor calmly whispered words like schizophrenia, bipolar disorder, and clinical depression to suggest that her loyalty to Christopher was helpful, but her denial about his potential problem was not. She was still adamant that the doctor was wrong.

Until he brought her back into the room.

The image was shocking. Christopher was sitting up in bed as pale as a ghost. He was almost catatonic, slowly blinking and licking his dry lips. His eyes were black like lumps of coal. It didn't feel like he was looking at her. It felt like he was looking past her. Through her. Through the wall behind her. All she could think about was Christopher's father. She met a healthy, beautiful man. And within five years, she would come home from work and find him muttering to himself. She would have given anything to find the right drug to help him. Maybe if she had this drug then, she would still have a husband and . . .

Christopher would still have a father.

"What does the drug do?" she asked, hating each word as it came out of her mouth.

"It helps control manic episodes. It's also effective in stopping self-injury, aggression, and quickly changing moods. If aripiprazole doesn't work, we can try others. I just feel it's a good first step because the side effects are mild compared to other drugs."

"What side effects?"

"The most common side effect in children is sleepiness."

The child psychiatrist scratched his hand and wrote the prescription, then immediately discharged Christopher from the hospital. Christopher's mother tried desperately to keep him there. She wanted another test. Another explanation. But the hospital had hundreds of people in the emergency room now, and they couldn't spare a bed for a crazy child (and what their expression hinted might be his crazy mother).

As they left the hospital, Christopher's mother was shocked by how much worse it had gotten. The building was beyond capacity now. Every room was filled. People were beginning to line the hallways. She asked the nurse pushing Christopher's wheelchair if she had ever seen anything like this. The nurse told her no, but at least no one had died yet.

"It is a miracle," she said in her broken accent.

They reached the parking lot. The nurse took away the wheelchair.

Kate Reese was on her own.

She put Christopher in the front seat and immediately drove to the Giant Eagle to fill the prescription. The hospital's pharmacy was out for some reason. The traffic was almost as psychotic as her son had been accused of being. The horns honked so often it sounded like ducks on a pond.

When she finally reached the supermarket, Christopher was so sick, he could barely move. She kissed his cheek, which felt like it was on fire. Then, she opened the car door to let the cold December air cut through the fever that the doctors assured her he didn't have.

"Can you walk, sweetheart?"

Christopher said nothing. He just stared through the windshield and blinked.

So, she helped him to his feet and carried him into the supermarket like a baby. He was too big to sit in the top of the shopping cart, so she took off her coat to soften the metal and gently laid him down inside. Then, she rushed to the pharmacy and handed the prescription over to the pharmacist.

"It'll be a few minutes," the weary pharmacist told her as he scratched his hand.

Christopher's mother knew they could be holed up for a while, so she quickly walked the rows of Giant Eagle, looking for enough supplies to get them through the next few weeks.

But there were none.

Christopher's mother had seen grocery stores picked clean before. She had traveled enough of the country to see what happens when a tornado or hurricane warning hits a community. Sometimes, she wondered if the supermarkets put a little pressure on the local news to sell the storms just to move some inventory.

But she had never seen anything like this.

All of the Advil, Tylenol, and aspirin. All of the skin rash and itching creams. All of the canned soup, the dried fruit, the canned meats and fish.

Gone.

If Christopher's mother didn't know any better, she would have thought that the town was preparing for a war.

She picked up what she could. Beef jerky, boxes of Lipton soup and cold cereal. At least Christopher would get his Froot Loops. She went to the refrigerator section. She got some cheese because it keeps well. Then, she went to the milk. Dozens of Emily Bertovich's pictures were keeping an eye on everything. She grabbed two half gallons and the last of the plastic jugs.

Christopher's mother gave a quick glance to the cart to make sure Christopher was comfortable. She saw that he was okay right before she realized that the people in the store were not. Everyone was short-tempered. Fighting over scraps. Yelling at the stock boys about not having enough supplies. Christopher's mother kept her head down. When she had filled the cart, she went back to the pharmacy to pick up Christopher's prescription. The pharmacist was in the middle of a heated discussion with an old man.

"I asked if there was any aspirin in the back," the old man said.

"What you see is what we've got," the pharmacist replied.

"Can you check the back of the—"

"What you see is what we've got," the pharmacist cut him off.

"I need my aspirin to thin my blood!"

"Next!"

The old man walked away, fuming. Christopher's mother noticed that he was scratching his leg. She turned back to the pharmacist, who gave her a "can you believe that asshole" look and put Christopher's pills in a white paper bag.

"Should he take this with or without food?" Christopher's mother asked.

"Read the directions. Next!"

After Christopher's mother paid for the pills, she took the groceries to the front. There was a long line and only one checkout clerk. She was a little teenage thing. Very pretty. A man in muddy boots was groaning his impatience.

"I've been here twenty minutes. Why don't you open a new fucking register?"

"I'm sorry, sir. Everyone called in sick," the teenage girl said.

"Then, maybe you could pick up the pace, you little—"

"Hey, why don't you leave the girl alone?!" a burly man said behind him.

"Why don't you go fuck yourself?"

"Why don't you try to fucking make me?"

A security guard stepped in to quiet the skirmish. Christopher's mother stood still, waiting for the storm to pass. The man in front of her in line turned around and started looking at some of the things in her cart. His eyes found the milk, and he smiled a very ugly smile.

"Nice jugs," he said.

Christopher's mother knew her way around dangerous men. There was only one way to handle a guy like this.

"Hey, little dick. You touch anything near my kid, and I'll break your fucking hands."

The man looked her dead in the eye.

"Cunt."

"Proud of it," she said with her best poker face.

The man finally turned back around, seething. Christopher's mother looked at the security guard. She made sure to give him a nice flirty smile to keep him around the checkout line. After the men bought their supplies and left, she went to the front of the line. As the teenage girl checked her items, Christopher's mother watched the "jugs" man walk out to his 4x4. The girl behind the counter coughed. She looked like she had the flu herself. Christopher's mother saw the girl's name tag. It read DEBBIE DUNHAM.

"Tough night, Debbie?" Christopher's mother asked.

"Hell," the girl said without a trace of humor. "Next!"

Christopher's mother waited in the store until all of the men from the line got in their pickup trucks and left. She knew the "jugs" man could have swung back and waited for her. Away from the security cameras. Away from the light. She had been in situations before. She had learned the hard way.

But she had learned.

The drive back from Giant Eagle should have taken ten minutes, but traffic had somehow gotten worse in the time she was in the store. It was backed up for a good three miles. A lot of people started blaring their horns. She heard windows rolling down and voices screaming into the night.

"Come on! Let's go!"

"I don't have all fucking night!"

When she finally reached the front of the traffic jam, she realized that it was all because of one accident.

"Rubberneckers," she thought out loud.

A deer had slammed into a pickup truck. The deer was wedged inside the driver's-side window. It looked as if the deer had rammed it on purpose, trying to kill the driver. The driver sat slumped down as EMT workers tended to the wound on his hand. The deer's antler had driven itself through his hand like a stake. After a moment, the driver looked up. Her heart skipped a beat when she realized the driver was the "jugs" man. She knew the man couldn't see her in the dark, but it still felt like he was looking right through her and thinking the word.

Cunt.

Christopher's mother quickly passed the accident and decided against getting back onto Route 19. She couldn't risk another traffic jam. So, she took the back streets to their neighborhood.

They passed the old Olson house on the corner. Christopher rested his head against the cold window. The heat from his forehead melted the fog off the glass. They pulled up between the log cabin and their house. The old lady sat in the attic, asleep in her chair.

Christopher's mother pulled into the driveway and parked the car in the garage. She quickly got out of her seat and moved to Christopher's side. She opened the car door.

"Come on, honey. We're home."

Christopher didn't move. He just stared out through the windshield. The only sign of life was him licking his dry, cracked lips. Christopher's mother bent down and picked him up in her arms. It had been years since the last time she carried him in from the car. He was so small then. He was so sick now.

Don't you fucking cry.

She carried Christopher into the house and brought him up to his bedroom. She took off his old school clothes that he wore to the Christmas Pageant. God, how long ago was that now? Two days? Two and a half? It felt like a year. The clothes were covered in so much sweat from his fever that she had to peel them off like snakeskin. She took Christopher to the bathtub and cleaned him the way she had when he was small enough to fit in the kitchen sink. She wanted to get the hospital off his body. Get the germs off. Get the crazy off. She scrubbed him from head to toe, then put him in his new favorite pajamas. The ones with Iron Man on them. He had stopped wearing Bad Cat a month ago for some reason.

Christopher's mother put him under the sheets. She went back to the bathroom and got the pain relievers out of the medicine chest. She expected to find enough for weeks. But when she looked, she had maybe two doses of Children's Tylenol and one of Children's Advil left.

"Christopher, have you been taking medicine on your own?"

Christopher just lay on the bed, looking out the window at the night sky. He said nothing. Christopher's mother figured he must have been hiding this from her. How long had he been sick? And why would he fake being well just to go to school? Didn't kids usually do the opposite? Christopher's mother sat her son up in bed and gave him the Tylenol. She could feel that the pillow was already hot under his neck, so she instinctively turned it over. She put him back down on the cool side.

"Honey, I'm going to make dinner now so you can have your pill. You just rest, okay?"

He just lay there. Not speaking. Not moving. Christopher's mother quickly headed downstairs. She opened a box of Lipton chicken noodle soup. His favorite since he was a little boy. "I like the small noodles, Mommy."

Stop it, Kate.

She shook her head. She would not let herself cry. Be strong. Weak doesn't help. She threw in some frozen vegetables for extra vitamins. She set the timer on the microwave for five minutes. Then, she took out the bread, butter, and cheese. She started the grilled cheese sandwiches. "I like mine brown, Mommy."

Stop it right now.

As the food cooked, Christopher's mother pulled out the bottle of aripipra-zole. She quickly read the directions. It could be taken with or without food, but he was so sick, she wasn't going to risk him throwing up the one thing that could help him. The one thing that might make the voices go away. "Daddy passed away." "What does 'passed away' mean, Mommy?"

Stop crying, God dammit.

But she couldn't. She could not stop her eyes from tearing any more than Ambrose Olson could stop his eyes from filling with clouds. She forced herself to read the directions. She saw the side effects for children. Fatigue. Sleepiness.

"He'll get some sleep. He needs to sleep," she assured herself.

Headache. Nausea. Stuffy nose. Vomiting. Uncontrolled movement such as restlessness, tremor muscle stiffness.

Your son is crazy like your husband was.

Christopher's mother kicked the cabinet. She kicked the hell out of the kitchen. She had been awake for over two days now. She wouldn't let herself sleep. She just held her son while he drooled on himself because no one knew what was wrong. This whole God damn system. A bunch of greedy people who will give away a child's bed so they can charge another person's insurance thousands of dollars a day for the same fucking bed and no fucking answers.

Stop crying, you God damn cunt!

DING.

The timer on the microwave went off. Christopher's mother looked around, confused. She'd set the timer five minutes ago. Where had the time gone? She took the soup off the stove. She flipped the grilled cheese sandwiches, seeing that they were the perfect shade of brown. She put it all on a tray along with one single aripiprazole pill. She poured a nice cold glass of milk to wash it all down. Emily Bertovich stared back at her from inside the refrigerator as she closed the door. Christopher's mother wiped all evidence of crying off her face, then went upstairs, fully prepared to feed her son the way she had when he was a baby.

But when she got to his bedroom, Christopher was gone.

"Christopher?" she said.

Silence. She put down the tray of food and medicine. She rushed to the bedroom window. She looked at the snow in the backyard. There were no tracks. Only a couple of deer chewing on the evergreens in the Mission Street Woods.

"Christopher?!" she screamed.

Christopher's mother raced to the bathroom. Images of her husband ran through her mind. Memories she kept locked away like an extinguisher in a glass case. Break in case of emergency. The day Christopher went missing. The day she came home to find her husband silent in a bathtub and her son crying next to it.

She opened the door. He wasn't in there. She moved to her room. To the other bathroom. He wasn't in there either. She ran down the stairs. To the living room. Was he watching television? No. Was he in the backyard? No. The garage? The kitchen? The front yard? He was nowhere to be seen.

"Christopher Michael Reese! You get out here right now!"

No answer. She looked at the door to the basement. It was open. She rushed down into the darkness. She turned the corner and flipped on the fluorescent light. And that's when she saw her son kneeling in front of the sofa. He wasn't catatonic. He was wide awake.

And he was talking to himself.

"What have you been able to find out?" he whispered to the sofa.

Christopher's mother couldn't speak. She walked to her son. She looked down at the sofa and saw her husband's old coat lying with an old pair of pants. A white plastic bag served as the head. A scarecrow, flat and terrifying.

"Christopher, who are you talking to?"

"Are you sure it's okay?" he asked the white plastic bag.

After a moment, Christopher turned around and smiled at her.

"This is my friend, Mom. The nice man," he said.

Then, Christopher put a finger to his lips.

"Now, shhhh. Or the hissing lady will know he's down here."

CHAPTER 62

Christopher's mother held the pill in her shaking hand. She watched as her little boy muttered to himself at the kitchen table. His nose had started to bleed again. His skin was so ghastly pale, it looked like his body didn't have any blood left. She tried to take him out of the basement without the white plastic bag, but he screamed bloody murder and fought her with all of the fury of the "terrible twos," "threenagers," and "fucking fours" put together. She finally gave in and let him bring the bag. And now, she willed her mouth into the shape of a reassuring smile like a trophy fish with two hooks in its mouth.

"I'll get you some milk, honey. You'll feel better after the pill," she said.

Christopher just whispered to the white plastic bag.

"Is she here yet, sir? Is she coming?"

Your son is crazy the way your husband was. You didn't do anything wrong, Kate. It's not your fault. You just need to deal with the problem.

You just need to love him.

Christopher's mother grabbed the glass of milk. Trying to keep her hands steady.

"It's going to be okay," she said in a calm voice.

She put the pill in his mouth and raised the glass of milk. She waited for him to swallow the pill. He kept it in his mouth for ten seconds and exhaled with the last ounce of his strength.

Christopher spit the pill on the floor.

"Mom," he said in a barely audible whisper. "The nice man says I can't have those pills. Please don't give them to me."

He's crazy, Kate. Just give him the pills. It'll help.

"Christopher, it's going to be okay. Trust Mom. I'm going to help you."

Christopher's mother picked up the pill bottle. She pushed down on the lid to unlock the childproof cap. It cracked a little under her weight. Christopher's mother shook a fresh pill into her hand. She looked up at her son, who was whispering under his breath.

"Mom, please. You have to believe him. Don't make me sleep."

Do you want them to take him away, Kate? Put him in an asylum?

"Take the pill, honey," she said.

"No!" he screamed.

Christopher pushed over the glass. Freezing-cold milk spilled down the table and all over her blue jeans. Fury ran through her.

"God dammit, Christopher! I'm trying to help you!" she hissed.

She hated herself for being angry. For yelling. For not seeing his illness earlier. She got up quickly and poured another glass of milk. She turned back and saw her little boy whispering to the white plastic bag. Blood poured out of his nose. He didn't even bother to wipe it away.

"I know I can't let her, but she thinks I'm crazy. What can I do?" he whispered.

Look at him, Kate. This is killing him.

Christopher's mother approached her son. She would have to force the pill into his mouth and hold it closed until he swallowed and asked for milk. It was the only way. She lost her husband. She wouldn't lose her son.

"Don't make me take the pill, Mom," he begged.

"Christopher, you have to take it. It'll help you sleep."

Christopher turned to the white plastic bag.

"Please, sir. Help me! Tell me what to say!"

He's going to hurt himself. Give him the pill.

"Honey, there's no one there! Just take the pill. It's going to be okay."

"No!" he cried to the white plastic bag. "She already thinks I'm crazy. If I tell her, she won't love me."

Christopher's mother stopped.

"I'll always love you, honey," she said. "Tell me."

"Mom . . ." he said. Christopher looked up at her. His voice was shaking with fear. Tears started to wet his eyes. They fell on his face like water on a hot skillet. "The nice man wants me to tell you something."

Don't listen to this, Kate.

"Tell me what, Christopher?"

Her little son took a deep breath and turned to the white plastic bag for strength. Then, he nodded and spoke softly.

"Mom . . . I know beer is not supposed to be on the rocks. I know everyone in your family was terrible to you except for one uncle. Uncle Robbie died when you were ten. Some men beat him up for being different."

His father told him, Kate. Give him the pill.

"At his funeral, you promised that if you had a kid, you would always believe them. No one believed you when you were little. You told your mom, aunt, and grandmother. But no one stopped it. And when you were a little girl, you were so mad, you thought you could close your eyes and destroy the world. But you never tried because you didn't know where you would live."

His father told him. You know that. Be strong.

Christopher's mother could feel an electricity rush through the house. She could smell ozone. Like lightning. Two clouds bumping together. The hairs on the back of her neck stood on end. Her son felt electric, like a balloon after rubbing it on a sweater.

"It's okay. We're going to get through this, honey. I promise," she said.

"You met Daddy when you were running away from home. You asked him to hit you when you first met because you thought no hitting meant no love. He didn't do it. He held you instead. You thought you would never stop crying."

Your husband was crazy, Kate. He told your son everything. Give him the pill.

"Mom . . . I know Daddy killed himself in the bathtub. I know you hurt a lot and hid most of it from me. You kept moving to get away from the blood, but it would never go away, so you kept moving. You felt really sad when you met Jerry. I know Jerry hit you, Mom. So, you took me away to keep me safe. Nobody ever did that for you."

"How do you know all that, honey?" she finally asked.

"Because the nice man told me."

What the fuck is wrong with you, Kate? He's crazy. Give him the pill!

"He asked me to build a portal to the imaginary world to help him. Because the hissing lady is going to shatter the glass between their side and ours. We have to stop her, Mom! She's dangerous. I was there in the kitchen with you and Jill. You thought you spilled your coffee, but it was really the hissing lady. She wants me to sleep. She wants me to lead her to the nice man and then kill me because I'm so powerful."

You want to lose another man? You want to be all alone again?

"But every time I go to the imaginary side, it hurts me. That's why my nose is bleeding. It's not my blood. It's your blood. It's Dad's blood in the bathtub. It's Mrs. Keizer's blood. Mom, please! I could feel the burn on your hand. I could feel all the old people at the pageant. The people in the hospital. I can feel all of their pain. All of their joy. What I know about people is killing me!"

Did you hear that? It's killing him, Kate! Give him the pill!

Christopher's mother stopped. She held her son and looked him right in the eyes.

"What do you know about people, honey?"

"Everything."

With that one word, Christopher fell into her body and began to weep. She held her son, who was too weak now to resist the pills. This was her chance.

Give him the pill, Kate.

Christopher's mother held her little boy as he convulsed with sobbing. Shaking from the sleep deprivation. A lifetime of motherhood flooded through her. Every pillow turned to the cool side. Every grilled cheese sandwich made just the way he liked them.

Give him the pill, Kate! Or you're a terrible mother!

Christopher's mother stopped. She listened to the voice again.

You're a terrible mother, Kate. Now give him the pill!

And that's when she realized that it wasn't her voice.

It sounded like her. It was almost perfect. The tone was right. She could be negative to herself. She had an internal monologue that had said some ruthless things over the years.

But . . .

Kate Reese was not a terrible mother. She was great. Being Christopher's mother was the only thing Kate Reese was ever great at. And some bitch was doing a perfect imitation of her voice to convince her otherwise. Something wanted Christopher to take those pills. Something wanted her son to sleep. Something wanted her son.

"Who is that?" Christopher's mother said out loud. "Who's there?"

The room was silent. But she could feel something creeping.

"Mom, do you believe me now?" Christopher whispered.

Christopher's mother looked down at the bottle of pills in her hand. In one motion, she dumped the entire bottle of aripiprazole down the sink.

"Yes, honey. Now, pack your things. We're getting the fuck out of here."

CHAPTER 63

Mary Katherine walked through the doors of the church. It was late, and the room was empty. The only light came from the streetlight pouring through the stained glass and a few candles lit by loved ones trying to keep family alive through faith. Otherwise, there was darkness. Mary Katherine dipped her fingers into the holy water and walked down the center aisle to the front. She crossed herself and sat in the pew usually reserved for the Collins family. But they weren't here. Right now, there was only Mary Katherine and God.

And the baby.

Mary Katherine choked back the thought. She barely remembered driving here. She thought about the first pregnancy test turning blue. She knew she couldn't be pregnant. It was impossible. So, she had convinced herself that the first test must have been defective. Yes. That was a much more reasonable explanation than a pregnant virgin. She'd torn open the next box and read the instructions by the light of her cell phone. With this brand, if there were two lines, she was pregnant. If there was one line, she wasn't. She squatted and peed on the next stick and waited like a prisoner in front of a parole board. The next few minutes felt like an eternity. Waiting for the one line. Waiting for one line.

Please, God. Make it one line.

When the two lines came, so did the tears. She immediately tore open the final box and quickly read the instructions. A plus sign (+) meant that she was pregnant. A minus sign (–) meant that she could wake up from this nightmare and go back to her life as if none of this had ever happened. She found her mother's bottle of water in the emergency kit and drank. And waited. After she peed on a stick for the third and final time, she looked at the test—God's test—and promised to study hard. Get into Notre Dame. Get married. Have a career. Have children with her husband like every woman in her family had for generations. Just please, God, make it a minus sign (–). She prayed harder than her father had during all Notre Dame and Steelers football games put together when the quarterback threw a long pass at the end. What did they call that again?

A Hail Mary.

She looked down at the stick and saw the plus sign (+) in her hand like the gold cross around her neck. And she sobbed. God's test was three for three. Father. Son. Holy Ghost. Mary Katherine would have a bump under her graduation gown. She would never be able to look at her graduation pictures. And once the admissions people heard, she would never get into Notre Dame.

Mary Katherine didn't know how long she'd sat there in the cold, weeping into her hands, but when she finally stood up, her knees were as sore as the passion play. She'd somehow managed her way to the car. And she somehow managed her way to the church. And now, she knelt down on the kneeling bench. She closed her eyes and prayed with all her heart.

God, I'm sorry. I don't know what I did, but I know I did something wrong. Please tell me what I did, and I'll make it better. I swear.

Silence. Her knees dug into the bench. She scratched her arm. She couldn't stop scratching. Her phone buzzed with a text. The noise startled her. She couldn't figure out who would text her this late. Maybe Doug woke up. Maybe her parents found her bed empty. She pulled out her phone. The text was from UNKNOWN.

The text read . . . **You peed on a stick, slut.**

Mary Katherine felt her heart go to her throat. "Mortified" was too small a word. Someone had been watching her from the woods.

Her phone buzzed again . . . **Hey, Virgin Mary. I'm talking to you.**

Mary Katherine deleted the texts. She wanted to make it all go away. She wanted to make herself go away.

God. Please. I don't understand why this is happening. Whatever I did to upset You, I promise to make it better. Just tell me what to do. I just need You to talk to me.

Her phone buzzed again. **I said I'm talking to you, slut.**

Mary Katherine stopped. She looked around the church. No one was there. She suddenly felt a terrible fear in the pit of her stomach. She shoved the phone in her pocket. The phone buzzed once. It buzzed twice. She finally couldn't help herself. She looked.

Why won't you write me back?

You think you're too good for me?

She typed back . . . **who is this?**

Her phone buzzed . . . **you know who.**

Her phone went silent. The room suddenly turned cold.

Her phone buzzed again . . . **I'm looking at you right now.**

Mary Katherine shrieked. She turned around in the church, but found nothing but the statue of Jesus and the saints frozen forever in stained glass. Suddenly every instinct told her to get out of this church. Get in the car. Now. Mary Katherine left the pew without crossing herself. She rushed down the aisle. Something was wrong. She could feel the danger all around her. She opened the door to the church.

Mrs. Radcliffe stood outside.

Mary Katherine let out a scream. Mrs. Radcliffe was scratching her own arm. Her eyes were bloodshot. Her forehead was wet with fever.

"What are you doing here, Mary Katherine? It's almost two a.m."

"Sorry, Mrs. Radcliffe. I was just leaving."

Mrs. Radcliffe walked toward her. Scratching her arm.

"There's something different about you."

"I'm just nervous about Notre Dame. I came to pray. Merry Christmas."

Mary Katherine forced a smile and rushed into the parking lot. She didn't care about what her parents would do anymore. She just had to get back home. She got in her car and turned on the ignition. She looked in the rearview mirror where Mrs. Radcliffe disappeared into the church. Mary Katherine didn't know what she was doing here so late. Maybe she was sad. Maybe she wanted to light a candle for her family. All Mary Katherine knew for sure was that for some reason, Mrs. Radcliffe wasn't wearing any shoes.

Mary Katherine started driving.

She knows, Mary Katherine. She's going to remember when you threw up after taking Communion. You were pregnant with morning sickness and the Communion wafer tasted like the flesh of Jesus. That's cannibalism. You're disgusting.

The inner voice was relentless. She looked down at the speedometer. She was driving 20 miles an hour. Her heart raced. She had to get home. Get safe. She put her foot on the gas.

She saw you drink the wine. Do you really think that you drank God's blood? That makes you a vampire. That's insane. The church wouldn't have cannibalism and vampirism. The church is beautiful. That makes no sense whatsoever.

Mary Katherine looked in the rearview mirror. She saw the steeple of the church getting smaller. She didn't notice, but she was now going 30 miles an hour. The voice inside her mind got louder, as if someone were turning up the TV.

It's not God's fault this is happening. It's yours. You're the one who thought about sex. It doesn't matter that you didn't do it. You know the rules...to think it is to do it. So, you're not a virgin at all. You're a slut.

Her phone buzzed. All the message said was . . . **I'm still here, slut.**

Mary Katherine scratched her arm. She couldn't stop scratching it and wondering who that was. She looked up at the sky. The clouds floated above her. The needle crawled up. 35 miles an hour. She just had to get home. 40 miles an hour.

And now you want God's forgiveness? After you threw up His body and blood. After you put Doug's thing in your mouth. After you didn't care about those old people because all you wanted to do was go to Notre Dame. After all of that, you think that God chose you? Go ahead, Mary Katherine. Go ahead and ask Him.

"God," she said quietly. "Am I having Your baby?"

Her phone buzzed. There was nothing but a smiley face emoji, laughing at her. Mary Katherine looked at the sides of the road. The deer began to creep out from between the trees and through the yards. 50 miles an hour. She shook off the text and kept praying.

"The reason I'm asking, God, is that um . . . that I'm thinking some very bad things. I can't stop thinking about throwing myself down a flight of stairs. I keep wanting to hit my stomach to have a miscarriage. And I don't want to think that anymore. So, just tell me, God. If I'm carrying Your child, make me hit a deer."

Her phone buzzed. This text had no words. Just that emoji, laughing. Mary Katherine started hyperventilating. She could see ahead on the road. The deer were gathering. Mary Katherine ran through a stop sign. Another and another. 60 miles an hour.

"Please, this one time. Just tell me. Because I keep thinking about killing myself. I would never do it, but to think it is to do it. So, I just did it. Did I just do it? Did I just kill myself? Am I dead? Did I just sin now? Am I damned forever? If I'm damned forever, make me hit a deer."

Mary Katherine flew through a red light. She passed a speed limit sign that read 25. She just couldn't get the sin off her. She couldn't outrun it. No matter how fast she drove. She couldn't get the sin clean. She looked down at the speedometer. 70 miles an hour.

"God, please. I need You to tell me right now if I am having Your baby because I keep thinking about having an abortion. And that's a mortal sin. But I keep thinking it, and if I keep thinking it, then I'm doing it. And I don't want to do it. I don't want to hurt Your child. Please! Please help me! God, if You want me to have an abortion, make me hit a deer. If You want me to kill myself. If You want me to die! If You want me to have Your baby! Just give me a sign, and I'll do it! I'll do anything for You, God."

Mary Katherine saw the red light up ahead. The deer watched her car from the side of the road. Rather than slowing down, she hit the gas harder. She flew into the intersection just as the light turned green. 80 miles an hour. 90 miles an hour.

Her phone buzzed one last time. **You're going to die now, slut.**

When she hit 100 miles an hour, Mary Katherine felt the world go quiet. She had no idea why she was doing this, but it felt like someone else was pushing the gas pedal. Someone else was picking up her phone. Someone else was furiously typing a text back to that random person who was bullying her.

WHO THE HELL IS THIS?! Mary Katherine typed.

She put the phone back down.

She was going 125 miles an hour.

She did not see the deer in time.

CHAPTER 64

Christopher's mother rushed through the house, throwing essentials into a suitcase. Food. Warm clothes. Batteries. Water. She could leave everything else. They could always come back for the rest. But when things got dangerous, she knew the smartest thing to do was run. And this was more than dangerous. Something in Mill Grove was making the town crazy.

And it was killing her son.

"We're leaving in one minute!" she yelled down the hall.

The wind howled outside. Christopher's mother slid the closet door open. She grabbed all the winter clothes she could find and stuffed them into her suitcase. She was just about to close it when she saw the one designer outfit she bought at the outlet mall. The one she wore on her date with the sheriff.

The sheriff. You can't leave the sheriff.

It was the voice again. Imitating her. Trying to slow her down.

"I'll call him from the road," she said out loud to make sure the thoughts were her own.

She passed over the designer outfit and high heels to grab a thick scarf, boots, gloves, and a thousand dollars in cash hidden in plain view in a fake aerosol can. She threw it all in her suitcase, then hurried down the hallway to Christopher's room. She found him sitting on his bed. His suitcase empty. He hadn't packed any of his clothes. Only the one picture of his father.

And the white plastic bag.

"What are you doing?!" she asked.

"Mom, the nice man says we shouldn't go. Something bad will happen."

"Tell him I'm sorry, but we're leaving."

"But, Mom—"

"This isn't a debate!" she yelled.

She started filling his suitcase. Christopher held the white plastic bag to his ear like a seashell and listened. After a moment, he nodded and turned to his mother.

"He says when you spoke out loud, the hissing lady heard. She won't let you take me away, Mom!"

"Watch me!" she yelled.

A tree branch scratched at the window.

"She's coming, Mom."

The wind howled outside. A branch brushed against the window like little baby fingernails.

"We're leaving right now, Christopher!"

Christopher's mother snapped the suitcase shut and grabbed it with her right hand. Christopher with her left. Christopher looked at the white plastic bag.

"Sir, you can't help us if she catches you. Run!"

He opened his bedroom window and threw the white plastic bag out. The wind took it like a kite. There were half a dozen deer milling about the backyard. They stopped nibbling on evergreens to start chasing the bag into the woods. There was a thud downstairs.

"She's at the front door, Mom!"

Christopher's mother held her son in her arms and rushed downstairs. She fished out her car keys and opened the door to the garage. The house dropped ten degrees. She ran into the garage and unlocked the car. She sat Christopher in the front seat.

"She's in the house!"

Pebbles hit the garage door as the wind picked up outside.

She threw the suitcases next to the emergency road kit and the Giant Eagle groceries that she'd never unpacked. She came back to the driver's side and climbed in. She hit the garage door opener.

"Mom, she's in the garage!"

Christopher's mother turned but saw nothing. She looked over at him. His eyes started to droop.

"Mom, I feel so . . . sleepy."

"No!" she barked. "Stay awake. You hear me? Stay awake until we are far away from this place!"

She flipped the key. The gears ground. The car wouldn't start. She tried again. The ignition caught, and the car roared to life. The garage door opened. Christopher's mother threw the car into reverse, then turned back to look through the rear windshield.

That's when she saw the old woman from the log cabin.

"Where are you taking him?!" she screamed.

The old woman rushed at the car. She tried to open Christopher's door. Christopher's mother hit the automatic locks.

"Where is my husband? We swam in the Ohio River together. He was such a beautiful boy!"

The old woman put her hands on Christopher's window. Christopher's mother hit the gas and tore back through the driveway. The old woman's daughter left the log cabin and ran to the driver's-side window, chasing the car like a dog. Christopher's mother hit the gas and raced down the street. Jenny Hertzog ran out of her house.

"Stop coming in my room! I'll drown you in Floods!" Jenny screamed.

Christopher's mother gunned the car past David Olson's old house on the corner. Jill was outside with her husband, Clark. They had moved the crib from the upstairs bedroom to the porch. Clark held Jill while she sobbed furiously.

"We asked you for a baby! Where is our baby?!" she shrieked.

Christopher's mother raced out of the neighborhood. Away from the madness. Away from the Mission Street Woods. She looked down at the gas gauge. It was near empty. She knew that if the grocery store was picked clean, the gas station wouldn't be far behind. She looked over at Christopher sitting in the front seat. His eyes were shutting.

"No, honey! She wants you to sleep! Fight her!"

She rolled down the windows. The air was freezing. It made her knuckles ache, but it did the trick. Christopher opened his eyes. They passed the gas station near the elementary school, but the line ran all the way down Route 19. Angry customers honked their horns and shouted at each other. She had to find something off the beaten path. She remembered there were two gas stations next to Kings Restaurant on McMurray Road. Only locals would know they were there. She turned off near the high school and headed straight for them. One of them was closed. One of them was practically empty.

It was a miracle.

Christopher's mother pulled into the gas station. She got out of the car and went to the pump. She swiped her card. Declined. She took out the Visa. Declined. American Express. Declined. She cracked open the fake aerosol can and pulled out five twenties. She raced inside the Mobile Mart. There was a teenage boy on the phone.

"Where's the party?" he asked his friend. "Is Debbie Dunham there yet?"

Christopher's mother grabbed a case of Coke and the last gallon of water. She threw the cash down on the counter.

"Pump seven," she said. "And I'd like a gas can."

The teenage kid flipped on the pump and gave her the last red gallon can. Just as she rushed out of the Mobile Mart, she heard the boy laugh into the phone.

"That girl is such a slut."

Christopher's mother rushed back to the car and gave her son one of the cans of Coke.

"Drink it, honey. It'll help you stay awake."

He cracked open the can and drank. She started pumping the gas. She quickly pulled out her phone. Call the sheriff and warn him. Call all the mothers and Ambrose and Mary Katherine and her friends at Shady Pines.

She looked down at the phone.

No bars. No service.

She would try calling again on the road. She would try all the way to West Virginia. She filled her tank, then topped it off. Then, she filled the red plastic can with one more gallon of gas. She knew this might be her last stop for a long time. She threw the gas can in the trunk and climbed back into the car.

"Mom? Am I asleep or awake?"

"You're awake, honey. Don't sleep yet. She wants you to sleep."

"Mom, I don't know where I am."

"I know, but I do. And I won't let you out of my sight."

Christopher's mother hit the ignition. She pulled away from the gas station and climbed onto the street. The wind had knocked a tree down on Fort Couch Road, so she turned around and headed west. Past the high school. There was a shortcut to the highway. She could get on it and be in West Virginia in less than an hour.

"Drink your Coke."

"I did."

"I know you're sleepy, honey. But you have to fight!"

"I just need to get in the backseat and sleep."

"We'll be in West Virginia in an hour. Then, you can sleep for days."

"The hissing lady will never let me go, Mom."

"Put your seat belt back on!"

"Don't worry. The nice man said he'd find me. I won't be alone."

He was too weak to move to the backseat. He closed his eyes. She shook her son frantically.

"NO! WAKE UP! WAKE UP!"

She grabbed the gallon of water and poured it on his head. His eyes snapped open. She gave him another Coke. His arms were too weak to hold it.

"Mom," he said.

"What, honey?" she asked.

"She's going to turn to avoid the deer."

"What?"

"Don't be mad at her. This was all meant to happen."

He touched her hand and calmly turned to the passenger-side window just as the deer ran in front of Mary Katherine's car. Mary Katherine turned to avoid the deer and Christopher's mother saw the two headlights rush right at her son in the passenger seat.

Christopher's mother looked out at the headlights. She could feel the tickle he left behind on her hand as time stopped.

Christopher was right.

This was all meant to happen.

She saw every coincidence strung together like popcorn around a Christmas tree. She could have unpacked the groceries, but they were still in the car. She could have lost her keys, but they were still in her pocket. One second here. Two minutes there. There could have been a line at the gas station. Or no more gas. Or a credit card that worked instead of cash from a fake aerosol can.

But that's not what happened.

Because it didn't want to stop her from leaving.

It wanted her to be on the road.

In that spot.

At exactly 2:17 a.m.

When Mary Katherine's car turned to avoid the deer
and crashed through the passenger-side door.

Part V

Asleep

CHAPTER 65

"Christopher, it's so nice to see you again," the voice said.

Christopher opened his eyes. He was in a hospital bed. A nurse stood above him, humming to herself. She was preparing a sponge bath. Her eyes looked familiar, but the white surgical mask covered her face.

The calm voice spoke again. "That's it. Don't be afraid."

Christopher couldn't tell where the voice was coming from. He looked around the room. The door to the bathroom was closed. He listened, but he couldn't tell if the voice was coming from behind the door. Was that breathing? Was that scratching?

"Oh. I'm not in the bathroom. I'm up here, buddy."

Christopher looked up and saw Bad Cat staring at him from the TV. It was one of Christopher's favorite episodes. The one where Bad Cat uses the fire hydrant to turn the neighborhood street into a water park. But the episode was all wrong. The fire hydrant wasn't shooting water.

It was shooting blood.

"Hi, Christopher," Bad Cat said. "Gosh, it's been a while. I've missed you a ton. How are you, buddy?"

Bad Cat smiled. His teeth were razor-sharp. Covered in meat. Christopher tried to sit up, but he was strapped down tight. He looked at his wrists and ankles. They were tied to a gurney with balloon strings.

"Don't fight, Christopher. We're trying to help you. We just need to know where he is, buddy."

Christopher panicked. He looked around the room for any escape. Bars blocked the windows. Was this the imaginary side? A nightmare? Where was he? How did he get here?

"Sorry, Christopher. We don't like locking you in, but we can't let you run away again until we find him. Gosh, no, we can't."

Christopher looked at the floor. It was stamped with bloody footprints. All shapes. Sizes. Men. Women. Mostly children. It looked as if people had been staring at him the way they would an animal at the zoo.

"Just tell us where he is, Christopher, and we'll let you go."

Christopher looked back at the television. Bad Cat made his tongue clack like playing cards in a bicycle tire. Tick tock. Tick tock. Then, somehow, he reached his claws out of the television and changed the channel. Christopher saw himself on the television now. Strapped to the bed. The nurse dipped the sponge into the bucket. When she brought the sponge back out and squeezed it, Christopher saw it was dripping blood like a bleeding heart. On the television, the door opened. Bad Cat walked to his bed.

"Hey, buddy," he said, leaning over. "Do you know where you are? Where do you think you are?"

Christopher thought he was on the imaginary side. Right? He had been here before. But how did he get here? Or was this a nightmare? Or was this both? Or neither?

"Where am I? That's what you're thinking, buddy. I can smell it on you. You didn't fall asleep, so this isn't a dream. No no no. You didn't go into your little tree house, either. But still, here you are. Yes yes yes. There are four ways in. Three ways out. You know two. We know more. She has the key. But where is the door?"

Bad Cat brought his paw to Christopher's forehead and began to pet him as if Christopher were the house cat. Not the other way around.

"I'll tell you how to get out, buddy. But you have to tell me where he is first," Bad Cat purred. "Four ways in. Three ways out."

Christopher's mind raced. The tree house and a nightmare. Those were two of the four ways into the imaginary side. What were the other two? He tried to remember how he got here. All he remembered was a bright light. And screaming.

"This is your last chance, buddy. We don't want to hurt you. Gosh, no, we don't. But if you don't tell us where he is, we're going to have to cut the words right out of your body."

"I don't know."

"I think you do, buddy."

"I don't! He ran away!" Christopher pleaded.

"No. You helped him escape. There's a big difference. He was going somewhere. He must have said where he was going."

"I don't know."

"Think real hard, Christopher. You must have a plan to meet up. Where will you meet him, buddy?"

There was no plan to meet. But he had to think of something fast. So, he lied.

"At the school."

"You're a bad liar, buddy."

"I'm not lying!"

Bad Cat dropped his smile. He let out a deep, resigned sigh.

"Nurse, please prepare him for surgery."

The television turned off, taking Bad Cat with it. The nurse took the bloody sponge and started to scrub Christopher's arms and chest with it.

"Please, ma'am. Help me," he whispered to the nurse.

The nurse did not respond. She just kept humming. She finished the bloody sponge bath, then unlocked the gurney and wheeled Christopher out into the hallway.

"Where are we going?!" he asked. "Where am I?! Is this the imaginary side?!"

The nurse said nothing. She just kept humming that tune. Blue Moon. She pushed Christopher down the hallway. The gurney wheels turned. One of them was crooked like a clubfoot. Squeak squeak squeak.

They passed a hospital room. Mr. Henderson sat up in bed, holding his bloody throat, trying to scream. But no words came out. Just blood. It poured from his neck in tiny bubbles, which floated like balloons in the air until they popped, letting out little screams. Suddenly the hospital loudspeaker woke up like an old radio filling with electricity. There was a moment of terrible feedback, and then the terrifying voice echoing through the hallway.

"Tick tock, buddy. You're almost there," Bad Cat said.

The nurse kept pushing the gurney. Squeak squeak squeak.

"This is your last chance, buddy. Oh gosh, yes it is. Tell us where he is, and we won't go into the next room."

"Where are we going?!"

"Oh, you don't want to see it, buddy. I'm counting to three. You ready? One. Two."

The nurse pushed the gurney toward a door. Squeak squeak squeak.

"Three!"

The door opened. Christopher was suddenly blinded. He looked around at moaning and slobbering faces lost in the flare of a bright light. His eyes slowly adjusted, and he saw that the faces belonged to children. All of their teeth were missing. The kids sat in a circle like ring-around-the-rosy. The center of the circle was completely clear with a large bright light hanging high above a cold, metal table filled with instruments.

He was in an operating room.

A doctor waited for him in full surgical scrubs, his face covered by a white mask. Christopher couldn't see the doctor's eyes. The nurse pushed Christopher through the circle as the children surrounded him. Their eyes glowing.

Christopher turned away, terrified. The kids began to howl, jumping up and down like monkeys at a zoo. They tried to scream "Just tell us where he is, Christopher!" but with no teeth, they sounded hideous.

"Juuuu elll uuussss whhherree hee izzzz chriiiituuuhhheer!"

The nurse wheeled Christopher into the middle of the operating room. She locked the gurney wheels right next to the cold metal table. The doctor held up his hand, asking the room for silence. The kids obeyed. The doctor slowly walked to Christopher on the gurney. His shoes made an echo with each step in the silent room. The doctor held up his scalpel, silver and gleaming.

"Christopher," the doctor said in Bad Cat's voice. "We don't want to hurt you, buddy, but we need a worm to catch the fish. Just tell us where he is, and it all goes away. We don't want to have to do this. Oh gosh, no we don't."

Christopher looked over and saw David Olson on the cold metal table. David's eyes were closed. Was he asleep? Was he dead? Did she find out that David helped the nice man escape? Was this his punishment? Was David being tortured?

"Christopher, we're running out of time. So, if you don't tell us where he is, we're going to cut out your tongue. Maybe it'll start talking, buddy."

Christopher searched the crowd, hoping to find his friends. His mother. The nice man coming to save him. But he was all alone.

"Oh, nobody can help you," the doctor said. "Not until you tell us where he is."

The whites of the doctor's eyes started to change as if someone were pouring black paint into them.

"So, use your tongue, or I'll cut it out," the doctor said.

"I don't know where he is! I swear!" Christopher said.

The doctor sighed. "Very well. Nurse . . . the gas, please."

The nurse nodded and wheeled over the gas tank. She took the plastic mask and opened the valve, which let the vapor out in a long snaky hssssssssssssss. She brought it to Christopher's mouth. He turned his head.

"NO! You won't put me to sleep!" he shrieked.

"This gas doesn't put you to sleep, Christopher. It makes you extra awake. We want you to feel this."

The nurse slammed the plastic mask down over his mouth and nose. The children jumped up and down, howling. Christopher held his breath, struggling against the mask. The doctor waited patiently for him to breathe. Christopher's face turned red. His lungs felt like they would collapse. He finally couldn't take another second of it.

Christopher took a deep breath.

The gas hit his lungs. Within seconds, he felt AWAKE! His eyes opened as if he'd eaten a million Pixy Stix. He tried to stop, but he filled his lungs with more and more gas, making his heart feel like it would explode. But there was something else he could sense. The gas reminded him of something. It smelled like . . . it smelled like . . .

It smelled like old baseball gloves.

Christopher looked back to the room, and that's when he saw her.

It was his mother.

She was dressed in the same outfit she wore when she was driving the car. *Yes. The car. That's where I was.* Her forehead was cut. Windshield glass in her hair. *From the accident.* And now she was crawling on the floor like a soldier. Past the kids screaming like monkeys. Using the shadows of their bodies to hide herself from the light.

Just as the doctor brought the scalpel to Christopher's tongue, Christopher's mother leapt up and rushed at him.

"Get away from him!" she shrieked.

Christopher's mother slammed her body into the nurse and grabbed the scalpel out of the doctor's hand. She drove the scalpel into his shoulder. The doctor screamed as his lab coat turned from white to a dark blood red. Christopher's mother unlocked the gurney. The children rushed at her, trying to stop the escape, but Christopher's mother was faster. She pushed the gurney out of the operating room.

"Are you okay, honey? Are you hurt?" Christopher's mother asked.

"I'm fine," he said. "Just get to the street!"

"What happened? What did they want?"

"They want to know where the nice man is."

"Where is he?"

Christopher's mother turned the corner. Following the signs for the exit. She made a hard right, running through the emergency room. Christopher saw Mary Katherine being wheeled into the ER from the parking lot on the real side. She was covered in blood.

"Where is the nice man?" his mother repeated.

"I don't know. He escaped."

Christopher looked at the next gurney being brought into the ER. He saw himself lying unconscious. He had a terrible gash on his arm. A bruise on his temple.

"Where are you supposed to meet him?!" she asked.

"I don't know!" he said.

"CHRISTOPHER! WHERE CAN WE FIND THE NICE MAN?!"

Christopher watched an EMT driver push the last gurney into the hospital. What he saw confused him. His mother was on the gurney. She wore the same clothes she wore while driving. She had a cut on her forehead. She had pieces of windshield in her hair. The memory of the car crash came rushing back. The shattering glass. The buckling metal. His mother's screams as he slipped away into unconsciousness.

That's how I got here, isn't it?

Christopher had refused to take the pill and sleep. He wouldn't go into the tree house. So, the hissing lady used a third way to get him back to the imaginary side. And this time, she brought his mother with him. They were both in the car. They were both in the accident. They were both unconscious in the hospital. But if that was true . . .

Why is my mother awake on the real side?

He saw her. Weak. Bloody. She was reaching out to Christopher, trying to will her broken body to get to him. Then, as she finally collapsed against the pain, a terrible question turned his blood to ice. If his mother was awake on the real side, then who was behind him on the imaginary?

"Mom?" he said, his skin suddenly crawling with fear. "How did you get here?"

Christopher craned his neck back and saw her.

The hissing lady. Smiling.

"I guess we'll have to cut out your tongue after all," she said.

CHAPTER 66

Christopher's mother opened her eyes. At first, she couldn't see anything clearly. There was a bright light above her head. Her vision was blurry. She blinked a couple of times until she realized she was in a hospital bed. There was a life monitor clipped to her index finger. She had an IV spike in her arm. She felt a little groggy from the painkillers they had given her.

Slowly, she sat up. Waves of nausea forced her stomach to her throat. She felt faint, but she didn't have time for that. She had to get to Christopher. She swung her feet over the side of the bed and stood on wobbly legs. She could instantly feel the cold air on her backside from the open hospital gown. She reached out to steady herself. That's when she felt the pain.

The memories came back to her in puzzle pieces. Her body slamming against the driver's-side door. Her ribs cracking. The jaws of life ripping them out of the car. Her son unconscious in the ambulance as it screamed its way to the hospital.

"Please sit down, Mrs. Reese. You were in a terrible accident," a voice said.

"My son. Where's my son?!" she said to the nurse.

"He's in the ICU. But you need to rest."

"Where's the ICU?!"

"Second floor, but Mrs. Reese, you need to—"

Without a word, Christopher's mother pulled the IV out of her arm, swallowed the pain in her side, and walked into the hallway.

"Mrs. Reese!" the nurse called after her.

Christopher's mother found the elevator and made her way to the second floor. When the elevator doors opened, she was shocked. The ICU was beyond packed. The waiting room alone had enough seating for ten. There might have been forty-five people in there.

"Christopher Reese," she said to the admissions nurse. "I'm his mother."

"Room 217," the nurse said while scratching her arm.

The security door buzzed like an angry wasp. Christopher's mother opened the door and moved down the hall. She saw that all of the beds were taken. Stabbing victims. Shooting victims. The madness or anger or whatever this was had been busy while she was asleep. She dragged herself to room 217 at the end of the long hallway. She opened the door without knocking.

And that's when she saw him.

Her little boy was lying on the hospital bed. He had a terrible gash up his arm. His body was covered in a hundred cuts from the explosion of glass. His eyes were closed. He had a huge tube sticking out of his mouth, connected to a jungle of monitors. Machines were breathing for him. Eating for him. Monitoring everything from his heart to his brain. Christopher's mother saw an ICU nurse enter numbers into Christopher's chart, stopping only once to scratch her shoulder.

"What's wrong with him?" Christopher's mother asked.

The nurse turned to her. Startled. Christopher's mother instantly flagged the look on the nurse's face. There was a moment of the nurse wondering who this woman was. Once she realized it was the mother, she plastered on a poker face and spoke like she was in church.

"Let me get the doctor, ma'am."

The nurse quickly left. Christopher's mother moved to the bed. When she took Christopher's hand, it felt like touching a hot stove. She moved her hand to his forehead. She figured he must have a fever of 106 degrees. She looked at the monitors and found his temperature buried in all of the numbers and lights.

According to the monitor, he was 98.6.

Christopher's mother grabbed a cup of ice chips from his bedside table. She shook the ice out on her hands and gently put them on his forehead. The ice melted rapidly, as if it had been left on hot asphalt. His skin turned the ice to water and quickly to vapor. She grabbed more ice and packed it under his armpits, neck, and chest.

"Mrs. Reese," the voice said.

Christopher's mother turned to find the doctor in the doorway. His face was covered by a surgical mask.

"Doctor, you have to wake him up!" she said.

"Mrs. Reese, please have a seat."

"No!" she said. "He needs to wake up! You have to wake him up now!"

The doctor took down his surgical mask. His poker face was not as good as the nurse's. Whatever the news was, it was not good.

"Mrs. Reese, I'm sorry, but we've already tried everything. I'm afraid nothing has worked. We can't revive your son."

"Why not?" she asked, panicked.

"Christopher is brain-dead, Mrs. Reese."

The words landed on her chest, taking away her breath for a moment. Then, she snapped back to anger.

"The hell he is! We need to revive him! WE HAVE TO DO IT NOW!"

"Mrs. Reese, you don't understand—"

"No, you don't understand! Somebody has my son!"

The doctor gave a quick glance to the orderlies in the hallway. They entered the room quietly.

"Somebody has your son? What do you mean, Mrs. Reese?" the doctor asked calmly.

She was about to talk about the hissing lady wanting her boy to sleep. And his imaginary friend, the nice man, who was disguised as a white plastic bag. Then she noticed that the doctor was obsessively scratching his ear. His face was sweaty with fever. She could feel the orderlies standing behind her. Security would come next.

You will sound like a crazy person, Kate.

She thought it again to make sure it was her voice and not the false one.

You will sound like a crazy person.

It was her. And she was right. She looked at the faces in the room. She had seen her husband get this reaction before. That strange mixture of calm and tense. That watch-spring ready to pounce if the patient is deemed unstable or dangerous. They were all scratching their skin, as if this were an opium den. Doctor. Nurse. Orderlies. Security. All waiting for her to give them an excuse to pounce.

She realized that Christopher was back in the hospital. Unconscious. Right where the hissing lady wanted him. And if the hissing lady was powerful enough to arrange that, then she could easily manipulate a doctor into locking up a grieving mother for a psychiatric "evaluation."

"Who has your son, Mrs. Reese?" the doctor repeated.

"No one. I'm sorry. I just . . . I'm just . . . " She feigned speechless grieving.

The room instantly relaxed as if some invisible sergeant said "At ease."

"We understand, Mrs. Reese," the doctor said gently. "I know how difficult this is. Please, take all the time you need. Then, we can discuss next steps."

Christopher's mother knew what he meant by "next steps." He meant a grief counselor, a lawyer, a piece of paper, a pen, and a funeral. Once she signed Kate Reese on the dotted line, Dr. Feel Bad would pull the plug on every machine keeping her son alive. Never believing her that Christopher was not brain-dead. Never believing that her son was simply lost. Right where the hissing lady wanted him.

"I'm sorry I lost my temper," she said contritely. "I know you've done everything you can."

"No need to be sorry, Mrs. Reese. We understand. We'll give you some privacy. Take all the time you need."

The peanut gallery left the room, including a burly security guard, who scratched his thigh with his nightstick and looked at her like she was a ripe piñata. When she was alone, she kissed her son's hot sweaty forehead and whispered in his ear so no one—not even the hissing lady—could hear.

"Christopher, I'll get you out of there. I promise," she said.

CHAPTER 67

Ambrose opened his eyes. For a moment, he couldn't remember where he was. He didn't remember falling asleep, but he had. Several times. Why the hell was he sleeping so much? Of course, he was used to taking catnaps. That was normal for a man his age. But this Rip Van Winkle shit was ridiculous. The last thing he remembered was sleeping all the way through the Christmas Pageant. He woke up a few hours later for dinner. But when he arrived in the dining room, nobody was there. The clock read 2:17 a.m. And somehow, the calendar on the wall had one additional X, taking away an entire day.

Ambrose had slept for thirty-six hours.

"Good morning, Mr. Olson," a voice said. "Welcome back from the dead."

Ambrose turned to find the night nurse adding another X to the calendar.

Make that sixty.

"Good morning," he said. "I seem to have missed dinner."

"And breakfast. And lunch. And dinner again," she joked. "No worry. We put a mirror under your nose to make sure. I'll fix you a plate. Why don't you get warm in the parlor?"

The nurse fixed him a bowl of leftover beef stew and brought it to him in his favorite chair in front of the parlor TV, all the while chatting away with the Shady Pines gossip, starting with the Christmas Pageant. It seemed Ambrose had missed quite a show. In addition to the usual favorites of "I Saw Mommy Kissing Santa Claus" and "Grandma Got Run Over by a Reindeer," this year's pageant must have been sponsored by a new children's division of the WWE. There was an epic brawl that ended with Kate Reese's son being attacked by Mrs. Keizer. The boy's nose bled really badly, and his mother took him to the hospital, but that wasn't the half of it.

"What happened next?" he asked.

"Mrs. Keizer . . . she stopped forgetting," she said in her broken English.

"What do you mean?"

"She no have Alzheimer's anymore. It is a Christmas miracle."

Or was it?

He ignored the thought and the wind outside as he opened his brother's diary.

<u>June 7th</u>

> We dissected frogs in school today. I put my hand on the frog and I felt that strange itchy feeling again. The teacher said the frog must have only been sleeping because it woke up right there on the table. I pretended that was true, but when I left the tree house yesterday, I saw a bird on the trail going back home. It was dead on the ground. It had a broken wing and a snake was eating it. I chased the snake away and picked up the bird. I closed my eyes and had that itchy feeling from the imaginary side. I brought the bird back to life. It made my nose bleed real bad. It terrified me. Because I know the power on the imaginary side equals pain on the real side. You can't have one without the other. So, the more things I make live, the more I am going to die. So, when my nose bleeds, it's the world's blood.

A chill ran down Ambrose's spine. He thought of the nurse's story of Christopher's nose bleeding after he touched Mrs. Keizer, just like David's nose bled after he touched the dead bird. Ambrose made a mental note to call Mrs. Reese in the morning, then went back to the diary. But he couldn't keep his eyes open. He felt like he was being drugged. As if something didn't want him to read. It reminded him of the time his buddies threw a pill into his whiskey and laughed when he threw off his clothes and stole a jeep. That time, he woke up to the sergeant's wrath and a month of KP duty.

This time, he woke up to terror.

Ambrose heard a noise outside. The beef stew was cold and uneaten in front of him. An hour had passed. The TV was still on and turned to the local news. Talking about the flu epidemic and the rise in violent crime. He looked out through the window and saw deer running down the road. He took a quick breath. Something was here. Something evil. He turned his magnifying glass around and adjusted his bifocals. His eyes were dry and tired, but he had to decipher David's handwriting. He had to get to the truth.

June 12th

The soldier is worried about me. I am pushing myself too hard. I am bleeding too much. He says that people on the real side aren't supposed to have this much power, so I need to slow down. But I can't. I was walking into school, and I touched Mrs. Henderson's arm. My brain cooked, and my nose bled. I knew everything about her in 2 seconds. But it was more than the things that happened to her. I knew the things she was going to do someday. I knew she would stab her husband. I could see it over and over again. They were older people, and they were in the kitchen, and the hissing lady made her grab the knife and stab him in the throat. I screamed, and Mrs. Henderson asked what was wrong. I lied because if I told her the truth, she would have put me in a nut house.

Ambrose stopped reading. He knew that name. Henderson. He couldn't place it. Where did he know the name Henderson? It took him a moment to finally turn to the television, where Sally Wiggins read the local news.

"...the ongoing investigation of Mrs. Beatrice Henderson, who stabbed her husband in the kitchen. She worked at Mill Grove Elementary School as a librarian..."

The hair rose on the old man's arms. Ambrose turned quickly. He thought he felt someone watching him. But the parlor was empty. He turned back around. He turned the page. The voice was trying to lull him to sleep again. He fought it off and read.

June 15th

I couldn't sleep last night because my mind works too hard. I was so restless, I got up and started reading the encyclopedia. I started with the A volume at 10:30 p.m. By 5:30 the next morning, I finished Z. The scariest part was knowing the mistakes the men who wrote the encyclopedia made. It's funny when people don't realize knowledge does not end in a particular year. People thought the sun revolved around the Earth and that the Earth was flat. There was a time before Jesus that people thought Zeus was God. Men were killed for thinking otherwise. They didn't know the hissing lady was there making them afraid of new knowledge. They didn't know that she's always been there making them hate other people for trivial things.

" . . . sad news out of the Middle East tonight as four Christian missionaries were attacked trying to deliver much-needed food and supplies to the refugees . . ."

June 17th

The nose bleeds will not stop. My mother keeps taking me to doctors, but none of them know what's wrong with me. The soldier and I are trying to figure out a way to tell Ambrose the truth that will make him believe me. I need his help. I need him to fight her if I fail. But he never believes me. He thinks I am talking to myself when I am talking to the soldier. He thinks I am insane.

Ambrose took off his glasses and rubbed his burning eyes. He suddenly felt sleepy, but he slapped himself across the face like he did in the army during guard duty. Nothing was going to stop him from reading this. He felt as if the world depended on it.

June 21st

I don't really know where I am anymore. I don't know what's real or what's imaginary, but we can't wait any longer. The hissing lady is everywhere disguised as the flu. We have to complete the training now before she takes over the tree house. I asked the soldier why the hissing lady wanted it so much, and he explained what it is doing to me. The power that she wants for herself. It was so simple. It explained everything I was going through. I wanted to tell Ambrose what was really happening to me, but I couldn't have him call me crazy again. So, I waited until he was asleep, and I got into bed with him. I whispered really quietly in his ear just in case the hissing lady was listening.

"Ambrose. I have to tell you something."

"What?" he said asleep.

"I have to tell you what the tree house does."

"Fine. Go ahead," he said in his sleep. "What does the tree house do?"

Ambrose turned the page.

And that's when it happened.

At first, he didn't understand. The pages were so blurry that they looked almost grey. He squinted his eyes harder, but there were no more shapes. No more outlines to the letters. He held the magnifying glass up to his eyes. It changed nothing. He took away his bifocals. Nothing again.

He had finally gone blind.

"NURSE!" he yelled out.

Ambrose heard the floor creak near him. Little tiny baby steps. There was only silence. He thought he heard breathing near his ears. He didn't know what it was, but he could feel it. Something was in here. A little whisper that made the hairs on the back of his neck stand up.

"Who is that?" he said.

There was no response. Only silence. Ambrose called out to the nurse again, and he finally heard her walking down the hallway from the kitchen. He was going to ask her to read the next line.

Until she started coughing with the flu.

"You okay, Mr. Olson?" the nurse asked calmly in her broken English.

There was something in her voice. Something wrong. If Mrs. Reese were working tonight, he knew he could trust her with the diary. But her son Christopher was in the hospital after he touched Mrs. Keizer and his nose bled...

Just like David.

Ambrose knew he needed to get to Kate Reese. He needed to get to the sheriff. Whatever was happening back then was happening right now. And his brother's diary might be the only clue as to how to stop it.

"You okay, Mr. Olson?" the nurse asked again suspiciously.

The old man held the diary in his arms like his high school coach taught him to hold a football.

As if your life depended on it, boy.

The old man folded his brother's diary in his lap and did his best to put on a casual voice.

"I need you to take me to the hospital," he said.

"Why, sir?" she asked.

"Because the clouds have taken my eyes."

CHAPTER 68

The sheriff opened his eyes. He must have fallen asleep. He didn't know where he was. He looked around the room, but he couldn't find his sight. He had heard the term "blinding headache" before, but he never knew it could be literal. He had to blink for a full minute to get rid of the fog.

He calmed his mind and tried to find his way with his other senses. He was fairly certain he was in the records room because of the dusty smell. He must have fallen asleep when he was going over records with Mrs. Russo. But he couldn't hear anything.

"Hello? Mrs. Russo? Are you there?" he said.

Silence. The sheriff tried to remember how he got down here again. He remembered that he hadn't left the office in days despite having that horrible fever. He knew that every time he tried to get to the hospital to be with Kate and her son, there would be another emergency. Another bad traffic accident. Another stabbing. Another bar fight.

It was as if the world were conspiring to keep him away.

The sheriff was the furthest thing from a conspiracy theorist, especially when the theory involved something as groundless as coincidence. But he also had an instinct to know when someone was fucking with him, and that instinct was flashing red. There were simply too many coincidences that kept him from getting to Kate Reese and her son. There were too many distractions that kept him from doing his work in the records room. There was too much noise that kept him from remembering that . . .

that name . . . that little boy . . . what was his name?

The sheriff couldn't remember, but his instinct told him that was wrong. The voice kept telling him that he couldn't remember, but the sheriff knew he had an exceptional memory. Not exactly photographic, but close enough when it counted. And this one counted...Somehow this mattered to Kate Reese and Christopher and...

that name...that little boy...his name was...

The sheriff's hand began to itch again. God, it was itchy. He looked down at his hand, and his eyes started to find focus. In the dim light, he saw that his hand was scratched raw. The skin was red and broken. Blood had dried on his fingernails. But there was something else on his arm. Hidden under his sleeve. He vaguely remembered hiding something there.

his name was...that little boy's name was...

The sheriff pulled back his sleeve and saw words written on his arm in black ink.

David Olson

The sheriff suddenly remembered what he had done. He had started writing clues on his arm. At first, he used regular marker, but the sweat from the fever erased the trail like birds picking up bread crumbs. So, he had switched to permanent ink. The sheriff pulled back more of his sleeve.

David Olson is the name of the boy.
Don't fall asleep again. Call Carl about the tools <u>NOW</u>.

The sheriff dialed the phone before he had time to think. After two rings, he recognized his friend's voice on the other end.

"Carl, it's me," the sheriff said.

"What the hell," Carl said in a groggy voice. "Do you know what time it is?"

The sheriff looked at the clock. It was 3:17 a.m.

"I know it's late. I'm sorry. But this is really important," the sheriff said.

"That's what you said last time."

"What?" the sheriff asked.

"You called me an hour ago."

"I did?"

"Jesus Christ. How sick are you? You called me an hour ago to ask about those tools. I can't keep doing favors for you. Tomorrow is Christmas Eve, for Christ's sake!"

"I know. I'm sorry. What about the tools?"

"Are you kidding me? You don't even remember."

"Just tell me!"

The sheriff could hear Carl giving him the finger on the other end.

"Okay, but this is the last time, so you better write it down. I gave the tools to my friend at the museum. The tools go back hundreds of years, but they aren't typical for coal miners or farmers of those times."

"What do you mean?"

"The tools were more of what a child would use. And that old two-by-four grey stone you gave me was not stone. It was petrified wood."

The sheriff grabbed the pen and wrote furiously on his arm.

Tools belonged to children.

"So, that's it. Last favor. I can't keep doing this, especially now. My caseload doubled in a week."

The sheriff stopped writing for a moment.

"What do you mean your caseload doubled?"

"Jesus Christ. Are we going to have the exact same conversation we just had?"

"I'm sorry, Carl. I'm just really sick."

"As I said before," Carl said, doing his finest impersonation of a sarcastic asshole, "there must be a full moon or something in the water because the whole city is either getting sick or going crazy. I haven't been home in two days. My wife says if I'm not home for her mum's Christmas Eve dinner, she won't give me my Christmas present this year. I can't lose that. It's my only blow job all year."

The sheriff smiled involuntarily.

"Well, I appreciate your help, Carl. You're a good man."

"Tell _her_ that. Now stop calling me. Merry Christmas," Carl said.

"Merry Christmas."

The two friends hung up. The sheriff picked up the pen again and started writing. The itch spread over his hand. Screaming for attention, but the sheriff wouldn't let it win. Not this time.

Stone was petrified wood.
Whole city either has the flu or is going crazy.
Just like...

When the sheriff woke up, it took him a moment to realize where he was. He was in the records room. Mrs. Russo was gone. He must have fallen asleep again. It took his mind a while to fight through the headache, but eventually he remembered that he was trying to figure out a connection to what was going on in town and that little boy . . . Ambrose's little brother . . . what was his name again?

That name . . . that little boy . . . his name was . . .

The sheriff's hand was terribly itchy. He aimlessly scratched it and realized that his uniform was soaked with sweat. Somewhere in the night, his fever must have broken. He moved to peel back his uniform sleeve and found a bunch of notes written on his arm in permanent ink.

David Olson is the name of the boy.
Don't fall asleep again. Call Carl about the tools <u>NOW</u>.
Tools belonged to children.
Stone was petrified wood.
Whole city either has the flu or is going crazy.
Just like . . .

The sheriff moved his sleeve back and saw that the notes kept going and going and going.

Just like the year David Olson went missing. The last flu epidemic ended the day after David disappeared. Did David Olson stop the flu somehow? What did he do to stop it? Did he save us?

The sheriff got to the end of his arm. The writing stopped. Instinctively, he moved to the other arm. He loosened the wet uniform sleeve on his right arm. The writing was now left-handed, so it was sloppy. But it kept going.

Call Ambrose Olson!

The town is falling apart. You don't have time for this shit.

The sheriff nodded to himself. This was ridiculous. He had more emergencies than he knew what to do with. What the hell was he doing reading old case files and accident reports?

You still haven't seen Kate and her son in the hospital, and you're going to call Ambrose Olson to tell him about his brother who's been dead fifty years? That's crazy.

The sheriff peeled back more of his sleeve.

Stop listening to the voice in your head. It is lying to you. It is making you forget.

Okay. That's crazy. You must be delirious to write something like that.
"Who is that?" the sheriff said out loud.
You know who it is. It's you. And you look like an idiot talking to yourself.

You are not an idiot. The voice is distracting you. It is making you sleep.

"Who's there?" he said again.

The voice went silent. The temperature in the room plummeted. The sheriff thought he could hear breathing. He turned around. The room was empty. He was suddenly terrified. He rolled his sleeve up past the elbow.

You know what the tools were for! Run to Kate now. What happened to David is happening to Christopher. Run now!

The sheriff woke up in the records room. He didn't know how he had fallen asleep again. But this time, he didn't listen to the voice in his head. He was not distracted by any blinding headache. And it didn't take him a minute to find the writing. He looked down at his arm. The sleeve rolled up past the elbow. And he knew there was one more message hidden under his shirt. The records room was freezing. The sheriff held his breath, then rolled the sleeve up to his shoulder.

Too late, Sheriff. I hit them with a car.

The sheriff was running before his feet hit the ground. His heart pounded as he raced through the records room. He didn't care if there were a hundred more bar fights to break up. He didn't care if a hundred people needed to be put in the holding cells. There was only one emergency that mattered. He was going to get Kate and her son. They were going to find Ambrose. Because somehow, they were the only ones with the information about how to stop this madness or flu or whatever it was from destroying the town from the inside out. The sheriff ran up the stairs and raced into the main office past the poster of Emily Bertovich.

That's where he saw Mrs. Russo and four of his deputies.

They were all shot and bleeding on the floor.

The sheriff looked around. The office was empty. There was no one in the holding cells. All of the criminals were gone. Instinct and training took over his body. The sheriff rushed to his crew. Mrs. Russo was the first.

He checked her pulse. Thank God she was alive. The sheriff made a field dressing out of Mrs. Russo's blouse as he grabbed the radio.

"Five officers down. I need backup!"

The radio crackled with silence. The sheriff forgot all about rushing to Kate Reese and her son as he triaged the four deputies.

"I need backup at HQ! Now! Somebody answer me!"

There was no response. The static was unsettling. It sounded like a deranged Geiger counter announcing that the police force was completely gone. Somewhere in the back of his mind, the sheriff began to make contingency plans as to how he was going to deputize people. Track down those criminals. Get to Kate Reese. Find Ambrose Olson. The only good news in this whole tragedy was that Mrs. Russo and all four of his officers were still alive.

"Hi, Sheriff," a voice said behind him.

The sheriff spun around. He saw Mrs. Henderson standing with one of his deputies' pistols. Her clothes were soaked with blood. Her bare feet making little crimson footprints.

"David Olson touched my arm a long time ago. He knew I would stab my husband," Mrs. Henderson said.

The sheriff took cover behind a desk.

"Drop the gun!" he shouted.

Mrs. Henderson took another step toward him.

"The lady said I could get my husband to love me again. She said he was going to take me on a trip, and if he didn't, I could stab him again. And again. And again."

The sheriff raised his gun.

"Mrs. Henderson, put the gun down!"

"Why should I put it down? Sheriff, it'll never end. Don't you understand what's going on?"

"Put the God damn gun down NOW!"

Mrs. Henderson calmly put the gun on the desk.

"Okay, Sheriff, but it won't make any difference. She has him trapped now. And once he's dead, it will never end."

"What are you talking about?"

"Crime. We'll just hurt each other forever until someone puts an end to it. And someone will. Do you know why?"

The sheriff was silent. Mrs. Henderson smiled.

"Because God is a murderer, Daddy."

With that, Mrs. Henderson grabbed the gun and ran at the sheriff, screaming. The sheriff raised his gun and fired.

CHAPTER 69

Christopher was strapped to the gurney in the operating room. The hissing lady smiled down at him as he writhed like a fish on a boat deck. Her trophy. Her prize. She went to David Olson, unconscious on the metal table next to him. She petted his forehead like she would a little dog.

"We need the worm to catch the fish. Your tongue will be the squirming worm."

Christopher slammed his mouth shut.

"Open your mouth, Christopher."

Christopher stared at her in terror. He saw the key around her neck, buried under her flesh like a ghoulish necklace. The key for all of them to escape.

"Four ways in. Three ways out," she hummed. "You know two. We know more. I have the key. But where is the door?"

She took her scaly left hand and pressed down on his nose with her thumb and pointer. Cutting off his air.

"Now let's see that tongue. This is for your own good."

One minute became two and finally, his lungs gave out. Christopher took a massive breath of air. The hissing lady jammed her left hand inside his mouth and grabbed his tongue. Her right pulled out the scalpel.

And Christopher bit down.

"AHHHHHHHHHH!" the hissing lady shrieked.

Christopher's teeth snapped her pointer like a breadstick. He could feel the rotten meat in his mouth. He spit her finger to the floor. The hissing lady looked at the stump of her finger shooting blood like a fountain. She turned to him. The look on her face bordering on amazement. Or was that fear? She bent down and grabbed her severed finger. She put the finger back in its place. Then, she brought both finger and hand to her forehead and used the heat to weld it back together. Good as new.

"Okay, Christopher. You want to keep your tongue. That's fine. You can keep it."

Then, she slammed tape over his mouth.

"We'll just get the answers where they're really hiding," she said, tapping on his forehead. "Nurse, may I have the bone saw, please?"

Christopher screamed under the tape. He saw the nurse give the hissing lady a gleaming metal saw with jagged baby teeth. It turned on with a whir, screaming like a dentist's drill. The blade rested inches from his scalp. He closed his eyes, preparing for death. Yet somehow, he didn't feel scared. He felt almost soothed.

My mother is . . .
My mother is . . . with me on the real side.

He could feel her in the room with him. Her hands on his skin. Trying to find the cool side of the pillow.

My mother is . . .
My mother is . . . saying she will get me out of here.

Just then, the lights cut out, leaving the hospital in darkness. Christopher looked around, but he could see nothing. He just heard screams. And running footsteps. The sound of a body slamming against the hissing lady. The bone saw hitting her skin.

And the nice man's voice.

"Don't worry. I've got you," the nice man said.

Christopher felt the gurney move. Racing through the darkness.

"GET HIM! HE'S OFF THE STREET!" the hissing lady screamed.

"Say nothing. Don't leave her a trail."

"STOP HELPING HIM!" the hissing lady screeched at the nice man from the darkness.

The gurney took a sharp right and raced down the hallway. The children howled behind them. The nice man turned the gurney like a skateboard and raced toward a dim light at the end of the hallway. Christopher felt the nice man's soothing hand rip the leather restraints from his wrists.

"Sit up, son," he said gently. "I need your eyes."

Christopher ripped the tape from his mouth and shook his hands loose. Then, he sat up and tore the straps away from his ankles. He was free.

"Now what do you see?" the nice man said.

Christopher squinted in the darkness, but somehow, he could make out shapes. Mailbox people and deer. Crouched low in the shadows. Waiting to ambush.

"They're blocking the exit," Christopher said.

"Good job, son."

The nice man turned the gurney. Running faster and faster down another hallway. His feet hitting the floor. Smack smack smack. Like a grandma's kiss. The gurney slammed through two doors, which swung like shutters in a storm. The nice man stopped and wrapped his belt around the door handles. The mailbox people threw themselves against the door. The belt stretched like saltwater taffy.

But it held.

They entered the maternity ward, and suddenly the gurney slowed to a crawl.

"Be quiet," the nice man whispered. "We can't wake them."

Christopher squinted in the darkness and realized where they were.

The nursery.

Row after row of babies. Some in incubators. Most in glass bassinets. All of them sleeping. The nice man pushed the gurney through the nursery like a boat through a swamp. Inch by painful inch. Christopher saw one baby stir as if having a nightmare. Then, another. They started to twitch like the first kernels of popcorn on a skillet. Pop. Pop. Pop. The nice man picked up his pace. More babies twitched. Christopher could feel the room waking up around them. The babies would begin crying soon. Sounding the alarm. As if left on a porch. One baby opened its eyes. It looked around in the darkness. It began to whimper. Another opened. Another. Christopher felt the gurney go faster. And faster. Racing to the other side. The first baby began to cry.

"Waaaaaaaa," it said.

It woke up its neighbor.

The sound traveled around the room like a pinball, waking up neighbor after neighbor. Baby after baby. The babies began to wail.

"WAAAAAAAAA!"

"It's the alarm," Christopher said.

"No. It's the dinner bell."

The lights turned on. Christopher saw them. Little babies with glowing eyes watching them. Drooling. Their mouths filled with sharp baby teeth. The babies began to crawl. Out of the bassinets. Cracking the walls of the incubators like serpent's eggs.

There was nothing left to do but run.

The nice man picked up the gurney on two wheels and raced to the exit. Babies climbed down from the glass and scurried on the floor like little spiders. The nice man crashed through the exit doors and aimed the gurney right at the end of the hallway. Christopher looked up and saw a laundry chute sitting in the wall like an open mouth. He felt the nice man pick up the pace. Three more thundering steps. Then, he climbed on the gurney behind Christopher like the anchor of a bobsled team.

"Hang on."

The gurney hurtled toward the wall. Christopher braced himself for impact. The laundry chute opened, and in a flash, the gurney went through it like a mat on a waterslide. Twisting and turning in darkness. Christopher screamed. Part fear. Part joy. Like the best and worst of all roller coasters. He looked up ahead and saw something dancing.

A reflection. Of stars. In water.

"Brace yourself," the nice man said, tensing his body.

Christopher clutched the nice man the way he used to cling to his mother after he saw Dracula. The water got closer. And closer. And then . . .

SPLASH!

The gurney hit the water like a skipping rock. It sliced through the creek bed, slowing, then stopping. The freezing water felt soothing on his feverish skin. For a moment, he thought that maybe the water was his mother putting ice cubes on his body. Christopher looked up. He saw the shooting stars in the night sky and the stones of the billy goat bridge.

They were back in the Mission Street Woods.

"What was that?" Christopher asked.

"Escape tunnel," the nice man said. "We have to get you out of here. They can see you at night."

The nice man is . . .

The nice man is . . . terrified.

"Hi, Christopher," the voice said.

It was the man in the hollow log. He was standing. Wide awake. His eyes black as coal. His face still scarred from the time Christopher saw the deer eating it.

"I've heard so much about you," the man said.

Then, he lunged at Christopher.

"Get me out of this!" he screamed.

The nice man grabbed Christopher's arm and ran. The man in the hollow log dropped and rolled after them. The nice man took a hard turn down a narrow trail. The man in the hollow log was about to run over them when he hit a thicket of branches and stopped like a fly in a web. The nice man jumped Christopher through a small space in the trees. Christopher heard the man in the hollow log's screams echo through the woods.

"GET ME OUT OF THIS!"

"He's sounding the alarm. Others will follow. Go!"

Christopher and the nice man reached the clearing. They raced to the tree house.

"How did you find me?" Christopher asked.

"Your mother," the nice man said. "She was right there with you. I just followed her light. She promised to get you out of here. And that's what I'm doing."

The nice man helped Christopher to the tree. It was warm like a mug of his mother's coffee.

"But what about you?"

"I don't matter. You do."

"You matter to me."

Christopher walked over and held the nice man, who flinched at being touched. It reminded Christopher of soldiers who listen to fireworks and can only hear bullets.

"Are you my dad?"

"No. I'm not your dad. Christopher, you need to go. Now."

Christopher nodded and climbed the ladder. He reached the top step and put his hand on the doorknob of the tree house. He turned it.

But it was locked.

"Christopher, stop stalling," the nice man said below.

"I'm not. It's locked."

"What?"

"The tree house door. It's locked."

"Oh, God!" the nice man said.

The nice man climbed the steps. He put his hand on the doorknob. He turned it with all of his might. It wouldn't budge. The nice man's face went white.

"NO!" he screamed.

"What's happening?" Christopher asked. "Why won't it open?"

"You're still in the hospital on the real side. You can't get back to your body. You can't wake up."

Fear pushed the word to Christopher's throat.

"What?"

The nice man banged on the door, turning his knuckles bloody. He bashed his fists on the windows. The glass didn't even bend.

"This is a trap. She arranged all of this," the nice man said. "She locked you in."

Finally, the nice man's arms gave out. He stopped hitting the tree house and slumped over with bloody fists.

"But what does that mean?" Christopher asked.

The nice man turned to Christopher. Unable to mask his despair.

"It means you're dying."

CHAPTER 70

Beeeeeeeep.

Kate Reese turned her attention from her son to the machines keeping him alive. They were suddenly flashing red.

Beeeeeeeep.

Before she could utter a word, the ICU nurses and doctor rushed into the room.

"What's happening?!" she asked.

"His pressure's dropping," the doctor said to the nurse, ignoring her. "I'm going to need ten cc's of . . ."

Thus began an assault of medical jargon that was too fast to follow. Christopher's mother didn't understand much, but she understood perfectly the doctor's "polite" request to . . .

"Get her out of here!"

"NO!" she shrieked.

The orderlies entered the room.

"That won't be necessary," Nurse Tammy said. "She was just going. Please, Mrs. Reese."

Christopher's mother allowed Nurse Tammy to persuade her into the hallway seconds before the orderlies dragged her out kicking and screaming. Broken ribs or not. She stood outside her son's room, trying to will herself through the walls.

"He'll be fine, Mrs. Reese," Nurse Tammy said gently. "It was just a sudden drop in blood pressure. They'll stabilize him."

After three minutes that felt like hours, the doctor came out and repeated what Nurse Tammy had said. Minus the compassion.

"Mrs. Reese, as long as your son is in the hospital, we are bound by law to resuscitate him, but I must say respectfully . . ."

Pull the plug already.

". . . your son shows no sign of brain activity. He will never wake up," the doctor said.

"Can I see my son now?" she asked, ignoring him.

His eyes narrowed to angry slits.

"No, Mrs. Reese. The nurses are turning the beds over. You can come back in half an hour," he said.

"Half an hour for a bed?! Are you kidding me?"

". . . or forty-five minutes. Your choice," the orderly said, scratching his arm.

He wants an excuse to call security. He wants you to lose it, Kate.

Christopher's mother saw the officious little look on the vicious little man. She wanted to punch him, but punching got her detained. Punching got her son killed. So, she swallowed her "fuck you" and forced a nod.

"Thank you, Doctor," she said.

I'll get you out of here, Christopher. I promise.

Christopher's mother set the alarm on her watch for thirty minutes. She didn't want to be away for a second, but she sure as hell wasn't going to waste this time. She ignored the pain in her side as she quickly made the long walk back through the ICU. She reached the end of the ICU hallway and waited to be buzzed out. She looked over as a nurse whispered to an orderly. Staring at her. Scratching. Their eyes swimming with thoughts. *That's the horrible woman who won't pull the plug. We need that bed for other people.* She saw Mr. Henderson, the librarian's husband, in one of the rooms. He was sitting up in bed with his hands on his throat.

The door buzzed.

Kate walked through the waiting room of the ICU. Everywhere she looked, people were desperate. Yelling about how the cafeteria was running out of food. Arguing about which channel to watch on the television. They flipped back and forth between the CNN coverage of the Middle East and a Bad Cat cartoon.

"My kid wants to fucking watch this!" a man yelled.

She saw a man viciously kicking the vending machine.

"Fucking thing took my last dollar!" he screamed.

The man kicked it three more times, finally cracking the plastic Coca-Cola swoosh. Then, he sat down and cried like a child.

"My wife is sick. I don't have any more dollars," he said.

Kate instinctively reached for money to help the man, then realized that she was wearing a hospital gown. Her backside was exposed. She covered herself with one hand and hit the elevator button with the other. Some construction workers looked at her from down the opposite hallway. She could see their eyes cross her bare legs as if sampling food at a grocery store.

"Hey, honey. What's your name?" a construction worker asked.

She reached for her cell phone. It wasn't there. No pockets.

"Wait. Don't go, beautiful!" the man called out, rushing toward the elevator.

The elevator finally opened. Kate hit the button. 1. 1. 1. 1. 1. 1. 1. 1.

"Stuck-up bitch!" the man yelled just as the elevator door closed.

Kate found her breath and focused. There had to be a way to get Christopher away from this hospital. She looked at her watch. Twenty-eight minutes. The elevator door opened. She walked back to her room on the east wing. The hallways were packed. There wasn't a free bench. A free chair. A free space on the floor. The people were scratching their arms. They all looked sick. And angry. And murderous. And desperate.

"What the fuck do you mean there are no pillows?!" a voice called out.

Kate reached her room. She quickly traded her hospital gown for street clothes, now torn and caked with her son's blood. She found her cell phone in her coat pocket. There was a little more battery left, but there was no signal in her room. She wandered back into the hallway. She kept walking down the hall, looking for a signal. She passed Mrs. Keizer's room. The old lady was still unconscious on the bed while her grandson Brady read to her from a chair.

"All the better to hear you with, my dear," he said.

Still no bars on the phone.

She passed an empty room that was being readied for the next patient as orderlies grabbed a middle-aged man holding on to the bed for dear life.

"My insurance didn't lapse! I have rights!"

Still no bars.

She walked through the emergency room entrance.

"We've been sitting here for forty hours, you son of a bitch!"

"So have I, asshole! Now sit down and wait your fucking turn!"

She walked outside to the parking lot.

She finally got a bar.

She dialed the sheriff. It rang once. Twice. Maybe the sheriff could call in a favor. Get an ambulance to take Christopher out of the hospital. Far away from Mill Grove. Far away from the hissing lady. She checked her watch. Twenty-four minutes.

The phone kept ringing. Three rings. Four rings. Five.

They could get out of here. Run away to some safe place. She would sell the house. They could send her the check. She would spend every dime of it on Christopher's medical care.

My son is not going to die today.

More rings. Six. Seven. Eight.

The voice mail clicked on.

"Bobby," she said. "I don't know how to say this in a voice mail, so you'll just have to trust me."

She heard an ambulance wailing. She covered her ears and shouted into the phone.

"I need to get Christopher out of here. Can you get anything? An ambulance. A medevac helicopter. I'll pay for it. I don't care."

The ambulance screamed into the parking lot. The EMTs rushed out.

"But I want you to come with us. I want you to be safe. Because something very bad is happening here. And right now, you are my son's only—"

She was about to say "hope" when she saw the EMTs wheel out the sheriff on a gurney. The sheriff's eyes were closed. His shirt cut open, his chest a mess of bloody bandages, an oxygen mask over his face.

Christopher's mother was speechless.

She looked on, dazed, as the ER doctor rushed out to meet the gurney. Through all of their shouting, she realized that there had been a shooting in the sheriff's station. Mrs. Henderson, the school librarian, had escaped from jail and shot the sheriff in the chest. The sheriff should have died already, but somehow he was hanging on.

Christopher's mother raced after the sheriff, but the orderlies stopped her. They would not let her into emergency surgery. It took a minute of stunned silence for her to realize that her phone was still on, and she was still leaving the sheriff a voice mail. She hung up and sat down outside. Her ribs like a toothache in the cold.

She didn't know what to do. So, instinctively, she just started calling friends. Anyone she thought might be able to help. Special Ed's mother and father. Mike and Matt's mothers. She got nothing. No voice mails. All texts were returned. No emails would go through.

She was completely alone.

Christopher's mother looked down at the phone in her hand. The time snapped her out of anything resembling self-pity. She had fifteen minutes until she could see her son. Her eyes darted back and forth, trying to think of what to do next. Was there another person to call? Someone she hadn't thought of? She looked back through the emergency room. She saw two men fighting each other for a chair. On the TV, the blond newswoman said that traffic accidents had already tripled the record high for December, and it was only the twenty-third.

"And now on to happier news. Christmas is only two days away. And what was the number one present kids asked for this year? Bad Cat dolls," she said with a smile.

"That's right, Brittany. The number one present adults asked for? Guns."

Someone turned the channel back to CNN.

"And now on to international news and the growing unrest in the Middle East..."

"I'm sick of this shit," a voice called out. "I don't care about the Middle East."

"My family is from there, asshole!"

"Then, go back to where you came from and help."

"The refugees are desperate, Anderson. The talk on the ground is that more bloodshed is imminent."

Christopher's mother closed her eyes. She didn't realize she was praying until she had finished.

"Please, God. Help us."

Suddenly, she sensed something. It wasn't a feeling so much as a smell. It smelled like baseball gloves.

Ambrose.

The name came to her from out of nowhere.

Ambrose Olson.

When you're in a war, ask a soldier. Who said that? Jerry of all people. Drunk and watching grainy footage of the Allies saving the world from ruin.

Ambrose could help us.

Christopher's mother dialed Shady Pines. As she waited for the phone to ring, the EMTs carried in the rest of the deputies, all of them gravely wounded. For a second, she had a chilling thought.

There are no police left. There is no law anymore.

"Shady Pines?" the voice said on the other line.

"Sheila . . . it's Kate. I need to speak to Mr. Olson."

"He ain't here."

"What do you mean?"

"He's in the hospital."

"What?"

"Sorry. I gotta go. Natives are restless with this God damn flu."

Click.

It took Christopher's mother all of five minutes with the ER admission nurse to find out that Ambrose Olson had been rushed to the hospital from Shady Pines after he had gone blind. Thanks to being a favorite among the hospital staff, he received a bed about thirty-nine hours ahead of schedule. He had been placed exactly three doors down from her son's room in the ICU. Kate Reese knew it could be fate. It could be coincidence. Or it could be help from the nice man. Whatever it was, she did not question it anymore. She needed whatever friends she could get.

Even imaginary ones.

She found Ambrose in his room. His eyes bandaged. Clutching his brother's old diary. She knocked on the door.

"Mr. Olson?" she said.

"Mrs. Reese? Thank God. I've been asking around for you."

"Me?" she said, surprised but somehow not at all surprised. "What for?"

"I need you to finish reading my brother's diary," he whispered.

"Why are you whispering?" she asked.

"You promise not to laugh?" he asked.

"Nothing is funny right now," she said. "Try me."

When Ambrose got done explaining about David's experience with tree houses and hissing ladies, it didn't take long for Kate Reese to realize it was happening again. But this time to her son. She sat down and took the diary.

*

Ambrose could not see Kate Reese as she read aloud to him like a mother to a child. But after everything she told him about Christopher's car accident and the sheriff being shot, he imagined this beautiful 110-pound woman looking a little like the last candle flickering in the eye of a hurricane.

Please protect her, God.

The prayer came out of nowhere. And it surprised him. But once he confirmed that it was indeed his own voice, he doubled down on it. Because somewhere deep in his soul, he believed that if something happened to Kate Reese, the world would come to an end.

CHAPTER 71

Whata fucking year.

That's what Jerry thought as he lay awake in bed. He looked outside the window. It was right before dawn. On the twenty-third of December. He couldn't remember the last time he had been up this early. Not since the last dream. Recently, he had been having these wicked dreams. He was always in his house or his neighborhood or getting some ribs at the Bone Yard, and he would see Kate Reese. She would be a little different every time, but always beautiful. With a key around her neck. And a wicked little smile. She would let him do everything that he ever wanted to her. Violent. Angry. Dirty. Hateful. It didn't matter. She loved it. She loved him. Every night, he would go to sleep to meet the Kate Reese of his dreams. Then, every morning, Jerry would wake up. He would turn over in bed, and he would see the empty space where the real Kate Reese used to be. And that fucking voice would ring in his ears.

You miss her, Jerry.

Every morning, his mind felt like his car parked in the front yard after a bender. The lawn looks like your driveway, and those dreams look like your life. But they aren't your life. Kate Reese was gone, and she was never coming back. He tried to let her go many times, but then he'd hear some God damn song or see some God damn girl in cutoffs and remember that this one time, he had been able to trick a legitimately good woman into loving him.

Until she left you in the middle of the night, Jerry.

Jerry turned over in bed. He didn't have a shift today, so he thought he'd go down to 8 Mile. The bars weren't open, but he knew an after-hours club that might let him in the back door. He could have a drink and maybe pick some low-hanging fruit. Sure, it was morning, but fuck it. There was no bitch telling him what he could do anymore. He got paid on Friday. What did he care?

He threw his jeans on and got in his Chevy. He was at 8 Mile twenty minutes later. He parked his car outside the infamous watering hole and walked inside. The jukebox was playing a great song. Hotel California by the Eagles. The room was covered in cigarette smoke. It was so thick, Jerry felt like he was walking through a cloud. He sat down and ordered a gin and tonic. He looked over at the girl at the bar, and he couldn't believe his luck.

Sally.

He knew Sally from way back in high school. She was always a good Catholic girl until one day, she most decidedly was not. Like most Catholics, she went from zero to sixty in about six seconds once someone put the key in the ignition. A year later, she was caught tag-teaming a couple of football players in the backseat of her daddy's Ford. She was forever known as "Mustang Sally" after that. Daddy's car was actually a Focus, but "Ford Focus Sally" just didn't have the same ring to it. Whatever the model, Sally wasn't the sharpest knife, but she still loved to have a good time. And he needed a good time. He had a few bucks in his pocket. He was free. He was young-ish. He could grab Sally, get in his old Chevy, and just drive to the casinos in West Virginia to whitewash Kate Reese out of his skull.

"West Virginia?!" Sally said. "You're crazy. It's snowing like hell outside. They have casinos in Detroit. Why the fuck would we drive to West Virginia?"

Good question.

Call it his gut. Call it a hunch. Call it a gin and tonic. But something told Jerry that his luck would change in West Virginia. Something told him that today could be his lucky day if he would just listen to the voice inside his head.

You can't lose, Jerry.

"You coming or not?" he asked Sally.

She was coming.

An hour later, his Chevy was sliding down a highway coated in snow. It was the worst snowstorm since that blizzard after Thanksgiving. Global warming his lily-white ass. Everywhere he looked, it seemed like one car was stalled out or another car got in an accident. But for him, it was smooth sailing. Sally kept flipping through the dial like a burglar trying to crack a safe. Top 40. Hip hop. An oldies station playing Blue Moon. He started to regret bringing Sally. All she seemed to know how to do was fuck up his radio and talk about how her co-workers were plotting against her. She worked at JCPenney for fuck's sake. Do women have nothing better to do than pretend the world cares about them?

"Sally, pick a fucking station already."

"Fine. Fine. Dick," she said.

She finally landed on a classic rock station outside of Cleveland playing the Eagles' Hotel California. Twice in one day.

He took that as a good omen.

When they reached the casino, he drove past the valet to self-parking. Sally gave him a dirty look for that one. Well, excuuuuse meeeee if he wanted to save a few bucks. They walked across the freezing parking lot, the sky opening up with a furious wind that whipped the snow around their heads like Dorothy's twister. How many times did he see The Wizard of Oz on those fucking Movie Fridays with Kate Reese and her weird son?

You miss her, Jerry.

But she doesn't miss you.

That voice. That pain-in-the-ass voice. It told him, go ahead. Drink all night. Gamble. Take road trips. Fish with the guys. Hunt with your cousins. Nothing you do will ever take this thought away.

She's the best you'll ever get, Jerry. And she's gone.

He knew that Kate Reese was out there, somewhere. She was probably with some new guy. Letting him have her body. Touching him everywhere. The feeling made him sick. It made his stomach angry. He had to get to the casino floor. Get a real drink. Make it stop.

"Sally, hurry the fuck up," he shouted.

"You try to walk on this shit in heels," Sally barked.

The doors opened to a cloud of cigarette smoke hovering over the white noise of slots and video poker. Sally had to pee. Of course. It was barely 10:00 a.m., but Jerry sat at the bar and guzzled a double Tanqueray with a little tonic water. The drink burned like a good workout, but it still wasn't enough. He needed a distraction to get rid of that voice. He looked around and found that someone had left a newspaper on the bar.

It was some Pittsburgh newspaper.

From a couple of months ago.

Jerry looked for the sports page, but of course, some low-life had already grabbed it. So, he leafed through the rest of the rag. The Middle East crisis was still going on. Jesus. That's still considered news? Tell me when the crisis stops. Then, I'll buy a paper. And the refugees? I have an idea. Get on your feet and start walking north. How fucking hard is that to figure out? Who sits still when the world is coming to an end around them? Fucking idiots. That's who.

Jerry turned the page to the life section and saw a headline, "Boys Find Skeleton in Woods." He was about to look down at the picture when Sally walked up with her caked-on face and an empty bladder.

"God, it smells like hell in there," she said.

Jerry threw down the newspaper and threw himself into blackjack. It wasn't usually his game, but something told him to sit down and start small. Call it a voice. He split two queens and remembered how Kate Reese told him that the queen's face on a playing card was the portrait of Queen Elizabeth. He got two aces and won a hundred bucks. He ordered another gin and tonic. Kate said that the drink was invented by British soldiers in some war or another. The tonic water prevented malaria somehow.

You miss her, Jerry.

She's fucking somebody else, Jerry.

Jerry ordered two more drinks over Sally's objections that it wasn't even noon, and he was already getting drunk. But he didn't care. Because that pain-in-the-ass voice had a different edge to it today. Something he couldn't quite put his finger on. Something that made him feel invincible.

So, he decided to take it out for a spin.

He looked at the cards on the table. The dealer gave him a pain-in-the-ass 13. But for some reason, he just knew it would be okay. *Fuck it. There's four 8s in the deck, right?* He hit, and he got his 8. Another 21. Another fifty bucks. He did it again with a 12. And again with an 18. A crowd began to gather around him. He knew what they were all thinking. Who is this low-life in the Lions cap with this trashy slut, who looks like she learned how to put on her makeup at a clown college?

I'll tell you who I am, assholes.

I'm the motherfucker who can't lose today.

The voice told him to only bet ten bucks on the next hand. Sure enough, he busted. His gut told him to play five hundred on the next. Blackjack. A girl clapped behind him. Some pretty Indian—Squaw, not Bombay—holding her own copy of that same old Pittsburgh newspaper in her sharp red fingernails. He wondered why everyone had all these old newspapers lying around until a voice brought him back.

"Blackjack!"

It went on like that for hours. The pit boss changed dealers to make his streak go cold. They shut down the table and made him move. They made it six decks instead of one, thinking maybe he was counting cards. Whatever they did, it didn't matter.

You can't lose, Jerry.

At 5:00 p.m., Jerry stood up on drunken legs and wandered over to the roulette wheel. Sally told him not to push his luck, but he stopped listening to anything but that voice in his head. The first number he played was 9. When he hit on 9, even Sally shut the fuck up. The guys at the bar had told him about this kind of streak. He had never seen one. Not even from the cheap seats. But right now, he was unbeatable. The voice told him to bet twenty bucks on black. Ten on red. Sit one out. It hit green. The hot Indian girl sidled up next to him. She put her newspaper down on the ground and locked her high heels into the chair for some serious gaming.

"Mind if I read your paper?" Sally asked, bored as a high school girl watching her boyfriend play video games.

The hot Indian girl handed it over. Sally looked at the paper. Nothing on Hollywood. Just some boring story about four little boys finding a skeleton in the woods in Western Pennsylvania.

"Oh, this little boy is so cute," Sally said, pointing to the picture. "Look, Jerry."

"Sally, would you shut the fuck up?" Jerry said, putting his money down on 33.

"Thirty-three!" the hot Indian girl yelled.

You can't lose, Jerry.

Jerry closed his eyes as the ball ran around the roulette wheel. He saw Kate Reese's face in his mind. The apartment empty the morning after she snuck away. What did he do that night that was so terrible? He hit her, yes, but he said he was sorry, and he actually meant it. So, fuck her if she didn't believe him. Fuck that bitch.

You miss her, Jerry.
You want to find her.

"Four!" the hot Indian girl yelled.

By midnight, the pit boss called over the manager, who comped Jerry a room on the spot with a politician's smile and a douche's handshake. The hot Indian girl got up and congratulated him on the streak of all streaks. She had spent the entire time losing, but for some reason, she kept playing right next to him. All day. With a seemingly never-ending supply of chips. Maybe she was another plant of the casino. Maybe she was a prostitute. All he knew was that she was hot as hell. She got up from the table, leaving the old newspaper at his feet. He picked it up and called out to her.

"Excuse me, miss? You forgot your paper."

She walked back to him and flashed him a smile and a dirty little look.

"Jerry, do you know what the numbers on a roulette table add up to?" she asked.

"No. Why don't you tell me over breakfast?" he said.

He couldn't believe his balls. But there it was. The invitation hanging in the air like the cloud of cigarette smoke. He thought Sally would claw his eyes out with her press-on nails for saying it. But "Mustang Sally" was oddly quiet. The hot Indian girl smiled at him so wide that he thought she'd run out of teeth.

You can't lose, Jerry.

The three of them went up to the comped suite and opened a bottle of complimentary champagne. The hot Indian girl turned on the television because she said she could be a "little loud." Around 3:00 a.m., the television station started playing the local news from the tristate area. Jerry could hear the news anchor blah blahing about a terrible traffic accident involving the boy who had won the lottery for his mother back in September and found the skeleton in November, but never turned around to see the actual footage. He was too busy watching the girls licking champagne off each other as the wind pummeled the large windows with the view of downtown Wheeling. Jerry crammed as much sex into one night as he possibly could, but every time he slowed down, even for a moment, the voice returned.

You miss her, Jerry.

You have to find her, Jerry.

Jerry woke up an hour before dawn. He might have had thirty minutes of sleep at most, but for some reason, he was wide awake. He drank the last of the warm, flat champagne to get rid of his splitting headache. He had been hungover before. Sometimes when he was still drunk. But this headache was different somehow. It felt personally pissed at him or something. Like he'd fucked the headache's wife. He heard Sally in the shower, but the hot Indian girl was long gone. He expected her to have robbed him blind, or maybe taken a thousand bucks for "services rendered" if she was indeed a professional, but she didn't even steal one poker chip.

But she did leave her old newspaper behind.

You miss her, Jerry.

You want to find her, Jerry.

She's fucking some other guy, Jerry.

The bitch is laughing at you right now, Jerry.

After the streak of streaks, the voice had come back as mean as a snake. The only thing he could do to get Kate out of his mind was read that old newspaper from the fall. He skimmed through a weather forecast predicting this would be an unseasonably mild winter. Great work, Kreskin. He was about to turn to the life section when he thought to skip ahead to sports. Luckily for him, the hot Indian girl's newspaper was intact.

About halfway through a story about the Pittsburgh Steelers' quest for another Super Bowl (try being a Lions fan, assholes), Sally came out of the shower, crying her eyes out. Jerry realized that when the booze wore off, so did the "Mustang" part of Sally. And whatever part of her was actually bi-curious was no match for her Catholic school upbringing in Flint.

"It's Christmas Eve. I need to go home," she said.

"Okay, Sally. Let's go," he said.

He left the newspaper in the hotel room. Facedown.

As he walked through the cloud of cigarette smoke on the casino floor for the last time, he looked around for the hot Indian girl. He realized he didn't even know her name. Maybe she was a mirage, like in that song, Hotel California. He hummed his own version. Welcome to the Hotel West Virginia. Such a shitty place. Such a shitty face.

The casino doors opened like a mouth and puked them outside. The fresh air was sweet. Pure, dry, and clean as the moonlight peeking through the clouds.

He walked slowly through the parking lot. The wind swept across his face. And it smelled like something. He was probably hungover still. But for some reason, he thought of being a little kid going hunting for the first time. That smell of the woods mixed with powder burns and beer. He couldn't stop thinking about his mom's old boyfriend who taught him how to shoot. The really bad one who also taught him how not to be afraid of a baseball by throwing them at his head.

He groaned when he saw his car. Some asshole had put one of those stupid flyers in his windshield wiper. When he got a little closer, he realized it wasn't a Jiffy Lube coupon or a We-Buy-Junk-Cars ad. It was a set of four index cards. They were attached to something hanging off them with strings. The wind kicked it up, and Jerry saw four colored deflated rubber things slapping the side of his Chevy.

They were four popped balloons.

Jerry looked at the cards.

Sir or Madam:

You have found balloons for the Mill Grove Elementary School Balloon Derby. Please contact us at your earliest convenience, so our students can see how far their balloons went. Thank you very much.

Jerry turned the cards over and saw a bunch of names that meant nothing to him. Matt something. Mike something. Eddie who-gives-a-shit. He was about to throw away the cards when the wind whipped a cold snap through his jacket. The hunting smell was all over him. And that little voice inside his head told him to just look at the last card before he threw them all away. His hands shivered as he turned it over and read the last name.

Christopher Reese

It's your lucky day, Jerry.

CHAPTER 72

The nice man led Christopher under a thick knot of trees and down an old path, worn and weathered by time. He moved some dead brush out of the way to reveal a fresh trail hidden behind it. Christopher looked at the clouds above the Mission Street Woods. The moonlight trapped inside them like a lantern. The hissing lady was spreading everywhere. Something terrible was coming.

It means you're dying.

The nice man's words echoed through Christopher's mind as they came to the old abandoned refrigerator. Big and white like an "icebox" in the old movies his mother loved. Its rusted chrome reminded Christopher of Jerry's old Chevy in the driveway.

Jerry is coming . . .
Jerry is coming . . . to kill my mother.

Christopher had to get out of the imaginary world. He had to get out and save her.

"Here we are," the nice man whispered.

The nice man opened the refrigerator door with a squeeeak. The refrigerator had no backing. Just a huge patch of dirt.

"What is this?" Christopher asked.

"My last hiding place," the nice man said.

The nice man got on his knees and wiped away the dirt, revealing a trapdoor. He opened it, and Christopher saw a long staircase leading to a room like a bomb shelter.

"She hasn't found this one yet," the nice man whispered. "I was saving it for an emergency. We have to hide you until daylight."

Christopher climbed inside. The nice man quietly closed the refrigerator door behind them. Christopher followed the nice man down the long stairs. When they reached the floor, the nice man folded the staircase like an attic door. The springs groaned as the steps locked together, leaving them hidden underground. The nice man lit a kerosene lamp. Then, he opened a portable cooler. There were bottles of water, Coca-Cola, fruit, cheese, and candy.

"Where did you get all that?" Christopher asked.

"People on a diet. Their nightmares are all about food. They don't mind when you take it. Trust me. You're doing them a favor," the nice man said.

Christopher filled his arms like a greedy shopping cart.

"Not the candy," the nice man cautioned. "We are only staying here until daylight. This is your last time eating for a while. We have to get you out of here before midnight. You'll need your strength."

Christopher begrudgingly traded a Snickers for applesauce and sat down on the floor. He looked around at the nice man's shelter. It was simple and bare. A cot. A locker. Some clothes. A clock on the wall. But the clock didn't measure hours and minutes.

It measured years.

Christopher looked at the number: 2,020. The number of months: 24,240. The number of days: 737,804 days of this terror. Of this torture. He looked at the nice man's scars. On his feet. On his hands. The crooked way he walked from his bones broken so many times over so many centuries.

"How old were you when she took you?" Christopher asked.

The nice man looked at him, surprised by the question.

"She didn't take me. I volunteered. Now eat."

The nice man opened a bottle of water and drank. Then, he screwed on the cap and swallowed, the water cutting through his battered body like a cold river.

"What happens at midnight?" Christopher asked.

The nice man said nothing. He simply put a finger in front of his mouth and mimed the word "Shhhhhh." He pointed above them. Christopher stopped and listened to the voices searching for him up above in the woods.

"Chrissssstopher! Chrissstopher! Where are you?!"

The nice man stood up. Tense and ready.

"I can't smell him anymore. Can you hear him?" the voices called out to each other.

Christopher watched the nice man, perched near the ladder, ready to strike if they came down. Everything in his posture made Christopher feel safe. The nice man was ready to defend Christopher to the death if that's what the night brought. Christopher had seen his mother like this before. He didn't know men could feel that way about children.

Finally, the voices moved on, and there was silence. Christopher was about to speak when the nice man held up one finger. Then, he picked up a piece of paper and scribbled quickly in number 2 pencil.

THEY ARE STILL UP THERE. IT'S A TEST.

Christopher took the pencil and scribbled. He handed the note back to the nice man.

What happens at midnight?

Christopher studied the nice man's face. Grave and haunted. The nice man shook his head with a silent "no" and wrote back.

I DON'T NEED YOU SCARED. I NEED YOU STRONG.

The nice man kept writing, but all Christopher could feel were his thoughts playing hide-and-seek between the words.

The nice man is . . .
The nice man is . . . afraid to tell me the truth.
The nice man knows . . . it will terrify me.

The temperature in the shelter dropped a couple of degrees. Christopher grabbed the pad out of the nice man's hands and wrote on the paper.

If you don't tell me, I'll just read your mind.

The nice man sighed, then took the piece of paper back. He wrote in big letters, never taking his eyes from Christopher's. He finished writing, and Christopher read the message upside down.

GIVE ME YOUR HAND.

Christopher searched the nice man's eyes. They betrayed nothing. Christopher's stomach turned. He suddenly wasn't very hungry. Not even for the candy. So, he picked up the pencil, and they passed notes back and forth like schoolkids.

What will that do?

IF YOU WANT TO READ MY MIND, I'LL OPEN IT TO YOU.

Christopher looked down as the nice man opened his hands like a book. Christopher studied the skin on his palms. Cut and scarred. Washed in the water countless times. He felt a weight on his chest. The answers to all the riddles. Four ways in. Three ways out. It was all etched on that hand like a palm reading. Christopher wrote one more time.

What happens at midnight?

The nice man took a deep breath and wrote a single word.

EVERYTHING.

Christopher grabbed the nice man's hand.

CHAPTER 73

hi. christopher. just breathe. we have to do this fast or your mind will cook. these are things i've seen over millennia. you are not supposed to know them this quickly. i'm sorry, but it can't be helped. breathe. or you'll die. breathe!

The nice man's words itched their way up Christopher's arm, spreading through his body like cracks in the windshield. He felt like the wind had been knocked out of him. But it was more than the wind. It was everything. His lungs frozen with fear. Or was that knowledge? Slowly, the breath returned to his chest. He looked up at the nice man's face, reassuring and friendly.

that's it, christopher. you're seeing it now. just keep breathing. no matter what you see, keep breathing.

Christopher blinked and looked around. Somehow, he was in two places at once. His left eye was still in the bunker with the nice man. His right eye was seeing what the nice man spoke. Not as words. But as pictures. Home movies and memories stuck together like peanut butter and jelly. It felt as if it were all happening in front of him. This was the world as the nice man had seen it. And it was terrifying.

breathe, christopher. it's okay. it can't hurt you. breathe.

Christopher saw the hissing lady torture the people on the imaginary side. The blood on the street. It was the world's blood.

this is what it looked like, christopher. just before the last time it hap-

pened. you see what she is doing. the ruin and the madness. look at the
street. see the blood. that is what it was. and that is what it was going to
be for everyone until something miraculous happened.

he was born.

Christopher saw a little boy in a bassinet. This was David Olson. Not how
his mother or father or even Ambrose knew him. This was how the nice man
saw him. How the nice man loved him.

things had been dark in here for decades. she was finding little cracks in
the glass between the real and imaginary sides. finding ways to creep into
the town through her whispers. and their dreams. i thought it was all over,
but then, I saw something. a bright light. it was david. i knew it the day
he was born. there was something different about him. he was talking
when most kids were crawling. he was drawing pictures when most kids
could barely hold a crayon. he struggled with reading because the letters
would not sit still for such an active mind. he thought he was stupid until
he realized he might be smarter than everyone. i watched him grow up. i
watched his classmates brutalize him for being special. i had never seen a
lonelier boy in all my time. but he was powerful. and SHE knew it. SHE
wanted him. i tried to keep him safe for as long as i could, but i was no
match for her. she lured him into the woods just like she did to you.

The nice man heard a noise above and stopped. For a moment, the circuit
was cut, and Christopher could only see the bunker. The nice man looked up
and waited for another footstep. But it was just the wind. Then, he took Christopher's hands again and gave him his mind.

i tried to help him at first. i showed him how the hissing lady could take
on different forms. i taught david how to stay on the street. i told him how
he could use his tree house to spy on her during the day just like i showed
you. but she was smarter than me. she knew what i was doing. she was
just waiting for the right moment to strike.

Christopher's perception split in two. In one eye, he saw a darkness fall over
the nice man's eyes. In the other eye, he saw the reason.

i was there that final night. she had captured me, but i managed to escape. just not in time. i tried to save him. david thought he was awake, but he was sleepwalking through a path that she had cleared for him. i saw the hissing lady walk over to the olsons' neighbor. the family had a senile grandfather. the hissing lady preys on the old. the old man didn't know where he was. so, he certainly didn't know why he was putting on gloves and walking to the attic to grab an old baby carriage. he didn't know why he recorded the sound of his granddaughter crying into an old tape recorder. he didn't know why he brought it to his neighbor's porch and pressed play for ambrose and his girlfriend to find. the hissing lady promised the old man that he would regain his memory. the next morning, he was dead.

Christopher could see the old man dead in a coffin. His family weeping over the open casket. He began to feel their tears. He had to push them away in his mind to stay with the nice man.

"What happened to David?" Christopher asked through his fingers.

at first, he didn't understand. he had escaped from the imaginary world through his tree house before. day and night. but this time, the tree house door was locked. he didn't understand that he was dying. he couldn't get out. so, he tried to rebuild the tree house door from the imaginary side. but it doesn't work that way. he would follow ambrose around, begging him to go to the tree house on the real side. 'just open the door, ambrose!' he would scream. but the hissing lady would just whisper in ambrose's ear and lead him in the wrong direction. it was all a game to her.

Christopher felt it all play out in front of him. David's anguish. Ambrose's grief. For a moment, he pictured himself in the same situation. He saw himself following his mother around. Begging her to open the tree house from the real side. Seeing her weep night after night with him unable to touch her. He could almost feel his mother's grief. It was unbearable.

i tried to give him things to make it easier. food. water. i showed him the stream to bathe in. i told him about safe places to go at night. places like this. if someone is dieting, their nightmare is a piece of cake. but to a little boy, a piece of cake is 5 minutes away from this horrible place. so, i showed him how to enjoy himself a little. i showed him how to survive. especially at night. but eventually, she caught me. she tortured me for years for helping him. but that's nothing compared to what she did to david.

"What did she do?" Christopher asked.

she broke him like a horse. then made him her pet.

Through both eyes, Christopher saw tears fall down the nice man's face. He felt the decades of torment. The guilt and the grief rushed through him in a single moment. His brain didn't know if it could take any more. Until suddenly the clouds parted, and the darkness found little cracks to let the light in. The nice man's hands warmed up.

i thought that was going to be the end of the story. but then you came along.

In his left eye, Christopher saw the slightest trace of hope on the nice man's face. In his right eye, he saw the moment his mother drove them into town in their old land shark. His mother wore that old bandanna. Christopher was there in the passenger side. But he was as bright as fireworks. He looked like magic.

when you showed up, it was like someone turned on a light switch. it had been so long since david, it took a while for my eyes to adjust to you. but once i blinked, there you were. as bright as the sun. your light took away her shadows. you were so powerful, she was afraid of you.

"Afraid of me? I'm just a kid. I'm not powerful. I'm not strong."

you're not powerful because you're strong, christopher. you're powerful because you're good.

Christopher saw his own light spread through the imaginary world. He saw the nice man squint from the glow of it. Then, smile. His eyes as blue as the sky.

i love all people, christopher, but I have no illusions about them. in here, we see their real thoughts. their secret wishes. their dreams. people can be loving. but people can also be selfish. they can be cruel. some are as dangerous as others are good. but no one is better than you. she can't touch your goodness. good terrifies her. she can't control it. can't predict it. so, she WANTED it. she put the mailbox people everywhere to keep us from helping you. i could only speak to you through hidden messages. but david . . . she didn't trust him to keep quiet . . . so david got the worst of it.

"How?" Christopher asked.

she cut out his tongue.

Christopher thought of the serpent tongue she had given David. He thought of all the messages David had to hide from her. The thought made him shudder.

and if we don't get you out of here, the same thing will happen to you.

Christopher's eyes began to fill with tears. He didn't know who the tears belonged to anymore. David. Himself. The nice man. Or all three.

christopher, we don't have much time, so listen very carefully. there are four ways into the imaginary world. you already know two of them. the tree house, which you control, and nightmares, which she controls. there are two more that no one controls, so she only uses them as a last resort. coma. and death.

Christopher could see all the nice man's words laid out in front of him. He saw himself walking into the tree house. Having the nightmare in school. Refusing to take the pill and being hit by the car on the highway and thrown into a coma like a bird hitting a glass window. When he felt his own death, he almost let go of the nice man's hand. The air left his lungs and didn't return. Like a corpse crawling through the dirt. Just get out. Get to the light.

there are three ways out of the imaginary world. the first way is the tree house, which she locked. the second way is waking up, which is much easier from a nightmare than from a coma. and then, there is the third.

The nice man was quiet for a moment as he gathered his thoughts. Christopher could feel him weigh each word carefully to make sure that he didn't scare him too badly.

"What is the third way out?" Christopher finally whispered.

we have to kill the hissing lady.

Christopher closed his eyes in horror. Suddenly, the bunker in his left eye and the nice man's words in his right were replaced by one vision. The hissing lady. Standing in front of him. Smiling with dog teeth. The most terrifying person he ever saw.

that is the only way to get the key that she has buried in flesh around her neck. that key will get you back to the real side. but we need to do it before midnight.

Christopher opened his eyes and saw the question that started it all. Written in a hurried hand on the notepad in the bunker. He didn't even need to say it anymore. He just needed to think.

What happens at midnight?

at midnight, the glass between the imaginary world and the real will crack. you will die. the town will go mad with fear. and they will blame your mother for it. they will torment her, ambrose, the sheriff, and your friends. you have already seen a lot of this beginning to happen. the town is like a frog that has been put in cold water and the heat has been turned up. the heat is her. disguised as the flu. i have seen her plant madness in people's ears like seeds. i have seen the seeds grow. and at midnight, the garden will bloom. the frogs will boil. and the real world will drown in its own shadow like floods. what happens at midnight, christopher?

EVERYTHING.

The nice man let go of his hand. Christopher blinked through the pain in his eyes. He had seen it all unfold before him. The death spreading over the town. The people insane with fear and rage and hatred. Torturing his mother, Ambrose, the sheriff, and his friends. Not knowing that it was all because of her. Not knowing that they were just little pieces on the hissing lady's game board. The nice man listened to the woods above them, and once he was satisfied that the imaginary people and deer had moved on, he finally spoke out loud.

"Remember," the nice man said in a comforting voice. "That hasn't happened yet. We can still stop it. I know you're scared. So am I. As she gets stronger, I get weaker. I used to be able to reach people on the real side. Now I scream until my throat becomes hoarse, and the only person who can hear me is you.

But I love people too much to ever give up hope that they can be saved. I just can't do it by myself anymore. But we can do it together. Someone is going to die tonight. It's either the hissing lady or the world as we know it. I know how she thinks tonight is going to end. But what she doesn't understand is that we have a secret weapon."

"What?"

"You. The tree house has been turning you into something extraordinary. I have never seen anyone from the real side who can be as powerful as you. Not even David. So, if we can use that power to save you from this terrible place, you will save your mother and everyone else in the town. Will you help me?"

"Yes, sir."

The nice man smiled. And patted Christopher's shoulder.

"Thank you, son."

Christopher smiled at the nice man, his teeth broken. His body battered.

"What is the tree house turning me into?"

The nice man stopped. Gravely.

"If I tell you, you have to promise me to be humble. Because David wasn't until it was too late."

"I promise, sir," Christopher said. "What is the tree house making me?"

The nice man offered his hand one more time. Christopher took it and saw the answer.

CHAPTER 74

It's making me goD.

Kate Reese stopped and looked at the childish scrawl on the paper. She couldn't believe what she had been reading. She quickly flipped back to the previous page to make sure she was understanding this correctly before speaking out loud to Ambrose. They were in Christopher's room. She had been there since the nurses finished turning over her son's bed. Reading poor David's terrified scrawl.

<u>June 21st</u>

I don't really know where I am anymore. I don't know what's real or what's imaginary, but we can't wait any longer. The hissing lady is everywhere disguised as the flu. We have to complete the training now before she takes over the tree house. I asked the soldier why the hissing lady wanted it so much, and he explained what it is doing to me. The power that she wants for herself. It was so simple. It explained everything I was going through. I wanted to tell Ambrose what was really happening to me, but I couldn't have him call me crazy again. So, I waited until he was asleep, and I got into bed with him. I whispered really quietly in his ear just in case the hissing lady was listening.

"Ambrose. I have to tell you something."

"What?" he said asleep.

"I have to tell you what the tree house does."

"Fine. Go ahead," he said in his sleep. "What does the tree house do?"

"It's making me God, Ambrose. The tree house makes you God."

"Jesus Christ," Ambrose said.

Christopher's mother stopped reading and looked at Ambrose. She couldn't see his eyes, but the rest of his face was frozen with grief. She turned to her son, unconscious next to her. She thought of the things he knew. The things he felt. His perfect test answers. His spontaneous genius. His healing touch.

"Keep reading, Mrs. Reese," Ambrose said.

Christopher's mother thumbed the page and continued reading in a whisper.

> "Fine. You're becoming God. Go back to sleep," he said.
>
> Then, my brother fell back asleep. I kept explaining that I wasn't becoming God all the way. I can't create or destroy worlds or anything like that. But I know everything, and I can heal things. The soldier said if I went any further than that, my head would explode. That's what the headaches are. It's God pushing on my skull like a baby chick tapping on an eggshell. It felt good to say all that out loud to Ambrose. I kissed his cheek and told him I loved him. I know he was asleep and didn't hear what I said. But it was wonderful to pretend that he listened to me and didn't think I was crazy. I want to think that he loves me like that because I know in 3 days I am going into the woods to kill the hissing lady. And if I don't stop her, she will shatter the glass between the two worlds. It's all up to me.

afTEr aLL, i AM god.

A chill ran down her back. It felt like someone was watching them. Christopher's mother would normally shrug off this feeling, but after reading David's diary out loud to Ambrose, she didn't think she would shrug off a feeling ever again. She thought that the hissing lady might be standing right there. Hovering over her unconscious son like a cat with a ball of string.

"Are you okay?" Ambrose asked her.

"Yes," she said. "I just need a minute."

Christopher's mother looked down at the sheets of paper where she kept her notes. If the orderlies saw them, they would definitely lock her up for forty-eight hours of psychiatric "evaluation." Words scribbled in a hurried hand. An imaginary world filled with hissing ladies and mailbox people with mouths sewn shut and eyes closed with zippers. Her son was trapped there right now.

June 22nd

BefoRe we kill the hissing lady, we need tO do Some rEcon...

It took a moment for Christopher's mother to adjust her eyes to David's illegible scrawl. She had never seen such disturbing handwriting. Not even from her late husband. It wasn't the handwriting of a child who was crazy. It was the handwriting of a child who was terrified. She read ahead to decipher the message. Then, she whispered it out loud to Ambrose.

June 22nd

Before we kill the hissing lady, we need to do some recon like they do in those war movies Ambrose loves. The soldier is worried I am pushing myself too hard with my training. He doesn't want my brain to give out. So, he didn't want me to come on this mission, but I did anyway. I followed her during the daytime. I could see her reaching into people. I could see people getting sick with her flu and changing. I watched her whispering into people's ears. Making them afraid of their own shadows. The shadow is just people without light. This place is starting to get scary. Even during the day. The town is about to go insane.

June 23rd

I asked the soldier what would happen to me if we failed. At first, he refused to tell me because he didn't want me to be afraid. But I am more powerful than he is now and I threw him a thousand yards until he told me. He said I will become the hissing lady's next pet. The final recon mission is tonight. The soldier says it's not safe because I won't be invisible. But I told him that Ambrose was in danger, and I am God, so I was coming. We found her hiding place. I can't believe where it is. It was so close the whole time.

<u>June 24th</u>

The soldier was captured by the hissing lady. I made a terrible mistake. I thought I was invincible. Now, I am alone. I am so stupid. I went into the imaginary world at night, and the hissing lady used me to set a trap for him.

The soldier ran to rescue me, but the mailbox people jumped on him, scratching him with their zipper eyes. I tried everything I could think of to save him. But every time I quieted my mind and got close to an answer, I felt someone hit a deer. Or beat their children. Or try to commit suicide. I should never have gone in at night like he said. Why didn't I listen? I should have been humble. I'm so ashamed. She is torturing him right now. I can feel him screaming even on the real side. I have to go in there and try to rescue him. It's all my fault. God, please help me. Please help me defeat her and save my big brother because . . .

Christopher's mother turned the page and looked at her son unconscious on the bed. The machines breathing for him. Eating for him. Living for him. The steady hum of the beep beep beep was the only sign of hope. She looked back at the page of David Olson's diary. The insane drawings. The terrified scrawl. Each word convincing her Christopher's survival and the world's survival were one and the same. That the madness then was the madness now. She thought of the seeds being planted by the hissing lady. The words whispered. The promises made. And what would happen to all of them if those flowers suddenly bloomed.

. . . the imagiNary world is almOst here.

CHAPTER 75

Special Ed opened his eyes just before dawn. He looked down and noticed that he had wet the bed. He had been doing that a lot lately. Then, he looked outside at the trees, and for some reason he could not understand, there was only one place he wanted to go today.

Chuck E. Cheese's

It didn't make any sense. He was only a little boy, but even he knew that for all of its merits as a video game and robot animal paradise, Chuck E. Cheese's pizza ranked just a notch above cafeteria. And today was Christmas Eve. They always went to his grandma's house for Christmas Eve after his other grandma died. They did it every year. But he just couldn't get it out of his mind. He just had to get to Chuck E. Cheese's.

Listen to Grandma.

He went to his father's bedroom and tried to wake him up, but his father just growled. "It's not even dawn, for Christ's sake. Go back to sleep." So, Special Ed left the room, but not before stealing his father's cell phone from the nightstand like his grandmother told him. Special Ed then went to the master bedroom. His mother was asleep in the bed. She always told him she needed separate bedrooms because his father snored. Special Ed knew it was actually because his mother drank too much and his parents fought about it and she said she could stop anytime and he said "prove it" and she said "fuck you" and told him to sleep in the guest room and he said "no you're the drunk you sleep in the guest room" and she cried and she won and so he finally did after she kept drinking from the flask in her purse that looked like a perfume bottle to make the sad in her head quiet down.

Listen to Grandma.

"Mom, can you take me to Chuck E. Cheese's?" he whispered.

She took off her cool gel sleeping mask. The one that kept her young.

"Honey, it's Christmas Eve. We're going to Grandma's house."

"I know. I just really want to go to Chuck E. Cheese's."

"What? Baby, I'm sorry, but that's fucking crazy. Go back to sleep."

"We could stop there for lunch on the way."

"Ask your father."

"I already did. He said it was okay."

"Okay. Fine."

But it wasn't fine. When Special Ed's father woke up, he caught Special Ed in the lie and said he was now on punishment. Especially after he got in that fight with Brady Collins at the Christmas Pageant. Enough was enough. The HBO he got in his room to celebrate Special Ed getting such a good report card was going to be turned off. No HBO for a month.

"But Dad! You don't understand! I have to go!" Special Ed protested.

"Stop being crazy. Get your clothes on. We're going to Grandma's house."

They were already off to a late start because his father couldn't find his cell phone. He asked Special Ed's mother to call him so he could trace the sound, but she couldn't find her phone, either. They didn't understand that their son had taken both of their phones and buried them outside in the snow. Special Ed's dead grandmother told him that he had to do it, or he would never get to Chuck E. Cheese's.

Listen to Grandma.

The family piled into the Ford SUV with the BUY AMERICAN sticker and left for Grandma's house. The weather had been particularly brutal overnight, and their normal route was blocked with fallen trees and a few car accidents. One of the accidents looked particularly bad. A station wagon had crashed into another car that looked vaguely like Kate Reese's car. Betty wanted to call Kate to check on her. She reached for her cell phone.

She forgot that she had lost it.

Without their cell phone maps, the family had to rely on the old GPS to find an alternate route to Grandma's house. Special Ed's father punched in the address, and the GPS lady told them to get on Route 79. Special Ed knew that his grandma was pretending to be the GPS lady to help him, so he relaxed a little in the backseat.

He watched his father take his usual shortcut around Bridgeville to get to 79, but this time, a deer ran across the road. When his father turned sharply to avoid the deer, he hit a bad pothole, and the two right tires blew out. Luckily, they were right next to a Sunoco station. The station attendant told them that most of his guys were out with the flu and the station had been picked clean of parts. But if they gave him a couple of hours, he could get his cousin to bring them used tires (for a small fee). So, he told the family to just grab some lunch and relax. Luckily, the Sunoco station was right next to a restaurant.

Chuck E. Cheese's

Eddie, bring your backpack. You're going to get prizes.

When the family entered Chuck E. Cheese's, Special Ed was so happy. The place was almost empty because today was Christmas Eve, but there was one birthday party in the corner. For identical twins. Special Ed's mother and father gave him a twenty-dollar game card, then ordered a pizza and a pitcher of beer. Special Ed wandered through the games and robots, looking over his shoulder. Wondering why he was brought here.

"Eddie," the voice whispered. "Eddie, psst. It's Grandma."

Special Ed turned around and saw a robot of Bad Cat, smiling at him.

"Grandma?" he said.

"Yes, Eddie. Listen to me very carefully," Bad Cat whispered. "Something very bad just parked in the parking lot. I want you to be ready, okay?"

Special Ed nodded and turned his gaze to the front of the restaurant. The door opened and a fat man walked into Chuck E. Cheese's dressed as a birthday-party clown.

"Stay away from him, Eddie. His wife just left him. Listen to Grandma."

Special Ed watched the fat clown walk over to the birthday party.

"HI, KIDS!" the clown yelled out.

"HI, UNCLE HAPPY!" the kids yelled back.

The fat clown pulled out a balloon.

"WHO WANTS TO HELP UNCLE HAPPY MAKE BALLOON ANI-MALS?!"

"ME ME ME!" the kids said.

The clown huffed and puffed and blew into long, stretchy balloons. He blew up one. And another. And another. Then, he twisted and turned all three balloons like femur bones until he made a beautiful animal shape.

"WHAT IS THIS, KIDS? WHAT DID UNCLE HAPPY MAKE?"

"IT'S A DEER! IT'S A DEER!" they shrieked in delight.

The clown pulled out a toy gun. He pointed it at the deer.

"THAT'S RIGHT, KIDS! AND IT'S TIME TO GO DEER HUNTING!"

He squeezed the trigger, and a long red banner shot out that read BANG! The banner hit the deer, and the balloons popped. The kids laughed and screamed.

"WANT TO MAKE ANOTHER ONE, KIDS?!" the clown yelled.

"YAY!" the kids screamed.

"Okay! But I need your help this time. This is a really hard one."

"I want to run away," Special Ed said.

"You can't, Eddie. There's a reason you're here."

Special Ed watched as the fat clown grabbed a handful of balloons and handed them out to the kids. The kids huffed and puffed like the Big Bad Wolf, blowing up the balloons.

"OKAY, KIDS! GIVE THE BALLOONS BACK TO UNCLE HAPPY!"

"Eddie," Bad Cat whispered. "Hide behind the pillar. Do it now."

Special Ed did as he was told. He was frozen in fear as he watched the kids scramble to hand back the balloons.

"GREAT JOB, MY LITTLE HELPERS! NOW, LET'S SEE WHAT WE CAN MAKE WHEN WE WORK AS A TEAM!"

Uncle Happy began to twist and turn the balloons, scraping and squeaking on each other like nails on a chalkboard. He ripped those balloons into a twisted shape and held it up like a head on a pike.

"WHAT IS IT, BOYS AND GIRLS?!"

"IT'S A CLOWN!" they all yelled.

"THAT'S RIGHT. WE MADE A CLOWN! AND NOW IT'S TIME TO GO CLOWN HUNTING!" the clown yelled out.

The fat clown reached into his bag and pulled out a different gun.

He put the gun against the balloon clown's temple.

The kids stopped laughing.

"THIS CLOWN JUST LOST EVERYTHING, BOYS AND GIRLS!"

Special Ed looked at Bad Cat. The robot said nothing. He just smiled the sickest frown upside down.

"THIS CLOWN FUCKED UP EVERYTHING HE EVER TRIED TO DO, KIDS! SO, AUNT HAPPY RAN AWAY FROM UNCLE HAPPY! AND NOW UNCLE HAPPY ISN'T HAPPY ANYMORE!"

The clown moved the gun from the balloon swiftly to his own temple.

"SO, WHAT DO YOU SAY WE PUT THIS CLOWN OUT OF HIS MISERY?!"

The parents were barely able to react in time. The bullet exploded in the gun and struck the clown's temple. The kids screamed and turned away as the clown fell in a heap on the floor. Uncle Happy's bag landed right at Special Ed's feet.

It was filled with balloons.

And bullets.

"Eddie, you have to do it now. No one is watching," Bad Cat whispered.

Special Ed instinctively bent over and grabbed as many boxes of bullets as he could. He quickly shoved them in his backpack (*Hulk…pack!*) as his parents fought their way to the scene. Special Ed felt really lucky because when he had finally opened his dad's gun safe, he hadn't found any bullets. Just a lot of drugs that Big Eddie pretended he didn't do just like Big Betty pretended she didn't drink too much.

"You see, Eddie," Bad Cat said. "I told you I would get you some prizes. Now you can protect Christopher from that awful Brady Collins. Listen to Grandma."

Special Ed smiled at Bad Cat as the robot's eyes suddenly went dull. Then, he zipped up his Hulk backpack with over two hundred rounds of ammunition.

CHAPTER 76

"Brady," the voice whispered. "Psst."

Brady Collins opened his eyes like a little bird and saw his grandmother sitting up in her hospital bed. She had been asleep ever since Christopher had touched her at the Christmas Pageant. The doctors didn't know if she would ever wake up again.

"Grandma?" he asked.

"Yes, sweetie."

Her voice was so dry and scratchy, it made his skin itch.

"How are you feeling?"

"Much better. Where is your mother?" she asked.

"Cafeteria," he said.

"What about your dad?"

"Working, probably."

"Good. That gives us a chance to talk alone."

She patted the chair next to her bed. Pat pat. Brady approached slowly and sat down.

"Look how big you are," she said. "I remember when you were so little, I could fit your whole head in one hand. You had no teeth, like a little old man. And look at you now. Brady, you're so big. Let me see a muscle."

Brady flexed his right arm. She felt his biceps with her arthritic fingers.

"Wow," she whispered. "You're so strong."

Brady smiled proudly. The old woman held the little boy's hand in her bony palm. Their hands began to heat up together like a mug of hot cocoa.

"Your dad is strong, too, Brady. You know, I can remember when he married your mother. I was happy that she was going to have a successful husband. I had an unsuccessful husband. He wasn't a nice man. Your grandpa was mean to your mom. He made her spend a lot of the winter in the backyard. Did you know that?"

"No."

"I wanted to stop him, but he was too big. She doesn't know that. She thinks I didn't try. It makes me sad. So, I know she is hard on you, but don't blame her, okay? She got it a lot worse than she gives it."

Brady was silent.

"You still hate her, though, don't you, Brady?"

Brady nodded.

"I know. It's hard. But she's trying to make you strong. So, try not to hate her too much, okay? Hating is really dangerous. It's like that boy. What's his name? The boy you were fighting with at the Christmas Pageant."

"Special Ed."

"Yes. He's a hateful boy, isn't he?"

Brady nodded. Mrs. Keizer looked into the hallway, and when she knew no one was coming in, she whispered,

"Special Ed's going to try to kill you. You know that, right?"

"Not if I kill him first," the little boy said.

"That's smart, Brady," she said proudly. "You see, that's what your mother has done for you. She's made you very strong and brave. Let him be the hateful one. You be the good one. That goes double for Christopher and his friends."

Brady smiled. The heat on their hands was warm like a campfire.

"Grandma," he said. "Do you remember things now?"

"Yes, Brady. I remember everything except my name."

"What do you mean? You're Grandma."

She laughed, revealing her toothless grin.

"I know I'm Grandma to you, but that's not my name. When I got married, I changed it to Mrs. Joseph Keizer. But I can't remember what it was before that. Your grandfather stole my real name. He hid it somewhere in the woods. But I'm going to get it back. Will you help me?"

"Of course."

"Good, Brady. You're a good, strong boy."

Brady smiled. The old woman put in her dentures and smiled back.

"We are going to win this war, Brady. Listen to Grandma."

CHAPTER 77

"Matt, they're going to kill your brother," the voice whispered.

Matt opened his eyes. It was right before dawn on Christmas Eve. And his body was shaking. He had been having terrible nightmares recently, but this one was the worst. He didn't know if he ever wanted to sleep again. Matt started to panic that maybe he was still having the nightmare. He didn't want those deer to come back.

"Hello?" he said to the darkness. "Mike?"

There was only silence. Matt sat up in bed. He was covered in sweat. All weekend, it didn't matter how many times he turned the pillow over. He could feel that horrible fever on his forehead. But his fever had finally broken. There was only sweat and that sweet baby aspirin smell. Matt had wet the bed again.

"Mike?" he said.

He heard nothing. Matt got out of bed and looked at the sheets. They were covered in urine. He felt so embarrassed. He couldn't let his big brother see him like this. So, Matt peeled off his pajamas and underwear, cold and clingy, and went to the bathroom to wash himself with a towel. When he got clean and dry, he went down the hallway to his big brother's room. He opened the door and tiptoed over to the bed.

"Mike?" he whispered.

His brother did not move under the covers.

"Mike? I had a nightmare. Can I sleep in your bed?"

There was no sound. Matt slowly pulled the blanket back, but all he found was a rolled-up sleeping bag and a baseball glove.

Mike was gone.

Matt looked around the room to see if something was wrong. There was a poster of the Avengers including Mike's favorite, Thor. The closet was messy. The floor was littered with balls from Nerf to Wiffle. Nothing was under the bed. Nothing was out of place. But it still didn't feel right. It felt like the street he saw in his nightmare. It just wasn't right.

Matt left the room and tiptoed down the hall to his mothers' room. He thought maybe Mike had his own nightmare and asked to sleep between them. But they were sleeping on opposite sides of the bed. Mike was nowhere to be seen.

Matt crept downstairs. When he reached the kitchen, he saw the carton of milk on the counter. Matt went over and touched it. The carton was warm. It had been left out for at least an hour. Matt looked at the picture of the missing girl. Emily Bertovich. For some reason, he could have sworn she was looking back at him.

He left the kitchen and went to the living room. He saw a half-eaten bowl of cereal on the coffee table. The spoon was still in the bowl. The TV was on, playing an old Avengers cartoon. Thor was speaking.

"Iron Man is in trouble, Captain America," he said.

Matt moved out of the living room and went to the entry hall. He looked up at the coat-tree and noticed that Mike's jacket was missing. The dead bolt on the front door was unlocked. Matt couldn't believe his brother would have left the house. They were still on punishment for getting in the fight at the Christmas Pageant. If Mike was caught outside, their mothers would ground him forever. Something was terribly wrong.

Matt opened the door.

The air was still and quiet. There had been a massive snowfall overnight, and from the looks of the clouds overhead, there was going to be an even bigger storm coming for Christmas.

"Mike?" he whispered. "Are you out here?"

Again, there was no sound. Just a deer staring at him from the lawn across the street. Matt started to feel a deep unease. He quickly threw on his coat and boots, noticing that his brother's shoes had been left behind. So, he tied them together and threw them over his shoulder. Then, right before he left their house, something inside him told him to go back to the kitchen and grab a knife.

Call it a voice.

Matt started walking down the street. He looked down and even with the dusting of snow covering it like powdered sugar on a doughnut, he thought he could see the slightest impression of his brother's bare feet. Normally, he wouldn't have been able to see very well because of his lazy eye. But ever since Christopher had touched his arm, his eye had been getting better. After a week, it was all healed. But it didn't stop at 20/20. It kept getting stronger and stronger. He could see for miles with it. The way that his grandmother said she was farsighted and could take off her glasses and watch drive-in movies a mile away from the back porch. She could never hear them. But she saw all the great movies. Then, they closed the theater. And she died of bladder cancer. Matt didn't know why he was thinking about his grandmother now. He followed the footprints all the way down the long hill.

Toward the Mission Street Woods.

They were covered in a slight morning fog. Like a cloud in the sky. Matt put his head down and kept walking on the street toward the woods. Following his brother's footprints. His eye began to itch and twitch the closer he got.

Matt gripped the knife tightly as he entered the Mission Street Woods. He followed the trail down the footpath. Past the billy goat bridge and the creek, which wasn't frozen anymore for some reason. He walked into the clearing. He could feel the deer looking at him through the spaces in the evergreens, their breath rising like steam from a manhole. Matt walked through the coal mine. All the way to the other side. He passed the abandoned refrigerator, which felt warm like a campfire. He finally came to the bulldozers and Collins Construction vehicles parked on the far side of the woods.

That's where he saw Mike.

His brother was crouched down in the mud with his bare feet and a knife. Matt watched as his brother slashed the rear tire of a bulldozer. Then, he moved to the front tire and unscrewed the cap. He slowly let the air out of the front tire with the knife. Matt silently approached his brother, who was turned away from him.

"Mike," Matt whispered.

Mike took the knife out of the tire.

"Mike, what are you doing?"

Mike didn't answer. For a long moment.

"It's Christmas Eve," Mike finally said. "The bulldozers will reach the tree house today."

"So?"

"If Mr. Collins tears down the tree house, Christopher will never be able to get out. So, we have to save him."

"Who told you that?"

"You did."

Matt turned his brother around and realized that Mike's eyes were closed. He was sleepwalking.

Matt gently took the knife out of his hand.

"Matt, we have to finish," Mike protested in his sleep.

"Don't worry. Lie down on my coat. I'll finish," Matt said.

Mike did as he was told. He laid his head down on Matt's coat and began to snore. Matt grabbed the shoes and covered his brother's freezing feet. Then, he took both knives to the Collins Construction Company fleet, and within minutes, the vehicles were rendered useless. On any other night, they probably would have been caught.

Luckily, the security guard was out with that terrible flu.

CHAPTER 78

Motherfuckers!"

Mrs. Collins watched her husband slam his cell phone down on the cafeteria table. Her mother was still unconscious upstairs in her hospital room, and somehow, his business had crept back into their lives. Even on Christmas Eve.

"What happened?" Mrs. Collins heard herself asking.

Mrs. Collins maintained a concerned, dutiful look on her face as she pretended to listen to her husband rant about how some "motherfuckers" destroyed the tires on his trucks and bulldozers. She vaguely heard him say that he should have broken ground on this "fucking Mission Street Woods project" a month ago, but someone was out to get him. He couldn't afford all the delays. They were leveraged to the breaking point. The loans were coming due. She better stop spending so much God damn money.

Blah blah blah blah blah.

How many times did he start this fight? Five times a month? Ten during the audit? She could have played a tape recorder and saved herself the time. "Kathleen, who do you think pays for all this because it's not your God damn charity work!" "But Brad, I turned Shady Pines from a tax shelter into a thriving business." "A thriving business?! That old folks home couldn't keep you in shoes!" When did the make-up sex stop? How can he stand the sound of his own voice all day? God, is he still talking? He is. He's still talking.

Mrs. Collins just nodded and scratched the skin underneath her diamond necklace. That itch just wouldn't go away. Mrs. Collins blamed the itch on being stuck in this hospital waiting for her mother to wake up. She was sweaty and sticky and could do nothing with her hair in that horrible hospital bathroom even if it was private. And she didn't know how much longer she could pretend that she didn't hate this man.

"Are you even listening to me?!" he barked.

"Of course, Brad. It's awful. Go on," she said.

As her husband continued to rant, Mrs. Collins looked over his shoulder and saw a room packed with people on gurneys. They had started moving the sick into the cafeteria like the dying soldiers in Gone with the Wind. She thought about her mother basking in comfort in the private room upstairs that could easily fit two more beds. She wondered why the poor people didn't get off those gurneys and just kill them. That's what she'd do. She wouldn't stand for this bullshit for five minutes. And she supposed that's what made her rich and poor people so hopelessly stupid.

For a moment, Mrs. Collins fantasized about the people on the gurneys standing up and marching into the cafeteria and tearing her husband's tongue out of his mouth. God, Mrs. Collins wanted it to happen. She quietly prayed for them to get up and just kill this man already, so she could stop humoring him that the world was out to screw him even though a casual glance at the facts and his numerous bank accounts would prove the opposite was 100 percent the case.

Then, when the mob was done with him, it could go into her mother's comfortable private room and rip her mother out of that bed with the thousand-thread-count sheets and hang her with them. Hang her for losing the memories that Mrs. Collins could never forget. The water bottle filled with vodka. The debt and the poverty. The brutal man who doused his own daughter with a hose and threw her in the backyard in December. And the mousy little mother who never did anything to stop it despite being given the opportunity dozens of times.

"If you want to be a dog, you'll stay out there like a dog," he'd say.

And from her mother? Nothing.

Thanks for the memories.

For eight years, Mrs. Collins watched each of her mother's memories follow the last down the rabbit hole. For eight years, Mrs. Collins worked that nursing home to give her mother a level of care that her mother never gave her. Why? Because that's what a Collins does. Not a Keizer. Keizers rot on gurneys in the hallway while the Collins family basks in private rooms.

Keizers drink themselves to death with vodka while the Collins family gets rich selling it to them. She was a Collins now. So, for eight years, Mrs. Collins did everything for her mother, and all she asked in return was for the old woman to just die already. Just die so that she could stop remembering everything for her. Just die so that she could stop sitting next to her mother in the parlor, watching endless daytime talk shows with endless parades of victims being interviewed by every sex, color, or creed of talk-show host about their abuse while studio audience psychologists babbled on about how their parents must have been abused themselves. Just die so she could stop watching silly tears spilling from silly people.

If these yokels had done three months of hard time being Kathy Keizer, they would have something to cry about. Try being your father's ashtray for a day. Try being called ugly every day. Try being called fat when you're anorexic. Try standing wet in the freezing cold, staring at the aluminum siding of the back of your little house every night. Then, see if you can bend your mind to turn that aluminum siding into a beautiful future.

See the house, Kathy. You're going to live in a bigger house someday.

The biggest house in town, Kathy. With a diamond necklace.

And a powerful husband. See the good husband. See the beautiful son.

You try digging your nails into your hands every night to keep from freezing to death in the backyard. You watch your father drinking in his warm kitchen. And then tell me about how that drunk bastard was abused himself. Because guess what? Some parents abused their kids who weren't abused themselves. Even in the grand design of chickens and eggs, not everyone has an excuse. Somebody had to be first. And just once. Just one time in the last eight years, she would have given a million dollars if one of those endlessly pointless talk shows had an honest father on the couch.

"I woke up and said, 'I'm going to burn her with cigarettes.'"

"Why? Because you were abused?" the talk-show host would ask.

"No. Because I was bored."

Mrs. Collins would send a check to that man to thank him for his honesty and another check to his children because they might understand what Kathy Keizer's life was really like. Everyone else, go ahead and try being Kathy Keizer for a day. And you see if by the end of it, you aren't a puddle on the God damn floor.

"Kathleen? What the hell is wrong with you?" her husband asked.

Mrs. Collins checked the clock on the cafeteria wall. Somehow, ten minutes had passed.

"I'm sorry, honey," she said. "I'm just feeling a little under the weather. Could you repeat that last thing?"

"I said I need to go to the Mission Street Woods to deal with this nightmare. I know it's Christmas Eve, but we're on a deadline."

He braced himself as if she would rip him a new polo chute for even suggesting he leave the family on Christmas Eve. But she just smiled.

"Of course, honey," she said. "I'll make you the best Christmas Eve dinner when you get back from work."

"Are you all right, Kathleen?" he asked.

"Of course I am," she said with a measured smile.

"You sure?"

"Go to work. I'll be waiting for you when you get back."

With that, she gave him a kiss on the lips. He couldn't have been more confused if she had given him a blow job without the minimum three glasses of Chardonnay on their anniversary. Mrs. Collins was many things to her husband. Understanding wasn't one of them.

"Okay," he said. "Call me if you need anything."

She nodded, and he left. The minute he was out of sight, Mrs. Collins looked down and realized she had dug her fingernails so deeply into her palms that they were bleeding. She hadn't even known she was doing it. She looked into the cafeteria at all the unwashed patients on their gurneys.

They were all staring at her.

She knew that without her husband there, these people might be coming for her instead. She had studied enough history to know what happens to rich men's wives during a revolution. Mrs. Collins knew that all these people were trying to intimidate her with their staring, but they didn't understand.

They were aluminum siding to her.

The staring contest lasted the better part of a minute. When the last person in the cafeteria blinked and looked down, Mrs. Collins moved out of the room. Call it common sense. Call it a voice inside her head. But something told her that she had to get her son back home. She needed a glass of white wine and a long hot bath. She couldn't wash herself off in her mother's private hospital bathroom again. So, she went back to the room and found her mother still unconscious and her son reading to her.

"All the better to see you with, my dear," he said.

"Brady, we have to go," she whispered.

"I want to stay with Grandma," he whispered back.

"Grandma is still asleep," she said.

Brady dug his heels in.

"No. Grandma is awake. We were just talking," he said.

"Stop lying. Get your coat."

"I'm not lying," he said.

Mrs. Collins looked at her mother, sleeping soundly on the bed. She had known her son to play some cruel jokes, but this was a new low.

"Brady Collins, I'm counting to three. At three, you sit in the doghouse."

But Brady wouldn't move.

"I swear we were talking," he said.

"ONE," she said.

"Grandma, wake up," he said.

"TWO," she hissed.

"Please, Grandma! Don't make me go home with her!"

"THREE!"

Mrs. Collins grabbed her son and spun him around. She looked him dead in the eye.

"If you make a scene in front of these people, I will leave you in the doghouse until Christmas morning. I swear to Christ."

Brady's eyes went black, and he stared at her for as long as he could bear it. But eventually, he did what everyone else did with his mother. Including his dad.

He blinked first.

As soon as they left the room, Mrs. Collins began to feel apprehensive. It wasn't the walk through the hospital, although the stares from the rabble were somewhat disconcerting. It wasn't even the drive home, even though the accidents and fallen trees and lines at the gas station were alarming.

No. The problem was Brady.

"Mom, what's your name?" he asked.

"Kathleen Collins."

"No. What's your real name? Before you met Dad."

"Kathy Keizer. Why do you ask?"

"No reason."

Mrs. Collins might not have been the warmest mother in the world, but she knew her son. And Brady didn't ask questions. He was exactly like his father in that respect. But right now, he couldn't have been friendlier. It was a sick friendly, though. A calculated friendly. He was giving the Stepford smile right back to her. A silence masking itself as peace. The two of them got home and climbed the long driveway through the estate. None of the servants' cars were there. While the cat was away, the mice did like to play. They were all alone.

"Mom, would you like a sandwich?" he asked.

"No, thank you. I just need a bath. And aren't you forgetting something?"

"What?"

"I counted to three. You can't fool me with this nice act. You know the rules. If you act like a dog, you'll be treated like one. Outside."

The air between them was silent. Mrs. Collins did not relish punishing her child. She was the opposite of her father in that way. She would never give Brady the hose. She would never let him stand in the elements all night. And she made sure he had a doghouse to keep warm in. But the rules were the rules for a reason. She needed to teach him to be better than her. She needed to give him his own aluminum siding on which to paint his own dreams. It was for his own good.

"One hour, Brady. Or do you want two?"

He was silent. Staring at her. Coiled like a snake.

"One," he said.

"Good. Then, sit out there for an hour while Mom takes her bath."

"Okay, Mother," he said.

She expected some rebellion. She felt guilty when she got none. Maybe he didn't deserve it this time. But she didn't want her son to learn the wrong lesson and end up on a gurney in a cafeteria, did she? Of course not. So she took him out to the doghouse in the backyard while the deer watched them. She let him keep his coat.

"I love you, Brady," she said before she went back into her warm kitchen to get her glass of cold Chardonnay.

*

Brady said nothing in return. He just sat in the doghouse and watched her like he was supposed to. His grandmother had told him this would happen. She had told him everything she wanted him to do right before she closed her eyes and pretended to be asleep for his mother's benefit. She didn't want his mother to get distracted by something as trivial as a lucid mother.

"Brady, when you're in the backyard, can you do your grandma a big favor?"

"Sure, Grandma."

"The next time she throws you in that doghouse, make sure it's the last. This family needs to heal. Okay?"

"Okay, Grandma."

The old woman smiled her toothless grin.

"Thank you, Brady. You're a wonderful little boy. I know it's been hard. Old people and kids are invisible to the rest of the world. But do you want to know a secret?"

"What?"

"It makes us unbeatable at hide-and-seek."

After Mrs. Collins went upstairs for her bubble bath, her son crept back into the house and snuck into the kitchen. He pulled the long knife out of the block with his little, freezing fingers. Then, he quietly moved up the stairs just like his grandmother told him to do.

CHAPTER 79

Mrs. Collins threw on her slippers and robe and walked to the master bathroom. She opened the door and looked at the beautiful room made of marble and glass. Her husband's construction crews were still working on the new cabinets and had left a few cans of paint and stain. But soon, this room would be all hers again.

She drew herself a nice, warm bath. She threw in the lavender soap chips and watched them bubble. While the bath filled, Mrs. Collins wiped the steam that gathered on the mirror like clouds on a windshield. She looked at the diamond necklace around her neck and felt a measure of pride that little Kathy Keizer had made it out of that cold backyard. Through sheer will, she had turned the aluminum siding into this beautiful bathroom and this beautiful bathtub with the beautiful marble floor.

See the house, Kathy. You're going to live in a bigger house someday.

The biggest house in town. See the good husband. See the beautiful son.

Mrs. Collins slipped her naked body into the tub. She didn't know what felt better: the hot water or the cold wine. She looked down at the cuts on her palms. The pools of apple-red blood that the tub carried through the water like soft red clouds. Mrs. Collins closed her eyes and let the hot water dig the cold out of her bones. The cold from that backyard that she could never get rid of. Not even on family trips to Hawaii when she tried to forget that she had ugly cigarette burns and scars on her palms underneath concealer. It was always there.

God, you're ugly, Kathy Keizer.

She wouldn't listen to the voice. Not tonight. She was not Kathy Keizer anymore. She remembered the moment when the priest told the flock, "I now present you Mr. and Mrs. Bradford Collins." She used the name Kathleen from that moment on. Mrs. Kathleen Collins.

Kathy Keizer was as dead to her as her father was.

When she got back from her honeymoon in Europe, all Kathleen Collins wanted to do was build her dream house. Her husband wanted a house in Deerfield that was close to Route 19 and his office. But the newly minted Mrs. Collins didn't spend all that time freezing in a backyard to buy somebody's "used" house. She wanted everything to be new. It would be elegant. Modern. Glass and steel. Not aluminum siding. A big fireplace to keep her bones warm. A beautiful bathroom to wash away the ugly memories. Mr. Collins agreed to everything she wanted because he loved her back then. His wife was as beautiful to him as that house was to her.

God, you're ugly, Kathy Keizer.

"My name is Kathleen Collins, God dammit!" she hissed out loud.

She listened to her voice echo off the imported marble floor. The floor she brought back from her third trip to Italy, which her father had never seen once. She closed her eyes and locked horns with the voice. She had done it before, and she had always won.

You'll never cover up the scars, Kathy Keizer.

You'll never get warm, Kathy Keizer.

God, you're ugly, Kathy Keizer.

Even through her father's burial, she beat the voice. She hated the man in the casket with all her heart, but she made damn sure to shed a tear for him because that's what a Collins would do. She watched him being lowered into the cemetery's ground in the dead of winter. He would be buried in a cold backyard for eternity. Buried with every secret because she wasn't about to turn her past into a daytime talk show to sell commercials to the people stuck on gurneys. She wasn't going to be one more God damn talk-show victim walking around with the idea that all parents who abuse their children were abused themselves. She would never be buried. She would be cremated. She would never be cold again.

"Mom?"

Mrs. Collins opened her eyes. She saw Brady standing in the doorway.

"Brady, what are you doing here?!" she asked.

"I was cold," he said.

Brady started to walk toward her.

• stephen chbosky

"What are you holding behind your back, Brady?"

"It's a secret."

"That's not an answer."

"It's the only answer I'm going to give you, Mom."

Brady took another step toward her.

"That's it, mister. You want to be out in the doghouse all night?! If you act like a dog, you'll be treated like a dog."

"You're the dog, Mom. Your diamond necklace is just a dog collar. You're just some rich man's bitch."

Brady took another step toward her. She looked into his eyes. She had seen him be willful before. But this was different. This was frightening. Something told her this was the final showdown with her son. Someone was going to blink first. This was the war.

And she was going to win.

"Mister, you march your fucking feet outside, or you will spend a week in that God damn doghouse, do you understand me?"

Brady said nothing. He just walked closer. His face was so calm. He had no fear of her anymore.

"Bradford Wesley Collins, I am counting to three."

"Good. I will, too."

Brady took another step toward her. Mrs. Collins had stared down everyone she had ever met, but Brady's face was filled with a dull, quiet rage that she had seen before. It felt like she was trying to stare down her own reflection.

"ONE!" she hissed.

Brady smiled the sickest frown upside down.

"TWO!"

Brady moved his hands from behind his back.

"THREEEEEEE!" Brady screamed.

With that shout, Brady raised the knife and jumped toward the bathtub. Mrs. Collins pushed him away and jumped out of the water. Any thoughts of disciplining her son were long gone. This was self-defense. Her feet hit the slick marble, and she tumbled over, slapping her head on the floor. She lay on the imported Italian marble. She saw her son walk over to her, towering like a giant. She began to feel woozy. She wasn't even sure if she was awake or still asleep in the bathtub.

"Mom?" Brady said. "Grandma is sorry for all the things Grandpa did, but we have to stop thinking about that now. Okay?"

Brady touched her arm. She could feel the tingle running through his finger-tips like the dying embers of a campfire. Brady handed her the knife. For a moment, she thought about cutting her own throat with it. Or maybe stabbing him. But that's not what the knife was for. No. It was for something else. Brady opened her makeup drawer and handed her all of her favorites. Eye shadow. Concealer. Lipstick.

"Grandma says it's time to stop feeling ugly. You're not Kathy Keizer any-more. You're Kathleen Collins. She told me to make you feel pretty now, okay?"

Brady reached his hand down to help her up. She still felt a little dizzy, but Brady gently took her hand to steady her as she stood. Then, he helped her over to the mirror. The two of them looked into her beautiful vanity with the custom lighting like a Hollywood starlet's. He slipped her beautiful silk robe over her shoulders to cover the cigarette burns.

"Grandma says you're not a dog, Mom. Listen to Grandma," Brady said.

Brady reached behind his mother and took off the diamond necklace. Mrs. Collins looked at her long neck. The skin used to be so tight when she was Kathy Keizer. But now Mrs. Collins had a wrinkly neck. It started to itch, so she scratched it. But the scratching did nothing. It just made her skin more itchy. So, she got another idea. She picked up the concealer and started to fill in the ugly red dimples the diamonds left in her skin.

"That's it, Mom. It's time to erase Kathy Keizer," Brady said.

Mrs. Collins could still see the ugly red, so she put on more concealer. When every inch of her neck was covered, she moved to her face. She needed to look presentable for Christmas. What would people think? She was Kathleen Collins now. She couldn't let anyone see Kathy Keizer.

God, you're ugly, Kathy Keizer.

She put bright-red lipstick over her lips, but it didn't look right. She didn't look like Kathleen Collins. She looked like stupid little Kathy Keizer, the first time she put on makeup and looked like a streetwalker. Like a hooker. Like a clown. A clown's face.

"Grandma wants you to feel beautiful," Brady said.

Mrs. Collins slathered the concealer over her skin. Layer after layer. Like butter on bread. But it still wasn't enough. She rummaged through her makeup drawer. She took out liquid bronzer and poured it into a pool in her palms. God, her palms. The scars on her palms. They didn't belong on Kathleen Collins' elegant hands. These were Kathy Keizer's hands.

God, you're ugly, Kathy Keizer.

She spread the liquid bronzer all over her hands. All over the scars. All over the memories. But it still wasn't thick enough. She could still see the little girl in the window outside of the warm kitchen. She grabbed more. Eye shadow. Eyeliner. Every shade of lipstick. She rubbed it all over her body. But there wasn't enough. She could still see the scars. Mrs. Collins poured and smashed every ounce of makeup she had onto her skin, but she could still see Kathy Keizer. She moved around in a blind panic, looking for more makeup.

But all she had left was paint.

Mrs. Collins grabbed the construction crew's paint cans and cracked them open with her son's knife.

"That's it, Mom," he said.

She moved to the mirror, lathering the paint on her face. A nice grey primer. A thick white paint. She poured the paint over her hair. Over her body. She couldn't stop the itch under her neck. She couldn't feel beautiful no matter how much paint she poured over her skin.

That's because you're ugly on the inside, Kathy Keizer.

The voice was back. She didn't think she could win this time. And maybe the voice was right. Of course, she thought. The voice is right. My insides are all scarred and ugly. That's where Kathy Keizer is hiding. That's where the paint belongs.

"Mom," Brady said calmly.

"Yes, Brady?" she asked.

"Do you remember how you thought that somewhere out there, there was a parent who abused their children who wasn't abused themselves?"

"Yes?"

"You said if someone could tell you that, you would die a happy woman."

"Yes," she said, the tears washing the paint down her cheeks.

"Well, I know for a fact there is," he said softly.

A great relief washed over her. Mrs. Collins smiled and stirred the paint with Brady's knife like soup over a campfire. Then, she brought the paint can to her lips. She thought she might be asleep. This must be a dream because how else could she explain her son's glowing eyes. Black as coal left in a child's stocking.

"So, Mom, would you like to know who the first parent was who abused their kids who wasn't abused themselves?"

"Yes, Brady. Please tell me."

Brady perched in front of her on the marble countertop. When his voice changed, her blood went as cold as that old backyard. Because she knew that voice. It was her father's voice. Slowed down like his old 45 records played at 33 speed.

"thE aNswer is goD."

Then, Mrs. Collins raised the can and painted over Kathy Keizer's insides.

CHAPTER 80

T hey had to kill the hissing lady.

They had to get the key.

The nice man lifted the attic stairs, and they climbed out of the shelter. Out of the refrigerator. Into the morning light. Christopher was invisible to all but the nice man, but that didn't take away the fear. The hissing lady had been out in the imaginary world all night. Waiting for them. Setting traps. Preparing.

"Come on," the nice man said. "We have to find her while it's still daylight. It's our best chance."

They started in the woods. Retracing their steps. The trail led to the clearing, which led to the tree house. The nice man climbed the ladder one more time to make sure the tree house was still locked. He found two words left on the door. Written in blood.

TICK TOCK

The nice man tried to hide his fear, but Christopher could see it. Growing with each step. It's not what they found. It's what they didn't find.

The woods were completely deserted.

It was as if the imaginary world were empty. Or hiding behind a corner. Waiting to strike. They searched for her in the woods for the better part of an hour, but found nothing. Except deer tracks. So, they followed them until the tracks went around in a circle like the beginning of the yellow brick road. It was all a trick. It was all a game. Christopher could feel the hissing lady's cat and mouse with every step. She was playing hide-and-seek like a little girl. Waiting out the daylight. Waiting for the night to come, so that she could yell . . .

"Olly Olly In Come Free!"

They left the woods. Christopher walked behind the nice man, who moved quickly through the bushes without making a sound. The streets were empty. No mailbox people. But the tracks were fresh. Thousands of footprints on the pavement. Little ones from high heels. Big prints from shoes or sandals or bare feet. Some from children. Some with an extra track left by an old person's cane. Some of them missing limbs. Or toes.

"Where do the mailbox people come from?" Christopher asked.

"They've always been here. They're her soldiers."

"Maybe we can turn them. Maybe we could cut the strings that hold them together and set them free," Christopher said.

"I tried that once. I cut the yarn that held a little girl and her sister's mouths shut."

"What happened?"

"They tried to eat me alive."

The nice man approached David Olson's old house on the corner. There was no one inside it. No hissing lady. No David. No mailbox people. Just words written in blood on David's bedroom window.

TICK TOCK

The nice man stared at the words bitterly. Christopher gazed at the same window where the hissing lady had led David Olson fifty years ago. He could almost see the boy sleepwalking into the woods. Never to return again. The nice man was quiet, but Christopher could feel some of his thoughts leaking out of his skin like a dripping faucet. Words laced with guilt and sadness. The last time the nice man tried to kill the hissing lady, David Olson died. Christopher could feel the burden weighing on the nice man's shoulders like a cross.

I can't let . . .
I can't let . . . this happen again.

The nice man looked at the sun getting higher in the sky. The clouds were getting darker and moving closer to the ground.

"Christopher, we're going to run out of daylight. You're God here. You have to quiet your mind. You have to find her."

Christopher tried to locate the hissing lady, but each time he closed his eyes, all he could feel was the real side's growing madness. With every blink, the picture changed like a vacation slide. He could hear the clown's bullet hit his skull. He could taste the paint going down Mrs. Collins' throat. He could feel Mrs. Henderson's blood-soaked nightgown as she drove the sheriff's car, listening to the radio. No police left to pick her up. The sheriff's blood dripping in surgery. Warm and sticky like the blood from the bullet wound in the clown's head. The bullets rolled to Special Ed. *He is loading the gun. He is preparing for war.* His friends were in danger. He had to get out. Christopher felt the nice man's hand on his shoulder.

"Don't let the real side distract you. Just breathe."

Christopher took a deep breath and finally felt the hissing lady's presence. But she wasn't in one place. She was everywhere. Whispering inside everyone's head. For a moment, Christopher thought she was hissing into his mother's ears. He could smell his mother's perfume and feel her warm hand on his chest. His mother was there. Somewhere. The hissing lady poisoning the town around her. If he didn't get out, she would be surrounded by them all.

"I have to get out of here and save my mother," Christopher said.

"Follow that thought," the nice man said. "Follow your mother."

Christopher did as he was told. He closed his eyes, and the light danced behind his eyelids like stars. The thought brought a memory, warm and soft as bread. His mother was driving him to the first day of school. They were in the old land shark. They pretended their address was different, so he would go to a great school. That's how much she loved him. She would do anything for him. She would die for him. Christopher's eyelids fluttered, and he saw the school in his mind's eye. Big and bright.

"Your eyes just twitched. What did you just see?" the nice man asked anxiously.

"My school."

"Come on," he said.

"Is that where the hissing lady is?" Christopher asked.

"I don't know. I just know we have to go there."

The nice man began to move down the street. Quickly and quietly. Always on alert. Always listening. Hunting her. Or being hunted. Christopher watched him crouch behind trees and bushes, studying every inch of the road, looking for a trap. But no trap came. Just two words written in blood on front doors and highway pavement. Two words scratched into cars.

TICK TOCK

The nice man led him up the hill to the school. They went to the boys' bathroom window. The nice man put his ear to the glass and listened to the sounds inside the school. Christopher thought he felt something inside. Cold and evil.

"Stay behind me," the nice man said. "If it's an ambush, you can still get away."

The nice man opened the window with a crrreak. He climbed down from the window and landed on the cold tile. The nice man studied the darkness like a soldier. Listening with his eyes. Seeing with his ears. After a long minute, he looked up and gave Christopher the nod that it was safe to follow.

Christopher climbed down, and the two walked through the boys' bathroom. Dark and dripping with water. The nice man opened the door and peeked down the hallway. Empty and quiet. They tiptoed past the metal lockers. Still and cold. Like vertical coffins in a mausoleum. Christopher remembered that first nightmare. The children coming to eat him alive. Christopher saw a familiar sight at the end of the hallway.

The library.

They walked toward it. Christopher could feel his heart in his throat. The nice man put his ear to the library door and listened. No sound. He opened the door slowly. The room was dark and seemingly empty. Christopher remembered talking with Mrs. Henderson in this room. She told him about David Olson's favorite book, then went home and stabbed her husband. Christopher tiptoed over to the stacks. To that one familiar shelf. To that one familiar book.

Frankenstein.

Christopher opened the book, and he smiled when he saw what David Olson had left them on the imaginary side.

Another Christmas card.

The two stared at it in silence. It was another message. Another clue from David. The front of the card was a picture of a beautiful home with a white picket fence covered in snow. Christopher opened the card, but there was no personal writing from David. Only the card's original inscription.

Over the river
And through the wood
To grandmother's house we go.

Christopher looked at the message again. He was puzzled by it. It didn't mean anything special to him. He studied the front picture. The white picket fence. The red door. Then, he turned to ask what it all meant. That's when he saw the nice man's expression. It curled Christopher's toes.

The nice man was terrified.

"What's wrong?" Christopher asked.

"I know where she's going."

"Tell me," Christopher said past the lump in his throat.

The nice man took a moment, then he whispered,

"Christopher, have you ever woken up from a nightmare that was so terrifying you couldn't remember anything about it?"

"Yes," Christopher said, already dreading where this was going.

"That's a place here. It's where she took you for six days."

Christopher took a long, hard swallow, trying to summon his courage. He tried to remember what happened to him. He could see nothing.

"So, we know where she's going," Christopher said, trying to sound a lot braver than he felt. "We can still get the key. We can still kill her."

"You don't understand. You don't just walk up to the path. It's surrounded by her guards. Hundreds. Maybe thousands."

"I'm invisible. I can do it. I can surprise her."

"That's just what David said," the nice man replied soberly. "Until she turned his tree house into the back door to this place. Her own sick little joke. And a warning to the rest of us."

"David wouldn't have left the clue for us if he didn't think it was possible to kill her there," Christopher said. "We need to get that key. What other choice do we have?"

The nice man nodded. There was nothing to argue.

"Come on," he finally said.

The nice man led Christopher outside. The clouds had cut off the sunlight, turning the day blood red. The temperature had dropped. And a great scream rose from the horizon, hitting the sky like a cue ball on a perfect break, scattering the clouds. It sounded like a thousand people thrown into a fire and burned alive.

"What is that?" Christopher asked.

"Her army."

He quickly led Christopher to the school playground. Christopher looked at the four-square court and the baseball field. The nice man got down on one knee.

"Christopher, listen to me carefully, because this might be the last chance I have to tell you this. The imaginary world is like a dream. And you can do anything in a dream, right? Just close your eyes, calm your mind, and use your imagination. That's how it works here. If you can see it in your mind's eye, you can do it. You can fly like Iron Man. Be stronger than the Hulk. Braver than Captain America. More powerful . . ."

"Than Thor?" Christopher asked.

"Than Thor's hammer," the nice man said. "So, if we are going to sneak into the gate, we have to do it quietly. Can you try?"

The nice man stopped speaking, but he didn't stop thinking. Christopher could feel the words tremble on his skin.

You can fly like Iron Man.

Christopher nodded. He closed his eyes and quieted his mind. He felt the itch crawl over his body like an army of ants. The fever broke out on his forehead. The heat felt like the fire under a hot-air balloon. He looked into his mind's eye and imagined himself floating like the balloons from the Balloon Derby. The air suddenly growing thinner. He imagined the world from ten feet above the ground. Twenty feet above the ground. Flying like a beautiful balloon.

Jerry found the balloons!

Jerry is going to kill my mother!

The voice came crashing through his mind. Christopher opened his eyes and saw that he was twenty feet above the ground. He panicked and fell, landing on the ground with a thud. The nice man picked him up.

"I'm sorry," Christopher said.

"Don't be. You haven't had enough training. That's my fault. We'll find another way."

The two of them were silent for a moment. Christopher looked at the horizon. He saw a bird flying into the clouds. Another bird dropped out of them. Christopher turned to the swing set. He thought about that day when he first saw the cloud face in the sky. He was swinging. He jumped and the Pirates won the World Series. He couldn't fly like Iron Man yet.

But maybe he could land like him.

"What about the swings?" he asked.

The nice man looked at the swings and their trajectory.

"Those will work," he said. "Let's go."

Christopher jumped onto one swing. The nice man took the one right next to him.

"Get to the hissing lady while it's still daylight."

Christopher nodded. The nice man reached into his pocket and placed a loose, leather sheath in Christopher's hand.

"My father gave me this," the nice man said. "Now, it's yours."

Christopher unfolded the leather to reveal a dull, silver blade. This was not a gleaming sword from the movies. It was common. Just like him.

"Use it wisely, son."

Christopher nodded, and they started to churn their arms and legs. Swinging higher and higher like he did with Lenny Cordisco a hundred times back in Michigan. Back then, they would swing as high as they could. Then, they'd let go and jump five feet into the sand. But this was more than five feet.

This was the horizon.

Christopher looked over at the nice man. He had never seen such a serene look on anyone's face before. It was a father's pride, but he wasn't a father. Other than his own mother, Christopher had never had someone look at him with so much love before.

"Close your eyes. Quiet your mind," the nice man said.

Christopher did as he was told. He took a deep breath and closed his eyes, losing himself behind the eyelids. Christopher imagined himself gripping the chains, whipping his legs, and swinging himself once. Twice. Three times.

Go.

With his mind's eye, Christopher saw himself let go of the chains and launch like a slingshot through the air next to the nice man. He imagined the world slowing down as they rose toward the clouds. Higher and higher. The school small as a child's model beneath their feet. He saw it all in his mind's eye. The baseball field. The highway on the real side. The overturned cars. The dead deer. The path of destruction was almost complete.

He saw his body hit the cloud before he felt it.

The cloud wasn't soft and pillowy. It felt like cold water vapor in the humidifier that his mother set up when he got sick. Christopher didn't know why he was thinking of her now. She must be in the hospital with him. Rubbing his hair and telling him it would be okay. He couldn't wait to get out and tell her about the clouds.

"They taste like cold cotton candy without any sugar, Mom."

They drifted higher and higher, their bodies rising above the cloud line. Christopher looked down and saw them, big and beautiful, moving slowly over the town. The clouds bumped into each other like a pillow fight. They cracked together, making lightning. Within a few seconds, there was a rush of warm soft ozone and the sound of thunder. A snow began to fall. A gentle snow washing away the fear.

In floods.

Christopher imagined moving up into the sky. The stars twinkling like snowflakes in the twilight. For a moment, he thought this must be what Heaven is. Sitting on a cloud. Looking at stars. Feeling his mother's warm hand on his forehead. Forever. He remembered when Father Tom explained that the Holy Trinity was God in three forms. Just like water can be water, ice, steam.

Or clouds.

They weren't flying so much as swimming through water in the sky. It was all the same now. His imagination was the limit of his power. For a moment, he thought that's why the hissing lady needed children. Adults are bad at remembering how powerful they can be because somewhere along the line, they were shamed for their imagination.

To think it is to do it.

"Get ready," the nice man said.

He felt them begin to fall, hitting the clouds again at a much faster speed. Christopher had no idea how far they'd flown. How long they had been up there. Time was lost in his imagination. He dropped faster and faster. He came out of the clouds and looked down. They were all the way across town.

Above the Mission Street Woods.

But the woods looked different. Bigger and meaner somehow. The sun had melted the snow on top of the trees, but the clearing was still covered in white. The tree sat in the middle of the clearing like a black dot. It took Christopher's mind a moment to realize what he was looking at.

The woods were a giant eye.

The eye looked up at heaven and watched the stars, shooting. A soul ascending or a sun dying. A son dying. The clearing was the white of the eye. The tree was its pupil. Its pupil. Its student.

They continued to drop. The nice man was heavier and fell faster. They were becoming separated.

"I'll create a diversion! Get to her before nightfall!" the nice man said, dropping out of the sky. "Remember what you are!"

With his mind's eye, Christopher saw the nice man fall hard on the street while Christopher flew to the side of the woods that Mr. Collins' construction crew had already cleared. He saw great hulks of trees lying in piles around a freshly dug clearing. The trees looked like teeth pulled out of gums by angry hands. Tree stumps like gravestones. They surrounded a massive clearing of torn earth and mud and equipment.

That's when he saw the hissing lady.

She stood in the middle of the muddy clearing, surrounded by a hundred deer. She didn't speak. She just touched their heads, and they bowed like worshippers. Thousands of mailbox people stood around them. They each held the string that kept the next in line. The line stretched beyond the horizon.

It was her army.

Christopher opened his eyes and fell to earth. His body hit the mud with a tremendous smack. The force knocked the wind out of him. His chest felt crushed, straining for breath like a goldfish flopping outside of its tank. He thought for sure they would have heard him, but the mailbox people's moans drowned the sound of the impact. Christopher looked up at the sky. The sun kissed the top of the trees.

Christopher was in the middle of the enemy's camp.

The nice man was nowhere to be seen.

He had ten minutes of daylight left.

CHAPTER 81

Christopher's mother looked up as her son suddenly stirred on the hospital bed. His eyes fluttered underneath closed lids. She took his hand and hoped with all of her heart and soul that he would open them. His perfect eyes. His father's eyes. But the hope faded with the sounds of the machines keeping his body alive with a cruel beep beep beep. She turned to the window and saw the sun beginning to set. A chill ran through her. Soon the terrifying night would come. And her son would be lost inside it.

Christopher's mother turned to Ambrose. His eyes covered in bandages. She looked down at the diary in her hands. Everything David had gone through Christopher had gone through. The itching, the headaches, the fevers. Both boys knew all of the answers to all of the tests. Both were hunted by the hissing lady. So, she knew that whatever David had done, Christopher was about to do. A sinking feeling came over her as she turned the page.

It was David's last entry.

The temperature in the room dropped. Her breath felt frosty in the air. She could almost feel her heart stop. The handwriting was now nearly illegible.

June 25th

Ambrose, I am going in to kill the hissing lady. If you read this diary, it means I didn't make it. But I want you to know how it was on my last day. When I got out of bed this morning, I felt peaceful. I know that's strange, but it's true. I felt like my whole life was leading up to this moment. Like I had been alive for 8 years for this one purpose. I know what I have to do. I have to follow her into my tree house. I don't know what's waiting for me on the other side. The place that's so scary that we don't remember our nightmares. But if I don't go there, I think everyone is going to die. I don't know if I am going to be alive tomorrow. I wonder what that will feel like. Ambrose, after you read this, please don't be hard on yourself too much. I understand you were just a 17-year-old kid. So, don't blame yourself for not listening because I wouldn't have believed me, either. That's the thing about being God here. It makes me know things. I know if you're reading this, it means you didn't die. I know it means I kept her inside the imaginary world somehow and away from you. And that's enough for me. I know you're a good person. I know you will miss me every day. But I will be there, Ambrose. I will be watching you from the imaginary side. I will make sure no nightmares get anywhere near you. So, even if you feel sad, you will always have a break when you sleep. And every time you smell a baseball glove, that will be me, Ambrose. I will be looking out for you every day until you go to Heaven. I will always keep you safe. I love you big brother.

Christopher's mother strained to make out the last sentence.

> *you are My best friEnd.*
> *DAVID*

Christopher's mother closed the diary. The two sat in silence for a moment. She grabbed Ambrose's hand for support and turned to the window. The bottom of the sun was touching the horizon. The sun would set within minutes with her boy stuck on the wrong side of the night. If history was hell-bent on repeating itself, she knew the hissing lady was leading him down a blind alley. She looked at her son lying on the bed, tubes sticking out of his mouth. Christopher's mother wanted to scream. Scream through the machines keeping him alive.

"Don't follow her, Christopher," she prayed. "Don't go into David's tree house."

CHAPTER 82

The sun was setting.

Christopher had ten minutes.

He saw the hissing lady in the middle of the enemy camp as she made her preparations for war. The deer were brought to her. She whispered in their ears. They moved back into the Mission Street Woods. Back to their positions.

Waiting for the mirror between the worlds to shatter.

Christopher crawled through the mud to get closer to her. He was only invisible in the daylight. This was his best chance. He had to get that key buried in flesh around her neck.

He took the dull, silver blade out of the leather sheath.

"What was that sound?" a voice hissed nearby.

Christopher held his breath. He watched the mailbox people cuddle next to the hissing lady like kittens on a leg. The people were all shapes and sizes. All ages and genders and colors. Her soldiers. Christopher wondered who they were before they stood in this clearing, letting the hissing lady unzip their eyelids and kiss their eyes.

"Chrissstopher," the voices said. "Are you there?"

Mailbox people and deer converged on the area around him, sniffing and circling. Poking the ground. Christopher made his body as small as he could. They walked closer. He raised the silver blade. The deer came right up to Christopher's face and looked through him. Nose-to-nose. One more step, and they would know he was there.

Suddenly, a great scream rose from the camp. They turned to see where the commotion was coming from.

It was the nice man.

He was bleeding. Running for his life. Fighting off the deer. One by one. Until finally an 8-point buck drove its antlers into the nice man's hands and feet and broke them off. Leaving the sharpest for his chest. The deer dragged the nice man in front of the hissing lady and left his body like a mouse offered by a cat to its master.

"NO!" the nice man screamed.

The scream was a little too loud. Christopher understood that this was the nice man's diversion. This was his sacrifice. The hissing lady left her perch and approached the nice man. Christopher crawled at them. The mailbox people stood the nice man up. The hissing lady grabbed one of the antlers broken off in his body. She ripped it out of the nice man's flesh.

"WHERE IS HE?!" the hissing lady screamed.

The nice man was silent. His arms spread. The deer bit his feet. The mailbox people clawed him, moaning. Christopher watched as the nice man smiled and took his punishment, knowing that Christopher was there, safe and invisible, hunting her. The hissing lady took the antler sticking out of his chest. She ripped it out violently and threw it on the ground. The nice man doubled over in pain. Christopher kept crawling. The blade in his hand. Get the key. Save the nice man. Save his mother. Save the world.

"WHERE IS THE BOY?!" she hissed again.

"You can make me scream, but you will never make me talk," the nice man said.

The hissing lady did not respond. She only smiled. Twisted. Cruel. And evil. She raised her arms and the entire camp opened their mouths. A tremendous scream ripped through the sky. The sound was unbearable. Christopher dropped the blade and covered his ears as the hissing lady made a slight motion with her head, and the entire camp picked up and started marching.

Deeper into the Mission Street Woods.

Christopher picked up the blade and followed behind the procession as it moved down a wide path. A mailbox person stood at every tree. The deer nipped at their ankles to keep them in place. Marking the route like guardrails down a highway. Christopher looked up through the trees into the sky. He had maybe three minutes of daylight left. He would be visible. He needed to get the key. Now.

Christopher looked up ahead. The nice man struggled to walk. His flesh was pierced. Blood poured from his wounds. He stumbled and fell. The deer bit him to keep him moving.

The army marched down a long, winding path that Christopher had never seen before. Or had he? He wasn't sure. The feeling reminded him of the dreams his mother used to have when there were suddenly three more rooms to their apartment that she had never noticed. She was there with him. Somewhere. Somehow.

The group walked toward the coal mine tunnel, which opened like a giant cave mouth. Its wooden jaws clicking. Click click click. The hooves of the deer. Click click click. Christopher followed closely. Or was he being led? He didn't know anymore. It could be a trap, but he had nowhere else to go. The procession left the coal mine through a different exit. One he had never seen before. One that was hidden on the real side. What he saw terrified him.

It was a lovely little garden.

A perfect little garden with flowers and grass and evergreens. The trees were so thick that the snow couldn't find its way to the ground. But the light could. The daylight was beautiful. The weather was unseasonably warm. A perfect spring day mixed with a crisp, balmy autumn. Christopher had never felt such perfection.

The procession stopped.

The hissing lady stood in front of a tall tree. Christopher looked up and saw something—beautiful and white—perched on the tree's thick branches ten feet off the ground. He saw a ladder descending below it like baby teeth. And a bright, red door.

It was David Olson's tree house.

"David!" the hissing lady called out. "Come out!"

The door to the tree house opened. David Olson stood in the doorway. He crawled down the tree like a serpent and slithered over to the hissing lady. She patted his head as if to say, "Good boy." She turned to the crowd and raised her hand. The drums sounded. The mailbox people dragged the nice man up the ladder. The hissing lady followed.

The last to go into the tree house was David. As he stood in the doorway, he looked back out into the woods. Maybe he knew Christopher was there. Maybe he thought his message didn't make it to Christopher in time. Whatever it was, he had the saddest eyes Christopher had ever seen.

"David! Now!" the hissing lady barked.

David followed her into the tree house like a dutiful little dog and closed the door.

Christopher looked at the red sky through the branches.

He had thirty seconds of daylight left.

There were still dozens of deer and mailbox people around the tree. Standing guard. Preparing for battle. Worshipping. Christopher had no time to lose.

He ran to the tree house.

"What is that sound?" the voices hissed.

Christopher didn't stop. He ran faster and faster to the tree house. He had to get into it before sundown. It was the only element of surprise he had left. He ran around the mailbox people. Jumped over the deer.

"Is he here? Where is he?" the voices yelled.

Christopher raced to the foot of the tree. He grabbed the ladder and began to climb the little baby teeth. The daylight was fading.

Christopher reached the tree house.

The little glass window was fogged from the cold. Christopher couldn't see in. He had no idea what was in there. He listened to the door. There was no sound.

Christopher turned the knob. He slowly opened the door. His heart raced. He looked into the tree house. There was no one in it. Just an old picture of Ambrose hanging on the wall. The only other decorations were scratches from fingernails. David trying to get out? Something trying to get in? The mailbox people and hissing lady were long gone. There was no trace of David Olson. No sign of the nice man. What was this tree house? A portal? A door to another level? A mousetrap?

He stepped into David's tree house.

Christopher turned back to the horizon. He saw the last sliver of sun touching the top of the earth. The clouds floated like an audience of faces. He could feel the whole town. Thousands of frogs trying to fight their way out of boiling water.

Christopher walked into the tree house. He had no idea what would happen when he closed that door and walked into the place where nightmares are so scary, we can't remember them when we wake up.

The world went quiet. Christopher thought that he might be walking to his own death. But he had no choice.

Christopher closed the door just as night fell.

beEp.

Christopher's mother was so focused on David Olson's diary that she didn't hear the machine at first.

beEp.

She read the last entry again. There had to be something they'd missed. Some clue to help Christopher. David went to his tree house that night. David went into the woods. He was never seen again. What happened to David Olson in the woods? How did he die that night?

beEp. beEp.

"What is that sound?" Ambrose asked.

Christopher's mother looked at Ambrose. Even with the bandages covering his eyes, she could read the fear on his face. A horrible weight pressed on her chest. The room sounded like she was lying in a bathtub. The world under water.

beEp. beEp. beEp.

The third sound was unmistakable. Something had changed. She turned to the life-support machine, her eyes searching for the reason. That's when she saw it. Christopher's temperature. It had been 98.6 every time she looked at it. Except now.

102 degrees

She sat up in her chair. She felt Christopher's hand. It was hot as a skillet.

"I'll get you out of there. I promise you. But you have to fight for me. Fight!" she said.

103 degrees

Thanks to WebMD and the panic of early motherhood, Kate Reese knew that any temperature above 104 degrees was dangerous. At 107, the brain begins to cook.

beEp. beEp. beEp. beEp.

104 degrees

The door opened. The doctor and nurse moved quickly into the room.

"Mrs. Reese, we need you to leave. Now."

"No," she said. "I can help."

"Security!" the doctor yelled out.

The guards ran into the room so quickly, Christopher's mother thought they must have been standing outside, waiting for this moment. Ambrose put a steady hand on her shoulder.

"That won't be necessary, Doctor," Ambrose said. "We were just leaving."

"The hell we were!" Christopher's mother shouted.

Ambrose squeezed her shoulder and whispered in her ear.

"You can't help him in a straitjacket."

Christopher's mother looked at the security guards. Two big guys with even bigger bellies. They were both obsessively scratching their faces, sweaty with flu. One held pepper spray. The other a nightstick.

"Doctor asked you to leave . . ." the bigger one said, swallowing the word "bitch" and pushing its replacement through the bile in his throat. ". . . ma'am."

Everything in her wanted to fight them, but she knew they would just lock her up.

Just give us a reason . . . bitch ma'am.

"Of course," she said as pleasantly as she could fake. "I'm sorry."

Then, she calmly left the room with Ambrose in his wheelchair, giving one last glance to the life-support machine as it ticked up.

105 degrees

beEp. beEp. beEp. beEp. beEp.

106

CHAPTER 84

When night fell, something changed. There were no words, but everyone felt it. The temperature dropped. The wind quietly picked up and left a little whisper on the backs of a thousand necks.

it's tiMe

"It's time, Eddie. Listen to Grandma." Special Ed sat in his bedroom with his father's gun in his hand. He looked outside at the tree in his backyard. One branch sagging like a smile gone sick. Load the gun, Eddie. It's time to go to the woods, Eddie. To Grandmother's house we go, Eddie. Special Ed loaded the gun. Each bullet slid into the chamber with a click sick click. Special Ed threw it in his backpack along with the rest of the supplies Grandma told him to pack. He zipped up his coat and opened the window. He jumped out of his window and grabbed the grinning branch, which lowered him safely to the ground like a snake. Go into the woods, Eddie. Brady is going to try to take the tree house, Eddie. Don't let them take the tree house, Eddie. Brady. Eddie.

"Listen to Grandma."

it's tiMe

"Did you hear me, Brady? It's time. Listen to Grandma," Mrs. Keizer said.

Brady Collins tried to help his grandma stand up, but her arthritic joints clicked, and she fell back into her hospital bed.

"Brady, I'm too old to walk to the woods, but you remember what Grandma told you to do, right?"

"Yes, Grandma," he said.

Brady walked to the closet. He put on his scarf and winter jacket. He grabbed his backpack that he had filled with supplies when he waited for the ambulance to bring his mother to the hospital. He found his father's hunting knife and a handgun that he collected from World War II. Brady zipped up the pack and walked back to the bed.

"I hope you find your maiden name, Grandma."

"I will if we win the war."

Brady Collins nodded, kissed his grandmother's whiskery cheek, and left. The hospital was so crowded that no one paid any attention to the eight-year-old boy with the backpack. Brady easily slipped out of the hospital and started the long walk to the Mission Street Woods. He wanted to say goodbye to his father, but his dad was at his mother's bedside in the ICU. Brady hoped that when his mother woke up, she would forget Kathy Keizer. She deserved that. After all, she sacrificed herself to distract Brady's father from tearing down the woods by midnight. Brady thought it a shame that nothing else had worked. But now it's time, Brady. Jenny. Brady.

it's tiMe

"Jenny?" the voice whispered. "It's time, Jenny."

The voice sounded like her mother. Soft and sweet. Warm as a blanket. Jenny Hertzog reached under her pillow and pulled out the knife. She looked at the reflection of her eyes in the metal and smiled when she pictured it disappearing into her stepbrother's skin. Then, she walked down the hall to her stepbrother's room and opened the door without knocking. He was on the computer, unzipping his pants.

"Scott?" she said. "Scott?"

"What the fuck do you want?" he barked, startled.

"I'm going to the woods. Wanna come?"

"Why the fuck would I go to the woods with you?" he said.

"Because I'll give you anything you want."

Her stepbrother immediately shut down his computer. Jenny walked up to Scott and took his hand. She moved the itch down her arm and into his skin. Just as she had every night while he was sleeping. For days, she breathed through her mouth, so she wouldn't have to bear the sour smell in his room. His socks and B.O. and acne medicine. For days, she touched that miserable sweaty hand. Preparing for this night. The war was here, and her mom told her that they needed soldiers. But her mom promised that as soon as the good guys won the war, Jenny would be allowed to cut off Scott's face and feed it to him. She could finally take her stepbrother's blood and drown him and the rest of the fucking world in Floods.

it's tiMe.

Ms. Lasko's face was in the toilet when she heard the whisper, sweet and wet on the back of her neck. She was in the women's bathroom at the bar, making herself throw up. Not because she felt sick. No. Because she still felt sober. She thought that if she emptied her stomach and filled it with a whole bottle of Jack Daniel's, she might at least get a little buzz. But it didn't work. So, she began to weep. It had been so long since Ms. Lasko felt drunk that she couldn't even remember the feeling. It's not that she hadn't had alcohol. On the contrary, she drowned herself in floods every night. But that God damn itch wouldn't let her feel it. And now she felt everything else. Life had become a merciless, dry drunk that made her remember every terrible thing that she had ever done. And every terrible thing that had ever been done to her. It got so bad that she got on her knees in front of the toilet and prayed to God to let her feel drunk again. And suddenly, to her delight and great relief, her prayer was finally answered. A little voice told her that she would finally be able to feel drunk again. All she had to do was go to a "little after-hours place" in the Mission Street Woods.

it's tiMe.

It went on like that for an hour or so. All through town, people stopped whatever they were doing and started walking to the Mission Street Woods. Doug was in the middle of Christmas Eve dinner when his phone buzzed.

She's cheating on you, Doug. She wouldn't let you go all the way, but she let everyone else do whatever they wanted. She loved it, Doug. She's pregnant, Doug. With another man's baby. But the woods will fix your broken heart. It's time.

Debbie Dunham was fucking the security guard in the parking lot of the Giant Eagle after all the supplies had finally been sold.

Stop fucking that man, Debbie. The woods will make the pain stop. It's time.

The old woman sat in the attic, rocking in her chair.

We know you swam in the Ohio River together. He was such a beautiful boy. And he's here in the woods. He wants to see you, Gladyssss. It's time.

Mike and Matt sat at the dinner table with their mothers. The Gabrielson-Scott Christmas tradition of Chinese food and a movie started one day early. When the feast was done, the boys cracked open their fortune cookies.

Mike, if they take the tree house, she's going to kill your brother.

Matt, please help me. Christopher is trapped. It's time.

Father Tom was in the middle of preparing midnight mass when Mrs. Radcliffe had the strange idea of holding mass in the Mission Street Woods. Father Tom didn't like that idea at all. He said it was an abomination. So, the choir jumped on him and bit him and stabbed him and left him on the altar bleeding as they started to sing. The song was one they had never rehearsed before, but somehow, they all knew the melody.

it's tiMe.

it's tiMe.

it's tiMe.

But perhaps the strangest of all thoughts occurred to Nurse Tammy while taking a much-needed smoke break after making her rounds in the ICU. The thought was so odd in fact that at first, she blamed it on having worked seventy-two hours straight due to the short staff. In the past week, she had seen more shootings, stabbings, and suicide attempts than she had since she graduated from Pitt nearly ten years ago. It started when some woman stabbed her husband through the throat. Then, Mary Katherine hit Christopher and his mother with her car. The sheriff had been shot in the chest. A clown shot himself in the temple. Mrs. Collins deliberately inhaled a gallon of house paint. But there were others. Drunk drivers. Bar fights. Car accidents. The worst was the school bus driver, Mr. Miller, who practically impaled himself on a deer's antlers while driving the bus back to depot after dropping off the last kid for the Christmas Pageant. It had been absolute carnage. But that wasn't the strangest part. No.

The strangest part was that nobody died.

For the life of her, she couldn't actually remember the last time somebody had. As a matter of fact, the coroner joked that he felt a little guilty that everyone else was working so hard, because the last dead body he saw was the skeleton of that little boy they found in the woods. What was his name again? David something. When was that? Maybe a month ago. A whole month and no death. Wow.

It's a Christmas miracle.

Nurse Tammy took three more greedy puffs and went back into the hospital. But not before thanking God that her shift finally ended at midnight. It was a few hours until she could drive home and share a nice glass of merLOT with her father. Only a few hours until Christmas.

Then again. If people just stopped dying, it would mean the end of the world.

CHAPTER 85

Mary Katherine opened her eyes. Her head throbbing. She looked outside at the sunset, and a horrible sick lodged in her stomach. It was Christmas Eve. But she wasn't going to Aunt Gerri's house for mushroom soup. She wasn't going to church for Father Tom's midnight mass. She had driven her car at 125 miles an hour. And in that crucial moment when the deer ran in front of her, Mary Katherine thought of nothing but saving herself. In order to stay out of Hell, she turned the wheel and hit a little boy and his mother instead.

You're selfish, Mary Katherine. You're so selfish.

The voice ate at her stomach as the memories came back in one large flood. The terrible impact. The violent ripping of metal and explosion of glass. The jaws of life prying both cars open like cans of soup. The EMTs pulling out Christopher and Mrs. Reese. They were such nice people. They were such good people.

You hit a child to stay out of Hell, Mary Katherine.

Mary Katherine would have given anything to trade places with him. But nothing happened to her that sleeping the day away couldn't fix. She had her seat belt and an airbag. She was fine. She wanted that airbag to kill her. She wanted that seat belt to strangle her. She deserved to die in that accident.

You deserve everything that's happening to you, Mary Katherine.

Mary Katherine finally forced herself to look down at her body. She saw the hospital gown. The life monitor clipped to her index finger. The heart monitor beeped and beeped and beeped. When they brought her into the hospital, an exhausted Nurse Tammy told her not to worry. Just rest. She would be fine. The doctor might have even sent her right home.

If it hadn't been for the baby.

The door opened.

"Mary Katherine?"

Her mother walked into the room. She rushed to Mary Katherine, crying and hugging her over and over again.

"Mom, I'm so sorry."

Mary Katherine had no way of understanding that her mother was not upset at her seventeen-year-old daughter because she was too relieved that the seventeen-week-old daughter that she remembered nursing hadn't died in that car accident last night. She had no way of knowing that no matter how big children feel, they will always look smaller to their parents.

"Thank God you're okay," her mother said. "Praise Jesus."

Mary Katherine looked up as her father walked into the room. His jaw was tight and clicky from hours of rage. Rage at her disobedience. Rage at her recklessness. Rage at the expense of hospital bills and insurance claims and the Notre Dame tuition that was now going to drown the family in debt.

"Dad," she said. "I'm so sorry."

He was silent as a statue. And he wouldn't look at her. He just stood there, scratching the dome of his scalp. When she was younger, she thought he had scratched away his hair like an eraser on the tip of a pencil. She waited for him to speak, but when he wouldn't, she asked him the one thing she cared about in that moment.

"How is Christopher?" she asked.

"He's in a coma," her father said. "He might die, Mary Katherine."

All the guilt she had ever experienced was a dry run leading up to that moment. Mary Katherine's face flushed with shame. Her eyes brimmed, and her voice quivered.

"I'm sorry, Dad. It's all my faul—"

"What the hell were you doing on the road at two in the morning?" he asked, cutting her off.

Her father's voice sounded different to her. She had never seen him this angry. Mary Katherine was silent. She looked at her mother.

"Don't look at her. Look at me. What were you doing, Mary Katherine?"

Mary Katherine looked into her father's eyes. She was terrified.

"I went to church," she said.

The minute the words left her mouth, her stomach began to churn. She wasn't lying. She did go to church. But only after buying three pregnancy tests. Only after peeing on three sticks. Only after testing positive three times. Father. Son. Holy Ghost.

"You went to pray?" her mother said, her eyes softening.

"Yes, Mom," Mary Katherine said.

"About what?" her father asked.

"Excuse me?" Mary Katherine stalled.

Her father stared at her. His rage only growing.

"You knew the family was going to midnight mass tonight, but you just had to sneak the car out at two in the morning to go to church to pray?"

"Yes, Dad."

"ABOUT WHAT?" he said.

Mary Katherine was a deer in the headlights.

"Um . . ."

"PRAYING. ABOUT. WHAT?" her father repeated.

Mary Katherine turned to her mother.

"Honey, please. What were you praying for?" her mother asked softly.

"Mommy . . ." Mary Katherine said, suddenly feeling about ten years younger than she was. "I don't know how this happened. I must have done something wrong, but I don't know what it is. Maybe I thought it because to think it is to do it, but I didn't know it could work that way, Mom. I swear to you I didn't."

"Just tell me what you were praying for, honey. Whatever it is, we'll figure it out together," her mother said.

Tears began to swell in Mary Katherine's eyes. Her father grabbed her hand.

"STOP STALLING AND ANSWER THE FUCKING QUESTION!" her father yelled. "WHAT WERE YOU PRAYING ABOUT?!"

"Daddy, I'm pregnant."

With the truth came the tears. Her mother held her as she sobbed. For a moment, Mary Katherine thought that maybe it would be okay. Her mother would still love her. She could still get into Notre Dame. She could get a great job and pay her father back and help Christopher recover. She promised them she would. Because her mother forgave her. Because when she deserved nothing, she was given love.

"When did you and Doug start having sex?"

Mary Katherine looked up and saw her father. He was so disappointed.

"When did you and Doug start having sex?" he repeated.

"We didn't."

"What? You're sleeping with other people?"

"No, Dad."

"Then, who is the father?" he asked.

Mary Katherine was silent. Her mother held her hand softly.

"Who is the father, honey?" she asked.

"I don't know, Mom," Mary Katherine said.

"You don't know? How many have there been?!" her father asked.

"None."

"What are you talking about?!" he said.

"I've never had sex."

"Then, how are you pregnant?"

Mary Katherine could not stand the look in his eyes. The confusion holding the rage back like fingers in a dam.

"I don't know. That's what I said. I don't know what's happening."

"Tell me who the father is!" he said.

Mary Katherine turned back to her mother.

"There is no father. That's what I'm saying. I don't understand what I did. Please help me, Mom."

"It's okay, honey. You don't have to protect anyone. Just tell us who the father is," her mother said kindly.

"Mom . . . there is no father. It's an immaculate conception."

Mary Katherine turned just as her father slapped her across her face.

"You stop this blasphemy right now! Who did you sleep with?"

"No one, Daddy," she cried.

"Who's the father?"

"I'm a virgin."

"MARY KATHERINE! WHO'S THE FUCKING FATHER?!"

Mary Katherine braced herself, but her father didn't hit her again. He just gave her a look of utter contempt and walked into the hallway, seething. Mary Katherine fell into her mother's arms and sobbed so deeply that it took her a few seconds to realize something horrible.

Her mother wasn't holding her back.

"Mom?" she asked. "Will you forgive me?"

She turned to her mother for support. But her mother couldn't even look at her.

"Only God can forgive you," she said.

Mary Katherine could have dealt with her father hitting her for the rest of the day. But she couldn't stand one second of her mother's disappointment. Within moments, her father returned with a doctor that Mary Katherine didn't recognize.

"Hello, Mary Katherine. I'm Dr. Green," he said. "We are going to give you a mild sedative."

He gave a look to the nurse, who began to clean her arm with a cotton ball and some antiseptic.

"It's just to help you with the move," Dr. Green continued.

"What move? Am I going home now?" she said.

"No. You'll be staying here for a while."

"Dad, what's going on?"

Her father wouldn't look at her.

"Mom?"

Her mother was silent. It only took Mary Katherine another moment to realize that they all thought she was insane. She started to struggle, but within seconds, some orderlies rushed in from the hallway.

"Please, Mom. Don't let them do this."

"We're going to get you help, honey," her mother said.

"Mom, it's an immaculate conception. You taught me this my whole life."

The orderlies grabbed her. She rocked her body backward to break their grip, but they were too strong.

"NO!" she screamed. "PLEASE!"

The doctor pulled out the syringe.

"I'M NOT LYING! I SWEAR ON MY SOUL! PLEASE! SOMETHING TERRIBLE IS HAPPENING!"

The doctor shoved the needle into Mary Katherine's arm. Within seconds, she went limp with the sedative, and right before she fell into a deep sleep, she looked at her mother.

"Mom," she said in a calm voice. "Please, don't let them take me."

She saw her mother turn away as the orderlies dragged her out of the room.

"You need help, Mary Katherine," the doctor said. "It's time."

CHAPTER 86

Mrs. Henderson drove the sheriff's car toward the elementary school. She kept the scanner on, listening for any sign of a manhunt. But there was none. In fact, the radio had been silent since she ran from the sheriff's office, leaving him and the deputies bleeding to death. Earlier in the day, she was confused by the silence. Then, she was elated. She realized she had done her job. At least the first part of it.

There were no police left in Mill Grove.

When she arrived at Mill Grove Elementary School, Mrs. Henderson parked the sheriff's car in her usual spot. She watched the sun disappear from the school playground. Such a big beautiful sun. Son. The son that Mr. Henderson never gave her. He said it was her fault, but when she went to the doctor, she learned her parts were fine. But would her husband get checked? Oh, no. He was too busy screwing around. God, she wanted to stab him again. She wanted to stab him again and again and have him never die. Just stab him again and again for eternity and have his blood run down the slide of the school playground. Right past the four-square court and the swing set.

Mrs. Henderson looked into the school. The hallways were empty. The doors locked. So, she reached back and broke the window to the library with her fist. The glass cut her fingers to ribbons, but she didn't mind. As long as her hands were healthy enough to stab, that's all that mattered. Mrs. Henderson pulled herself through the window and walked into the library.

She'd only been in jail for a little while, but the library was much smaller than she remembered it. The little desks and tables. The bookshelves placed a little lower so that smaller hands could find bigger words. The art projects from poor, drunk Ms. Lasko's class. Little handprints dipped in paint and turned into little paintings of Thanksgiving turkeys. She saw that one of them was made by Christopher.

Such a shame what was about to happen to him.

Mrs. Henderson climbed on top of her old desk. She removed a white panel in the ceiling and pulled out an elegant leather suitcase. She had hidden the bag in the ceiling right after the blizzard. She didn't know why at the time. It seemed strange, but a little voice told her that she might need it. A little voice told her that it was very romantic to hide a little weekend bag in the library just in case Mr. Henderson ever wanted to surprise her with a spontaneous trip.

For weeks, she had pictured her husband saying, "Darling, I want to whisk you away to a little bed-and-breakfast. I want to thank you for giving me the last fifty years of your life. It's just too bad we aren't packed already."

And she would reply, "We are!"

Then, she would show him the little weekend bag. He would be proud of how perfectly packed it was. He would be moved by his thoughtful wife. He would realize that he couldn't love her more when he saw what she packed for them.

1 change of clothes
2 pairs of fresh underwear
1 pair of hiking boots
And of course, a butcher knife, duct tape, rope, zippers, thread, a dozen sewing needles, and 300 yards of black yarn that she got on sale at
Jo-Ann Fabric

Perfect for a weekend getaway.

The getaway never happened, of course. Fridays came and went, and Mr. Henderson never asked to whisk her away to a B&B for some red wine, birdwatching, and lovemaking. There was no ballet. No symphony. No Broadway musical at Heinz Hall. Not even a first-run movie. God, she wanted to stab him. Still, it was lucky that she packed away this little romantic bag because she needed these supplies for tonight.

Mrs. Henderson climbed off her old desk and said a proper goodbye to the library. She had spent fifty years in it, and she knew she would never see it again. At least with her own eyes. She walked past the bookshelves and grabbed one book as a souvenir. One book for eternity. The book was Frankenstein. The copy that Christopher had read.

Mrs. Henderson, Christopher is on the computer.

Mrs. Henderson, write to Christopher on the computer.

Mrs. Henderson, get the copy of Frankenstein.

Mrs. Henderson, underline these letters.

Mrs. Henderson, make them think David Olson is helping them.

The voice promised her something in return. This time, her husband would respect her. This time, her husband would appreciate her. This time, her husband would love her. And it could still happen if she did a good job tonight.

Mrs. Henderson brought the book and her weekend bag to the nurse's office. She stripped off her bloody clothes and rinsed her body off in the sink. She cleaned and dressed the wound that the sheriff's bullet left in her side. She cleaned up her sliced fingers. Then, she opened up the bag and put on the fresh clothes. Ahhhh. The soft cotton and sturdy boots felt good against her skin. She felt like herself again. That young girl of twenty-three who came to this school with all of her passion and education. The young girl who was going to change the world one student at a time. Starting with that first class. And that one special little boy. David Olson. And her last class. With that other special boy. Christopher Reese. She remembered when he first came to school. He couldn't read a book for first graders. And now, he was more than a genius. Now, he was almost God. So much to ask of a little brain. So much to ask of a little body. It's such a shame what would happen to him.

But they all had their jobs to do.

Mrs. Henderson put the copy of Frankenstein next to the rest of the supplies and went back to the broken window. She jumped out and looked up at the moon rising in the sky. It was full. Big and blue. Just like she knew it would be.

"Excuse me, ma'am?"

There was a handsome man leaning on a truck parked behind the school. She didn't know when the truck had pulled up.

"Yes?" Mrs. Henderson asked.

The man approached her. There was something very dangerous about him. Her body tensed.

"Do you work here?" the man asked.

"Why do you ask?" she said.

The man looked at the broken window and her bandaged hand. He put two with two and smiled.

"Because I need to know where this school keeps records," he said.

"That's confidential information," she said.

"I can always beat it out of you," he said with a shrug.

"In the principal's office. Down the hall," Mrs. Henderson told the man.

"Thank you, ma'am," the man said.

"You're welcome, Jerry," Mrs. Henderson said.

"How did you know my name?" Jerry asked.

Mrs. Henderson smiled and left without an answer. She passed his truck with the Michigan plates and walked off the playground, but not before seeing the swing set one more time. For some reason, she pictured Christopher jumping from those swings. And then, a thought came to her. Quiet as a whisper.

Christopher was such a nice little boy. It was too bad that he was going to die now.

it's tiMe.

CHAPTER 87

Christopher opened his eyes.

At first, he didn't understand. The minute he closed the door to David's tree house, he expected to open the door and see the woods again.

But he was back at home.

In bed.

At night.

Christopher looked around his room. Everything seemed normal. He turned to the antique bookshelf that smelled like baseball gloves. The one his mother filled with his very own books. Everything looked to be in perfect order. The picture of his father rested safely on top. His closet door was closed. The door to his bedroom was locked from the inside. He was in the imaginary world. It was night when the imaginary people were supposed to wake up. But he felt perfectly safe. Christopher breathed a sigh of relief. He threw off the blanket and sat up, getting ready to swing his legs to the floor.

That's when he heard the breathing.

Coming from under the bed.

Christopher froze. He looked at either side of the bed, waiting for a hand. A claw. Something to reach out and pull him under the bed by his ankles. But nothing came. The person just waited. Breathing. Licking its lips. Christopher thought he could jump and run out of his bedroom. But the door was locked. Not to keep anything out. Locked to keep him in.

Scccratch. Scccratch. Scccratch.

The noise startled Christopher. He looked at the window. The tree in his backyard had somehow moved closer to the house. The tire swing hung like a noose. The tree reached an old withered branch to the glass. Scraping back and forth like an arthritic finger.

Scccratch. Scccratch. Scccratch.

The breathing got louder under the bed. Christopher had to get out of here. Right now. He stood on his bed and brought himself up to his tiptoes. He looked out of his bedroom window into the backyard. He thought he could jump off his bed, land, and climb out.

But the entire backyard was filled with mailbox people.

They stood like laundry drying in the breeze. A hundred deer waited next to them. Lying on the ground. Lurking in the shadows.

Scccratch. Scccratch. Scccratch.

Christopher frantically looked around his room for a way out. His bedroom door was locked. The backyard was filled. He had nowhere to go. Christopher quieted his mind. The nice man said he had powers here. Use them!

Christopher saw a hand reaching up from under the bed.

Christopher jumped off the bed just as the hand grabbed for him. He landed off balance and tripped. He turned back to see hands crawling out from under the bed. The hands were not attached to bodies. Just voices screaming from the shadows.

"COME HERE, CHRISTOPHER!"

They grabbed his feet and ankles and began to pull him back under the bed. Christopher twisted blindly, shaking the hands loose like spiders off a back. A dozen screams erupted as Christopher kicked the hands back to the darkness. He struggled to his feet and ran to his bedroom door. He reached to unlock the doorknob.

Until it began to turn from the other side.

"Can he hear us?" the voices whispered.

Christopher froze. He backed away to his bedroom window and looked down into the backyard. The mailbox people moved the strings linking them together from the right hand to the left. Then, they took their free right hands and reached up like synchronized swimmers to unzip their eyelids at the same time. The metal gleaming in the moonlight.

The mailbox people were waking up.

Christopher turned back into the room to find his bedroom door open. People stood next to the bed with their arms folded behind their backs. They smiled. Chunks of the wood door still stuck in their teeth.

"Hi, Christopher," they said.

They brought their arms in front of them. Their arms were stubs. Rounded flesh. Chopped off and cauterized.

"Where did you put our hands? Thief!"

They started running at him. Christopher threw open the bedroom window. The deer circled the backyard like piranhas in a tank. If he jumped down, they would tear him to pieces. There was nowhere to go . . .

. . . but the roof.

Christopher grabbed the ledge of the bay window and pulled himself up just as the people behind him jumped at him. They reached for his feet, but their bare arms betrayed them, and they slipped, falling into the backyard.

The deer were on them in seconds.

Biting. Ripping. Clawing.

Christopher climbed onto the roof and hid behind the chimney. The first sliver of the blue moon rose above the horizon as night descended. He looked out over his neighborhood. The grey concrete of the street was slowly turning red. The pavement looked squishy. Like after a rain. But this was not rain. It smelled too much like a copper penny. And it ran down the street like a waterslide into the sewers.

The street was bleeding.

He saw the man in the Girl Scout uniform.

Waking up.

The man opened his eyes. He was at least forty or maybe even a young fifty. But his eyes were innocent. And he was happy. He yawned and rubbed away the sleep like a baby. Then, he stood and began to skip down the street, kicking blood puddles all over his bare legs. The man kept whistling a song. Blue Moon. He bent down to tie his shoes near the bushes. Whistling. And tying. And whistling. And tying.

Until two hands reached out and grabbed him.

The man let out a bloodcurdling scream. When Christopher saw who pulled the man into the bushes, he couldn't believe his eyes.

It was the man himself.

They looked like identical twins. But the other man wasn't wearing a Girl Scout uniform. He wore glasses that were missing a frame. And a whistle around his neck. He was bald and his hair was too thin to comb over, but he did it anyway. As the balding man ripped off the Girl Scout man's uniform, Christopher finally understood the words he was screaming.

"GET ME OUT OF HERE! PLEASE!"

Christopher saw another man jogging down the street. Out of nowhere, a car turned the corner and ran into him, knocking the man into the grass. The car screeched to a halt. The car door opened to reveal that the person driving the car was the man himself. He held a flask. When he saw what he had done to himself, the driver ran back into his car and drove away. Then, the man who got hit with the car dusted himself off and stood up. He jogged back into the street. Out of nowhere, the same car turned the corner and ran into him.

"PLEASE MAKE IT STOP!"

Christopher looked around his neighborhood. Everywhere he turned, he saw people hurting themselves. Over and over again. He saw a man cheating on his wife with one of their neighbors. The man and woman were kissing, their arms intertwined like candles melted into each other. They couldn't stop kissing.

"PLEASE! PLEASE! MAKE IT STOP!" the couple shouted, blood running from their lips.

The screams pounded Christopher's mind. It felt as if someone had put earphones on his head and turned up the volume to 10. Then 11. Then 12. Up and up and up to infinity. He felt like his brain was cooking. It was beyond a fever. It was beyond a headache. It was beyond any pain he knew possible. Because it wasn't his pain. It was the world's pain. And there was no end to it. Christopher's mind raced for answers inside all of this madness.

I was here for six days.

Christopher looked across the bleeding landscape. The mailbox people fanned through the neighborhood. Climbing chimneys. Gutters. Cable lines. Breaking glass and doors while the deer sniffed the bloody ground. Sniffing for him in the shadows. He heard screaming in the house next door.

"Stop! Don't hit me, Mom!" a woman said to herself over and over in a little girl's voice.

"Spare the rod! Spoil the child!" she replied in her mom's voice as she pulled off her belt.

Christopher felt the woman's shrieks as she hit herself over and over. The belt connecting with flesh. Christopher calmed his mind as much as he could. He pushed the screams out of his ears and thought quickly.

You have to get the key.
You have to kill the hissing lady.
You have to save the nice man.

He searched his mind for the nice man, but the screams came back, louder than before. Just when he thought his mind would crack in half, there was a great silence. It looked as if someone pushed the OFF button on the street. Every person went limp like a robot at Chuck E. Cheese's. Every mailbox person. Every deer. Christopher stood, perched on the roof of his house. Waiting. Not breathing.

Something is coming.
What is it?

Suddenly, a familiar sound broke the spell. An ice cream truck was coming down the street. The truck was playing a song, but the little music box sounded warped. Like an old record left out in the sun.

> All around the mulberry bush
> The monkey chased the people
> The monkey thought that it was a joke
> Pop! goes the weasel.

The truck drove closer and closer. The doors of the houses opened, and little children started walking outside. Rubbing their eyes like moles. Squinting in the moonlight. The little children poured into the street and ran at the ice cream truck. They all wore different styles of dress. Some kids looked like they were from old movies that he watched with his mom. Little boys in caps and suspenders. Little girls in poodle skirts. Some of the boys wore Amish hats. Some of the girls wore dresses like the Pilgrims. They moved to the ice cream truck, singing along to the song with their serpent tongues.

> A penny for a spool of thread
> A penny for a needle
> That's the way the money goes
> Pop! goes the weasel.

The ice cream truck stopped. All of the children moved to it, clamoring for their treats with shouts of "Me! Me! Me!"

"Okay, kids," the voice said. "Pay up."

Christopher watched the children reach into their pockets and each pull out two silver dollars. All of the children lay on the bloody street and put the coins on their closed eyelids. The ice cream man reached his burnt skeleton hand down to collect the money. When all the coins were collected, the hand went back into the shadows of the truck and threw the kids Popsicles and Screwballs and Push-Ups. But they weren't ice cream.

They were frozen deer legs.

All around the mulberry bush
The monkey chased the people
The monkey thought that it was a joke.
Pop! goes the weasel.

The music slowed down as if stuck on flypaper. The kids wrapped their tongues around the frozen treats like snakes. Some kids got Screwballs that didn't have gum on the bottom of the ice cream. They had eyeballs. Other kids got delicious vanilla soft serve with sprinkles on top. But they weren't sprinkles. They were little teeth. There was only one kid who didn't have any coins to give the ice cream man.

It was David Olson.

He stood away from the group. All alone. Christopher had never seen such a sad face in all his life. David Olson walked over to the other kids and gestured for a lick of their ice cream. The kids all pushed him away. David walked over to the truck, raising his hands up to beg for free ice cream. The skeleton hand reached out and smacked David's hand away. Then, the truck started up and moved down the street, bringing the horrible music with it.

A penny for a spool of thread
A penny for a needle

When the ice cream truck was gone, the street came alive. The other children surrounded David and started to hiss at him. Like a pack of wolves surrounding a fawn. Their teeth exposed. Their eyes glowing. Christopher could feel David's fear. The panic moved from his stomach to his throat. The pounding in David's chest.

But there were no words.

For the life of him, Christopher could not read David's thoughts. Every time he tried, his nose bled, and his eyes threatened to push their way out of his skull. A fever broke out on his brow. Sweat poured like the blood rushing down the street into the sewers, dark and filled with voices.

Without warning, the streetlights turned on. The street looked like an old amusement park right when the clangs and bells of the rides wake up. The light illuminated something slithering in the shadows.

It was the hissing lady.

She was perched on the roof above David Olson's old house like a gargoyle. Surveying her kingdom. Watching the procession. The children walked in a circle, following David like the tornado after Dorothy.

"You better pray, prey."

The children spoke in unison. A choir of voices repeating the same phrase like a Sunday mass. David faced them and hissed back. The others backed away, frightened and jittered. The fear only adding to the pleasure of their chase. They moved around him like a carousel, pushing David down the road into the cul-de-sac. His heels reached the very edge of the street.

Don't leave the street.

They can't get you if you don't leave the street.

The hissing lady followed them from the rooftops. Watching. Waiting. Christopher wondered why she didn't intervene since David was her pet. But maybe they were all her pets. Maybe David was just the runt of the litter, and she was going to let him be torn apart or starved by the others.

Maybe this was her version of dogfighting.

Or maybe it's all a trap.

For David. Or for me.

Christopher watched David Olson step off the street and walk through the field. The children giggling behind him. Fifty yards away, hidden in shadow, Christopher saw the hissing lady move through the backyards and enter the Mission Street Woods from another angle. Like she was stalking prey.

You better pray, prey.

Christopher knew that it all could be a trap, but there was no other trail of bread crumbs left to him. The nice man was imprisoned somewhere. David Olson was his only friend left in this horrible place. And there was only one way out for all of them.

We have to kill the hissing lady.

We have to get the key.

Christopher backed away from the chimney and looked in his backyard. The deer were picking the last of the meat from the people's bones. He couldn't climb down, or he would be the next course. Christopher looked at the log cabin across the street. It was a far jump, but it was his only choice.

And he had been trained now.

Christopher closed his eyes and quieted his mind, priming his imagination like a water pump. In his mind's eye, he ran as fast as he could to the front of the house. He planted his foot right at the gutter and jumped. He saw the street below him, covered in blood gushing down the sidewalk. Christopher landed on the log cabin's roof, opened his eyes, and backed into the shadows. Almost slipping on the icy shingles.

He looked at the Mission Street Woods standing tall right in front of him. Branches swaying in the breeze like arms in the air on Sunday. He quickly turned his gaze down to make sure the lawn was clear. Then, he climbed down the gutter, landed quiet as a feather, and sprinted as fast as he could through the field. He looked back at the street as the mad carnival raged on. People hurting themselves over and over. Their screams falling like trees in the middle of the forest where no one was left to hear them.

Except Christopher.

He listened for a moment to make sure there wasn't a trap right behind the trees. He checked his pocket for the dull, silver blade. Then, Christopher followed David Olson into the Mission Street Woods.

CHAPTER 88

106.1 degrees
beEp.

Christopher's mother stood outside of her son's room. She could have broken the glass window with her bare hands to get to him. She promised herself that when he hit 107, and his brain began to cook, she would. But the orderlies stood like two sentries on either side of the door. Scratching their sweaty, feverish faces. Looking for a reason to drag her away.

106.2 degrees
beEp.

The entrance door buzzed like a hornet's nest, and Nurse Tammy walked back into the ICU, cigarette smoke stuck to her scrubs like Velcro. Christopher's mother approached her just as she started washing her hands, then slathering them with a sweet lotion that made her smell like a lavender ashtray.

"Excuse me, Nurse?" Christopher's mother said as gently as she could manage. "I need to get back in to see my son now."

Nurse Tammy rubbed her tired eyes and looked through the window. The doctor shot back a loaded shake of the head. Any child would have known that the answer was a decided NO. And GET YOUR ASS IN HERE.

"I'm sorry, hun," she said in her kindest Western PA.

Then, feeling sorry for her, she studied Christopher's vitals through the window with a trained eye.

"Mrs. Reese, I know his temperature is high, but don't worry. He won't die."

"How do you know that?" Christopher's mother asked.

Nurse Tammy dropped her voice to a whisper, making sure that none of her colleagues could hear her.

"Because no one has died in over a month. And I can't imagine God will start again with yours."

"What?"

"Yeah. No one has died since they found that little boy's skeleton in the woods. It's a Christmas miracle."

"Jesus," Ambrose said.

The word was right, but Nurse Tammy's expression seemed to indicate she found the old man's tone rather odd.

"Yes, sir," she said, wrinkling her nose. "Praise Jesus."

With that, Nurse Tammy went into Christopher's room, leaving the two in the ICU. Their silence had its own pulse. Kate Reese's mind instantly moved from her son's struggle for life to something far bigger in scope. She gripped Ambrose's wheelchair and began to walk them around the ICU. The feeling was palpable. In the hours that they had been reading David's diary, the number of people crowding the rooms had tripled. There were no more gurneys. No more beds. Just screaming and illness. So many sick people. So many angry souls. Sweaty faces. Itchy. Feverish. The itch wouldn't stop. The hospital was on the verge of mutiny.

"Does it look as bad as it sounds?" Ambrose asked from his wheelchair.

"Worse," Kate Reese said. "She's everywhere."

Be a victim or be a fighter, Kate.

She shook off her own fear and focused. Fear did Christopher no good. Action did. Answers did. No one had died since they dug up David Olson's skeleton. Maybe there was an answer in the diary. Maybe there was an answer in the woods where they found him. And nobody knew those woods better than Christopher or . . .

The sheriff.

She didn't know if the words led her eyes to his room or the other way around. But Kate Reese found herself looking at the sheriff in his room in the ICU.

"The sheriff," Ambrose said, as if his own mind were on a three-second delay from hers.

Kate Reese looked down at Ambrose. He might have been blind, but he was sharp as a tack. She pushed him into the sheriff's room. The sheriff was terribly pale. His lips shivering. Even in his sleep. She moved to his bedside and took his hands. The same hands that sweated on their first date. His hands were now freezing. Not from cold. From blood loss.

"How is he?" Ambrose asked.

She looked at the wounds in his chest, stitched with a practiced, if hurried, hand. He had been shot point-blank in the chest. One of the bullet wounds was right above his heart. But it was still beating.

"Alive," she said.

She looked at the IV bringing morphine into the sheriff's arm. The same arm that had been scrubbed within an inch of its life by the surgical team. But she could still see little impressions of words left behind by permanent ink.

"There's a message on his arm," she said.

"What is it?" Ambrose asked.

She moved her hands over the words like Braille as she spoke them aloud to Ambrose.

David Olson—boy. Don't—sleep. Call Carl—NOW. Tools— children. Stone—wood. Whole city—the flu. The last flu— ended—David disappeared. Did David—stop the flu? Did he save us?

Suddenly they heard screaming down the hall. A man was hungry, and he didn't understand why the meals were only for patients. They could hear shouts of "Calm down, sir," from the nurses and shouts of "Help my wife!" from the man. Eventually, there was the sound of metal crashing on the floor, and the man being pulled out by security, kicking and screaming.

"That will be us soon," Ambrose cautioned. "Keep reading."

Kate Reese found the other arm, deciphering each faded word.

Call Ambrose! Stop listening—the voice—is lying to you— making you forget. You know what the tools were for! Run to Kate. What happened to David—happening to Chris- topher. Run now! Too late, Sheriff. I just hit them with a car.

"You have to get out of here," a voice whispered.

Kate Reese almost screamed. But the voice belonged to the sheriff. He was forcing himself awake. Barely audible.

"It's not safe here. There are no police left."

The sheriff tried to sit up, but he was too weak. Kate put a loving hand on his forehead and brought him back down with a soft shhh.

"Christopher is right next door. We're not leaving you," Kate assured him.

The sheriff let go and allowed himself to melt back into bed. The morphine falling like raindrops on a glassy pond. Drip. Drip. Drip.

"Bobby," she whispered. "What were the tools for?"

"Huh?" he said, his voice as high as a kite from morphine.

"The tools," Kate repeated desperately. "What were they for?"

He took a hard, dry swallow and pushed through the pain.

"The construction crew found tools and petrified wood. My friend Carl ran the tests. There are dozens of tree houses out there. Kids have been making them for hundreds of years."

"What does that mean?" Ambrose asked.

"It means David and Christopher are not alone in there," Kate Reese said.

Kate settled back in thought. There were other children. She didn't know if that was a good thing or a bad thing. Ambrose's voice broke the silence.

"Were the tree houses all in the same place?" Ambrose asked.

"No," the sheriff said. "They were spread all over the woods. Why?"

The old soldier wrinkled his brow under his bandages. "Maybe they're all linked," Ambrose said. "Maybe she's using them to build something bigger."

106.3 degrees

beEp.

CHAPTER 89

Christopher tiptoed down the path, bending his body to avoid every twig. Every branch. He was not invisible at night. He couldn't make a sound. The hissing lady was in these woods. Somewhere. Christopher saw David a hundred yards up ahead on the trail. The little children surrounded him like a maypole. Skipping and clapping. Christopher saw the footprints David left behind. Muddy and bloody. Christopher remembered following footprints into the Mission Street Woods for the first time. The cloud had winked at him. He followed the cloud and followed the footprints and went missing for six days.

What did I do here for six days?

What did she do with me?

SNAP.

A twig cracked under Christopher's feet. The children looked behind them. David used the distraction to take off running. The children turned and followed.

"Daaaavvvviiid," they hissed.

David put his head down and ran faster. Trying to outrun their voices.

"Dooo yooouuu knowwww wheerrrreee yoouuu areeee?"

David broke into a sprint. Two little girls ran in front of him.

"Oh, David. You're back! We've been waiting for you! It's almost finished!"

David screamed and made a hard right. It was all Christopher could do to keep pace. David sprinted over the billy goat bridge and jumped into the cold water, trying to lose the girls. Three mailbox people rose from the water. Their zipper eyes open. Moaning and reaching for him. David jumped over their outstretched fingers. Rancid and rotting. He landed near the old hollow log. The man in the log popped his head out.

"Hi, David! It's almost finished!"

David jumped over the man just as two deer came out of the woods. Three more deer hit the trail. David turned left again. Three more. David turned right. Five more. David stopped. He was surrounded.

"Do you know where you are, DavId?!"

Suddenly dozens of mailbox people came from the shadows. They opened their mouths, struggling against the stitching. The deer walked closer. Baring their teeth. Christopher picked up a rock. He didn't care that it would give away his position. He had to help David. He wound up and was about to throw it at the leader just as the deer jumped for David's throat.

That's when it happened.

The moment lasted the blink of an eye, but Christopher could still see each step clearly. He saw David Olson close his eyes. He felt the boy's mind go quiet. Then, he sensed a charge in the air as his mind was filled with imaginary thoughts. Suddenly the sound around him died as if the quiet of his mind had absorbed it like a sponge. And there was nothing left but imagination. Christopher could not hear David's thoughts, but he knew what they were from the result.

David Olson began to fly.

It didn't look like anything Christopher expected. David wasn't flying around like Superman. He wasn't a superhero. He was just a little boy who found himself in the air as if floating on a thought. An invisible cloud instead of a cape.

The deer crashed heads into each other, locking antlers.

You can fly like Iron Man.

Christopher closed his eyes and calmed his mind. He didn't have David's level of training, so he didn't think he could fly without the nice man there. But he tried to picture himself weightless anyway. He tried to see himself floating on the wind like a leaf. Or a feather.

Or a white plastic bag.

Christopher felt his feet lift off the ground for a second. He tried to gain his balance like a tightrope walker at the circus. But this tightrope didn't go across.

This one went up.

With his eyes firmly shut, Christopher pictured himself moving past one branch. Then another. Climbing the tree with his imagination instead of his hands. He saw himself above the treetops. The trees standing under him like green fluffy clouds. The moon full and bright and blue. The sky above it filled with stars. Space reaching out as wide and deep as time is timeless. Deep space the ocean, and Earth a life raft. The stars not shooting. The stars still.

The stars dying.

In his mind's eye, Christopher looked up ahead and saw David flying toward the clearing. Christopher pictured himself planting a foot on the tops of the trees. Running across them as if walking on water. Gaining speed. The leaves falling like petals under his feet. The fever breaking out over his body like whispers on his skin.

David Olson is...
David Olson is...terrified.

Christopher could feel David begin to fall up ahead. He looked exactly like the birds Jerry used to shoot out of the air. But it wasn't a bullet that brought David down.

It was something in the clearing.

Christopher opened his eyes and lowered himself under the treetops to hide. He moved quietly, branch to branch. He heard movement under him on the path. Running. Whispers. Christopher moved to the edge of the clearing and stopped. His eyes searched the ground for any sign of David, but there was nothing except one mark in the dirt where he fell. A few footprints. And then, nothing. Christopher looked up, trying to see if David had started flying again.

And that's when he saw it.

For a moment, Christopher didn't understand what he was looking at. He had come to the clearing so many times, he took for granted what he would find. There was the grassy path. The perfect circle. And the old withered tree that looked like an arthritic hand.

The tree was still there.

But it was gigantic.

Like two skyscrapers standing on top of each other.

At the base of the tree, Christopher saw there was now a door carved into the trunk. With a large doorknob and a keyhole. Hundreds of mailbox people stood on either side of it, standing guard. Keeping something in. Or something out. Was this a prison? What was this place?

Christopher stood breathless. He found the tree house that he built with Special Ed, Mike, and Matt. But it wasn't alone. There were hundreds of other tree houses hanging on the giant branches, each swinging like a body in a noose. Little birdhouses. A big angry hive.

He stared at it, remembering somewhere in his belly that he had been here before. He had been in one of those little birdhouses for six days. Being scratched. Being whispered to. Being warmed like a baby in an incubator. An egg ready to hatch.

Do you know where you are?

CHAPTER 90

106.4 degrees

beEp.

Christopher's mother sat by the sheriff's bedside, looking across the way at her son helpless on the bed. His brain less than a degree away from being cooked. The security guards and orderlies keeping her out. Or maybe keeping Christopher in. She didn't know anymore.

The sheriff and Ambrose sat with her inside this pregnant silence. Their minds raced. People had stopped dying. People were going mad all around them with the flu. That wasn't the flu. It was her. There were other children in the imaginary world. The children were building something. They had been building it for hundreds of years. Their tree houses linked. Including David's. Including Christopher's. There had to be an answer.

"What does the diary say?" the sheriff asked weakly.

Christopher's mother snapped it open, her eyes racing over the pages.

"We already read it cover to cover. Nothing," she said.

"No word about people not dying, Sheriff. No word about other children," Ambrose concurred.

"May I see it?" the sheriff asked.

Christopher's mother handed him the diary. The leather binding cracked a little when he opened the brittle, faded pages. She heard the sound of the liquid morphine falling into his IV bag.

Drip. Drip. Drip.

The sheriff turned the pages, his eyes darting across the words in a way that only a trained professional would read. After a few minutes, he looked at Ambrose.

"David was a smart kid, right?" he asked.

"Yes, sir," Ambrose said.

"Then, why is his handwriting so bad? It doesn't make sense."

He handed the diary back to Christopher's mother, closed his eyes, and drifted back to sleep. She looked at him. His body so weak and fragile. She had no idea what forces were at work right now, but she knew that the sheriff was here for a reason. So was Ambrose. So was she. Christopher's mother opened David Olson's diary again.

Drip. Drip. Drip.

She studied the diary over and over. Not reading the words. Just looking at the handwriting. That disturbing, terrified handwriting.

afTEr aLL, i AM god.

Drip. Drip. Drip.

"Mr. Olson, did David always have bad handwriting?"

Ambrose thought, then furrowed his brow and shook his head.

"No," he said. "It only got worse as he started to lose his mind."

"But he wasn't losing his mind," she said.

She flipped to the next page and studied that strange combination of capital letters, lowercase, cursive, and printing.

BefoRe we kill the hissing lady, the sOldier said we needed to do Some rEcon...

"What does it mean, Mrs. Reese?" Ambrose asked.

Christopher's mother suddenly felt a chill run across her skin. A whisper brushing against her ear like an insect. She flipped back to the previous page.

afTEr aLL, i AM god.

Flipped forward.

BefoRe we kill the hissing lady, the sOldier said we needed to do Some rEcon...

Drip. Drip. Drip.

Christopher's mother flipped back and looked at only the capital letters.

afTEr aLL, i AM god. BefoRe we kill the hissing lady,
the sOldier said we needed to do Some rEcon
lIke They do in thoSe wAr movies ambrose loves … i
followed her during the dayTime. i could see her
ReAching into People.

The letters spelled … TELL AMBROSE IT'S A TRAP

CHAPTER 91

Christopher approached the tree.

Somewhere deep in his soul, he knew he had been here before. He had been kept in one of those tree houses for six days, dangling like a Christmas ornament on a massive branch. What did he do here? What did she do to him?

Do you know where you are?

Christopher searched the tree, looking for David. His eyes darted from ground to branch. Tree house to tree house. A green one. A blue one. Different colors. Different styles. Different eras. A teepee next to a Craftsman next to a miniature barn next to . . .

The one with the red door.

It looked so familiar to him. Why? Was that where she took him? Christopher finally found David Olson, hiding in the shadows, perched on the roof of the red-door tree house. He looked exhausted. His nose bleeding as if his own imagination squeezed him out like a sponge. Christopher remembered all those times he had left the imaginary world. How each power on the imaginary side turned to pain on the real. The nice man's warning came back to him.

The power comes at a price.

He looked at David Olson drained like a battery. To David, this was the real side. To David, this was the only side. David quietly moved to the window. The deer and mailbox people stirred below. Christopher watched as David opened the curtains.

The nice man was inside the tree house.

He was beaten and battered. Lying on the floor. Unconscious. David inched closer to him. Suddenly a terrible shriek shot through the clearing. The woods came alive around them. The stars shooting up above the clouds. The sky burned bright, and when the clouds moved aside, the moon lit the clearing with piercing white light. That's when Christopher saw her.

The hissing lady.

She walked into the clearing surrounded by the little children. Squealing like piglets begging for milk. She led them to the massive tree. Christopher looked at the key twinkling in the moonlight. The key still buried in her neck.

We have to kill the hissing lady.

We have to get the key.

"Davvvviiiiid!" she screeched.

Christopher felt David Olson look back from his perch, suddenly terrified. Any thoughts of helping the nice man escape were quickly abandoned. David rushed away from the tree house with the red door and ran deep into the woods to hide.

It was up to Christopher to save him.

You can be braver than Captain America.

Christopher closed his eyes and imagined himself beginning to run. His feet hitting the treetops, throwing down leaves. He had never moved this fast in his life. Not even on the highway. He saw himself race toward the giant tree. The deer and mailbox people standing guard around it. He couldn't make a sound, or they would see him. If he jumped with all of his strength, he might be able to reach the tree. If he missed and landed in the clearing, they would tear him to pieces. He moved faster and faster. The clearing was right ahead of him. One step. Two steps. Three steps.

Jump.

In his mind's eye, Christopher sailed over the clearing like a slingshot. He stretched his body as far as he could. He saw a low-hanging branch ahead of him on the giant tree. He reached his fingers out. He could feel his knuckles click click click.

Christopher grabbed the branch with his outstretched fingers and opened his eyes.

One of his knuckles popped out. He wanted to scream, but he swallowed the pain. He reached up with his other hand and pulled his body safely on the branch. He popped his finger back into the socket.

Christopher looked down. The hissing lady was on the ground below. She saw the pine needles fall around her. She looked up, smiled to Christopher, then turned to the little children behind her. Their heads bowed.

"There he is. Climb," she whispered.

The children began to climb.

Christopher had to get to the nice man. He climbed as quickly as he could, his fingers aching. He pulled himself to the next branch. He heard screams coming from the tree house next to him. Christopher looked through the little window in the green door and saw a woman putting a noose around her own neck. The woman locked eyes with Christopher. She ran straight at him. "Help me!" she shrieked just as the noose snapped her neck back. Within seconds, she was putting the noose back on her neck to do it all over again.

Christopher looked down. He saw the children giggle and climb. They were thirty branches below him. Spreading out through the tree like baby spiders hatching. Christopher forced his aching fingers to climb. Branch after branch. Tree house after tree house. He saw one man through a peephole. The man stabbed himself over and over again. "Who's laughing now, bitch?!" he screamed at himself. In the next house, he saw another man eat a large piece of cake. The man couldn't stop. He just kept chewing and chewing until his jaw broke and there were no teeth left in his mouth. But the cake wouldn't get smaller. "Make it stop! Please!"

Do you know where you are?

His mind raced. There was something familiar about all of this. What was this place? The hissing lady's home? Her prison? Her zoo?

Christopher reached the tree house with the red door. The nice man was unconscious on the floor. Christopher tried to open the door, but it was locked. He scurried to the side window. Covered in prison bars.

"Sir! Wake up!"

The children were twenty-five branches below.

The nice man stirred. Christopher reached through the prison bars and touched the nice man's hand. The heat began to warm up in his mind, and he gave the nice man all the energy he had in a single burst. The shock was electric.

The pain was instant.

It coursed through Christopher as he kept his hands on the nice man's hand, trying to revive him.

Sir! Please wake up!

Christopher pushed his thoughts deep into the nice man's mind. Trying to jump-start him like an old car.

We have to kill the hissing lady!

He felt the nice man's heart. Slowly beating. Then, faster. And faster.

I can't kill her alone! Please!

Suddenly the nice man's eyelids stirred. He forced his eyes open and bolted upright.

"It's a trap, Christopher. Run!"

"No! I'm not leaving you!"

"You have to! You have to kill her before midnight!"

Christopher looked down. The children were fifteen branches below.

"Can you get free?" Christopher whispered breathlessly.

The nice man rushed to the door. It was bolted shut.

"No. You have to kill her without me! Get the key!" the nice man said, pushing him away. "You can't let them take you! Go!"

Christopher looked down. The children scurried up the tree like rats. He had no choice. He had to escape. He left the nice man and climbed. All the way to the top of the tree. Until there was nowhere left to go.

Except his own tree house.

It was there above the others. Right at the very top. Like the angel on a Christmas tree. How did it move? Did it move? What was this terrible place?

Do you know where you are?

The children clambered up. Pulling at his feet. He grabbed the doorknob to the tree house. He threw the door open and looked inside. But the tree house didn't look like itself anymore.

It looked like Christopher's old bathroom.

Slowly filling with steam.

A figure sat in the bathtub, lost in the cloud.

"Hi, Christopher," the voice said.

It sounded just like his father.

CHAPTER 92

DEAR AMBROSE,

I HOPE YOU CAN SEE THIS. I HAVE TO HIDE THIS MESSAGE BECAUSE I AM BEING WATCHED ALL THE TIME. SO ARE YOU. SO IS EVERYONE. BUT IT'S NOT WHAT YOU THINK IT IS. IT'S SO MUCH WORSE. I CAN'T SAY WHAT WE FIGURED OUT IS HAPPENING HERE OR ELSE I WILL BE DISCOVERED AND YOU WILL BE TORTURED FOREVER. I TOLD YOU WHAT YOU NEED TO KNOW IN THE ONLY PLACE I KNOW THAT'S NOT BEING WATCHED. ONLY YOU KNOW WHERE THAT IS. YOU USED TO HIDE MAGAZINES THERE. PLEASE GO TO IT NOW, AMBROSE. BECAUSE IF YOU ARE SEEING THIS, IT MEANS THE WORLD IS GOING TO END. AND IF THIS IS NOT AMBROSE OLSON, PLEASE TELL HIM YOU FOUND HIS LITTLE BROTHER DAVID. TELL AMBROSE IT'S A TRAP. BUT THE NEXT CHILD DOESN'T HAVE TO DIE. THE WHOLE WORLD DOESN'T HAVE TO END. SO RUN NOW. PLEASE. YOU DON'T HAVE ANY MORE TIME.

DAVID

Christopher's mother held the deciphered diary in her shaking hand. She turned to Ambrose and lowered her voice to a desperate whisper.

"Mr. Olson, where did—"

But the old soldier was way ahead of her.

"I hid magazines under David's bookshelf," he said.

"Where is the bookshelf now?"

His brow furrowed. Thinking. She looked into the hallway. The orderlies were watching them with a suspicious eye. They moved into Christopher's room to discuss something with the doctor.

106.6 degrees

beEp.

"Please, Mr. Olson. Where is the bookshelf?"

"I don't know anymore. I sold it."

"Where?!"

When the orderlies were finished speaking, the doctor turned to Christopher's mother. He whispered something to the security guards. The lighting made them all look like ghosts. Pale sick and green. Staring at her. She felt as paranoid in that moment as her husband the night before he died.

I can hear voices, Kate! Make them stop!

The security guards nodded to the doctor and left Christopher's room to approach her.

"Antiques shop," Ambrose said like a lightbulb. "David ruined the bookshelf, but the lady who owned the shop knew my mother years ago. She took it out of sympathy."

"Why? How did he ruin it?"

"He covered it with duck wallpaper."

Christopher's mother was struck silent. The only sound in the room was the sheriff's morphine trickling into the IV bag with a drip drip drip.

"Mr. Olson," she said in a whisper. "Will you stay with Christopher for me?"

"Of course," he said, confused. "Why?"

"I know where the bookshelf is," she said.

Christopher's mother looked across the hallway at her son. His broken little body. His poor feverish mind. At the rate he was going, his brain would hit

107 degrees and begin to cook by midnight. And the answer was on the other side of town.

"You can have any bookshelf you want. Why do you want that one, honey?"

"Because it smells like baseball gloves."

That bookshelf was in her son's bedroom.

CHAPTER 93

The figure sat up in the bathtub. Hidden in clouds of steam.

Christopher stood, frozen. He looked around the bathroom. It was exactly as he remembered it. The foggy mirror. The Noxzema smell on his skin. His father's shirt resting on the sink. Sweet with tobacco.

"Do you know where you are?" the voice asked.

Christopher couldn't speak. He shook his head. No.

"Would you like to know?"

Christopher nodded. Yes.

"Okay, but it's a secret. I could get in trouble. So, come here. I'll whisper it to you."

Christopher didn't move.

"Don't be afraid, honey. I would never hurt you. Come here."

The figure patted the tub. Little trickles of blood ran from his wrists down the porcelain in tiny red rivers. Christopher wanted to run away, but his feet moved without him. He began to walk. Through the steam. Through the clouds.

"That's it, honey. Walk to your daddy. It'll all make sense soon."

Christopher took a baby step. A second. A third. The figure reached out for him. The hand was warm and smooth with tobacco stains between the fingers.

"That's it, Christopher. Come and give me a hug."

Christopher felt a hand on his shoulder. The figure wrapped him up like a blanket.

"Where am I, Daddy?" Christopher asked.

Christopher was so close, he could smell the tobacco on his breath.

"You're off the street."

Christopher looked back into the tub as the clouds cleared to reveal the smiling figure.

It was the hissing lady.

CHAPTER 94

106.8 degrees

beEp.

Christopher's mother looked through the window at her son, struggling for life across the hall. She had to help him. She had to save him. She had to get the message David Olson left on his old bookshelf back at home.

But Mary Katherine had destroyed her car.

The two security guards raced across the hallway and opened the door to the sheriff's hospital room. They scratched their red faces. Bloated and sweaty. Blocking the door. A nurse Christopher's mother had never seen before entered the room behind them.

"Mrs. Reese, is everything okay?" the nurse asked.

"Yes. Fine," Christopher's mother lied.

The nurse smiled and coughed with the flu that wasn't the flu. She looked at Christopher's mother a little too long.

"What's that you're reading?" she asked.

The question hung in the air for a tense second. The nurse scratched her arm.

"This is a little embarrassing," Ambrose said. "She's reading a scrapbook of letters from my late wife. Some of them are a little racy. You can read them out loud to me next if you want. Mrs. Reese was just about to get me something from my car."

Then, Ambrose dug into his pocket and held the key up.

"You remember where I usually park it, right? The old beat-up Cadillac in the corner? Scraped and dented, just like me."

"Yes, Mr. Olson," Christopher's mother said.

"Good. I'll sit right by Christopher's bedside while you're gone."

He handed her the key in exchange for his brother's diary.

"Thank you, Mr. Olson," she said.

"No. Thank you, ma'am," the old soldier replied.

Christopher's mother took the car key and left the room, squeezing past the dubious security guards. She went straight to the ICU door, waiting to be buzzed out. She winced from the pain in her ribs. Her medication was wearing off, but there was no time to stop now.

Come on. Open up, God dammit.

She turned to see the nurse wheel Ambrose back into Christopher's room. Her son lay in the bed.

106.9 degrees

beEp.

The door buzzed like a swarm of locusts. Christopher's mother ran out of the ICU.

CHAPTER 95

Mrs. Henderson felt something shudder through her. A horrible cold breeze that ran from the inside out. Like a toothache. She knew she was behind schedule. That was unacceptable. The voice told her.

Unacceptable.

Mrs. Henderson quickened her pace. She passed the Collins Construction bulldozers and cranes, lying still like her husband back in the hospital. Big useless hunks of metal like the ones keeping that bastard alive. The doctors had no idea why he hadn't died, but she did. She knew what all of this meant. She knew what was coming next. For everyone. Especially Christopher.

Mrs. Henderson parked the sheriff's car and entered the Mission Street Woods.

She had never been there before, but she knew exactly where to go. The voice told her where. Left at the tree. Right at the boulder.

Right down the path, Mrs. Henderson.

Mrs. Henderson looked down at the dirt. She saw footprints of all sizes. All of them heading to one place. The same place Mrs. Henderson was going.

Hurry. You have to hurry.

Mrs. Henderson picked up her tired legs and started running. It was slightly uncomfortable because each step ripped the wound in her side back open. But no pain, no gain, as the kids liked to say. Her pair of hiking boots cut through the snow and mud. She ran through the coal mine tunnel, passing a dozen deer who bounced behind her like puppies. The voice rang louder and louder in her mind.

Hurry now. You don't have much time.

Mrs. Henderson reached the clearing and stopped.

It was so beautiful. It was more beautiful than her husband standing at the altar. More beautiful than her vows. Or their wedding night. Mrs. Henderson had never seen anything so beautiful in all her life. There was a magnificent old tree and the most beautiful little tree house resting on its branches.

There were hundreds of people around the tree.

As silent as church.

She knew some of the people from school, like Ms. Lasko and Brady Collins and Jenny Hertzog. Some students from the past who went from adorable little boys to bald middle-aged men in the blink of an eye. But there were other people she didn't know. Random faces she might have seen once at the grocery store or gas station or during her brief time in jail. But she may as well have known them all. That's how comfortable she felt.

That's how comfortable they all felt.

She walked through the clearing, and the crowd parted for her like the Red Sea. All faces turned to her. All faces smiled. They were all so happy to see each other. This was a glorious day. There was no more pain. No suffering. In all of her life, Mrs. Henderson had never seen the Christmas spirit this beautiful.

Mrs. Henderson walked up to Ms. Lasko. The two women smiled at each other and nodded their greetings before laughing at their own silly formality. Then, they hugged as if they were long-lost sisters. And really . . . weren't they? Weren't they all? Mrs. Henderson held Ms. Lasko in her arms. Then, they each put a maternal hand on the shoulders of the young ones—Brady Collins and Jenny Hertzog. They all felt so much better. In one moment, they all had the same thought.

Someone finally understands me.

Ms. Lasko knew she didn't need to feel sober anymore just like Brady Collins knew he didn't need to sleep in the doghouse just like Jenny Hertzog knew she didn't need to strip for her stepbrother. And if anyone said otherwise, well, the community could put their foot down, couldn't they? If some awful people like Christopher's mother or his friends or the sheriff or Ambrose Olson got in the way, they could be stabbed again and again. The group would rid itself of anyone who didn't understand. And when the war came, they would win.

Because good guys always win wars.

They all knelt down and put their hands on the tree together. The tree was warm like a baby's bottom. The serenity they felt was unlike anything they'd ever known. The cold side of the pillow mixed with a hot bath. In one moment, all of their fevers broke. All of their arms stopped itching. They were finally at peace. The calm before the storm.

The peace before the war.

"It's time," Mrs. Henderson said.

Mrs. Henderson picked up her weekend bag. She felt the soft leather in her hands. The cold zipper gave way like vertebrae snapping. She opened the bag and pulled out the sharp butcher knife.

"Can I help?" Brady Collins asked.

"Of course, Brady. Thank you. You're very polite. Your grandma would be very proud," she said. "Why don't you stand guard?"

Brady Collins smiled and pulled out his gun. He began walking back and forth to protect them from Special Ed, who he knew was hiding somewhere in the woods.

"Me, too?" Jenny Hertzog asked eagerly.

"Of course, Jenny. That's why you're here, sweetie."

Jenny smiled proudly and reached into the bag. She pulled out a dozen sewing needles and as much black yarn as her little arms could hold. Then, Mrs. Henderson turned to the gathered congregation and surveyed the eager faces.

"Can my stepbrother go first?" Jenny Hertzog asked quietly.

"Are you sure you don't want to save him for last?" Mrs. Henderson asked.

"No, ma'am," Jenny said.

"Very well. Scott . . . Front and center."

Jenny's stepbrother stepped up and smiled.

"Yes, ma'am?" he said eagerly. "What can I do?"

"You can fucking feel everything you've ever done to Jenny for eternity and no one will ever stop it. How does that sound?"

"Super," he said.

Scott nodded in his trance as his little stepsister looped a strand of black yarn through the needle and handed it to Mrs. Henderson. The old woman kindly patted her on the head and moved to Scott. She clamped his lips together with her left hand, and she began stitching his mouth shut with a practiced right hand that she'd learned in home economics.

As she sewed Scott's lips together, she couldn't even hear his bloodcurdling screams through the white noise of her own mind. Mrs. Henderson smiled, waltzing with a memory. It was a simpler time back then. Back when girls took home ec and boys took shop. Back when men were loyal to their wives and never thought about divorce. Back when the good old days were the good new days. It was better then. Things would be that way again. The little voice promised her they would. This time, her husband would respect her. This time, her husband would appreciate her.

All she had to do was play her part.

And get them all ready for theirs.

As she stitched, she looked up at the tree house. Such a beautiful little tree house. Her husband was on the other side of that door. She could almost hear him whispering.

"Honey, let's go away for a long weekend."

"What?" she asked, surprised.

"I want to spend some time with my wife. I just wish I'd packed a bag."

"I have one. I have a bag! I hid it in the library. I brought it with me! It's right here!"

"You're the greatest wife a guy could ever have."

This time, they could throw that bag in the trunk of his car and drive away. It didn't matter where. Because she was young again. Her hair was red. Her body was beautiful. And she knew she would live this day for eternity. Maybe she wouldn't even need to stab him.

"Where should we go, darling?" she finally asked.

"The tree house, of course. It's so beautiful in here."

Mrs. Henderson was so lost in the dreams of her new future that she didn't realize she had already finished turning Scott into a mailbox person.

"Scott, it's Christmas Eve. The tree is so empty. We need to decorate it with ornaments," she said.

Jenny handed Scott a length of rope, which Ms. Lasko cut to size with the butcher knife. Scott took the rope and climbed up the tree on the little 2x4s like baby teeth. He reached the first thick branch and climbed out to the edge of it. Then, he tied the rope to the branch and wrapped the other end around his neck. When he jumped off, his neck snapped like a wishbone, but he didn't die. Just like Mrs. Henderson knew he wouldn't. No one would ever die again.

"When can I drown him in floods?" Jenny asked.

"As soon as we've won the war, Jenny," Mrs. Henderson said and smiled. "Next!"

Mrs. Henderson turned to the Collins Construction security guard who thought about all the overtime he would be getting for guarding the property so late on Christmas Eve. As the old woman closed his eyelids with thick black yarn, she didn't hear his screams over the sound of her own anxious thoughts. If a lifetime in public education taught Mrs. Henderson anything, it was to make do with what she had. She looked at the hundreds of townsfolk waiting to be turned into mailbox people. She would have loved to stitch all of them by hand like she did Scott, but alas, they were behind schedule. Midnight was coming. They had to be ready for Christopher's sacrifice. So, she would have to let go of the controls and let people stitch their own mouths and eyes shut while Ms. Lasko, Jenny, and Brady passed around the needles, zippers, yarn, and thread.

Or else, I'm never going to get all this sewing done.

"Next!"

CHAPTER 96

The hissing lady stood up from the bathtub. She was naked. Covered in bullet holes and knife wounds and burns. Christopher screamed. He ran to the door. The hissing lady moved to the wet tiles on the floor. Christopher reached for the doorknob. Locked.

It was all a trap.

The hissing lady grabbed Christopher from behind. She brought him up, thrashing like a fish. She kicked open the door and threw him onto the branch. He tried to crawl away, but his hands stuck to the tree like flypaper.

Christopher looked back as the hissing lady emerged from the tree house. She put on her finest Sunday dress, streaked with blood, torn up like rags. Then, she closed the tree house door behind her. She studied Christopher with her dead doll eyes.

"Chrissstopppheerrrrr. Itttt'ssss tiiiiiimmme," she said.

The hissing lady walked slowly down the branch toward him. Christopher screamed,

"NO! PLEASE!"

The hissing lady smiled and grabbed Christopher by the ears. She wrapped him up in both arms and slithered down the tree trunk like a snake.

H
  S
    S
  S
    S
      S
    S
  S

Christopher looked down at the clearing. Her entire army was there. Staring up at him in silence. The hissing lady kept slithering. Down. They passed dozens of tree houses. The doors were closed. The curtains drawn. Christopher couldn't see inside, but he could hear voices. Children were giggling. A doorknob began to turn.

"Not yet. Let's surprise him," the little voice whispered.

The doorknob stopped. The hissing lady kept crawling down. They passed another tree house. One with a pink door. He heard breathing behind it.

"He'll make such a fine pet," a little girl whispered.

Her fingernails scratched the door like a school blackboard. He passed another tree house. Blue-and-white curtains like Dorothy's dress.

"Does he know where he is?" a man's voice whispered.

"He will soon," a woman's voice whispered back.

The hissing lady landed at the base of the tree. Right in front of the large door cut into the giant tree trunk. She stared at her army in triumph. She raised Christopher's arms. The crowd roared like Times Square on New Year's Eve. Christopher heard drums beat in the distance. Four mailbox people grabbed Christopher by the arms and legs. They pinned him against the tree. It wasn't bark. It was flesh. Sweaty and warm. Christopher started to scream.

"Please! Don't kill me! Please!"

"I'm not going to kill you," the hissing lady said calmly.

"What are you going to do?" Christopher asked, terrified.

"I can't tell you that." She smiled.

The hissing lady dug into her own flesh with long, dirty fingernails. She ripped the key from her neck. She shoved her hand into the flesh of the tree. Her hand looked like it was squishing into a garbage disposal. Blood. And meat. She found the keyhole inside the tree's rotten flesh. She turned the key and opened the lock with a . . .

Click.

A chorus of screams rose up from the people in the tree houses above. The voices ripped through Christopher's mind. His eyes searched the clearing. He looked for an escape. The mailbox people guarded all of the paths out.

"It's time! It's time!" the voices cried.

The hissing lady put the key back into her neck like a hand in wet cement.

In an instant the flesh healed. The key was protected. The hissing lady opened the door. Light poured from inside the tree trunk. Christopher looked into the light. It was blinding. A cold tremor ran through his body.

"What is this place?! Where am I?!" Christopher screamed.

"I thought you'd remember," the hissing lady said.

Christopher could feel the energy coming from the tree. The static electricity from a million balloons. He remembered following the footprints. The tree felt like flesh. He remembered. He was put on this tree for six days. Cooked here. Incubated here. Made smart here. Left on top of this tree to soak up everything.

But he had never gone inside it.

"Christopher," she said. "This is for your own good."

The hissing lady moved him toward the light. It was blinding. Steam came out of the tree like fluffy white clouds. Christopher screamed, digging in his heels. Scratching. Clawing. She picked up his legs. Kicking. He could smell things inside the light. A kitchen. Rusty knives. The water from his father's bathtub. The smell of the hospital.

"NO! NO!" he screamed.

Christopher dug his hands into the flesh of the tree. Hot like feverish skin. The hissing lady ripped his hands free. He squirmed out of her grasp. He planted his feet on both sides of the door. The mailbox people swarmed him. Christopher held on for dear life. He pushed the mailbox people back. He was too powerful for them. The hissing lady grabbed Christopher in her scarred hands. They were coarse like sandpaper. She held him tight to her body and brought his face to hers until their noses were touching. She looked him dead in the eye. Furious and insane.

"IT'S TIME!!!!!!!"

Christopher looked down at the clearing. He saw dozens of footprints materialize. The people themselves invisible to him. But they were there. He could feel them. The townspeople on the real side. Their eyes being stitched up. Being turned into mailbox people. The world screaming in pain. It was blinding. The worlds were blurring. The imaginary and the real. The glass was about to shatter.

Christopher looked up into the sky. He saw the stars shooting. Constellations falling apart like a puzzle dropped on the floor, shattering into a million pieces.

It was six minutes to midnight. Six minutes to Christmas. Christopher closed his eyes. He let his mind go quiet. And he whispered,

"Please, God. Help me."

Suddenly Christopher saw a cloud coming on the horizon. The face in the cloud. As big as the sky. In an instant Christopher felt a great calm wash over his body. It was as if someone hit the MUTE button around him, and there were no more screams. There was only the sound of his own heartbeat. The beeps of hospital machines. A voice on the wind.

"Christopherrrrr," the wind whispered.

The hissing lady shoved him. Christopher felt his left foot cross into the light.

"Don't go into the light, Christopher. Fight her," the whisper said.

I can't. She's too strong.

Christopher's arms felt so heavy. His right foot crossed into the light. He just wanted to sleep. So sleepy.

"You have to kill her by midnight!" the wind screamed.

I can't kill her by myself.

"Yes, you can. A nightmare is nothing but a dream gone sick. Say it, Christopher!"

"A nightmare is nothing but a dream gone sick," Christopher said out loud.

Christopher saw the hissing lady's eyes shift.

"Who are you talking to?!" she asked.

"Say it again!" the wind whispered.

"A nightmare is nothing but a dream gone sick," Christopher shouted.

Christopher saw the hissing lady scream, "Who are you talking to?!" over and over, but he could not hear her. All of her screams were gone. There was only silence. There was only peace. The air was cool and fresh. He could only hear the whisper of the wind.

"And I can do anything in a dream!" the wind said.

"And I can do anything in a dream," Christopher repeated.

"Because in here . . ." the wind said.

Christopher closed his eyes. In his mind's eye, he imagined himself groping in the darkness behind his eyelids until he finally found the switch. He flipped on the light and there, laid before him, was more than knowledge. It was power. Raw and furious. Christopher opened his eyes and looked right at the hissing lady. Christopher saw her eyes move. She was terrified.

". . . I am God," Christopher said.

Christopher pushed back with all of his might, and the hissing lady went flying backward in the air. She landed on the edge of the clearing a hundred yards away. The deer and the mailbox people watched, stunned. Christopher looked at his hands as if they belonged to someone else. He couldn't believe his own strength.

The hissing lady sat up. Insane with rage. Or was that surprise? The deer and the mailbox people turned to Christopher. A thousand eyes stared. Furious at him for harming their queen. But Christopher did not blink. He did not run. He did not hide. He just slowly reached into his pocket and pulled out the leather sheath. He unfolded it to reveal the dull, silver blade.

"You're off the street," Christopher said calmly.

He looked at the key buried in her neck. Then Christopher raised the silver blade above his head and charged right at her.

CHAPTER 97

Christopher's mother raced down the highway. It had taken her fifteen minutes to run to Shady Pines, where Ambrose kept his old beaten-up Cadillac. Fifteen minutes passing burning stores and hiding behind cars left abandoned and smashed as frightening men looted in the shadows. There were no cabs. No police. She was all alone with nothing but violence all around her. Her ribs fractured. The pain medication now a memory. Christopher's mother looked at the clock on the dash.

Ten minutes to midnight.

She turned off Route 19 and slowed to a crawl. She expected to see her neighborhood filled with Christmas decorations and lights and families enjoying a final drink on Christmas Eve. Children needing to be corralled back to bed with warnings that Santa might pass by their house if they didn't go to sleep.

But that's not what she saw.

The place was eerily silent. All of the streetlights turned off. She looked on either side of the road. Deer stood like telephone poles. Their black eyes gleaming in the moonlight. Watching her. Waiting.

She turned onto Hays Road.

She looked inside all of the houses. The lights twinkled on the Christmas trees, making the ornaments glow. But there were no people in the living rooms. No people watching the televisions playing Christmas specials. No people anywhere.

Just the deer.

She turned onto her block. Christopher's mother passed the old Olson house on the corner. There was no sign of Jill and Clark. She drove by the Hertzog house. She did not see Jenny Hertzog or her stepbrother. There were no cars in the driveways. She looked down the street at the Mission Street Woods, and she saw nothing.

But she felt it.

On the hairs of her neck. Impossible to ignore. There was something horrible in those woods. Something spreading. Something running.

She moved down the street.

Toward her driveway.

Just then, the old woman who lived across the street ran out of the log cabin. She wore a white nightgown. Cotton and lace. She had no shoes. She darted in front of the car, the headlights catching her face. Her eyes and mouth were stitched together with black yarn. Christopher's mother screamed and slammed on the brakes. The old woman moaned through the stitches...

"Eeee waaas uch a eautiful oy!"

...and bolted into the Mission Street Woods like a deer on its hind legs. Christopher's mother looked into the woods to see if anything else was coming. But there was nothing. Just that feeling. Death is coming. Death is here. We'll die on Christmas Day. Christopher's mother looked at the clock.

It was six minutes to midnight.

Six minutes to Christmas.

CHAPTER 98

Mrs. Henderson stitched as fast as her fingers could fly. She looked at the long line of mailbox people waiting patiently for her to finish. She looked up at the night sky through the tree branches. The branches sagged from the weight of all the lucky ornaments. They kicked their legs and twisted their necks, leaving rope burns. But no one died. No one would ever die again.

"Next," Mrs. Henderson said.

It was six minutes to midnight, and there were only a few souls left. They were going to make it. They were going to be ready in time! Mrs. Henderson looked over at Ms. Lasko. The young teacher stitched the eyes of Jill and Clark, a lovely young couple who wanted to fill the tree house with children like a womb. They were going to have what they wanted tonight. Everyone was going to have what they wanted tonight.

11:54

Ms. Lasko could taste it. Every time she licked her lips, it only got stronger. The taste was alcohol. But it wasn't just any alcohol. It was the whiskey her mother put on a metal spoon when Ms. Lasko was a little baby, teething. The whiskey made her gums stop hurting. Ms. Lasko ran her tongue over her lips. The whiskey turned into the most delicious wine when her mother took her to Communion. Ms. Lasko took the sip of the red wine, but by the time she swallowed, it had turned into champagne. Her mother toasted her on her graduation. "You're the first to go to college, honey," she said. Her mother was in the tree house waiting for her. There was a big party happening inside the tree house to celebrate her. She would get to feel drunk again. She would get to feel hopelessly numb and happy.

"Next," Ms. Lasko said, finishing the last stitch on Jill's eyes.

11:55

Jenny Hertzog led Jill and Clark to the end of the long line of people waiting at the bottom of the ladder for Mrs. Henderson to finish. Jenny looked up at her stepbrother Scott, his legs twitching on the bottom branch. Jenny looked up at the beautiful tree house above him. She took a deep breath through her nose, but it didn't smell like the woods anymore. It smelled like her mother. Perfume and lotion and hair spray and her soft warm skin. She could hear her mother whisper to her, "Come in, Jenny. We will have a slumber party together. We'll make popcorn and watch movies in your room. Scott will never bother you again. You will be safe forever and ever and ever."

"Next," Mrs. Henderson said.

11:56

There were only two people left in line. Debbie Dunham and Doug. Doug had been so sad until he came to the woods. So sad until he saw Debbie Dunham. She was smiling at him. It was the most delicious slutty awful smile he'd ever seen. "What's wrong, Doug?" she asked. "Mary Katherine cheated on me," he said. Debbie Dunham nodded sympathetically. "I've been cheated on lots of times," she whispered. "Do you want to cheat back?"

Doug was quiet. He thought about Mary Katherine, and the sadness grew in his stomach like the baby some other guy put inside her. "Do you want to see me naked, Doug?" Debbie asked. He nodded, hoping she would take his mind away. The air was freezing, but she slowly stripped away her uniform from the Giant Eagle. He looked at her naked body, fresh like ripe fruit. She went in for a long, licky kiss. Her tongue like a snake. "Doug, aren't you tired of doing the right thing for the wrong girl?" she asked. Her words were as sweet as her breath. And when she reached down and brushed her hand against him, whatever shame he felt stepped aside to reveal what was playing hide-and-seek behind it. Rage.

All those years of being a good boyfriend. All those years of respecting Mary Katherine's morals. Obeying her wishes. Pretending to bump into her breast over her sweater instead of doing what he really wanted. And then finding out that it was all a lie. The good girl on her knees in a car. The good girl being knocked up by some stranger. "We have to go into the tree house and then you can have every inch of me," Debbie said. Then, she let go of Doug's hand while Mrs. Henderson stitched up her mouth.

Finally, Debbie thought. Finally, she had a nice boy to treat her right. Finally, Doug thought. Finally, he had a bad girl to treat him wrong. At midnight, they would belong to each other, and he could forget about Mary Katherine. Forever.

"You're next, Doug," Mrs. Henderson said, finishing Debbie's eyes.

11:57

Brady Collins led Debbie Dunham to the end of the line. He had never seen a naked girl before, but all he could think about was that she must be freezing. He had been cold in his doghouse so many times. Brady Collins took off his jacket and handed it to her. It was too small, but she wrapped it around her freezing legs. The beautiful naked girl patted the top of his head and tried to smile, but the stitches stopped her. Brady felt cold without his jacket, but he wasn't worried. His mother was up in the tree house. He could hear her voice calling out to him. "Brady, come in from the doghouse. Mommy's in the warm kitchen. Come in from the cold. Your mother loves you."

11:58

Mrs. Henderson finished the final stitch on Doug's eyes. Then, she put down her needle and thread. She looked around the tree and realized that their work was done.

There was no one left but each other.

The four of them locked eyes and smiled proudly. They had finished before midnight. Mrs. Henderson handed Ms. Lasko her own needle and thread. The young teacher barely screamed as she sewed her own mouth shut. But Mrs. Henderson wouldn't have heard it anyway. She had to help Brady Collins and Jenny Hertzog with their stitches.

Little hands make for sloppy work.

Soon, the children were done, and Mrs. Henderson had no one left but herself. The needle sliced through her skin like the knife through her husband's throat. Her screams sounded like their wedding night. Pain mixed with pleasure. Funny that her mother never told her how much it would hurt and how much she would love it.

"I'm waiting for you, honey," her husband called from inside the tree house. "Let's go on that trip now."

With her eyes and mouth stitched, Mrs. Henderson grabbed hold of the first 2x4 of the ladder. The first little baby tooth.

And she started to climb the ladder to the tree house.

With her congregation right behind her.

It was one minute to midnight.

One minute to Christmas.

CHAPTER 99

beEp.

Ambrose sat in the wheelchair. He listened to the sound of the machines keeping Christopher alive.

beEp.

He had promised Kate Reese to never leave her son's side, and he was a man hell-bent on keeping promises.

Help him, David.

The thought was quiet and solemn. He didn't notice that the door behind him had opened.

beEp.

But he felt the temperature change.

"Hello?" he said.

Silence. Breathing.

"Nurse, is that you?"

beEp.

"Doctor?" he asked. "The boy's hand is hot as a skillet. What is his temperature?"

There was a long moment of silence. Then . . .

"One hundred seven," the voice whispered. "But I'm not the doctor."

Ambrose furrowed his brow. He tried to remain calm.

"His brain is beginning to cook," Ambrose said. "Call someone."

"We have, Mr. Olson," the voice replied.

Ambrose listened to the voice. He couldn't tell who it was. A man. A woman.

"When is the doctor coming?" he asked.

"Soon," the voice replied.

Ambrose could hear the person circling him. Little pit-pats on the balls of their feet. Then, a slight echo. There was more than one person in the room.

"How soon?" Ambrose asked.

"I'm not sure. The hospital is understaffed. Everyone has the flu," the voice said.

The voice was closer. More footsteps. Circling.

beEp.

"That's okay," Ambrose said calmly, gripping the side of Christopher's bed. "I understand."

Suddenly Ambrose heard mocking laughter from a half dozen people.

"He understands," "That's okay," "He understands," the voices cackled.

"I guess you're not that understaffed," Ambrose said.

The laughter stopped, revealing a familiar sound underneath it. Hissssssss.

It was gas.

"Mr. Olson," the voice said.

Ambrose's blood went cold. He finally recognized the owner of that voice.

"Yes, Mrs. Keizer?" he asked.

"Death is finally here, Ambrose. You can't say I didn't warn you," she said.

Suddenly he felt a dozen hands on him. He held up his arms to defend himself, but the mob grabbed him. He felt the cold plastic of the gas mask cover his mouth. The gas hissed out of the tank like a serpent. Hissss.

"Get the fuck off me!" Ambrose shrieked.

The old soldier pushed back, flailing blindly. He grabbed one head of hair. He tore at another person's eyes. The army of hands pinned him back. His wheelchair tipped, and Ambrose crashed to the ground. The mob was on him in seconds. He fought back with all of his strength, but there were too many. He felt his arms and legs give. He was an old man. Blind. Helpless. It took everything to push the gas mask off his face. But it was back within seconds. And there was nothing to do but wait for his lungs to cry mercy.

"Now breathe deeply and count back from ten," the voice said.

It was one minute to midnight.

As he took a huge drink of air.

And heard Christopher flatline.

beeeeEEEEEEE

CHAPTER 100

Christopher charged at the hissing lady.

Her army circled him like a spiderweb. The deer snapping. The mailbox people blocking his path. Their bodies created a hurricane, and Christopher was the eye.

"GET HIM!" the hissing lady shrieked.

Christopher looked at the key buried in her neck. He held the silver blade and jumped through the air. He landed on one of the deer, planting his feet on its back. He jumped onto the mailbox people's shoulders. They reached for him. He moved quickly. Running farther and faster. He could feel his body change with each step. The light from the tree had stayed with him somehow. The headaches were different. The fever was knowledge. He couldn't believe how fast he was moving.

"NOW! WE HAVE TO GET HIM NOW!" the hissing lady screamed.

The deer closed in from every direction, but they were too slow. Christopher slid through their legs. Jumped over their antlers. He couldn't believe how quickly the trees whipped by. He felt outside of his own body.

But not the pain inside it.

With each step, he could feel it growing. Like hands tightening around his throat. Blood began to trickle out of his nose. He thought of David, drained like a battery. How long did he have until the power was gone and the pain remained? Midnight was coming. He was either going to kill or die.

He saw the hissing lady up ahead, her gaze tracing the blade in his hand. For a flash, he thought he saw fear in her eyes. She covered the key with her burnt hand. Then, she turned and retreated into the woods. Christopher raced behind her. He looked down and saw her tracks on the muddy, bloody trail.

Christopher followed her footprints into the stream near the billy goat bridge. The water soaked through his boots and turned his feet freezing. For a moment, he thought he was cold in the hospital on the real side. Cold in a hospital gown.

Do you know where you are?

Christopher raced through the freezing water. The cold soon turned to numb, and the numb soon turned to heat. His legs were as hot as his forehead. He jumped out of the stream and back onto her trail. The streetlight far in the distance. Christopher saw a fork up ahead. He looked down to know which direction to turn.

Suddenly the footprints were gone.

Christopher stopped. Panicked. It was a trick. A trap. Another way to kill him by killing time. He looked around him on all sides. All he saw were trees. The hissing lady could be anywhere. He was a sitting duck. Christopher listened for any sign of her. He heard nothing. Just the wind and the sound of his own breath.

Crack.

Christopher looked above him in the trees. He saw hundreds of mailbox people, waiting quietly in the shadows. Hanging on the high branches like icicles. Christopher turned to run, but all at once the mailbox people jumped into the path.

Christopher was surrounded.

The mailbox people swarmed over the woods. The deer rushed at him. Christopher grabbed a branch to climb his way out. He moved up one branch. Two branches.

But the hissing lady was in the tree like a serpent.

She grabbed his hand. Slithering.

Christopher screamed and fell down onto the trail. But the deer were on top of him. Their teeth punctured his skin. They smelled like the hospital. Like antiseptic. Christopher was too tired to scream. He knew this was the moment of his death. He closed his eyes for the inevitable when suddenly, he heard deer being picked up and thrown. Christopher looked up.

It was the nice man.

"GET OFF HIM!" the nice man screamed.

The deer snapped at the nice man. Taking chunks of flesh from his shoulders. Blood poured down his shirt. Down his arm. He grabbed Christopher's hand.

"COME WITH ME!" he yelled.

"NO!!!!!!!" the hissing lady shrieked. "STOP HELPING HIM!!!!!"

The hissing lady swooped down from the trees just as the nice man and Christopher took off running. The deer and the mailbox people giving chase.

"How did you get away?" Christopher asked breathlessly.

"David."

"Where is he?"

"Bringing help. There are others who want to be free. Come on!"

They ran together. Down the path. The streetlight was right in front of them. Blue like the moon. They jumped out of the woods onto the field. They raced toward the street. Christopher looked ahead and saw his neighborhood laid out like a circus.

The imaginary world had gone completely mad.

He saw clouds move over the town like a brushfire. Hundreds of people screamed. The man in the Girl Scout uniform pulled himself into the bushes. Another man pulled himself into a van. The couple couldn't stop kissing each other. People he had never seen before. All of them were screaming the same thing.

"Get us out of here, Christopher. Please!"

Christopher and the nice man raced toward the street. The mailbox people fanned out through the smoldering yards, surrounding it. The hissing lady crashed through the trees with the deer and ran at them at blinding speed.

"GIVE HIM BACK TO ME!" she hissed.

The hissing lady jumped on the nice man just as he threw Christopher over the mailbox people and into the street to safety. Christopher hit the cul-de-sac with a hard thud, scraping his body on the pavement. He immediately jumped up. He saw the nice man being torn apart by the hissing lady. Her burnt hands ripping at his flesh like two claws.

"Stop helping him!" the hissing lady screamed.

The nice man pushed her back and crawled to the street. The hissing lady slipped onto the pavement. Her foot started to smoke and burn. Leaving liquid skin on the concrete, which was carried away by the blood. She immediately jumped back onto the driveway, screaming and cursing.

The hissing lady motioned for the deer. They laid their bodies across the pavement like chips on a roulette table. The hissing lady jumped on them and moved to the nice man crawling on the street. She pulled up his head and sank her teeth into his neck. His throat crunched like a wishbone. She was eating the nice man alive. It was now or never. Christopher felt it. It was ten seconds until midnight. Ten seconds until Christmas.

10

The deer jumped on the nice man. Snapping and biting. Christopher knew he had to kill the hissing lady now. He looked at her body. Shot. Stabbed. Burned a hundred times with fire.

Her whole body was practically scar tissue. But nothing had been able to kill her. Yet.

9

Christopher gripped the dull, silver blade. He closed his eyes to summon his power, but all he heard were screams. The voices ripped through his mind. The people hurting themselves. Over and over and over.

8

He could feel the two worlds bleeding into each other. The glass cracking between the imaginary and the real. His mother was running into his bedroom.

7

Christopher suddenly felt the wind rustle down the street. "Christopher, look at me." Christopher locked eyes with the nice man. The nice man was being torn apart, but he had a calm smile on his face. There were no words. But Christopher could feel the whisper scratch and the nice man's thoughts on his skin.

The street.

6

"Stop helping him!" the hissing lady screamed as she scratched his eyes.
She will burn on the street.

5

The clouds parted ways and Christopher saw the key gleaming under the flesh of her neck. It sparkled like a diamond in the blue moonlight.

4

The nice man kicked the hissing lady back. More mailbox people rolled into the street to catch her fall. Her hand slipped into the street. It sizzled on the pavement.

3

Christopher looked at the hissing lady's burnt hand. Then, he closed his eyes and quieted his mind. One second an eternity. God had built a river of salvation into this nightmare. And he was going to baptize her in it.

2

In his mind's eye, he ran at the hissing lady, perched on top of the nice man. Christopher saw the deer charge at him. But it didn't matter anymore. To Christopher, they might as well have been crawling. That's how slow it all felt now.

You can be smarter than Tony Stark.

Christopher jumped over the deer.

You can be stronger than the Hulk.

Christopher jumped over the mailbox people on the ground.

You can be more powerful than Thor's hammer.

1

Christopher slammed the full force of his body into the hissing lady. He felt her bones shatter from the impact. She flew back through the air and landed in the street in a heap.

"NOOOOO!" she screamed.

Christopher watched as the hissing lady began to burn.

CHAPTER 101

The house was quiet and still.

Christopher's mother would have run through the house, but there was something wrong. She could feel it all around her.

She started to walk up the stairs. Slowly. Don't make a sound.

Where are you going, Kate?

Christopher's mother cast the voice aside. She could feel her son. Fighting for his life. The air was cold, as if the world had left a window open. It was in the house. It was everywhere. She had to help her son. He needed her.

She reached Christopher's bedroom.

What are you doing, Kate?

She looked at the old bookshelf resting in the corner. Wrapped in wallpaper the way that a child would wrap a Christmas gift. All tape and no corners.

She walked to the bookshelf.

You left your son in the hospital. What kind of mother are you, Kate?

Christopher's mother looked at the photograph of her late husband on the top of the bookshelf. His picture stared back at her. Frozen in time. She could barely breathe. The danger was closing around her son. She could feel it like the day when he swallowed a marble. She was in the next room, but she knew it. She ran to him. He would have choked to death. She saved her son's life.

Christopher is dying, Kate. You have to go back to the hospital!

Christopher's mother picked up the photograph of her late husband, then dumped the rest of the bookshelf on the floor. Books scattered everywhere. Her eyes found the clock on the wall. It was ten seconds to midnight.

Christopher's mother tore at the duck wallpaper with her fingernails. She ripped away the first slab underneath the bookshelf. There she found three words written in David's handwriting. There was no mixture of cursive and print. This was David's real handwriting. Every letter was perfectly clear.

DO NOT KILL

What is that, Kate?

THE HISSING LADY

Stop reading, Kate.

SHE IS THE ONLY THING KEEPING

You should really stop now, Kate.

THE DEVIL IN HELL

CHAPTER 102

*D*o you know where you are?

Christopher watched the hissing lady burn, crying and screaming in what he thought was her rage and madness.

But something felt terribly wrong.

"Who is she?" Christopher asked.

It was such a simple question that the nice man was taken off guard for a moment. He looked over at Christopher as the hissing lady screamed.

"Who is she?" Christopher repeated.

"She's evil," the nice man said. "We have to kill evil people."

The sky thundered. The clouds bumped into each other like koi in a crowded pond. The mailbox people tore at the stitches in their mouths, trying to say something to him, but all he could hear was their moaning.

"Now, go get the key, son," the nice man said gently.

Do you know where you are?

Christopher gripped the dull, silver blade. He looked at the hissing lady fighting to drag her shattered bones to the lawn. He saw the rope burns around her neck. The chemical burns on her skin.

"But she was a baby once. Where did she come from?" Christopher asked.

"She was born here."

"I don't think she was. Look at her."

Christopher pointed to the hissing lady again. Her eyes seemed filled with agony. Not rage. Not madness. She crawled desperately over the street. Trying to get to the lawn. And for some reason Christopher couldn't understand, no one would help her. No mailbox people. No deer. They seemed frozen in the light of the fire.

"Christopher, I know you feel sorry for her. But don't be fooled. She tortured me for centuries, just like she tortured David. Just like she would have hurt you and your mother. But you stopped her. Only you."

Christopher looked at the nice man, smiling through his broken teeth. His skin and clothes torn apart from centuries of torment. There was something so kind about him. Something that reminded Christopher of his dad. Maybe it was the tobacco smell on his shirt. Christopher didn't remember the nice man ever smoking, but it was there nonetheless.

"We can't let her get off the street until she's burnt completely. Come on, son. You need to get that key," the nice man said, putting his hand on Christopher's head.

The nice man's hand felt so comfortable to Christopher. Like the cold side of the pillow. All of the screams around them fell away, and the air became fresh and clean. It didn't smell like the nightmares anymore. It smelled like the forest in winter. It smelled like . . . like . . .

Like Heaven.

The nice man smiled and led Christopher across the street. The hissing lady stretched her fingers to the lawn. Christopher knelt down, blocking her path. She groped at him wildly, her scarred fingers coarse against his skin.

"STOP HELPING HIM!" the hissing lady screamed at the nice man.

"Don't let her leave the street, Christopher," the nice man said calmly.

"She's still too strong. I need your help."

"No, son. It has to be you. Only you. You're God here."

Christopher held the silver blade. The hissing lady burned, her eyes wild with fear. She tried to crawl around him, but her body crumpled. Christopher knew she would never make it to the lawn.

The hissing lady was going to die.

"You saved us, Christopher," the nice man said. "Your father would have been very proud of you. Now, get the key, son."

Christopher felt the nice man's hands on his shoulders. Rubbing them. Christopher smiled. He moved the silver blade to her throat. He was just about to carve the key out of her scarred, burnt skin when something caught the corner of his eye.

A shadow figure.

Walking out of the woods.

It shuffled its feet through the field, dazed and delirious. Its hands and legs shaking. Christopher looked as the shadow figure stepped into the streetlight.

It was David Olson.

He was ashen. Christopher could see the scratches on his neck. The gash across his cheek. The blood pouring out of his nose. The bruises on his arms.

"David!" Christopher screamed in triumph. "It's over! You're safe! You're free! Look!"

Christopher pointed to the hissing lady burning on the street. David opened his mouth and unrolled his serpent tongue. What followed was a cry of such anguish that it made Christopher shudder. David ran to the hissing lady. He took one of her hands and desperately tried to drag her off the street with his battered body.

"David? What are you doing?" Christopher asked.

David pulled with all of his strength, but he was too weak. Christopher looked into the hissing lady's eyes, illuminated by the streetlight. For the first time, he realized her eyes were filled with tears.

"Stop helping him," she pleaded.

Christopher suddenly realized that the hissing lady wasn't talking to the nice man.

She was talking to <u>him</u>.

Christopher felt the nice man's hands on his shoulders. Rubbing. His ears went flush. His heart began to pound. He turned around. The nice man was in a grey suit. He looked flawless. Not a mark on his skin. Not a scar on his body. He smiled a kind smile, his teeth perfectly intact. He wore a bow tie. And he had green eyes—sometimes.

"hI. Christopher."

His voice was so pleasant. Like a warm mug of coffee.

"Your mom is going to be safe, and everything iS going to be okay now, son."

The hair stood up on the back of Christopher's neck.

"Who are you?" Christopher asked.

"What do you mean? I'm your friEnd."

"But you don't look right."

"Don't worry about my clothes. You broke her curse. That'S all. As she gets smaller, I get bigger. It's always been like that."

The nice man walked closer, his perfectly polished shoes leaving footprints in the blood on the street. Each footprint was a different size. A little girl. A grown man.

Do you know where you are?

Christopher started to back away from the nice man. He felt the screaming of the world break his eardrums. The man in the Girl Scout uniform being pulled into the bushes. The couple kissing so hard their faces began to bleed. The mailbox people held together with string like men on a chain gang. And that screaming. It never ended.

This wasn't the imaginary world at all.

"Where are we?" Christopher asked, terrified.

"It's just a dream, chrIstopher," the nice man said calmly.

"No, it isn't."

"It's a nightmare. A nightmare is nothing but a dream gone siCk."

"This is no nightmare."

Christopher felt the fever on his skin. The heat of the flu inside everyone. It wasn't a fever. It was a fire.

"This is Hell. I'm in Hell."

Christopher remembered the six days he spent in the woods. The six days he lay on that tree, being whispered to by the nice man. "Chrissstopher. Chrissstopher." Soaking in as much knowledge as his little brain could take. Being made powerful. Being turned into God. Or a soldier. Or a murderer. For one purpose. To kill the hissing lady. To get the key. To free the nice man. He thought he was asleep. He thought he was dreaming.

I was in Hell for six days.

"Of courSe you weren't," the nice man said, climbing out of Christopher's mind. "This is just a nightmare. A nightmare is just a few hours in Hell. So, we need to get you out of here. Now go get that key."

The nice man smiled, so calm and reassuring. But his eyes weren't smiling. Christopher backed up toward the hissing lady and David Olson. The nice man spoke in a measured voice.

"Where are you going?" the nice man asked.

He walked toward Christopher with calm little steps.

"We need the key, son. Do you want the mirror between the worlds to shatter? Do you want the hisSing lady to get out?"

Christopher saw the thoughts playing hide-and-seek between his words.

There was no mirror between the worlds. There was no glass that could shatter. The nice man only wanted to escape through his tree house. He only needed the hissing lady dead and the key buried in her flesh to open the door.

"She doesn't want to get out. <u>You</u> want to get out."

The nice man took a step closer. The smile frozen on his face. Christopher looked at David Olson, desperately pulling on the hissing lady's hand. He looked into the hissing lady's eyes, filled with tears, delirious with pain.

"Stop helping him," she wept.

Christopher took her right hand, coarse from centuries of torment. He felt the truth move like a whisper from her hand to his. He saw how the nice man tortured her. How the nice man turned all of her words into terror. This whole time, she wasn't trying to scare Christopher. She was trying to warn him. The light inside of the tree was not death. The light inside of the tree was life.

She was trying to save his life.

Christopher tried to pick her up, but she was as heavy as the world she protected. It didn't matter how hard he strained, he was never going to be able to carry her back to the lawn by himself. So, he moved side by side with David Olson, and the two little boys began pulling her off the burning street.

"Don't do that, christopHer. Please dOn't."

The nice man smiled a frown gone sick.

"Attack!" the hissing lady screamed.

Upon her command, hundreds of deer rushed at the nice man. Their fangs exposed. Charging like an army. Ready to rip him to pieces.

The nice man did not move.

He simply held up his hand. The deer instantly stopped and moved to his side. One by one. Their teeth bared. But they weren't biting this time. They were bowing to him. Rubbing on his legs like house cats. Christopher saw the hissing lady's expression change from hope to horror.

"They aren't your army, dear. They're mine. Did you forget tHAt?"

The nice man calmly walked across the street. The deer turned around and walked behind him, baring their teeth. Christopher and David strained against the hissing lady's weight.

"Come back here before I get upset, soN."

Christopher dragged her over the river of blood in the street. The river of blood in his nose. The clouds bumped together. Lightning ripped the sky. The nice man inched toward them.

"Come back here before I have to hIt you."

Christopher's heart raced. The nice man stepped closer. Christopher looked down. The soldier's legs were wrong. He had deer legs.

"I don't want to do that. Don't maKe me do that."

Christopher's feet reached the lawn. The hissing lady closed her eyes. She was seconds from death.

"If you pull her off the street, I will hurT you."

One more step.

"If you save her, I'll kill your motHer."

Christopher and David Olson pulled the hissing lady onto the lawn. Her skin instantly stopped burning. She got up, her legs shaking, her body still broken. She stood between the two boys and the nice man. A mother lion protecting her cubs. The nice man walked toward them, shaking with rage. The deer stalked behind him. Christopher saw their shadows in the moonlight. They weren't deer anymore. They were hounds. With glowing eyes. The hissing lady turned to the boys. She ripped the key from her flesh and put it in David's shaking hand. Then, she screamed.

"Get him out!"

CHAPTER 103

Mrs. Henderson crawled up the ladder to the tree house. The bullet wound in her side made the climbing slow. Each step excruciating. She would have stopped climbing, but her husband was calling to her from inside the tree house.

Come on, honey. Let's go on that weekend trip. I want to show you how much I love you.

Ms. Lasko put her hand up to help the old woman climb faster. They had to hurry. She had to help her because it was waiting for her inside the tree house. She could taste it, cold and sharp and burning on her lips. That beautiful buzzy butterfly feeling in her belly and blood. The flush on her face.

You can feel drunk again. It's waiting right in here.

Brady Collins felt so thankful. Mrs. Henderson said he did such a good job keeping the mailbox people in line. And now it was his turn to climb up those stairs to the tree house. He heard his mother in there. She was standing inside the warm kitchen, surrounded by the smell of hot soup and bread.

Come in from the doghouse, Brady. Mommy loves you. You'll never be cold again.

Through the stitches on her eyelids, Jenny Hertzog watched Brady climb the ladder. He passed the first branch, where her stepbrother Scott was still twitching. Jenny was happy, but she still wondered why Scott didn't die. Jenny looked up at the tree house and realized that she could hear her mother's sweet voice calling down to her. The woods smelled like her mother's old room. Sweet perfume and buttery popcorn.

Come inside, Jenny. We will have a slumber party together.

We'll make popcorn and kill your stepbrother and watch movies.

And no one will come into your room again to hurt you.

We'll drown Scott together in Floods. Floods.

Forever and ever and ever.

The four souls climbed past the branches, sagging from the weight of all the bodies hanging like Christmas ornaments. They just had to get to the tree house. They just had to walk into the light.

Then, they would be free.

CHAPTER 104

The hissing lady blocked the nice man as David and Christopher ran toward the Mission Street Woods. The nice man smiled, his teeth little daggers. The hissing lady squared off, burnt and bleeding. A coiled animal. Ready to strike.

"I'm off the street," she smiled through broken teeth.

"He made me strongeR," the nice man smiled back.

The two circled each other. The hissing lady felt the deer crawl toward her. She knew the window was closing. She launched herself at him, screaming at the top of her lungs, her fingernails ready to gouge out his eyes.

The nice man did not blink. He simply stood and waited for her as if she were a leaf falling in slow motion. He pivoted his body and hit her like swatting a fly. She flew back a hundred feet and crashed through Christopher's front door. The splinters flew like shrapnel. Within seconds, the deer were on top of her, biting and scratching.

And the nice man chased the boys into the woods.

*

Christopher ran down the path with David Olson. The key in David's hand. The silver blade in his own. They passed the billy goat bridge. Christopher knew the clearing was right in front of them. He felt David's hand on his. Moving him off the path.

"No! We have to go to the clearing!" Christopher yelled.

David shook his head no. He grabbed Christopher's hand and made a hard right through the thickest tree branches. Christopher looked back at the path just as the deer poured out from the clearing like fire ants from a hill. It was an ambush. David knew it. David knew every hiding place. Every shortcut. David had been here for fifty years.

The deer spread out behind them like dogs chasing mechanical rabbits.

Christopher followed David through the trees until the path was so thick that only children could move inside it. The deer slowed behind them. Their bodies too big to follow. But they did not stop, pushing themselves through the thickets until their skin scraped on the branches.

Suddenly the sky grew dark. Christopher heard branches snap like twigs behind them. He turned and saw murderous green eyes in the distance. It was the nice man. Tearing the trees apart to find them. Christopher felt David Olson's hand grab his. The itch moved from David's skin to Christopher's. Along with the fever. Christopher felt every hair on his body stand up like pine needles.

The boys closed their eyes and quieted their minds. They pictured themselves beginning to fly. The deer screaming behind them. The nice man tearing the path apart with his bare hands to get at them. They imagined flying higher and higher. Farther and faster. Up through the clouds. The wind in their hair.

Two rockets heading to the moon.

Until David began to sputter. The blood trickled out of his nose like a plane leaking fuel. He barely managed to put the key into Christopher's hands.

The power comes at a price.

Christopher could feel the pain through the boy's skin. The cuts and lashes on David's neck. Christopher felt it all unfold from David's point of view. The nice man breaking out of the tree house. The nice man savaging the boy to keep him quiet. They weren't cuts on his neck. They were bite marks.

David began to fall.

Christopher used all of his strength, but he could barely keep himself afloat. Let alone both of them. He curled himself around David's body to cushion the blow, and the two boys dropped like children playing cannonball in a swimming pool with no water.

They fell out of the clouds and into the sky right above the clearing. Christopher looked down and saw the angry eye cut in the middle of the Mission Street Woods. The giant tree stood in the middle like a demented pupil. Staring. Furious with rage. The deer poured into the clearing. Little veins turning white snow into a bloodshot eye.

The boys landed, the wind knocked from their bodies. They were a hundred feet from the tree. A hundred feet from the door. A hundred feet from life. Christopher jumped up, pulling David to his feet. The boys raced across the clearing to the tree. The nice man crashed through the woods, cracking the branches like bones. He reached the edge of the clearing.

"Hi, boys," he said.

The boys turned. David Olson opened his mouth to scream. Christopher froze. The nice man smiled. So gentle.

"Christopher, I'm sorry I lost my temper. I didn't mean to. I just need to get out of here. Please."

The nice man's voice sounded so desperate. It was as soft as thunder.

"I've been here for millennia. I don't get to wake up from this nightmare. I'm here. Every day. Every night. I never sleep. So, give me the key, and I promise I'm not going to hurt anyone. I just need to get out."

He moved toward Christopher. Little baby steps.

"You know me. I saved you over and over, Christopher. I gave your mom a house. And I did it because you are a good boy with the kindest heart. I have never seen anything like you. You can save the world from itself. Please, Christopher."

His voice sounded so sincere. Everything he said sounded right and true. The nice man did save Christopher. He did give his mother a house. He was the only man Christopher ever knew who didn't leave him.

"You are my best friend," the nice man said.

Christopher felt out of his body. Like the dreams he used to have after his father died when he would fall down in the street and not be able to move. He held up the key with one hand. The dull, silver blade with the other. The nice man took another step. Smiling.

"That's it, Christopher. That'S it, son."

Just then, David Olson grabbed the silver blade from Christopher's hand. He cut an invisible string and threw Christopher back to the tree. The bark like flesh. The world's flesh.

"No!" the nice man yelled and began to charge.

David grabbed the key with shaking fingers. He moved his hand to the tree trunk. The bark was slick with blood. The world's blood. He reached into the tree's rotten flesh and found the keyhole. David shoved the key into the lock and turned it with a CLICK. The door began to open. The light poured from the tree.

— Death is coming —

Mrs. Henderson climbed the ladder to the tree house. The freshly made mailbox people moaned behind her as her husband called out from the tree house. "Climb, honey! Let's go on that weekend trip! Just open the door, honey. I'm waiting in bed for you. It's time."

— Death is here —

Christopher looked into the light. He moved his foot over the threshold. He felt something running at him from the other side. He couldn't see it, but the sound was deafening. It was a stampede. They were coming. The people on the real side. Rushing to get in.

The worlds began to blur.

If he didn't get out, they would all come in. The door between the two worlds would be open. The layers of Hell and Earth would bleed together in "FLOODS! FLOODS!"

— We'll die —

Mrs. Henderson put her hand on the tree house doorknob. "You don't need to stab me, honey. Just come into the hotel room," her husband said on the other side of the door. "I love you more than I ever did."

Mrs. Henderson turned the doorknob.

— on —

The nice man ran at the tree. His eyes exactly like the eye of the clearing. Christopher could feel the cold around him. The light was life.

"David, come with me!" Christopher yelled.

David shook his head sadly and touched Christopher's hand. The boys locked eyes. In an instant Christopher understood. David couldn't leave. He had no body to go back to. David put the key in Christopher's hand just as the nice man ran at the tree, screaming at the top of his lungs.

— *Christmas* —

Mrs. Henderson turned the doorknob and opened the door. She looked into the tree house and saw Special Ed, Mike, and Matt, crouched down and waiting for her.

"It's ours. We built it," Special Ed said.

Then, he pulled out his father's gun and shot her between the eyes.

Mrs. Henderson fell backward, taking Jenny, Brady, and Ms. Lasko down to the ground with her.

— *Day* —

David shoved Christopher back into the light and closed the door just as the nice man crashed into the tree. Christopher put the key in the other side of the door, locking it.

Click.

Christopher had escaped from Hell.

CHAPTER 105

tHe nIce Man stared at the tree. the moment lasted a second on earth. but for hIm, it was just another eternity. hE had been right. this child was the child. hE had not seen anything like the boy for two thousand years. hE needed him. hE knew that after he broke the boy, hE would get out. and hE knew how to break the boy. hE knew how to get that key. hE was going to be free. finally.

hE turned to the woods as the deer swarmed David Olson. hiS petS biting the boy and dragging him back like a mouse for their master. hE took David's neck in hiS hand and held him up, squirming like a man in a noose. tHe nIce Man grabbed the dull, silver blade from David's hand and put it back in hiS pocket.

"i told you what would happen if you betrayed me, david," hE said.

hE left a part of himself to stitch David's eyes and mouth closed. then, he walked over to mrs. henderson. sweet mrs. henderson. she was on the ground on the real side, still stunned by the bullet that bounced off her forehead. she was lucky hE made people stop dying, or she would never get the chance to see her husband again.

"get up, honey," hE called out in her husband's voice. "we can still go on that weekend trip."

"we can?" she said hopefully.

"yes. i want to show you how much i appreciate the home you've given me. the body you've shared with me. but i need you to do something first. okay, honey?"

hE left hImself to whisper to mrs. henderson and moved to brady collins. hE turned hImself into the smell of a warm kitchen.

"brady, get up now. come into the kitchen. you'll never be cold again."

"I won't?" the little boy said.

"of course not. mommy loves you. i just need you to do something for me. okay?"

hE stayed with brady collins as hE became the smell of a safe bedroom for jenny hertzog . . .

"do you want to drown Scott in floods?" hE asked as jenny's mother.

. . . just as he became the smell of jenny's bedroom for her stepbrother scott.

"you can have me, scott," hE said in jenny's voice. "i just need you to do something for me first."

hE slithered up the giant tree to christopher's tree house—his latest and most prized ornament. hE looked through the window at the three little boys, three little pigs, crouched behind special ed's father's gun, still smoking in his little hand. hE knew that christopher's love protected these boys. that was the risk with making someone god. but still, hE was surprised by this turn of events. hE had gone to a lot of trouble to get special ed bullets. hE had turned him into a zealous little sentry to keep the tree house door open. not closed. and now, hE had a problem. but there were solutions. christopher's protection wouldn't last forever. those who couldn't be turned could be tricked. it was so easy to trick boys into playing war. almost as easy as grown men. the tree house would be hiS when it really mattered. just keep whispering. and waiting. whispering and waiting.

"nice guys win wars, eddie. listen to grandma."

"they're going to kill your brother, matt."

"you have to protect the avengers, mike."

hE left hImself outside of the tree house and slithered back down the ladder.
h

  s

   s

    s

  s

hE crawled around the rest of the clearing, leaving impressions of hImself like little wisps of clouds. whispering to each person as hE did to mary katherine as she drove her car straight into christopher. whispering to mrs. henderson to underline the book. whispering to christopher as he slept on the tree for 6 days. stroking his hair. always smiling. always calm. always gentle. touching people's arms. that little itch. people think it's dry skin. it's not. it'S mE. hE was the taste of alcohol on ms. lasko's lips that was so pure that she wept when hE took the drunk feeling away from her. hE was the ecstasy for debbie dunham that she always felt before the shame and loneliness returned. hE was the thought racing through doug's mind.

she cheated on you, doug. she's a whore and she cheated on you.

do you want a virgin? you can have a virgin, doug.

you know what you have to do. you know where you have to go.

hE was the promise of 72 virgins and the hAhA on the 73rd night.

no more vIrgIns. just 72 unhappy wIves and time. it's tiMe.

hE was their memories and dreams and secret desires and thoughts.

as hE had been for centuries.

but it was different with christopher.

it was better with christopher.

at first, hE didn't recognize it. that's how long it had been. but after a few seconds, it was unmistakable. hE could smell again. it wasn't the memory of smell. it was an actual smell. pine needles fresh and wet as sex. hE hadn't felt this alive in decades. not since david olson. david could have taken him out of this place. but hE had made mistakes and david slipped through hiS fingers like sand. so hE had to search for the next child. not search land. but search time. watching the real world through the glass. waiting. whispering. how long had hE waited for this one. decadeS the way that children wait for the school bus. and the bus finally came. to tHis day. to tHis boy.

the nice man walked back through the clearing. hE could feel the wet grass on hIs feet. the cold snow crunching. it was glorious. hE passed the billy goat bridge. the man who buried the prostitute in the hollow log screamed as the deer ate his face. again. "please! make it stop! i'm sorry."

hE walked out of the woods.

hE looked across the landscape. lit by the blue moon. hE walked across the slick field to the street hE created to burn her. the street warmed hIs cold feet like stockings hung over a fireplace. the man in the girl scout uniform pulled himself behind the bushes and screamed. the couple stopped kissing long enough to look at hIm through the madness in their eyes.

"please. we're sorry!"

hE whispered in their ears. they forgot. and they kept right on cheating with each other. feeling the heartbreak they caused their dying spouses with each kiss. just like the man opening the door to the police and hearing how his child had been found murdered. 10 minutes of worry. 10 minutes of devastation. 30 seconds of joy when the child is born. then, 10 minutes of worry. 10 minutes of devastation. forEver. by hIs count, the man who murdered that child had experienced the pain he caused those parents 1,314,000 times by now. people thought that they would eventually get used to eternity. didn't they realize that you can't get used to something that you can't remember experiencing? of course the answer was no. but hE thought someone would have realized how it works by now.

every day was the first day here.

and soon, it would be on earth.

hE looked at the mailbox people on the sides of the street. waiting for their turn at eternity. not knowing what they would see when the zippers keeping them blind were finally opened. the top of a cloud. or this place. forEver.

then hE saw

her.

she crawled across the lawn. desperate to get back to david's house on the corner. she had already begun to heal. she always could. she always did. hE could make her insane. hE could turn all of her words of warning into terrifying screams. hE could take all of her maternal gestures and shouts of "run away. he is evil. you must not help him." and twist them into hisses and nightmares and rage that terrified the very children she was trying to save. hE could turn all of her kindness into terror as easily as hE could turn men's love into mankind's wars. but it didn't matter how many times hE stabbed her. how many times hE shot her.

hE could not kill her.

and she kept hIm in here.

forEver.

they balanced each other like two children on a seesaw. the energy between them intertwined like an ocean's ebb and flow. neither of them owned the power. they simply channeled it like the moon's gravity through water. some decades her. others hIm. except in those rare times when hE could find that even rarer child. so pure. so kind. so trusting. with enough intelligence to know everything except the one piece hE had to keep hidden like a rabbit straining for breath inside the hat.

which one of them was actually holding the strings.

hE had tried many stories over the centuries. and hE had learned from hIs mistakes. in the end, hE found it somewhat ironic that honesty was the best policy. christopher was too smart not to find the inconsistencies in the story otherwise. so, most of what hE told the boy was true. there was indeed something of a one-way mirror between the worlds. there was a way to whisper to people on the real side. the tree house was in fact a portal between the worlds. there were 4 ways in. 3 ways out.

but

the imaginary world was not exactly imaginary. the 3rd way out did not exactly require anything more than the key. and the hissing lady was not exactly the one who would be considered evil between the two of them.

except by hIm.

hE picked her up, broken and bleeding. she spat at hIm. cursed hIm. stared at hIm. eye-to-eye. i-to-I. hE pulled out the dull, silver blade. hE sharpened it on his teeth like a barber's razor on a leather strap. hE plunged it into her chest. then hE pulled the blade out of her flesh. the wound healed instantly. hE plunged the silver blade into her over and over and over again, stabbing her like a woodpecker. he could feel her bones crunch, dulling the blade until the silver was no more. just like she did. Every time. ForEver.

"why don't you just fucking die already?" hE sighed.

then hE kissed hEr.

hE left hImself with the hissing lady as hE broke apart and spread through the town like a cloud. walking down the hallways of the hospital. marveling at the pieces on the game board. there was no coincidence. everyone was where they needed to be. all of those people sick with it. so much anger. so much flu. all of that heat. the frogs were squirming in the water.

do you know why you all stopped dying?

he walked through the old folks home and the church.

do you know what that means?

hE walked past the rubberneckers on route 19. hE sat in the passenger side of each and every car. whispering. rubbing up against people like two sticks making fire.

you all stopped dying.

do you know what that means?

hE had been in solitary confinement for two thousand years. watching. waiting. testing the fence until hE found this night. this boy. for one moment, hE brought all of the pieces of hImself together. from the middle east where the next shot of the endless war was just fired, through europe and africa to this little out-of-the-way no-one-would-ever-notice town in pennsylvania. the perfect place to hide hIs back door. hE hadn't done this in decades. hE looked up at the heavens through hIs eye. past the blue moon lying there like a ball of yarn for a lion. hE stared at his Father hiding Himself inside one hundred billion stars. the one hundred billion people who had lived and died. hE always lost the people to his Father. hE always lost the people to those stars. they could be taken away from hIm when they died. because goD is a murderer, daDdy.

> *but you all stopped dying.*
> *do you know what that really means?*
> *it means that the frogs will live.*
> *boiling.*
> *forEVEr.*

> *that's all eternity is*
> *just the absence of death*
> *and soon, i will be tHere*
> *to make you all understand*
> *that hell has come to earth*
> *all it needs now is its kIng*

hE was so close. hE knew it. hE would get out. out of the woods. out of the shadows. out of the creeps up and down a person's neck. this was hiS chance to finally look god's children in the eye and introduce hImself to all of them. hE would take over hIs Father's little blue planet. hE would rip the blue right out of hIs Father's fucking eyes. those eyes filled with clouds. and all hE needed to do was make it possible for a small group of people to die.

christopher and everyone he loved.

all around town, hE walked, spreading hIs word like the flu by every means available. a whisper. a hint. a forgotten dream. a family's touch, the fear that keeps the old awake at night. the anger that haunts the middle aged. and slowly, over the past several months, through the very milk that emily bertovich's father had spent a fortune to turn into hope of his daughter's return.

only hE knew she never would.

all over town, people had memories and heard whispers from loved ones long dead. those who were touched by christopher shook it off. to them, it was a strange little whisper or a terrifying warning. but to everyone else, the whisper grew and grew until it was screaming in their ears. the thing they could all blame. the reason they were unhappy. the reason their lives never worked. finally, something made sense. finally, something explained all of the problems of the world. this was the answer to all of their prayers. the people finally admitted to each other out loud . . . they didn't know why . . . they just knew what had to be done to finally make heaven on earth . . .

"We have to kill that little boy Christopher and everyone who gets in our way. Because he is the enemy. This is a war. And good guys win wars."

hE smiled so wide that hE almost ran out of baby teeth.

Part VI

Run foR Your Life

bEEp.

Christopher opened his eyes.

He blinked through the harsh fluorescent light. He strained to see where he was. His eyes found a life-support machine breathing for him. In and out. Up and down.

Beep.

The sound came to him. And with it, the pain. All of the power he'd felt on the imaginary side came crashing into his body like the break of a wave. He had never known such agony. He felt like he had been hit with a car—because he had. His eyes were sore as if he hadn't used them since the car accident—because he hadn't. His eyes had been closed. He had been lying in a hospital bed, unconscious. He had come close to death, but he was still alive. For now.

Beep.

Christopher took a hard swallow. His throat felt like sandpaper. The breathing tube pushed cold air down his throat like hard plastic vomit. He had to get this breathing tube out. He looked around the room for help, but all he could see was the white curtain around his bed.

He saw the button for the nurse to his right. He reached up to press it, but something stopped him.

The hissing lady's key was still in his hand.

Beep. Beep.

Christopher heard muffled voices outside in the hallway. He knew what was happening. He could feel it swarming around him.

The nice man is . . .
The nice man is . . . starting the war.

Beep. Beep. Beep.

Christopher's heart began to pound. He had to slow it down, or the nurses would know he was awake. He reached with his right arm, still battered and bruised from the car accident, and picked at the gel holding the sensors to his chest.

My mother is . . . in the house.
My mother is . . . in danger.

He gripped the breathing tube and ripped it out of his mouth. He immediately turned over and threw up all the air from his stomach. The retch smelled like acrid bile. Acidic and awful.

Beep. Beep. Beep. Beep.

Christopher kept the clip on his finger and swung his legs out of the bed. His bare feet hit the freezing tile. He put the pillow under the covers to make it look like he was still sleeping. Then Christopher slowly slid the white curtain open. He saw that another person had been moved into his room.

It was Mrs. Collins.

She lay perfectly still. Her eyes closed. The ventilator moved up and down for her lungs, rattling like the ball inside a can of spray paint.

Hsssssss.

Christopher wanted to run. Get to the closet. Get his clothes. Get out of here. But there was the clip on his finger. If the clip came off, the nurses would come running in. There was only one way to fool them.

He had to put the clip on Mrs. Collins' finger.

Christopher slowly ripped away the blood pressure Velcro strangling his arm. Then, he tiptoed to her bed. He heard voices right outside the door. He only had a few seconds. He spread out her fingers and put the index on top, big like a cherry. All he had to do was unclip and reclip. But it had to be done instantly. He took a big breath. This was it. His only chance. He grabbed the clip from his finger, his heart beating like crazy.

Beep. Beep. Beep. Beep. Beep. Beep. Beep.

Christopher snapped it back on Mrs. Collins' index finger.

Beep. Beep.

Hssssss.

The voices outside were getting louder. Christopher put the white curtain back around his bed and moved to the closet. But not before snatching Mrs. Collins' cell phone from her nightstand. Half a charge left. No bars. No service. He quickly stripped off the hospital gown and put on his clothes. The phone went into his pocket along with the key.

The door to the room opened.

"Christopher? Are you awake?"

Christopher looked through the crack in the closet door. He saw Nurse Tammy walk into the room with a tray of food. She moved over to his bed and gently rolled the white curtain back. She saw the pillow under the blanket. It must have looked very convincing. She took the tray of food and carefully set it down.

"I just talked to my dad, Christopher. A deer frightened him in the backyard, and he dropped the bottle of merLOT. It broke, and the state store is closed. Now he'll never have his Christmas merLOT. He worked night shifts to put me through school and you took his favorite thing."

Nurse Tammy pulled out a scalpel from her pocket.

"I could have bought him more merLOT, but I had to work a triple. You made everyone sick. You made me miss Christmas. I have to stay here because of you."

Nurse Tammy brought the scalpel down and violently stabbed the sheets. When she didn't see any blood, she ripped them off. She found the pillow in place of the boy. She turned and whispered.

"Christopherrrr, where are youuu?"

Beep. Beep. Beep. Hssssss.

Christopher turned to Mrs. Collins in the bed. Her eyes were wide open now, staring at him through the crack in the closet. The wet paint rattling inside her lungs.

"Iiiiiiiizzzzzzz," she groaned, trying to push the word "Christopher" through the breathing tube.

"What is it, Mrs. Collins?" Nurse Tammy asked.

Nurse Tammy rushed to her bedside. With her back turned, Christopher crawled out of the closet door and silently moved to the hallway.

The hallway was empty.

But he knew it was only temporary.

He could feel the people in bed.

Waking up for the hunt.

The ICU doors began to open. Christopher saw Mr. Henderson sit up in bed and point right at him. He screamed to alert the others, but no sound came out. He put his hands to his throat. The place where his wife stabbed him. He began pushing over the machines and equipment to wake up the floor.

There was no time to lose. Christopher ran to the supply closet at the end of the hall. He quickly shut the door behind him just as the people in the hallways spilled into the ICU. He turned around and looked at the room, expecting to find it empty. But there was a big black shape in the middle of the floor. It took him a moment to realize what it was.

A body bag.

It inflated and deflated like a bag of popcorn in the microwave. Someone was inside it. Breathing. Christopher was trapped. He couldn't leave the room. The hallway was swimming with people.

"He's around here somewhere, Doctor," Nurse Tammy said.

Christopher needed to hide. He knew they would check the closet. There was only one place left. He walked over to the body bag. He moved his hand over the plastic and slowly opened the zipper. Heat rose from the figure inside. Christopher saw small pools of blood on the hospital gown and a five-day beard.

The sheriff.

He looked pale. Dead asleep. Barely breathing. Christopher touched his hand. The itch fluttered on his skin.

"Wake up," Christopher whispered.

The sheriff did not stir.

"What's in this room?" Nurse Tammy asked.

The footsteps came closer. They were right outside the door. There was nowhere to go but in. Christopher opened the bag and climbed inside next to the sheriff, zipping it up behind him. He could feel the sheriff's heartbeat. His shallow breathing.

"Please wake up, Sheriff," he whispered.

The door opened. Someone walked into the room.

"Is he in here?" a voice said.

"No, Doctor," Nurse Tammy said.

"Okay. Let's keep looking."

The footsteps walked out of the room and closed the door. Christopher was about to open up the bag when he realized he could still hear breathing.

They were still in the room.

After a long moment of silence, a man groaned through a sliced throat.

"You're right, Mr. Henderson. That body bag is moving," Nurse Tammy said.

The footsteps got closer.

"Hi, Christopher. Are you in there?"

Christopher did not breathe. He felt the body bag being lifted.

"That's heavy. The sheriff must have put on fifty pounds in the last hour."

Christopher felt the bag laid down on a hard table. The table began to move. They were on a gurney. Being wheeled to God knows where.

Squeak. Squeak. Squeak.

"Come on, everyone. Let's bring Christopher to the rest of them," Nurse Tammy said.

Christopher heard someone hit the button on the ICU wall. The security door opened. A murmur ran through the hallway. Christopher grabbed the sheriff's hand and focused his mind. The fever broke out on his forehead. He let the heat from his own body move to the sheriff. Healing the wounds. Giving color to pale skin.

Wake up, Sheriff.

The gurney went into the elevator.

"Could you hit the button for the basement, please, Mr. Henderson?"

Mr. Henderson groaned through his sliced vocal cords. The elevator beeped and started moving down.

Please! They're going to kill us!

The gurney stopped with a squeak.

"We're here, everyone," Nurse Tammy announced.

A hand reached down and unzipped the body bag. The cool air hit Christopher's lungs. He saw instruments. Metal tables. And drawers so big the wall looked like a massive filing cabinet.

He was in the morgue.

CHAPTER 107

Christopher's mother stood in her son's bedroom. She stared at David Olson's bookshelf and the little boy's terrified scrawl.

DO NOT KILL
THE HISSING LADY
SHE IS THE ONLY THING KEEPING
THE DEVIL IN HELL

She felt a prickle on her neck. An electricity running through the house. The hair on her arms stood up as if someone rubbed a balloon against an invisible sweater.

hI, kate. Remember <u>him</u>?

She turned to the photograph of her late husband. Lifeless in the silver frame. Her husband stared back at her. That same smile. The same pose. Frozen in time.

But something had changed.

His flannel shirt was getting wet.

His wrists were turning red.

He began to walk toward her.

I have your husband, Kate.

Her husband's smile never left his face. He moved toward the glass of the frame. Getting bigger inside the picture. Reaching his arms out. Banging on the glass. Desperate. Let me out! Let me out!

I have your son, too.

Christopher's mother ran out of the room. Down the stairs. She had to fight the voice. She had to get to Christopher. She passed the photographs on the stairs.

You let all of your men die.

In every photograph, her husband was walking right at her. Bringing his hand up to the glass of the frame. Ready to knock. His wrists slashed. The blood streaking down the glass from the inside.

Knock. Knock. Knock.

Christopher's mother stopped. Someone was on her porch. She saw her husband in the photographs. He banged on the glass just as she heard a bang on the front door.

Knock. Knock. Knock.

Ding dong.

Christopher's mother tiptoed away from the door. She had to get out of here. She had to get to Christopher. The doorknob turned. Stopped by the lock. She backed away into the living room. Never taking her eyes from the front door.

Until she walked straight into a body.

She spun around. She saw him. Standing with a gun.

"Hi, Kate," Jerry said.

CHAPTER 108

The boys were surrounded.

Matt looked down at the clearing and saw Mrs. Henderson on the ground. His lazy eye began to burn as if his doctor had just put drops in it. The same lazy eye that Christopher had healed. Through it, he could see the shadow of a man moving through the clearing from person to person. Whispering.

The flock's random movements began to unify. The people hanging from the sagging branches freed their necks from the nooses. They dropped to the ground like acorns and gathered around Mrs. Henderson, who lay on the ground with a deep gash in the middle of her forehead left by Special Ed's bullet.

"Jesus. She's still alive," Mike said.

"That's impossible," Special Ed said, moving to the window.

The boys watched in silence as the town picked her up gently. Mrs. Henderson nodded her thanks to the mailbox people. Then, she put a loving hand on the shoulders closest to her and pulled the thread from her lips as if unraveling a sweater. She spoke calmly.

"Kill Christopher and bring him back to the tree," she said.

Half of the flock began to run silently through the woods. The other half stayed, waiting for her next command. Mrs. Henderson snipped the thread from Doug and Debbie Dunham's lips.

"Go to Mary Katherine. She is laughing at you both. Make her stop."

The two teenagers nodded and ran back through the woods. Mrs. Henderson put down the knife. She took a little needle and thread from her sewing kit. She looked up at the tree house, staring at Special Ed while she stitched the bullet wound he left in her forehead like a thumbprint on Ash Wednesday.

Then, Mrs. Henderson led the charge up the ladder.

"Oh, my God," Matt said.

Special Ed checked his gun. Five shots in the cylinder. Two hundred rounds in his backpack. He threw open the door and pointed his gun down. Like a deranged video game, dozens of people were climbing the ladder, with hundreds waiting to take their place. Special Ed shot. Slowing the tide. Bodies fell backward. But no one would die. No one would stop.

Matt watched the madness, his lazy eye burning. He could see the shadow man everywhere. Whispering to people. His shadow transforming into a warm kitchen. A hotel room. A dream house. The boy who finally loved them back. The girl who finally said yes. The long-lost father. The prodigal son. Whispering. All they had to do was open the door. Take the tree house. Hurt those three little kids blocking their way, and then, they could be happy.

Forever.

"We're never going to have enough ammunition," Special Ed said.

Matt looked down. Eddie was right. Two hundred rounds would come and go, but the bad guys would keep coming. Mike grabbed the hammer and started to climb down.

"Cover me," he said to Special Ed.

"No, Mike!" Matt screamed.

"They can't climb if there isn't a ladder. I'm not going to let them hurt you."

Mike moved quickly down ten steps. The clearing went wild beneath him. Mike swung the hammer, knocking the first 2x4 loose. Matt took the gun out of Special Ed's hand. He waited until the first mailbox person reached out for Mike's leg.

Then, he shot.

The mailbox person fell, taking down people like dominoes. Mike threw the 2x4 up to the tree house for Special Ed to catch. Then, Mike climbed up another step, prying each 2x4 loose. Throwing them up. Taking the ladder up with him.

"Knock him off the tree!" Mrs. Henderson shouted.

The people in the clearing threw rocks. Stones. Whatever they could find. The debris hit Mike, but nothing could stop him. He took another step. And another. He reached the last 2x4. The last step. There was a good twelve feet under him. Nobody could reach the tree house from there. They could wait for Christopher to bring help. They could wait for the sheriff. They had won.

Until Brady pulled out his gun.

Matt watched in horror as the shadow man twisted himself around Brady like a tree root.

"That's it, Brady," the voice whispered. "Come in from the doghouse."

Brady lifted the gun as Mike dislodged the last 2x4.

"Get that boy out of our kitchen."

Mike handed his little brother the hammer.

"You never have to be cold again."

Brady Collins shot.

*

tHe nIce Man smiled as the clearing began their little fight to the death for the tree house. hE watched the bullet hit mike's shoulder. hE watched mike fall. and mrs. henderson stalk over with her needle and thread. hE whispered to Matt that his brother could still be saved. hE watched Matt lower the secret rope ladder and climb down into the fog. hE watched matt's expression when he saw his brother had turned into a mailbox person, running at him with the needle and thread. a minute later, hE watched as special ed heard screams in the distance.

eddie.

"Matt? Is that you?"

yes. send down the ladder.

"What's the password?"

chocolate milk.

hE watched special ed lower the ladder. the ropes tighten. the hands climbing out of the darkness. the expression on special ed's face when he saw it wasn't matt.

it was brady collins.

tHe nIce Man smiled at the two dogs growling at an invisible whistle. soon, hE would have them chasing each other through the woods. guns drawn. just two little boys playing war. it was so easy to make men kill each other over territory that only time could truly own. so easy to make them all think they were the good guys.

with that, the tree house was left empty and unguarded. just as hE needed it to be. hE could not go to earth. noT with the hissing lady still alive. but the portal was opeN.

all hE needed now was christopher.

and that key he kept in his pocket.

hE just needed to take care of some other people first.

CHAPTER 109

J esus, help me."

Mary Katherine was on her knees looking up at the only window in her padded cell. The white cotton nightgown left her feet cold. She was in the hospital.

No, you're in the mental hospital.

Mary Katherine shook off the voice, which had been there like a virus ever since her parents let the doctors drag her to the psychiatric ward. The doctors gave her a sedative, and when she woke up, she was inside this padded room. Ten by ten. With a single window. And white walls. She was starving.

Because you're pregnant. Your parents didn't believe you.

They left you here, Mary Katherine.

Mary Katherine called out for someone to give her food and water. The baby was famished inside her. Kicking the walls of her stomach. But no one called back. No nurse came. No doctor. No parents. She was alone.

"Jesus, please help me."

Mary Katherine stared at the blue moon shining through the window. Then, she stood on her tiptoes and looked out across the town. There were fires on the horizon. Buildings burned.

Something terrible was happening.

Yes, your parents put you in an asylum, and you're never getting out.

Mary Katherine tried to breathe through the panic. She reminded herself that "asylum" meant something else. It meant safety. She had much better conditions than the Virgin Mary had in a barn two thousand years ago, right? She could be grateful for that, right? Jesus helped her there, right? He loved her, right? Just calm down, Mary Katherine. Calm down. You're in a safe room.

Do you feel safe?

Mary Katherine heard footsteps down the hallway.

"Hello?" she said.

She waited for a response. None came. The footsteps got louder.

"Hello? Who is that?" she yelled out.

The person stopped right outside the thick padded door. Mary Katherine looked at the doorknob. Turning. She thought it must be the doctor. The nurse with another shot for her arm. She wanted to scream. The door opened.

It was her mother.

Mary Katherine burst into tears. She ran to her mother, hugging her. In her mind, she said everything perfectly.

"I need to eat, Mom. The baby is so hungry. But I swear I never had sex. I don't know how I got pregnant. Thank you for coming for me. Thank you for helping me. Thank you for saving me. Thank you for still loving me."

But the words came out completely unintelligible in between sobs and snot. To her mother, she must have sounded crazy because she held her like the cold side of the pillow.

"We have to go now, Mary Katherine," she said sadly.

Mary Katherine finally found her breath enough to speak clearly.

"Where are we going, Mom?" she asked.

"To church. It's time."

CHAPTER 110

Jerry stepped into the light. A bottle in one hand. A gun in the other.

"Why did you run away from me?" he said.

Kate backed away from him. Jerry finished the last swallow of whiskey and carefully put the bottle on the counter.

"I don't want you to be afraid," Jerry said. "I've cleaned up. I'm sorry. Hey, where's Christopher? I want to throw the ball around with him."

Her mind raced. She had to get away. Get back to Christopher in the hospital. Jerry pulled out four stacks of bills, each neatly wound in a white paper band.

"I know you don't believe me, but I promise . . . I'm not a loser anymore. I can take care of you both. I won over forty-one thousand bucks. I still have most of it. All I bought was this gun."

Knock. Knock. Knock.

Ding dong.

"Kate, are you in there?!" a voice screamed outside. It was Special Ed's mother.

"Betty! I'm here!" she yelled out.

Jerry took a step closer.

"Don't open the door, Kate," Jerry slurred. "Don't run away again. I'm sorry. I was crazy. I've been sitting here for hours. I came here with all these thoughts in my head. But the balloons led me to the school. The principal's office was trashed, but I found your address."

Knock. Knock. Knock.

Ding dong.

"Open the door! Something's wrong in the town!" Betty cried out.

Jerry reached out with the money in his hands.

"Please, Kate. I want to be a better man for you. Your son is so great. I can be his father. I can teach him things. And when he misbehaves, I can be a lot nicer to him than my dad was."

Jerry had a hundred pounds on her. But she had one advantage. The woman Jerry knew back in Michigan was long gone.

Be a victim or be a fighter.

Her hands reached inside her pocket. Where was her pepper spray? It was in her purse. Where was her purse? The car. She had Ambrose's car keys.

The panic button.

He took another step. She hit the panic button in her pocket. The alarm roared to life. Jerry turned to look outside. She ran past him and threw open the front door.

The chain caught.

She couldn't get out! She saw Special Ed's mother through the three-inch gap. There were more people behind her. Special Ed's father. Mike and Matt's mothers.

"Where are our kids, Kate?" Betty asked.

"Yes. We woke up, and Eddie was gone."

"Mike and Matt, too."

"I don't know. Help me!" she yelled out.

"Help you? Your son took our children. Where the fuck is he, Kate?"

"Yes. Hand Christopher over before he gets our boys killed," Betty cried.

The parents moved to the door. Banging and screaming. Pushing against the chain. Kate pushed back to keep them out.

Jerry stood, staring at her.

The gun in his hand.

"I told you not to run away again, and you didn't listen," he said coldly, rubbing his bloodshot eyes. "Are you with someone new? Is that it? Is he better than me? Do you two laugh at me? Is that what you do when he fucks you? Are you laughing at me right now? Stop laughing at me."

Kate Reese heard the glass of the sliding door in the backyard. She turned. The backyard was filled with people coming from the woods. The old woman from the attic stood there with a large butcher knife.

Tink. Tink. Tink. Her knife on the glass.

Jerry raised the gun.

"Get out of my head, Kate. Stop laughing at me. Who the hell do you think you are? I drove all the way from Michigan just to be with you, and you think you're too good for me?! You want something to laugh at, bitch?!"

Jerry cocked the hammer back.

"You're right, Jerry!" she yelled. "I was a bitch. I was testing you. I made it impossible to find me. But you did. Let's go to Michigan right now."

"What?"

"I didn't think you cared, but you passed the test. You're a real man, Jerry. I want you to take me back to Michigan, but we have to go right now. Where's your truck?" she said.

Knock knock knock.

Tink tink tink.

"Truck's outside," he said, dumbfounded.

"Then let's pick up Christopher and go back to Michigan."

"You're lying to me," Jerry said.

"I'm not lying. I was just mad. You hit me. I had to make you pay."

The chain began to splinter.

The sliding glass door began to crack.

"This is your last chance, Jerry. If you don't take me away right now, you will never have me again."

The mailbox people crashed through the sliding door. The glass slicing their hands. The old woman ran through the shattered glass with her butcher knife.

BANG!

Jerry shot the old woman in the leg.

The chain behind them gave. Betty fell into the entry hall, the other parents rushing in behind her. Kate grabbed Jerry by the hand and led him into the garage, locking the door behind them. She hit the garage door opener. Coiled. Ready to run.

The chain lifted the garage door with an aching groan. Kate saw legs in the driveway. Blood pounded in her ears. Christopher was alone in this madness. Her survival was now Christopher's survival. She had to get to her son.

"Jerry," she said. "Take me home."

Jerry smiled as the garage door opened. He led her through the crowd.

BANG! BANG! BANG!

He shot one man in the hand. Two others in the chest. Kate saw Ambrose's Cadillac in the driveway. The tires were slashed. The windshield shattered. She ran to Jerry's truck parked down the street and threw open the door. Jerry slid into the driver's seat.

"Start the truck, Jerry," she said.

He took out his keys. They slipped in his hand.

"Start the God damn truck!"

Ms. Lasko ran from the woods. Her eyes insane with sobriety. The truck roared to life. Jerry threw it into first gear. He drove straight into the cul-de-sac. There was no time to reverse. Dozens of mailbox people rushed toward them, Ms. Lasko leading the way. Jerry whipped around the circle. The truck's tires skidded, then found pavement, and he drove out of the cul-de-sac, leaving the madness behind them.

The adrenaline left their bodies, and the two ex-lovers looked at each other as Jerry laughed and laughed and laughed. Kate kept a smile plastered on her face as the pain returned to her side. Her eyes went to the gun in Jerry's hand.

The hospital was ten minutes away.

CHAPTER 111

Christopher looked up from the autopsy table.

All the people in the morgue stared at him. Nurse Tammy. Mr. Henderson. The doctor with his scalpel. The security guards with their guns. All waiting in a deli line for Christopher's death by a thousand cuts.

Christopher looked around for help. The tables to his left were covered with bodies. The deputies from the sheriff's office. Some old people from Shady Pines. All of their eyes closed. All of them breathing. Still alive.

The old people began to sit up. Moaning.

Christopher turned to the slab next to him. He saw the faded eagle tattoo on leathery skin. The bandages over the eyes. It was Ambrose Olson. The old man looked as if he had been stabbed.

"Mr. Olson! Wake up!" Christopher cried.

He grabbed Ambrose's hand. Blood poured from his nose as he tried to heal the old man. But Ambrose was lost somewhere deep in sleep.

"Chrissstopppheerrrrr," the voices whispered behind him.

The old people rose up on the tables. Their eyes mean with cancer. He saw them stand. One by one. Their withered feet hitting the cold tile floor. Their hips clicking like insects.

"Why won't you let us die? We are in pain."

The old people moved toward him. He could feel their bodies. All the throbbing in their joints. The black molasses in their lungs. He could feel their breath on his forehead. The sour smell of age. Old fingers pried his eyelids open while withered hands ripped him from Ambrose. They spun him around to face the room.

"How should we proceed, Doctor?" Nurse Tammy asked.

"Let's give Christopher to <u>them</u>," he said.

"Yes! Give him to them!" the old people agreed.

The security guards moved to the wall lined with cold metal drawers for the dead bodies. They banged on the drawers with the butts of their guns.

"Wake up in there! Wake up!"

The old folks surrounded Christopher, lifting him off the table.

"NO!" he screamed.

Christopher fought back with all his strength. He grabbed the sheriff's hand with his right. Ambrose with his left. Desperate. Clinging. He threw his loudest whisper into both of their arms. The electricity hummed inside the fluorescent lights. The room filled with the smell of ozone. The smells of clouds bumping together.

Sheriff! You have to wake up!

Mr. Olson! We can still save your brother!

The old people pried his fingers off one by one until he was loose and kicking. The drawers began to open. Hands clawing at metal. The bodies were inside. Squirming. Screaming, "Let us die!" Christopher saw a body in the middle drawer. It was draped with a white sheet.

The group shoved him inside the drawer and locked it. The drawer went pitch black. Christopher's cries echoed off the cold metal walls. He could see nothing, but he could feel the body inside the drawer. Was it moving? Was it breathing? Christopher reached back and felt the skin of the body's hands peeking out of the sheets. They were cold and lifeless. No electricity. And that smell. He remembered that smell from his father's funeral. It was like talcum death. Was it alive? Dead? Christopher focused his mind. He had to find a way out. He reached down and patted his own body.

The phone.

He almost forgot. Mrs. Collins' phone. It was still in his pocket, right next to the hissing lady's key. Christopher turned on the phone. The light reflected off the metal drawer, making it glow. He looked to his sides. He saw old, withered hands. And no bars on the phone.

The light went dark.

Christopher turned the phone on again. He looked back down. The hands were palm-side up now. The body had moved in the darkness.

The phone went black. Christopher turned it back on. The hands were moving.

Twitching. The fingers reached up. Brushing against the back of Christopher's neck.

"Chrisssstopher," the voice whispered.

Christopher screamed. The corpse sat up.

"What's my name? Give me back my name, Christopher."

Mrs. Keizer's hands went around Christopher's neck. Christopher fought back against the old woman, but her grip was inhuman. He felt the air leave his body until a voice boomed through the morgue.

"NO! HE'S MINE!"

The morgue fell silent. Christopher felt Mrs. Keizer's hands leave his neck. The drawer opened with a click and slowly slid back into the room. Christopher looked up and saw the eyes staring at him from the center of the morgue. Bloodshot and black. The face was pure evil.

It was the sheriff.

"Why did you kill her, Christopher?"

Christopher was stunned. The sheriff looked so hateful. His skin pale and waxy. The whisper scratched his hand. He had already broken the skin. He was going to scratch his way to the bone.

"She was only a little girl. Why did you kill her?"

"I didn't, sir. Please."

"Why did you kill him? He was just a little boy," a voice said.

Christopher turned. He saw Ambrose Olson rise off the gurney. His eyes black with rage.

"I didn't kill David, sir. We can still save him!" Christopher pleaded.

The sheriff and Ambrose reached down with powerful arms and lifted Christopher out of the drawer. Struggling for their sanity.

"You kill her every time I go to sleep. I can't watch her die again. I have to stop you before you kill her again!" the sheriff yelled.

"You kill David every time I go to sleep. I can't watch my brother die again. We have to stop you before you kill him again!" Ambrose hissed.

The sheriff held out his hand to the group.

"Somebody give me a gun," he said.

The security guard handed his gun to the sheriff. Mr. Henderson took Christopher's right hand. The doctor and Nurse Tammy took the left. Mrs. Keizer rose out of the drawer, the vertebrae of her spine curving like a vulture.

Ambrose backed through the crowd and joined the sheriff. They stood with their backs to the exit door. The rest of the morgue stood behind Christopher. The sheriff raised his gun.

"You brought this on yourself," the sheriff said. "This has to end now."

With those words, the sheriff pulled back the hammer and shot four times. Christopher felt the bullets whiz past his ears on their way to hitting the doctor, Nurse Tammy, Mr. Henderson, and Mrs. Keizer. The four fell back into the mob, blocking their way. The sheriff grabbed Christopher and brought him through the exit doors. Ambrose quickly locked the mob inside the morgue and turned to Christopher with a gentle hand on the shoulder.

"Come on. We need to get you out of here."

CHAPTER 112

Mary Katherine sat in the backseat of her father's Mercedes, looking out the window. It was quiet outside. The roads were empty. The Christmas lights twinkled on every house and storefront. But it didn't feel like Christmas. It felt eerie. Not a soul in sight. Just the smell of those fires far away. She would have said so, but her parents hadn't spoken a word since they took her out of the hospital, and she wasn't going to say the wrong thing to make them turn around now.

"We're here," her father said calmly.

The Mercedes turned into the church parking lot.

Mary Katherine looked up at the church. It was especially beautiful tonight. An oasis in the middle of the eerie night sky. Christmas was always such a special time for the family. For one day every year, her mother and father relaxed. Mom would have her red wine. Dad would have his eggnog, and he would get drunk enough to give her a hug.

The Mercedes parked in the family's usual spot.

"Let's go," her father said.

"But——" Mary Katherine said.

"But what?" her father said curtly.

Mary Katherine wanted to say that she was still in her hospital gown. She wanted to ask for a pair of shoes or a coat. But she was so afraid of rocking the boat that she didn't utter another word except . . .

"Nothing."

The three got out of the car. Mary Katherine walked behind her parents. The parking lot was chilly. The pavement and dirty snow freezing under her bare feet.

Mary Katherine knew something was terribly wrong, but she didn't want to go back to the hospital. She just wanted her parents to love her again. So, she focused on the church. It was silent inside even though the parking lot was filled with cars. The decorations were beautiful. She remembered being a little girl and making up stories about the people inside the stained-glass windows. They were her imaginary friends.

They arrived at the church.

They opened the door.

Mary Katherine looked inside. The church glowed with soft, warm candlelight. She saw the entire congregation gathered as if for midnight mass. But they weren't talking among themselves. They weren't singing with the choir. They weren't even kneeling in prayer.

They were just staring at her.

Mary Katherine searched the room for a friendly face. She recognized old classmates from youth group. Kids she'd known since CCD with their parents. The only person she still talked with was Doug, sitting there next to Debbie Dunham. Doug held Debbie's hand. His face looked wrong. As if there were needle marks around his mouth. This was all wrong. Mary Katherine instinctively backed away toward the door.

Until she ran into someone behind her.

"Mary Katherine," the voice said.

She turned to see her CCD teacher, Mrs. Radcliffe, smiling pleasantly.

"Don't be afraid. We're here to help you. We even saved you a seat," Mrs. Radcliffe said, gesturing.

Mary Katherine nodded and forced a smile. She didn't know what to do. So, she walked toward her family's usual spot in the second row.

"No. Not in the pews, dear," Mrs. Radcliffe corrected. "At the altar."

Mary Katherine turned to her father and mother for guidance. Her father looked stern. Her mother looked away nervously. Mrs. Radcliffe grabbed Mary Katherine's hand and gently led her to the altar. Mrs. Radcliffe's skin was blistering hot with fever.

"Get on your knees, dear," Mrs. Radcliffe said.

Mary Katherine turned to her mother, who couldn't bear to look back.

"Please get on your knees, Mary Katherine," her mother pleaded.

Mary Katherine knelt down. The pit inside her stomach fell lower. An itch broke out on her skin.

"Thank you, Mary Katherine. Now . . . confess," Mrs. Radcliffe said.

Mary Katherine began to stand. Mrs. Radcliffe put a feverish hand on her shoulder, keeping her on her knees.

"Where do you think you're going?" she asked.

"The confession booth," Mary Katherine replied.

"No. You will do it here," Mrs. Radcliffe said.

"Um . . . okay, Mrs. Radcliffe . . . but where is . . . where is Father Tom? He needs to hear my confession."

"Don't worry about Father Tom. You can confess to us."

Mary Katherine nodded. She was in terrible danger. She looked up at the beautiful statue of Jesus on the cross just as she had every Sunday she had ever known.

"Confess," Mrs. Radcliffe said gently.

Mary Katherine swallowed. The pit in her stomach grew. Out of the corner of her eye, she saw Mrs. Radcliffe walk to the side entrance of the church. She opened the door. Mary Katherine saw Father Tom lying on the sidewalk outside in the cold. He had been stabbed repeatedly. Heat rose from each cut like steam from a sewer grate.

"Who is the father, Mary Katherine?" Mrs. Radcliffe asked calmly.

Mrs. Radcliffe ripped the collection basket from Father Tom's hands. She began walking back into the church, passing around the collection basket.

"I don't know who the father is," Mary Katherine said.

Mary Katherine turned to her mother. Her mother looked terrified.

"Please, tell them, Mary Katherine," she begged.

"I can't tell them what I don't know."

"Please! Just tell them who the father is!"

"I don't know. I'm a virgin."

Mary Katherine turned back as the collection basket was passed around the room. But this time, the congregation wasn't putting money into the basket.

This time, they were taking out stones.

"TELL THEM! PLEASE!" Mary Katherine's mother screamed.

"Mom, I'm a virgin. Like Mary."

"Blasphemy!" the congregation shouted. "Confess!"

"Just give them a name, Mary Katherine!" her mother cried.

"Mom, don't make me lie in church. Please."

"CONFESS TO US! NOT HER!" Mrs. Radcliffe shouted.

Mrs. Radcliffe wrenched her head back to the altar. Mary Katherine knelt in her hospital gown. Her back exposed to the church. Freezing like Mary in the manger. Nothing but a slip of underwear. She heard the congregation rise out of the pews and stand behind her. The basket being passed down the row. Stones being picked like apples.

"Oh, Jesus. Help me," she prayed.

"Confess!" Mrs. Radcliffe shouted, throwing the first stone.

The stone shattered a stained-glass window in front of her.

"CONFESS!" the congregation echoed.

The word chanted over and over. Confess. Confess. Confess. Mary Katherine held her hands up above her head in surrender. She faced the congregation. The stones in their hands. Father Tom outside caked in blood. The flock had taken over. The lunatics were in charge of the asylum. Ready to stone her to death.

"OKAY! I'LL CONFESS! I'LL CONFESS!" Mary Katherine screamed.

The congregation went silent. Waiting. Mary Katherine turned to her mother.

"Mom," she said, her voice quivering. "I was going to be late that night."

When the truth came out of her mouth, Mary Katherine burst into tears.

"What?" her mother asked.

"The night I found Christopher. I wasn't going to make it home by midnight. I lied to you and Dad. I just didn't want to lose my license, so I lied. But it was wrong. I am being punished for it."

"That's not your sin. Who's the father?!" Mrs. Radcliffe screamed.

"Mom, if I hadn't lied about being late, you would have taken my license. And I never would have been on the road. I never would have turned away from the deer and hit that little boy with the car. I hurt a little boy because I was afraid of going to Hell. I was selfish. THAT is my sin. But I swear . . . I don't know who the father is. I swear on my soul that I am a virgin. Do you believe me?"

She looked at her mother through her tears. Her mother's face softened as if remembering the little girl she raised. She nodded.

"Yes, honey."

"Daddy?" she said.

"I believe you, Mary Katherine," her father said.

The dam inside her broke as the congregation moved closer, the stones raised for death.

"DAN!" her mother screamed.

Her father's instincts returned in an instant. He ran to protect his little girl, but the congregation jumped on him and beat him bloody.

"Leave my family alone!" her mother screamed as the congregation wrestled her to the ground.

Mary Katherine ran to help her parents, but Mrs. Radcliffe and Debbie Dunham grabbed her. They stood her up in front of the cross.

"Doug," they hissed. "It's time."

Doug rose from the pews. His eyes were black and distant. Insane. He held a stone in his hands.

"Doug! Please help us!"

Doug said nothing. He just walked to her. Mary Katherine looked at her boyfriend with tears in her eyes. That face she had loved since they were eleven years old. She saw the marks around his mouth. Little pieces of yarn hanging out of his skin. He covered his mouth self-consciously until he realized she wasn't looking at him like a monster.

"What did they do to you, Doug?" she asked, concerned.

"Don't listen to her. She made you look like a fool, Doug," Debbie Dunham said.

"Stone her, Doug," Mrs. Radcliffe hissed. "Stone the whore!"

The congregation spoke as one. "Stone her. Stone her." All of his friends from CCD and youth group chanted his name. Doug held the stone and looked Mary Katherine in the eyes.

"I love you, Doug," she said. "I forgive you."

He looked at her with tears in his black eyes. He raised the stone above his head and threw it as hard as he could.

Right into the middle of Mrs. Radcliffe's forehead.

"RUN!" he screamed.

Doug threw his car key into her hand and turned to block the mob. Mary Katherine raced into the parking lot from the side exit. The lot was so packed, she couldn't find Doug's car. A terrifying scream rose up from inside the church. She heard stones shattering the stained glass. She hit the panic button. Doug's car flashed to life on the far end of the parking lot.

Mary Katherine ran to the car, her bare feet cut on stones and gravel. She opened the car and turned the key in the ignition. The motor froze in the cold.

The congregation crashed through the main doors into the parking lot. They raced toward her. Screaming. She turned the key again. The engine roared to life. She threw it in drive and hurtled through the parking lot. The congregation threw stones, shattering the windshield. Mary Katherine turned onto the road. She saw the congregation in the rearview mirror. Car doors opened. Headlights came to life like sick, glowing eyes.

"Please, Jesus," she said. "Help us."

CHAPTER 113

Ambrose and the sheriff ran down the hall. Christopher limp in the sheriff's arms. Ambrose could hear the people locked in the morgue behind them. Banging on the doors. Breaking glass with their bare hands. The sheriff held on to Christopher a little tighter as they ran faster than Ambrose had ever run in his life. It was more than fear. More than adrenaline. He had run for his life before. But this speed didn't come from him.

It came from Christopher.

An hour ago, the sheriff had been in a hospital bed with a gunshot wound in his chest. Ambrose had been crippled and blind on a slab in the morgue. Now, Ambrose was moving like a man half his age, and the sheriff was sprinting like a man who had never felt better. The only thing they had come into contact with was Christopher's hand. One touch, and they looked like they could take on an army by themselves.

But Christopher looked like he was dying.

"We need a car! Follow me!" Ambrose yelled.

Ambrose ran ahead, opening the door for Christopher and the sheriff. He still couldn't believe what was happening. The last thing he remembered was a plastic mask thrown over his mouth. The next thing he knew, he felt a child's hand on his own, generating heat that moved up his arm to his neck, finally settling

On his eyes.

There had been no surgery. But he still saw halos around lights as bright as an eclipse. He felt like a soldier again, dissecting the hospital like a battlefield in war. He never thought he would be grateful for all those trips to the eye surgeon, but he may as well have been a spy for how well he knew this place. The back doors. The shortcuts. The basement corridors that led to the laundry. His men were outnumbered, but he could force the enemy into a bottleneck.

He had done it before.

Ambrose led them to the back staircase. They sprinted up the stairs toward the garage floor.

Click went the door above them.

Mr. Collins stood there, holding a nail gun from his construction site. At least two dozen people behind him.

Click went the door below.

The people from the morgue looked up the stairs. Their hands torn apart from breaking through the glass.

Ambrose led the sheriff up. They had to get to the garage floor first. A terrifying screech echoed off the staircase as Mr. Collins began running full speed down the stairs with the people from the morgue running up.

Ambrose reached the garage floor and ripped open the emergency door. The alarm shrieked through the hospital. They ran down the empty hallway, the two mobs narrowing into a single line behind them. Two fronts now one. The perfect bottleneck. Ambrose led them to a fork in the hall. He was about to turn right when suddenly, Christopher whispered,

"Go left."

The sheriff made a hard left, and Ambrose followed. He looked back, seeing the ambush crash into the hallway behind them. Somehow, the boy had known. Ambrose turned to Christopher. Blood dripping from his nose and eyes like tears. They came to another fork.

"Go right," he said weakly.

Ambrose turned right. Christopher led them down a labyrinth of back hallways and side doors. Putting some distance between them and the mob. They finally reached the back entrance to the parking garage. They closed the door behind them.

The parking garage was empty.

The silence was eerie. Their footsteps echoed off the cement walls. The sheriff instinctively began to run down the ramp toward the exit.

"They're waiting for us down there," Christopher said.

"Then go to the roof," Ambrose said.

"They're up there, too," Christopher said.

"We need a diversion," Ambrose said. "Follow me."

He began to sprint. Legs and lungs straining. Ambrose ran through the garage, kicking cars, setting off alarms. How many times had he set off munitions to serve as a diversion? He never thought he would do it again. Especially with a Ford. He led them into the maternity ward entrance, leaving behind a half dozen blaring alarms. The three ran down the hallway. Past the nursery. All of the babies were crying. They reached the first fork.

"Which way, Christopher? Left or right?"

*

Christopher closed his eyes. He didn't need to use them anymore. He just felt the people's rage like white-hot fever on his skin. The screaming tore itself through his mind as the mob tore apart the shrieking cars in the parking lot looking for them. The headache pounding like blood trying to claw its way out of his veins. The imaginary world and the real were the same to him now. He didn't know where he was.

"Which way, Christopher?!" the sheriff screamed.

Christopher opened his eyes and saw nothing but dark angry space. There were too many voices now. Bodies running through the parking lot. Others scattered through the hospital. The mobs like tumors in the hallways all around them. There was so much darkness, he didn't know which direction to run.

"He's slipping," Christopher heard Ambrose say.

"Christopher, can you hear us?" said the sheriff.

Christopher could say nothing. There was too much rage to guide them through it. They were enveloped by darkness. There was no light left in the world.

Except one.

In the middle of all that hatred, he felt a light. Warm and kind. It was racing to the hospital.

It was his mother.

He could follow his mother's light.

"My mother is coming for us. Go to the ER," Christopher whispered.

"But—" Ambrose cautioned.

"Trust me," Christopher said.

So they did. They made a hard turn back into the belly of the beast. Christopher felt the light getting closer. His mother was coming. He could feel Mr. Collins crash into the maternity ward behind them. They turned the corner into the ER. It was flooded with people, angry after waiting a week for a bed that would never be empty again. The vending machines were now debris on the ground. People sifted through the rubble. Looking for food. Looking for drink. Looking for vengeance. When they saw Christopher, the ER opened into a primal scream and joined the chase.

The three rushed outside into the icy parking lot. The storm swirled above them. A big angry sky filled with clouds. Giant faces moaning.

"Mr. Olson! Look out!" Christopher screamed as Mrs. Keizer rushed at them.

"Help my daughter forget her name!" she screamed.

The old woman raised a scalpel. Ambrose reached out and grabbed her before she could stab Christopher. Mrs. Keizer slipped on black ice, landing on her hip, which cracked like a wishbone. A scream rose from the other direction. Mrs. Collins wheezing through her paint-coated lungs.

"Look what you did to my mother! Give my mother back her name!"

The sheriff turned as Mrs. Collins charged from the other direction in a wheelchair. She ran her hands quickly over the wheels, then jumped up onto her feet and broke into a dead sprint. She raised a scalpel. The sheriff winced as the scalpel sliced into his side. He dropped Christopher and fell to his knees. Bleeding profusely. Mrs. Collins inched toward Christopher. Coughing and hacking white sludge. Nothing could stop her.

Except Christopher's mother.

Kate Reese reached over and turned Jerry's truck on the black ice. The truck slammed into Mrs. Collins, who flew backward across the icy parking lot. Christopher's mother threw open the passenger door and rushed to her son.

"Help me, Jerry!" she screamed.

Jerry left the engine running and jumped out of the truck. He ran behind Kate. Gun reloaded and drawn. Firing at everyone to save Kate Reese as she ran to save her son. She grabbed Christopher and raced him back to the truck. Ambrose and the sheriff behind her. She laid her son in the passenger seat and jumped into the driver's just as the sheriff and Ambrose climbed into the flatbed with Jerry. Mr. Collins led the mob out of the hospital and ran at Christopher in the passenger side, his nail gun raised.

Bang.

The last bullet left the sheriff's gun. Mr. Collins fell backward next to his wife and her mother. The truck powered through the black ice, and Christopher's mother raced her son away from the hospital.

"Are you okay?" she asked.

Christopher looked up and smiled at his mother, who didn't know she was covered in the light from one hundred billion stars.

CHAPTER 114

The sheriff looked back as the hospital emptied itself into the parking lot like a rattlesnake uncoiling. He turned and saw Kate Reese hold the wheel with her left hand. Her son with the right. She looked down at her little boy, sick and pale.

"You hang in there," she said.

Kate reached into the glove compartment and found a box of ammunition. She handed it back to the sheriff in the flatbed of the truck. She said nothing. She merely nodded to him through the rearview mirror. The sheriff nodded back and watched as she returned her eyes to the road.

He promised himself that if they lived, he would ask that woman to marry him.

Suddenly, the sheriff felt Ambrose Olson tighten the field dressing for the scalpel wound in his side. The sheriff winced. His teeth chattered.

"Are you cold?" Ambrose said.

"No. I feel warm, actually," the sheriff said.

"You're going into shock."

Ambrose quickly rummaged through Jerry's pickup and found coveralls and an old construction jacket.

"What about you?" the sheriff said.

"I'm fine."

The sheriff knew the old man wasn't lying. Ambrose should have been freezing in those hospital clothes, but somehow he felt no cold. Somehow as the world went insane around them, he and Ambrose were both immune to the madness. He didn't know if this protection was from Christopher or David.

Or maybe both.

Whatever it was, he only felt the warmth from the fresh clothes and a sense of loyalty to the little boy in the passenger seat and his mother in the driver's. Ambrose did not speak of the brother he could not save. The sheriff said nothing of the little girl with painted nails who called him Daddy. But he knew the two men understood each other.

For all of their failures, they were going to save Christopher and his mother.

Or they were going to die trying.

"Hi, Christopher," the voice said.

The sheriff watched as Christopher looked up at Jerry, crouched in the back of the flatbed. His chin on the small window partition. The gun in his hand.

"Cat got your tongue?" he said, laughing. "Don't worry. I've already worked it out with your mom. We are going to be a family. Her, me, and you are driving to Michigan now. Right, Kate?"

The sheriff saw Christopher choke down a swallow.

"Right, Jerry, we're going to Michigan," she said, her body tensing.

Jerry smiled. He looked back at the descending mob trailing in their cars. He turned to the sheriff shivering under the blanket and Ambrose in the hospital gown.

"Hey, Kate, who's that?" Jerry asked.

"Mr. Olson," she said absently.

"No. Not the old man. Who's that?" he said, gesturing to the sheriff with his gun.

"The sheriff."

"Huh. How do you know him?" Jerry asked.

"He helped us."

"Why?"

"That's his job."

"Hmmm," Jerry said with a coiled smile. "Does he come over a lot?"

The sheriff could feel the silence. Eerie and black.

"No, Jerry," she said.

"Christopher, does the sheriff come over to your house a lot?" he asked.

"Leave him out of this," she said.

Jerry nodded. Smiling. Silently. Then, he turned to the sheriff and Ambrose.

"Great family, right?" he said.

The sheriff and Ambrose nodded to the man in the flatbed with them. The sheriff instantly recognized the face. He remembered researching this man as a suspect when Christopher first went missing back in September. He remembered the domestic abuse. The violence. This was the animal who hit the woman he loved. The sheriff looked at the gun in Jerry's right hand. The sheriff's gun was still empty.

"The best," the sheriff said. "Who are you?"

"Jerry. I'm Kate's fiancé."

The sheriff offered his hand. Jerry moved the gun from his right hand to his left. The two men never taking their eyes off each other. Never blinking.

"And who are you?" Jerry replied suspiciously.

"Ambrose Olson," Ambrose said, shoving his hand into the mix like a salesman's foot in the door.

"I wasn't talking to you, old man," Jerry said. "I was talking to him."

"I'm Sheriff Thompson," the sheriff said.

Then, he took Jerry's hand. The two men shook.

"Are you fucking her, Sheriff?" Jerry said.

Before Jerry knew what hit him, the sheriff did. He planted the butt of his palm in his throat. Jerry landed in the flatbed. Writhing in pain. Furious, he grabbed his gun and rose up.

"I knew you were fucking him!" Jerry screamed.

Then, the sheriff saw the reflection of Kate's eyes in the rearview mirror.

"Goodbye, Jerry," she said.

She slammed the brakes. The truck stopped, but Jerry kept going. His body slammed into the cab. He doubled over.

"Fucking bitch!" he said.

In another split second, Kate Reese hit the gas, and the sheriff watched Jerry tumble out of the back of the flatbed. He hit the pavement and rolled down the side of the road.

The hospital convoy passed him as dozens of cars chased after them. The quiet was over.

Here came the storm.

CHAPTER 115

Christopher's mother looked up as a gust of angry wind spread the clouds over the town. The wind blew the trees over. The branches fell like severed arms, blocking the road ahead. She took a hard left through a front yard. Cars tangled in the trees behind her, slowing down the assault. Her mind raced. She had to get to the highway. She turned on the radio, desperately searching for a traffic report.

"...a great snowstorm through the tristate area..."

"...Bad Cat 3D now on video is the purrrfect last-minute Christmas present..."

"...blue moon I saw you standing alone..."

"...what is being called the refugee war in the Middle East..."

"...local traffic every fifteen minutes on the hour..."

She stopped the dial and turned up the volume.

"Traffic through the Fort Pitt Tunnel is jammed. Excellent work. We can't let them escape. They are trying to get to 79. So, look for them around the high school."

Christopher's mother quickly did a 180 and turned away from the high school. There had to be one path open. She had to find it.

"They did a U-turn," the radio voice said. "They are turning away from the high school."

Christopher's mother looked through the windshield and saw the cars back on her tail. They were hurtling toward the truck. She was never going to be able to outrun them.

"Turn off your headlights, Mom," Christopher said weakly.

"What?" she said.

"Don't worry. I'll tell you where to go."

Without a moment's hesitation, Christopher's mother turned off the headlights. The DJ's voice crackled through the radio.

"We lost them. They might be able to hear us. Go to the alternate station."

The radio went dead. Christopher closed his eyes and began to describe what he saw. Christopher's mother could almost see it. A giant maze of streets filled with cars, searching for them like the ghosts in Pac-Man. Jerry wiping the blood from his road rash. Hitching a ride from the caravan. Hell-bent on finding her. And killing her in front of the sheriff.

"Turn left," Christopher said, coughing blood into his hand.

Christopher's mother made a left. Then, a sharp right. Whatever he said, she did blindly. She looked in the rearview mirror. They were starting to lose the hospital mob. It was working. They were going to make it. She turned back to the front windshield. Her eyes adjusted to the blue moonlight. She floored the gas pedal as deer began to crawl into front yards and driveways. Behind bushes and trees. Waiting for the order to strike.

A deer ran in front of the car.

She slammed on the brakes, and the truck skidded in the snow. Christopher's mother turned into the skid. She straightened out and raced toward Route 19. She saw the on-ramp right in front of her. There was still a chance.

"Go straight, Mom. Faster," Christopher said.

The deer broke through the yards ahead of them. Christopher's mother floored the truck, trying to make it to the on-ramp before the deer overtook it. The speed climbed. The wind howled. The entire street began to fill with cars all converging on that one intersection.

Christopher's mother pushed on the pedal so hard, she thought her foot would break through the floor. They barreled toward the on-ramp, but the cars beat them to it. Colliding in an explosion of glass, metal, and flesh.

Their escape route was blocked.

"Where do we go now, Christopher?!" she asked.

Christopher was silent.

"We need to get to the highway. Where do we go?!"

"The highway is gone," he said.

The news hit all of them. Without the highway, the town may as well be an island. They were stuck in Mill Grove. Kate Reese's mind raced. There had to be a way out on surface streets. They could get to a neighboring town. Things would be better in Peters Township or Bethel Park or Canonsburg.

i will never let hIm leave, kate.

She shook off the voice and kept driving. The snow fell, making the streets slick like glass. Everywhere she went was a new dead end. An abandoned car. A fallen tree. Roads turned into parking lots. Everywhere she drove, the car simply returned to the streets she knew all too well.

They were driving back to their neighborhood.

They were going to the Mission Street Woods.

i will kIll him, kate.

"Where do we go, Christopher?!"

"There is nowhere to go, Mom," he said weakly.

"Yes, there is!"

Christopher touched her leg with his hand, burning with what felt like a 108-degree fever.

"He will never let me leave, Mom," Christopher said.

The deer galloped like horses with an invisible rider. Dozens of them broke through the lawns. There were too many of them. Christopher's mother refused to accept the inevitable.

The deer were going to overtake the car.

i'm going to kill your son now, katE.

Christopher's mother raced to the crossroads. A stampede of deer charged in front of them. Dozens more charged from behind.

There was no escape. It was over.

They were never going to survive.

CHAPTER 116

Mary Katherine slammed her foot on the gas pedal. The engine redlined. There was no extra gear. No extra speed. She looked in the rearview. The congregation chased her. Blaring their horns. Stones in their hands.

"Jesus, please save us," she cried.

A deer ran from the woods. Mary Katherine screamed. She swerved left, barely missing the deer. Barely missing Hell. Terror gripped her heart.

"God, why is this happening?"

The voices on the wind wailed as the snow fell from the sky. The world was coming to an end. She knew it. This was the end. She turned sharply toward Route 19. The highway that she was never allowed to drive on. Another deer raced in front of her. Mary Katherine skidded right, barely missing it.

"God, why are You letting this happen?"

Two more deer ran into the road, blocking her from turning onto Route 19. God wasn't going to let her escape this time. She had sinned too greatly. He was going to force her into hitting a deer. He was going to force her into Hell. She gunned the car up the hill. The blue moon hung on the horizon like an angry eye.

"What did I do to deserve this?"

It started as a dark little seed in her heart. Every question she never dared speak. Every doubt she ever had.

"I told my mother the truth. What else did I do? I didn't do anything. I know I thought about it, but thinking it is not the same as doing it. It's not fair. Why do You give us bodies we don't get to use? And we can't even think about it? I don't understand. I have confessed every sin. And it's still not good enough?"

The cars flew behind her. Horns blaring. She saw the deer creeping out from behind houses on both sides of the road. Her lips curled up in anger.

"Well, what the hell is that about? I'm sorry, but why did You make these rules that no one can follow? Why do you give us these tests that we can only fail?! Well, do You want to know what I think?! I think when Eve bit the apple, she didn't commit the original sin. YOU did!"

Mary Katherine was so angry she didn't know how to stop it. She felt more horrible with each word. But it was intoxicating at the same time.

"You didn't have to banish her! She loved You! You were her Father! When you love someone, you don't test them. You trust them. You talk to them. And You never talk to me! You just sit there silent, and I do all the talking. I do all the work, and You do nothing! And I'm supposed to feel bad for YOU?!"

Mary Katherine looked up at the sky. The clouds like angry faces.

"I did everything You told me! I believed everything You said! I prayed to You every day, and to thank me, You had my parents bring me to a stoning?! You had me get on my knees in front of You?! Why do You want me on my knees?! Why don't you want me on my feet?! What the hell are You afraid of?"

Mary Katherine hit the next street.

"God, please make me understand because I am starting to hate You, and I never want to hate You! I need You to talk to me this time! I can't do it by myself! I know You keep silent because of free will, but You can't this time! I've lost everything. My mother. My father. My boyfriend. My priest. Church. Home. Town. Freedom. And I deserve an answer. TALK TO ME, GOD DAMMIT! WHY DID YOU DO THIS TO ME?!"

Because I don't love you, Mary Katherine.

The voice was so calm. So sure. So gentle.

"What?" Mary Katherine asked.

I don't love you.

Mary Katherine felt a chill crawl down her spine. She saw the deer running out of the woods up ahead. Ready to hurl themselves in front of her car.

"You're not God," she said.

I am God, Mary Katherine.

"God loves everyone, so you can't be God. You're the devil."

Mary Katherine thought about her plight, and it suddenly dawned on her.

"And I'm not the Virgin Mary," she said plainly. "I'm Job."

Mary Katherine looked up ahead. She saw a truck barreling down a side street. Dozens of deer were chasing the truck. Her car raced toward the intersection at a ninety-degree angle. Somehow, she knew who was inside that truck.

It was the little boy.

Christopher.

Mary Katherine realized it was all a test. Three times she drove near Christopher. Three times she was brought to a crossroads. The first time, she stopped at the stop sign. The second time, she barreled into the little boy. And this was the third. The holy trinity.

Father. Son. Holy Spirit.

Ice. Water. Clouds.

She didn't know why God needed to test her, but she knew the world was ending, and He didn't have a lot of soldiers left. She was just one dot of paint on His massive canvas.

And it wasn't about her, was it?

Mary Katherine wasn't kept alive for herself. She was kept alive for Christopher. The minute she understood that, the voice went away. The imposter was gone.

And a great comfort fell over her.

She realized that she was living everything she had ever feared. She was pregnant. Shunned. Hunted. Hell had come to Earth. She was in the valley of the shadow of death.

But she feared no evil because the Lord was with her.

The car raced to the crossroads. There was no way out. She either had to hit the deer or let them rip Christopher to pieces. Mary Katherine lowered her head.

"Jesus, I am a sinner. I am vain. I am narcissistic. And my biggest sin was that I have been so afraid of You that I never really loved You until this moment. But I'm not afraid anymore because heaven and hell are not destinations. They are decisions."

Christopher's truck ran through the intersection. Her car flew down the street.

"I love You, Jesus," she said.

Mary Katherine turned the wheel and barreled through the herd of stampeding deer. The car buckled under the weight. Antlers ripped through the windshield and windows. Then, they ripped through her flesh. The car rolled a dozen times before finally landing on four thrashed tires. Mary Katherine looked through the blood running past her eyes at Christopher and his mother racing away. For the moment, they were safe.

Mary Katherine smiled.

"Take care of them, Jesus," she said.

Before she went unconscious, she could feel Him sitting next to her. His hand as warm as the blood running down her arm. She felt at peace because she would believe in Him for the rest of her life. Not out of fear. But out of love.

Mary Katherine was free.

CHAPTER 117

Christopher's mother looked through the rearview mirror as Mary Katherine's car flipped down the road. The girl had saved them from the deer.

They still had a chance to escape.

She floored the truck. The Mission Street Woods loomed in the distance. She saw doors open and dozens of mailbox people run into the street from the houses. Screaming.

"... Givvve him toooo ussssss ..."

She looked in the rearview mirror. The mailbox people began to crest the hill. They were coming from everywhere. Clogging every road like the arteries of a man minutes before a fatal heart attack. There was no street left.

Except one.

Monterey Drive.

For a moment, she remembered turning onto this road with their real estate agent back in September. For the first time, she would have her very own house. She could finally give her little boy a safe home with a good school and good friends. She looked down at Christopher. He was pale as a ghost. Blood pouring from his nose.

"I will never let them take you," she said.

She looked ahead at the Mission Street Woods as the clouds moved like a cancer across the sky. The fog coming to take back the earth and drown it in floods. The whole world was being replaced by its own shadow. She felt no fear for anything other than her son. She would live for him and die for him and kill for him. She would do anything to keep him alive.

They reached the cul-de-sac. She slammed the brakes and picked up her little boy's sick body like a rag doll.

We can escape on foot.

There's still a chance.

Christopher's mother carried him from the truck. Ambrose jumped out of the flatbed. He helped the sheriff to his feet. The sheriff winced, the wound coming apart in his side. The four stood in the cul-de-sac as the clouds rolled toward them like a battleship. The thickest fog she had ever seen. Cars appeared in the distance, their headlights illuminating the street like a ghostly lantern. Garage doors opened. Mailbox people appeared on the horizon. Their screams traveling down the street like a game of telephone. Running at them full speed. They were surrounded. Backed into a corner.

They had nowhere to go but the Mission Street Woods.

They ran off the cul-de-sac. Across the field. The clouds made a thick fog, glowing in the blue moonlight. All visibility died. Christopher's mother heard the voices getting stronger. People pouring into the woods from every angle.

"Where do we go, Christopher?" she asked.

Her son held her a little tighter. Terrified.

"The Collins family parked near the construction site," he said in a hoarse whisper. "Mr. Henderson entered the woods from the north with the doctor and Nurse Tammy. The car that picked up Jerry just stopped. Jerry just ran into the woods with a gun, Mom."

Christopher's mother rushed on with her son in her arms. Ambrose and the sheriff at her side. The trees whipped by at a staggering pace. She couldn't see where they were going. But she knew Christopher could. All the eyes. The people watching. The woodland creatures. The birds. The nice man had eyes everywhere.

It would take a miracle for them to escape.

CHAPTER 118

Ambrose looked through the halos in his eyes. He saw the frozen path ahead of him. His feet pounded the snow with every step. Something compelled him to run. Faster. The smell of baseball gloves. The voice in his mind.

My brother went into these woods fifty years ago.

I can still save my brother.

The fog was unworldly. He could barely see an inch in front of his face. But the old soldier knew that camouflage works both ways. If he couldn't see them, they couldn't see him, either. He finally caught the silhouette of a child running up ahead. Ambrose turned back.

"Sheriff, did you see that?" he asked.

But the sheriff was gone.

"Sheriff?" he repeated.

Ambrose stopped. He could hear nothing but his own heart pounding. He searched the halos in his eyes, but he could see nothing but fog all around him.

"Mrs. Reese? Christopher?"

It was dead silent. He couldn't see Mrs. Reese or her little boy. Somehow, Ambrose had run too far. Too fast. He had lost them. He was all alone. Suddenly, he felt the wind on his neck.

"Ammmmbrrroooseeee," the wind whispered. "ittt'ssss daaaavvviiiddddd."

Ambrose listened to the wind, his heart gripped with terror and hope in equal measure.

"David?" he said.

"yesssSsssss," the wind whispered.

"Where are you?"

"hhhheEeeErrrreeee," the wind said.

Ambrose felt a chill on his skin. The mist of the clouds danced down the path, the fog floating like smoke from his father's old pipe.

"hheelllllppppp meeee, ammbrrosseee," the mist pleaded.

Ambrose followed the voice. Even with the halos in his eyes, all he could see was the fog in every direction. He heard whispers around him. Something was in here. He didn't know what, but he could feel it. This little whisper on the hairs on the back of his neck.

He heard a footstep.

"thhhheyyyy'rrreee cominngggg ammmbrrrosssse," the wind wheezed through the branches.

Another footstep.

Ambrose picked up his pace. He moved through the fog as the wind got louder around him. It sounded like the woods were taking a deep breath through lungs filled with paint.

Another footstep.

Something was running straight at him.

The branches suddenly disappeared. There were no more trees above him. Just the blue moon, lighting the fog like a lantern above a massive clearing. Ambrose saw a trace of something. The outline of a body. It could be a deer. One of those people. He squinted through the halos in his eyes and finally saw what it was.

A little boy ran past him.

"David!" he screamed.

But the little boy did not stop. He was not David. Another boy ran past him, chasing the first and screaming.

"It's ours! We built it!"

The boys sprinted through the clearing. Right past a giant shadow in the fog. At first, Ambrose could not make out the shape. It seemed too impossibly big. He took a few steps closer and finally recognized what it was.

A tree.

Every instinct in Ambrose's body told him to run away from that tree. But his feet kept going toward it. Toward the voice.

"David?" he said.

"iii'mmm upppp heeerrreee," the wind howled.

He knew he could be walking into an ambush. He knew it probably wasn't true. The voice wasn't David. But something compelled him to take the next step. The thought Christopher had planted in his mind.

I can still save my brother.

The wind whipped through the branches. Ambrose could make out the faint outline of a rope ladder leading up to what looked like a tree house.

"heelllllppppp! hellllpppppp!" the voice whispered from above.

Ambrose began to climb. He looked up into the trapdoor above. The light glowed inside the tree house. David could be behind that door. Somewhere. He could be in that tree house. Ambrose could finally know what happened to his little brother.

"helllllpppp meeee ammmmbrossssse! helllpppp!" the little voice called.

Ambrose reached the tree house. He climbed up through the trapdoor. Something pulled at the rope ladder below him. Giggling. Climbing. Ambrose slammed the trapdoor shut. The tree house went pitch black. He could see nothing in the room. His hands groped the wall, hoping to find a lantern or a flashlight.

He heard breathing in the room.

"ambbbbbbrossse . . ." the voice whispered from the darkness.

"David?" he said.

The voice did not speak. Ambrose's hand trembled along the wall. He finally found something. A plastic bump. It was a light switch. The hair on his neck stood up. It didn't make any sense. Why was there a light switch in a tree house?

"ambbbbbbrossssse . . ." the voice whispered. "doooo yooouuu wannnt toooo know????"

Ambrose searched the darkness. The wind stopped howling. And started hissing.

"doooo yooouuu wannnt toooo seeeeeee wherreee heeee issssss?"

Ambrose swallowed past the dry lump in his throat.

"jussssttttt turn on the lighttttt."

Ambrose braced his body, his face flush with terror.

"turnnnn onnn theeee lighttt, ammbrossssssSeeee."

Ambrose turned on the light. He wasn't in the tree house anymore.

CHAPTER 119

Christopher clung to his mother as she carried him through the fog, her feet pounding the mud back into the earth. The sheriff ran next to them, wincing from the pain in his side.

"Christopher, where do we go?" she asked.

Christopher closed his eyes and looked for a way out. He saw nothing but darkness. Ambrose was lost. They were being cornered. Forced like rats through a maze. His mother's light was all that remained.

"Run past the bridge, Mom," he whispered.

Christopher felt the billy goat bridge ahead of them. He knew a way out of the woods from the bridge even if he couldn't see it. They could still make it. He could still save his mom. They passed the billy goat bridge. Christopher looked into her light. There was a path back to his house. As long as they had the tree house, he could always find the way out of the woods.

but i have the tree house now.

The voice tapped on the glass inside his mind. Suddenly the world went silent. His mother's footsteps disappeared.

i'm waiting for you.

Christopher looked down the path just as they passed the billy goat bridge again.

"We just passed that bridge," his mother said, confused.

"Where are we?!" the sheriff asked.

"Turn around, Mom," Christopher said.

She raced past the billy goat bridge again. Running faster and faster down the path to their house.

Until they passed the bridge again.

you will never leave, christopher.

Everywhere they turned, they just ended up going back into the woods. Deeper and deeper. The shadow all around them. The voices in the fog. Hunting them. He remembered how the cloud lured him into the woods for the first time. He remembered when the child cried and then giggled. The child ran on all fours.

Like a deer.

There were two children on the path ahead of them. The children didn't move. They just stood there.

"Mike! Matt! It's me!" Christopher called out.

The boys turned around. Their eyes and mouths stitched together. They pointed and screamed through the thread.

"...HISTOPHER!"

The M&M's ran straight at them. Christopher's mother turned off the path. He could hear the pounding of feet coming at them. Hundreds of townspeople hunting them like rabbits. Jenny Hertzog and her stepbrother Scott jumped out with knives. Ms. Lasko ran behind with a broken bottle, scratching her own skin like a junkie. Christopher's mother raced down the path, but there was no escape anymore. There was only the instinct to survive. The people were everywhere in the fog. Christopher could feel their rage. The woods were scorching with it. The voices were getting closer. The wind carried the chant.

"Death is coming. Death is here. You'll die on Christmas Day."

He felt Jerry running through the woods with a gun. The Collins family carrying saws and hammers from the construction site. The nice man's voice twisted people's minds like a knife. The blood ran from Christopher's nose and eyes. His body getting hotter with every new voice. Every new person running through the woods.

"Mom," he said weakly. "You have to save yourself."

"No!" she screamed as her legs found another gear. "Tell me where to go!"

"There is nowhere to go, Mom."

But she kept running. She would never give up. She looked for a tree to hide behind or climb, but suddenly, there were no trees. There was only light and fog. Christopher looked up and saw the moon. Brilliant and blue.

Twigs cracked all around them. The voices came from all directions. Chanting.

"Death is coming. Death is here. You'll die on Christmas Day."

A body came out of nowhere and jumped on the sheriff. Christopher's mother turned. The sheriff was gone. She cried out for him.

"Death is coming. Death is here. You'll die on Christmas Day," the voices chanted. Getting closer.

Christopher searched his mother's light, but he could see nothing but clouds. Nothing but darkness. The chanting turned into a single voice on the wind.

death is coming. death is here. you'll die on christmas day.

The voice blew the wind through the woods and took the fog with it. Great twisting tornadoes carried the clouds back into the sky like a giant exhale. There were no more branches. No more trees. Except one.

They were in the clearing.

They were surrounded by the entire town. The sheriff had been thrown to the ground next to the tree. Every inch of the clearing was filled with a townsperson.

The tree house was lost.

There was no escape.

The mailbox people pulled out knives and rocks. Guns were pointed at Christopher from every angle. Christopher's mother stood in front of him.

"Stand back!" she screamed.

The mob kept coming. Mrs. Henderson stepped to the front of the pack. Mrs. Collins walked next to her husband, her lungs wet and wheezing. Mrs. Keizer limped on her shattered hip. Christopher began to tremble in his mother's arms.

"Mom! They don't want you! They only want me! Please, run!"

She held him tighter and stood her ground. The mob walked closer. She backed up toward the tree. The sheriff staggered to his feet.

"Everyone back!" the sheriff yelled. "I am still the law!"

The mob stepped closer. Walking as one. Breathing as one. Christopher looked into the faces of the people drowning in their own fear and hatred. The pain was too much. He stumbled against the tree and fell backward when he saw the most terrifying sight of all.

Special Ed and Brady Collins.

The little boys raced into the middle of the clearing, their guns drawn. Their eyes white with murder. Each spoke in the voice of his grandmother.

"Brady is going to kill your mother, Eddie! Shoot him!" Special Ed said.

"Special Ed is going to kill your mother, Brady! Shoot him!" Brady Collins said.

In the final moment, they raised their guns and pointed them at what they thought was each other.

But the guns were pointed directly at Christopher.

"Listen to Grandma!" they said in unison.

And each boy pulled the trigger.

Christopher closed his eyes, waiting for the bullets to strike.

But the bullets never reached him.

Somebody got in the way.

It was the sheriff.

He threw himself in front of Christopher and his mother, taking the two bullets in his shoulder and back. He fell to the ground. The sheriff reached up for Christopher's mother. His eyes lost like a child left alone. He tried to say her name, but the words caught under the blood in his mouth. He fought to stay awake. Stay alive. For her. For her son. She cried out his name just as he collapsed, bleeding and unconscious. The mob screamed in unison just as Jerry ran to the front of the crowd. Jerry looked at Christopher, his face twisting into a jealous rage.

"You took her from me," he said. "She can only love one of us."

Jerry raised his gun at Christopher.

Christopher's mother grabbed him and threw him to the ground. Christopher felt her wrap her body around him like a blanket just as Jerry opened fire. The bullet ripped through her body.

But nothing touched her son.

Nothing but her light.

Christopher saw her light flash before him. One hundred billion pictures of a little girl thrown away by the world. The girl became a young woman through sheer force of will. The young woman met a man who was kind to her. The woman saw that man give up in a bathtub. But he gave her a son.

Her son was her light.

Christopher looked into his mother's eyes. He could see with her light. He could see the answer. As long as she had that light, there would always be a chance.

The light began to dim.

"No, Mom!" he cried.

Her body started to give. Blood ran from her nose.

"Please, don't go!"

The candle flickered in the wind of the hurricane.

"I love you, Christopher," she whispered.

Then, the light of one hundred billion stars burned out.

CHAPTER 120

Christopher closed his eyes. The only sound his tears.

"Wake up, Mom. Please, wake up."

He held her body close to his, praying that his fever was warm enough to heal her. The mob kept coming. Christopher heard them loading their guns one bullet at a time.

"Don't go," he sobbed. "Please, don't go."

Suddenly the mob wrenched her body from him and stood him up against the tree. They weren't people anymore. They were a hive. The rage pushed their fingers against the triggers. But they didn't point their guns at Christopher. They pointed them at his mother. Christopher held up his hand and screamed,

"LEAVE MY MOTHER ALONE!"

Christopher's voice boomed through the clearing. The mob froze, terrified. Their trigger fingers stopped for a moment. Then, Christopher felt a little prickle on his hair like static electricity from a balloon. He watched in horror as Mrs. Henderson spoke with a strange calmness, as if she were a ventriloquist's dummy.

"What do you mean leave her alone, Christopher?" Mrs. Henderson said.

But it wasn't Mrs. Henderson's voice.

It was the nice man's.

"Don't you understand? This will never stop," the nice man said through Jenny Hertzog.

"This is eternIty," Brady Collins mimed. "I can make them do anything."

Brady ran at Christopher's mother, pulling the hammer back on his gun. Brady was about to pull the trigger when he froze. The whole group spoke at the same time. Every voice belonged to the nice man. The town was his conduit. A thousand stereo speakers.

"I will make them do this forEver," he said. "I will kill your mother over and over and the world will never run out of bullets."

Christopher felt his fever rise. He finally understood what it was. Hell bubbling under his skin. He saw Special Ed walk through the crowd with Mike and Matt. The three of them opened their mouths at once.

"I have all of your friends. I have your tree house. Watch what I can do with it now that it's all mine," the nice man said.

Special Ed walked over to the sheriff and helped him to his feet. The sheriff's eyes never opened. But he looked in Christopher's direction, trying to pry them open in absolute desperation.

"Please don't let me sleep anymore, Christopher. Every time I go to sleep, she's waiting for me, but I don't save her. I'm late every time. Please make it stop. I can't hear her say Daddy again."

The sheriff fought against his own body, but he couldn't stop it. He climbed the tree against his will. Little 2x4s returned at jagged angles like a broken smile.

"No! I don't want to go!" the sheriff screamed.

Christopher moved to help him, but the crowd engulfed him.

"No! Stop!" Christopher yelled.

Invisible hands moved the sheriff's limbs like a marionette. He climbed to the top of the ladder and opened the door to the tree house.

"Please! I can't watch her die again!"

"Let him go! Wake up, Sheriff!" Christopher screamed.

But the sheriff was lost. The tree house glowed. The sheriff went inside and closed the door behind him. His screams began immediately.

And then there was silence.

The nice man spoke next. His voice buzzing in Christopher's mind so sharply that he felt it in the fillings in his teeth.

now who iS going in next?

Christopher watched the town move toward his mother's body. They picked her up like pallbearers and carried her toward the tree.

"NO!" Christopher yelled.

Christopher fought through the crowd to get to his mother. Mr. and Mrs. Collins each grabbed one of his hands. They hissed,

"Do you know what your mother will see when she wakeS up?"

"NO! YOU CAN'T! PLEASE!" Christopher screamed.

Christopher wrenched his hands free and ran toward his mother. Jerry tackled Christopher to the ground.

"She is going to wake up with Jerry. GuesS what happens next?"

Christopher scrambled back to his feet. He clawed to get to his mother. His fever rising.

"She will notice someone iS watching her from the bathtub. It's your father. He will rise up from the bathtub with the knife."

"YOU CAN'T. NOT MY MOM. PLEASE!"

"But he isn't going to kill her with it. He iS going to kill you."

The crowd dragged his mother up the ladder by the hair. She dangled like a pocket watch.

"She will watch you dIe and the next morning, she will wake up with Jerry. She will notice someone is watching her from the bathtub. It's your father. He will riSe up from the bathtub with the knife. But he isn't going to kill her with it. He iS going to kill you. She will watch you dIe and the next morning . . ."

"NO!"

Christopher ran to the tree and grabbed his mother's legs. Trying to pull her down. Christopher dropped to his knees, swimming in pain. He couldn't hold her anymore. Mike and Matt walked up to him. They each put a loving hand on a shoulder and opened their mouths as one.

"christopheR. i aM donE chasinG yoU. i havE waiteD twO thousanD yearS tO geT ouT oF thiS prisoN. yoU eitheR brinG mE bacK thaT keY and kilL thE hissinG ladY oR i wilL keeP youR motheR aS mY peT iN herE foreveR. therE iS nO otheR choicE. somebodY wilL diE oN christmaS daY. iT iS eithEr thE hissinG ladY oR youR mothEr. noW . . .

"choosE."

Mr. and Mrs. Collins opened the tree house door, ready to throw her in.

"Okay! Stop! I'll do it! Just let her go!" Christopher cried.

There was a moment of silence, then a whisper came in from a thousand mouths.

"thanK yoU, christopheR . . ."

The town gently lowered Christopher's mother down the ladder to the ground. Christopher looked at her lying next to the tree. She seemed so peaceful. After everything she had been through. Everything that life had done to her.

He knelt next to her body and stroked her forehead like she always did for him when he was sick with a fever. He took her hand. If there was a pulse, he couldn't find it.

"Mom, I have to go now," he said quietly.

The fever started. It was unlike anything he had ever felt before. The hairs on his neck stood up. His stomach got warm and crackling with electricity. The whisper scratch heated up all over his body, but for his mother, it didn't start in his mind or in his hands.

It started in his heart.

He closed his eyes and held her to his chest. The whisper scratch moved through him like the clouds moving above. He could smell the Vicks VapoRub she put on his chest when he was sick. The beer on the rocks he poured like Mary Katherine's altar wine like the blood running out of Christopher's nose.

There was no difference anymore.

Christopher felt as if he would have no blood left, but he would never let go. No matter how much it hurt. Whatever he had left he would give to her. The whisper scratch made Christopher feel the bullet in her body. Every hope and every fear that pulled the triggers. Every broken promise and broken life.

His fever climbed. Christopher's head screamed. His skull felt like it would snap in half. He knew everything now. Everything his mother had been through. Everything his mother had ever done for him. He looked at her life, and he finally understood this feeling inside him.

The feeling was not pain.

It was power.

He was omniscient. He was omnipotent. He was as close to God as a mortal could be. He healed her broken ribs. Every cavity. Every wrinkle. Every little ache and pain. It all ran through him and disappeared into the clouds.

Christopher's mother opened her eyes. She was alive.

"Christopher?" she whispered. "What's happening?"

"Nothing, Mom. You're okay now."

He kept touching her chest. Giving her more and more life. He saw all of her memories. Not only the fact of them. The feeling of them. The tears. The rage. The self-hatred. The invisible scars.

"Mom, I can take away all of your pain. Will you let me do it?"

"What?" she said softly.

"You don't have to feel any hurt again. Will you let me do that for you?"

"Yes, honey. Whatever you want," she said.

He brought his hand over her shoulder and touched the skin between her breast and collarbone. For a moment, she didn't feel any different.

And then, it started.

She looked up at her son, blood pouring out of his nose.

"What's wrong, honey?" she asked Christopher. "Do you have a nosebleed?"

"I'll be okay, Mom. Just watch," he said.

She instinctively reached up and wiped the blood from his face. He took her hand in his and smiled. His warmth spread all over her skin, and she saw her life pass in front of her eyes. Every time she hid her tears because she was not going to teach her son how to be afraid. Every time she smiled to make him feel safe, then went into the next room and counted the thirty-one dollars they had left. All the hits she took for him. All the things she gave up for him. Every time she tucked him into bed at night. Every time she dragged herself out of bed because she would never give up on Christopher the way that everyone she ever knew gave up on her. She felt every moment she ever spent with her son all over again.

But not the way she saw it.

The way <u>he</u> saw it.

At first, she didn't recognize the feeling, but when she realized what it was, tears began to pour from her eyes. She felt what it was like to be put first. What it was like to be loved without condition by someone bigger who could protect her and make things right. She was her own parent. She was safe. She had never been so happy in all her life. But it was more than happiness. It was more than safety. It wasn't what she felt. It's what she didn't feel anymore.

There was no pain.

It was gone. All of the guilt. The fear. The blame she took for his dyslexia. For their poverty. For their situation. It all melted away. There was no failure. She saw herself only as he saw her. A hero. All powerful. All knowing. The most amazing person who ever walked on the face of the earth.

She looked up at her son smiling down at her like he had every Movie Friday. Every time he picked up a book for her. Every time he pretended to love a movie for her. Every time he made her a beer on the rocks. She felt her own smile. Her hugs. Her cooking. Her beauty. An eternity of moments stretched out in front of them as they looked up at the light of one hundred billion stars.

"Mom," he said. "This is who you really are."

In that moment, Christopher closed his eyes and gave his mother back all of the love she had ever given him.

She was in Heaven.

Christopher's nose stopped bleeding. He put a warm hand on her forehead, and she curled up like a little girl ready to fall back asleep.

"Go to sleep, Mom," he said. "It's all a bad dream. It'll be okay in the morning."

"Okay, honey. Good night," she said.

"Good night."

Christopher bent over and kissed her warm forehead. She would be dreaming now.

"I will never let them hurt you," he said.

Then, he stood up. Christopher had taken in all of her pain. His joints swelled. His knees creaked. His arms felt skinny and weak. He looked back through the clearing. The town stared back at him with their dead eyes. The nice man had taken them all. All but his mother. There was no one left. Christopher was all alone.

He took his broken body and limped toward the tree.

The town parted like the Red Sea. Hundreds of frogs not understanding why they were suddenly starting to feel so bad. Christopher knew that he was walking to his own death, but he had no choice but to walk. For her. For them. For everyone. He reached the bottom of the tree. He moved his skinny arms up and climbed the little 2x4s like baby teeth.

Christopher reached the tree house.

He opened the door and looked inside. It was just a little room, empty and cold. With nothing but the sheriff and Ambrose lying on the floor, twitching unconsciously, muttering horror in their sleep. The smell was all wrong. The light was too bright. Something had changed. The nice man controlled the portal now. Christopher didn't know what would be different once he closed that door. All he knew for sure was that the nice man couldn't kill the hissing lady without him.

And that Christopher was the only thing keeping Hell from Earth.

Christopher stepped into the tree house, holding the hissing lady's key in his pocket like a lucky rabbit's foot. He turned and looked at his mother sleeping peacefully on the ground. The only light left in the world.

"I love you, Mom," he said.

Then, Christopher closed the door and walked into Hell.

Part VII

The Shadow oF Death

CHAPTER 121

Christopher opened his eyes.

He was still in the tree house. He saw his physical body still lying next to Ambrose and the sheriff, lost and twitching. But something was different. Something had changed. Christopher moved to the door. He put his ear to it. He listened for any signs of the nice man. All he heard was whispering. Voices he'd never heard before. Hissing his name.

"Chrissstopher."

"We know you can hear ussss."

He turned to the windows to see who was whispering, but the windows were so fogged over that he couldn't see out. The clouds were all around them. Covering both sides of the world like a blindfold.

"Chrissstopher . . . you're running out of air."

The voices were right. The air inside the tree house had become hot and thick like breath under a blanket. The whispers scratched at the tree house.

"This is what happens to people in coffins."

"They run out of air."

"They are alive down there, Christopher."

"They are squirming."

"If you don't come out, you'll die just like them," the voices whispered.

Christopher had no choice. He reached for the doorknob. He opened it just enough to let fresh air into the room. The breeze outside was charcoal-sweet, like cotton candy barbecued on an open spit. He peeked one eye through the door crack. What he saw horrified him.

The imaginary world was beautiful.

The grass was green. The sky was blue. And black. And starry. And clear. All at the same time. The sun was as bright as the moon right next to it. A breeze rustled through the tree leaves, green and ripe as fruit. The weather was a perfect mixture of warm and cold. Balmy and dry. A beautiful spring day mixed with a crisp autumn night. The best of all seasons. The best of all times. Not quite day. Not quite night. The best of both and the worst of none.

The Mission Street Woods were heavenly.

Christopher looked down into the beautiful world and saw.

Hundreds of deer.

In the clearing.

Staring up at him.

Voices hidden in the wind.

"Hi, Christopher."

"Hello, friend."

"Just come down. We won't eat you. Not this time."

Christopher felt the whispers on his neck. He whipped around and saw a tree branch reach down like a snake in Medusa's hair. The branch offered its hand to him and helped him down to the ladder. Light as a feather.

"Right this way, Christopher," the friendly voice said.

The voice was everywhere. The voice was nowhere. He looked up at the blue moon next to the orange sun. They lit the clouds above the clearing like a lantern. The stars above were twinkling like Christmas lights.

Christopher held the ladder. It felt wet and slick. White and shiny. The 2x4s were now baby teeth. He climbed the ladder.

Down the giant tree.

With every step, Christopher's body ached. He felt weak after healing his mother. The only thing he had left was his mind. He knew the sheriff was lost somewhere inside here. Ambrose, too. They were running out of time. He looked down at the clearing and saw the deer standing there. Trying so hard to not look like their ribs were sticking through their skin from starvation. They licked their noses with long, scratchy tongues.

"That's it, Christopher. Careful now," said the voice.

Christopher kept moving. For his mother. For his friends. For his town. He reached the ground and stared at the deer approaching. Bowing to him. Nibbling the ground around his feet. Nuzzling his hands.

Christopher was too weak to outrun them. Too weak to fly. But he forced himself to walk. They surrounded him like guards. To keep him safe. To keep him walking. He looked ahead at the woods. The tree branches were smiling now, slithering like cat tails. A frown gone sick.

The breeze did its best to cover the sounds, but he could still feel the screaming in the distance. The cries of "Make it stop!" on the imaginary side mixing with the shouts of "Here we come!" on the real. The worlds were bleeding together. The frogs were starting to itch.

Ms. Lasko just opened a bottle of whiskey. She put it to her nose. It smelled delicious. She moved it to her mouth. But her mouth was sewn shut.

Christopher could feel Ms. Lasko cry through her stitches. He didn't have much time. Christopher walked through the beautiful woods. The branches rubbed his shoulders. Ruffled his hair. Gently nudged him down the path.

"Mom?" he could feel Mrs. Collins scream. "Mom?! Why won't you let me in the kitchen now?! You promised! Please! I'm so cold!"

Christopher hobbled down the path. He looked down and saw footprints. Every foot was different. Men. Women. Boys. Girls. The feet were getting smaller. Human beings disappearing.

"Mom?!" he could feel Brady Collins cry. "Mom?! Why won't you let me in the kitchen now?! You promised! Please! I'm so cold!"

Christopher walked past the billy goat bridge. He felt something splash in the creek on the real side.

Jenny Hertzog just pushed her stepbrother into the creek to drown him in floods. She didn't understand why the creek became his bed. "Mom! Please! Make it stop!"

Christopher looked at the billy goat bridge. It was all up to him. He had to save Jenny. He had to save them all. The splashing in the creek got louder.

The old lady across the street just went swimming with her husband, but she doesn't understand why he keeps getting tired. "You have to swim, honey! Please! Oh, God! He's drowning!"

Christopher knew he had to defeat the nice man, or this would be the world's eternity. The people in the clearing would blame each other. Turn on each other. The nice man had gathered them all together to play a game of pickup war. Shirts and skins. Tribes could be made out of something as small as a sports team. It would start at this clearing. One neighbor would strike another neighbor. And that neighbor would have a cousin somewhere who would join in. Then, another. And another. Until everyone knew a mother or father or brother or sister or spouse or son or daughter who was wronged by some other mother or father or brother or sister or spouse or son or daughter. And the two sides would begin fighting and they would never stop. They would never die. They would never listen. They would just bleed. Hell would come to Earth.

Christopher looked up ahead as flowers lined the path leading out of the Mission Street Woods.

Christopher reached the street.

He stopped the moment he saw it. His neighborhood. His house. The log cabin. The cul-de-sac with a beautiful night fog mixed with the morning dew. All of it was trying desperately to look happy despite the fact that it was burning. He heard muffled screams coming from the houses. Thousands more trapped behind stitches. Trying to sound so cheerful.

"He's back! He's back! Hello, Christopher," they said.

He saw the man in the Girl Scout uniform tip his softball visor. The couple made yum yum sounds as they kept kissing until their teeth landed on the street like pebbles. The mailbox people stood next to each other like passengers crammed into a train. No doors. No seats. No hope. The street stretched forever as the mailbox people lined the sides, keeping everyone in their place as the damned screamed the same thing under their smiles.

"Make it stop! Please, God!"

There was only one person not smiling. She lay on the lawn next to the street. Her feet and hands bound. Surrounded by deer.

It was the hissing lady.

"You're off the street," she said, defeated.

Christopher stepped onto the cul-de-sac. Deer started to walk around the circle like a snake hugging its young. A shrouded figure walked toward Christopher. It reached its hand out. Then, it slowly took off its shadow the way others take off clothes at the end of a long day.

It was the nice man.

He looked so handsome. So clean. A charming man in a grey suit. He smiled so pleasantly. His mouth full of baby teeth.

"Hello," he said. "I'm sorry, but you need to kill her now. it's tiMe."

Christopher looked at him. The nice man had no weapon in his hand. Just a pleasant expression. And a paternal nod.

"because god iS a murderer."

CHAPTER 122

*D*addy.

The sheriff opened the door.

He looked down the hallway of an old tenement building. For a moment, he wondered why he wasn't in the tree house. He was sure he opened the door to the tree house, but this was definitely an old tenement building. The door closed with a heavy click behind him.

Ding.

The elevator opened down the hall. A teenage couple walked out of the elevator. The boy was about sixteen. The girl was seventeen. He was black. She was white. She held their baby.

The baby was crying.

"Daddy!"

The sheriff stopped for a moment and felt like he had been here before. Like this had already happened. But he quickly shook off the feeling.

He had a job to do.

"Excuse me. I received a complaint about a smell coming from room 217. Do you know who lives—"

The couple quickly looked away and slipped into their apartment without a word. The sheriff heard them dead-bolt their door with a Click. Click. Click. The sheriff was used to people not wanting to talk to police officers, but he hadn't heard three locks since he moved to the suburbs. It gave his stomach a sinking feeling.

He walked down the hallway toward the elevator. It was one of those old lifts with a gold-plated mechanical display. It looked like the top half of a clock with an arrow that moved from 9 to 3.

But this one was pointing straight down at 6.

It must have been broken.

The sheriff pushed the button. He watched the gold-plated arrow move through the semicircle in the wrong direction.

Ding.

The elevator door opened. He saw a middle-aged couple in the elevator. The man was black. The woman was white. They walked with their little girl, who was dressed in a beautiful white dress for church. The little girl was crying because she spilled something on it. It looked like grape juice. Or blood.

"Daddy!" she cried.

"Excuse me," the sheriff said. "I received a complaint about a smell coming from room 217. Do you know who lives there?"

"No," the mother said. "But you dO."

The mother smiled. She had no teeth. Her husband put a gentle hand on his family and quickly moved them into their apartment and locked the door. Click. Click. Click.

The sheriff walked into the elevator and pushed 21. The doors closed and the Muzak came on. Blue Moon. The sound almost distracted him from the smell of urine and feces. The sheriff was used to tenements smelling like piss and shit, but this smelled like the inside of a baby's diaper. The baby was crying.

The elevator doors opened on the twenty-first floor.

The sheriff left the elevator and entered darkness. The lights flickered. The carpet was threadbare. He turned and saw room 217 at the very end of the long hallway.

The door was ajar.

The sheriff walked toward it. He heard scratching behind all of the apartment doors. He listened for the familiar sound of dogs or cats, but there was no sound. Just scratching. And breathing.

He reached room 217.

The sheriff tried to see inside, but the room was black.

"Hello. Sheriff's Department. We've received a complaint about the smell."

Silence. The sheriff opened the door to a smell that made him nostalgic for the elevator. Sweet smoke and rotten meat mixed with spoiled milk. The sheriff gagged and covered his face. His eyes watered so badly that he felt like he was looking through a fog. Wasn't he just in a fog? He thought he was. He couldn't quite remember.

He turned on the light.

He looked into the cold kitchen. A milk carton sat on the table. He saw some roaches. A box of Cheerios and a bowl.

That's when he saw the woman.

She was facedown inside a bowl of cereal. The woman's body was bloated and rotting. A needle stuck out of her arm. The belt was still loose around her shoulder. It looked like she had been here for days without anyone noticing.

Except the family dog.

The sheriff rushed over to the woman. He pushed the dog, all skin and bones, away from the snack he was making of her legs. Then, the sheriff lifted her out of the cereal bowl. He quickly checked her pulse to confirm the woman was dead.

There was a sound in the bedroom. Squeak. Squeak. Squeak.

The sheriff stood up. Gooseflesh crawled across his body.

"Hello?" he said.

The sheriff walked to the bedroom door.

Squeak. Squeak. Squeak.

"Hello?!" he said.

The sheriff opened the door slowly. He peered into the room and saw her. Her hands and feet were each bound with a neck tie to an old rusty bed frame. She was filthy and starving to death. She might have been fifty-five pounds. She had struggled so much that her wrists and ankles were caked with blood. But somehow, her hands and feet were still clean.

It was the girl with the painted nails.

At first, he thought she had been kidnapped, until an old photograph made it obvious that she was the daughter of the dead junkie in the kitchen. The sheriff didn't need to do a lot of work to guess that she had been sold to perverts to pay for the needle in her mother's arm.

The sheriff rushed over to the little girl. Her pulse was faint. But she was still alive! He could save her this time! Had he been here before? He reached for his radio, but it was gone. He looked for a phone, but there was none. There was no way to call 911. He untied her hands and bent down to untie her feet. Suddenly he felt her little hand on his arm.

"Daddy?" she whispered.

The sheriff looked back up. He looked outside the bedroom window and saw the little Charlie Brown Christmas tree through her window in Mercy Hospital. Something was wrong. They were in her bedroom. Or was this a hospital room? Where were they?

"Daddy?" she whispered.

"No, honey. I'm a police officer. I'm the one who found you."

"You can't fool me. I always knew you'd rescue me, Daddy," she said.

He untied her feet and picked her up. She was a rag doll in his arms. He laid her back on the hospital bed and tucked her under the covers. She smelled so warm and clean.

"Will you read me a story? No one has ever read me a story," she said.

The sheriff picked up a worn copy of Little Red Riding Hood that had been left in the hospital room. As he began to read, the little girl looked up at the television on mute. She asked him why the picture was so clear. She had never been outside of her apartment. She had never gone to school. She had never learned to write her name.

He heard the morphine going into her arm.

Drip. Drip. Drip.

He reached the last page of the story. What big teeth you have.

"Daddy, can you get me some milk?"

"No, honey. I can't," he said.

"Why not?"

"Because that's when you died," the sheriff said.

"I won't this time. I promise."

"But you have to hear the end of the story. You have to know that the wolf doesn't win."

"Please, get me some milk, Daddy."

The sheriff looked down into those big beautiful eyes. He heard the morphine fall like raindrops.

Drip. Drip. Drip.

The sheriff handed her the book and walked into the hallway. He quickly found a nurse and asked for a carton of milk. While he waited, he decided what he was going to do. The sheriff was the first grown man the little girl had ever met who didn't hurt her, so she thought he was her daddy. So, why couldn't he be? He wasn't a praying man, but this one time, he could make the world right. He could bring her home in time for Christmas. He could get her presents. He could adopt her. After everything she'd been through, she was still innocent. She was the best little kid he had ever seen.

"Here is the milk, sIr," the nurse said.

The sheriff looked at the little carton of milk. Emily Bertovich was there, smiling in her second-grade picture.

The sheriff walked back into the room.

"Okay. Let's finish that story now, honey," he said. "Honey?"

The little girl was lifeless on the bed.

"NO!" he yelled.

He ran over and held her in his arms. He screamed for the nurse, but no nurse came.

"PLEASE!"

He began to sob. Suddenly, the sheriff remembered everything. He had already been here. He had done this. He had already seen her die fifty times tonight.

"MAKE IT STOP!"

The sheriff ran to the door. He knew what came next. He would run out into the hallway to get the doctor to save the little girl. But instead, he would open the door to the tenement building. He had done this fifty times already. But this time, he promised himself he would remember. Christopher was in terrible danger. So was his mother. So was Ambrose. He had to help them. He had to get to her faster. He had to save her this time. To get out of here. He couldn't watch her die again.

but god iS a murderer

Daddy.

The sheriff opened the door.

He looked down the hallway of an old tenement building. For a moment, he wondered why he wasn't in the tree house. He was sure he opened the door to the tree house, but this was definitely an old tenement building. The door closed with a heavy click behind him.

The sheriff turned back to leave the building, but the door was locked.

Ding.

CHAPTER 123

Ambrose turned on the light. He looked around, expecting to see the tree house. But he wasn't in the tree house anymore.

He was in his old house.

The basement.

Something was terribly wrong. Ambrose knew it instinctively. He was behind enemy lines. He looked around the basement. Something was in here. He couldn't see it, not even through the halos in his eyes, but he could feel it. There was something too familiar about it all. The hairs on the back of his neck stood up like antennas.

Ambrose moved to the stairs.

He climbed, the wooden stairs creaking with each step. He could feel something in the basement behind him. He quickly looked back, but he saw nothing. Just the wood paneling that he'd put up with his father one summer. His little brother begged the two men to help them. His father said no. Ambrose said yes.

Ambrose opened the basement door.

He walked into his mother's kitchen. He saw the doorframe where his mother measured his height with pencil marks. Ambrose was 6 foot even. David was frozen at 3 foot 5. There was something boiling in a pot on the stove. Something that smelled like . . . like . . . venison.

Ding dong.

Someone was at the front door. Ambrose's blood went instantly cold. He slowly moved to the door. He stood in his mother's living room. The old RCA Victor was in the corner right next to the sewing machine.

"Hello?" he whispered.

That's when the baby started crying.

Ambrose quickly went to the window and pushed his mother's old curtains down the brass rod with a squeak. He craned his neck to see who was at the front door, but all he saw was the baby carriage. Ambrose's heart stopped when he realized what was happening. He didn't know where he was. But he knew <u>when</u> he was.

This was the night that David went missing.

"David?" Ambrose called upstairs. "David, are you up there?"

There was no answer except a . . .

Clunk. Clunk. Clunk.

As a baseball slowly rolled down the stairs.

Ambrose caught the ball. It smelled like David's baseball glove. Ambrose began to run up the stairs as fast as his old legs would take him. He passed the family portraits and the wedding pictures. A hundred years of Olson family history decaying on the walls like faded Missing posters. There was no one left to remember. No one left but him. He reached the top of the stairs and moved to David's bedroom. Ambrose opened the door and peered into the dark room.

"David? Are you in here?" he said.

He flipped the light. The room was empty. The walls were covered in scratches left from madness when their father locked David in this room with nothing but his fear to keep him company. Ambrose saw a lump underneath the covers on the bed. It looked to be the size of a child.

"David? Is that you?" he whispered.

Ambrose studied the lump in the bed. Was it moving? Was it breathing? He moved to the bed and ripped off the covers before fear could talk him out of it. There was no one there. Just two pillows left under the covers to trick a grown-up.

And David's baby book.

Ambrose picked it up slowly. The leather cover had the scent of old baseball gloves. It still smelled like his brother. He opened the book and ran his fingers over the little beads from the hospital. D. Olson. He studied the little footprint and the pictures that every family seemed to take.

David laughing naked at the tub.

David floating in a pool looking cranky.

David opening his presents on Christmas morning.

Ambrose had looked at the photos so often, he didn't need to look at them again. He knew the last photo in the book. David with his big brother's baseball glove. Ambrose stared at the picture, then turned the page.

But this time, the album kept going. There were more pictures.

David climbing out of the window.

David running through the woods.

David screaming in his grave.

Ambrose turned to the window. He saw his brother's fingerprints on the glass. The wind using an old tree branch to scratch the window. Ambrose threw the window open and looked down at the ivy scaling the walls. His little brother used it to climb down the night he went missing. This was that night.

I can still save my brother.

He climbed through the window and down the ivy walls. His feet found the mossy grass. Ambrose looked down and saw his little brother's footprints in the lawn. He knew it could be a trick, but he had no other option. He followed the trail. He had to find his brother. He had to save him this time.

Someone buried my brother alive.

Ambrose quickened his pace. He could see nothing except his little brother's footprints squished into the wet street. He thought he could hear David's voice far off in the wind. David was crying. Ambrose raced after his brother's footprints until he saw the cul-de-sac in the distance.

And the Mission Street Woods.

The old soldier braced himself and moved across the field. He could feel the woods come alive in front of him. The wind moving in and out through an invisible mouth. Making clouds.

Ambrose followed the footprints into the woods.

Immediately the path went dark. Ambrose would have been blind had it not been for the halos in his eyes. His heart was in his throat. This was where his brother was killed. This was where he was lured. David was in here somewhere.

I can still save my brother.

Ambrose searched for any sign of abduction. A hole in the ground. A trapdoor. But all he saw were his brother's footprints. Leading into the old coal mine. Ambrose walked into the darkness, clutching to memories like a child to a night-light. He had heard stories about this mine. His grandfather's grandfather had been a child laborer here. Hard work made for hard men. Not to mention families. Ambrose would be the last Olson. Unless he could save his brother.

"David! Are you in here?"

His voice bounced off the walls. He could feel something in the dark. A silent presence. Watching. Waiting. Slithering. Ambrose steeled himself against the darkness and walked until he reached the light on the other side. The path led to an overpass. A hidden clearing. Ambrose followed the footprints into a little garden. He looked up and stopped dead in his tracks when he finally saw it.

David's tree house.

Ambrose looked through the dense fog and saw the shadow of a little boy carrying something to the tree house.

"DAVID?!" Ambrose called out.

The word was right in Ambrose's mind. But when it left his mouth, it was silent.

The little boy didn't turn.

Ambrose started to run to him, but his legs became so heavy, he couldn't move. He couldn't speak. He could only watch frozen on the ground. The little boy turned, and Ambrose finally saw his face. His beautiful face. And that perfect head of hair. It was David. My God. It was really him. He was still alive.

And he was crying.

Ambrose tried to scream, but the word was trapped in his throat like a marble. David could not hear him. David thought he was all alone. David wiped the blood from his nose with one hand and grabbed a hammer from a pile of tools near the tree house with the other. Ambrose watched as his little brother tore the tree house apart. Plank by plank. Throwing the wood in a pile like a dog stacking bones.

Until there was nothing left but the ladder.

The boy tried to move up the ladder by himself, but he was too weak. He lifted the hammer in his brittle hand and tried to pry one of the ladder rungs off the tree, but the hammer was too heavy. He finally lost his grip and fell to the ground with a thud. The little boy stood up and held his throbbing head.

"Help me. Somebody," he cried. "I have to destroy it all."

"DAVID!" Ambrose yelled. "I'M HERE!"

Ambrose screamed until his throat burned, but there was only silence. He tried to get to his feet, but he could only watch helplessly as a man walked into the garden. The man looked so handsome. And clean. In his grey suit and smile. The only thing that looked off about the man was the fact that he only stood in the shadows. His voice the wind.

"Hello, David," he said. "What are you doing?"

David backed up to the tree. Terrified.

"I . . . I . . ." David stammered.

"Don't be afraid. We're still beSt friends."

The man slowly moved to David, who hid the hammer behind his back.

"What do you have behind your back, davId? Is that a hammer? Are you destroying the tree house?"

"Yes," David said, finally finding his voice.

"But we built it together," the man said. He seemed hurt. "The tree houSe is the we houSe. Remember?"

David quickly wiped his tears and pretended they had never been there.

"No one on the real side will ever know it was here," David said defiantly.

The man walked like a serpent on hind legs. Swallowing his smile.

"But how can you destroy it? The tree house made you goD. I gave you that power to kill her," the man said in a friendly voice.

"I won't kill the hissing lady for you," David said. "I won't let you escape."

Then, David walked to the tree and ripped the ladder out like a dentist pulling teeth. He threw the 2x4s on top of the woodpile. The man's smile dropped. He followed David. Calm and dangerous.

"You know the ruleS, david. Someone is going to die. It's either the hissing lady or your brother. There iS no other choice."

"Yes, there is," David said. "There is someone else who could die."

Ambrose watched his little brother throw the last 2x4 on the pile. Then, he picked up a shovel.

"You're on the real sIde," the man said with a laugh. "You can't even see me right now. I'm just in your mind. How are you going to kill mE with a shovel?"

"I'm not going to kill <u>you</u>," David said.

Then, David turned the shovel down and jammed the spade into the dirt. The man's laughter instantly stopped. The calm in his voice cracking.

"WhaT are you doinG?"

David said nothing. He just kept digging more and more earth. The man ran to him.

"StoP thaT!"

But David would not stop. The bones in his thin arms looked like they were going to break from the weight of the shovel.

"If you don't stop, I'm going to kill your brotHer."

"No, you won't. If I die, so does the power you take from me. She will be stronger than you again. And she won't let you get to Ambrose."

Ambrose watched helplessly. He could smell the scent of baseball gloves. It was getting weaker. The man walked up and put a kind hand on David's shoulder.

"Please, David," the man said in Ambrose's voice. "I will never find you. It will destroy me. How could you do this to your own brother?"

"You're not my brother," David said. "You're nothing."

The word fell like a bird from the sky. The man closed his eyes in rage. Light like fireflies danced through his skin. Constellations of stars crawled over him, and he took one finger and moved it into David like a needle.

"This is what eternity has been for the hissing lady, and if you don't kill her, thiS is what it will be for you."

David's nose began to bleed. His eyes. His ears. He screamed as if he were being burned alive, but he wouldn't stop digging. Not until the hole was complete. Then, he threw the shovel on top of the woodpile and pulled something out of his back pocket.

Lighter fluid.

He opened the cap and poured the liquid on the tree house's bones. Then, he brought a trail of it back to the hole with him. The man screeched into David's ear, and David fell to his knees in agony. All the boy could do was crawl, dragging his broken body into the grave.

Then, David pulled out a book of his brother's matches. Lucky Strike. He lit the match with a

Hiss.

The man looked at it. The flame the color of hIs eyes. He spoke like a policeman talking to someone on a ledge.

"David, if you kill yourself, you will wake up here and never leave this place," he said. "You will relive this night forever."

"So will you," David said and threw the match.

The trail crossed the garden to the tree house. The fire roared up, casting a glow, making his little brother look like he was lit by the sunrise.

Ambrose watched frozen on the ground as David stood in his grave and pulled the dirt back in. Sacrificing himself. For the family who ignored him. For the town who would forget him. The man in the grey suit watched incredulously as the little boy put the world in front of himself.

"Why did you do this, David?" hE asked.

"Because I love my brother."

Then, David grabbed one last handful of dirt and covered his mouth and eyes, drowning in earth and the world's blood. Ambrose searched for the scent, but the baseball-glove smell was gone forever.

David had buried himself alive.

"No!!!" Ambrose shouted, but his voice was drowned out by the man, railing against the sky.

"nO!!!"

The man in the grey suit smashed David's tree to kindling. Great hunks of wood ripped the man's flesh until there was nothing left of the tree. Just an empty space that made the clearing around it that much bigger.

When the tree house was charcoal, and the wood of the tree dust, the man dragged his depleted body back out through the garden. His handsomeness was gone. He was old and haggard. And his suit suddenly looked to Ambrose like prison greys.

When the man was gone, Ambrose's body finally returned to him. He ran to his little brother's grave and shoved his hands into the fresh earth. He dug feverishly. His brother was here. It wasn't too late.

I can still save my brother.

Ambrose dug through the dirt. Foot after foot. Looking for his brother's body. But he couldn't find him. He kept digging. Faster and faster. He felt the dirt in his mouth. His eyes. Worms crawling on his body. His lungs screaming for air. This was what his brother felt. This was eternity.

forEver and eVer and evEr

Suddenly there was darkness. He reached inside the dirt and found something hard and cold. Plastic. A light switch. Ambrose turned on the light. He looked around, expecting to see the tree house. But he wasn't in the tree house anymore.

He was in his old house.

The basement.

CHAPTER 124

Christopher's mother opened her eyes.

She was in a nice, warm bed. Clean sheets fresh from the dryer. She looked up at the white ceiling with the cracks that greeted her every morning. She stretched and yawned, feeling the little aches and pains dissolve like butter on a pan.

"Jerry?" she called out.

There was no answer. It was just as well after last night. If he had been there, she would have just seen that same sheepish smile that greeted her the morning after the first time it happened. She thought about leaving him that first night he hit her. But better judgment calmed her down. Men could be changed. Men could be saved. Didn't her mother always say that?

Christopher's mother got out of bed.

She looked down at the pillow, white and fluffy like clouds. For some reason, that first night wouldn't get out of her mind, like the chorus of an annoying song. Why didn't she leave him that first time? Just pack her things, get the Visa he didn't know about, the hidden cash from the drawer, and just go?

Because.

That single word sat there like his car on blocks in the driveway. What would have happened if she had left that first time he hit her? Who knew? Her mother always said that when something bad happens, think about the worse. If you get a flat tire, it's just God saving you from a fatal accident twenty seconds later. That sentence helped her mother endure (or allow) two decades of men coming in and out of her life so quickly that she joked that she should have installed a revolving door and saved them all the trouble. Christopher's mother didn't know what the accident would have been if she had actually left Jerry, but there are worse things in the world than a black eye. Or two.

Right?

Right. It's not like the world came to an end. Plus, she reminded herself that her own mother had known a lot worse than Jerry. Little Kate had listened to more than her fair share of kisses mixed with fists through the bathroom walls of their studio apartment. The little girl she was hated those men. Especially when she was left alone with them. But the woman she became hated her mother more. Kate may have had low standards for herself. But no one touched her son. No one would fucking dare.

If only Christopher could give her credit for that.

Christopher's mother went to the window. She looked at herself in the glass. It was fogged a little. Just enough to soften the wrinkles that marked time. Thank God for small favors. She got out the concealer she kept in the nightstand.

Then, she covered up the fresh black eye with a practiced hand.

It didn't look so bad, she told herself. Not in the opaque window, anyway. And it's not like she was leaving the house today. He cried last night after it happened. Real tears. Jerry wasn't a bad man. His childhood was almost as bad as hers. Maybe that's what made them understand each other. Maybe that's what made him propose and her say yes all those years ago.

When she was done, she looked down into the backyard at the swing set that she had begged him to buy. The swings were rusted now, but they were moving in the wind like they did back when Christopher and his buddy Lenny Cordisco played on them.

Back when her son would still talk to her.

Christopher's mother put on her favorite house dress and left the room. She looked down the hall at her son's old bedroom. How long ago did Jerry finally insist that she get his stuff out of it? She put her foot down. But so did he. That was a bad night. She didn't like to think about it anymore.

She walked down the stairs. She stared at pictures of a lifetime together greying like her hair. Their wedding photo. The honeymoon in West Virginia at that casino. What was the name of it again? She couldn't quite remember. She couldn't quite remember anything outside of this house anymore. She shook off the feeling with more photos. Christopher's graduation. High school. Then, military academy. Then, wedding. Then, her first and only grandchild. And somewhere along the line, he or his wife decided it was best if Jerry wasn't in their life anymore.

"It's me or him, Mom," he said, two decades too late.

She reached the bottom of the stairs, where Christopher's belongings had been thrown when she finally lost the argument.

Not argument! Fight, Mom! Wake up!

She suddenly got a terrible feeling. A chill ran down her back as if she were lying on the ground in the dead of winter. That's what she got for remembering things. Just forget it.

Christopher's mother shook off the past and brewed herself a pot of coffee to get through the morning. Jerry had left the living room in shambles. Again. She told him a million times that she wasn't put on this earth to pick up after him like his God damn mother as she spent the best years of her life picking up after him like his God damn mother. But that's what marriage is. Clothes are only new once. So are vows. So are kisses. Didn't her mother always say that?

Christopher's mother busied herself with the living room first. Then, the dining room table that his pension check kept filling with empty beer bottles and overflowing ashtrays. She made herself eggs. She watched her stories. For some reason, she could never remember what happened in yesterday's episode. But it was still better than silence. She finished her eggs, and during the commercial break, she put the paper plate in the trash can.

The one right next to the drawer.

She promised herself that she wouldn't do it this time. Don't open it. It's only going to make you cry. But she couldn't help herself. It was the closest thing she had to him anymore. She opened the kitchen drawer and looked at the stack of letters. The first one she wrote angry. The second desperate. The third insulted.

Every emotion from A to Z with one message in common.

"Please, let us back into your life, Christopher."

Every unopened envelope—from faded yellow to fresh white—with the same indifferent stamp.

RETURN TO SENDER.

Christopher's mother closed the drawer with a snap. She wouldn't let herself cry. Not today. She had too much to do. Like sitting in the warm kitchen and looking out into the cold. And remembering her son as a little boy who worshipped her. Not the grown man who looked at her with the same disdain with which she looked at her own mother.

All of these lifetimes stuck in her mind like the end of a record turning over and over in the wax. Going nowhere. Hadn't she been here before? Hadn't she sat in this warm kitchen all alone staring out the window, waiting for him to come home out of the cold? Even settling for the mailman to just come with a message? Hoping. Praying. Just one time to bring her an envelope not marked RETURN TO SENDER. One letter from her grown son's own hand. Mom, I'm sorry. Mom, I know it was hard for you. Mom, you gave up your life for me, and I don't hate you anymore for that. I understand you. And you are still a little boy's hero.

Christopher's mother put her head in her hands and wept. Her voice echoed off the kitchen walls, and for a moment, she thought of her tears like trees falling down in the middle of a forest with no one there to hear them.

Knock. Knock.

Christopher's mother looked up. Her heart leapt. She ran to the door. She had installed a mail slot in the front door because she couldn't bear to walk to the mailbox anymore. Or did Jerry just not let her leave the house without him? She couldn't remember.

"Hello?" she called out.

But the mailman said nothing. He never did. He simply slipped the mail through the slot like a schoolkid passing notes and walked away. She had never even seen his face.

Christopher's mother dropped to her knees and grabbed the stack of mail scattered on the floor. She waded through coupon books and catalogs until she found what she was looking for. Her hopes and dreams took their familiar place in her throat. She turned over the letter, and she saw it.

RETURN TO SENDER.

The envelope was blurry through her tears. Like cataracts in an old man's eyes. Why did she always think of an old man when this happened? She picked herself up with whatever dignity she had left. She went to the kitchen and opened the drawer. She was just about to throw another log on the fire of her lifetime of disappointment and go upstairs for her afternoon nap, hoping that this time she wouldn't have that terrible nightmare of Christopher's father stabbing him with the knife again.

When she stopped.

She looked outside again. The cold backyard. The swing set moving in the breeze. Reminding her of Christopher. Reminding her of something important. His hand on her chest. When did that happen? She looked at the light behind the swing set. The sun had risen. It reminded her of Christmas morning for some reason. Christopher asking if the word "sunlight" came from son's light? And if so, what is a mother's light?

Christopher's mother held the envelope up to the sunlight and looked at the shadow inside it like a child looking for a check inside a Christmas card. She remembered writing it. She remembered Jerry saying that it wasn't worth the price of a stamp right before he gave her a black eye in their last argument.

Not argument! Fight, Mom! Wake up!

She remembered she had put a one-page letter into the envelope.

But there were two pages inside.

Then, Christopher's mother did the one thing she had never thought to do in all those years of disappointment.

She opened the envelope.

She pulled out her original letter. Then, she pulled out the second and began to weep when she saw her son's handwriting. The way it used to be. Back when he was a child. Struggling to read. Back when he needed her. Back when she was still her little boy's hero.

Mom. I love you. Now, open them all. Everything you need to know is inside.

CHAPTER 125

Christopher stood in the middle of the cul-de-sac, the key in his pocket, looking at the nice man. So calm. So gentle. So patient and polite. There was no terrifying face. There was only his reassuring smile with rows of perfectly white, perfectly straight baby teeth.

"All you have to do is kill the hissing lady, and I promise you, everything will be okay," he said.

Christopher looked down the street. The man in the Girl Scout uniform was happy and innocent.

"I don't want to hurt anyone, Christopher," the nice man said. "I just want my freedom. It's all I want."

The man in the Girl Scout uniform pulled himself into the bushes.

"I just want out of this prison, so I can do some good. You see that man in the bushes? Do you know what he did to a little girl?"

"Make it stop!" the man in the Girl Scout uniform screamed.

"It was terrible. And he knows it now. I just want bad people to stop hurting good people. That's all I'm trying to do."

The mailbox people moaned and pulled at their stitches. The street was so loud, Christopher couldn't hear anyone in the woods, but he knew they were there. He felt Mrs. Henderson on the real side. She saw her husband sitting in the kitchen. She cried tears of joy. He was home! Her husband finally came home! She ran across the kitchen to hold him in her arms. Then, for some reason, she couldn't stop herself from picking up a knife and stabbing him.

"NO! I don't want him to die now! He's finally home!"

Christopher looked up. The street went silent as the nice man's eyes changed to a beautiful green color. He smelled like pipe tobacco. This was the man Christopher remembered. The man who got Christopher's mother a house.

"What about the people in the town?" Christopher asked.

"You want to save the people who hurt you and your mother?" the nice man asked.

"Yes, sir," Christopher said.

"There will never be another like you." The nice man smiled. Then, he looked at the little boy and nodded.

"Once you free me, you can free them."

Christopher looked into the nice man's eyes, pained and wise.

"How can I trust you?" Christopher asked.

"You don't have to trust me. You are all powerful. All knowing. You are God here. You can save anyone you want. But someone has to die for the rest to live. It's either the hissing lady or your mother. There is no other choice. I'm sorry."

He spoke the words, then went silent. His face remaining still and solemn. But Christopher could feel the thoughts playing hide-and-seek. He would not let Christopher kill himself like David did. The choice was set.

The hissing lady or his mother.

Christopher looked at the nice man, then over to the hissing lady bound in a heap in his yard just off the street. She panted like a deer that had been hit by a car.

"I'm sorry," he said to her.

Christopher began to walk toward the hissing lady. She screamed in her restraints. Terrified. Writhing in pain.

"NO! DON'T! STOP!" she begged.

Christopher walked to the lawn and grabbed the hissing lady.

"YOU'RE OFF THE STREET!" she cried.

Christopher felt the fate of the world as he held her, and she struggled. He felt her torment. The world's torment. All the moments the hissing lady tried to scare him away. She had been here forever. She was exhausted. Tortured beyond recognition. Christopher began to drag her to the street.

"NO! NO!" she screamed.

The street came alive like a hot skillet. The man in the Girl Scout uniform pulled himself into the bushes at a frenzied pace. The couple kissed harder and harder until they began to eat each other. The frogs couldn't get out of the pot.

The pavement was as hot as one hundred billion suns. One hundred billion sons. Burning.

"STOP HELPING HIM!" she begged.

Christopher looked down and saw a reflection in her eye. She was running through the woods, desperately searching. She found David Olson buried under the earth. She dug him out with her bare hands and held him in her arms. David was terrified. She kept him safe. She gave him food. She showed him where to hide. Where to sleep. Where to bathe. For fifty years, they were always together. She was his guardian. In here, David was her son.

"Who are you?" Christopher asked.

"YOU'RE OFF THE STREET!" she screamed.

"Please, tell me who you are," he begged.

"STOP HELPING HIM!" she yelled, the words barely recognizable anymore.

Christopher brought her to the edge of the lawn. The street was an inch away.

"You have to tell me!" Christopher said.

She reached up and gently touched his hand. She had no words anymore. The words had been tortured out of her. But he felt something. He turned around and saw his neighborhood through her eyes. Not as it was today. As it was two thousand years ago when there were no people here. No houses. Nothing but quiet and stars twinkling in a clear sky untouched by people. The clouds were pure. In a blink, Christopher saw the world grow up and people spread over the continents like trees.

God had a son who served on Earth.

The hissing lady looked at him. A spark of recognition filled her eyes.

But He also had a daughter.

Christopher held her hand and felt the truth flow through his skin like electricity.

And she volunteered to serve here.

Christopher felt the last of her pain with whatever strength he had left. Which wasn't much. The warmth from his body left him. Then, he stood, shriveled and empty, and faced the nice man.

"No," Christopher said.

The nice man turned to Christopher.

"What dId you say?" he asked calmly.

Christopher said nothing. The nice man walked over to him.

"The tree house made you God. I gave you that power to kill hEr. Are you refusing me?"

He smiled. His baby teeth trying hard not to look like fangs.

"I wouldn't do that, Christopher," he said kindly. "I can make this so much worse."

He picked Christopher up in a warm, paternal hug.

"No!" the hissing lady cried helplessly.

He smiled and studied Christopher like a dissected frog.

"You think you've seen this place, son, but you haven't. Do you know what the imagInary world looks like wIthout my protection?"

The nice man's wrinkles began to spread from his eyes like the earth cracking in a drought as rage coursed through his veins.

"thiS iS whaT iT reallY iS!"

Christopher looked up in horror as the white clouds burned with souls crying out for murder and blood. The clouds twisting into the faces of the damned. The people there were not screaming, "Make it stop!" The people there were screaming, "More! Give me more!"

"i wilL pasS yoU arounD tO thE reallY baD peoplE anD telL theM thaT yoU arE a gifT froM heaveN whilE youR motheR watcheS theM. i wilL leT theM torturE yoU untiL yoU arE unrecognizablE tO goD."

The nice man curled his lips and turned to Christopher. The little boy looked into the nice man's eyes and saw them burn in different colors. Mountains melted. An eternity of warfare. It would spread and rage on and no one would ever die. They would just kill and watch helplessly as every square inch of the earth was covered with people stuffed like cattle on a train. The door locked. The fever burning inside their skin. Forever.

"i gavE yoU thE poweR oF goD tO kilL heR. usE iT anD geT mE ouT oF herE!"

"But I can't kill the hissing lady, sir. I don't have the power anymore."

"whaT diD yoU dO?! wherE diD yoU puT iT?!"

"I gave it away, so you couldn't get it," Christopher answered defiantly.

"wherE iS iT?!?!?! wherE diD yoU hidE iT?"

"I didn't hide it. I used it to make something far more powerful than you."

The nice man laughed.

"morE powerfuL thaN mE. whaT iS thaT?! goD?!"

"No, sir," Christopher said. "God's mother."

Christopher saw the nice man stop, sensing the presence behind him. He turned and saw her.

Christopher's mother.

Her eyes glowed with the light of one hundred billion stars. Her voice boomed.

"GET AWAY FROM MY SON!"

CHAPTER 126

When I was a little girl, I was so angry I thought I could close my eyes and destroy the world.

Kate ran at hiM.

Her instinct had taken over, like the women she heard about who turned over cars that trapped their children. But what she felt was more than adrenaline.

This was omnipotence.

She launched herself through the air. Their bodies collided. The nice man fell back, dropping Christopher.

"Mom!" he yelled out.

"Run!" she commanded.

The nice man tackled her to the street. They fell down into the river of blood. Scratching. Clawing. All the fury of a mother lion surged through her. A lifetime of bastards. Beating her. Leaving her. Everyone who ever put her down. Everyone who left her behind. They all had one face now.

"Come on, fucker," she said. "Pick on someone who KNOWS who you are."

She threw her body at him. There were no words anymore. Only instinct. She opened her hands, nails sharp as knives, and tore through his face like a farmer plowing a field. The nice man screamed. Blood gushing down his neck. He moved back to her, swinging wildly. His fist landed on her jaw, knocking teeth loose. But she had learned to take a punch a long time ago.

Now she was learning how to throw one.

*

Christopher moved to help the hissing lady just as a terrible whisper ran through the streets like a leaf floating on a breeze. It was the nice man. His body was fighting Christopher's mother. But a little piece of hiS voice whispered through the wind.

wakE uP . . .

Christopher looked as the man in the Girl Scout uniform stopped stabbing himself.

wakE uP, everyonE . . .

The couple stopped kissing. The little children put down their ice cream and deer legs. The man stood at the door, having just learned about his dead child. A woman looked down at her watch, waiting for her blind date. The clock had only moved a second in seventy-five years.

dO yoU wanT iT tO stoP?

"YES!" they cried.

Christopher tore at the ropes binding the hissing lady's hands. She was terrified.

"You're on the street!" she warned.

dO yoU wanT thE tormenT tO stoP?!

"YES! PLEASE!" they begged.

dO yoU seE thaT littlE boY oveR therE?

Every eye turned to Christopher. The hissing lady cried out, pulling at the rope frantically.

"Get off the street!" she commanded.

hE iS thE onE whO tortureS yoU.

"Run, Christopher!" his mother screamed.

Christopher's mother jumped on the nice man. She put her hand over his mouth to silence him. He bit into the flesh of her hand.

hE iS thE onE whO won'T leT yoU leavE.

Christopher saw the adulterous couple turn to him.

"hI, christopheR," they said.

Christopher's mother wrapped her legs around the nice man and squeezed. The nice man screamed, blood pouring out of his mouth. But the whisper kept coming.

becausE goD iS a murdereR!

The man in the Girl Scout uniform came out of the bushes. Knife raised.

"hI, christopheR," he said.

sO yoU havE tO kilL hiM noW!

Christopher loosened the knot around the hissing lady's hands. She tore herself free and went to the ropes around her feet.

thE firsT onE whO killS goD iS freE!

The man in the Girl Scout uniform pushed the cheating couple out of the way.

"coMe hEre, christopheR. i wanT tO shoW yoU soMething."

The nice man looked Christopher's mother dead in the eye. His whisper was gone. He opened his mouth and howled so loudly the ground shook.

"kilL goD anD you'rE freE!"

With a wave of his hand, the nice man turned the blue moon a fire red. The street boiled over with blood. The frogs jumped out of the pot and turned to Christopher, their eyes furious. Screams came from inside the houses. Hands shattered windows. The doors of the houses opened. All of the damned rushed outside.

"hI, christopheR," the voices said. "caN wE talK tO yoU?"

They started running at him. Fighting each other to be first.

Christopher's mother raced to save her son. The nice man tackled her to the ground. She turned and bit a chunk out of his shoulder. The nice man yelled in pain and ecstasy. The deer poured out of the woods. The damned ran at Christopher. There was only one group not moving.

The mailbox people.

They stood still like a fence surrounding the street. Their eyes sewn shut. Their mouths frozen. Each holding the string that kept the next in place. The street was completely blocked in.

Christopher was surrounded.

The hissing lady finally ripped the ropes from her body. She stood in front of Christopher as the nice man's army moved toward him. Her eyes darted, looking for any means of escape.

There was nowhere to go.

But down.

The hissing lady bent and grabbed the sewer grate. She planted her foot on the side of the street, her shoulder muscles ripping in tiny fibers as her foot sizzled. The sewer grate gave. She pried it open, the metal scraping.

The air poured out. Rotten air. Christopher looked down into the sewer. It was pitch black.

"Off the street!" she said, pushing him into the darkness.

Christopher's feet hit a puddle of blood with a squish. Immediately he realized that the sewer was not a sewer at all. It was the coal mine. Running underneath the street like veins through a cadaver. He looked up as the hissing lady turned and the nice man's army grabbed her. He saw the deer and the damned striking. Biting. Clawing. She fought back with everything she had. She wouldn't let them anywhere near Christopher. But there were too many of them. They swarmed her. Christopher watched as the hissing lady used her last ounce of strength to drag the grate back into place with a clank. Just before hands groped into the darkness and dragged her away, screaming.

Christopher ran down the coal mine. His legs almost buckled under him. He listened for any sound, but all he heard was the shuffling of feet. He was in complete darkness. What was down here? He reached into the blackness like a blind man without a cane.

He stopped when he touched the hand.

Christopher screamed. His voice echoed off the cement walls.

"he'S dowN therE!" the voices screamed above. "liSten."

Christopher groped into the darkness. He felt another arm. Another hand. He turned back around. A hundred feet behind him, he saw the dust kick up as the damned dug their way down. A shaft of moonlight lit the tunnel. He saw shadows of the damned running through the coal mine.

"hurrY! he'S dowN herE somewherE!"

Christopher ran deeper into the tunnel, his hands reaching out. He heard bodies stirring. A bare leg rubbing against the wall like a cricket. A finger reached out and touched his hair. Another grabbed his hand.

More digging behind him. More digging below. The tunnel was filling with the damned. Deer hooves clacked and squished in the bloody street above him. Christopher felt more hands on him. Moaning. His eyes adjusted to the darkness. And he finally saw what was reaching out and grabbing him.

The mailbox people.

They stood side by side like bats hanging upside down in a cave. They held each other in place with one long string.

The string.

The thought came out of nowhere. Maybe he could follow the string out of here. Christopher saw it running down the tunnel in every direction. Tunnels that went into themselves. He was in a labyrinth.

"christopheR?" the voices said behind him. "wE caN seE yoU! wE caN smelL yoU!"

He looked back and saw the man in the Girl Scout uniform leading the charge. Christopher followed the string deeper into darkness. He ran past the smells. The decay. The earth, coal, and wood mixed together like cement. He looked up through the cracks in the tunnel and saw the bottoms of people's homes. Pipes and basements. Crawl spaces hidden away for rats and glowing eyes. Then, the houses were replaced with tree roots hanging like stalactites on the ceilings of caves. He was under the Mission Street Woods now. Running deeper into the labyrinth. He saw what looked like an opening up ahead. He ran through it and saw a bedroom carved into the tunnel underground. It was filthy. Hateful. Pictures of naked ladies and men with cigarette burns where their privates would be.

A man was asleep on the mattress.

Next to a little kid's night-light.

Christopher saw a door at the other end of the bedroom. This man must be a guard. There was something on the other side of that door. He had to get to it. It was his only way out. He tiptoed past the mattress. He passed a mirror and looked at his reflection. But he didn't see his face. He saw the back of his own head. The man in the bed began to stir behind him.

"i'M huntinG thE sherifF noW, christopheR," the man said in his sleep. "ambrosE iS burying hImselF alivE again. and Again. gueSs whaT wiLl happeN to yoU! herE i comEEEEEEEEEEE!"

Christopher turned back and saw the shadows of the damned racing to become the first to kill him.

He would need an army to escape.

Christopher reached the door on the other side of the guard's bedroom. He opened it, the thick metal squeaking on its hinges. He slammed the door shut and locked it with a heavy click.

Then, he stepped into the darkest place he had ever been.

The air around him suddenly changed. It felt like being inside an oven. He stood breathless for a moment, listening. He heard rustling like bugs on a screen door. He called out to get any perspective, but all he heard was the sound bouncing off the walls in a giant echo. It reminded Christopher of old war movies when men were far from the battlefield. Miles away, people were in agony. But for him, the world was quiet.

Until his eyes adjusted to the darkness.

And he looked up to find the most horrible thing he had ever seen.

A giant hive of mailbox people.

The hive was as large as the clearing. Christopher looked above them and realized they were underneath the giant tree. These people were the roots. They guarded the only door to the surface. He was trapped. Christopher's eyes followed the string that held the mailbox people in place. He had to find the first person who held the string. Where did it all start? It could take him out of here.

Christopher walked down the line. Each person held the string. Their bodies swayed like trees, their arms branches dancing in a sick breeze. Puppets and strings. They were all connected. Christopher ran and saw the next hand holding it. And the person after that. And the person after that. Adults. Children. All ages. All genders. He had to find the master. The one holding all of the marionettes. He kept running. Faster and faster. Frantic for the exit. He heard banging on the locked door behind him and realized he was back at the entrance.

It was a circle.

A chain.

There was no master.

They were all holding the string.

Christopher stared into the darkness. There was no life here. There was no death. There was only eternity. A life sentence after everyone stops dying.

He was in the valley of the shadow of death.

Christopher closed his eyes and fell to his knees. He clasped his hands together and prayed for deliverance. For his mother. And the hissing lady. And David Olson. And the sheriff. And Ambrose. The list of names stretched out as long as the line of mailbox people. Mrs. Keizer. Mrs. Collins. Mr. Collins. Brady. Jenny. Eddie. Mike. Matt. Even Jerry. Especially Jerry.

"Please, God. You can have me if you need me. Just save them."

Suddenly a hand reached out from the darkness and held Christopher's arm.

Christopher screamed and turned quickly. The hand wouldn't let go, so it took him a moment to realize there was something different about it. There was no ripping or grabbing. There was only a soft touch. Christopher found the hand and the wrists with the scars. He moved his gaze up the body until he saw the face of the final mailbox person in the hive.

It was his father.

CHAPTER 127

Hist eyes were sewn shut.

Christopher's father stood in a porcelain bathtub. He wore hospital clothes. The bottoms of his pajamas were wet. Not from water. But from blood.

youR daddY iS crazY

Christopher took a step closer. His father's wrist scars were still wet. Still dripping. Filling the bathtub forever.

CLANK. CLANK.

The metal door banged behind them. The damned were coming.

"Dad?" Christopher said.

Christopher reached out and took his father's hand. He remembered the funeral. The viewing. The room with the ashtrays. He had kissed his father's dead forehead. It was so lifeless. There was no electricity. His hand was so cold.

But now his hand was warm.

"Dad, is that really you?" Christopher said.

His father twitched. Moaning through the stitches holding his lips together. Christopher felt the nice man's warning burning his ears.

I cut the yarn that held a little girl and her sister's mouths shut.

They tried to eat me alive.

Christopher reached into his pocket, looking for something to cut the string. He found it, coarse and jagged.

The hissing lady's key.

He stood on his tiptoes and brought the key to his father's mouth. He sawed through the strings holding his father's lips together. His father moved his jaw, frozen and stiff from years of bondage.

"Christopher?" he asked weakly. "Is that you?"

"Yes, Dad," Christopher said.

"You're alive?"

"Yes."

The man began to cry.

"I've seen you die a thousand times," he said. "You keep drowning in a bathtub."

"No, Dad. That wasn't me."

His father thought for a moment. His brow furrowed until he found the memory.

"Was I the one who died in the bathtub?"

"Yes, Dad."

"I'm so sorry I left you."

"I know you are."

"Let me look at you, honey."

Christopher brought the key to his father's eyes and sawed through the thick thread keeping his father blind. He pulled the thread out through his father's eyelids and dropped it to the ground. His father opened his eyes, bewildered, as if this dark cave were the brightest sun he'd ever seen. He blinked like a newborn until his eyes adjusted to the light. He looked down at his son. Then, he smiled.

"You're so big now."

His father reached out to hold him, but the string held his arm in place. Christopher moved his hand to help him. When he finally touched the string in his father's hand, he was surprised. There was nothing special about it. It wasn't made of steel. It reminded him of the time he watched the old movie about the circus with his mother. He saw a baby elephant tied to a post with a steel chain. The baby ripped and scratched and tried to get free, but the chain wouldn't break. Then, he saw a grown elephant tied to a post with nothing but a little piece of rope. He asked his mother how the little piece of rope held the big elephant in place. She explained that they chain the babies until they give up.

The elephants think that little piece of rope is still a chain.

Christopher thought. He didn't know if it would work or not, but he had to try.

"Dad," he said. "I think you can put the string down now."

"I can?"

Christopher gently held his father's hand. He felt the moment of his death. The final second when his father changed his mind. He wanted to live. He couldn't bear to be away from his family. But it was too late. But it wasn't too late. It was never too late.

Christopher's father let go of the string.

He stood still for a moment, waiting for a sky to fall. But it never did. He stepped out of the bloody bathtub. He knelt down and held his son with both arms. His shirt smelled like tobacco. Christopher held his father as he looked around the hive at hundreds of mailbox people. They were all connected. The town and the tunnels. All connected by an invisible string. No one was holding the mailbox people in place. They were holding themselves. The mailbox people weren't the nice man's soldiers.

They were his slaves.

Christopher heard the moaning. All of the mailbox people were actually asking for deliverance. Christopher finally understood the screams. The anger. The madness. All he could hear anymore were the words "Help me." He felt the heat being turned up. The frogs stuck in a boiling pot not understanding that the fire was a fever under their skin. They were inside the valley of the shadow of death, but the valley was not a place outside of them. It was inside.

The valley is us.

Christopher picked up his father's string and held it tightly in his hands. He brought the string to his lips, took a deep breath, and pushed the words down the string. Like a child making a telephone with two tin cans.

"You are free now."

CHAPTER 128

The sheriff felt the blood rush through his temple. He saw the girl with the painted nails dead in her hospital bed. He turned to run through the door to find a doctor as he had a hundred times already. He was a hamster on a wheel, trying to outrun a past that was always right in front of him. It had never occurred to him that he didn't need to run.

Until now.

"You are free now."

He didn't know where the voice came from. But there it was in his mind like a seed in soil. The sheriff stopped running. He turned and walked back to the hospital bed. He faced her. His heart in his throat. He knelt down. A bear of a man who suddenly felt so small. The sheriff closed his eyes and held her like a father. He saw light dance behind his eyelids.

When the sheriff opened his eyes, he looked at the girl with the painted nails. But she wasn't a little girl anymore. She was a grown woman. Maybe thirty years old. With bright eyes and a warm smile. She was in a white hospital gown. She held a baby in her arms. The little baby was sleeping.

"Where are we?" the sheriff said.

"We're in Mercy Hospital," she said. "You're a grandpa."

"I am?"

She smiled a patient smile. He saw the color in her blue eyes. Little flecks of light stretching into their own universe.

"Don't you remember?" she asked. "You came back into the room with my milk and you finished reading that story. You took me home for my first real Christmas. You moved me away from the city, so I would be safe. I grew up in that little house in Mill Grove. I went to a real school. I was in the school plays.

I even got to be Annie one night when Mary Kosko got sick. I graduated from high school. I went to Pitt. You cried at all of my graduations. You walked me down the aisle. We danced at my wedding. Don't you remember?"

She slipped her arm through his. Her arm felt warm and soft. Like an angel.

"I do now," he said. "I remember all of that."

"Then, you remember when I told you that you were going to be a grandfather. And you remember when I told you he was a boy. And my husband and I decided to name him Bobby . . . after the man who saved my life."

The sheriff looked down at his grandson, sleeping peacefully. A lifetime of memories flooded through him. All of the life she would have had. She got to live it every day. Forever. The sheriff looked up at his daughter, who smiled back at him. She put her hand on his. She slowly rubbed his hand where he had scratched himself to the bone. In an instant, the itch was gone. The skin was healed.

"God is not a murderer, Daddy," she said.

The sheriff nodded and felt the tears wet on his face. He didn't realize he had been crying.

"Can I stay with you here?" he asked.

"Not yet, Daddy. You have to live your life before you get to live your Heaven."

The sheriff held her and sobbed.

"We need your help, Daddy. This is a war. And the good guys have to win the war this time. You have to wake up right now. You have to help her. She's right next to you. You have to open your eyes."

"They are open."

"No, Daddy. I'm behind your eyelids. You have to open your <u>eyes</u>."

The sheriff slowly reached up and touched the thread holding his eyelids closed. He felt the thread keeping his mouth shut. The string in his hand.

"Drop the string, Daddy. She's standing right next to you. Save her."

The sheriff nodded to his adopted daughter and smiled. He dropped the string and pulled the thread that held his eyes closed.

"You are free now."

The sheriff opened his eyes. His real eyes. He looked around the woods and saw thousands of mailbox people stretching to the horizon. They were all moaning and twitching. Trying to find the way to get free. He dropped the string and turned to his right, expecting to find Kate Reese.

Instead, he saw a little girl with her eyes and mouth stitched up. He knelt down and gently took the string out of her hand. He slid the stitching out of her mouth and took the thread away from her eyes.

"I'm a police officer, honey. I'm here to help you."

The little girl opened her eyes and fell into his arms, crying. The sheriff held her. He would have known that little girl anywhere.

Her name was Emily Bertovich.

She held him, the warmth from her hands washing over him. In an instant, he saw the pictures unfold. The man who took her from the driveway. The fear she felt. The pain. The place where her body was buried. And finally, the peace.

"Will you tell my parents all that?" she asked.

The sheriff nodded, his eyes wet with tears.

"Yes, Emily," he said. "You are free now."

CHAPTER 129

Ambrose's hands ripped through the dirt of his little brother's grave. He felt himself getting lost in the cold ground. The dirt in his mouth. His eyes. Worms crawling on his body. He was burying himself alive, but he couldn't stop. He had to find his brother's body. He could save David this time. He could finally hold his brother again.

"You are free now."

Ambrose didn't know where the voice came from. Was it in the woods above him? The earth below? Was it inside his mind? He didn't know, so he dismissed it. His hands kept digging through the dirt. He couldn't let his brother die again. He couldn't let—

"You are free now."

It was unmistakable that time. The voice was clear, blowing out through the branches. A child's voice. Soft and innocent. Compelling him to do the only thing he had been unwilling to do for the last fifty years.

Let go.

Ambrose stopped digging. He knelt silently in the dirt, and rather than use his hands to tear the earth, he put his head in them and sobbed. The grief and guilt flooded his body as the memories returned. The baby his mother brought home from the hospital. "His name is David." His brother crawling then walking then running then climbing down the ivy wall. Going to the woods to save a world that had failed him so completely.

"David, I'm sorry I couldn't save you."

The old man stood, the dirt falling off his shoulders. His face found the surface, and he filled his lungs with fresh air. He looked through the halos in his eyes and saw something come out of the shadows.

A light.

It stopped in front of him and floated like a cloud with all of the lightning trapped inside. Ambrose moved his trembling fingers to his mouth and pulled a piece of thread stuck in the corner. He felt his lips pinch with a little stab of pain. Then, his jaw loosened as he realized that his mouth had been sewn together. Ambrose reached up and felt his eyes. They were sewn shut with the same evil string.

Ambrose pulled the thread and finally freed his eyes. He saw where he really was. There was no garden. No tree house. No grave. There was only the woods with what looked like thousands of other people. They were all freeing themselves of that string. A great quilt unraveling itself back to thread. And the light that stood in front of him was not a light at all.

It was David.

He was still a little boy. Scrawny. Missing those two front teeth. But his tongue had been replaced by a serpent's. Ambrose saw his brother cover his mouth, ashamed. Just like the men he served with who lost limbs or more after fire or shrapnel made them strangers to their own mirrors. Ambrose shook his head and gently moved his brother's hand away from his mouth.

"There's nothing to be ashamed of. You're a hero."

David smiled. Ambrose held his arms open, and his little brother melted into them. He smelled like baseball gloves. And he still had that amazing head of hair.

"I'm sorry, David. I'm sorry."

David pulled away and shook his head. No. Then, he knelt down and dragged his finger in the dirt. Ambrose saw four words. He would have known his brother's real handwriting anywhere.

YOU ARE FREE NOW

The words drifted on the wind. They moved through the clouds and the clearing, spreading from the imaginary world to the real.

Mrs. Keizer stood in the middle of the clearing. She thought she saw her husband in the fog.

"Please," she begged him. "What was my name before I met you? I can't live without knowing my name."

"Are you sure you don't want to be Mrs. KeiZer anymore?" the voice asked.

"Yes!" she screamed.

Her husband stopped and smiled and snapped his fingers.

"Okay. You're not Mrs. KeiZer."

In an instant, he took away the name Keizer, leaving her no name at all. She had never gotten married. She had never had her beautiful daughter Kathy. Her body began to shrivel. Her arthritic hands and broken hip. She felt like she aged fifty years in fifty seconds. Her hearing began to fail. Her mind. Her memory. Mrs. Keizer stood in the middle of the clearing. She thought she saw her husband in the fog.

"Please," she begged him. "What was my name before I met you? I can't live without knowing my name."

"Are you sure you don't want to be Mrs. KeiZer anymore?" the voice asked.

But this time, Mrs. Keizer didn't hear it. She heard something else. Words on the wind. Or were they inside her own mind?

"You are free now."

Mrs. Keizer stopped. Something felt so familiar about this moment. She was sure she had done this only five minutes ago. She had said yes, and her husband took away the name Keizer. She had never gotten married. She had never had her beautiful daughter Kathy.

"Are you sure you don't want to be Mrs. KeiZer anymore?" her husband repeated.

Mrs. Keizer turned around. She looked into the clearing at her little girl freezing in the backyard.

"No. I want to be Mrs. Keizer," she said. "My daughter is cold."

Then, she picked herself up and walked back toward her Kathy.

"whaT?! iF yoU leT heR iN thE kitcheN, i'lL breaK youR fuckinG necK, lynN!"

Mrs. Keizer didn't listen to her husband. He could beat her all day this time. She didn't care anymore. Her daughter was freezing in the backyard. Her daughter would never be cold again.

"iF yoU leT heR iN thE kitcheN, yoU arE ouT oF thiS housE. yoU caN gO backK tO beinG thaT dumB littlE worthlesS bitcH, lynN—"

"Wilkinson," she said aloud. "My name was Lynn Wilkinson."

She opened the door and brought her freezing little girl back into the warm kitchen.

"Kathy," she said. "You are free now."

Mrs. Collins looked back at her mother. She suddenly felt like a little girl again. She remembered the feeling of her mother wrapping her up in a towel after a bath. The steam from the shower covering the mirror like a fog. Mrs. Collins wasn't cold anymore. But someone else was. Someone in her own backyard.

She turned and saw her son Brady in the doghouse, shivering in the cold. She opened the door and brought her freezing son into the warm kitchen. Her husband joined her. They were a family again.

"Brady, I'm sorry," she said. "You are free now."

The word spread through the clearing. Mrs. Henderson dropped the knife and held her husband. Ms. Lasko put down her drink. Jerry stopped swinging his arms and hitting himself.

Jenny Hertzog heard her mother's sweet voice. "Stop, Jenny! Stop drowning him!" Jenny stopped pushing her stepbrother and used her hands to rip the thread from her mouth instead. In an instant, the truth poured from her mouth to her father in floods. Her father took the threads from his eyes. The silence was over. The healing began.

The words traveled through the clearing from Special Ed to Matt to Mike, their parents, and their town. Freeing their minds. Their bodies followed. The fevers broke. The itching stopped. The fear melted away with the madness. The frogs stood safely away from the boiling pot of water that each carried under the skin. The flu was no more.

"You are free now."

CHAPTER 131

Christopher's mother and the nice man fell to the street. Her hands ripped at his eyes. His fingers tore through her flesh. She fought back, but she was running out of strength. Christopher's warning echoed in her mind.

The power comes at a price.

She staggered back and the nice man wrapped himself around her like a snake. His skin stretching over her mouth as he prepared the needle and thread for her eternity. He whispered in her ear. She felt the world's madness. The evil that made God cry at night. With every word, she grew weaker and weaker.

"Kate, your son is about to be eaten alive. There iS only one way to save him now."

She saw the hissing lady. The deer swarmed her like sharks in a feeding frenzy. The damned jumped on her back. One after the other. Biting. Scratching. Clawing.

"Christopher gave you his poweR. If you kill hEr with it, I will let you go."

Christopher's mother could feel the backs of her eyelids licking her eyes moist. Her eyes boiling with fever. With vision. She was omnipotent, but this was his world. She could see him. He was terrified. And terrifying. Burning with cold fury.

"I've known too many men like you," she said.

"No, you haven't, katE."

Then, he sewed her mouth shut.

"You've never met anyone like mE."

Then, the nice man bit a chunk out of Christopher's mother's neck. He was everywhere and nowhere. Everyman and no man.

"So, if you won't kill her, you will become heR."

She fought back with everything she had. Broken and bleeding. Until he choked the blood out of her like water from a sponge and threw her on the street like trash. Her skin scraped off on the pavement, and she landed in a heap right next to the hissing lady on the lawn. The deer and the damned began to circle the two women. They couldn't battle all of Hell by themselves. They would need an army. But at least her son got away. That's all that mattered.

"Mom."

Christopher's mother turned and saw her son.

Walking out of the woods.

Alone.

"NO!" she screamed, ripping the threads from her mouth. "LEAVE ME! RUN! RUN!"

The deer ran at him.

"It's okay, Mom," Christopher said.

"OFF THE STREET!" the hissing lady screamed.

"Don't worry," he said. "I'm here."

Christopher's mother struggled to move as the man in the Girl Scout uniform climbed out of the tunnel with the rest of the damned and charged at her son.

*

Christopher paid them no mind. He just walked out of the woods. Fearless. He felt the voices come back to him through the string. The voices didn't rip his head apart anymore. There were no headaches. There was no fever. All he did was listen to the voices on the string. Everyone's past. The secrets. The lost innocence. The pain. Identity. Disappointment. Rage. Confusion. The regret. The guilt. The love. The loss. Of all humanity. It wasn't pain. It was power. Fear is not fear. It is excitement afraid of its own light. The whole world stretched out in front of him. All of the people on Earth. Christopher never felt such love. Such hope. Such gratitude. Every single soul in that line. He knew their names and their loves and their hopes and their dreams. He knew them, and he was them. Just as they were him.

"You are free now."

Christopher felt the mailbox people tear at the strings like elephants who suddenly remembered that a rope is not a chain. They opened their eyes like miners seeing the sun after a hundred years underground. They tore the strings from their mouths. The words spilled through the valley. The woods. The clearing. This fight wasn't over. The nice man had not won. It was still a war, and the good guys would keep fighting this war until there were no good guys left. They didn't need an army.

They <u>were</u> the army.

CHAPTER 132

Christopher emerged from the woods with Ambrose, David, the sheriff, and a thousand mailbox people behind them. They looked down the street where the other mailbox people stretched as far as the eye could see. The threads from their mouths now resting on the ground around their feet. Their eyes unzipped. Finally opened.

In silence, they turned their gaze to the nice man. They glowed with the rage of centuries. For all of the misery. For the million times he made them see a loved one die. A mother suffer. A child harmed. Christopher took the string in his hand, and the energy shot through him as he spoke.

"We are free now," he said.

The string dropped.

And the mailbox people ran at the nice man.

Starting with Christopher's father.

Kate was speechless. For a moment, she forgot where she was. Even with everything she had seen, she still didn't know if he was real. Until their eyes met, and she felt the whispers travel from his gaze to hers. She knew he was sorry for forgetting what he had in her. She knew that he thought the sheriff was a good man. She knew he was saying goodbye. For now.

"Wait. Where are you going?" she asked.

"I'm going to protect my family this time," he said. "I love you, Katie."

With that, he kissed his wife. All of her regret and loss gone in an instant of peace. Then, he turned and ran at the nice man, yelling to the rest of the mailbox people,

"FOLLOW ME INTO THE LIGHT!"

He launched himself at the nice man. The moment he hit skin, Christopher's father transformed into light. Burning hot like the sun. The son. The star. The soul. Ascending to Heaven.

The nice man screamed, his skin burning.

The dominoes fell. The mailbox people followed Christopher's father, running full speed at the nice man. They jumped on his back like fleas on a dog and burst into light. Floating up to the sky like embers from a campfire. The message spreading to everyone.

"We are free!"

The mailbox people kept coming. Trampling the damned in a stampede. The nice man hit back. With each swing of his powerful arms, dozens would burst into sparks. But they kept coming. Faster and faster. The light inside cracked them open and pulled them into the sky. Forever free. He swung his fists, but there were too many. They jumped onto his body, burning him with light. Filling the sky with shooting stars.

The nice man got weaker with each soul. With each sun. Son. Daughter. Father. Mother. Emily Bertovich smiled at the sheriff, then ran straight at the nice man's heart, breaking into a million pieces of light. The sky burned so brilliantly that the deer froze, staring into this massive headlight. The bodies piled on faster and faster until they couldn't see the nice man anymore. He was screaming in pain, buried in a pile of light.

Christopher looked up into the sky. He saw a cloud begin to gather.

"Mom?" he said, terrified.

The sheriff saw the deer blink and adjust to the light. They began hissing as the damned staggered to their feet. Ambrose felt his little brother tug at his sleeve.

"What is it, David?"

David pointed to the sky. Ambrose looked through the halos in his eyes at the clouds that were forming into a face. It looked like it was smiling. With big teeth. The man in the grey suit.

"MOM! WE HAVE TO GO RIGHT NOW!" Christopher screamed.

Before he could finish his sentence, Christopher's mother picked up her little boy and took off running back to the woods. The sheriff followed. David and Ambrose ran with the hissing lady as dark angry clouds began to twist behind them.

"chrisSstopheR!" the voice boomed.

Christopher looked behind his mother's shoulder and saw tornadoes of fire, spinning at impossible speeds. Each tornado looked like a fang in the nice man's mouth.

"yoU wilL neveR leavE mE!"

A wall of fire rolled in a tidal wave. Burning through the neighborhood like a house made of straw. There was a grinding sound, then a fantastic BOOM as the nice man stood up, scattering the bodies of the mailbox people like fireflies into dusk. He saw Christopher, his mother, the sheriff, David, Ambrose, and the hissing lady run into the woods. He put his feet down on his beautiful street and climbed down into his tunnel.

Into the passage that no one else knew.

CHAPTER 133

Christopher's mother ran with her son in her arms. The deer and the damned behind them. Christopher felt the panic in the hissing lady, her eyes darting down each path. Something was wrong. She knew it. The woods were different.

Where is the door?

Christopher felt David's terror. In fifty years, he had never seen the woods like this. The trees woke up. The branches reached out. Violent arms trapped for centuries. He could sense David trying to quiet his mind and fly Ambrose above the tree line, but the branches locked arms above them, creating a tunnel. They were being herded like cattle through a slaughterhouse.

Christopher looked back. The clouds were not just clouds anymore. They were smoke from one horrible fire. He felt the heat coming for them. He tried to find his mind's eye, but the string and the mailbox people left him drained, helpless in his mother's arms. He felt her, weakened by her battle with the nice man. Only her maternal instincts kept her legs moving as fast as they did.

"WHERE IS THE DOOR?!" his mother screamed.

Christopher looked down the path and saw a wall of trees up ahead. The woods had closed in on them. They were running into a dead end. He felt the ground tremble beneath them.

"dOoo yOuU knOw wHy wE burY bodIes siX fEet deEp?" the voice asked.

Christopher saw the dirt moving under his mother's feet.

"sO wE doN't heAr theM whEn theY wAke uPpp, chrIstopheR. theY're aLl wAkIng uPpPpP nOwwww! theY aRe cOminnnng!"

He could feel all the people under the earth. Roots tilling the soil.

"WHERE IS THE DOOR?!" his mother repeated.

Christopher quieted his mind. And found the memory. He had been here before. He had been here for six days. He knew this place.

"Keep running," he said.

The group looked ahead at the wall of trees. The branches like giant spears ready to impale them.

"It's a dead end!" his mother said.

"No, it's a trick. Trust me."

Without hesitation, Christopher's mother did. She ran straight into the wall of trees, ready to be torn apart by the branches.

But the trees weren't there.

They were only reflections in a mist of water. An illusion inside the nice man's maze. The group ran through the fog like a waterfall and reached the clearing on the other side. It glowed under the fire-red moon. They looked up and saw it.

The giant tree.

The tree of knowledge. Broken and tortured. The branches moving like marionettes. Each branch with a tree house. The shadows inside them scratching and clawing the doors. Little seeds in acorns squirming. Ready to be born.

"KEY!" the hissing lady yelled.

Christopher pulled the key from his pocket. She grabbed it and led them to the door carved into the trunk. The clouds descended. The faces moved in them like ghosts.

The wind blew the key out of her hand.

"NO!" the hissing lady screamed.

The key carried on the wind, swirling around the tree. Christopher watched as David Olson closed his eyes. He felt David push himself past the pain and find his mind's eye. Picturing himself flying after the key. Jumping from branch to branch. The tree house doors opening behind him. The shadows crawling out of the tree houses and slithering up the tree, giving chase.

"davvvvvviidddddddd . . ."

More tree house doors opened. Shadows leaked onto the branches. Some of them moving up toward David. Others moving down.

"chrisstttopppherrrr . . ."

A fog bank crept in from all sides of the woods like camouflage. The deer and the damned playing hide-and-seek in the mist. The last of the nice man's army.

The man in the hollow log. The couple. The man in the Girl Scout uniform. All of their eyes glowing like coals from a fire. Christopher felt them descend from all sides of the clearing.

They were completely surrounded.

The adults made a circle around Christopher as the deer and the damned attacked. The two women turned back to back. Christopher between them. The deer swarmed, tearing the hissing lady's flesh with razor-sharp teeth. The man in the Girl Scout uniform jumped onto Kate's back. Licking her neck. Ambrose looked through the halos in his eyes as the shadows dripped off the tree onto the ground like sap. Creeping toward them.

"Sheriff!" he yelled.

The sheriff turned as the ground opened up. Little skeleton hands reached up from the soil. The missing souls that built the tree houses over centuries. The bones of children approached the sheriff.

"sheriffffffffff . . ." the children giggled.

The children threw themselves onto him, biting, leaving their skeleton teeth in his skin. The sheriff fell to the ground as more hands broke through the earth and started pulling him down.

Christopher. Help!

Christopher felt David's plea on the wind. He looked up and saw the key moving through the air faster than David could fly. Christopher needed to grab the key for him, but he was too weak to follow. He needed thousand-foot arms. He needed hands.

He needed the tree.

Christopher had given all of his strength to his mother.

But he still had his mind. Christopher closed his eyes and let the whisper take his body. He touched the tree, pulsing like a heartbeat. It didn't feel like bark. It felt like flesh.

I was here for six days.

Christopher pushed the whisper from his mind into the tree's flesh. He spread his fingers, moving the top branches like fingers in a glove. Christopher watched the key flying up past the branches. David Olson behind it. The shadows chasing. Everything slowed down. The wind. The air. The tree branches above them. The key raced in the wind. It was almost at the top. It was now or never. Christopher reached out with the top branch like a fishing line.

Christopher snagged the key out of the air.

He held it for David, who snatched it away from the branch, the shadows right behind him. Christopher opened his eyes and saw David crest the top of the tree.

Where the nice man floated.

"hI, davId."

He brought his hand down like a thunderclap, striking David Olson, who fell like a clay pigeon out of the sky. David crashed on the ground at Ambrose's feet, blood pouring from his mouth and eyes.

"NO!" the hissing lady screamed in anguish as David dropped the key.

CHAPTER 134

The key lay on the ground. Ambrose watched in horror as the clouds descended. He saw the nice man through the halos in his eyes, hidden in the fog. The nice man jumped through the air and landed quietly on the ground. He reached for the key. Ambrose hit back with all of his rage at the man who took his brother. The man who tortured him for fifty years.

But he was no match.

The nice man grabbed his arms and drove his thumbs through the old man's eyes. Ambrose felt his body go. His fingers shriveled with arthritis. His back. His knees. His feet numb from the trenches. Whatever Christopher had healed was gone. He was an old man again, blind and helpless.

The nice man reached for the key.

Ambrose heard the hissing lady throw off the deer and tackle the nice man to the ground. The two battled, her screams filling the night with red. All he could do was listen helplessly as the damned attacked Christopher and his mother. The giggling skeletons of the children dragging the sheriff to his grave.

Ambrose reached blindly for the key. His hands digging through the dirt until he found it buried in blood. He picked up his little brother's body and moved to the door on brittle knees. He held the key in his arthritic hand and searched for the keyhole with the clouds in his eyes.

"yoU wilL neveR finD iT, olD maN," the wind taunted.

"I know how to be blind, motherfucker," Ambrose said.

Ambrose's hands found the keyhole. He put in the key and turned it with a click. Ambrose opened the door to . . .

Light.

"Come on, David!" he yelled.

Ambrose held his little brother and rushed into the light. With every step, the halos in his eyes returned. Along with the joy. He had found his brother. He was going to rescue him. He was going to get him out of this horrible place. Suddenly Ambrose felt them hit an invisible wall. An invisible fence. His brother dropped from his arms. He turned around and found David, staggering to his feet. Desperate.

"Come on, David!"

David shook his head. No.

"You can't leave?" Ambrose asked.

David nodded yes. He pushed against his brother. Pushing him into the light to save him.

"It took me fifty years to find you. I'm not leaving you," Ambrose said.

David began to cry. He pushed on his brother like an oak tree, but Ambrose wouldn't budge.

"David, stop. I'm never leaving you again."

Gently, the old man lowered David's hands until the little boy stopped pushing. Ambrose knelt down and put his hand on David's shoulder. He felt the light inside him. He looked through the halos in his eyes.

"David . . . can you go to Heaven?" Ambrose asked.

David nodded. Yes.

"Then, why aren't you there already?"

David looked at Ambrose.

"You stayed here for me?" Ambrose asked.

David nodded. Yes.

"You were protecting me?"

David nodded again. Ambrose looked back at the clearing. He saw the hissing lady being torn apart by the nice man. The shadows and skeletons crawling on the sheriff. The damned ripping Christopher from his mother as the deer attacked. All was lost.

"David, do you want to see Mom and Dad?"

David stopped. He knew what Ambrose was asking. The little boy nodded. Yes.

"Come on, David," Ambrose said. "Let's go home."

He took David's hand, and they ran at the nice man. With every step, Ambrose's body felt like it did on that night when he was seventeen. His bad knees.

Arthritis. The scars from the wars. All the little aches and pains. They all melted away. There was no more pain because there was no more flesh to hold it.

The two Olson boys raced through the clearing.

And then . . . impact.

They hit the nice man, who fell to the ground in agony. Their light spreading like buckshot through his skin. It was so bright that the shadows were vaporized. The deer attacking Christopher's mother were blinded. The skeletons and the damned were knocked away from the sheriff and Christopher like a house made of cards.

Time seemed to slow. Ambrose opened his eyes. There were no halos. It was all a halo. All of the grief. The worry. Fifty years of an empty room. It was gone. He finally found his little brother. He could stop being lost now. In a blink, he saw David turn to the hissing lady. His protector. His guardian. The woman who kept him safe for the half century Ambrose could not. He waved goodbye to her and smiled with his missing front teeth. She cried in joy as she watched him leave this place forever. Her David was finally going home. The two Olson boys rose up. Two sons. Two suns. The light was brighter than anything Ambrose had ever seen, but it didn't hurt his eyes. The lights came on in his bedroom. Ambrose looked up from his bed and saw his little brother at the light switch.

"Hey, Ambrose. You want to have a catch?" David asked.

CHAPTER 135

Christopher watched as the last of their light flickered in the wind, and then, darkness descended. The woods were coming back to life. Christopher ran to his mother, bleeding on the ground. He helped her to her feet. She put her weight on her leg, bitten to ligaments by the deer. Christopher helped his mother over the graves left by the skeletons as the hissing lady grabbed the sheriff and threw his arm over her neck like a soldier.

The four limped to the tree.

The door opened to light. The hissing lady threw the sheriff into the trunk. Back to life. Back to the real side. She turned to Christopher's mother. One look a lifetime.

"Go!" she said.

Christopher's mother moved her son into the light. Christopher looked back at the hissing lady when suddenly, he saw the nice man charging them. Christopher knew both of them couldn't get out. It was either him or his mother. He threw his mother into the light.

"No!" she screamed.

The nice man grabbed Christopher and yanked him back into the clearing. The hissing lady rushed at him. In his fury, he threw her down like a chew toy for the deer.

"chrisssStopherrrrr," hE said. "iF i can'T leavE, yoU can'T leavE."

The nice man shoved Christopher against the tree.

"yoU tooK alL oF mY petS."

The nice man locked the door, then held the key in front of Christopher's face.

"i wilL starT oveR witH yoU."

He put the key in his mouth and swallowed. Christopher saw the metal poking inside the skin of his throat. The door was locked. The key was gone. Christopher was trapped.

"yoU wilL neveR leavE mY sidE."

Christopher looked for an escape, but there was nowhere to run. He had given all of the power to his mother. David was gone. The hissing lady was passed from deer to damned. The man in the Girl Scout uniform pulled out a knife. The kissing couple regrew their teeth to twice the normal size. The man in the hollow log giggled like a child. They stood, waiting for their turn.

Christopher looked to the horizon and saw soft light begin to break above the trees. The sun was rising. Something would change in the dawn. He felt it all around him. The voices chanting.

Death has come.

Death is here.

You die on Christmas Day.

Christopher saw the sun break over the horizon. Suddenly, he felt a voice. A little voice cutting through all of the others. He would have known that voice anywhere.

It was his own.

"I forgive you," he said.

"whaT?" the nice man asked.

Christopher looked at the nice man in the light of dawn. He realized he was a magician. He always had people looking in one hand while he moved things in the other. That was his only real power.

Christopher looked down into his hand. He saw a string. Invisible. He had carried it his whole life. He never knew it was there. He hadn't given all of his power to his mother, because the power of God was not omniscience. The power of God was not omnipotence.

The power of God was love.

"I forgive you," he repeated.

Christopher knelt down in front of the nice man. He loved everyone. All the people above. All the people below. He knew it was his destiny to die in these woods. To keep the nice man unaware of the fact that to get out, he only needed to look in. Because in was out. To keep power you give it away. It doesn't take violence to kill evil. It takes good.

"I forgive you," Christopher repeated.

The nice man ran at him like a howling dog.

"sssStoP sayinG thaT!" he hissed.

"You can kill me," Christopher said. "I will take all of their places."

Christopher lowered his head, ready for death.

"i won'T leT yoU diE! yoU wilL neveR escapE! i havE lockeD thE dooR."

"You can't lock the door," Christopher said.

"whY?!" the nice man laughed.

Christopher looked at the hissing lady and smiled. All was quiet and calm.

"Because there is no door."

Christopher reached up and felt his eyes. It was so easy to see in everyone else, and so hard to see it in himself. His eyes were sewn shut. Christopher reached up and tore the stitches from his eyes. He looked at everything in the plain light of day. The clearing. How small it seemed now. Like going back to his old school and seeing the tiny lockers. The shadows were not terrifying. They were the proof that light exists. The fire and brimstone were all a mirage. The clouds nothing but steam inside a bathroom. All he needed to do was wipe away the mirror.

He didn't need a key.

He <u>was</u> the key.

Christopher turned to the nice man with his real eyes. For the first time, he saw . . .

The d

evil.

Calm. Still. Ready to strike. Abandoned. Insane. Inside a trap that hE could not see. hE was all alone. hiS eyes were sewn shut. hiS mouth was zipped tight. hE held the string around hiS own neck. hE did nothing but gaze into the reflection of hiS own smoke and mirrors and call them clouds. hE wasn't a God. hE was a coward.

Christopher reached up and unzipped his mouth. Christopher loosened his jaw and spoke for the first time out loud.

"I am free now."

Christopher dropped the string. The door inside the tree opened.

"nOOOO!" the devil screamed.

The tree opened everywhere. The light broke through the cracks in its skin, cascading out of the giant trunk. The deer and damned ran from it. Their eyes wild with panic. All Christopher heard were two words inside all of their madness. Inside all of their screams.

"Help me."

The light absorbed them all and took them away in floods. Some wept. Others screamed. And in an instant they were gone. Leaving the hissing lady safely on the ground, the light already beginning to heal her.

Christopher looked at the nice man.

"I love you."

Then, he turned and walked back into the light.

*

The nicE maN ran at him. Murderous.

"yoU'rE noT goinG anywheRe . . ."

hE ran blindly into the light and reached in to pull Christopher back. hiS skin burned when hE hit the invisible fence. hE pushed through with all of hiS rage.

"wherE iS thE dooR?!"

It burned hiM, but hE wouldn't stop. Christopher left an opening. Somewhere. hE could feel it. Where was iT?! hE could get out! hE ripped the key from hiS throat. hE kept testing the fence, burning hiS body. Looking for the door. Where is it?! Where is it?!

"geT mE ouT oF herE!"

hE saw Christopher walking back to earth. Christopher was in his tree house on the real side. hE could smell the fresh winter air. The pine trees. Christopher left the tree house. hE saw it.

The tree house door was open!

"leT mE ouT!"

hE could feel the surge of energy outside. The wet grass and winter. hE could get out! hE squeezed hiS body through an opening in the fence, burning hiS skin to scars. hE was inside the tree house on the real side. Christopher slammed the door. hE looked out to the real world through the windows. Wild-eyed and insane. Freedom was on the other side of the door. hE ran at the tree house door. hE was going to escape!

"i aM freE noW!" hE screamed.

Christopher threw his body against the door. The nicE maN pushed against the other side. Ripping the wood. Clawing. Trapped like a caged animal.

"leT mE ouT! leT mE ouT!"

The sheriff joined Christopher. The whole town pushed back. The nicE maN moaned and scratched the glass windows.

"yoU arE all goinG tO burNNN!"

Suddenly hE saw water pouring down the windows in thick streams. hE thought it was rain, but hE hadn't brought the clouds. hE didn't know what it was until he took a deep breath through his nose. The mossy pines and the winter air were replaced with another smell.

Gasoline.

hE saw Christopher's mother climb down from the roof to the ladder with the gas can. Three words stenciled on its side. COLLINS CONSTRUCTION COMPANY. She held a match in her hand. The nicE maN frantically scratched the window to put out the flame. Christopher put his palm against the glass, the whisper scratch touching the nicE man'S hand.

"You are free now," he said.

Christopher's mother threw the match onto the tree house.

The dEvil screamed.

Christopher looked at the nicE maN with no malice. No hatred. Nothing but compassion and forgiveness. Christopher took hiS hands and gave the dEvil back everything hE had ever given the world. hE was Mrs. Henderson alone and unwanted in the kitchen. hE was Mike sewing hiS own brother's eyes shut. hE was Scott and Jenny drowning in floods. hE couldn't drink enough for Ms. Lasko. hE couldn't get warm in the freezing backyard with Brady Collins or his mother. hE was the first parent who ever abused hiS child and every child since.

"makE iT stoP!"

The fire ate through the window frames. The door. hE ran everywhere to get away from the feeling. hE screamed through the tree house windows. Every word in another voice.

"puT ouT thE firE! gooD guyS wiN warS. listeN tO grandmA!"

And a quiet voice from centuries ago.

"To kill in the name of God is to serve the devil."

Light poured into hiS eyes. Blinding hiM. The nicE maN felt the light surround hiM. The tree house was a wooden straitjacket. The burning was too great. The hissing lady pulled hiM back through the light. Back to the giant tree in the blood-soaked clearing.

The devil was back in Hell.

hE looked at the hissing lady, who reached down and took the key from hiS charred hand. She locked the door behind her with a click. Then, she put the key back around her neck. There were no more doors. No more escapes. There were no more deer. No more damned. No more shadows.

There was only him and her.

"You're off the street," she smiled.

hE looked at her. Defeated. Broken. hiS eyes blurry from rage baptized in tears. hE ran at her with all the hatred in hiS heart. The hissing lady stood quiet and still. She was at peace.

"diE!" hE screamed.

hE swung and hit her with all the force of Hell.

*

She felt no pain. She only heard a voice. A sweet, gentle voice.

"Come home. I'm sorry. Your Father loves you."

Her brother died on Earth. It was her choice to die here. The hissing lady broke into a million pieces of light. The nicE maN watched the hissing lady ascend to Heaven. Stars streaking across the sky. We all become the ocean. We all become the stars.

"Please, come home. You've done enough. Your Father misses you so much."

The hissing lady approached her Father's house. A grown woman freezing in the backyard. She knocked on the door and waited until He opened it. She felt the warm kitchen air. The hissing lady looked up at her Father. He opened His arms and held her.

"I'm sorry for what I did," she said.

"I know you are. I'm sorry, too," He said.

"I love You, Father," she said.

"I love you, too, Eve," He said, kissing her forehead. "Welcome home."

tHe nIce Man looked through the kitchen window from the freezing backyard. hE felt so much hatred in that moment that hE thought he could break down the door and kill them both. hE ran at the door and hit it.

"leT mE iN! leT mE iN!"

Silence. hE hit the door over and over until hiS hands were bloody and broken. But no one heard hiM. hE was the tree in the middle of the forest. All hE could do was watch those shooting stars. Every star a sun. Every sun a soul. Within a moment, all of the stars were gone. The planets around earth had no more light.

And hE was alone.

The nicE maN was suddenly terrified.

hE realized hE had been here one hundred billion times.

The faces always changed, but the ending never did. God had abandoned hiM in this trap. hE had to find a way out of this torment. hE looked through the vastness of the universe and saw nothing but a 6x6 cell. hE looked around at hiS white walls, not seeing that hE alone held a string. hE would never reach up and feel the thread on hiS eyes. hE would never feel the zipper on hiS mouth.

"You are free now," the voice said.

But hE could not hear it. hE could only sit in hiS solitary confinement. Watching the town. Looking for the next child.

hE walked through the clearing. Staring at them. The frogs were still waking up, staggering, getting sober. They looked at hiS tree house as it burned into smoke that disappeared into

Clouds.

hE knew some would dismiss this experience as a bad nightmare. Some might even force themselves to forget. But hE would always be there. In their ears. In their dreams.

"mrS. hendersoN . . . psst . . . mrS. hendersoN . . ."

hE whispered into the old lady's ear so closely that she mistook hiS breath for a breeze. She scratched her ear, but she still did not hear hiM. She was too focused on her husband, who looked at the tree and found himself holding his wife's hand. Now that the nightmare was over, all he wanted to do was take her away for a weekend trip. Luckily, she had already packed a bag.

"jennY, honeY. scotT iS stilL therE. let'S drowN hiM iN floodS."

But Jenny could not hear hiM. She was safe in her father's arms, being carried far away from her stepbrother. She promised herself that she would report Scott to the police because she deserved justice more than silence. What she couldn't know was that Scott would confess to the sheriff later that night. It was the only way to make himself stop drowning in that creek. In floods.

"bradY . . . kilL thaT boY . . . listeN tO grandmA."

Brady Collins was too busy listening to his actual grandmother to pay the voice any mind. Lynn Wilkinson apologized to her daughter for not stopping her late husband just as Mrs. Collins promised her son she would never put him in the backyard again.

"eddiE . . . psst . . . eddiE . . . listeN tO grandmA . . ."

Special Ed scratched his ear, then went right back to being showered with kisses and promises of cakes and pies and HBO <u>and</u> Showtime in his room forever. That night, he would put his father's gun back in its case. He would slip himself under the covers and look at the tree outside with the branches like a smile gone sick. The tree would frighten him, and he would go to his mother's room only to find that his mother was sleeping in the same bed as his father again. Special Ed would sleep between them that night, and when he closed his eyes, he would dream of his grandmother. His real grandmother.

"I am so proud of you, Eddie. You won the war."

The nicE maN walked through the clearing, getting angrier and angrier as other children were scooped up by their families. hE saw Mike and Matt's two mothers wrap their boys in their arms. hE knew that Matt and Mike would grow up together. They would always be there for each other. Matt would always keep his magic eye on his brother. No one would ever split up the M&M's again.

"lisSsteN tO mE . . ."

hE whispered to Ms. Lasko about the beautiful buzzy butterfly feeling on her skin, but she didn't need it anymore. That would leave more merLOT for Nurse Tammy, who had vague memories of falling asleep at work before waking up in the middle of nowhere with the doctor, who figured it must have been a fever dream brought on by the flu. She called her father and told him she would come home for Christmas as soon as she and the doctor helped the town get back on its feet. Her father kidded, "Is that the cute doctor you always talk about?" "Shut up, Dad."

"listeN tO mE!"

hE screamed into their ears but all they did was scratch hiM away and make the peace they needed to make. Jill and Clark returned home. The old lady returned to the log cabin. She would sit in her room that night and look out at the beautiful stars twinkling like sunlight on the Ohio River. She would see her husband beckon her to come into the water with him so they could be together forever. She would be reunited with him soon. He was such a beautiful boy.

"jerrY! she'S goinG tO fucK thE sherifF, jerrY. thE bitcH iS laughinG aT yoU."

But even Jerry was beyond hiS reach. After hE had moved Hell and earth to lure him here, all hE could do was watch Jerry utter two simple spineless words . . .

"Goodbye, Kate."

Jerry nodded to Christopher. Then, he took his casino winnings back home to Michigan. Back home to Mustang Sally.

"buT goD iS stilL a murdereR, sherifF. goD wilL kilL the woMan you lovE . . ."

The sheriff looked over at Kate Reese covered in mud and blood. He had never seen anyone so beautiful in his life. He knew they didn't have all the time in the world, so he didn't want to waste a minute of it. He wanted to make memories with her. He wanted to have a child with her. He wanted to spend every Christmas and every holiday for the rest of his life with her and Christopher.

"he'lL leavE yoU, katE. jusT likE youR husbanD."

Kate Reese turned to the sheriff and gestured for him to come and join the family. For a moment, she thought of her late husband. The memories of her life returned but the pain did not. She looked at Christopher, sober and present. His fever was gone for now. So was hers. Children do not cry at happy endings, and he was never going to learn how to do it from her. She kissed the sheriff.

She knew she would marry that man. She knew they would be a family. Everyone gets an ending. Whether or not it's happy is up to them.

"i aM watchinG yoU."

hE watched the sheriff kiss Kate Reese goodbye and go back to his job to help the town get home without further incident. The sheriff promised himself that in the morning, he would make the drive up to Erie, Pennsylvania, to give Emily Bertovich's family some peace. But for now, he was needed right where he was standing. The nicE maN watched the sheriff help the crowd disperse and return to their homes safely. It amazed hiM how people always did that. No matter how big the war. How bloody the battle. In the end, the frogs always kept going. Like little seeds sprouting from the soil of a burnt forest. They always went home.

Rubberneckers.

"i aM watchinG yoU."

hE watched the town leave the clearing and walk back out through the Mission Street Woods. hE looked around at hiS world. Empty. Silent. The tree had fallen in the middle of the forest, and there was no one left to hear it.

Except Christopher.

He was looking straight at hiM.

"i aM watchinG yoU, chrisSstopher," hE said.

Christopher looked through hiM. To the cloud. The face. The blue moon. The eclipse. The end of days. The shooting stars across the brittle sky. Another. Then another. Every one a daughter. A son. A sun. A soul. A fleck of color in God's eyes.

"I am watching you, too," Christopher said.

hE saw Christopher's mother turn and look hiM right in the eye with all of the fury of Heaven.

"So am I," she said.

Then, she took her little boy's hand, and the two walked out of the Mission Street Woods. The nicE maN stayed at the tree for a moment. The last of the tree house was now charcoal on the ground. The smoke rose into the air, and hE followed it.

hE floated into the cloud, rising above the woods. Higher and higher. Until hE saw the clearing and the tree looking back with itS giant angry eye.

hE saw the horizon. The single sun. The earth was the head on the giant's body. Human beings were the bugs crawling on hiS face. hE looked out into the world. Watching. Waiting. Looking for the next soul.

hE hovered above the town. Following the sirens. hE saw the ambulance race down the road. hE followed it all the way back to the hospital and saw the paramedics rush the gurney down the hall into the operating room.

While the doctors did their best to play God, hE floated down the hallway. hE saw Father Tom resting in a bed. Mrs. Radcliffe held his hand from his bedside. Thank God he is still alive, hE heard the woman pray. Thank God they are all still alive. The mother. The father. The teenage boy. It was a Christmas miracle.

When the girl's operation was over, hE quietly floated into the hospital room and lay down on the ceiling. hE watched her sleeping. Deeply and peacefully. All day and all night as the world kept itself busy turning.

When Mary Katherine woke up, she looked up into the bright white light above her bed. She looked down at the bandages and gauze covering her legs and arms. Suddenly she remembered the accident. The deer antlers ripping apart her body. But she saved Christopher's life. Somehow in her heart, she knew Christopher was still alive.

The door opened.

Mary Katherine saw a doctor and a nurse enter the room. Mary Katherine's eyes were still a little blurry, but she saw that the nurse's name tag read TAMMY. Behind Nurse Tammy, her mother and father entered the room with Doug. They had escaped from the church. Their nightmare was over.

"Is this Heaven?" she asked.

Everyone in the room laughed.

"No, honey," her mother said kindly. "We're in the hospital."

"You had a close call, honey," her father said. "We all did."

Her father choked back tears and held his daughter's hand. Mary Katherine suddenly felt as warm as if she were in her mother's kitchen. The doctor stepped up and started explaining the operation to her, but Mary Katherine's mind drifted on the cloud of painkillers. She heard a word here or there, but she was too focused on her family "*blood loss*" to put her full attention "*ruptured*" anywhere else. She just felt so grateful to be alive. To be here with her family and Doug. Beautiful Doug. Maybe she would get into Notre Dame after all. The possibilities of life suddenly seemed "*full recovery*" endless. Mary Katherine closed her eyes and began to drift away when she felt her mother's loving hand.

"We will help you, Mary Katherine," her mother said.

"That's right," her father agreed. "We're in this together as a family."

"I'll be here, too, Mary Katherine. You're not alone," Doug said.

Mary Katherine was confused. She opened her eyes and looked at her mother.

"Alone with what, Mom?" she asked.

Her mother cried tears of joy.

"They were able to save the baby. You're still pregnant."

hE watched as the news spread over the young girl's face. hE watched as she held her mother. hE watched as the young man professed his love and promised to raise the child as his own. hE watched as the father wondered what his grandchild would be.

A daughter

A son

A sun

A soul

After a few minutes, the doctor ushered her family out of the room to let Mary Katherine get some much-needed rest. After all, she was sleeping for two now. As she lay on the pillow, she felt a little prickle on the back of her neck that she blamed on the air-conditioning. She scratched her neck and curled up into the blanket. She closed her eyes, and right before she fell asleep, she could have sworn she heard a sweet whisper in her ear.

"Mary Katherine . . . " the sweet voice said.

"You are having a Son."

READING GROUP GUIDE FOR

IMAGINARY FRIEND

DISCUSSION QUESTIONS

1. "I will protect you," Christopher silently resolves to his mother at the end of Chapter 1 of *Imaginary Friend*. Discuss the various ways that Christopher protects his mother over the course of the novel, as well as the ways Kate protects Christopher. What does it mean to protect those you love? From what should one's loved ones be protected? Does this impulse ultimately do more harm or good, whether in your own personal experience or in Chbosky's novel?

2. *Imaginary Friend* is a different genre than Chbosky's acclaimed, celebrated debut novel, *The Perks of Being a Wallflower*. Have you read both books? If so, in what ways are the novels similar? In what ways are they different? If you haven't read *The Perks of Being a Wallflower*, do you think you'll now be seeking it out after reading *Imaginary Friend*? If you've already read *Perks*, do you think you'll be rereading it after reading Chbosky's second novel, or will you think of Chbosky's debut in a different light?

3. What other novels, TV shows, or movies do you feel share a kinship with *Imaginary Friend*? Where in the canon of horror and contemporary literary fables does Chbosky's novel fall, in your estimation?

4. What or who do you think was the cloud with the smiling face who first led Christopher into the Mission Street Woods?

5. Kate chooses to raise her son Catholic, so he can grow up the same way his father had grown up; Mary Katherine, who plays an important role in the story, is also religious. Discuss the role of religion and spirituality in the novel.

6. Discuss the phrase "To think it is to do it," which Chbosky uses to explore a handful of different themes in the novel. What does the phrase mean to Mary Katherine? What does it mean to Christopher?

7. Discuss the role that nightmares play in *Imaginary Friend*. What does Chbosky's novel seem to suggest about the things that haunt us, whether during our waking hours or when we're asleep?

8. What conclusions can you make about the nature of evil as Chbosky describes it? Of good as Chbosky describes it?

9. *Imaginary Friend* takes places in the months leading up to Christmas. Why do you think Chbosky chose to set this story then? What effect does the countdown to Christmas lend to the overall mood and tone of the read?

10. *The Perks of Being a Wallflower* is, in part, famous for a handful of quotable lines like "I feel infinite" and "We accept the love we think we deserve." If *Imaginary Friend* becomes, like Chbosky's debut, a novel that readers continue to discuss for years to come, what lines from Chbosky's newest seem most likely to you to stand the test of time? What about this novel might readers remember long after finishing it?

11. How does this book help you to better understand people with mental and/or social disabilities? Does it make you think differently about the young or old people, or see them in a different light?

12. What do you think is the scariest part of *Imaginary Friend*? Explain why.

13. What was your favorite part of *Imaginary Friend*? Explain why.

In *Imaginary Friend,* the townspeople sew their own mouths and zip their eyes closed as Christmas Day approaches, blinding them from the reality of their struggle. What message did you want to send the reader with this imagery?

Evil requires silence to spread. In the case of Mill Grove, sewn eyes and mouths make it painfully easy to "see no evil" and "speak no evil."

Did you have an imaginary friend when you were younger? How old were you? How did you meet them? What did you do with him/her/them?

No comment. :)

What were some of your childhood fears? How did they come about? Did any of them find their way into the pages of *Imaginary Friend*?

Growing up just south of Pittsburgh, I was surrounded by woods. Deer were everywhere. Shadows. Shapes. My street—Carmell Drive—had this one especially terrifying hill. On the crest of the hill sat two houses. They were directly across from each other. Each house had a massive front yard and trees that hid the houses from the world.

It wasn't so bad during the day.

So, every now and then, on Saturday afternoon, I would walk to my friend Kevin Dorwart's house. I would reach the crest of the hill, but in the daylight, I was fine. I'd arrive at Kevin's house to eat dinner with his family and watch horror movies on *Chiller Theater*, hosted by Pittsburgh legend, Bill "Chilly Billy" Cardille of *Night of the Living Dead* fame.

Then, after the movies, it was time to walk home.

Between those two houses.

One night in particular, I walked home, and the houses were especially quiet. Especially dark. The trees obscured whatever streetlights Carmell Drive provided. I ran away from the houses, then I fell. I couldn't get up. A car slowly drove up the road. The car stopped. The door opened with a creak. I saw two high-heeled shoes under the door. A lady with eye shadow looked down at me. It was my fourth-grade teacher. She said nothing. She just walked toward me and when she was two feet from me, she reached out her hand with her long nails and HISSED at me.

That's when I woke up. Because unbeknownst to me, I was asleep. And unlike all the other times I walked over that hill, this was a nightmare. And in that moment, thirty years later, the hissing lady was born.

Which authors have influenced your work the most?

My favorite author of all time is, was, and will always be Stephen King. When I was a kid, I was a very slow reader. If I'd been tested, I would have probably been diagnosed somewhere on the dyslexia spectrum. So, all of the books that my friends loved were too difficult for me. Except Stephen King. *Imaginary Friend* is my tribute to him and how his work convinced a kid from Pittsburgh that someday, he could be a writer.

What are some of your favorite books of all time? Any recent favorites?

The Stand by Stephen King

To Kill a Mockingbird by Harper Lee

The Great Gatsby by F. Scott Fitzgerald

1984 by George Orwell

The Handmaid's Tale by Margaret Atwood (The sequel was great, too!)

The Long Walk by Richard Bachman

. . . and one recent favorite . . .

The Fireman by Joe Hill

Religion plays a role in *Imaginary Friend*. Did you grow up with a religious background? How has your relationship with spirituality grown or changed as you've gotten older?

I was raised Catholic. As I've gotten older, I've become more spiritual, but my definition of what spirituality is has changed. I now know people of all faiths. All religions. In the end, I believe that faith is as good as the person who practices it. History has taught us time and time again that the same words have inspired charity and love in one soul. Hatred and war in another.

What inspired the character of the hissing lady?

My nightmare about my fourth-grade teacher. Fun fact . . . she was also my first writing teacher, and I absolutely adored her. Ms. Caridis was the first person to ask me to stand up and read a story in front of the class. The story was called "Two Killers in Snug Harbor." It was about a serial killer and a killer whale terrorizing the small town of Snug Harbor. (SPOILER ALERT: the whale eats the killer in the end.) Yes, I was nine years old. Yes, I watched too many scary movies on HBO!

What is your writing process like? Do you have set hours when you write, or only when inspiration strikes? Do you have any special places you like to write?

When I was younger, I let inspiration come to me. Now that I'm older and have two kids, I have to go to it. I have set hours (more or less). I have an office where I write on what was once a dining room table. It is my favorite place to work.

What advice would you give to aspiring writers hoping to be published for the first time?

First, to never use the word aspiring. If you write, you are a writer. It is not up to any agent, editor, or publisher to tell you who you are. Case in point . . . my first novel, *The Perks of Wallflower*. After I finished the manuscript, I could not find an agent for over a year. Then, I got lucky, and the right people read it (thank you, Chris and Heather McQuarrie!), and they sent it to three more of the right people (thank you, Greer Hendricks, Eduardo Braniff, and Jack Horner!). Suddenly, I had a deal. Same book. Two different times. So, I do not believe in aspiring. I believe that if you are writing, you are a writer. And if you keep writing, you will get better.

What advice would you give to writers working on their second book?

Don't take as long as me to do it. (Actually, that's a cheeky answer because it took me twenty years *and* I wrote a lot of movies and television shows in between.) In the end, I think writers put too much pressure on themselves to think that each book has to be THE book. I think second novels might the hardest to write because usually, writers spend a lifetime living their first books. And by the second, authors may feel like they're running on fumes.

So, if it helps, look at legendary artists. Maybe your first work is your greatest. But maybe you are like Bob Dylan and your second is when it really clicks (*The Freewheelin' Bob Dylan*). Or maybe you're Bruce Springsteen and the third time is the charm (*Born to Run*). Or you are Stephen King and your third published book makes you a household name (*The Shining*) and the fourth makes you a cult legend (*The Stand*). It might even take many more to finally find your greatness (George Orwell). The point is, write as many books as you can with your own standard of excellence and let history rank them.

Which of the characters in the book do you relate to the most?

When I started writing the book, I related to Christopher since he was based so much on my childhood growing up in Pittsburgh. By the end of writing the book, however, my wife and I had two kids. So, Kate Reese became my touchstone. In many ways, I feel like I began writing the book as a boy and finished as a man.

In addition to your career as a novelist, you've had a successful career in Hollywood, directing the film adaptation of your debut novel *The Perks of Being A Wallflower* and the film adaptation of R. J. Palacio's *Wonder*. Do you plan to adapt *Imaginary Friend* for the screen as well? Why or why not? If so, is there what part of the story do you think lends itself best to the screen? What do you expect to be the most challenging aspect of the story to adapt?

Absolutely. I have had some of these images in my head since I was nine years old. I can't wait to put them on a screen. As far as challenges go, I have to decide between making a movie or a TV series, and then work on what to keep and what to let go. In the end, my hope is that it will be both a movie series and a TV series before all is said and done. Even if I only do one of them personally. I would love to see both versions.

What are you working on now?

I am writing this answer two months into quarantine here in Los Angeles during the COVID-19 crisis. So, right now, I am working on being a good father and husband.

 @grandcentralpub @grandcentralpub @grandcentralpub

YOUR
BOOK
CLUB
RESOURCE

VISIT
GCPClubCar.com

to sign up for the **GCP Club Car** newsletter, featuring exclusive promotions, info on other **Club Car** titles, and more.

 @grandcentralpub

 @grandcentralpub

 @grandcentralpub